READER'S DIGEST
SELECT EDITIONS

READER'S DIGEST
SELECT EDITIONS

The condensations in this volume
are published with the consent of the authors
and the publishers © 2008 Reader's Digest.

www.readersdigest.co.uk

The Reader's Digest Association Limited
11 Westferry Circus Canary Wharf London E14 4HE

For information as to ownership of
copyright in the material of this book,
and acknowledgments, see last page.

Printed in Germany
ISBN 978 0 276 44432 6

SELECTED AND CONDENSED
BY READER'S DIGEST

THE READER'S DIGEST ASSOCIATION LIMITED, LONDON

CONTENTS

In the wake of the Second World War, a clandestine Jewish organisation set out to punish all those involved in the horrors of the concentration camps, not just Nazi leaders. The Avengers, as the conspirators were known, provided the inspiration for Sam Bourne's powerful new thriller in which a murdered man's daughter and a UN lawyer unravel dark secrets at the heart of the establishment.

The raw excitement of horse racing and the high tension of legal battles fought in the Old Bailey are cleverly interwoven in this vintage mystery from the Francis team. A jockey framed for murder and underhand dealings at a stud farm are just part of a web of clues that young barrister Geoffrey Mason must untangle with the help of his girlfriend, equine vet Eleanor Clarke.

Dogs can often be extraordinarily comforting, as newly widowed Roxanne Pelligrino discovers when she takes a job as an animal rescue warden. An injured Labrador finds his way into her heart when she gives him temporary shelter, and soon she can't face life without him. To keep Lloyd, she must enlist the help of new friends to find out why the dog was hurt and abandoned in the first place.

James Holland's novel *The Odin Mission*, set during the Second World War and starring Jack Tanner of the King's Own Yorkshire Regiment—the first of a new series—will be a treat for all those who like exciting action tales based on real events. The author promises that the stories will follow the timeline of the conflict, moving book by book from the fjords and mountains of Norway, and the scorched deserts of North Africa, to the rocky outcrops of the Apennines, the islands of the Mediterranean and the jungles of Burma. In these different campaigns and theatres of war, Tanner will be tested and gradually find himself. He is, James Holland explains, 'an intelligent, experienced and independently minded soldier, who often gives voice to the despair of the men on the ground. From reading contemporary diaries and letters, it's interesting to see how often these men knew when their commanders and generals were making ill-judged, unsound decisions. I hope this sub-theme will be educational as well as exciting.'

Already there has been interest from a film production company, so Jack Tanner may soon be joining the ranks of iconic book and screen heroes such as Sharpe and Hornblower.

THE ODIN MISSION

JAMES HOLLAND

425

JAMES HOLLAND
THE ODIN MISSION
Introducing Sergeant JACK TANNER

James Holland in the cockpit of a wartime Hurricane.

THE FINAL RECKONING

SAM BOURNE

Tom Byrne has come a long way since
his days as an idealistic young lawyer.
Now he'll work for anyone, as long
as the money's right. So when the UN
ask him to take on a dubious job,
he doesn't hesitate.
A suspected suicide bomber, shot by
UN security staff, has turned out
to be a harmless old man and Tom
must placate the family. But when
he travels to London to do so,he
finds out that the elderly victim
was not quite the
innocent he
seemed to be . . .

Chapter One

The day that changes a life, or ends a life, rarely comes with a warning. There are no signs in the sky, no dark ravens on a post, no soundtrack in a minor key. For Felipe Tavares, security officer at the United Nations building in New York, September 23 had started as a regular Monday.

He had come in on the Long Island Expressway on the 6.15 train, picked up a cappuccino, waved his permit at the guys on the door and headed to the basement, where he opened up his locker, pulled out the blue uniform of an officer of the UN Security Force, and dressed for his shift.

Next, he went to the armoury to pick up his weapon, a 9mm Glock, standard issue for most serving members of this miniature police force charged with protecting the international territory that was the UN compound and everything within it. Felipe loaded the gun and holstered it on his belt. After being inspected by an officer and deemed fit for duty, he headed back to the main entrance on First Avenue to begin what he assumed would be another long day checking permits and answering tourists' questions. The work would be boring, but he didn't care. Felipe Tavares had yearned to escape from the drudgery of small-town Portugal, where he had grown up, and he had made it. He was in New York City and that was excitement enough.

AT THAT SAME MOMENT, across town in a Tribeca side street that was no more than an alley, Marcus Mack conducted his own morning routine. African-American and in his late twenties, wearing loose, frayed jeans, with a full head of dreadlocks and a grungy computer bag slung across his shoulder, he checked on his parked car. Anyone watching would have assumed he was merely proud of his souped-up, if aged, Pontiac, and that when he knelt down by the driver's side rear wheel he was checking the tyre pressure. They probably wouldn't have seen him feeling in the well above the wheel and finding, stuck there with duct tape, a cellphone. He took it and walked on.

A minute later the phone rang, as Marcus knew it would. The familiar voice said just four words—'*Athens coffee shop, seven thirty*'—then hung up. At the corner of the street, Mack dropped the phone into a garbage can.

The café was full, the way his handler liked it. Marcus spotted him instantly, on a stool at the window, just another grey-suit reading his newspaper. Marcus took the seat next to him and pulled out his laptop.

They made no eye contact. The handler's phone rang and he pretended to answer it. In fact, he was speaking to Marcus, whose eyes remained fixed on the computer screen in front of him.

'We've picked up activity in Brighton Beach. The Russian.'

He did not have to say any more. Marcus knew about the Russian, as did the other member of his unit in the NYPD Intelligence Division. The Russian was an arms supplier who had been spotted a year ago. The Division had enough to shut him down immediately but the order had come from on high: *Keep him in play*. It was a familiar tactic. Leave a bad guy in business, watch who comes and goes, and hope he leads you to some worse guys.

'Surveillance caught a man entering the Russian's place last night, leaving an hour later. Traced him to the Tudor Hotel, 42nd and Second.'

Marcus did not react, just kept tapping at his keyboard. But he knew what the location meant. The Tudor was the nearest hotel to the United Nations building. And this was the UN's big week. Heads of government from all over the world were in New York to address the General Assembly, and US Secret Service were crawling all over the place in preparation for the President's visit later in the week. At a time like this, anything was possible.

'Placed a tap on the Tudor Hotel switchboard last night. Recorded a guest calling down to reception, asking about visiting times to the UN. "Is it true tourists can go right into the Security Council chamber itself?"'

'Accent?' It was the first word Marcus had spoken.

'Part British, part "foreign". You need to get down there now. Watch and follow.'

'Description?'

'White male. Five eight. Heavy black coat, black woollen hat.'

'Back-up?'

'There's a team.'

FELIPE TAVARES was now outdoors. Behind him was the temporary white marquee that served as the UN visitors' lobby—still up after five years. Not much tourist traffic yet, too early. So far it was just regular UN staff, permits dangling like necklaces. Not much for him to do. He looked up at the sky, now darkening. Rain was coming.

MARCUS STATIONED HIMSELF on the corner of 42nd and Second Avenue, tucked into the doorway of McFadden's Bar. Diagonally opposite was the Tudor Hotel. The first drops of rain were a help; the shelter gave him an excuse to be standing there, doing nothing. And it meant the Tudor's doorman, in cape and peaked cap, was too busy fussing with umbrellas and cab doors to notice a shifty guy in dreads across the street.

That was how Marcus liked it: to go unnoticed. It had become a speciality of his, back when he was doing undercover work in the NYPD's narcotics squad. Since he had moved over to the Intel Division a year ago, it had become a necessity. The thousand men and women of what amounted to New York's very own spy agency, a legacy of 9/11, kept themselves secret from everyone—the public, the bad guys, even their fellow cops.

He had been waiting twenty-five minutes when he saw it. A blur of black emerging through the hotel's revolving door. Just as it turned towards him, the doorman stepped forward with his umbrella, blocking Marcus's view of the man's face. By the time the umbrella was out of the way, the blur of black had turned right. In the direction of the UN.

Marcus spoke into what those around him would have believed was a Bluetooth headset for a cellphone. 'Subject on the move.'

Without waiting for a response he started walking, keeping a few paces behind the man on the other side of the six traffic-filled lanes of 42nd Street. A voice crackled into his ear. 'Do we have a positive ID?'

Marcus shot another look. The man was swaddled in the thick, dark coat the handler had mentioned; his head was covered in a black woollen hat pulled low, and he was no more than five foot eight inches tall. Marcus pressed the button clipped to his sleeve. 'Affirmative. We have a positive ID.'

Suddenly the man in black began to turn, as if checking for a tail. Marcus swivelled quickly, switching his gaze to a small playground. In his peripheral vision he could tell that the subject was marching onwards.

Something about the man's gait struck Marcus as odd. Was he limping slightly? There was a restriction to his movements, something slowing him down. He walked like a man carrying a heavy weight.

Suddenly the East River came into view. They had reached the corner of First Avenue; UN Plaza was visible through the rain.

The man in black crossed First Avenue at the pedestrian crossing. Marcus hung back on his side of the street, keeping his eye fixed on the subject, who now stopped by the first entrance to the United Nations. He was reading the sign: STAFF, DELEGATES AND RESIDENTS. CORRESPONDENTS ONLY. The subject moved on, separated by a black iron railings from a procession of empty flagpoles. Further back loomed the trademark curve of glass and steel that was the UN headquarters.

Marcus pulled up the collar of his leather jacket to stop the rain running down his neck. The man in black moved past another UN gate, and another sentry box. Marcus stopped for a moment in the doorway of the Chase Bank. The second he did so, a tourist bus pulled up into the slip road that fronted the UN between 45th and 46th.

'Lost visual, lost visual!' Marcus said urgently into his mouthpiece.

'I got it,' said another voice over the air, instant and calm. 'Subject has halted outside main gate.'

Marcus walked on, trying to get ahead of the tourist bus.

His headset crackled again. 'Subject back on the move.'

OK, thought Marcus with relief. A false alarm. The man in black was not trying to enter the UN building after all.

At last the bus pulled out, giving Marcus a clear view of the subject, now walking farther down First Avenue. But this was no relaxed stroll. Marcus could see him studying the garden on the other side of the railings intently. He drew level with a large sculpture—the slaying of a dragon—and stopped as if looking for something. Was he searching for another, unguarded, way into the UN compound? If so, he clearly had not found it. Now, with renewed purpose, the man turned and headed back towards the main entrance.

FELIPE TAVARES'S RADIO was bulky, low-tech and, in this rain, barely audible. But the word 'Alert' came through clear enough above the static.

'This is the Watch Commander to main entry points.' Felipe recognised the accent: the guy from the Ivory Coast who'd started three months ago. 'We have information on a possible threat to the building. Suspect is male, five foot eight, wearing a heavy black coat and dark woollen hat. Please stop and apprehend anyone fitting that description.'

Felipe had barely digested the message when he saw a blur of black striding, head down, towards the gate he was guarding.

MARCUS WAS NOW halfway across First Avenue, struggling to hear the voice in his ear above the traffic.

'. . . compound. Repeat, agents are not to enter the UN compound.'

He stopped as he reached the kerb of the slip road, now just yards away from the man he had been following, and watched him walk through the gate and up the few steps to the small piazza in front of the white marquee. He had crossed into UN territory; he was now officially beyond reach.

FROM THIS ANGLE, at the side of the piazza, Felipe could see only a little of the man's face in profile, the hat and the collar of his coat obscuring even that. But he fitted the Watch Commander's description perfectly.

The man stopped, as if contemplating what stood before him. Felipe felt his palms growing moist. He was suddenly aware of how many people were around, dozens of them crossing between him and this black-coated figure. His gaze fixed on the coat. It was raining, but it was certainly not cold. Why was the coat so thick, so heavy? Answering his own question prompted a wave of nausea that started in his stomach and rose into his throat.

Felipe wanted to use his radio—'Believe suspect could be armed with a bomb. *Repeat, believe suspect could be armed with a bomb!'*—but what if that only provoked him to act? The security man was paralysed.

The man was on the move again, now just yards from the marquee. Felipe thought that perhaps he should wait, let the man go through the doors and be stopped by Security. He'd never get past the detectors or a frisk. *But he wouldn't care.* That, Felipe realised, was the horror of it. Nothing would scare this man.

Now the subject turned to face the street. Felipe wanted to cry out, demand that the man freeze and put his hands in the air, but he understood that that would be no less fatal. Once the man knew he'd been discovered, he would push the button immediately. And there were so many people around . . .

Felipe did not *decide* to do it. He simply reached for his gun. And at that moment he saw ahead of him, through the iron railings, two men, one of them young, black and dreadlocked, both raising their hands as if in surrender. The alarm on their faces, the mortal panic etched on them, settled it for him. He pulled out his weapon and aimed it squarely at the man in black.

The next moment was one Felipe Tavares would replay over and over until his last breath, the image he would see each night and when he woke up each morning. At the centre of it were the faces of those two men, frightened and shocked by what they saw. Both of them shouting the single word '*No!*'

Felipe was certain of what had happened. The man in black had obviously undone his coat, revealing an explosive vest. The two men on the other side of the railings had seen that he was about to blow himself up. The sound of that cry, the look of horror on the dreadlocked man's face, coursed through Felipe, sending a charge of electricity down his right arm and into his finger. He squeezed the trigger twice, and watched the man collapse at the knees, falling slowly, even gracefully, like a chimney stack detonated from below.

Felipe couldn't move. He was fixed to the spot, his arms locked into position, still aiming at the man now lying five yards away from him.

He heard nothing for a while. Not the echo of the gunshots. Not the cries of the crowd. Not the alarm that had been set off inside the UN building.

Unsteadily, dumbly, Felipe walked over to the pile of black clothes now ringed by a spreading puddle of blood. And, in an instant, he understood. There, at his feet, was not the body of a suicide bomber. There was no explosive vest filling that jacket. All it contained was the broken corpse of a white-haired old man.

THERE WAS A MOMENT of silence, lasting perhaps two beats, and then the noise erupted. There were screams, of course—a man first, yelping in a language few around him understood, and then the cries of three women who had been posing for a photograph by the pop art sculpture of a gun, its barrel twisted into a knot. Soon there was shouting and the sound of the fire alarm. The officers in the marquee abandoned their posts at the scanning machines and rushed to stand at the doors of each entrance, their pistols brandished. The United Nations headquarters was going into lockdown.

Felipe Tavares was now flanked by two colleagues, guiding him away from the corpse. Tavares was talking feverishly, babbling about the men he had seen at the gate, describing the horror on their faces, but when his fellow officers looked, they could see no one.

Less than ninety seconds after the shooting, the first of forty NYPD squad cars converged on UN Plaza, their lights flashing, their sirens wailing: this was the 'surge' they had practised nearly a dozen times since 9/11. Several cars disgorged SWAT teams, who soon ringed the entire UN perimeter, their assault rifles trained on the terrified men and women within.

First Avenue was free of traffic now, thanks to the NYPD officers armed with 50mm machine guns who had sealed the road from 30th Street all the way south to 59th. In the air, four NYPD Agusta A119 helicopters equipped with high-resolution, thermal-imaging 'super-spy' cameras hovered, policing an impromptu no-fly zone over the entire area. On the East River, police launches had taken off from their bases in Throgs Neck, Brooklyn and along the Queens shoreline. No one would be able to enter or escape the United Nations compound by air or by water.

Not much later, the NYPD's Chief of Detectives arrived with his own lights and sirens. To his pleasure, he had got there ahead of Charles 'Chuck' Riley, the Police Commissioner, whose motorcade pulled up a few moments later. Both nodded with satisfaction as they observed a lockdown utterly complete. But as they stepped out of their cars and shook hands with each other, the two men saw the nature of their problem. They could approach the now-locked steel gate of the UN but could go no farther. They had reached the limit of the NYPD's authority, the very boundary of United States sovereignty.

EIGHTEEN MINUTES after Felipe Tavares had fired his fatal shot, Henning Munchau, the United Nation's Under-Secretary-General for Legal Affairs, was standing beside the lifeless body. It had not been touched, save for the waterproof cape placed over it. The rain was still coming down.

Munchau saw the small army of NYPD men that surrounded the UN compound and felt like the inhabitant of a medieval castle on the first day of a siege. Then, on the far side of the railings, he saw a face he recognised, one rarely off the front page of the city papers.

'Commissioner, I am Henning Munchau, the UN's chief lawyer.'

'Good to meet ya, Henning,' the Police Commissioner said, his face and tone conveying nothing of the sort. 'We appear to have a situation.'

'We do.'

'We cannot enter these premises and respond to this incident unless you formally request that we do so.' The language was officialese, the accent down-home Southern.

'Looks like you've already responded in quite a big way, Commissioner.' Though German, Munchau spoke his eerily fluent English with a hint of Australian, the legacy of his service in the UN mission in East Timor.

Riley shrugged. 'I'm assuming you don't have the resources to handle a terrorist incident.'

Munchau tried to hide his relief. It meant the NYPD had not yet heard about the dead man. That would give him time. 'You're quite right,' he said, struck by the strangeness of speaking through metal railings in the rain, and envying the Commissioner his umbrella. 'But we need to agree some terms.'

The policeman smiled wanly. 'Go ahead.'

'The NYPD can come in but only at the request and at the discretion of the United Nations.'

'No discretion. Once you let us in, it's our investigation. All or nothing.'

'Fine, but none of this.' He gestured towards the SWAT teams, their guns cocked. 'This is not the UN way.'

'OK, minimal show of force.'

'I'm talking one or two armed men only, to accompany your detectives.'

'Done.'

'And your investigation is to be shadowed at all times by a representative of the UN. A lawyer. From my team.'

'A lawyer? For Christ's—'

'Those are the conditions.'

Munchau saw the Commissioner weigh it up, knowing he could hardly refuse. A suspected terror attack in New York: the NYPD had to be involved. The 'Commish' couldn't go on television saying that the department was sitting this one out, whatever the explanation. He would want to be on the air within the hour, reassuring New Yorkers that he had it all under control.

Now a black limo pulled up, with a whole new battalion of lights and sirens, and behind it were two satellite TV trucks. The Mayor had arrived.

'OK,' the Commissioner said, glancing over his shoulder. 'I accept.'

Munchau offered his hand through the railings and Riley took it hurriedly. Munchau nodded to the UN guard on the gate, who fumbled with the lock until it opened.

Watching a TV reporter heading his way, Munchau raised his voice to declare, 'Mr Commissioner, welcome to the United Nations.'

IT TOOK TIME for the Chef de Cabinet of the Secretary-General of the United Nations to convene this meeting. The UN's most senior officials, the elite quintet of USGs—Under-Secretaries-General—had been on their way to the building when the shooting happened. Thanks to the shutdown of First Avenue, none reached UN Plaza much before 10 a.m.

They were gathered, at last, in the Situation Center, a heavily armoured, lavishly equipped and top-secret meeting place modelled on the legendary Situation Room of the White House. At its heart was a polished table, each place round it fitted discreetly with the sockets and switches that made all forms of communication, including simultaneous translation, possible.

The Chef de Cabinet, Finnish like his boss, began by explaining that the building remained in partial lockdown, with authorised access and egress only. No one would be let in or out without the express permission of the Legal Counsel, as agreed with the NYPD, who wished to interview all witnesses, even if that meant interviewing the entire UN work force.

The Chef de Cabinet went on to confirm that the Secretary-General himself had not been inside UN Plaza at the time. He had been at a breakfast held in his honour at the Four Seasons and was now heading over through horrendous traffic. 'In the meantime, I suggest we establish what we know and work out some options that we can present to the Secretary-General. Can I start with you, Henri?'

Henri Barr, the Under-Secretary responsible for the security of UN personnel across the globe, glanced down at the notes he had hastily written when being briefed by the Watch Commander. 'We understand that a man was shot at eight fifty-one a.m. today by a member of the UN's Security and Safety Force in front of the main visitors' entrance between 45th and 46th Streets. He had been monitored by a team from the NYPD Intelligence Division, who had cause to believe that he posed an imminent danger to the United Nations. That information was passed to the Watch Commander and he passed it on to the guards on duty, including the officer who fired his weapon, believing the man to be a suicide bomber.'

'And the man is dead?'

'Yes.'

'And what else do we know? Is the building in any danger?'

'The lockdown procedure was followed perfectly. The building is now secure. We do not believe this to be the start of a series of attacks.'

'And why is that?'

Barr looked at Henning, who gave a small nod. 'Because we strongly suspect that the man killed does not match the profile put together by the NYPD.'

'What the hell does that mean?' It was the USG for Humanitarian Affairs, a white South African ex-communist who had made his name in the anti-apartheid movement. His bullshit detector was famously robust.

'It means that the man who was shot was old.'

'Old?'

'Yes, he was an old man.' Barr gulped oxygen. 'But his clothes fitted the description and they seemed to be the clothes of a suicide bomber.'

'Oh, come on. He was *dressed* like a suicide bomber, so we killed him?'

The Chef de Cabinet stepped in. This was no time for grandstanding. 'When you say "old", Henri, what do you mean?'

'We estimate seventy, perhaps more.'

'Did he even look Muslim?' It was the question that several of them had wanted to ask but had not dared. Anjhut Banerjee, the Indian Under-Secretary for Peacekeeping, had none of their inhibitions.

'No,' said Barr, looking down at his notes. 'It seems not.'

'Good God,' Banerjee said, falling back into her chair. 'You know what this means, don't you? I was in London when the police shot a Brazilian electrician on a train because they thought he was a suicide bomber. Completely innocent man.' She exhaled sharply.

'What is our liability, Henning?' The Chef de Cabinet looked at the lawyer.

'I don't think we should get too hung up on compensation claims and the like,' the German replied. 'The problem's not legal. It's political.'

'So what do you suggest we do about it?'

'I think I know what needs to be done. And I know just the man to do it.'

TOM BYRNE was jolted awake by a sound both unfamiliar and unpleasant. It was a repeating chime, with a long, echoing sustain, the sound lingering in the air. Tom could feel his heart thumping in his chest. Then he saw the culprit: his new BlackBerry, fresh out of the box just yesterday. He hadn't got round to setting it to silent.

He squinted at his watch: 10.30 a.m. That was OK; he hadn't got to sleep till five, having worked through the night on the Dubai contract. He swung his legs out of the bed and headed for the blinds, which he louvred open.

The BlackBerry sounded again, a single high-volume chime to herald the arrival of a message. Bound to be his new clients; he had sent them the first draft of the paperwork in the middle of the night, and here they were, already demanding revisions. You could say what you liked about organised crime, but you had to hand it to them: they worked long hours.

The Fantonis were what you'd call 'a family of Italian-American descent with long and historic roots in the New York construction industry'—that is, if you were their lawyer. They were now seeking to expand into property in the Persian Gulf, all legal and legit, but a pile of international papers had to be filed first. A friend of a friend had recommended him, and the family were happy to have him—they liked being represented by a big-shot international lawyer, British-born and with several years at the United Nations on his résumé—and he was happy to have them, earning more in a week than he had earned in a year working for the blue-helmets of UN Plaza.

He looked back down at the BlackBerry. *1 Missed Call*. He pressed it to see a single name displayed: *Henning*.

Now there was a surprise. Henning Munchau hadn't called Tom from his personal cellphone all that often even when Tom worked for him. But that had been more than a year ago. Tom listened to the message.

'Hi, Tom, it's Henning. We need to talk. Meet me at that coffee shop as fast as you can. Tom, I . . . Don't call me back.'

Not even a 'long time no speak'.

So the UN's most senior lawyer needed to discuss a topic so sensitive he didn't dare do it on the telephone or in his own building. That was hardly news; everyone knew there was not a word spoken in UN Plaza that was not monitored, by the Yanks at NSA, by the Brits at GCHQ and by God knows who else. But *Meet me at that coffee shop* was especially interesting. That meant Henning didn't even want to give away a specific location.

If it had been anyone else from the UN, Tom would have hit delete and not given it another thought. But this was Henning.

He walked into the closet, reviewing the line of suits. A big meeting like this would normally call for the Prada or Paul Smith. But Tom didn't want to rub Henning's public-sector salary in his face; he'd go for something plainer. Pink shirt and cuff links? No, the blue would do. He caught a glimpse of himself in the mirror: wrong side of forty, but he could still scrub up all right. No time for a shower today, though. He shot two bursts of Hugo Boss aftershave onto his neck and ruffled his close-cropped, dirty-blond hair.

He gathered up his things, admiring again the vast, open space of his loft apartment, and headed for the door.

Chapter Two

The cab driver shook his turbaned head, muttering that he would get there as fast as he could, but the road had been blocked for the past hour. 'On the radio, they say something about terror attack,' he said.

Tom handed him a ten-dollar bill and got out at 39th Street. He could see the clutch of police cars, their red lights winking, and behind them the glare of TV bulbs already illuminating a jam of trucks bearing satellite dishes. In itself that was no surprise during General Assembly week. But now he could see a city cop, a woman, turning people back from the first entry gate to UN Plaza. Along the railings, encircling the entire compound like a ribbon on a Christmas gift, was a continuous thread of yellow-and-black plastic tape: POLICE LINE, DO NOT CROSS. He walked on, noticing how each successive entrance was blocked off.

The gate used by the public was thronged by reporters and cameramen. Tom was tall enough to peer over their heads, to see, in the middle of the paved area in front of the security marquee, a small tent constructed from green tarpaulin. Around it fussed police officers, a single photographer and a forensics team in overalls, masks and white latex gloves.

He crossed the road, threading his way through the cars. Facing him was the concrete phallic symbol that was the Trump World Tower. The Nations' Café was just next door.

He saw Henning Munchau immediately, earnestly studying the map-of-the-world pattern that decorated the vinyl table top. To Tom's surprise, Henning rose the moment they made eye contact, leaving his coffee untouched. His eyes indicated the door: *Follow me*. What the hell was going on?

Once outside, Henning raised his eyebrows, a gesture Tom took a second or two to understand. 'Of course,' he said finally. Munchau was one of those smokers who never carried his own cigarettes; he believed that if you didn't buy them, you didn't really smoke them. Tom reached into his jacket pocket, pulled out a pouch of Drum rolling tobacco, inside which was a small blue envelope of cigarette papers, and in a few dexterous moves conjured up a neat, thin stick, which he passed to Henning. He did the same for himself, then lit them both with a single match.

'That's better,' said Henning, his cheeks still sucked in, refusing to exhale the first drag. He looked hard at Tom, as if seeing him for the first time. 'It's been a long time. You doing OK?'

'Never better.'

'That's good.' Henning took another drag. 'Because you look like shit.'

Tom let out a laugh, which triggered a broad Henning grin, the smile that made Tom instantly like the man when they had first met all those years ago. That and the Munchau patois, flawless English with an Australian lilt and the earthy vocabulary to match. Tom had seen it take shape when they served on the Australian-led East Timor mission together.

'So, Henning, we're both busy guys. What is it you need?'

'It's about . . .' He trailed off. 'About what happened here this morning.'

'Yeah, what *is* all this? I saw the police line and—'

'You don't know? Christ, Tom, all those fat corporate fees and you can't afford a radio? A man was shot here two hours ago, a suspected terrorist.'

'OK.'

'Not OK,' said Henning. He exhaled a plume, then checked left and right. 'Turns out we got the wrong guy,' he whispered. 'Apparently we killed some pensioner in a woolly coat.'

'What do you mean, "we"?'

'The shooter was from our own bloody security force.'

'Jesus.'

'Jesus is right.' Henning took a long, final drag, then threw the cigarette to the ground. 'Just unbelievable bad luck. NYPD Intelligence tipped us off about a suspect who'd been visiting an arms dealer. Dressed in thick black coat, black hat. Which just so happens to be what the old boy was wearing when he went out for his morning stroll. Can you imagine tomorrow's *New York Post*? "Now the UN kills geriatrics on the streets of New York."'

'Picked the right week to do it.'

'Yeah. Not exactly the start Viren wanted, is it? Imagine, the new Secretary-General spending his first General Assembly on his knees apologising.'

'He knows?'

Henning nodded. 'For the past hour, we've been in the Situation Center with his Chef de Cabinet, all the USGs. Secretary-General wasn't there; he was at some society breakfast. The building's in complete lockdown. USGs are the only ones allowed out.'

'What are you going to do?'

'Well, that's what I wanted to talk to you about. I know you said you'd never work for us again. I understand that, but—'

'Good. So you'll understand me when I say, "Nice to see you, Henning, but I've got to go."'

'But this is not working for the UN.'

'Who's it for, then?'

'It's for me. A personal favour. I think I have the right to ask for that.'

Tom examined Henning's face. It was the one argument to which he had no response, the same unarguable fact that had made him drop everything and come straight here. It was true: Tom owed him everything.

'What do you need?'

'One good thing about the situation is it turns out the dead guy was British.'

'Why's that good?'

'Because the Brits are the only ones who won't go ape about the Yanks murdering one of their citizens. Inside America, it'll be the pinko faggot UN who fucked up. Everywhere else, it'll be America who gets the blame.'

Trigger-happy cowboys, all that. Not the British government, though. Your boys will bend over and bite it.'

Tom would have liked to argue, but he remembered the campaign to get British citizens released from Guantánamo. The British government had barely raised a peep in protest, lest it offend the Americans.

'So? Was it an American who pulled the trigger?'

'No. Portuguese. Name of Tavares.'

Tom digested this. 'So what do you need me to do?'

'First, I need you to shadow the NYPD guys on the case. By now they'll know we screwed up. I need you over their shoulder. Just for this first day— I made a big deal of it, so I can't send out some novice to do it. Get a sense of what they're doing, then hand it over.'

'And then?'

'Then I need you to close this thing down, Tom. Make it go away. We can't have the grieving family on television holding up pictures of Grandpa, wanting to send the bloody Secretary-General to jail. You need to go to England, find the family and do whatever it takes to make it go away. Offer a gushing apology, massive compensation package, whatever. But no grandstanding, OK? No photo ops with the Secretary-General or any of that bullshit. He's new. We can't have him associated with this.'

Tom took a drag of his cigarette. He could see the politics clearly enough: his departure a year ago had left no Brits in the Office of the Legal Counsel. Plus it would probably help to have an outside lawyer do this—arm's length, so that the UN itself would be less tainted by whatever shabbiness Tom would have to resort to. But it was hardly a top-flight legal assignment.

'There are plenty of other Brits around who could do this, Henning. Perfectly capable lawyers. Why me?'

'Because you're a safe pair of hands. Someone I can rely on.'

Tom raised an eyebrow. A lawyer who'd left the UN the way he had was not what you'd call a safe pair of hands. *Come on*, the eyebrow said. *Flattery isn't going to work. Tell the truth.*

Henning sighed. 'OK, you're not a conventional safe pair of hands. But you know what they're like, the young lawyers here, Tom. Full of idealistic bullshit about the UN as "the ultimate guarantor of human rights" and all that crap. We don't need any of that right now. We need someone who will do what needs to be done, and not be afraid to put the rule book to one side.'

'You need a cynic.'

'I need a *realist*. Besides, I know that you'll regard the interests of the

United Nations as paramount.' There was a hint of a smile around Henning's mouth. He couldn't risk some British lawyer who might give a call to his old pals at the Foreign and Commonwealth Office, just to keep them in the loop. But Tom Byrne, graduate of Sheffield Grammar and the University of Manchester, could be relied on not to betray the UN to his old-boy network for one simple reason: he didn't have an old-boy network.

'You know me. I'm a citizen of the world.'

'I knew I could rely on you, Tom.'

'You did a lot for me, Henning. I haven't forgotten.'

'After this, we're even. Really. Which is not to say you won't be properly rewarded. There's a separate budget for this, Tom. Emergency fund.'

'So I'm to give the family whatever they want.'

'Yep. Your job is to make sure that, after today, none of us ever hears about the dead guy again. I want this whole thing buried with him.'

HENNING LED TOM through the press gauntlet, the pair of them using their shoulders to carve a passage. He said nothing until they reached the entrance of the makeshift tent that contained the dead man's body.

'Tom, this is Jay Sherrill. The Commissioner tells me he is one of his elite, first-grade detectives.'

'First grade? That sounds junior.' He couldn't help it: the guy looked about nineteen. Maybe early thirties, tops. Neatly pressed shirt; studious absence of a tie; sleek, hairless, handsome face. Tom could have drawn up a profile of Jay Sherrill there and then: one of the fast-track Ivy Leaguers favoured by all urban police forces these days. They were the young guns who spoke and dressed more like management consultants than cops. He had probably done a fortnight on the street and was thereafter catapulted to the first rank of the force. Men like him were the new officer class.

'Young, sure. But with a ninety-six per cent conviction rate.' Sherrill's accent was posh Boston; he sounded like a Kennedy.

'Ninety-six per cent, eh? Which one got away?'

'The one with the best lawyer.'

Henning stepped in. 'All right. As you know, Commissioner Riley and I have agreed that the UN and NYPD are going to work closely on this one. And that means you two fellows. Are we clear?'

'We're clear,' said Sherrill, making a pitch for the high ground of maturity. 'Mr Byrne, I'm on my way to meet the head of security for this building. You're welcome to come with me.'

Tom raised a palm in farewell to Henning and dutifully followed, noting Henning's schoolmasterly gaze as he did so. He would behave himself. 'Let's hope you're the first person he's spoken to,' he offered, in a tone he hoped suggested a truce.

'You worried he might have talked to the press?' Sherrill asked.

'No, I'm worried he might have talked to someone in this building. It leaks.' Tom was thinking of his own mission to London. He didn't need a whole lot of rumours reaching the family before he did.

They walked through the visitors' marquee, now closed to the public, and into the eerily quiet foyer of the main building, then rode in an empty elevator to the first floor, where Harold Allen was waiting for them. Tom recognised him. He'd once been the most senior African-American officer in the NYPD, before he had famously sued his own force for racial discrimination. He showed his guests to a round table in the middle of his office, anxiety carved into his face. Tom noticed the multiple framed NYPD citations for bravery on the wall.

Sherrill wasted no time on pleasantries. 'As you can imagine, I've got a few questions for you, Mr Allen.'

'Yeah, you and this whole goddamn building.'

Tom took notes as Allen talked through the sequence of events: the tip-off from the NYPD about the Russian; the recorded phone call from the hotel room to reception; his own instruction to his watch commanders to be on the lookout for a man fitting the description the police had provided; how that message had been passed on to the guards at the gate, including Tavares; and finally the shooting. A tragic case of mistaken identity.

'Where is Officer Tavares now?'

'He's with one of the NYPD support officers, getting counselling.'

Tom's forehead crinkled. 'Counselling?'

'Yes, Mr Byrne, counselling. Tavares is in a state of grave shock.'

'How's he bearing up?' It was Sherrill, his voice softened.

'He's in a bad way. He's a good man.'

'Do we know how old the dead man was?'

Allen glanced down at a sheet of paper. 'Seems like he was seventy-seven years old. Name of Gerald Merton. Place of birth, Kaunas, Lithuania.'

'Lithuania? Not many Gerald Mertons there,' said Sherrill with a smug smile. 'May I ask, what is that you're looking at, Mr Allen?'

'This is a photocopy of his passport.'

'His what?' No softness now.

'His passport. One of my men removed it from the pocket of the deceased, just after he was killed. Wanted to check his ID.'

'I strongly hope you're joking.'

'I'm afraid not, Mr Sherrill. We put it back, though.'

'Have your men never heard about preserving a crime scene, about contamination of evidence? My God!'

'Handling a homicide is not what we do here. It's never happened before.'

Tom saw an opening. 'Can I see that?'

Allen handed over the piece of paper, and Tom stared at the copy of the photograph. It was grainy, but distinct enough. The man was clearly old, but his face was not heavily lined, nor thin and sagging. His head was still firm and round, with a close crop of white hair on each side. None on top. The eyes were unsmiling, tough. Tom's eye moved back to the place of birth: Kaunas, Lithuania. Under nationality, it stated boldly: *British Citizen*.

He passed it to Sherrill, who scanned it for a few seconds, then said, 'We'll need to speak with Officer Tavares.'

'That may be difficult. He's not in a state right now—'

'Mr Allen, this is not a request.'

Allen's temples were twitching. 'I'll see what I can do.'

WHEN SHERRILL AND TOM returned to the makeshift tent, the corpse had already been zipped up in a body bag and dispatched to the Office of the Chief Medical Examiner. The post-mortem would begin immediately.

Sherrill gestured to one of the police cars still idling outside UN Plaza, its driver clearly a personal chauffeur, indicating that Tom should get in and join him on the back seat. The car zipped south along First Avenue. Just past the Bellevue Hospital, Sherrill tapped on his driver's shoulder and he and Tom leapt out when the car halted.

'Ordinarily no one's allowed to witness an autopsy,' he explained to Tom. 'But they don't usually say no to first-grade detectives.'

They waited only a few minutes at reception before a woman in scrubs appeared. When Sherrill introduced Tom, she gave him an expression he translated as *OK, Mr UN Lawyer, prepare yourself for an eyeful . . .*

She opened a pair of double doors by punching a code into a keypad and led them down one corridor, then another. At last she took them into what seemed to be a hospital ward. The odour of disinfectant was strong.

'All righty, let's put these on.' She handed them both green surgical gowns and hats, pulled back a green curtain and there it was. A slab on a trolley, under a rough sheet. 'Here's where I got to before I was so rudely interrupted,' she said, pulling back the sheet.

The body was on its side, a vast hulk of pale white flesh like the underside of a fish, though now tinged with green. Strangely, Tom's eye found the unbroken flesh first. The wound, the torn opening in the back, he saw only later, and when he saw it he could not look away. It was the depth of it that appalled him, the deep, red depth of it.

'. . . consistent with severe trauma to the trunk, shattered shoulder blade, ruptured lung and exploded right ventricle . . .'

Tom was not listening. He was still gazing at the congealed crimson gash.

'Let me turn him over for you.'

The two men had been standing opposite the pathologist, with the body between them and her. Now, they moved round so they were alongside her.

'You can see the exit hole here. Which means you'll be looking for a bullet.'

Feeling a hint of nausea, Tom focused on the dead man's face. The passport photograph must have been recent; the same full, roundness of head was still visible. 'Can I see his eyes?' he asked.

She stepped closer and, with no hesitation, pulled back both eyelids, pinning them with her latex thumbs and holding the position.

The inert lump of dead flesh was suddenly transformed back into a man. The eyes seemed to look directly at Tom's own.

'Pretty striking, huh?'

Tom knew what she meant. The eyes were a bright, piercing blue.

'He was strong, wasn't he?' Tom pointed at the thickness of the dead man's upper arms.

'You bet. Look at this.' She pulled back the rest of the sheet, revealing a flaccid penis, its foreskin drooping limply, before prodding the man's thick thighs. 'That's some serious muscle. He must have been a fitness freak.'

'What about that?' It was Sherrill, anxious not to be forgotten—and to remind Tom who was in charge here. He was gesturing at a patch of metal bandaged to the dead man's left leg like a footballer's shin-pad.

'That appears to be some kind of temporary support. When plates are used in reconstructive surgery, they're inserted under the skin. Maybe this was used as a splint after a muscle strain. Odd to use metal, though. It will probably become clearer once we see the deceased's medical records.'

'And that?' Sherrill asked, pointing at the left foot. There was a big toe, one next to it, then a space where the other three should have been.

'I hadn't got to that yet.' The doctor moved to the end of the trolley, so she could examine the foot from above. 'These are old wounds,' she said. 'At least sixty years old, I'd estimate. Maybe an industrial accident.'

Sherrill resumed with a battery of technical questions, most of which seemed to centre on ballistics. He and the pathologist were now trading in a technical dialect Tom didn't speak, all calibres and contusions, and that was when Tom noticed, lying on the top of a small cabinet of drawers, several clear, ziplocked plastic bags. One contained a plain white plastic card that looked like a hotel room key; another, a clunky, outdated mobile phone. These had to be the possessions of the deceased. There was also his passport and a few dollar bills.

As casually as he could, Tom picked up the first plastic bag. Sure enough, the card inside bore the imprint of the Tudor Hotel, suggesting once again that this poor old buffer was no suicide bomber; he probably planned to go back to his room after his 'mission' to UN Plaza, to have a nice cup of tea.

Sherrill's stream of technicalia was still flowing when a head popped round the door, summoning the pathologist outside. Tom seized the moment to beckon the detective over and show him the bag containing the phone. Through the plastic he reached for the power button, then brought up the last set of numbers dialled, recognising the familiar 011-44 of a British number and then, below that, a New York cellphone, beginning 1-917. Instantly, Sherrill pulled out a notebook and scribbled down both numbers. Tom did the same. He was about to bring up the 'Received Calls' list, when a 'Battery Empty' sign flashed up and the screen went blank.

Sherrill waited for the pathologist to return, peppering her with a few more questions before making arrangements for a full set of results to be couriered over to him later that afternoon. Then he and Tom went back to the UN security department to interview a pale, trembling Felipe Tavares.

Despite himself, Tom had to admit that Sherrill was a class act. He spoke to the Portuguese officer quietly and patiently, as if they were simply chatting, cop to cop. Unsaid, but hinted at, was the assumption that, if Sherrill had his way, no police officer was going to be in trouble simply for doing his job. All Felipe—can I call you Felipe?—had to do was tell Jay everything that had happened. When Tavares reached the point where he received the alert from the Watch Commander with the description of the potential terror suspect, Sherrill pressed him for the precise wording. Tavares protested that it was difficult to remember; the rain had been coming down so hard he had struggled to hear properly.

The detective did his best to sound casual when he asked what was clearly, at least to Tom's legal ears, the key question. It came once Felipe described the moment he pulled the trigger.

'At that instant, did you reasonably believe your life was in danger?'

'Yes. Not just *my* life. Everyone's life. I thought he was a suicide bomber.'

'And you thought that because you saw some kind of bomb?'

'No! I told you. I thought it because of the warning we had about a man who look like this. And because of the faces of those men I saw. Looking so shocked, and screaming, "No!" like they were desperate.'

'And you now think they were screaming because they could see that the man was, in fact, old. Not a terrorist at all. They were shouting, "No!" not to him, but to you, urging you not to shoot.'

Felipe Tavares's head sank onto his chest. Quietly he replied, 'Yes.'

'Yet when you looked later, you say there was no sign of the two men?'

'No sign.'

'Isn't that a little strange? That they just vanished into thin air?'

'It is strange, sir. But that what happen.'

'So to conclude, Felipe, you have no idea why the Watch Commander gave his warning then? At that particular time?'

'No. I just heard the message and then I saw the man they describe.' Tavares looked down at his feet again. 'Well, I thought I saw the man.'

Tom could see the cogs in Sherrill's mind turning, as if he was getting what he needed. Quite what that was, Tom had not yet worked out.

BY NOW TOM HAD DONE what Henning had requested: he had overseen day one of the investigation. It was time to say his goodbyes if he was to make the overnight flight to London. To his surprise, the detective promised to let him know whatever the forensics guys and the medical examiner turned up. He took Tom's cellphone number, then insisted that Tom take his—at which point the nature of Sherrill's collegiate generosity made itself apparent. With no men of his own in London, he wanted Tom to pass on whatever he discovered about the victim.

In a cab on the way back to his apartment to pack, Tom called security head Harold Allen to get details of the next of kin. 'How are things, Harold?'

'Not great, Tom, I'll be straight with you.' He sounded rough, like a man whose career was flashing before his eyes.

'Have the family now been notified?'

'The Under-Secretary-General made the call nearly an hour ago. There's no widow, just one daughter, apparently. I'll email the coordinates.'

'Press?'

'They haven't got the name yet. Just confirmation of a Caucasian male.'

'Has his age been announced?'

Allen sighed. 'Not yet.'

Tom felt sorry for the man, who was shaping up to be the obvious fall-guy. Just senior enough to be culpable, but not so senior that his sacrifice would actually cost the high command.

He offered some bland words of reassurance and hung up, wondering who to phone next. No need to speak to the Fantonis; BlackBerry and cell-phone contact would be fine for them, no matter where he was. He should tell the guys from his five-a-side team that he'd miss Wednesday's game. Otherwise, he had no one else to call.

The traffic on the Van Wyck Expressway was heavy. Tom reached into his pocket to check his passport when he felt the hard cover of his notebook. He probably ought to call Sherrill, tell him that the family had been informed, which meant the press would soon get the dead man's name. He flicked through the pages looking for the detective's number, but instead came across the scribbled note he had made at the medical examiner's office.

Now, in his other hand, he fired up his BlackBerry. A message from Allen's office, as promised. A name, a London address and two phone numbers, the second clearly that of a mobile. Rebecca Merton, it said. Tom glanced at the UK number he had seen on the phone in the Ziploc bag. Sure enough, they matched. Merton's last call had been to his daughter.

Tom tapped out the second number he had found on the dead man's cell-phone, beginning 1-917, thinking it would probably just be the number for a taxi service the old guy had used to collect him from the airport.

He put the phone to his ear, hearing it connect and then the long tone of a first ring. A silence and then one more ring. And then a male voice, speaking to someone else. At first Tom assumed it was a wrong number, that he had scrawled the digits down too fast. He was about to apologise for his mistake when instinct silenced him. He heard the voice again, first winding up another conversation, then calling out 'Hello, hello'—and a shudder passed through him, making even his scalp turn cold.

It wasn't the accent, or even that telltale half-sentence Tom had heard, spoken in a language Tom had studied back in his university days. No, it was the tone, the brusque hardness. Tom quickly disconnected. With relief, he remembered that these new BlackBerries came with an automatic block on Caller ID. That man would not be calling back.

A quick call to Allen—and from him to a friend in NYPD Intelligence who took pity on a former comrade clearly in the wringer—confirmed Tom's hunch. When Allen asked why Tom needed the number, he deployed an old party trick, speaking a few broken words, and then hung up. It would sound to Allen as if Tom had disappeared into a tunnel and lost the signal.

The choked roads gave Tom Byrne some time as the car crawled the final few miles to John F. Kennedy Airport. He knew he should relay his discovery to Jay Sherrill immediately, but he hesitated. He wanted to think this through. Besides, Sherrill would get there himself soon enough. When he dialled the number they had both written down, he would hear what Tom had heard. And he would be able to confirm that the man whose number had been in the late Gerald Merton's mobile telephone was the arms supplier the New York Police Department had branded long ago as 'the Russian'.

Chapter Three

They never did say welcome home. Tom always imagined they did, or that at least one day they would, but they never did. The immigration officer on the dawn shift at Heathrow had simply glanced down at the passport picture, glanced back up, then nodded him through.

He wasn't to know that this was always an unsettling moment for an Englishman who had made his home in New York since his late twenties. Whenever he returned, Tom felt the same curious mixture: the familiarity of a native and the bemusement of a stranger.

When Tom had left London, it had been in the doldrums of a recession. Now it seemed to crackle with energy. Each time he came back, the skyline was filled with new buildings or cranes putting up new buildings. You only had to look at the shop fronts, the hoardings, the cafés to smell the money.

Tom took the Heathrow Express into town, one thought still preoccupying him: why was the Russian's number on Gerald Merton's mobile phone? The only reasonable explanation seemed to be that Merton had phoned the Russian arms dealer and gone to see him on Monday, just as the Feds said he had. The very thought made Tom smile. It meant that his old friend Henning Munchau might not be in such deep trouble after all. If Tom could prove that the UN had not shot an entirely innocent man, they could put aside the sackcloth and ashes. His debt to Henning would be discharged.

Sure, it was unusual: a suspected terrorist aged seventy-seven. But, hey, these guys were crazy. Why couldn't Gerald Merton have been the first pensioner accelerating his entry to paradise? He might not have been wearing an explosive belt when he was shot, but Tom could argue that Merton's stroll to the UN had been a reconnaissance mission to see what obstacles he would encounter. He was probably planning to return the very next day, strapped into a bomb supplied by the Russian.

Motive was the big problem. What cause could this old man have believed in so passionately that he was ready to wreak havoc in the headquarters of the United Nations? Perhaps he had been promised a cash payment for the family he would leave behind.

At Paddington, Tom took a cab straight to Merton's daughter's address; there was no time to check into the hotel. He needed to see her as soon as possible, before the entire membership of the Amalgamated Union of Lefty Lawyers and America Bashers had descended on her doorstep.

He had imagined her living in a tidy suburban semi, with a husband and a couple of kids. But this was not that kind of area. He was in Clerkenwell, the residential pocket just southeast of the sleaze and grime of King's Cross, where most of the old Georgian houses had been divided into flats.

As the cab turned into her street, he saw immediately which house was hers. People were emerging from a front door with baleful expressions; clearly they'd been making an early-morning condolence call. He paid the driver, jumped out and headed for the open door. From the hallway he could hear voices on the stairs, saying goodbye. He headed up.

For a second, he was confused. In front of him stood a man plus two women in an embrace, one of them sobbing loudly, the other, taller woman offering comfort. Yet he felt certain that this calm, tearless woman was Rebecca, the daughter of Gerald Merton. It was her eyes that confirmed it. They were as striking as those that had stared at him on the mortuary slab in New York.

'Hello,' he said, extending a hand. 'I'm so sorry to come unannounced like this. My name is Tom Byrne and I'm from the United Nations.'

She fixed the extraordinary eyes upon him, then said in a clear and penetrating voice, 'I think you'd better leave.'

Taken aback, it took Tom several seconds to realise that she was not speaking to him, but to her departing guests.

'Call us if you need anything,' said the man, whom Tom guessed was roughly Rebecca's age, in his early thirties. The woman tried to say something, too, but her eyes welled up again and she shook her head in defeat.

Throughout, Tom kept his gaze on Rebecca, who stood tall and straight-backed in this wobbling, sobbing huddle. Everything about her was striking; nothing was moderate. Her hair was a deep black; her nose was strong and somehow proud. Most arresting were those eyes of clearest green: not the same colour as her father's, but with the same shining brilliance. They seemed to burn not with the grief he had been expecting but with something altogether more controlled. He found that he could not look away from her.

'You can come in here,' she said.

He followed her into a cluttered room, which he rapidly tried to interpret. The polished wooden floors, the battered TV in the corner were predictable enough: urban bohemian. The books surprised him. Not the first couple of shelves of fiction, but the rest: they seemed to be medical journals. He took a glance round the flat. No sign yet of another person. No sign of a man.

She sat down in a plain wooden chair, gesturing for him to take the more comfortable couch opposite. He was about to speak when a phone rang—hers, a mobile. She looked at the display and answered it without hesitation.

'Not at all; I said you could call. What's happening?' She began nodding as she received what appeared to be a burst of information. 'She's hypotensive now, you say? Despite good gram-negative coverage? . . . Poor girl, this is the last thing she needs. I'd make sure she's on Vancomycin and let intensive care know she may need pressors. And, Dr Haining? Keep me posted.'

Tom waited for her to close the clamshell phone, then began, his opening line now duly revised. 'Dr Merton, you know why I'm here. I've flown into New York this morning because of a grave mistake.'

'London. You're in London.' She showed him a brief glimpse of a crooked smile. He felt his pulse quicken.

'Sorry. London. Yes.' He tried to collect himself. 'The Secretary-General of the United Nations asked me to convey his personal sorrow and regret at what happened to your father. He speaks for the entire—'

'You can save the speech.' She was staring right at him, her eyes dry. 'I don't want a string of platitudes. I want answers.'

'OK,' he said. He had not planned on this.

'Let's start with this. How on earth could any police force in the world not recognise a seventy-seven-year-old man when it saw one?'

'Well, identification is one of the key issues that—'

'And what the hell happened to shooting in the legs? Even I know that when police want to immobilise a suspect they shoot in the legs.'

'Standard procedure in the case of a suspected suicide bomber is to shoot at the head—'

'Suicide bomber!' She stared at him. 'Have you ever come across a seventy-seven-year-old suicide bomber, Mr Byrne?'

'Look. Perhaps I should walk you through the events of Monday morning, as best we know them.' He was finding it hard to concentrate; every time he looked at this woman, he felt he was being shoved off his stride.

'OK. So my dad's on a little retirement holiday and decides to be a tourist and visit the UN. Then what happened?'

Tom reached into his bag for the sheaf of papers he had brought, the timelines and FBI reports that he and Sherrill had got from Harold Allen so that he would be able to maintain at least the pretence of full disclosure.

'Don't start giving me some presentation, Mr Byrne. I don't want you trying to blind me with science. I'm a doctor, I know that trick.'

'All right.' Tom put the papers back. 'Tell me how we can help.'

'I want an apology.'

'Of course the United Nations feels the deepest—'

'Not from you. From the man at the top. I want a face-to-face meeting with the Secretary-General. I want him to look me in the eye and admit what the United Nations has done. A full apology, in person.'

Tom remembered Henning's sole condition: no grandstanding, no photo ops. 'Look, a tragedy happened yesterday. We know that. And the United Nations wants to show that it recognises the scale of that tragedy. We'd like to make a gesture, to establish a fund available to you for whatever purpose seems appropriate. It could be a memorial—'

'Sorry, I think I misheard you. What did you say?'

'I said that the UN is willing to acknowledge the life of Gerald Merton with a one-off payment.' He immediately regretted *one-off*.

'Christ.' Her full lips slowly coloured a deep red, as if her rage was filling them with blood. 'Do you really think you can buy us off with blood money?'

'I don't underst—'

'You think this is what Jews are like? That we'd let you kill our parents so long as the price is right?'

'I had no idea—'

'That's right. You have no idea at all.'

Her mobile rang again. He was trying to digest what she had just said, but as she stood up, all he could focus on was her shape. She was wearing jeans and a loose black top, but it was clear that she had the figure of a real woman, not like the anorexic dolls he saw in Manhattan.

'Hi, Nick. How's her chest X-ray look? . . . That's not good.' She began nodding, murmuring her assent to the voice on the phone. 'Sounds like she's developing acute respiratory distress syndrome. Tell the parents I'll call them soon. They've been through the wringer; they need to hear a familiar voice. Thanks, Nick.'

He was trying not to stare, but it was an unequal struggle. The intensity of this woman seemed to be burning up all the oxygen in the room.

So Gerald Merton was Jewish. Tom had never even considered it. Everything had thrown him off course: the name, the passport—*Place of birth: Kaunas, Lithuania*—and especially the corpse. Tom Byrne knew what a circumcised penis looked like and Merton's was not it.

She finished the call and turned to him. 'I have to go: there's an emergency at the hospital. Anyway, I don't think we have anything more to talk about, do you?' She turned round and disappeared into the kitchen, where he could hear the jangle of car keys being scooped up.

He began pushing the pile of unused documents back into his case when he saw it: a small, black notebook on a side table. For a moment he thought it must be his own Moleskine, but then he saw it was thicker. It was hers. On impulse, he shoved it into his bag. He would say he'd taken it by mistake; that way he'd have an excuse to come back.

He stood up and followed Rebecca Merton down the stairs and out of her front door. 'Here's my card,' he said, repressing his surprise that she took it. 'If you think of anything more you'd like to discuss, call me.'

She studied it for a moment, then looked back up. 'So you're not even a UN lawyer. You're the guy they brought in to do their dirty work. Goodbye, Mr Byrne. I don't think we'll be seeing each other again.'

TOM WATCHED HER cross the road, get into her old-model Saab and drive off, then stood as if paralysed, trying to work out the effect she had had on him. It wasn't the usual feeling he would often get at a Manhattan party when he spotted some young beauty and lazily decided he wanted her, the way you might pick a delicacy off a menu. This was different. His pulse was elevated and he felt the same palpitating excitement he had felt when he had his first crush at sixteen. For God's sake, he told himself firmly, grow up.

A sudden deep need for coffee prompted him to walk to the top of the street, where there was a small parade of shops. Mercifully, one was a café. He went in, sat at a table and ordered an espresso.

When it arrived, he downed it in two gulps, sat back, closed his eyes and breathed deeply. Only then did he remember the book in his bag. Could it be Rebecca Merton's diary? He knew he shouldn't, but he opened it.

The notebook was filled, page after page, with tiny, neat blue handwriting. Instantly he knew this was not the diary of a thirty-something woman. It had been a mistake to pocket it. But he only had to read the first few sentences to realise that he—and not only he—had made another, graver mistake.

My name is Gershon Matzkin and I was born in a village near Kovno in Lithuania. If you look on a map now, you will see no such place. Today they call it by its Lithuanian name: Kaunas. I was the second of four children of Meir and Rebecca Matzkin. I was different from the others. My sisters had dark hair, their features proud, while I was blond with blue eyes and a small nose. I did not look like a Jew at all.

My father would joke that maybe my mother had been too friendly with the goatherd in the village. He could joke about such things because he knew they were impossible.

I was born too early; they said my life was hanging by a thread. When I was eight days old, the rabbi said I was too weak to have my brit milah, too weak to be circumcised. Afterwards, because of every-thing that happened to our family, it was delayed. Maybe my mother did not want to think about it. And after that it was too late.

Our village did not have many Jews. We kept ourselves quiet, trying to get by. But every now and then there was trouble . . .

Gershon's Diary

I was frightened even before it started. At that age—I was perhaps seven years old—the sound of the rain on the windows was enough to scare me: it sounded like fingers, tapping, demanding to be let in. There was no rain that night, but it was very dark and that scared me, too. My sisters, also, were awake and crying. Local Lithuanians were running through the streets where the Jews lived, shouting, *You killed Christ! Come out, you Christ-killers!*

This happened every now and then, especially at Easter. But there were more voices than usual, and they did not fade as they went past. They remained loud and near. My mother sat on the bed with us—all four of us children shared a single bed back then—telling us to hush. She thought my father was downstairs, peering through a gap in the curtains, watching for the moment when the thugs grew bored and moved on. She was partly right: that was why he had gone downstairs, so that he could look. But then something had caught his eye. He had seen smoke coming from the barn.

We were not farmers, but like most people in our village we kept a few chickens and a cow. And now he thought only that he had to rescue the animals. So he ran into the barn.

I don't know when my mother first realised what had happened but she suddenly called out, 'Meir?' Then she saw the first orange flames. '*Meir!*' When there was no reply, she ran downstairs and fled out of the house towards the barn. I was so frightened that I stopped crying.

We saw her tugging at something, bent double, as if she were dragging a sack of seeds from the barn. In the dark it was almost impossible to see that she was, in fact, pulling at the ankles of a man. My sister Hannah made out the shape first. 'It's Daddy,' she said.

We never knew for certain what had happened. Perhaps the smoke was too much. Maybe one of the thugs had followed him into the barn and beaten him. Whatever had happened, our mother had been too late.

She was never the same person after that. Her hair went grey and she let it fall loose; her clothes were sometimes dirty. She no longer laughed and if she smiled it was a strange, misshapen smile, crooked with regret and sadness.

She decided we could no longer live in that place. She had a cousin who had once lived in Kovno, so we moved there. She felt we needed to be in a big city, a place where we would not stand out. A place where there were not just a few Jews, but thousands of us.

We arrived when I was eight years old, and I have happy memories of our first two years there. My sisters and I went to school, and I discovered that I was good at learning languages. The teacher said I had an ear for it. Russian and, especially, German. I only had to hear a word once to remember it.

In the village, we had followed only the essentials of Jewish tradition, and not even all of those. But in Kovno it was different. Nearly a quarter of the people of this city were Jews, and in the area where I lived, everyone was. There were synagogues on every street, Yiddish schools, Hebrew schools, even a Jewish hospital. There were people to teach me how to say Kaddish for my father. We did not feel like outsiders here, even if I now looked like one.

We lived in two dark rented rooms on Jurbarko Street. I do not know how my mother paid for them. During this time, her eyes were always empty.

And then, one day in 1940, the Russians arrived to make Lithuania part of the Soviet Union.

At school, the teachers seemed nervous. My Russian teacher vanished. Hannah explained to me that the Russians were arresting people. They shut down some of the Jewish buildings because they were against 'the revolution', whatever that was. Some of the men were taken to Siberia.

We were frightened of the Russians, but it was not they who scared us most. We heard there was a resistance movement against the Communists, local Lithuanians determined to kick the Soviets out. They said the Jews were to blame for the Communist occupation. Hannah showed me a leaflet she found in the street. It said: *Without the Jews, we would be a free people!*

'We must not let Mama see this,' Hannah decreed. I was not yet eleven years old and I knew nothing of Communism or occupation, but I understood that my mother was frail. She never did see that leaflet.

A year later, I thought our troubles were over. At school, the headmaster announced that the Russians had gone. They had simply run away. Good, I thought, now the Lithuanians won't be angry with us for bringing the Soviets here. But the headmaster seemed more worried than ever.

This was June 1941. It was only when I heard the boys in my class talking that I understood that the Russians had not just left because they wanted to leave us in peace. They had vanished because they were frightened: the Germans had begun an invasion of the Soviet Union.

The next day I was in the street, playing catch with two other boys, when I heard the sound of faraway whistles and drums. We thought that people were celebrating, a marching band parading through the streets because the Russians had gone. But then there were new sounds: women screaming and children crying. My friends ran off. I stood there on my own for a few seconds before a man grabbed my wrist and told me to get out of the street. 'Go home,' he said. '*Go home now!*' I must have looked dumb and uncomprehending because he stared at me hard. 'Pogrom,' he said. '*Pogrom.*'

I ran as fast as I could back to Jurbarko Street. The screams were getting louder: the Lithuanians were marking the great occasion of the Russian withdrawal the best way they knew how, by attacking any Jew they could find. They were wearing strange uniforms, ones I had never seen before. They were black, with the flag of Lithuania on their sleeves. These jackets were not all identical, like the uniforms of real soldiers. And the men did not march in columns, but rampaged through the streets, shouting slogans: 'The Jews and Communists have brought shame to Lithuania!' They called themselves the Lithuanian Activist Front.

Later we found out that they took dozens of Jews to the Lietūkis garage, in the centre of Kovno. They killed hundreds of men there. Afterwards, I learned from a book that on that night of June 23, 1941, and on the three nights that followed, they killed more than 3,800 Jews.

Just outside the tenement where we lived, I ran into my sisters. Hannah was so relieved to see me that she clutched me in a long, tight hug. She bundled us into the building and up the stairs so that we could warn our mother what was going on. But she already knew.

I understood what had happened when I heard Hannah's cry. So small, as if she were just a little girl, which of course she was. She tried to stop us, my other sisters and me, from seeing it, but I can never forget what I saw.

My mother's feet were in the air, her body dangling from a beam in the ceiling. She was hanging there, swinging like the pendulum in a clock—a clock that said we had reached the end of time.

Tom closed the notebook and looked up. This was a nightmare. Truly, a waking nightmare.

He checked his watch. Too early to call Henning. He imagined what he would tell him. 'I've got good news and bad news. The good news is that the dead guy may not be so innocent after all. The bad news is, you killed a Holocaust survivor.'

PR calamities didn't get much worse than this. Rebecca Merton could simply pop this notebook into an envelope and send it to any newspaper in London. He could see the headline, across a two-page spread: 'MY FATHER'S WARTIME HELL', BY DAUGHTER OF UN SHOOTING VICTIM, complete with full-colour photo of 'raven-haired Rebecca Merton, 31'.

Tom ordered another espresso and went back to the notebook, girding himself for the next revelation.

Gershon's Diary
I remember little about those next few days. We moved around as if in a kind of trance. My sister Hannah the least. She had to be our mother now.

My job was to be the provider of food. I was a child, but I looked older, and with my colouring I could pass for one of the local Lithuanian lads. I would scavenge wherever I could, turning up at a baker's shop just before closing time, my hand out for any scraps. Women would take pity on me. 'Such a sweet face,' they would say, handing me a loaf-end of bread or a hardened rock of old cake. 'Where are your parents?'

'I'm an orphan.'

'What happened to your mum and dad, little one?'

'The Russians.'

'Oh, those evil animals. And here I am giving you a hunk of stale bread. Irena, fetch that meat we have in the back. Come on, quick now. Here you are, young man. Now you be on your way.'

None of us told the truth. If anyone ever came near Hannah, she would say, 'My father will be back soon,' or 'My mother has just popped out'. She did not want people to know there were only children in our two rooms. She must have worried that someone would steal what we had or send us away.

This time, between the Russians and what followed, did not last long. The books say that an advance group of Germans was already there, from the very beginning, even organising the pogroms the night my mother ended her life. But when the Germans arrived in force, we knew it.

I was in the apartment, watching Hannah carve up the crust of bread I had brought. We heard them before we saw them. At first, I thought it was a storm. But the sky outside was bright and clear.

There it was again, the rumble of distant explosions. 'Shhh,' said Hannah, closing her eyes so she could concentrate. 'Aeroplanes,' she said eventually.

Soon there was a different noise. It was the thunder of an army marching into a city. Then the hard, mechanical sounds of motorcycles and infantry and mammoth field guns on wheels and finally tanks, all rolling into Kovno.

I edged towards the window. What I saw confused me. The windows of the building opposite ours, and the one next to it, were opening. Out of them people were unrolling large, billowing pieces of cloth: flags. Girls were leaning out, smiling and waving, throwing flowers at the men below.

We went to school the next day and I knew immediately that even if our Lithuanian neighbours were glad to see the Nazis, we Jews were not. Everyone was tense. The headmaster spoke to the whole school, his face carved with anxiety, and told us that we were being tested.

I'm not sure if it was that day or the next, but very soon notices went up in German. I read the one posted on a lamppost near the school, translating it for the boys in my class. The sign said that from now on all Jews would have to wear a yellow star on their outer clothing, to be visible at all times. And there would be a curfew: after dark, every Jew was to be indoors.

I don't know whether I was scared, even then. If this was all they planned to do to us—make us wear a yellow star and stay home after dark—then it was better than being beaten on the streets by the Lithuanians.

But I could not comfort myself like that for long. A few mornings later, we were woken by a loud banging on the door. I sat bolt upright, and must have been about to say something because Hannah, who was also now sitting up, placed her finger over her lips and glared at me.

The banging on the door started up again, louder and more insistent. We could hear the same noise repeated up and down the corridor and outside on the street: Nazis pounding on the doors of the Jews. Hannah got up, grabbed something to cover her nightclothes and opened the door.

He was tall, his back straight. I couldn't stop staring at his boots. They shone like glass, and when they moved, the leather creaked. 'You have ten minutes to gather everything,' he barked in German. 'You are moving!' He turned and headed for the next door.

When Hannah turned round her face was serious. 'Get dressed. Rivvy and Leah, wear as many skirts as you can, one over the other. Do the same with sweaters. You too, Gershon. As many clothes as you can.'

Then she scurried around the two rooms, shoving whatever she thought essential into suitcases. Finally she removed a picture of my parents from its frame and placed it in her pocket. Then she ushered us to the door and closed it, for the last time. We waddled down the stairs. I was wearing four or five shirts and two coats, as well as carrying our largest suitcase. By the time we reached the street, I thought I might boil with heat.

We saw many Jews like us, trying to carry as much as they could. Many had bags of food. Hannah scolded herself. She had not thought of that.

Within a few minutes, we were ordered to walk. We would be crossing Kaunas, they said, to our new homes. We were surrounded by men with guns and, more frightening to me, dogs. We did as we were told.

A lady began to walk beside us. She said to Hannah, 'I hear they're taking us across the river, to Viriampole. We're all going to have to live there.'

'All of us? But Viriampole is tiny.'

The Jews of Kovno numbered in the tens of thousands. What Hannah did not know then, none of us did, was that Jews from all the surrounding villages would be crammed into those few small streets of Viriampole, too.

The walk was long and hard. I kept shifting the suitcase I was carrying from one hand to the other, but I did not stop. Finally we came to the narrow concrete bridge that marked our crossing into Viriampole.

'Quickly, quickly,' Hannah said, shooing us over. I think she was hoping we would not notice the barbed wire and the watchtowers, or perhaps that I would not have time to translate the German signs that marked the entrance. 'Plague! Entry forbidden!' one said. 'Jews are forbidden from bringing in food and heating supplies—violators will be shot!' said another.

Once we were inside, the soldiers were no longer walking beside us. Now that they had herded us into the ghetto, their job was done. Everyone waited for a few minutes, for instructions. But slowly the penny dropped. One man broke away from the crowd and dashed into the first entrance he saw. He then appeared at a ground-floor window and beckoned the rest of his family to join him. Immediately another family followed, then another and another. It took a second or two for Hannah to understand: this was to be a free-for-all; you lived in whatever corner you could find.

We went to Linkuvos Street with the lady Hannah had been talking to, and her family. Hannah understood even then that there would be times when she would need someone else to keep an eye on us. And so we crammed thirteen people into two rooms, the other family and us.

I LIED ABOUT MY AGE and got a permit to work. I was twelve now but tall enough to pass for sixteen. So each morning I would cross the narrow bridge out of the ghetto in a detail of thirty men. We were given yellow armbands to wear, then loaded onto trucks and driven to Aleksotas, where we were to build the Germans a military airbase. We worked from dawn till dusk, twelve hours or more, until every sinew was screaming for rest. We stopped for only a few minutes, to drink thin soup and eat a crust of bread.

But at least it was food. Hannah, though, was struggling to find enough for the others to eat. That was when she decided that she too would have to get a work permit. If she had one of those precious yellow pieces of paper, she would earn food for herself and our sisters, Leah and Rivvy.

I don't know what she did to get that permit. I like to think she met up with the resistance, who were forging papers all the time. But sometimes I think something else. Because Hannah was a pretty girl, and when you are hungry and your family is hungry, you will do desperate things.

And so Hannah began to leave the ghetto each morning, along with me and the rest of the workers. There were checks at the gate, but the guards were Lithuanian, not German. In fact there were very few Germans in places like Kovno. They relied on the local people to help them.

Then came the cruel day that changed everything. Hannah never told me about it in so many words, but I have pieced together what happened and set it all down here so that the memory of it will not die.

Hannah went through the checkpoint, and worked in the normal way. But at some point she must have broken away from the work detail to steal some bread. Perhaps in the queue at the gate she looked nervous. Something gave her away. Not to the policemen on duty, who were too drunk to notice. But to the son of one of the Lithuanian guards, a boy not much older than me, who often hung around at the gate. We called him the Wolf, because he was as cruel as a beast. His face seemed to shine with evil. That night he asked his father to let him search Hannah.

I can imagine how she trembled as he pushed and prodded at her clothes, feeling at her bony frame. He was about to let her go when he gave one last poke, under her armpits. And it was there he found the lump of bread.

The Wolf turned round to the cheering guards like a novice fisherman who has just reeled in a prize trout. Nodding, he soaked up their applause.

'So what will be your reward, son?' his father said, beaming. 'Name it.'

The Wolf paused while Hannah stood there shivering. The rest of the ghetto inmates stared down at the ground, wanting this moment to be over.

'Let me punish her myself.'

There was a loud, lecherous roar from the guards, and they began chanting a Lithuanian song about a boy becoming a man. The Wolf led Hannah to the ghetto cells, where the jailer recognised him and stepped away.

'Take off your clothes,' the Wolf told Hannah.

Hannah stood still, unable to move.

'I said, take off your clothes, Jew!'

She was cold, her fingers like shards of ice. She did not move fast enough. He punched her in the face. 'I won't tell you again! Take off your clothes!'

Hannah did as she was told, and stood there naked with her head down. She would not have seen the Wolf reach for his truncheon and hold it high before bringing it down onto her arms, her back and thighs. When she fell to her knees, crying out in pain, the Wolf kicked her in the face, in the ribs, in the place she had always cherished as the womb of her future children. Soon she lay prone on the floor, waiting for unconsciousness, or death.

Then it stopped and Hannah let out a brief sigh. But her ordeal was not over. Now she felt two cold hands on her hips, hauling her up from the floor, forcing her into a kneeling position. She heard the unfastening of a zip, and screamed in protest, but he brought his hand down over her mouth, clamping her jaw tight so that she could not bite, and thrust himself inside her.

Her mind left her; it fled to the same place it had gone when she had seen her mother's corpse hanging from the ceiling. She vanished from herself. But then, as his assault endured, she saw, on the ground just a few inches away, a bent and rusty nail.

She reached for it and curled it into her right hand. She did not hesitate. In a single movement, she pushed back, pulling his arm away from her face with one hand and wielding the nail between her fingers of the other.

She found his left arm, the one that had been gagging her, its underside exposed. The nail tore through the cotton of his shirt and scored down the flesh. She had never known such strength and resolve. It made her roar, louder even than the scream he let out as he felt his arm ripped open.

She shook him away, and fled as fast as she could, grabbing her clothes from the floor as she ran. She was three streets away before she noticed that no one was chasing her. Later she told me she believed the Wolf was too ashamed to admit that he had allowed a snivelling Jewess to get the better of him. He would claim the deep gash in his arm was the result of an accident.

After that, Hannah could not be our mother any more. She would stay all day and all night in our small room. I kept on working, bringing back what food I could, deciding at the gate whether I could risk bringing it in. If the guards were drunk, I would try it. If the Wolf was anywhere near, I would pass what I had hidden to someone braver, or more foolish, than me.

Then, in late October 1941, all inhabitants of the ghetto were ordered to gather at six o'clock the next morning at Demokratu Square. I was the one who took charge, collecting a few scraps of food, ensuring the girls wrapped up warm. We left our doors unlocked. Those were the orders: so that no one would try to hide.

A light dusting of snow lay on the ground that morning. We waited in the damp cold for three hours. Then an SS sergeant stepped on top of a mound and nodded for the first column of people to be brought before him. I noticed there were machine-gun nests all around the square. On the hillsides stood local Lithuanians, getting a good view of proceedings.

With the tiniest movement of his hand, the sergeant would send some people to the left, some to the right. My sisters and I were near the front of the queue. We picked up Hannah and stepped forward. The sergeant made a parting gesture: he wanted the girls to go to the right and me to the left. I protested that we had to stay together. 'As you wish—to the right!' he barked, with what I thought was a smile.

And then I felt a hand grip my shoulder. 'Not you,' a man's voice said.

I turned round to see a policeman. Not a German or a Lithuanian, but one of the Jewish policemen who worked in the ghetto.

I tried to wriggle away from him and join my sisters, who were now being shoved ahead. Rivvy was reaching out for me. Leah began to cry.

The policeman held me back. 'Not you,' he said again.

I began to cry out, pushing and punching at him, but he would not let me go, no matter how much I struggled. My sisters were disappearing deeper into the scrum of people moving to the right. The last thing I saw were Hannah's eyes, vacant and staring.

The policeman finally pulled me off and frogmarched me away, down a side alley, until we were gone from the square altogether. Then he left me there, alone in the silent street.

I WALKED BACK to Linkuvos Street, past buildings that were now empty and still. I felt as if I were the last child on earth. Four thousand people had gone that day. Everyone else was either outside the ghetto, doing forced labour, or they were hiding. I was twelve years old and I was all alone. I felt jealous of my sisters, imagining them living somewhere new.

I carried on working, still pretending I was sixteen. And I lived in the same room, though I shared it with a different family. The other lady and her children had been on the convoy with my sisters. Nobody I knew was around. My school friends were all gone. The only familiar face belonged to the policeman who had stopped me getting on the convoy, that pig of a traitor.

Then one night there was an urgent knock on the door. The woman in the apartment looked terrified. Believing it was the Gestapo, she glared at me in terror. What misfortune had I brought down on them?

Then we heard the voice on the other side of the door. 'Polizei, open up!'

It was the Jewish police of the ghetto. Before I could make a plan, the woman had opened the door, and there he was, the policeman who had pulled me off the convoy some three weeks before.

'You, boy, come now,' he said.

I was frozen with fear. I did not move.

'NOW!'

I was still wearing all the clothes I had. You did not dare take them off at night because they might be stolen. I let the policeman lead me away.

He marched me downstairs and into the street, loudly promising to take me to the authorities for what I had done. I did not know what I had done. Eventually, he led me into an alley, then down some steps to the entrance of a cellar. This, I knew, was not the police headquarters. I felt my stomach tighten.

The policeman knocked on the door: three quick knocks, two slow ones.

'*Wer geht dort?*' came a voice on the other side. Who goes there?

'*Eine Sohn die Macabi.*' A son of the Maccabees.

The door creaked open and the policeman darted in, pulling me with him. Inside were three other men, their faces lit by a single candle on a small table. They stared at me. I thought they looked old, their eyes sunken, their faces gaunt. But now I know they were young, one of them barely twenty.

Finally, the one who seemed to be the leader said, 'It's a miracle.'

Then another nodded and said, 'He's perfect. Our secret weapon.'

The leader spoke again, his face harsh. 'Take off your trousers.'

I hesitated, but I realised I had no choice. I lowered my trousers slowly.

'All the way down! So we can see.'

And once they had seen, the three men all gave a small smile. One even managed a brief laugh. 'Well done, Shimon,' they said, and the policeman nodded proudly. 'You have truly brought us a Jewish miracle.'

I had heard about the Jewish underground, about a resistance that was coming, but we had seen no sign of it. I believed it was a fairy tale. Now, though, I understood where I had been taken. The policeman, Shimon, had called himself a 'son of the Maccabees'; that had been the password. I knew that the Maccabees had been great Jewish fighters.

I was blond-haired, blue-eyed and uncircumcised. I could pass for an Aryan. Perhaps they would use me to smuggle food into the ghetto. I was excited; I knew I could do it.

But then the leader sent Shimon away and began whispering in Yiddish with the other men, seemingly oblivious to the fact that I was still there.

Finally, he raised his hand, as if the discussion were over. He turned to me and told me his name was Aron. 'Are you brave?' he asked.

'Yes,' I said.

'Are you brave enough to perform a task that carries with it a grave risk?'

'Yes,' I said, though of course I had no idea of such things.

'I am going to give you a task on behalf of your people. You are to travel to Warsaw, to an address I will give you, with a message. Are you ready?'

I nodded, though I was not ready.

'You will say these words, "Aunt Esther has returned and is at Megilla Street 7, apartment 4." Do not change the words, not even one.'

'But I don't understand—'

'It's better you don't understand. Better for you.' He meant that if I were tortured I would have nothing to reveal. 'Now repeat it back to me.'

'Aunt Esther has returned and is at Megilla Street 7, apartment 4.'

'OK.'

Shimon came back into the room and led me away. Standing in the alley outside, he went over the plan in detail.

The next morning I left the ghetto with my work company as always. Except this time that same Jewish policeman was on duty at the gate, to ensure there was no trouble as I peeled away from the others.

A few seconds after I had crossed the bridge over the river, I did as I had been told. I removed the yellow star from my coat and walked towards the station. I held my head high, just as I had been told.

When I reached the railway station, a small group of guards was standing outside, with a man in an SS uniform supervising them. I spoke in Lithuanian. 'My name is Vitatis Olekas,' I said, 'and I am an orphan.' I asked for permission to travel to Poland, where I had family to look after me.

As Shimon had predicted, the SS officer took charge. He circled me, assessing me, as if I were a specimen that had been placed before him.

Finally, I felt a tug on the waistband of my trousers. '*Runter!*' he said. Down. I looked round and saw that he was gesturing at my trousers.

'He wants to see you,' said one of the Lithuanian men, a smirk on his face.

I looked puzzled, as Shimon had said I should.

The officer barked, 'Come on, come on.'

Hesitantly, I lowered my trousers and my underpants. The SS officer eyed my foreskin, then waved me away.

So began my journey, a twelve-year-old boy armed with the right Aryan identity papers and a travel document for Warsaw. I showed my *Kennkarte* to Nazi border guards in Marijampolé and Suwalki and Bialystok, over and over again. The *Kennkarte* made everything possible. It was not a forgery, but the real thing. No document was more precious.

Finally I pulled into Warsaw. It was midday and the place was bustling, but no one was going where I was going. My destination was the ghetto.

I dug into the hole I had made in the lining of my coat, the place where I had hidden my yellow star, and pinned it back on. I waited for a group of workers to return, and I tagged along. Shimon had promised that workers had to show papers only when they went out, not when they came back in.

I walked along streets as crammed and filthy as the ones I had left behind, and found the house I was looking for. I told them who I had a message for.

'Tell us and we'll tell him,' they said.

'I can't,' I said. 'I have to give the message to him alone.' And so I waited.

It was only after the war that I discovered what had prompted my mission, why those three men in the candlelit cellar sent me away that night. It was a response to something that had happened three days earlier.

Some Jews working outside the ghetto had seen a young girl, barely clothed, her eyes wild and staring. She was covered in dirt and smeared with blood, and her face twitched and shook. They brought her back to the ghetto, and eventually she began to speak, though the words came slowly.

She had been one of those sent to the right at Demokratu Square, along with my sisters. The selection had gone on all day, until there were 10,000 of them. Then they were pushed through a hole in the fence into an area known as the 'small ghetto'. At dawn the next morning, Lithuanian militia-men herded the Jews into a column and ordered them to march. They were to make the four-kilometre trek to the Ninth Fort, an old encampment built in Tsarist times to keep the Germans out.

It was an uphill walk and many of the aged and the sick fell by the wayside, sometimes helped to their deaths by the rifle-butt of one of the militiamen. The Nazis had a name for this route. They called it *Der Weg zur Himmelfahrt*. The Way to the Heavenly Journey.

The Jews did not arrive till noon. Once they had got there, the Lithuanian thugs grabbed all their jewellery, then ordered them to strip naked. Only then did they lead them to the pits.

These were vast craters dug into the earth, perhaps a hundred metres long, three metres wide and two metres deep. Each was surrounded on three sides by small mountains of earth, freshly dug. On the fourth side was a raised wooden platform, where the SS men stood with their guns.

Those who had survived the march now began to scream; they under-stood where this heavenly journey had led them. Some tried to escape but they were shot instantly. And so the killing began.

First the Nazis tossed the children into the pit, then the waiting machine-gunners opened fire. The women were lined up at the edge of the crater and shot in the back, so that they would fall in on top of the children. The men were last. They killed them in batches of 300, with no guarantee that one batch was finished when work began on the next. Ammunition was rationed, so they could not afford more than one bullet to the back per victim. And most of the gunmen were drunk. The result was that many Jews were not dead when they fell; they were buried alive. Those who saw it told of how the pit moved for three days, how it breathed.

This is the event they call the 'great action' of October 28, 1941, when 10,000 Jews were driven out of the Kovno ghetto and put to death.

And this is how my sisters were killed.

The girl who had found her way back to the ghetto covered in dirt and smeared with blood was one of those who had been buried but not shot. She had passed out as she fell, but had woken to find corpses all around her, above and below. Others who managed to haul themselves out were spotted and shot, but this girl was cautious. She had waited till the middle of the night, when the drunken singing of the Nazi gunmen had faded into sleep. And so she had escaped.

This was the story she told once she was clothed and fed and could speak. And this was the story that had reached the leaders of the Jewish underground in Kovno, those men in the cellar. Perhaps for the first time they understood what kind of threat they faced. They had decided they must spread the word to those who were also trying to fight back.

And so, many years later, I came to understand the meaning of the message I had carried. I waited for three hours for the man I was to give it to. He was the leader of the underground in the Warsaw ghetto.

When I said the words 'Aunt Esther has returned and is at Megilla Street 7, apartment 4', he looked bemused. But then he asked for someone to bring him a book, a holy book rescued from the ruins of a synagogue in the ghetto. It was the Book of Esther, which Jews call the Megilla of Esther. It is the book we read for the festival of Purim, which commemorates a plot many hundreds of years ago to destroy the Jews.

This leader of the underground turned to Chapter 7, Verse 4, and then he understood everything. He read it out loud: '"For I and my people are sold to be exterminated, slain and lost; but if we were only being sold as slaves and maidservants, I would have stayed silent."'

AS HE READ Gerald Merton's life story, Tom realised that the bind from which he was meant to extricate the UN was getting tighter. The man they had killed was not only a survivor of the Holocaust but one of its heroes: the young boy who had carried word of the Nazi plan to exterminate the Jews.

His phone rang, a New York number.

'Tom? It's Jay Sherrill. I have some news. That New York number we saw on the cellphone? Belongs to the Russian, to the arms dealer.'

'Really? Wow.'

'I know. Incredible, isn't it? That's not all. Overnight I had a team do a deep search of Merton's hotel room. They found something hidden in a wall cavity in the bathroom, by the extractor fan. Very professionally concealed. It's a state-of-the-art, plastic-build revolver, designed to escape detection by security scanners. Russian, .357 Magnum calibre. All you have to conceal are the steel inserts and the bullets; the gun frame itself gets through unnoticed. Apparently it's the weapon of choice in the assassin community.' Tom could hear Sherrill's amusement at his own joke.

'Hold on, Detective.' There was the beep of a call waiting. Tom looked at the display: a London number he didn't recognise. He put Sherrill on hold and took the new call.

'Tom Byrne? It's Rebecca Merton. You need to come here right now. Do you hear me? *Right now!*'

Chapter Four

'I want to go to the funeral.'

'I can see the case for that, Secretary-General,' said Munchau.

'So you think it's a good idea? I'm glad. My political staff say it would be an admission of liability. That is why I was so keen to see you. If you see no legal problem, then we can go ahead. You're the boss.' At that, the Secretary-General dipped his head in a small, courtly nod.

The *Time* magazine profile had been right: 'The world's top diplomat has world-class charm.' Once Asia and Africa had had their turn at the top UN post, the long-standing foreign minister of Finland became the obvious choice. To everyone's surprise, Paavo Viren had glided into the job unopposed.

'Well, sir. There is no legally meaningful admission implied by your visiting the family. But such a move will inevitably be seen as an act of contrition. Secretaries-General ordinarily attend only the funerals of heads of government or heads of state. Your going to London would be such an extraordinary gesture, it would imply we had something to apologise for.'

'Well, we do.'

Henning Munchau smiled tolerantly. 'That's not something we would want to say publicly at this stage, sir. Not until we have all the facts.'

'We killed an innocent man!'

'But, sir, the UN guard did not know that at the time. He seems to have believed the man posed an immediate threat to the life of our personnel.'

'OK, so it was a genuine mistake, but we apologise for it.' The boss sat back. 'Look, I'm not naive. I see the risks. But you're not thinking politically.

If I'm photographed with the widow, or daughter or whoever it is, showing humility, that makes me look good. Transparent, honest, human. A new approach from the new man at the UN. This could be wonderful PR.'

Over my dead body, thought Henning. 'Sir, let me speak with my man in London. If he's managed to square it with the family, then your idea could be a very good one. I'll get in touch with him right away.'

THE FRONT DOOR was open, just as it had been earlier, but this time there were no other voices. Tom reached the landing where he had first met Rebecca Merton three hours earlier. Now, as she surveyed the wreckage of her apartment, all he could see was her back.

The floor was covered with books, their pages flung open, their bindings ripped; every shelf had been emptied. On the wall hung frames denuded of pictures; canvases lay torn among broken glass. The sofa had been slashed, its stuffing bursting out like unkempt hair. Even the plants had been shaken from their pots. Tom had never seen a place so comprehensively trashed.

Suddenly she wheeled round, her eyes ablaze. 'Well, this bloody confirms it. Did you watch them do it, then? Did you stand and watch?'

'What the hell are you talking about?'

'I'm talking about the fact that my home happens to have been smashed up straight after you came here. And five minutes after I call you, you're back. Were you waiting on the corner, making sure they did a good job?'

'Are you mad? This had nothing to do with me.'

'It's a bit of a coincidence, isn't it? First the UN kills my father and the next day my flat is wrecked.'

'You think the *UN* did this?'

'What were you looking for? Dirt?' There was a hint of the crooked smile. 'Is that why you sent the boys in? To see what discrediting filth you could dig up, in case I dared to demand justice from the organisation that killed my father? Jesus, and this is the holier-than-thou United Nations.'

'You think the UN goes round smashing up people's houses? Aren't we in enough trouble with the Merton family without this?' He gestured at the debris. 'Besides, the UN doesn't have the people to do burglaries in EC1.'

She looked at him hard, scrutinising his face. Then she seemed to remember something and sprinted upstairs. Seeing his chance, Tom reached into his briefcase and pulled out Gershon Matzkin's notebook, ready to throw it onto the pile in the centre of the room. But something stopped him. He wanted to be straight with her. He put the book back.

A few seconds later, she was back, brushing past him into the kitchen, and he caught the musky smell of her. The arousal was instant. He felt as if his powers of reason were shrinking, the space filled by a growing desire.

She returned, and he followed her on her tour of devastation. What on earth had happened here? It would have been rapid; they had barely been gone an hour. And the superficial items of value—TV set, stereo—were still in place. This wasn't the work of crackheads out to make fifty quid.

Rebecca was searching, clearly panicked that some precious object had been stolen. She went back up the short flight of stairs, past a bedroom, to a study. There were box files on the floor, their contents scattered.

She stood still for a while, then turned to Tom. 'If you're behind this in any way, I will drive to the nearest newspaper office and give them the story that will ruin the reputation of the UN—and you. Do you understand me? After that, I'll make sure you're prosecuted for murder and robbery.' She shook her head in disbelief. 'No wonder you wanted to cut a deal.'

'Just calm down. If anyone should be trying to cut a deal here, it's you.'

'What the hell is that supposed to mean?'

'It means that there are a few things for you to explain, too.'

'Like what?'

'Like the fact that the number of a known arms dealer was on your father's cellphone. Like the fact that a gun favoured by assassins and hitmen was hidden in his hotel room.'

Something passed across Rebecca Merton's face, but it was so brief, so fleeting, that Tom couldn't catch it. Was it doubt or shock or panic?

The pair of them stood facing each other, saying nothing. Finally, she sighed heavily. 'Listen. I think you need to know the truth about my father.'

At last, thought Tom.

'There's something you need to read, but I can't—'

'Is this it?' Tom produced Gershon Matzkin's journal from his case.

'Oh, thank God.' She grabbed the book and clutched it to her chest. Then her eyes opened into a wide stare. 'Where did you get this?'

'It was a mistake. I thought it was mine.' He took out his own, near-identical notebook and held it up. 'I was going to come and give it back to you.'

She looked at him hard, her gaze powerful enough to make his muscles weaken. 'I don't know whether I can believe a word you say.'

There was silence before she spoke again. 'Did you read it?'

He hesitated. 'Bits.'

'Well, I'd like you to read it properly.' She placed the book in his hands.

Tom went back downstairs. He could hear the scraping and banging of furniture being moved and objects being returned to their rightful places above him. He wondered if Rebecca's plan had been to keep this book, this story, a secret. Had it taken his mentioning of the concealed weapon, the assassin's gun, to make her feel the need to exonerate her dead father?

He flicked through the pages, finding the place he had reached when Sherrill phoned.

I carried the same message to ghetto after ghetto: 'Aunt Esther has returned'. Everyone understood what it meant, that we Jews did not face mere slavery or a random death here and there, but a plan of complete extermination. My job was to tell the Jews of Europe that the Nazis wanted there to be no more Jews in Europe . . .

Tom scanned the next few pages for anything that might shed light on the circumstances of Merton's death.

I somehow found my way back to the forests outside Kaunas. I met up with the handful of resistance fighters who had survived, and we did what we could, blowing up a bridge here, derailing a train there. We killed the enemy in ones and twos. On a very good day, tens . . .

It was in the forest that I met my Rosa. She was older than me, but I was an old man, no matter my age. To be a Jew in Europe in those years was to be old in the world . . .

Rosa had met someone who survived the Ninth Fort. They said that the Nazis had not even needed to press-gang the local Lithuanian boys to take part in the mass killings; they had volunteered eagerly, including, of course, the Wolf. They all wanted to take a turn, firing bullets into the backs of naked Jews.

There was a space on the page, as if to denote the passage of time. Good, thought Tom: after the war.

Those of us who had survived were the only ones who understood each other. We saw the same darkness in each other's eyes. We wandered across Europe, looking for each other. Those of us who could not forget what we had seen. Those of us who were determined to—

The facing page was blank. Tom turned it, only for it to fall out in his hand. As he wedged the page back in, he noticed that the next page and the one after that also came loose. As he examined the book's binding, he remembered the same problem with his childhood exercise books: tear out one page from the front and a corresponding page from the back would become loose. To be sure, he followed the page he was reading, to see if its other half was intact. It wasn't. Indeed, each of the last five or six sheets was ragged along its edge. Several pages of this notebook had been ripped out.

'HAS IT HAPPENED?' his boss asked, in that trademark baritone.

'Yes. They sent people in a couple of hours ago. It's done.'

'Did they find anything?'

'So far, nothing. They took some papers, a computer with a few files, which they're examining. But, so far, none of it seems to relate to the, er . . .' As he struggled to find the words, he wished his boss had kept him out of this operation. If they were back home, he'd have relied on his chief of staff, who'd been with him since the beginning. But here in New York the only one the boss trusted to get this done was him. The aide finished his sentence. 'They have no bearing on this issue.'

'Damn,' the boss said quietly. 'I thought this had gone away decades ago. I mean it, decades ago. Even in death, he's come back to haunt me. Gershon Matzkin, the man who comes back from the dead.'

TOM WENT INTO THE KITCHEN, sidestepping the shattered crockery on the floor, and put the kettle on. Eleven years in the States had not muted his appreciation of the value of a cup of tea in moments of crisis.

He was looking for an unbroken mug when his cellphone rang. Henning. Tom glanced up at the ceiling. Too near: Rebecca would hear everything. He headed downstairs, rolling a cigarette—an excuse to stand on the pavement outside—and answered. 'Hi, Henning.'

'Too early to ask what you got?'

'I've got good news and bad news.'

'Bad news first, please; I like to have something to look forward to.'

'Bad news is, Gerald Merton was a Holocaust survivor.'

'Good God.'

'A hero, in fact. As a boy he travelled under cover across occupied Europe, going from ghetto to ghetto, warning the Jews what was about to happen.'

'I think I need to hear the good news now.'

Tom was watching a man across the street, also talking into his phone. Was there something odd about the way he was pacing?

'Merton may not have been just an elderly tourist,' he went on. 'He had a gun concealed in his hotel room. A polymer-framed revolver, designed to escape detection. Seems he got it from a Russian arms dealer in New York.'

'You want me to claim we didn't make a mistake? We got the right guy?'

'I think it could fly,' said Tom.

'No way. Not with his history. Court of public opinion, mate. That's where we'd lose this case before we'd said a bloody word. The gun's circumstantial. What's the link with the arms dealer?'

'His number was on Merton's phone.'

'Also circumstantial. Back to Plan A, Tom: pay the daughter whatever she wants and come back home.'

'She's rejected that out of hand. Says it's blood money. She wants an apology from the SG, in person. Which I've obviously declined.'

Henning let out a sigh. 'Can't you turn on the legendary Byrne charm? I've never known a woman refuse you anything.'

'Somehow I don't think that's going to work.' Tom heard the slight wobble in his own voice. 'She's not like that. She's very, I don't know, unusual—'

'Don't tell me you've gone and fallen for the grieving daughter.'

'Seriously, Henning. I need to work out why Merton was in New York. I'm trying to do what's best for the UN. If he was up to no good, we can see off any legal claim against us. The UN would be completely in the clear.'

'All right, then. Do what you have to do. But I stress: my overwhelming preference is that you close this thing down. It's the bloody General Assembly this week, remember. I don't have time for another headache.'

Tom went back inside and returned to making tea. Carefully he carried the two warm mugs upstairs. In the doorway he watched Rebecca replacing chipped and broken picture frames onto the shelf.

'You should leave that,' he said as gently as he could. 'For the police.'

'I'm not going to call the police.'

He tried to hide his relief. The last thing he needed was for this to become public knowledge, with a thousand online conspiracy nutcases jumping to the same conclusion as Rebecca: that the UN was behind this break-in. 'Why not?'

She looked right at him, the green clarity of her irises so bright it was hard not to look away. 'In the last twenty-four hours,' she said quietly, 'I've discovered that my father has been shot down in cold blood. My home has been burgled and I've surrendered my father's life story— which I've spent my life guarding—because it was clearly the only way to persuade you that my father was not a terrorist.' The volume was louder now, the face redder. 'Do you think I can cope with yet more people traipsing all over my home, asking me more questions and more questions and *more fucking questions*!'

'Listen, Rebecca—'

'No, you listen to me. You wanted to cut a deal, so let's cut a deal.'

'I'm listening.'

'I want to find out the truth of what happened to my father in New York and what it has to do with all this.' She gestured at the detritus of the room. 'I can't do that alone. But you're a lawyer; you've got the UN behind you. You know how these things work. I want you to help me.'

'Deal,' he said. 'But no police means we'll have to do this ourselves. We have to start at the beginning. Can you see anything missing?'

They looked around, surveying afresh a room in which every item had been either displaced or smashed. She caught his eye, and the hint of that wonky smile appeared around her lips. He smiled back. The absurdity of his question now hung in the air, and at last she released a laugh, a laugh powered by tension and grief coiled up for too long.

The sound coming from her changed. He could see a tear falling down her cheek. He stepped forward, hesitated, then put his hand on her arm and drew her towards him. She let her head rest for a moment on his chest.

But then, just as suddenly, she sprang back, dabbed her eyes and signalled that the moment had vanished. 'Let's get on with it.'

She started methodically, in the far left corner of the room, picking up books not to replace them but to divine a pattern. Tom watched her, noting the concentration on her face. After a few minutes, she walked over to the desk. She tugged at one of the drawers and it moved easily.

She looked up. 'The lock's been broken,' she said.

'What was in there?'

'My father's papers—legal documents, bank details, things he wanted me to look after. In case . . .'

Tom was about to mention the missing pages from the notebook when he saw something that made him start: two words, filling a sheet of A4, pinned to the corkboard above the desk. Though clearly scribbled in haste, they were in the same hand as the notebook he had read that afternoon. The message read simply: *Remember Kadish*.

'What's this? Was it here before?'

Rebecca glanced up and for a moment looked startled. 'Oh, yes, it was here before,' she replied. 'It's something my father wrote a while ago. He's reminding me to say the memorial prayer for my mother.'

'For your mother?'

'Yes. She died six years ago. My father was always very insistent that we do the prayers on the anniversary of her death.'

No wonder she had looked so shaken: that piece of paper must have looked like a message from the grave, her father pleading to be remembered.

Luckily, she didn't hear the dull vibration of Tom's silenced BlackBerry, tucked inside his jacket pocket. He waited till she had turned back to the bookshelves before pulling the device out and reading the message from Jay Sherrill. It consisted of a single line: *Prints on gun match Merton's.*

'THANKS FOR SEEING ME, Commissioner.'

'No need to thank me. I asked you to report direct to this office. So what you got, Sherrill?'

'Well, some of our early findings shed doubt on our basic assumption that Gerald Merton's death was a tragic case of mistaken identity.'

'Do they indeed?'

'Yes, sir, they do. The first alert Intel Division had was a meet-up at the premises of an arms dealer—'

'The Russian.'

'Yes. His phone number appears on the cellphone of Gerald Merton. Second, an overnight search of the deceased's hotel room has produced a weapon, a polymer-framed revolver, with steel inserts, Russian-made.'

'Hitman's friend.'

'Precisely, sir. It was secreted in Merton's hotel room. And third, the gun has his fingerprints on it, sir. All over it.'

Riley sat back in his chair, testing its recline mechanism to the full. 'That's fascinatin', Sherrill. Anyone else in NYPD know about this?'

'No, sir. You asked that I report only to you.'

'Good work, Sherrill. Let's keep it that way.' He let his seat spring forward. 'How'd your interview with Watch Commander Touré go?'

Sherrill hadn't expected this. The Watch Commander's testimony had been nothing compared to what Sherrill had found on Merton. Why had the Commissioner not reacted to what was clearly the biggest news here?

'Watch Commander Touré reported that a phone call had come to him from his liaison at the NYPD, suggesting a heightened state of vigilance in respect of a man wearing a dark black coat, woollen hat and—'

'And when'd this come through?'

'At approximately eight forty-nine a.m., sir.'

'And when was the shooting?'

'Eight fifty-one a.m., sir. Two minutes later.'

'And what does that tell us, Detective?'

'Well, it could be a coincid—'

'No coincidences in police work, Mr Sherrill. It tells us there was *live* intelligence, that's what it tells us.'

'You mean that someone saw the suspect approaching the building?'

'That's exactly what I mean. Now, what was the precise wording of the message received by the Watch Commander at the UN?'

Jay Sherrill turned back to his notebook. 'It was an urgent warning, sir. Urging the UN to be on the lookout for a possible terror suspect.'

'Urgent, you say. Almost as if they knew he was on his way.'

'But that makes no sense. Anybody who actually *saw* Merton would have seen that he was an old man. The opposite of a terror suspect.'

'You'd think so, wouldn't you, Mr Sherrill?' Riley was enjoying himself.

'What do you want me to do, Commissioner?'

'An excellent question, Detective. I want you to find out who fed that urgent advisory to Watch Command and on what basis. Because a crucial mistake was made, a mistake that led that unlucky Belgian policeman—'

'Portuguese.'

'Whatever. It led an unlucky, terrified cop to make a fatal error. We need to find the *precise* source of that original error. I want to know which part of the law-enforcement apparatus of this city—'

'But it may not have been a mistake, sir. The gun, the fingerprints—'

Riley held up his right palm, in a gesture of hush. 'All in good time, Mr Sherrill. All in good time.'

NOW WAS NOT the time to tell Rebecca what Sherrill's text had said. Tom didn't want to break the mood that had been established by his sighting of the message on the notice board, the plea for the remembrance of a dead mother.

'Your mother, was she the girl I read about in your father's book?' he asked. 'Rosa?' It was the first chance he'd had to speak about what he'd read.

'Oh, no.' She smiled, the warmth of it moving across the table and spreading through him. 'I never met Rosa. She and my father did stay together after the war. Then she came here with him, to England.'

'But?'

'But I'm not sure they loved each other in a normal way. They clung to each other. They needed each other.'

An image floated before Tom's eyes: two teenage children who had witnessed the gravest horror. He pictured young bodies and old faces.

'She died in 1966. My father grieved, but he was not a man who could be alone. A few years later, he met a woman in London. They married and a few years after that they had me. He was forty-five.'

'Did that make a difference, having a dad who was a bit older?'

'Not as much as having a dad who survived the Holocaust.'

Tom nodded.

'Besides,' she went on, 'he was always really fit. Took great care of himself. He swam, he ran, he used to lift weights.'

I saw that for myself, Tom thought. 'Did the experience of the Holocaust leave a physical mark on him of any kind?' he asked.

'Well, he didn't have a number on his arm, if that's what you're asking. He was never in Auschwitz, or in any death camp.' She paused. 'But he was missing three toes from his left foot. He lost them to frostbite in the forests, when he was fighting with the partisans.'

'And did that affect him? Missing those toes?'

'Not really. He walked with a slight limp.'

There was no point hinting at it. He would have to ask directly. 'I'm told that your father was found with some kind of metal plate on his leg, taped to his shin. Why might that be?'

She looked at Tom again, her gaze lingering. 'I saw my father regularly, and I can tell you he had nothing wrong with his leg. You must be mistaken.'

Tom wouldn't push it. He would just file the metal shin-pad among the ever-lengthening list of mysteries attached to this case.

'And what about you?' she said. 'Do you have family here?'

'I have a mother in Sheffield. My father's dead.'

The phone rang, the land line this time: another condolence call. Rebecca took the cordless phone and headed out into the hall.

While she was gone, Tom surveyed the damaged kitchen. Who had turned the place over with such brutal efficiency? What had they been looking for?

He looked up to see her, breathless, in the kitchen doorway.

'I just saw this downstairs, on the doormat.' She was holding up a large white envelope. 'Hand-delivered.'

She passed it over, sitting herself on the bench next to him, so close their thighs touched. Inside the envelope were two sheets of paper, almost furry with age, held together by a single staple. Each of them bore the distinct print of a manual typewriter. The first page featured only a list of names, no title or explanatory heading, apparently arranged alphabetically:

Wilhelm Albert
Wilhelm Altenloch
Hans Bothmann
Hans Geschke
Paul Giesler
Odilo Globocnik
Richard Glücks
Albert Hohlfelder
Friedrich Wilhelm Krüger
Kurt Mussfeld
Adalbert Neubauer
Karl Puetz
Christian Wirth

Each name had been neatly crossed out by two inked lines forming an X. Tom turned to the next page. The names were not sorted alphabetically:

Hans Groetner
Hans Stuckart
Joschka Dorfman
Otto Abetz
Theo Dannecker
Karl-Friedrich Simon
Fritz Kramer
Jacob Sprenger
Georg Puetz
Herbert Cukors
Alexander Laak

They too had all been crossed out, though this time less neatly and in strokes that were not uniform, not even in the same colour of ink. It seemed as if the first list had been marked in one sitting, the second at different times.

Other than that, the document in his hand gave no clues. Yet Tom felt sure that this list would explain the mystery of Gershon Matzkin.

'This is all that came?' he asked. 'No note?'

'That's it. Nothing else.'

Tom went to the window, looking for the man he had seen before. No sign. He began to pace. 'Do any of those names look familiar to you?' he asked.

She looked unsure. 'No.'

'Might they be friends of your father's, business associates?'

'My father owned a dry-cleaning shop in Stoke Newington.'

'Right. So not much in the way of business associates, then.' He attempted a smile. 'Could any of them be relatives, distant family members?'

'I'm telling you, I don't recognise any of them.'

Tom looked back at the list. A hunch was beginning to form.

Her computer was gone, but the cables and modem were still in place. He took out and connected his own laptop and Googled the first name. An entry on Wilhelm Albert, Fifth Duke of Urach, born in 1957, appeared: not what he was expecting. He tried the second name. Wilhelm Altenloch was a major in the Nazi SS in Bialystok. He looked up at Rebecca, standing at his shoulder.

Hans Bothmann was identified as the Kommandant of the Chelmno death camp, where he had directed mass killing operations from spring 1942 to March 1943. Google drew a blank on Hans Geschke, but Paul Giesler had a Wikipedia entry all of his own. He was an early recruit to National Socialism, signing up to Hitler's fledgling movement in 1924, rising to be Gauleiter of Westphalia South and, by 1942, Munich and Upper Bavaria. His claim to fame was the supervision of the Dachau concentration camp.

Rebecca leaned forward to get a closer look at the screen, a loose curl of her hair brushing Tom's face.

Odilo Globocnik had an entry too, one befitting a senior SS apparatchik, credited with overseeing the Einsatzgruppen, the mobile killing units who massacred Jews throughout Poland from 1942 to 1943.

The pattern grew clearer with each entry. SS Colonel Albert Hohlfelder, decorated for his work sterilising Jews through mass exposure to X-rays. SS Lieutenant General Dr Friedrich Wilhelm Krüger, member of the planning staff responsible for the liquidation of the Jewish ghettos of Poland. SS Lieutenant Kurt Mussfeld, supervisor of Auschwitz crematorium number two in 1944. Christian Wirth, assistant to Globocnik, and responsible for implementing the T-4 euthanasia project, in which disabled people were gassed or killed by lethal injection in state-of-the-art, industrialised factories of death.

'So we have a list of big-time Nazis,' Tom said finally, pushing his chair back from the desk. 'Can you think of any reason why anyone would want to hand-deliver this to you? Anonymously?'

Her eyes were aflame with something Tom could not quite interpret. Was it grief, anger or fear? Tom could have looked and looked into those eyes without ever being certain.

'I have no idea what any of this means, Tom,' she said, shaking her head. 'But I know someone who might.'

Chapter Five

Rebecca drove them through a northeast London landscape that would
have been utterly alien to the Tom Byrne who grew up in Sheffield
more than three decades earlier. A single, endless street seemed to
pass not through neighbourhoods so much as entire continents. Turkish
newsagents and kebab sellers gave way to clusters of Vietnamese restaurants, which in turn were replaced by Polish delicatessens, then shop fronts
promising Internet access and cheap calls to Nigeria and Sierra Leone.

His expression must have been obvious, because Rebecca said, 'I see this
is your first visit to the Kingsland High Street.'

They parked the car, and Rebecca led the way to a shabby shop front that
announced itself as the Kingsland Law Centre. She pushed the door open in
a manner that suggested she had been there before. Inside, a bicycle was
propped up in the corridor, which led to a staircase and, Tom guessed, some
above-the-shop flats. They went through the second door on their left.

The front half of the office was laid out like the waiting area of a down-
at-heel doctor's surgery: three chairs arranged round a forlorn, fake wood
table. The chairs were taken by men whom Tom, expert in these matters
after eleven years at the UN, guessed were Somali. One was holding a
leaflet entitled YOUR ASYLUM RIGHTS IN THE UK.

Behind a flimsy partition, a conversation that was clearly meant to be
private was audible. 'Sorry, Lionel, I need to ask you again. Have you
stopped taking your medication? Do I need to call someone for you?'

Even without trying, Tom could see over the screen. Seated in front of a
desk like a customer visiting a bank manager, was an unshaven man in a
baseball cap, surrounded by half a dozen plastic bags, muttering to himself.
Behind the desk was a handsome man no more than thirty years old, with a
head of dark curly hair and tortoiseshell glasses.

Rebecca smiled in the man's direction with a look that suggested the
indulgence of an older sister; he held up a hand in silent greeting, without
interrupting his discussion with Lionel.

The unanswered phones, the threadbare carpet, the chaos: it all combined
to trigger a wave of memory. Tom had briefly worked in a legal-
aid practice like this one when he had returned to Sheffield soon after

graduating. His father's emphysema had finally caught up with him, and his mother had asked Tom to return, to 'give your old man a decent send-off'. The clientele was not quite as diverse, but the atmosphere was the same.

'Rebecca, I'm so sorry.' The lawyer had come over now, leaving Lionel to gather up his bags. 'I've been trying to call, left a couple of messages. I guess you've been swamped. We're all so shocked.'

Rebecca waved the apology away, then swivelled to make introductions. 'Julian, this is Tom Byrne from the United Nations. Tom, this is Julian Goldman, legal linchpin of the Hackney community—and the grandson of one of my father's oldest friends.'

Julian's smile, basking in Rebecca's recognition, told Tom all he needed to know: this bright young man was in love with Rebecca.

'Lequasia, can you get us some coffee?' he called out to a secretary Tom hadn't noticed.

Seated at a desk next to Julian's, Lequasia was surely no more than eighteen, with a current commitment to admiring a set of improbably lengthy nails rather than answering the phones. She looked up now with an expression that combined indolence and derision in equal measure.

'Come, sit over here.' Julian grabbed a couple of stiff-backed, plastic chairs and arranged them in front of his desk. 'What about funeral arrangements? Is there anything I can do?'

'When they rang to tell me what had happened, they said there'd be a delay. For the autopsy.'

Rebecca was speaking softly, Tom noticed. He wondered how much she would tell Julian; they had not discussed a game plan on the way here. In New York, Tom Byrne never went into a meeting to discuss the monthly stationery order without a game plan. Yet here they were, winging it.

'Are you thinking of taking action against the'—Julian shot a glance at Tom—'the people responsible for this?'

'I'm not thinking about that right now,' Rebecca said. 'But there are some things I need to find out. About my father.'

'Well, you know it all, Rebecca. You were everything to him, anyone could see that.' He turned to Tom. 'You have never seen a father and daughter who were closer.'

'What about the will?' she asked.

For the first time, Julian turned upon Rebecca an expression that was not undiluted adoration. 'You can't be thinking of that now, surely.'

'I want to know if there's anything he left for me.'

'Oh, Rebecca.' He looked shocked.

'I don't mean money, Julian,' she said with an impatience that pleased Tom. 'I mean anything else he might have left here for safekeeping. To be given to me in the event of his death.'

Julian recovered himself. 'You know he arranged his affairs when my father was still his lawyer, before Dad retired. I didn't actually do any of that with him myself. But I'll check.' He got up. 'I won't be a minute.'

Tom looked at Rebecca and raised his eyebrows. 'What's the story?'

'My father was sentimental. He and Julian's grandfather came to this country together. I think he was also a partisan, though much older. When his son became a lawyer, my father became his first client. Out of loyalty. Then, when the son retired, Dad moved on to the grandson.'

'Did your father need a lawyer for any reason?'

The steel returned to Rebecca's eyes. 'Not once.'

Julian emerged at last from a back storeroom carrying a container structured like a shoe box, though double the width, made of strong cardboard with metal reinforcements on the corners. The colour, once red, had faded to a pale pink. He laid it on the desk.

'How long has this been here?' she asked, not touching it.

'We had it transferred over here from my father's practice about two years ago, when my father retired. It looks pretty old, doesn't it?'

Slowly, Rebecca lifted the lid. Julian removed himself to the reception area, where he could be heard apologising to the three Somali men.

The moment the lid was off, Tom felt a surge of disappointment. He did not know what he had been expecting, but it was not this: a collection of once-important documents of the kind you might find in the homes of most pensioners. What had he hoped to find in there, a gun?

Carefully, Rebecca took each item out, as if handling precious stones. The old passports were bundled together with a rubber band. Next to them she placed a document that elicited a wistful smile. It was entitled 'Certificate of Naturalisation', the sheet of paper issued by the Home Office in 1947 that accepted Gershon Matzkin as a loyal subject of King George VI and magicked him into a new creature: Gerald Merton.

There were more certificates, including the incorporation of his dry-cleaning business in Stoke Newington. The long-gone world of postwar Britain seemed to rise from this box like a cloud of dust.

'Tom, look at this.'

Crumpled at the bottom was a thin pile of yellowed newspaper cuttings.

Rebecca lifted them out gently, to prevent them disintegrating in her hands. Only a couple were in English. Several were in Spanish, two in Portuguese and half a dozen in German. Handwritten at the top of each was a simple date. Almost all of those in German were clustered in the same period: the second half of 1945, with the rest spread throughout the 1950s and 1960s.

Rebecca turned the first fragile clippings over, until she came across one from *The Times*, a faded pencil line boxing a story just a paragraph long.

Odilo Globocnik, former SS leader, was found dead yesterday in an alpine hut, high in the mountains near Weissensee. Occupying authority sources said that Globocnik, notorious for overseeing the Einsatzgruppen in Poland, had most likely taken his own life . . .

There was one from *Die Welt*, originally published by the British occupying forces after the German surrender. It too was a single-paragraph item. Tom's schoolboy German was just about adequate to translate.

The military spokesman yesterday announced that a high-ranking official of the Third Reich had been found dead. SS Lieutenant Kurt Mussfeld had been a senior officer at the Auschwitz and Majdanek death camps . . .

Tom reached over Rebecca for the envelope that had come through her letterbox an hour earlier. He laid out the list of names, then looked through the cuttings at the top of the pile, the 1945 ones, pulling out of the German news accounts the names of the men reported dead. He saw a Wilhelm Albert and a Karl Puetz. He glanced back at the list: there they both were, a cross by each of their names. He went deeper into the pile, finding names from the 1950s. They were on the list, too, also crossed out.

An image of Gershon Matzkin floated into his head: prematurely old, scouring newspapers, visiting the local library, recording the deaths of ageing Nazis the world over. The deep tragedy of it—a man consumed by such grief and hatred, living only to hear of the faraway deaths of others—struck Tom. How powerless Gershon Matzkin must have felt, a boy whose family had been destroyed by these men, now grown up and waiting for the day when a road accident here or a faulty electrical cable there might leave one less Nazi in the world. Is that why he had stayed fit, so that he might live to see the day when there were none of them left?

Or was that not how it was at all?

'Rebecca, pass me the passports.'

Tom peeled off the rubber band—and he saw it straight away. There were three old, black, hard-cover British passports, each in the name of Gerald Merton. But there was also a large, stiff, navy-blue passport of the French Republic, issued in the name of Jean-Luc Renard—with a photo that was unmistakably the young Gerald. There was a travel document for Hans Borchardt, loyal citizen of the Federal Republic of Germany, and passports for Paraguay and Argentina. Tom stared at one passport in particular. Issued in 1952, it identified one Fernando Matutes as a Spanish citizen—even though the picture inside showed the same, unsmiling face of Gerald Merton.

Flicking quickly through the pages, Tom saw that the first and last time it had been used was in August 1952. Quickly, he pored over the pile of newspaper cuttings until he found one in Spanish. And there it was. Faded and yellowing but nevertheless clear: *El Correo*, the newspaper of the Basque country, from the second week of August, 1952.

Tourist found dead in San Sebastián hotel; wife discovers body
Police in San Sebastián have launched an inquiry into the mysterious death of a holidaymaker, whose body was discovered by his wife in their room in the Hotel Londres. Mrs Schroeder said she and her German-born husband had been enjoying a week's vacation and that he had shown no signs of distress or depression. 'I had only been out shopping for an hour or so, and when I came back he was, he was—' a grief-stricken Mrs Schroeder told a reporter, before breaking down in tears . . .

When they'd both finished reading, he said, 'Rebecca, I'm afraid there's no other way to understand it. Don't you see the pattern? For every date stamp on a passport, there's a cutting. Look.'

Methodically, Tom set out the pile of newspaper clippings alongside the passports. There was a news report of a corpse found hanging in a Rio suburb in late 1952. Tom checked the date and, sure enough, 'Fernando Matutes' had arrived in Brazil four days before the hanging and had left the same day. There were reports of men killed in car accidents, some of them only months apart. One was found dead in a gutter. The pencilled note identified him as *Hans Stuckart, Ministry of Interior*. An account from 1953 reported police bafflement after a driver was burnt alive, his car having suffered a rare steering failure that sent it spinning across the highway. The handwritten note added that the deceased was *Otto Abetz, deported Jews of France*.

Now Rebecca began working through the cuttings herself, turning them over rapidly, in date order. After the first set from 1945 and 1946, they jumped to 1952, then paused again before the final item, which dated from the early

1960s in the *Winnipeg Free Press*. It reported the death of an Estonian immigrant, found hanged in his home. In pencil, the suicide was identified as *Alexander Laak, commandant of the Jägala concentration camp in Estonia.*

Silently, Tom tucked each news story into a passport, inserting it alongside the page where there was a matching stamp.

'Rebecca, what languages did your father speak?'

'Lots,' she said quietly, staring down at the table. 'German, Russian. French, I think. Maybe Spanish.'

Some words from the notebook surfaced. *I discovered that I was good at learning languages. The teacher said I had an ear for it.*

Tom didn't know what to say. First the shooting in New York and now this: the father Rebecca thought she knew had been killed twice over.

She fell into a chair, biting her lip so hard he thought it might bleed.

He dragged his gaze away. 'Look, Rebecca, this is—'

'Don't say anything. I need time to think.'

Tom retreated, putting the items from the table back in the box.

At last, Rebecca stood, picked up the box and strode over to Julian. Tom watched her hand it back to him, then ask for what appeared to be a favour. Julian scribbled down a number, kissed her on the cheek and said goodbye.

Tom ran after her as she went out the door and onto the street, feeling like a dog on a lead. 'Where are we going now?'

'To see the one man who might know the truth about my father.'

THE CONVENIENCE STORES and fast-food restaurants rapidly gave way to the sparkle of steel and glass as Hackney receded and the glistening towers of Canary Wharf became visible.

'You drive,' Rebecca had said as they walked away from the Kingsland Law Centre. 'I want to think.' And she had sat there in the passenger seat, her face grim with determination.

In a court of law, Tom could have argued that all the evidence they had uncovered was circumstantial, that there was no ironclad proof connecting Gershon Matzkin to any of the killings, let alone all of them. And yet, neither he nor Rebecca doubted that Gershon Matzkin had been an assassin. Who else would keep a score sheet, a roll call of war criminals, their names crossed out on the occasion of their deaths, but the man responsible?

As they drove on, Tom began to see everything slip into place. He thought back to the corpse he had seen in the Office of the Chief Medical Examiner, how he had been struck by the toned muscle, the body of a strong man who had fought to keep his shape. Now that strength made sense. He had been a human weapon, deployed to hit back at those who had nearly wiped out his entire people. Of course, Gershon had always eschewed publicity: he dared not risk his story slipping into public view. But carried away by the human impulse to shape the narrative of his life, he must have begun to set down his story in full—only to realise that he had written a confession of serial murder. Tom could picture him frantically tearing out the incriminating sheets of paper from the notebook, shredding or burning them.

Is this what had taken Gerald Merton to the UN, one last assignment, one last Nazi to kill? Back in the 1980s, the Secretary-General from Austria, Kurt Waldheim, had been exposed as having lied about his military service in the Wehrmacht, glossing over his knowledge of Nazi war crimes. But there was no one who could possibly fit that bill now, no one old enough, for a start. He thought about Paavo Viren, the new Secretary-General. Now in his late sixties, he would have been a toddler during wartime. Besides, he was Finnish; the country had stayed out of the Nazis' clutches. Tom couldn't think of anyone on the UN staff who came into the right age range.

On the other hand, it was General Assembly week: the place was teeming with large numbers of representatives of every country . . .

They were in Canary Wharf now, an area that had built up a serious high-rise skyline since he had left London, something the capital had always lacked. They found a parking space, and while Rebecca fumbled for change for the meter, Tom stepped a few paces away and dialled Henning's number.

'Munchau.'

'Hi, Henning. It's Tom. I won't bore you with the details, but there's some information I could use.'

'Bore me.'

Tom looked over at Rebecca, now placing the pay-and-display ticket on the windscreen. 'It's just a hunch at the moment, nothing more.'

'Don't really have time for hunches, mate. At the risk of repeating myself, General Assembly, General Assembly, General Assembly.'

'That's what I'm thinking about, too. Could you get someone to compile a list of every official either in New York for the GA already or due to arrive this week who's aged seventy or above?'

'Are we still on the hitman theory?'

Tom paused. 'It's a bit difficult to explain right now.'

'Oh, she's with you! Why didn't you say? Is she unbelievably gorgeous?'

'Thanks, Henning. I appreciate it.'

'All right, I'll see what we can get. Seventy? That's the cut-off?'

Tom did his sums once again: even seventy was pretty young. Still, best to err on the side of caution. 'Yes. Seventy. Heads of government, foreign ministers, ambassadors, obviously. But anyone else: aides, translators, too.'

'What about the entire UN staff, while we're at it?'

'Actually, that's not a bad idea. Start with—'

'Tom, I was joking.'

Tom hung up and hurried to catch up with Rebecca, already walking towards the offices of Roderick Jones & Partners, one of the grander City law firms that had moved into Canary Wharf in the late 1990s. The recently retired senior partner was Julian Goldman's father, Henry. But Goldman *père* couldn't quite make the break, Julian had told them, so spent at least two days a week in the office, nominally as a 'consultant'.

Tom smiled to himself as they walked into the lobby. It gave him the measure of the young man they had left behind in Hackney. The vast steel and glass atrium was tall enough to house an impressive, if vaguely absurd, indoor tree. The marble floor stretched for acres before reaching a wide white desk, with three receptionists. It was a textbook example of the paradox of corporate relations: the easiest way to impress clients was to show them just how profligate you were with their money.

Poor Julian Goldman—born on the top of the mountain, where could he go but down? He had clearly turned his back on Daddy's riches and gone the ethical route, opening his battered legal-aid practice in deepest Hackney as a rebuke to Henry Goldman; he would be a lawyer driven not by money but by conscience. Tom smiled to himself at the predictability of it all.

When they stepped out of the lift, Henry Goldman was waiting for them. He stretched his arms open to embrace Rebecca, then shook Tom's hand and ushered them into a conference room more plushly furnished than even the grandest meeting place in the United Nations.

'Rebecca, I was so sorry to hear of your news. We all were.'

Rebecca nodded. 'My father always said your father was his best friend.'

'That's true. I think my father regarded Gerald as a younger brother.' A wounded expression briefly flitted across his face. 'Maybe even another son.'

'I presume he told you things. As his lawyer.'

At that, Goldman stretched out his legs and smoothed a hand over his tie. Tom recognised the colours of the Garrick Club.

'You've come here from Julian's office, you say? You know the key'—Goldman paused—'*materials* are kept there now.'

'I know,' said Rebecca. 'I've just seen them.'

'I see.' The lawyer got to his feet and began to pace. 'I cannot claim to be wholly surprised by this turn of events. No matter what we tell our clients, nothing can stay secret for ever. Isn't that right, Mr Byrne?'

Tom was barely paying attention. He had not got past the clipped English accent, straight out of a Kenneth More movie. *This* was the son of a Holocaust survivor and underground fighter—this stuffed shirt in a Garrick Club tie?

Rebecca didn't give Tom time to answer. 'Can you tell us what you know?'

There'd be no mistaking Rebecca Merton for a lawyer. Let the guy warm up, Tom thought. But he needn't have worried; Goldman simply talked on.

'Of course, my father knew it all and he brought me into his confidence on some of the key aspects. I shan't deny that it became a source of great tension between us. And I've often imagined Julian and me rerunning some of those arguments, with my son in the role of my father.'

Tom asked, 'And has Julian ever confronted you about this?'

'No. Perhaps he never worked it out, never even opened the box.' Goldman sat down at the table and looked them both straight in the eye. 'It's difficult for me to talk about this without letting my own views show. So perhaps it is best if I simply pass on the arguments advanced by my father.'

'Actually, a few facts at this stage would be an enormous help,' Tom said.

'Very well.' Goldman leaned forward. 'As you now know, Rebecca's father was involved in the'—he searched for the right word—'*removal* of certain men associated with the events of the Second World War. Well, he did not do this work alone. He was part of an organisation. We would call them Holocaust survivors now, men and women who had seen unspeakable horrors.' Goldman gave a little shake of his head. 'At the start, in the final weeks of the war and immediately afterwards, there were no more than fifty of them. Almost all had been involved in the resistance in some way.'

An image floated into Tom's head of the young Gershon Matzkin, hopping on and off trains as he crisscrossed occupied Europe, cheating death and desperately trying to warn others so that they might live.

'They were ghetto fighters, my father included. And I suppose this effort evolved naturally out of that. They had been trying to kill Nazis before and they were killing Nazis now. Churchill and Roosevelt had declared the war over, but it wasn't their war to finish. The Jews had their own score to settle.' He paused. 'But there was more to it than that. More to what we'—he meant Tom and him, fellow lawyers—'would speak of as *motive*. To understand that, you have to start from first principles.'

Tom didn't have to look over at Rebecca to know she was squirming, desperate for Goldman to get to the point. But Goldman had no appreciation of the urgency of their situation. They hadn't told him about the break-in for fear it would make him clam up. They would have to be patient.

'You must remember that Jewish resistance to the Nazis was impossible.' Goldman raised his palm, anticipating an objection. 'I know, I know. There *was* resistance. My father and your father, Rebecca, were part of it. But the Jews lacked the essential requirements of any plausible resistance. They had no arms, no tradition of fighting. They had no army, no barracks, no arsenals. Above all, they had no friends. I'm sure you know the stories, the lengths the Jews had to go to, the bribes they had to pay, to get the Poles or Lithuanians or Ukrainians to sell them so much as a single pistol.'

Rebecca was shuffling in her seat. 'Could I—?'

The raised palm again. 'You'll soon see where this is leading.' He cleared his throat. 'Add to this the fact that the Nazis did not exactly advertise their plans. They hid behind euphemisms: "resettlement in the east" and so on. And the Jews swallowed it. "Never underestimate a man's inability to imagine his own destruction." Those were the words of a member of the group. A rabbi, as it happens. Yes, there was a rabbi. A poet, too. A couple of journalists. Farmers, merchants, doctors. They were a mixed bunch. Anyway, Rebecca, this is the context in which your father and mine acted. They believed that the Jews had accepted their fate too passively. And they could not stand that Jewish life had been extinguished so cheaply, without punishment. So they looked back into history and found an ancient vow: *Dam Israel Nokeam*. "The blood of Israel will take vengeance." They took the first letter of each Hebrew word of that slogan to form another word, DIN. A word in itself: it means "judgment", and that became the name of this group. Your father and my father, they were both in it. And I believe, Rebecca, that your father was its very last member.'

Tom was thinking hard about everything he had seen: the passports, the press clippings, the evidence in New York. Had there been any pointer to this word DIN, some clue he had missed?

'In the beginning, it was quite straightforward. By the middle of 1945, the Allies ruled Berlin and DIN could operate relatively freely. They cultivated informants in the British and American bureaucracies, especially in the prosecutors' offices, finding men who for their own reasons were more than happy to leak information on Nazis who had melted back into civilian life. One way or another, DIN acquired a target list. Then they used all the old techniques of the ghetto resistance to acquire the uniforms and IDs they needed. My father was good at this work. He would follow a military policeman, knock him out cold and steal everything he had: wristwatch, wallet, belt. When the soldier came to, he was unaware that the only things his attacker had really wanted were his uniform and military ID.

'Posing as military police made the job easy; they could walk right up to a target and "arrest" him, bold as brass. Or they could do a "snatch", an abduction. They could do all this because DIN were wearing the uniforms of the Allied authorities—and the Allies were the masters now.

'Then they would act like a court, reading out the prisoner's crimes. Only then would they announce themselves, "We act in the name of the Jews and we have come to administer justice." Afterwards, they would hide the body. Ideally, the death, once discovered, was recorded as a suicide.'

Tom thought back to the cuttings he had seen in the box that afternoon: most of the deaths reported there were either car accidents or suicides.

Goldman continued. "I must stress that they went after only those who had a hand in the Final Solution: SS men who had staffed the extermination camps, those who had served in the mobile killing units, the Einsatzgruppen. You know about those, Mr Byrne?'

Tom nodded, remembering the story in the notebook, the story recounted in countless history books: the pits, the shooting, the piles of bodies.

'Mr Goldman,' Rebecca cut in. 'What we saw today suggested the actions my father took were some time after the war, in the 1950s and 1960s.'

Henry Goldman fell back in his chair, the air escaping from him like a punctured tyre. 'I'm sorry. I've talked too long.' He gave a forced smile, an expression of containment. 'I have not shared this story with my wife or my sons. I have carried it, as it were, for many, many years. I don't know how else to tell it, except as I heard it from my father.'

'There's no problem with the way you're telling it, Mr Goldman. You take your time,' said Tom.

Goldman nodded his silent thanks, cleared his throat and went on. 'The killings I have referred to were known as "the first hunting season". They arose out of the strong belief that there would be no other kind of justice. The Allies had promised it, of course, in fine speeches about bringing every last Nazi killer to book. But soon there came the suggestion that only those in charge of the Third Reich would face prosecution. Which is how we came to have the great show at Nuremberg, in which a grand total of twenty-four men were brought to account. DIN were repelled by the pretence that only two dozen men were responsible for this massive, international crime. They had seen with their own eyes the men who had whipped Jews to death for sport, who had shot them into pits and shoved them into gas chambers, and they knew it was not the work of *twenty-four* men. It was the work of tens of thousands, hundreds of thousands, maybe even millions!'

There was no interrupting Goldman now; the words poured out of him.

'When the crimes began to be revealed, and newsreel footage was shown of those mountains of naked bodies, people in the West demanded better. The Russians were executing Nazis by the thousands; people here and in America expected something similar. The Allies felt they had to do something. By the end of 1946, they had jailed nearly half a million Germans, holding them before trial on charges of direct participation in mass murder, with another three and a half million listed for "significant criminal complicity".

'At last it seemed as if they were going to get justice after all. The group had a hard debate, but concluded that, if justice was truly on its way, they had no business carrying on as judge, jury and executioner. They decided to lay down their weapons, to disband and go their separate ways, start their own lives. My father and yours came here to London. Some went to America, many to Israel. They believed it was all over. But it was not to be.'

He paused, as if remembering himself. 'There's a revealing table of statistics in a book by Raul Hilberg, one of the great historians of the Holocaust. My father would look at it often. It starts off with the *Fragebogen*, the "registrants", those thirteen million or more who were part of the Nazi apparatus. One line down is the total number of men charged: three million, four hundred and forty-five thousand, one hundred, if I recall. The figure on the next line relates to those who, having been charged, were released without so much as a trial. A blanket amnesty, if you like. It's large, this number: two million, four hundred and eighty thousand, seven hundred. They just walk away. That left just under a million Nazis still in the prosecutors' sights.

'How are they punished? Just look at the table. Five hundred and sixty-nine thousand, six hundred of them are fined. The slate is wiped clean with a cash payment. A further one hundred and twenty-four thousand, four hundred men had to suffer the indignity of employment restrictions. Unfortunately, for certain jobs, being a Nazi mass murderer was an immediate disqualification. The same was true of eligibility for public office. Twenty-three thousand, one hundred Nazis were told their political careers were on hold.'

Goldman's eyes were bright. 'If memory serves, another twenty-five thousand, nine hundred had their property confiscated. I say "their", but this was property acquired through a rather unorthodox route. Those deemed guilty had seen their neighbours in Hamburg or Frankfurt dragged off to the camps, shed a tear and then ransacked their homes once they were gone. The table also speaks of "special labour without imprisonment": I suppose we'd call that community service now. Thirty thousand, five hundred get that. And nine thousand, six hundred are sent to labour camps.

'If you tot it all up, it leaves less than two hundred thousand convicted Nazi war criminals with sentences of up to ten years. But then we look at the very last figure in the table: "Assignees still serving sentence." And that figure is'—he paused, as if expecting a drum roll—'three hundred. When this little table was compiled in 1949, out of more than thirteen million men once deemed complicit in the horrors of the Third Reich, we have eleven death sentences at Nuremberg and three hundred men in jail. That's all.

'And when the West Germans took over responsibility for war-crime prosecutions, they were no better. They convicted, to take just one example, Wilhelm Greiffenberger for involvement in eight thousand, one hundred murders—and sentenced him to three years' imprisonment and three years' "loss of honour". Almost every man convicted melted back into German society. These men walked free from those prisons, as if they were guilty of nothing more serious than a parking infringement. They were so arrogant, so certain there would be no consequences, they didn't even hide what they had done. They were in the phone book.

'And this, you see, is the dirty little secret of the Second World War. We're told, over and over again, that the attempted extermination of the Jews was the greatest crime in human history and yet hardly anybody was punished for it. It was a crime that was unavenged.'

At last, Goldman slumped back in his chair; he seemed exhausted, emptied out, like a medium once the spirit has departed.

Rebecca and Tom sat in silence. It was Rebecca who spoke first.

'And that's why DIN re-formed.'

'Yes,' he said softly. 'In 1952.'

'And the killing started then. Except now it was all over the world. Wherever the Nazis were hiding.'

Goldman nodded. 'I found one of their lists. I was looking for something else, and I came across a file for the poker club. That was the cover they used: five Jewish men who met on Thursday nights to play poker. My father always said it was a secret society because if their wives knew how much they gambled there'd be hell to pay. So we could never know who was in it.

'When I saw the file I had to look. I wanted to know about this secret gambling world of my dad's, a man who did nothing more interesting than sell ladies' outerwear to department stores. Little did I know.' He gave a rueful smile. 'Inside the file was a wad of foreign currency, several passports and a list of German names, crossed out one by one. I understood immediately. I was twenty years old, I think.

'We had a fierce argument. We never stopped having it, until his dying day. I said I would alert the authorities. I was a newly qualified lawyer. It was my duty.' Tears began to appear in his right eye. 'But I never did.'

'But they were hardly murderers,' Tom said quietly. 'They were ensuring that a grave crime did not go unpunished.'

Goldman looked at him anew. 'I confess I am amazed to hear a man like yourself speak in such a manner, Mr Byrne.'

Tom could feel the veins on his neck begin to throb. 'I'm sorry. But I'm just thinking of what you said a moment ago. That the men behind this monumental crime got off scot-free.'

'Mr Byrne, as you well know, I was merely doing the job of an advocate, putting the case for DIN so you might understand it. The right course of action was the law. That was the course these men should have pursued.'

'Except the law often leads nowhere. We both know that, don't we, Mr Goldman?' Tom could hear a tremor in his own voice. 'Because, when all's said and done, there's no such thing as "the law". We like to imagine some wonderfully impartial, blind goddess of justice—but the truth is, there's only politics. And politics never finds it convenient to pursue the guilty.'

'Tom, *really*—' Rebecca interjected.

'I'm sorry, but it's true. The bigger the crime, the less convenient it is. When there's a clash of "reconciliation" and justice, reconciliation wins out every time. I've seen it again and again.' There was that crack in his voice again. 'So, inappropriate though it might be for a lawyer to say this, I have some sympathy for what this group, what DIN, were feeling. They had seen their whole families wiped out. Of course they wanted to hunt down those responsible. The law had let them walk free. I do wonder if, on this point, Mr Goldman, your father got it right and you got it wrong.'

Goldman was about to respond when Rebecca stood up. Glaring at Tom, she cried, 'That's enough.' Her eyes were burning. The unspoken reminder that she had just lost her father shamed them both into silence.

In the calm, she turned to Goldman and asked in a manner that conveyed the desire for a brief, straight answer to a straight question, 'Is there anything else at all, any other element in the DIN story, that you haven't told us? Some secret, perhaps, that someone might not want to come out?'

Tom could see that Goldman was weighing up his answer. As he leaned forward to speak, the air was filled with the brain-splitting sound of an alarm, coming from inside the building.

JAY SHERRILL would have admitted it to no one, not even his mother, but today, as he sat in the waiting area of the office of the man formally titled Deputy Commissioner for Intelligence, he was feeling his inexperience.

He had followed the Commissioner's cue and made contact with the NYPD Intelligence Division. He had asked to see those involved in the surveillance operation of Gerald Merton. He had heard nothing back. He called again, adding that his request related to an ongoing criminal investigation designated as the highest possible priority by the Commissioner himself. No one returned his call.

Then, this morning at 8.30 a.m., the call had come. The head of the Intelligence Division, Stephen Lake, would see him at 10 a.m. It made no sense. Sherrill had made a request to see a field officer. That request had apparently been refused. Instead he was due to see the man at the very top.

Lake had been top brass at the Central Intelligence Agency, a wholly political appointment made by the city after 9/11, when New York decided that it could no longer rely on the federal authorities and had better make its own arrangements. Sherrill had searched the archive of the *New York Times* website that morning, and discovered that the Intel Division had up to a thousand officers at its disposal, a force within the 40,000-strong force of the NYPD itself. The *Times* had reported a slew of complaints from civil liberties groups that the Intel Division was not catching foreign terrorists but watching domestic political activists and bugging the phone calls of US citizens. It only added to the unfamiliar sensation now brewing inside Jay Sherrill that he was badly out of his depth.

At last a secretary gestured for Sherrill to follow her into an office he instantly assessed as being slightly larger than the Commissioner's.

Lake was short by alpha-male standards, five ten at most. His silver-grey hair was cut close and his eyes were chilly. He rose slightly out of his chair to acknowledge the detective's arrival, extended a hand, then began speaking even before Jay had sat down.

'So what is it we can help you with, Detective?'

'Well, sir, I really didn't mean to trouble you with this. It's a matter way below—'

'My pay grade, Detective?' There was a mirthless smile. 'Why not let me be the judge of that? What are the questions you have for this department?'

'Sir, the UN security force opened fire on Gerald Merton at eight fifty-one a.m. yesterday. Two minutes earlier, the Watch Commander of that force had received a warning from his liaison within NYPD, offering a description of a terror suspect said to be about to enter the United Nations compound. It was on the basis of that description—for which Gerald Merton presented a complete match—that the UN officer opened fire.'

Lake rubbed his chin, apparently deep in thought. 'And your question to me is what exactly?'

Sherrill could see that Lake was going to extend not the slightest help.

'I want to know how the NYPD was in a position to pass on what could only be live intelligence to the UNSF, sir.'

'*Live intelligence?* Are you sure you're not getting a little ahead of yourself here, Detective? Is intelligence an expertise of yours?'

Sherrill could feel a burning sensation in his cheeks. He reminded himself that this tactic of intimidation—the invocation of specialist knowledge—was just that, a tactic. 'I don't think it requires any great expertise, sir. Just as it would have required no great expertise to see that Gerald Merton was a man in his late-seventies—hardly the profile of a terrorist.'

At that, Lake's eyes turned to steel. 'There are two answers to that, Mr Sherrill: the official one and the unofficial one. The official one is that this department never comments on operational matters, lest we compromise those working in the field to protect the great city of New York and, with it, the entire United States.'

'Of course, sir,' Sherrill said. 'And what's the unofficial one?'

'We may have had our eye on the UN for a while, with evidence of a ticking time bomb over there. Or we may not. But this was one hundred per cent a fuck-up by the Keystone Kops at UN Plaza. You try to roll the blame ball over to this department for that and I will personally make sure that it crushes you into the ground so hard you'll think yourself lucky if you end up writing out parking tickets in Trenton. Do I make myself clear?'

Sherrill swallowed hard. 'Doesn't this count as coercion of a law-enforcement officer, sir?'

'Save it for the Kennedy School, Detective. The only words I have uttered to you in this meeting are as follows: that this department never comments on operational matters, lest we compromise those working in the field to protect the great city of New York and, with it, the entire United States. Any other words imagined by you will be denied by me. I will swear an affidavit to that effect and submit it to any court—along, of course, with a copy of your medical records showing your past history of mental illness.'

Jay Sherrill could feel the wind exiting his stomach as surely as if he had been punched. 'What are you talking about?' he said.

Stephen Lake looked down at a sheet of paper he now held between his thumb and forefinger. 'Seems that you once sought counselling for depression. Is that compatible with the role of a first-grade detective in the New York Police Department? Hmm, I can't recall. Perhaps we should just check with the Chief of Detectives.' He reached for his telephone.

'No! It was years ago; I was a student! My brother had just died!'

'My condolences, Detective. I'm sure the NYPD human resources department would have been real sympathetic when you applied to be a fast-track, high-flying, big swinging dick detective. Except, for some reason, you forgot to share that piece of information with them, didn't you? I've got your form right here in front of me.' He reached for another document. '"Have you ever sought professional help for a mental-health problem, including but not confined to . . ." blah, blah, blah, oh there it is, "depression"? And here's the little check box you've marked with an X. It couldn't be clearer. N-O spells no. That counts as a lie in my book. Might even count as perjury.' He fixed Jay Sherrill with a fierce stare. 'You go take your blame ball and roll it onto someone else's yard, Detective, because this one's full of land mines and one of them will blow you right out of the sky. I guarantee it.'

Chapter Six

The instant the fire alarm sounded in the Canary Wharf offices of Roderick Jones & Partners, the conversation halted. A secretary popped her head round the door to say that she was terribly sorry, but they had to evacuate the building immediately. Henry Goldman composed himself, packed his papers into a leather portfolio case and followed the secretary out.

Outside, there was a crush of employees, two of them donning fluorescent bibs, and a mood of nervous excitement. Tom and Rebecca walked the fifteen flights downstairs, neither daring to speak about what had just happened. One of the fire wardens peered at their visitor labels and shepherded them to a different meeting point from the rest of the Roderick Jones staff. They stood there for twenty minutes in the early evening cold. Then, with no announcement, merely directed by the herd instinct that grips every crowd, people began to drift back into the building. Apparently a false alarm.

They were soon back in the conference room. The secretary reappeared. 'Can I help?' she chirped, as if she had never seen them before.

'We were here before the alarm,' Rebecca said. 'Meeting Mr Goldman?'

'Oh, but Mr Goldman's gone, I'm afraid.'

'Gone?'

She shrugged. 'I assumed you'd finished your meeting.'

At Tom's request, she called down to Security, who checked the executive garage: Mr Goldman's parking space was now empty.

Tom gave a full-wattage smile: charm mode. 'And that was a regular fire drill, was it?'

'Oh, no. We only have those on Mondays. Janice—she's one of our fire marshals—said someone broke one of the "In case of emergency" things in the basement. Used one of the plastic hammers to smash the glass. Security have no idea who did it, but they're checking the CCTV already.'

'Perhaps it was a high-spirited prank,' Tom said, recalling the language the Dean had used back at Manchester when he and his mates had let off fire extinguishers. 'By one of the younger members of staff.'

The secretary looked appalled. 'But we don't have anyone like that here,' she said. And Tom believed it.

Rebecca was in no mood to prolong this chitchat with Henry Goldman's secretary. They excused themselves and headed out of the building. Letting Rebecca walk on ahead of him, Tom made a quick call to Jay Sherrill; he didn't like the guy, but he ought to look like he was cooperating.

'Hello, Detective Sherrill. It's Tom Byrne here in London.'

'Any leads on that weapon we found?'

'I do have something, as it happens, yes. It's sketchy, nothing firm, but it's possible that Merton may have had a past in some kind of armed group.'

'Jesus. What kind of armed group?'

'Like I said, it's sketchy at the moment. But I think he may have been one of a group of men acting as vigilantes, punishing criminals.'

'When you say "punishing" do you mean—?'

'Yes, Detective Sherrill, I do. But it was a long time ago and I'm not sure it sheds much light on the finding in the hotel room or the Russian—'

'No, but still. This is useful. What's the evidence?'

'A hint or two in some documents Merton left behind. Nothing explicit.'

'Is the group still active?'

'That's the million-dollar question. I'll check in when I get more.'

He hung up and sprinted to join Rebecca, now unlocking the Saab. Once in the driving seat, she let out a gale of pent-up rage. 'Christ, he's finally on the brink of telling us something we don't already know and you start *ranting*.'

'I did not rant. I was just making a point—'

'I don't want to talk about it.'

'—that sometimes justice—'

'I mean it,' she said, glaring. 'I *don't* want to talk about it.' And with that, she pulled out of the parking space and into traffic, the ferocity of her silence filling the car.

The arguments Tom wanted to make were running through his head, but they did not get very far. Rebecca was probably right; he had indeed scared Goldman off. He knew that voicing his own views was an elementary mistake, but what unnerved him was why he had done so.

The daylight was fading now. Rebecca was gripping the steering wheel furiously, her gaze fixed on the road ahead. Tom stared into space. Neither of them paid attention to the wing mirror on Tom's side of the car. If they had, they might have seen the manoeuvre of the Mercedes three cars behind them—the move that confirmed it was following them.

NOW OFFICIALLY ELDERLY, the boss could still outrun his staff. Given how little sleep he had had, he should have tired hours ago. It was always like this. While the men in their thirties and forties were already aching for a hot bath and a night's sleep, the boss was ready to crack open a bottle of Scotch malt whisky, loosen his tie and begin some serious talk.

For the aide, it was a reminder of what everyone had said about his future employer when he took the job: that power was the purest form of adrenaline and this guy had it running through his veins in neat form. Forget adrenaline, he thought now; it was more like embalming fluid. Somehow, the decades this man had spent at the top of his nation's politics seemed to have halted the ageing process entirely.

'So what do we have?' the boss began. His usual opening gambit.

'Well, our people in London managed to follow the subjects—'

'Subjects? Let's cut the bullshit intelligence language, shall we?'

'They followed Rebecca Merton and Tom Byrne to a meeting at a law firm. Fortunately, it was in a tall, steel-and-glass building, so, thanks to a highly directional shotgun microphone, we were able to carry out surveillance of the meeting.'

'And?'

'The guy at the law firm spoke at length about the group—'

'DIN?'

'Yes, sir. But he did not touch on, er . . . our aspect of the matter. At least, not in the part of the conversation monitored.'

'What the hell does that mean? You missed some of it?'

'The very beginning, sir. But everything that came afterwards suggests our aspect was not touched upon. And when there seemed to be a risk that they might stray into, you know, sensitive territory, we took action.'

'What kind of action?'

'We terminated the conversation.'

'How the hell did you do that?'

'We activated the fire alarm, sir.'

At that the boss gave his first smile. 'The fire-alarm trick, eh? Always a winner. Perhaps we should use it at the UN.'

The aide laughed loyally.

'And now?'

'It's under control, sir. Subjects are—sorry, the people involved are all under close watch. If the information we are concerned about is known at all, which I strongly doubt, then we will ensure it does not reach either Ms Merton or Mr Byrne. And if it does, we will make sure it goes no further.'

THE SILENCE DID NOT BREAK, even as Rebecca parked the car, unlocked the front door and stormed up the stairs into her flat.

'Seriously, Tom, what the hell was all that about?' she said, once he had followed her into the kitchen. 'You wrecked that meeting at the most crucial stage. There we were, listening to Goldman drone on, telling us what we already knew, and then, just as he's getting to the—'

'You already knew all that?'

Her face formed into an expression Tom couldn't understand. 'No, of course I didn't. But we'd worked it out, hadn't we? From the box.'

'Sure, but we didn't know any of that detail. Or the motivation. I thought you'd be fascinated to hear all that. To understand your father.'

'This is not therapy for me, OK? Someone trashed my place today. And we have no idea who they are or what they want. No idea if they're going to come back.'

'I understand. This is very frightening—'

'You're damn right, it's frightening.' The volume was getting higher now. 'And then you start sounding off, defending vigilante murderers—'

'Well, can you blame them? Given everything that had happened to them. They were right: they weren't going to get justice any other way.'

'How can you say that? You're meant to be a lawyer, for God's sake.'

'That's exactly why I'm saying it!' He was shouting now. 'Oh, yes, I used to believe all that crap about "the law" and "justice" and all the fine words. Why do you think I went to work for the UN? Because I was one of those saps who was going to change the world.'

He was startled to hear himself talk like this; he hadn't voiced these thoughts, even to himself, for so long. But now he couldn't stop. 'I was right there, at the very top. The United bloody Nations. And then I was asked to lead for the UN on the Rwanda tribunal. It was a massive job; I was thrilled to get it. I'd be fighting the good fight. I began by reading the witness statements, page after page of them; they were just like your father's notebook. Stories that would make you weep. You know what happened there. Minimum of eight hundred thousand people killed in the space of three months. Fastest genocide in human history, they reckon—even faster than the Nazis. And as always, everyone, but everyone, is up to their necks in blood. Nuns stood by while children were herded into churches and torched alive. *Nuns*, for Christ's sake. And all the stuff that happens every time: teenage girls getting raped, boys having their balls sliced off, men forced to kill their wives. Thousands of pages of it.

'On the evidence we had, at least a million people should have been in the dock. But guess how many Tutsis have been convicted?'

Rebecca looked down at the floor. 'I don't know.'

'Just *guess*, Rebecca!'

'Five thousand? A thousand? I don't know!'

'Twenty-six. That's the grand total after a decade and a half of legal work by dozens of lawyers and millions of dollars. Twenty-six people. You know what they say about lies: the bigger the lie, the more people will believe it? It's the same with mass murder. If you kill ten people, you'll never get away with it. But kill a thousand and you'll never see inside a dock, let alone a prison cell. That's what I learned in Rwanda.' His voice was trembling.

'So what did you do?'

Tom steadied himself against the kitchen table. 'The usual. Drinking, smoking, drugs—the things you do when you want to throw your life away.'

'You had a breakdown?'

'You could say that. In fact, the UN personnel department *did* say that. *Byrne, Thomas—indefinite leave on health grounds.* They would have fired me, but Henning—my boss—looked out for me. Kept me on the payroll. I think he was worried that if they cut me loose I might do something to myself.'

'And would you?'

'I thought about it.'

The silence hung in the air—until he broke it. 'And then I decided I wouldn't be a sap any more. I got wise. Law's a racket, so you might as well enjoy the benefits. Everyone else was doing it, so why not me?'

'What do you mean, it's a racket?'

'Put it this way, Rebecca. You wouldn't want to meet my latest clients on a dark night.' He tried to smile, but all that came was a wince. 'That's the difference between me and Julian. He hasn't learned the lesson yet.'

'What's the lesson?'

'There's not going to be a brighter tomorrow, and no one cares what happened yesterday, so you might as well live for today.'

'No one cares what happened yesterday? You really believe that?'

'I do now. And it seems your father did, too; he looked around the world and saw that no one gave a fuck what happened to the Jews. Not enough to bring the guilty to justice. So he and his friends did it themselves.'

'You think it was OK to go around killing and killing like that?'

'They were Nazis, for Christ's sake!'

'What if they'd got it wrong, Tom? Eh? What if they'd accidentally killed the wrong man? And who gave them the right to do it? Who set them up as judge and jury and executioner?'

'Oh, for God's sake. If they didn't have the right, who did? It's a bit much for us to sit here, judging the people who lived through all that. It was different for them, they—'

'Lived through it?' Her eyes were wild now. 'You don't think I've lived through it? Are you kidding? I lived through every *hour* of that war, over and over since the day I was born. Can you imagine growing up in a house that's dark with sorrow even when the sun's shining?'

'I . . . I thought . . . You told me your father didn't like to talk about it.'

'He didn't. He didn't have to. It was in every room, without him saying a word. So don't tell me I didn't live through it. I lived through . . .'

And the sentence faltered, as she choked back tears. Without a conscious thought he closed the gap between them, placing his arms round her, trying to calm her with his embrace. But she would not be calmed, hammering instead at his chest, her fists two hard balls.

He could not help himself now. He lifted her chin and guided by an impulse he had held back too long, moved his lips to touch hers.

The kiss was urgent, powered by the desire that had thumped through him from the first instant he had laid eyes on her. At first she resisted, her hands clutching at his shirt, but it did not last. Her mouth was just as ravenous as his. The first touch of her tongue sent a current through him.

The smell of her was strong now. She pulled off his jacket and set to work on his shirt buttons, letting out a moan as she touched his warm skin. Tom's hand was on her waist, feeling the naked flesh above her belt, when he heard it, a trilling sound. Breathless, she pulled away—and reached for the phone.

'Oh, hi, Julian.'

Of course, thought Tom, suddenly aware of the blood pulsing round his entire system. Julian's lovelorn antennae had probably been twitching the moment they had kissed. He watched Rebecca nod and 'uh-huh' her way through the conversation, then reach for a pad to scribble down an address.

She hung up. 'That was Julian, calling to ask how it went. He'd spoken to his father. Said he seemed "fired up" by our conversation.'

'Fired up? Is that good or bad?' It was a struggle to speak.

'Julian couldn't tell.' She was biting her lip. 'But he reckoned we should try to see his father tonight. He said he got the distinct impression he wanted to tell us something. Something important.'

As REBECCA DROVE up the Holloway Road and into the well-heeled charm of Highgate Village, Neither of them spoke. But the silence was different now. The tension between them had been building steadily, like a darkening sky on a close summer's day. Thanks to the stand-up row, and the kiss that followed it, the weather had broken. Tom sat alongside her, no longer fighting the urge to stare or, occasionally, touch her.

'Rebecca, we talked about the injury on your father's leg, didn't we?'

'There was no injury; I told you. Why?'

'His body was found with a kind of metal shin-pad.' He reached round to the back seat. 'Can I get your father's notebook from your bag?'

She nodded, giving him another flash of the crooked smile whose power over him she surely understood. Tom thumbed through the pages.

There. He had found it: a passage describing young Gershon's involvement with the partisans, hiding in the forests. It was one of the passages Tom had had to skim-read, but something had lodged. And here it was.

For those months, I did not often serve as a fighter. As usual, my great value was my Aryan looks. So instead of simply firing a gun, I was involved in procuring guns. I became a smuggler. I would run from our place in the woods to a meeting point, pick up a pistol or grenade or detonator, pay for it with whatever I had—sometimes cash, usually a watch or a ladies' necklace—and then creep back to camp.

The trick with smuggling is to be prepared for getting caught. You need to let them find something on you. Then they will congratulate themselves on having done a good job and let you go on your way. And only you will know that the real thing is hidden somewhere else. So whenever I bought a gun, I would also pick up some cigarettes or perhaps some meat and these I would hide—but not so well. If I was stopped, they would find the cigarettes, maybe beat me a bit—but the gun strapped to my back by bandages, this they didn't find . . .

Tom smiled to himself. So that explained the metal shin-pad. Gerald Merton was preparing himself for the metal detectors he knew would be at the entrance to the United Nations building. The alarm would go off and, with an apologetic shrug, the old man would reach down, roll up his left trouser leg and show the security staff the metal plate he had to wear for medical reasons. He would probably crack a joke—'Airports are the worst'—and they would smile and nod him through, without checking for the state-of-the-art weapon he had disassembled and bandaged to himself, along with the steel inserts and ammunition.

The gun hadn't been on him that day; it was still in the hotel bathroom. The Monday-morning trip to the UN had surely been a reconnaissance mission. It would have been a smart plan: if Merton had returned the next day, and the metal detectors had gone off again, chances are, one of the security staff would have recognised him and waved him through, no need to roll up his trousers a second time.

But who was the gun meant for? Tom had still not heard back from Henning with that list. Who would have warranted DIN's last, aged warrior to don his assassin's cloak one more time? Tom wished that those missing pages from the old man's notebook would somehow reappear. Had Gershon destroyed them, or had he hidden them somewhere? Was that what the thieves were after when they had turned Rebecca's apartment upside-down?

Now they were driving alongside Hampstead Heath, the vast park on their left, houses of extraordinary opulence and size on their right.

When Rebecca slowed down, Tom said, 'Don't tell me he lives here.'

Rebecca nodded. 'Here we go,' she said, signalling a right turn into a steep, sloping driveway. The house was vast and absurdly palatial. She pulled the car up alongside a sleek Mercedes and turned off the engine. 'Remember, all charm this time.'

She pressed the doorbell. No answer.

'Try the knocker,' he said. 'Really hard.'

Rebecca reached for the brass knocker, and banged it firmly down.

The door swung inward. It had not been locked at all.

Rebecca furrowed her brow at Tom, then stepped in. He followed her into a wide hallway. 'Hello?' she called, and walked farther in, to a large reception area bordered on all sides by cream sofas.

Rebecca tried again, 'Mr Goldman?'

'Perhaps we should leave,' Tom suggested, glad of an excuse for an early exit—and perhaps a return to Rebecca's flat. 'We can call him tomorrow.'

'But Julian said he was definitely home. I'm just going to try the study, and if he's not there, we'll go.'

She stepped gingerly into the gloom, calling out, 'Mr Goldman? Henry?' as she moved. She reached a door, and as she opened it the corridor was filled with light. Behind her by several paces, Tom felt vaguely disappointed: if the lights were on in the study, then the old boy was clearly home. He'd probably nodded off in his chair.

Rebecca's scream tore the air. She stood frozen in the doorway, then darted forward. Tom ran after her, only to find her hunched over a slumped body, her ear clamped to the chest of Henry Goldman, whose cold white face was staring upwards. He looked aghast. Rebecca straddled his body and began pounding at his chest, bringing both hands down in a series of massive thumps. Tears streaked down her cheeks like rain on a window pane.

After several minutes, she climbed off the unmoving body and let her head fall onto Tom's shoulder. 'He's dead,' she sobbed, the tears soaking into his shirt. 'He's dead, he's dead, he's dead.' Finally, she pulled back so that Tom could see her face. 'He's dead—and we killed him.'

Chapter Seven

Jay Sherrill stared at the Post-it Note stuck to his computer screen. He had gone to the vending machine for a cup of Styrofoam coffee, could only have been five minutes, and when he got back, there it was. The message was marked in block capitals: *SUBWAY. ACROSS STREET. 4.15.*

He looked at his watch. It was 4.06 p.m. It could be a trap. But how could someone have possibly got in here, one of the most heavily secured buildings in New York City, and got out again that quickly? Besides, he would have to go. You couldn't ignore a direct message like this; no cop would.

Sherrill walked out of the main entrance and was about to turn left for the subway station when he saw it. Subway, the sandwich bar. Right opposite headquarters, it served as an alternative police canteen.

He pushed the door open and scanned the room: a line of customers, either cops or secretaries on their lunch hour; a couple of middle-aged men on cellphones. None of them seemed to recognise him.

'Excuse me,' Sherrill said, still scoping the faces, as a blue-overalled cleaner shuffled into him. One of those ridiculous, preppie habits Sherrill couldn't shake: apologising when someone bumped into him.

'No problem, Detective,' the cleaner murmured back.

Sherrill wheeled round to see a black, dreadlocked man with headphones in his ears. 'You wanna take a walk?' the man said.

Sherrill watched, stunned, as the man propped his cleaning equipment by the front door and headed outside. The cleaner did not wait for Sherrill to catch up. He remained a half-pace in front, looking ahead, so that he and the detective might just be two New Yorkers hurrying about their business.

'Thanks for coming, Detective Sherrill. Sorry about'—he made a small movement with his hand—'all this.'

'Who are you? How do you know my name?'

'I'm an agent with the NYPD Intelligence Division. Undercover.' Still looking straight ahead, he smiled briefly. 'In case you hadn't noticed.'

'How did you—?'

'Get into your office? That was easy. I've got an NYPD pass. Hey, Sherrill, pull out your cellphone.'

'My cellphone, why?'

'Just pretend you're talking into it. And don't keep looking at me.'

For the second time in six hours, Jay Sherrill was coming face to face with his own inexperience. He had never done undercover work, didn't know even the basics. He did as he was told and tried to fake a phone call.

'OK, what do you want?'

'I don't want anything. What is it with you people? I'm risking my fucking job here because I have some information that might help you.'

The pitch of Sherrill's voice lifted. 'Information?'

'On the killing of Gerald Merton.'

'What kind of information?'

'The eyewitness kind.'

Sherrill couldn't help but shoot a glance at the man walking just ahead of him. Then, guiltily, he returned to the blank middle-distance stare adopted by all those talking on cellphones in the street. 'You were there?' he asked.

'I saw it all. From the beginning.'

'FIRST, I NEED YOU to calm down. We need to be really calm here.'

'We need to get away.'

'We can't do that. We need to stay and call the police.'

'I mean it!' Rebecca pulled away from Tom's embrace. 'Something very bad is happening here and it's following us. First my flat and now this.' She pointed at the corpse of Henry Goldman, stiff on the floor of his study.

'I know, I understand,' Tom said, his mind jamming as one thought skidded and crashed into another. It was becoming impossible to deny: danger was stalking them. The important thing was to stay focused. They had met Henry Goldman that afternoon, and his secretary would tell detectives about the raised voices she had heard. Then Julian would confirm that his father had sounded agitated when they spoke that evening. 'We have to report this. You need to call the police right now. It will sound better coming from you. You're a friend of the family. You have a reason to be here.'

He picked up the cordless phone charging on Goldman's desk and instantly regretted it: fingerprints. Too late to undo his mistake, he dialled 999 and passed the phone to Rebecca. 'Ask for the police.'

She spoke within a few seconds. 'I'm calling to report a murder.'

'No!' Tom mouthed the word with desperate urgency. He shook his head and stage-whispered, 'You're calling to report a dead body!'

She tried to correct herself but the damage was done. Once the call was over, she looked at Tom. 'I'm sorry,' she said. 'I don't know—'

'You need to call Julian.' Any delay there would look even more suspicious. She took the phone and left the room, though he could still hear her speaking in the corridor.

Through the study windows he could now see the blue light of a police car and two uniformed men emerging. Tom went to the door, opened it and gestured for the two men to come in.

They introduced themselves as constables, showed their ID and pulled out their notebooks. Rebecca came in and the four of them stood together in the hall like hosts welcoming guests to a dinner party. The older of the two men asked them to describe what had happened.

The policemen nodded as Rebecca explained that Henry Goldman was a friend of her late father's. They listened as she said that she had come here to carry on a conversation started earlier today. Then they both picked up their pens and scribbled furiously when she said that they had found the front door unlocked.

Of course, thought Tom. That was the crucial detail, the awkward fact that would turn this from the unfortunate discovery of a dead old man into a murder inquiry. He noticed the older officer firing regular glances his way. Wait, thought Tom, till you find out that I have known Rebecca Merton for less than twelve hours. Wait till you discover why I'm in London in the first place. He fought hard the urge to sink his head into his hands.

Soon a doctor arrived, to confirm that Henry Goldman was dead, followed by a second police car, containing a photographer and a plain-clothes detective. While the photographer went directly to the study, the detective asked them all to step outside; he did not want any more footprints in the hallway than were there already. So they stood outdoors, in a huddle on the drive, and the detective asked Rebecca the same questions all over again, though now he loaded some with extra and, Tom felt, threatening emphasis.

'So you came here and let yourselves in, and you felt comfortable doing that because you had visited this house often as a child, am I right?'

'No, that's not—'

'And once you're in, you find the body. In the study, which means you had to go exploring to find it. And then you, Miss Merton, once you see it, you start trying to revive Mr Goldman. Kiss of life and so on, am I right?'

'CPR. Cardiopulmonary resuscitation.'

'All right, Miss Merton. And this is because you suspect what?'

'I suspected major cardiac arrest. A heart attack.'

'And Mr Goldman was in what state when you made this effort?'

'He was dead.'

'I know that, Miss Merton, I know that.'

'Dr Merton,' Tom interjected. She placed a hand on his. *Don't*.

The detective gave a hard look at Tom before turning back to Rebecca. 'What I am driving at is that he obviously hadn't been dead for very long or you wouldn't have tried reviving him. Am I right?'

'He was still warm, if that's what you mean.'

'That is exactly what I mean, *Dr* Merton. Exactly. Thank you. Now what about you, Mr Byrne? What were you doing all this time?'

'I watched Rebecca try to bring him round. I consoled her once we realised that it was too late. And then we phoned the police.'

'Yes, the phone call. I'm curious about that. The note I have says that the call that came at nine fifty-five was to report a *murder*. Now what I don't—'

'Can I ask you a question, Detective?' Tom now drew up himself to his full height, several inches taller than the policeman. 'Are we being interviewed as witnesses or as suspects?'

The detective suddenly allowed his expression to harden. 'That's exactly what I'm trying to work out, Mr Byrne.'

THE AIDE KNOCKED on the door of the boss's suite and let himself in. The old man was sitting at a table set for afternoon tea, with a clear picture-window view of Manhattan easing its way towards dusk.

'Any news?' he asked, before the aide had even crossed the room. No hello, not even a look round. These were not good signs.

'Good news and bad news, you might say.'

'What's the bad news?'

Damn. He cursed himself for not having rehearsed how to present this. 'Well, it only really makes sense once you've heard the good news, sir,' the aide began, incredulous that he'd walked into so obvious a cul-de-sac. 'Which is that Henry Goldman will be giving us no further trouble, sir. He did not manage to pass on the, er, critical information to the subj— sorry, the people we're following, sorry, I mean the people we're interested in—'

'You're babbling. What's happened?'

'Goldman is dead, sir.'

'What? How?'

'Tonight. At his home, sir.'

The old man's face was reddening. 'Are we responsible?'

'Not in any way that could be proved, I don't think, sir.'

'You don't *think*?' The boss slammed his fist on the table, sending cutlery, plates and a milk jug leaping into the air. 'What do you mean, you don't *think*? What the fuck happened there?'

The aide swallowed hard. 'The trouble is, Goldman had a weak heart. The minute he saw them, there in his house, he started shouting, then clutching his chest. They didn't touch him. It just happened.'

The old man slumped in his chair. 'Did they find anything?'

'Yes. As it happens, Goldman was going through a box of papers when our men arrived. It appears that they relate to our issue.'

'And those papers are safe now?'

'Perfectly.'

'Any mention of . . .' His voice trailed off. 'By name, I mean?'

'Don't yet know that, sir. There's some translation work to be done.'

The old man rubbed his chin, processing the information, calculating.

Finally, he threw down his napkin and pushed back his chair. Then, barely audibly, he muttered, 'What have we started here?' And with that, he waved the aide away.

A HARSH BEAM of light swept across the driveway. That would be Julian, Tom thought. Without waiting for permission, Rebecca broke off and walked towards his car. Tom saw the look of apprehension on the detective's face: if he regarded Rebecca as a potential suspect, he wouldn't want her chatting with the son of the deceased, filling his head with her version of events.

'I'll tell you what,' the detective said suddenly. 'Why don't we all go down to the station? We can take statements from you both and then we can see how things look in the morning.'

'After the autopsy, you mean.'

'Yes. That should make things much clearer. We have a car here. We can take you right away.'

'We'll be fine. We've got our own car.'

'You've both undergone a traumatic experience tonight. Our guidelines on victim support say that often people who have experienced trauma are too shocked to drive. Even when they don't realise it.'

Tom acquiesced, though he suspected that the detective's primary, if unauthorised, purpose was to give the Saab a quick once-over.

They were taken to Kentish Town police station, a poky hole of a place, where they were interviewed separately, as Tom had expected. No less predictably, the lead detective decided to interview Tom first, and soon realised

Rebecca Merton's connection to events in the news. Tom explained that that was why they had been to see Goldman, because he was an old friend of her father's. To Tom's relief, the detective pressed the point no further.

Finally, a junior officer led them both to some electronic gismo, where they pressed their fingers on a glass plate to have their prints taken, 'to exclude them from the inquiry'. Tom guessed that any intruder would have taken the elementary precaution of wearing gloves. Which meant the only prints that would be found in Goldman's study would belong to him and Rebecca.

Some three and a half hours after they had first driven past Hampstead Heath, the detective told them that if the autopsy showed that Goldman had died from natural causes, this would not be a murder inquiry at all. Tom and Rebecca would hear no more about it. Then he sent them on their way.

Outside the police station, they hailed a taxi and headed east.

Tom looked out of the window, too tired to talk. He didn't want to be here, bouncing once more up and down the speed-bumped streets of the London Borough of Hackney. He had wanted to go back to Rebecca's flat or, more ambitiously, his hotel, if only to get some rest, but she had rejected that idea instantly. In the police car, he had tried to touch her hand, but she had brushed him away—not angrily exactly, but with a sort of suppressed irritation, as if now were not the time.

He was in danger of forgetting that not yet forty-eight hours had passed since her elderly father—her only family in the world, by the looks of things—had been shot dead in circumstances that remained baffling. Her home had been the target of a violent robbery, and now an old friend of the family lay dead—hours after revealing the secret life of a shadowy, lethal organisation in which both their fathers had been players. He might try to reassure her that Henry Goldman's death was surely a coincidence, but the minute he saw the corpse, he had succumbed to the same nauseous fear that she had. The old lawyer had surely been murdered—and she could be next.

'I've worked one thing out,' he said finally, breaking the exhausted silence that had held since they had left the police station. 'The fire alarm.'

'What about it?'

'It wasn't a coincidence. The timing,' he said. 'It's an old tactic. The Trots did it all the time when I was a student. A meeting wasn't going their way, they'd just yank the fire alarm: meeting abandoned.'

'You're saying that Henry Goldman pulled the fire alarm because he didn't like what we were asking?'

'Not him.'

'But no one else was in that meeting, Tom.'

'No one else was in the room, I grant you that. But that doesn't mean no one was listening. I don't know how they did it, but they did it.'

'And who's "they"?'

'I wish I knew.'

Tom's phone rang. He looked down at the display: *Henning*.

'Hi.'

'You don't sound pleased to hear from me.'

'Sorry. It's been a tough few hours.' Tom closed his eyes in dread at the mere thought of Munchau discovering that he'd been in the custody of the Metropolitan Police in connection with a suspected homicide. He wondered how long he would be able to keep it quiet.

'Well, maybe this will help. We've come up with a few names.'

'What?'

'You know, for your geriatric club? Seventy and over?'

'Oh, that. Right.' He had clean forgotten about it; that phone call to Henning, that hunch, felt like it happened years ago. 'What have you got?'

'Well, first, you won't be surprised to hear that there are none on the permanent UN staff. Retirement at age sixty, strictly enforced.'

'Sure.'

'But there are three visitors in town this week who are over seventy.'

Tom nodded, unseen; his pulse quickened.

'The Chinese have brought a veteran interpreter, Li Gang. Legend has it he did Mao and Nixon, though I don't believe it. I mean, they—'

'What about the other two?'

'The President of the State of Israel is here. He's eighty-four.'

'And the other one?'

'Foreign minister of Ivory Coast. Seventy-two. Been in the job on and off since the 1970s, apparently.'

'Thanks, Henning.'

'No use?'

'It was only a hunch.'

Tom almost smiled at the irony of it. If you wanted to pick three people less likely to be Nazi war criminals, you couldn't do much better than representatives of China, Ivory Coast and—just to put it beyond doubt—Israel.

By now they had arrived at Kyverdale Road, home of the late Gerald Merton. Rebecca had insisted on it; if they couldn't find out whatever it was Goldman wanted to tell them from Goldman himself, they would have to see if there was some clue, some hint, that her father had left behind. As Tom paid the fare, he braced himself to see Rebecca hit by yet another emotional freight train. How much could one person endure?

He watched her produce a ring of keys, choose one and turn it in the lock. She did not linger in the hallway but strode up the thinly carpeted stairs to the third floor. Tom noticed Rebecca's hands trembling as she unlocked the door. She switched on the main light and gasped.

He peered past her. The place had been ransacked, worked over just as thoroughly as her own apartment. The cushions were slashed, the books strewn on the floor like casualties in a battlefield. Even the carpet had been rolled back to expose the dirty, dust-caked floorboards underneath.

Tom waded through the wreckage, trying to construct an image of how the place would have looked. The kitchen was small and off-white, the appliances museum pieces from the 1970s. There was a basic two-person table by the wall, and a radio, a vase and several framed photos, lying broken on the floor. Tom peered closely at one holiday snap showing a tanned man, his shirt off, with his right arm round a woman and his left round a girl of about twelve, all seated at a table in an outdoor café in bright sunshine. Tom focused on Gershon. He looked at least ten years older than his wife, but his body was in remarkable shape, the muscles firm and toned, the chest and stomach hard and flat. And his eyes were as luminous as his daughter's.

Tom went back into the living room, and examined the slashed remains of a single well-worn armchair by the window. Next to it stood a table bearing a telephone and a radio-cassette player, a relic of the 1980s. All over the floor, emptied out from a large, glass-fronted cabinet, were assorted silver knick-knacks, a few books and many more family photos.

He found Rebecca in the bedroom contemplating another depressing scene: clothes strewn across the carpet, cupboard doors flung wide open. Tom expected her to sink onto the bed and burst into tears, but instead she went back into the living room.

A look of relief passed across her face. 'They're still here.'

She knelt down and began poring over the framed photographs dumped on the floor. She studied one of these images closely. It was in that peculiar shade of dull orange that seemed to veil all colour photographs from the 1970s, and it showed five middle-aged men beaming widely, four of them wearing large square glasses. All five were in black tie, though they had their jackets off. The one on the far right was raising a glass. She angled the picture for him to look at it properly. 'This is the poker club.'

Looking at this photograph, no one would have guessed what these men had been capable of, or what they had endured to make them do it.

'Joe Tannenbaum and Geoffrey Besser, they're both dead now,' she said quietly. 'And there's Henry Goldman's father. The only one I don't know about is this bloke here. Sid something, he was called.'

Tom looked hard at the man she indicated, the one with the raised glass. Now that he knew the story of this band of brothers, was he deluding himself, or could he really see something else in these five faces? Gerald Merton had a wariness in his eyes discernible in every photograph Tom had seen. But there was something like it in the gazes of the other men, too. A steel below the surface, despite the apparently avuncular smiles.

'Sid Steiner! That was his name. Sid Steiner.'

'Is he alive?'

'I have no idea. But I think we'd better find out.'

THEY SAT NEXT to each other, in the dead of night, on the slashed remains of Gerald Merton's couch, and searched the online archive of the *Jewish Chronicle* obituaries on the BlackBerry. Tom was struggling to concentrate against the noise of the TV set. Turning it on had been his idea; if someone was eavesdropping on their conversations, as he was convinced they had been at Goldman's office, then at least they could make the eavesdropper's job a little more difficult.

At Rebecca's suggestion, he had typed in the single word 'Steiner', and the website had come up with hundreds. They scrolled through looking for Sids, and to Rebecca's dismay they found one easily, dated six years ago. But when she had read the family's death notice, she shook her head.

'Those are the wrong names. His wife wasn't called Beryl. And they had a son called Daniel. Dan. I remember because I had a crush on him when I was about seven.'

They searched again and found three more Sid Steiners, but none struck Rebecca as the right one. Either the age or the family names were wrong.

Tom put the machine to one side and shifted position to face her. 'Is it possible he died quietly, without an announcement?'

'No. If you're as Jewish as Sid Steiner, you die in the *Jewish Chronicle*.'

'So where is he?'

'I don't know.'

'OK,' said Tom. 'We'll do this the old-fashioned way. We'll get some sleep, and in the morning we'll start working the phones.'

ON AN IMPROVISED BED of slashed cushions and a torn sofa, Tom tried to slip into sleep. Though he was exhausted, his mind was still sprinting. Rebecca was next door, in her father's bedroom.

A succession of images was flipping through his head like the pages of a child's flickbook. He saw a boy in ghetto rags, then an old man shot on the steps of the UN, then a woman's body swinging from a rafter, then Rebecca's crooked smile and then, without warning . . . Rebecca.

There she was, framed in the doorway. She was wearing only a shirt.

Tom brought himself up so that he was resting on his elbows. He didn't say a word, and neither did she.

Their kisses were as hungry now as before—hungrier for having been thwarted. The touch of her skin, the scent of her, sent such a voltage through him that he felt he might be burning. And there in the shadows, their sweat and their taste mingling, the moment he entered her was as if they had entered each other. The intensity of it was so great that it frightened him.

Afterwards, the silence seemed to bind them together. Her head lay on his chest, and he suddenly felt the sensation of a tear falling onto his skin.

'Rebecca?' He could feel her trembling now. 'What is it?'

'I just wish this hadn't happened like this.'

He stroked her hair, certain that his first instinct had been right: it was madness for them to have made love here, in the home of her dead father.

She spoke again. 'With all this going on, I mean. I wish it could have happened another way. I'm so sorry.'

'I can handle it if you can.'

The silence returned, but this time Tom knew it was the prelude to another question. 'How come there's no Mrs Byrne?' she said.

'Is it that obvious?'

'It is to me. Was there ever one?'

'No. I used to be married to the work. And then, after everything that happened, I sort of shut out the future, along with the past. Made my home in the present. I couldn't plan much beyond dinner reservations.'

'You're speaking in the past tense.'

'Maybe I've changed.'

She got up, headed for the kitchen and returned with a glass of water. She drank from it, passed it to him, then lay back down, skin touching skin.

'How come there's no Mr Merton?' he asked. 'Sorry, I mean—'

'It's OK. Well, there's the patients. They take a lot out of you.'

'But that's not the whole story.'

'No. The truth is, it was hard with my dad. I was his only child. And then, after Mum died . . . Well, marrying someone would have felt like I was—'

'—leaving him.'

'Maybe.'

'What would he have thought of me?' Tom asked.

'Well, you're not Jewish, for a start.'

'So?'

'So, let's not get into it.'

'Rebecca—'

She placed a finger on his lips. 'Don't. Don't say anything.'

'Why not?'

'Because I'm trying to be like you. I grew up my whole life either drowning in the past or worrying about the future. I want to see if I can enjoy the present. Just for once.'

WHEN HE WOKE a little after eight, Rebecca was no longer lying next to him. She was up and dressed, explaining that she had been too impatient to sleep. She wanted to start the search for Sid Steiner immediately.

She reached for the phone, tried directory enquiries first, and in vain, then turned to the phone book. She circled one number and dialled it, only for the call to be fielded by an answering machine. The voice belonged to Sid Steiner—but it was an accountancy practice in Hendon, no connection.

'What about this Dan, then?' Tom asked. 'Haven't you stayed in touch?'

She shook her head. Then she brightened, and said, 'I know. He'll be on Facebook.' She reached over for Tom's BlackBerry.

Tom felt a sudden awareness of the age gap between them: he relied on old-fashioned email. Still, at least he knew what she was talking about.

Sure enough, once logged on, it took a matter of seconds in the search box to generate an image of a depressingly handsome man of about Tom's age, with a full head of dark hair.

'I could just poke him,' she said. When she saw Tom's startled expression, she smiled. 'That's not what it sounds like. It's a Facebook thing.'

THERE WAS ONLY ONE SPACE left in the car park; the rest were taken up with three minibuses, which, Tom noticed, were equipped even on the outside with assorted ramps and handles for wheelchair access. The building itself was large, fashioned out of the grey concrete that seemed to have been the only material available to architects working in the 1970s.

Rebecca had 'poked' Dan Steiner only an hour ago. He had responded immediately, supplying Rebecca with a phone number. She had rung him from a phone box three streets away. After expressing his condolences, he had been happy to give her the address of the retirement home on Stamford Hill where his father now lived. It was a five-minute drive from her own father's place; the last two boys of the poker club had somehow stuck together.

They had not phoned ahead, but Dan had: the lady at reception said she was expecting two visitors for Sid. As it happened, they had picked a good time to come: Sid was playing bingo in the main hall. Before they could ask where that was, a large woman in her mid-fifties came striding towards them. From her ID tag, Tom could see that her name was Brenda.

'Hello! We haven't seen you at the centre before, have we?' She sounded breathless. 'You're here to see Sid?'

'We are,' said Rebecca, back in doctor mode. 'We're not family, but he and my father were very close.'

'And has your husband met Sid before?'

'I'm not—'

'He's not—'

They shot each other a quick look.

'Well, I'm glad anyway. Visitors, he doesn't get so many.' The voice was musical, almost singsong: a Jewish melody. 'The sons come every now and then, but you know how it is. Everyone's busy.'

She led them through double doors into a large hall. At the head of the room was a man at a table of his own, clutching a microphone and, with no expression in his voice, reading out a series of numbers. Occasionally, one of the old folks would scratch away at a card. Despite the absence of patter or laughter, Tom realised that the man was a bingo-caller.

'Ooh,' said Brenda. 'I thought Sid would be here. I hope he hasn't gone wandering. You know about his condition? His son explained, yes?'

Rebecca flashed Tom a look of panic. 'No. No, he didn't. He said it might be difficult to talk to his father, but he—'

'Oh, I expect he didn't like to talk about it. But Sid's not the only one here, you know. Lots of them have it. I sometimes think it's a bless—'

'Can we meet him, do you think?' Rebecca was getting impatient.

Brenda led them out of the hall and up a flight of stairs. She stopped to catch her breath. 'I think I can hear someone,' she singsonged.

She pushed open a pair of double doors and they walked into a large room in which the floor was almost entirely covered in a mat the colour of a billiard table. At the far end was a solitary upright piano, and, hunched over it, a man with white hair on both sides of a bald head, playing scales.

'This is the room we use for mat bowls and line dancing. And there, at the piano, is Sid.' She smiled. 'Sid, visitors for you!'

The old man's gaze remained fixed on his left hand as it moved up and down the keyboard.

'I say, Sid, these nice young people have come for a chat.' She turned to Rebecca and Tom, her back deliberately to Sid Steiner. 'Maybe now's not a good time. Could you come back tomorrow? Or at the weekend?'

'We'd love to, we really would.' The doctor voice again. 'But unfortunately I lost my own father this week and there's something urgent that has come up. I think Sid might be the only person who can help us.'

'I wish you long life, dear.' Brenda took Rebecca's hand. 'And you need to ask Sid something? You need to find out information?'

Rebecca nodded. Brenda's mouth formed itself into an expression suggesting scepticism. 'Let's see what a cup of tea can do.'

At the mention of tea, Sid halted mid-scale. Gently, Brenda turned him towards Rebecca and Tom.

His face was liver-spotted and veined but he was still recognisable as the man who had toasted the poker club's collective good health thirty years earlier. When DIN were in their first hunting season, Sid Steiner would have been in his twenties: fit, strong and fearless.

'Hello, Sid,' Rebecca said gently. She gestured towards a column of stacking chairs, and Tom pulled out two of them. Once she was seated, she spoke again. 'I'm Gerald Merton's daughter, Rebecca.'

'Who?'

'I'm Gerald Merton's daughter.'

'What do you say?'

'Gershon Matzkin.'

'Gershon Matzkin? Gershon's a good boy.'

Rebecca dipped her head, and Tom could see that the sides of her eyes were wet. Was it despair at the pitiful state of Sid Steiner or the notion of her father as a boy that had done that? He squeezed her shoulder and, in thanks, she touched his hand briefly.

'Do you remember when you last saw him?'

'My mother won't like me talking to a girl like you, you know. She's warned me not to talk to girls like you. From across the river.'

Rebecca reached out and placed a hand on Steiner's sleeve. 'Can you tell me anything Gershon said to you recently?' she asked. 'Did he come and visit you here?'

'Now, did you get married in the end? Or wouldn't he have you?'

'Who?'

At that moment, Brenda pushed her way through the double doors, back first, holding a tray of tea. She must have caught Rebecca's expression, because she gave a small nod, as if to say, *This is what I meant. Dementia.*

'It's tea time, Sidney.'

'What's that?' He was pointing at the tray.

'That's a cup.'

'I know that's a cup. What's that?'

'Guess.'

The old man scrunched up his eyes in concentration. Eventually, he said three words that made Tom's eyes prick. 'I can't remember.'

'That's milk, Sidney. That's a jug of milk.'

Rebecca got to her feet and spoke quietly to Brenda. 'I'm sorry to have taken your time, but I don't think this is going to work. We made a mistake.'

'What is it you need him to remember?'

'We need him to remember something from long ago,' Tom said quickly, pulling an answer out of the air. 'Maybe fifty or sixty years ago.'

Brenda smiled. 'You should have said. Now come with me.'

THEY PASSED THROUGH a door set with patterned glass, the way front doors used to look. Next to it was a brass plate: THE Y DOVE REMINISCENCE ROOM.

The space had been divided into two areas. The first was wood-floored and done up like a hallway with a hat stand and a sideboard cluttered with objects: a wind-up gramophone, a Philips wireless, a Frister & Rossmann sewing machine and a heavy, black mechanical cash register. Opposite was a small kitchen area, including a big square sink, a washboard and a stack of battered enamel saucepans. Sitting on the counter were products from decades ago: Flor Brite Mop Furniture Polish and Lipton's No.1 Quality Tea.

The main part of the room boasted a floral carpet the like of which Tom had not seen since childhood visits to his grandparents. There was a fire-place, its surround made up of beige ceramic tiles, and on a side table a heavy, black Bakelite telephone. Beside it, Sid Steiner sat in a big armchair.

This was the place residents with dementia came for sessions aimed at giving their ravaged memories a workout. Because, while short-term memory was the first casualty, the experiences of long ago tended to be forgotten last, with recollections of childhood clinging on until the very end.

Rebecca cleared her throat. 'So, Sid, when did you come to this country?'

Brenda shook her head. 'Try to avoid factual questions,' she whispered. 'Use the objects in the room, try to get him talking.'

Tom looked round and grabbed a packet of Park Drive cigarettes. He passed it to Rebecca, who put it in Steiner's hands.

'Do you smoke, Sid?'

'We all do.'

'Did you ever smoke these, Sid?'

He looked down at the packet and shook his head. 'It's not easy to get cigarettes. Besides, when you get them, you don't smoke them; you use them. Don't you know that? Didn't they teach you anything in Warsaw?'

Rebecca leaned forward; it was the most coherent response they had yet heard from Sid Steiner. 'What do you buy with them?'

'Anything. To get in, to get out, to get past a guard.'

Neither Tom nor Rebecca knew where or when in his memory Sid had landed. Was it whichever ghetto he had been locked up in, or was it the occupation zone of 1945, scene of DIN's first hunting season?

'What about this?' Hung up on a wall, among a display of photographs, was the jacket of a British Army uniform. Rebecca passed it to him.

'Not bad.' He assessed the three stripes on the upper arm. 'Sergeant. That could be useful. But what we need are MPs. Can you get me one of those?'

Tom squeezed Rebecca's wrist in excitement: MPs were military police. This fitted precisely with the testimony Henry Goldman had given them, that MPs' uniforms were the ones DIN prized most.

'Use it for what, Sid?'

'I'm not going to tell you that. If you don't know, then you're not meant to know.' Tom smiled: it was a smart answer.

'Did you work with Gershon in DIN?'

'You some kind of spy? I don't answer questions like that.'

'I'm with Gershon.'

'He's too young for a girl like you. He's only a boy.'

It must be 1945. Sid Steiner must have transported himself back to Allied-occupied Germany, probably the British zone. Maybe the uniform had done it. Tom scanned the walls and shelves for another prop, something that might trigger a useful memory.

Then Sid spoke unprompted. 'I know how to use that.' He aimed his withered finger until it rested on a rolling pin. Tom sighed: and just when we were getting somewhere.

'What did you use it for, Sid?' It was Brenda. She had pulled the rolling pin from its case and was handing it over.

'Well, I had to train as a baker, didn't I? If the plan was going to work.'

Rebecca leaned forward once more. 'What plan, Sid?'

'Ask Gershon, he'll tell you. He trained too. We both did. Kneading the dough, glazing the cakes. I was very good at doughnuts.'

'What's the name of the plan?'

'Plan B.'

'B for bakery?'

'No. Wrong again.'

'Did Plan B work?'

'It made the papers, you know. *New York* flipping *Times*. Nuremberg, April 1946. But we could have done more.'

'What was the plan?'

'Everyone needs bread, no?'

'You were making bread. Who for?'

'You may be pretty, but Gershon's picked himself a bit of a dunce, if you don't mind my saying so. Who do you think it was for?'

Chapter Eight

Gershon's Diary

Our first task was to decide a target. This was not a decision for me; I was just a teenage boy. Others took those decisions. One of them was the man I had met in the cellar in the ghetto at Kovno, on that night of the candles: Aron. The other two were dead by the spring of 1946. Nearly everyone was dead by then.

But a few leaders of the resistance had survived, and they, along with a few from the camps, were the men who started DIN. I was still a teenager but I wanted them to think of me as a warrior, a man who had proved himself. And anyone who had lived through what we had lived through was no longer a child, no matter how young you were. Your childhood was gone.

We were in a safe house in Munich, and one night, as I was clearing away the dishes from our meal, I heard one of the commanders mention that the Allies had set up a prison outside the city, to hold Nazis for 'questioning'. 'There are eight thousand SS in there,' Aron said. 'No small fry. They're being held for *major* war crimes. They're all in there: senior staff at the camps, *Politische Abteilung*, Gestapo, Einsatzgruppen, everyone.'

Aron had done some research, using a DIN volunteer who had ended up in Nuremberg. He had tracked down the source of all the camp's bread, a medium-sized bakery on the outskirts of town. The leaders talked some more, their voices becoming hushed. Then they fell silent. I looked up from the dishes I was washing to see that they were all looking at me, with that same look I had seen before, three years earlier, in the cellar in the ghetto.

THEY GAVE ME an address and described the man I was to speak to at the bakery: the works supervisor. I recognised him as soon as I walked in.

'My name is Tadeusz Radomski,' I began, 'and I need to learn how to be a baker.' I told him I was a Pole, with an uncle in Montreal who was himself a baker and was ready to give me a job. 'All I need is a visa, but it takes time. While I'm waiting, I want to learn. My uncle says I need experience—'

'I'm sorry,' the works supervisor said, wiping a flour-dusted hand on his apron. 'There are no jobs here.'

'My uncle said I should show you this.' I reached inside my canvas satchel. As soon as the man got a peek of what was inside—a bottle of Scotch whisky and two bars of chocolate—he gestured for me to come into a back office. 'My uncle says you can have this now and there will be more for you when I have done a month's work.' I started that afternoon, with no pay.

And so I began as an apprentice baker, learning everything from kneading and rolling the dough to icing cakes. I said little and worked hard. I wanted the manager to trust me completely, so that he would let me work anywhere in the bakery. My job was to find out exactly how the system worked, to understand every aspect of it. Above all, I needed to discover how the thousands of loaves for Stalag 13, the holding centre for Nazi prisoners, were baked, and when and how they were transported. I did as much as I could, never asking a single direct question. I just watched and listened.

Then one day, the American Army trucks arrived as usual, just before dawn, to pick up the bread. I had been doing the night shift, and when one of the American drivers complained that his partner was off sick and that he needed someone to help unload at the other end, the manager took one look at me and gestured me towards the truck. 'He'll go.'

And so I rode up-front in the cab, next to the American. When we got to Stalag 13, waved through by the American guard on the gate, I felt prickles on the back of my neck. This site, I knew, had been a concentration camp.

'OK, here we go,' the driver said in English, parking outside the prisoners' kitchen. He told me, in gestures and signs, to start unloading the wheeled trolleys, each stacked with a dozen racks, each rack containing two dozen loaves. I estimated that, along with the other trucks, we delivered around 9,000 loaves of bread. All black bread.

'What about the white bread?' I asked in German.

The driver shook his head. He did not understand. Somehow, through a combination of hand signals and pidgin German and English, I got the question out. He pointed into the distance, at a single truck unloading at the other end of the camp. So that was how it was done: 9,000 loaves of black bread for the Nazi prisoners taken in several trucks to the prisoners' kitchen, and a separate truck carrying 1,000 loaves of white bread, delivered to a different kitchen for the American guards. The driver pointed at the black loaves and made a retching expression. Then he gestured in the distance, at the white loaves, and patted his stomach. He was telling me that the Americans couldn't stand the coarse black bread and wanted white.

I worked hard to hide my smile as we drove back to the bakery. This will be easy, I thought. This will be easy.

I briefed the commanders that night, proud of my discovery. We had only to direct our attention to the black loaves; anything we did to them would not affect the Americans. It would be DIN's simplest, but greatest, operation.

But then Rosa brought bad news. All of us had had to get jobs. Rosa's job was to find an American boyfriend. No one asked whether she minded being used in this way; it was her duty, as a soldier for DIN. No one asked me, either, even though, by that time, Rosa and I were together. Perhaps no one knew; perhaps people assumed I was too young for such things.

She had set about throwing herself at the GI Joe responsible for the guards' canteen at Stalag 13, and she had heard this sergeant joking about some of his officers, health-conscious types from Boston, who refused to eat white bread. 'They want the brown stuff the Krauts eat!' he said. So he had to arrange for one hundred loaves of Nazi bread to be separated from the rest and delivered each morning to the American kitchen. 'Crazy, they are.'

I received this news as you would word of a disaster. If we tampered with the black bread, we would hit some Americans, and they would not let such an attack go unpunished. They would hunt us down.

There were more complications. In what I imagined was an idle moment of pillow-talk, Rosa's boyfriend explained that he'd had a rough day, having to do a spot-check on the prisoners' kitchen to make sure no knives had been stolen, and that the food supplies were not being used as cover for any smuggling. These inspections, done weekly, meant there was no guarantee that any tainted bread would not be examined and, possibly, discovered.

Rosa and I did as we were told, uncovering every detail of the process and relaying it to our commanders. I was asked to come up with a thorough blueprint of the bakery, including all measurements. And of course I had to bring back several loaves of bread, black and white, to be studied.

After two months of this, we were summoned for another meeting. This time, though, a man I had not met before was there. He had come from Paris and was never introduced to us by name, but he was treated by the commanders with respect. It turned out that he was an experienced player of the black market—and that he had made contact with a chemist. This man told us that as we could no longer introduce the poison into the mixture for the black bread, it would have to be painted on to the loaves so that those that were separated out for the Americans would not be tainted.

'You're sure the poison will have no taste?' Aron asked.

'No taste.'

'No colour?'

'No colour. It's an arsenic mixture, odourless and colourless.'

I was nervous about speaking, but as the only baker in the room I felt I had some authority. 'Won't the crust on the top be moist?'

The Frenchman widened his eyes into a smile and pointed at me. 'Our young friend has asked a good question! This, for me, is our biggest problem. But we think that after an hour or so it will have dried out.'

'You *think*?'

'If there is some slight dampness, no one will think anything of it. Remember, this is not the Ritz Hotel. What are the Nazis going to do, ask their waiter to take it back?'

Aron ignored the joke and turned to Rosa. 'What time do they start eating breakfast?'

'At six fifteen a.m.'

Now to me. 'And the loaves are picked up at five?'

'Yes. But most are baked by three.'

We waited for Aron to give his verdict. Looking at each of us, his gaze steady, he said, 'The first night with a full moon, we do it.'

AS IT HAPPENS, we did not choose the very first moonlit night. We waited for a Saturday. That was because on Saturday nights half the workers went off for a drink when the work was almost finished.

We had discussed how best to do it. When the commanders first hatched the plot, they assumed it would be a simple business. I would smuggle some poison into the bakery and tip it into the vat of flour. But painting poison on to 9,000 loaves was a mammoth task. It would take hours and many people. Luckily, Aron had a plan.

When Saturday, April 13, 1946 came, I was more nervous than I had ever been before. I had been on shift since five o'clock that afternoon and the hours had dragged. I did my work but I kept asking myself, Will we have enough of the arsenic mixture? Will we have enough time to apply the poison to the loaves? Will this crazy scheme work?

At 2.53 a.m., I heard the words I had been waiting for, spoken by the manager himself, 'Come on, the beer is calling!' He and seven others took off their overalls and headed for the tavern down the street. They said goodbye to me and the other 'saps' who had to stay behind.

I knew what was happening outside. Once the lookout signalled to Rosa that they'd gone, she would appear from the opposite direction, wearing a short black and red dress. I can picture her strolling up to the gate in high heels, waiting for the German night watchman to emerge. She would have had just a few moments to make her impression. I can see him unlocking the gate, then stepping forward to give Rosa a proper look over. She would have probably let him grope her a bit, so she could move close, and she would only have had to push the blade a few inches forward to find his heart.

Then Manik, the lookout, would run from his hiding place and help Rosa drag the dead body out of the way. They would give the signal to the truck over the road. The vehicle was from the British Army transport pool, signed out by a friendly member of the Jewish Brigade, using forged papers. With its lights switched off, it drove through, Manik closing the gate after it.

That was when I headed for the outside loading area. By the time I got there, they were all out of the truck, five of them, their faces blacked up. With Manik and Rosa, it made seven. All were armed.

I guided them through the drying room until they were huddled around the far door that led into the bakery proper. Silently, Aron counted the group off, then one, two, three—they burst through, shouting, '*Achtung!*' and training their guns on the half-dozen bakers they found within.

I watched through the window in the door. The bakers raised their arms in the air, a group of Germans surrendering to a gang of Jews. It should have been a sweet moment, but it had come at least three years too late.

While three of the group bound and gagged the bakers, I emerged from the drying room to show Aron where the supplies were kept. The eyes of the men tied up all around me were aghast with surprise, and some were ablaze with hatred, at the Polish boy who had betrayed them. Aron and one other set about emptying the storeroom, filling up the truck that was waiting outside. They took their time, making sure this activity lasted as long as necessary.

Back in the drying room, I started to prise open each memorised floorboard, bringing out the bottles of poison I had concealed beneath them. Rosa and I then began filling the metal mixing bowls I had brought in. The Frenchman had been right: the fluid was clear and smelt of nothing.

The other four in our group opened up their bags, pulled out paintbrushes and began methodically painting on the poison, loaf by loaf.

Soon we had a production line, as Rosa and I ensured that five bowls were full of poison at any one time. Every ten minutes Aron passed through the drying room, but he could not stop for long: he had to maintain the charade of loading up the truck with sugar, yeast and flour. He could not let the bakers know that anything was going on inside the drying room.

The two hours flew by, each of us possessed by the same fierce desire: to poison as many of those loaves as we could in the time. I counted the racks we had done and I estimated we had painted arsenic on to about 3,000.

Then Aron joined us, gesturing at his watch. It was a quarter to five; the American trucks would arrive in fifteen minutes. He urged us to pack up.

We rinsed out and hid the mixing bowls, filled our bags with the empty poison bottles and put the unused bottles back under the floorboards. By the time they were found, it wouldn't matter. I was the last to leave, and was already in the loading area when I saw it, lying on a steel counter, close to the loaves. An oversized paintbrush, too large and crude to be used for glazing pastries. I rushed back and grabbed it. When I turned round I saw our leader, now crouching with the rest of the team in the back of the truck, glaring at me, his hand on his pistol.

It was 4.59. Any further delay would have been too costly. Aron could have shot me, and left me there, and it would not even have looked suspicious. The apprentice boy killed in the course of an armed robbery on a bakery. That, after all, was our cover story.

The Americans would conclude that the armed thieves had come to steal the flour, sugar and yeast they knew were held within. It would be no great surprise. Foodstuffs fetched a good price on the German black market of 1946. The workers would tell them all about it. 'It was an inside job,' the manager would say. 'That little Polish bastard let them in.'

The Americans would offer consolation and, perhaps, call for a military policeman to come and investigate. But they would not be diverted from the task of the morning. They had thousands of men to feed in Stalag 13 and— yes, look over here—as luck would have it, the intruders had not stolen the bread. Well, our sympathies, gentlemen, but we need to be on our way.

That, anyway, was the plan, dreamt up by the Frenchman and pushed and pulled, kneaded and twisted, over the previous weeks.

The truck travelled south, where Manik found a deserted spot to hide it. The rest of us got out a few miles from the bakery and simply waited by the roadside. Before long, a taxi came by. Aron handed the driver a wad of notes and told him to take us to the Czechoslovak border.

Eventually, we read the official accounts of the mysterious attack of food poisoning in the newspapers. We knew they were censored and suspected the Americans would want to cover up what had happened. If they had not managed to protect the men they were holding, it did not look so good. But the reports left no doubt. The poisoned loaves had got through and the Nazis, in their thousands, had eaten them. How many had died? We never knew for sure. Aron said the exact number did not matter. What was important was that the Nazis held in Nuremberg would have understood that the Jews had not accepted their fate, but had come back for revenge.

I tried to accept what Aron said, but I cannot lie. I wanted to know, and I never stopped wanting to know, exactly how many Nazis had tasted that bread I had helped to bake, and how many had died from it. I wanted to know if their death was painful. Above all, I wanted to know that among the dead was the man who had killed my Hannah, my Leah and my Rivvy, my sisters.

JAY SHERRILL wanted nothing more than to sit down. The information from Agent Marcus Mack of the NYPD Intelligence Division was coming too fast to take in, especially walking on a busy Manhattan street, pretending to talk into a cellphone. This was not how Detective Sherrill liked doing business.

'So you say surveillance had been monitoring him since the previous night, when he met the Russian?'

'Right.'

'And they put that together with his location near the UN, and on that basis he became a suspect. A terror suspect.'

'Which is why I was following him.'

'You say there was another man, another agent?'

'Well, I saw one other guy when I got to UN Plaza. But when I asked my handler whether there was back-up, he told me, "There's a team." Now, he coulda been shitting me; it may have just been me and this other guy I saw.'

'Did you speak to him, this other agent?'

'Well, we didn't exactly have a conversation, but we spoke.'

'To each other? To someone else? Who?'

'No, we said something at the same time. That's when I realised. Look: back up a second. When I got to the Plaza, I could no longer tail the guy, because he was on UN turf. So I hung back and watched. I see the suspect walk into the centre of the Plaza. Then I see the UN guard reach for his weapon. And exactly at that moment, the suspect turns round. That's when I see it. What I hadn't been able to see the entire time I was tailing the guy.'

'You saw his face.'

'Exactly. I saw his face. And I realised it instantly, the mistake we'd made. I meant this guy was old. There was no way he was a terrorist. And I know the guard's just had the warning, my warning, that the suspect is about to enter UN territory, and this old guy fits the description: black hat, black coat.'

'So you try to stop the guard from shooting him?'

'I wanna shout, "You got the wrong guy!" But there's no time. The only word that comes out is "No!"'

'And at the same time, another man does the exact same thing.'

'Right. The same word at the same moment. And that's how I know that that guy, maybe five yards from me down the street, is also a cop.'

Jay clenched his teeth. He was remembering Felipe Tavares's testimony two days ago. Why had he started shooting? *Because of the faces of those men I saw. Looking so shocked, and screaming 'No!'*

'Did you talk to the other agent?'

'No. We kinda looked at each other, as if we both understood. Then we did what the rules say you do in that situation. You scoot. Opposite directions.'

Sherrill remembered Tavares saying that both men had vanished. 'OK,' he said. 'And you've been thinking about this ever since?'

'You could say that. Look, it was me who called in that the "suspect" had moved into UN Plaza. And who freaked out the UN guy by shouting "No?"'

'So you feel guilty?'

'The word I would use is *responsible*. But it's not just me.'

'Who else?'

'Who do you think? I'm talking about the New York Police Department Intelligence Division, that's who. I can see what's going on here. They've suddenly gone quiet. Letting a few friggin' cops over at the UN take the rap. That, my friend, ain't right. And I don't intend to let them get away with it.'

It had been Tom's idea to come here after leaving Sid Steiner to his memories, rather than risk going back to Rebecca's flat. And now he was staring. Not, for once, at Rebecca, but at the man sitting two seats away from her, in the Internet café on Kingsland High Street, just a few hundred yards from Julian Goldman's legal-aid practice. He was just another guy tapping away at a computer keyboard, but he seemed out of place here: too well dressed, not poor enough. The rest of the café's customers, Tom guessed, were Kenyan, Somali or Sudanese. He watched over Rebecca's shoulder as she clicked through her emails: a deluge of condolence messages. Then she called up the *New York Times* website, and found the archive search page.

'Sid told us it was April 1946,' Tom whispered. 'So let's start with that.' She filled in the date fields. 'What about keywords?'

'Try "Nuremberg and poison and bakery".'

She typed in the words. Instantly, two items filled the screen. Tom reached over and clicked on the first.

Poisoned Bread Fells 1,900 German Captives in US Army Prison Camp Near Nuremberg

FRANKFORT ON THE MAIN, Germany, April 19 (AP)—Nineteen hundred German prisoners of war were poisoned by arsenic in their bread early this week in a United States camp and all are 'seriously ill', United States headquarters announced tonight.

Tom turned to Rebecca, whose eyes were wide. He shot another look at the man two seats away: if he was watching them, he was doing a good job of concealing it. Tom clicked on the second item, filed three days later:

Poison Plot Toll of Nazis at 2,283; Arsenic Bottles Found by US Agents in Nuremberg Bakery that Served Prison Camp

NUREMBERG, Germany, April 22 (AP)—United States Army authorities said tonight that additional German prisoners of war have been stricken with arsenic poisoning, bringing to 2,283 the number taken ill in a mysterious plot against former Nazi elite guardsmen confined in a camp near Nuremberg.

TOM HESITATED before suggesting a return to her father's flat. Hard enough to be among the worldly remains of a dead parent, harder still to be in a place that had been trashed. Besides, it was making things easy for their pursuers, returning to a place they had already targeted. And yet, if they had intended to kill them, why had they not done it? Whoever was after them was patently efficient enough to have followed their movements over the past twenty-four hours, to have bugged their meeting with Goldman and terminated it at the crucial moment. For all he knew, they were aware of everything he and Rebecca had discovered since. Were they meant to lead these people somewhere? Were they meant to find out something they didn't already know? Could that explain the envelope that had mysteriously arrived at Rebecca's flat yesterday?

After they had left the Internet café and hopped on the 76 bus, Rebecca took the decision out of his hands. 'The answer is somewhere in his flat, I'm sure of it. And anyway, there's nothing else we can do. We don't have a Plan B.' Even then, despite everything, that 'we' warmed him.

And so they returned to Kyverdale Road, to see if there was something that, however improbably, had been overlooked by the burglars. Rebecca stayed in the bedroom, working through her father's jacket pockets, while Tom started on the old man's books, shaking each one by the spine in case some long-forgotten note tumbled out. All the while he was thinking of what had happened in that room just a few hours earlier.

He was flicking through the pages of an *Antiques Roadshow Compendium* for 1981 when he came across something: yellowing, handwritten and impossible to understand. 'Rebecca! Come here!'

She ran from the bedroom and was by his side in seconds. She took the paper from him, bringing it closer to her eyes. 'These are the names of dry-cleaning fluids.' She smiled. 'This is one of my dad's old shopping lists.'

Tom scrunched it up and fell into a chair. Suddenly he sat forward. 'What's that?' he asked.

Rebecca turned to face a picture in the hallway. Barely lit in the windowless space, and obscured by the coat rack, was an abstract painting, a formless collection of greys and blacks, at least three feet wide and two feet tall. Tom had not paid attention to it before. Nor, it seemed, had the intruders.

'Oh, Rosa did that. I think it was the only thing my father had left of hers. My mother hated it. She'd only let him have it in the basement.'

'But when he had his own place, he hung it on the wall. That's interesting, isn't it?'

'Maybe he felt he owed her something, I don't know.' Rebecca moved closer to the painting. 'As a child I resented the idea of Rosa: you know, "the woman who came before Mummy" and all that. But you look at this, and realise what an awful life she had.'

'What's it called? The painting.'

'It's called *Aleph*. See the grey lines? They just about make the shape of an Aleph. The first letter of the Hebrew alphabet.'

'Right.'

They stood gazing at it, the shape of the letter now obvious. Tom tried to imagine the world Rosa and Gershon inhabited those sixty years ago. A world of massacres, death and cruelty that, they believed, could be redeemed only by more death. He imagined Gershon in the bakery, doubtless praying that the tainted bread would poison the man who had murdered his sisters.

And then an idea thudded into his brain. He turned to Rebecca. 'What was it you said before, when you talked about coming here? On the bus.'

'I said that we had to come, we might have overlooked something—'

'Not that, something else, keep going.'

'I said, we didn't have any other option. We had no Plan B.'

'Exactly! That's it: Plan B. What happened at the bakery wasn't the main operation after all. It was Plan B. That's what Sid called it.'

'I thought B was for bakery, or bread.'

'So did I. *Brot*, German for bread, or *Bäckerei* for bakery. Remember, that's what I said to Sid. "B for bakery." And he said, "No. Wrong again." Think about it. Why would all those Jews use German for a code name? They wouldn't. They'd use Hebrew. What's the Hebrew for bread?'

'*Lechem.*'

'Right. No "b" there. What's the second letter of the Hebrew alphabet?'

'*Bet.*'

'You see! Plan Bet. Plan B. The fall-back plan.'

'So what was the main plan?'

Tom smiled. 'Plan A. Or as DIN might have called it, Plan Aleph.'

Slowly, they both turned to contemplate Rosa's assemblage of baleful blacks and night-time greys.

THEY TOOK THE PAINTING down as carefully as their impatience would allow, and carried it into the centre of the room, where they leaned it against a chair, and looked at the back. It was in a thick wooden frame, and the backing board was secured by layers of binding tape. Using a steak knife that

Rebecca had brought in from the kitchen, Tom raised the edge of the tape, then slowly removed it all. Finally, he lifted the backing board off.

They could both see that the work had not been in vain. Stuck to the back of the painting, not glued but pressed there by time, was a set of papers. His hands trembling, Tom reached in and peeled them loose. There were five large sheets. Tom turned the first one over. To his surprise, it was a drawing, something between a map and an architect's blueprint. The next was similar, and so was the next and the next.

'What the hell are these?' he said, but Rebecca was too stunned to answer.

Tom stared hard at the first drawing. He wondered if it was an electrical diagram, or a map of an underground railway. He looked more closely, and saw tiny numbers written at various intervals. Measurements, he decided.

And then Rebecca spoke. 'Of course,' she said quietly.

'What is it?' Tom said, his voice rising. 'What?'

'Remember from the notebook, how Rosa escaped from the ghetto?'

Tom shook his head. That must have been in the section he had skimmed, the pages dealing with the flight into the forests.

'Sewers. Rosa and the others, the leaders of the resistance—they all got out on the last day of the liquidation of the ghetto. The Jews were being rounded up and sent to the camps. But the resistance always had a plan for the last day, when there could be no more fighting back.

'So Rosa and the rest, they went down into the ground. Not my father. He was already on the road by then, spreading the word. The others had to crawl through those stinking pipes for nearly two miles, until they got to an opening outside the ghetto walls, where fighters from the Communist underground were waiting to pull them out. These must be the maps of the sewers.'

Tom ran his fingertips across the paper. What an extraordinary document this was, a testament to almost superhuman resourcefulness. He squinted at what had seemed to be a printed stamp, in the bottom right-hand corner. Now he could see that it was a block of words, written in a tiny, fine-point script. He could decipher none of them, except for one in block capitals: NURNBERG. He looked in the same place on the next map. München. The next three were Weimar, Hamburg and Wannsee, a suburb of Berlin.

He gestured for Rebecca to take a look and her brow instantly furrowed.

'There were no ghettos in Germany itself, were there?' Tom asked.

'No, the ghettos were in Eastern Europe.'

They both stared at the diagrams, trying to decipher their meaning.

'But we do know your father was in Nuremberg after the war,' Tom said at last, pointing at the Nuremberg drawing. 'And we know that this, all of this, somehow relates to Plan A. That's why it was hidden in the painting.'

But Rebecca was no longer listening. Something had caught her eye. Taped to the discarded backing board was a square of card, so flat as to be barely visible. With great care she pulled at one corner, and the card came away.

She turned it over, and Tom found himself staring at a line of random squiggles, half-squares and incomplete hieroglyphs.

'What is it?' he said.

Rebecca was gazing at it intently. 'It's either one or the other.'

'I don't understand.'

'The characters I recognise,' she said. 'I'm just not sure of the language.'

THE NOISE of the TV was distracting, but it was his own fault. He had turned up the volume as soon as Rebecca had realised the card carried a message: if someone were listening, now was the time to stop them.

Tom prided himself on his facility for languages, and he would have liked to think he could have identified a sentence of Hebrew when it was put in front of him, but Rebecca had had to explain that in Hebrew the printed alphabet was not the same as the script used in everyday handwriting; the shape of each character was vaguely related, but not identical.

Although Rebecca could make out each character, she wasn't sure she could do much more. 'I can just about read Hebrew,' she said. 'The problem is, this might not be Hebrew. It could be Yiddish.'

'I thought Yiddish was like German.'

'It is, mostly, but it's written in Hebrew characters.'

Tom had to smile at that. Yiddish was surely tailor-made for undercover communication. How many non-Jews knew the Hebrew alphabet at all, let alone in this handwritten form? It meant DIN would have had no need of cryptography; their own language, written down, was sufficient.

'OK,' Rebecca said finally. 'This much I've worked out: *Fargess nicht!*'

'Right,' said Tom. 'That's simple enough. That means "Don't forget".'

She read on. '*Yir-mee . . . Yirmiyahu!* It's a name, like Jeremiah.'

'Keep going.'

'*Yirmiyahu vet zine*—and now there's the number twenty-three—then there's the word *dem* and then another number, fifteen. And then it finishes with another exclamation: *Lomir zich freien!*'

'*Lomir zich freien.* It's some kind of exhortation, like "Come, let's party. Come celebrate". Read the whole thing again.'

'*Fargess nicht! Yirmiyahu vet zine* twenty-three *dem* fifteen. *Lomir zich freien!*'

'Don't forget, Jeremiah turns twenty-three on the 15th. Let's celebrate!'

Rebecca frowned. 'Don't tell me all we've got is a party invitation.'

Tom got up to pace, but it was no good. Finally he marched over to the TV set and stabbed at the off button. In the quiet, perhaps twenty seconds later, it came to him. 'Oh, that's very neat. Very neat indeed.'

'What's neat?'

Tom turned the TV back on. 'Do you remember, in your dad's notebook, the message they gave him to take to the other ghettos?'

' "Aunt Esther has returned and is at Megilla Street 7, apartment 4." ' She paused. 'Oh, I see. We need a Bible.'

It took them a while, wading through the rubble of books and junk heaped on the floor, but eventually they found one. Rebecca turned the pages hesitantly, like someone narrowing down to a single reference in a dictionary.

'Here we go. The Book of Jeremiah, Chapter 23, Verse 15.'

'Read it out.'

' "Therefore, this is what the Lord Almighty says concerning the prophets: 'I will make them eat bitter food and drink poisoned water, because from the prophets of Jerusalem ungodliness has spread throughout the land'." '

Gershon's Diary

In the autumn of 1945, Aron told me that DIN was over, that from now on, justice would be up to the courts and the lawyers. We were to put down our guns and head off to the next front in the war for Jewish survival: Palestine. The Jews would need all the soldiers they could get in the coming struggle. I was barely fifteen, but I counted as a veteran.

I was ready to leave when Aron called me in to see him. He asked me, for the first time, how my family had been killed. I told him how my father had been burnt to death in his own barn by a mob; how my mother had hanged herself the day the Nazis arrived in Lithuania. Finally I told him about my sisters, shot into the pits at the Ninth Fort. I did not cry as I told my story, and he nodded, saying nothing. When I finished, he stared at me for many minutes, occasionally rubbing his chin. Eventually, in a quiet voice, he told me I should stay in Europe, that DIN had one last mission for me.

It had all begun with the Frenchman, then idling in post-liberation Paris. He had run into a former resistance fighter, a scientist, who had told him the greatest threat in the second half of the twentieth century would not be the atomic bomb but something much smaller, a weapon that could be deployed not on the traditional battlefield, but on the morning commuter train or in a theatre or in a soft-drinks factory. Poison, that was the weapon of the future. The Frenchman's curiosity was piqued. Discreetly, he began his own enquiries, speaking to chemists who told him of toxins that retained their potency even when mixed with great volumes of water. It was as a result of those conversations that *Tochnit Aleph*, Plan A, was born.

The day after Aron told me that I should stay in Europe, he sent me for what he called 'training', with a man I had not met before, a Jew from Palestine. He came from Germany but had left in the 1930s. The moment I learned this, I hated him. What did he know of DIN and of vengeance, this man who had saved his own skin and got out early?

But I had to keep silent and be his pupil. This man, who introduced himself as 'The Engineer', spread a number of complex blueprints on the table and explained that this was the water system for the city of Nuremberg and that I was to seek employment with the Department of Filtration.

'But I don't—'

'I know. You know nothing. That's what I'm here to teach you.'

And so this engineer taught me to speak of regularised pressures, saline clearance and filtration residues. At night, one of the DIN commanders drilled me in German, ironing out weaknesses in my vocabulary and accent. We devised yet another cover story—that my late father was Polish and that we had lived some time in the east—to explain any lapses, and I was handed a set of forged papers, including documents showing sterling service in the Wehrmacht. We worked out the youngest age that would be compatible with this life story and decided I was eighteen. Luckily, I was not just blond, blue-eyed and uncircumcised, but also tall for my age.

On all this I was tested and tested again, until finally, after six weeks, Aron said, 'Apply for the job tomorrow.'

Even though I had done it so often, I never got used to lying. The interview was mainly about my war service. The boss was in his early fifties and had missed the draft himself; he was envious of me, blessed with a chance to serve the Fatherland. I nodded but did not smile. I let him think I was a hardened soldier. And at the end of it, he said how much he had enjoyed our conversation, and that I could start at the beginning of the following week.

I still did not know what I was supposed to do. The commanders had told me nothing. Dressed in the overalls of a lab technician, I checked pressure gauges, lowered dipsticks and entered figures onto a form attached to a clipboard—and wondered what it was all for. When I finally understood that DIN's plan was to poison the water supply not only from the plant where I worked in Nuremberg but in four other German cities—Munich, Hamburg, Weimar and the Wannsee suburb of Berlin—I did not baulk, so deep had my hatred become. This is what Aron must have seen in me. He must have seen that mine were the eyes of a man who had seen his own blood spilt too often. That is why he trusted that I would not hesitate when I discovered the truth of *Tochnit Aleph*.

For this was Plan A. It aimed to kill, in a single stroke, no fewer than a million Germans. And I did not question it for a moment.

Chapter Nine

The aide marvelled at his boss's ability to do this. He was on his fourth meeting of the morning, listening, nodding sagely, leaving each person he met convinced that the great statesman had focused on his or her problem to the exclusion of all else. No one would have had a clue that the great man was, in fact, distracted beyond measure, that he was thinking throughout of a topic a world away from the one under discussion.

In the intervals between meetings—the 'bilaterals' that always took place in the margins of UN General Assembly week—the boss would turn to his aide, letting his rictus smile disappear, and pick up the conversation they had been forced to abandon some twenty or forty minutes earlier. Always, the aide noticed, at the exact same point.

'There's no point waiting for definitive proof,' he said now.

'Why not, sir?' asked the junior official.

'Because if you're able to get definitive proof, it usually means you've left it too late. An example: if you're worried I'm going to kill you, then a bullet in your chest is definitive proof.' He smiled coldly. 'But you wouldn't want to wait that long. So if we even suspect—'

Instinct made him stop before he could have heard the knock on the door. It opened to reveal the pretty assistant who was handling logistics.

'The Italian foreign minister is here, sir,' she said.

He showed her the hand gesture, peculiar to his country, that indicated she would have to wait a moment. She closed the door quietly.

'If we even suspect that they are getting close, we will have to act.'

'Act?'

The boss inspected his counsellor, his eyes scoping upwards, starting with the younger man's shoes. His mouth curled in derision. 'Try not to make your squeamishness quite so obvious. By act, I don't mean anything rash. I mean only that we should'—he paused, ostentatiously searching for the right word, part of his standard performance—'open up a dialogue.'

The aide knew better than to ask how he was meant to do such a thing. He would find a way to ask after the next meeting was over, using some form of words that would not expose his own lack of worldliness.

So he got up, opened the door and gestured at the neatly moustached man waiting, with leather portfolio case on his lap, to come forward. He gestured him into the room, where the boss, the elder statesman, was already standing, his arms outstretched in readiness for a politician's hug.

'*Signor Ministro degli Esteri!*'

Gershon's Diary

My job in the filtration plant in that winter of 1946 should have been boring, but it never was; I had to concentrate too hard for that. I had to make sure my German did not let me down. I had to avoid letting slip a remark that would contradict my false life story. And most of all, I had to watch my face, to be sure I did not betray what I truly felt about the German murderers who surrounded me. I kept turning up each day, doing my shift, eating my sandwiches, listening to the jokes in the canteen—including the ones about the kikes and the yids. Then I would return to the safe house and wait for my orders. In the end it was other news that came.

First, a message arrived that the plan had changed. The DIN man in Berlin had failed to get inside the water plant there; he had gone for an interview but he hadn't got the job. We were down to four cities.

Three weeks later, more bad news, this time from Weimar. Our man there had been shifted to a desk job that allowed no access to the filtration areas. To get near them would run a high risk of being caught, thereby jeopardising the entire mission. He was ordered to stand down.

Not long afterwards came word from Hamburg. Our most qualified man, an engineer in his own right, had been sacked when a discrepancy was discovered in his documents that convinced them the papers were forged—which they were. Luckily, they assumed he was a common criminal seeking to hide his past. They did not guess he was a Jew.

The plan of five cities was down to just two: Nuremberg and Munich. The commanders did their sums and calculated that a total of 1,380,000 people drank the water supplied by the plants in those two cities. The target of reaching—poisoning—a million Germans could still be achieved.

But when I was established in my post in Nuremberg, and Manik was installed in the water plant in Munich, the commanders hesitated. As they stood on the brink of a decision that they knew would reverberate around the world, they paused. I look back on it now and realise what I could never see then: that they were only young men.

They decided they could not make such a fateful decision themselves. They needed to act on some higher authority. But they were not religious men; they would take orders from no rabbi. The higher authority they had in mind was the sovereign Jewish people: the men and women fighting for Jewish independence in Palestine. They were three years away from statehood then, but the apparatus of Jewish sovereignty was already in place.

It was decided to seek the guidance of the elders of the Jewish nation before they acted in that nation's name. In their quest for a blessing, Palestine would be their destination.

The limit on Jewish immigration that the British had imposed in 1939 was still in force. The only way in was via the secret and illegal network that crisscrossed Europe, a system that relied on backwood paths through forests, then midnight rendezvous at tiny fishing ports, followed by perilous voyages dodging storms, sickness and British gunboats.

That was Aron's journey to the promised land. His reputation, as a leader of the Jewish underground in Nazi-occupied Europe, preceded him, and they honoured him as a hero. He told none of them that the work of resistance had become the work of vengeance. They knew nothing of DIN.

He would reveal that to only one man and, after two weeks of moving in the circles of those set one day to govern the new Jewish state, he came face to face with him. He was seventy, a founder of the movement for a Jewish homeland, regarded first as its chief emissary and now, in old age, as its figurehead. No man carried greater moral authority.

The younger man sat with him in the private study of his home and told him what, until then, this elder had only read about. He told him how the Germans had set out to remove the Jews from the face of the earth in the death factories of Auschwitz and Treblinka. He told him of the 'experiments' conducted without anaesthetic on terrified women and children in the name of science. He told them of the world of death he had inhabited for nearly five years—and how the men who had created it had emerged unpunished.

And then he told him of *Tochnit Aleph*.

Now, there was a reason why DIN's leader had chosen this man in particular. It was not just his seniority, the power his blessing would carry. It was also because this man, this leader, had earned distinction in an earlier life as a great scholar, specifically in the field of chemistry. Indeed, he had now retired from front-line politics and returned to his laboratory.

The elder listened throughout, his eyes darkening with each new tale of catastrophe. His head seemed to bow lower. By the time Aron spoke of *Tochnit Aleph*, the elder did not wince or recoil or tell him to get out. He simply nodded. And then he spoke.

'If I had travelled the road you have travelled, if I had seen what you have seen, then I would do the same.'

Aron dipped his head, as if in grateful acknowledgement. But the elder's statement had been ambiguous. Was he simply expressing understanding for DIN's rage, or was he doing what Aron needed him to do, namely offering moral approval for the plan to extinguish a million German lives?

An ambiguous answer was not sufficient, but Aron would not push the old man. He would have to tell the others that the plan was off. If the blessing did not come easily, then it was not a real blessing.

By the time Aron was standing, he could see that the elder had removed a fountain pen from his breast pocket and was writing a note.

'Here,' the old man said eventually. 'This is the name of the finest bacteriologist in Palestine. He is a student of mine, at the Institute in Rehovot. I have written him a message, telling him what you need. And I have told him it his duty to give it to you.'

'Thank you,' Aron said.

Then the elder clasped Aron's hand, like a grandfather on his deathbed. His eyes closed and he began to incant what Aron thought was a prayer. He said, '*Dam Israel Nokeam*.' The blood of Israel will take vengeance.

TOM LOOKED UP at Rebecca and saw that the faraway distraction of a few moments ago had vanished. He followed her gaze to the blueprints.

'Tell me the quote again,' she said.

Tom reached for the piece of paper he had scribbled on. '"I will make them eat bitter food and drink poisoned water."'

She nodded, still staring at the diagrams of the waterworks.

'It can mean only one thing, Rebecca. It would have been so many people.'

'I know.'

Tom got up from the chair he had been sitting on and moved across to her. She leaned into him, welcoming his touch.

'Look, we know it didn't happen,' he said. 'Everyone would know about it if it had. We know that Plan B happened because Plan A failed. The key question is, why did it fail? What happened?'

Gershon's Diary

Aron went to meet this young scientist, whose name was Eliezer. He took the note as if he were a pharmacist handling a prescription. He read it quickly, glanced up at Aron, then looked back at the note. At last he said, 'This will take some time. You will hear from me when it's ready.'

Perhaps a fortnight passed—time presumably spent in further meetings with the leaders of the Jewish state-in-waiting—before Aron met again with Eliezer. The young chemist handed him the canisters filled with toxin, steel flasks cased in a protective netting. They could pass for camping equipment: Aron would be able to take them back to Europe in his rucksack.

With the help of the Jewish underground, he was smuggled onto one of the British transport ships that sailed from Haifa, with forged papers suggesting he was one of the Free Polish soldiers who were in Palestine at the time.

The voyage was nearly over, the ship about to dock in Toulon, France, when Aron heard a noise from above, the footsteps and the barked enquiries as British military police boarded the ship. Did his instincts tell him what they were there for? Did Aron know, as they rattled down the stairs to the lower decks, that they were after him? I bet he did. Did he reach for the rucksack? What did he do with the canisters of lethal liquid?

They dragged him off the ship without explanation and later sent him to a jail in Jerusalem. The British interviewed him but their questions were vague, unfocused. Aron concluded that they knew little about him or about *Tochnit Aleph*, that they had picked him up on a tip-off. But who was the source? I know the question gnawed away at him through those endless days and nights he spent alone in a dank prison cell. He would have assumed that the informant was someone he had trusted. He would have drawn up lists in his head of all those who knew of *Tochnit Aleph*: the elder who had given his blessing; the young chemist; the most senior underground leaders he had met in those last weeks. Had they blabbed to the British inadvertently, or had it been deliberate? If on purpose, why? Why would any Jewish patriot have sabotaged this audacious attempt at justice?

We—Rosa, Manik and I, even the DIN commanders—knew nothing of this, of course. We were simply waiting for Aron to return with the poison. Finally, a messenger arrived with a note that Aron had somehow smuggled out. It said simply: *Arrested. Proceed with Plan B.*

'BUT IF IT DIDN'T HAPPEN, what's the connection with everything that's been going on?' Rebecca asked. 'It doesn't make any sense.'

Tom wished he had an answer for her, but she was right. It lacked all logic. Plan A had not happened. There had been no mass poisoning of Germany's major cities. How could it possibly matter now?

'Let's go back to basics,' he said, pacing. 'Your father was obviously after someone in New York. This person reckons your father had evidence against him, that maybe your father had a list of names—like that list that came to your flat, though consisting solely of Nazis who are still alive. Maybe the person in New York knows he's on this current list. He needs to have that document, and that's why he was so frightened of Goldman talking. Because this person, this old Nazi, suspects Goldman had the list, too.'

They had reversed positions, Rebecca now perching against the sofa. 'So this won't stop until we find that list.'

'If there is such a list. There might not be. Let's face it, Rebecca. If we haven't found it yet, where's it going to be? It probably doesn't exist.'

'Not any more, anyway. There can hardly be any ex-Nazis left now. They'd have to be too bloody old.'

'Exactly. Which means whoever your father was after was probably just one person whose name he kept in his head. We have to find out that name.'

'How the hell are we going to do that?'

Tom was all but forming his reply, that he had no idea, when it struck him. Of course: what an elementary mistake. *Too bloody old.*

Tom quickly folded the blueprints and cards back inside the picture frame and crudely taped the thing back together. 'Come on. We're going.'

'Where? I don't understand.'

'Neither do I. Not yet. But I think we're about to.'

HE WOULD HAVE PREFERRED to have gone somewhere else, somewhere with more people, but without the car they couldn't be choosy. So they would take their chances and simply make the ten-minute journey back to the Internet café on Kingsland High Street.

The second Tom walked out of the front door, he scanned the street. He saw two women pushing buggies, one on a mobile phone. It could be an ingenious cover—or nothing at all. He looked in the other direction. A post-man—or was that a disguise for a lookout? Tom was aware that all he could do was keep looking over his shoulder, and stick to busy streets.

'I've been thinking,' Rebecca said, looking left and right as they crossed Cazenove Road. 'Shouldn't we have heard about the autopsy by now.'

'No news is good news. If they'd found drugs or poison in Goldman's bloodstream, we'd know about it.'

'So the police will say he died of natural causes?'

'And therefore it's not a murder inquiry.'

'But it should be.'

They'd reached the High Street now and Tom was gratified to see the same melancholy clientele gathered in the café for the afternoon shift. As he handed over a couple of pound coins, reserving the machine at the end of the row, an older, bearded man in ultra-orthodox Jewish garb got up from the seat next to it. Now there were two spaces, one for each of them.

He went straight to Google and typed in the two words that had struck him with such force in Gershon's flat. It had been such a basic error of logic he was almost embarrassed by it. What had been his request to Henning Munchau in New York? To come up with a list of everyone over seventy who was present for the week-long General Assembly. He had drawn a blank, presented with a roll-call that included a Chinese interpreter and an Israeli head of state. The opposite of a list of Nazi war criminals.

But when Rebecca had complained that 'They'd have to be too bloody old', he had instantly seen it. Just as she had been raised in the shadow of the events of the Nazi era, so had many others of her generation. But not all of them were children of the victims; the children of the perpetrators, too, might have been drawn into this strange, unresolved riddle. Except these people, the ones Tom was imagining, would be fighting on the other side.

Which is why Tom so badly wanted his hunch to be wrong as he typed into the Google search field the two words that made his heart heavy.

'Henning Munchau.'

MOST OF THE PIECES that appeared were in German, starting with a news story from the *Frankfurter Allgemeine Zeitung* when Munchau's appoint-ment at the UN was announced, as well as several others from the specialist legal press. In English there was an interview with *New World*, the maga-zine of the United Nations Association in Britain, and a diary item from the

New York Observer, noting Munchau's legal summons for the failure to pay a parking fine. Not what Tom was looking for.

Tom decided to narrow it down. Not allowing himself to stop, lest he change his mind, he re-entered the name into the search field—'Henning Munchau'—this time adding one more word, 'Nazi'.

It took the machine less than a second to scour the world and find the sentence Tom had dreaded. But there it was, the first few words of an entry intelligible even in the opening list of results. It came from a website attached to the Department of History at the University of Maryland.

Captain Wilhelm Henning Munchau, 1898–1975; served in the SS's Totenkopfverbände, or Death's Head units, responsible for guarding concentration camps; received suspended sentence from West German court in 1966 for service at Theriesenstadt (Terezín).

Now he pushed back his chair and reached, instinctively, for the pouch of tobacco in his inside pocket. With his eyes still on the screen, he rolled himself a cigarette and put it between his lips. Even this sensation, before he had lit a match, felt like a hit of soothing nicotine.

Jesus Christ. What part of his brain had not thought of this earlier? He'd been dispatched to shut down the case of an aged Nazi-hunter by—guess who—a German! Why had he been so stupid? He had allowed his personal affection for Henning to cloud his judgment. Or perhaps it was simply that Tom no longer even saw Henning as German, but rather as some internationalised quasi-Australian.

His mind sprinted ahead, trying to keep up with the implications. Surely it meant that Henning not only knew everything that mattered about Gerald Merton, starting with the old man's motive, but had also masterminded an intelligence operation in a foreign capital, to say nothing of eavesdropping on, then murdering, Henry Goldman. How would Munchau possibly have such power? Unless he was part of something much bigger.

Tom turned to Rebecca, expecting her to be looking over his shoulder, reading the potted history of Munchau Senior that still glowed on the screen. But Rebecca wasn't looking at his terminal. She was looking at her own. And her face was white.

'What is it?'

She simply pointed at the display, open to her Facebook page. She indicated the Friends column down the left-hand side.

'I don't understand,' Tom said.

Rebecca made a few key strokes, going back several pages. 'See this guy here?' She was pointing at a square filled not with a photograph but with a question mark. 'He asked to friend me earlier.'

'To *friend* you?'

'It's a Facebook thing. Anyway, I said yes.' She saw Tom's look of disbelief. 'Lots of people were getting in touch, mainly to send condolences about Dad. It just seemed easier to say yes to everyone.' She pointed to one of the entries on the Facebook page. 'That's him.'

Richard needs to meet Rebecca urgently—so he can explain everything that's going on.

Tom had barely read the words when Rebecca began typing furiously.

Who are you? How do you know what's going on?

Tom rubbed his chin. 'I wonder if you should say—'

'Too late,' Rebecca said. 'I've already sent it.'

'For God's sake, we needed . . .' He stopped himself: he couldn't afford to pick a fight now, not with what he was about to tell her. He glanced round; there was a man sitting at the end of the row with his head down, banging away at the keyboard, apparently oblivious to them and everyone else. 'Rebecca, there's something you need to look at.' He turned his screen towards her, so that she could see his discovery for herself. 'Remember my old boss, Henning Munchau? Legal Counsel to the Secretary-General of the United Nations and all that? OK. Take a look at this.'

He watched as Rebecca's eyes skipped across the few lines of biography. 'You think this could be what this is all about?' she asked.

'I don't know. It seems crazy. OK, Henning plays hardball, no doubt about it. But underneath the cynical exterior, he's on the side of the angels. Serious humanitarian. If you'd seen him in East Timor, when—'

'But it would explain a lot. His father's a Nazi—'

'Probably grandfather.'

'—and he doesn't want it to get out.'

'I know. But I can't believe he would go to those lengths: sending men over here to wreck your father's home, to bug our meetings—'

'To kill Goldman.'

'Even if he wanted to do that, he wouldn't have the capacity. People always imagine the United Nations is some global power, but it's got nothing. If it wants ink for the photocopier, it has to go begging.'

'Have you got a better explanation?'

Tom rubbed his eyes until they emitted an audible squeak. Despite everything they had learned, he still could not even be certain what Gerald Merton had been doing in New York two days ago. 'No. I can't think of—'

'Aha. Here we go. He's replied.'

I'm a friend and I really want to help.

Instantly, Rebecca hammered out a reply: Of my father's?

It took perhaps thirty seconds, but then Facebook announced a new message had landed. She clicked it open. I never had the privilege of knowing your father. But I knew his work.

She turned to Tom. 'What does that mean? My father was a dry-cleaner.' She pounded the keyboard. What 'work' do you have in mind?

The reply came back in a matter of seconds. I am an admirer of DIN.

Rebecca looked back at Tom, hesitating. 'What should we do, Tom?'

Again, that 'we' sent a thrill through him. 'I think we should meet him,' he said. 'Somewhere public, somewhere safe.' Tom glanced over at the man at the end of the row, squinting to make out what was on his screen: he appeared to be immersed in some kind of gothic video game.

Rebecca was typing again, breaking off for a moment to check her watch. We'll be in Starbucks, Portland Place, at 6 p.m. How will I recognise you?

The reply took only a few seconds to come back.

Don't worry about that; I'll recognise you.

IT WAS TOM'S IDEA to be early. You always had an advantage in any negotiation if you owned the room. That's why, back at the UN, there was such an elaborate protocol over where colleagues would meet, even for the most mundane exchange. By being here ten minutes early, Rebecca and he could simulate the office politics of UN Plaza, if only a little bit.

'There,' said Tom, pointing at a round table that could just accommodate three people. It would be awkwardly intimate, but had the advantage of ensuring that they could talk with this 'Richard' quietly. And the place was so full that any eavesdropper would struggle to hear the conversation.

Now that the territory was marked as theirs—jackets hooked over backs of chairs—Tom went over to the counter to order a cappuccino and a latte. While he waited for them to pour, scoop, froth and steam the concoctions, he looked over at Rebecca—on the phone, no doubt checking in with the hospital—and he had to marvel at her resilience, marching forward as if there was no time to rest, as if she would bind her wounds later when the battle was over. He realised that he felt for her a sentiment that he had rarely felt for a woman. Not just desire or affection or even love, but deep admiration.

Maybe she sensed his eyes on her. She came over to the counter, and he was about to open his arms to her when the girl announced that his drinks were ready, gesturing towards the side table where they placed the coffees once brewed. He picked up the two mugs and had turned back to Rebecca when he saw a man standing directly in front of her.

'Rebecca Merton?' He stuck out a hand in greeting. 'It's Richard.'

He was, Tom would have guessed, a couple of years older than her and several years younger than him. His brown hair was longish, almost tousled, and he was wearing a suit. He looked healthy, as if he worked out.

He turned to Tom. 'Where are you sitting?'

Tom paused. With his hands full, he used his head to indicate, twisting a look over his right shoulder and saying, 'Just there.'

'Great. I'll just get a drink and join you.'

They took their seats, Tom furrowing his forehead into a question for Rebecca. She shrugged, as if to say, *I don't know. Not what I expected.* They sipped their coffee and waited.

'Thanks for meeting me here, and at such short notice,' the man said once he had come back with a mug of his own. 'I'm sorry about the whole Facebook thing. I just couldn't see any other way to get in touch with you.'

'That's OK.' To Tom's surprise, Rebecca smiled.

Don't reward him too early; he hasn't given us anything yet.

Tom extended a hand. 'Tom Byrne.' He shot a look over at Rebecca, who seemed happy for him to take the lead. 'So you say you know what's going on with all this mess?' He had vowed not to sound aggressive and he was pleased with the result: his question had come out casual rather than rude.

'Yes, and we will talk about that. About that and everything else. I have to say, Rebecca, you do look very tired. Do you feel tired?'

'As a matter of fact, Richard, I'm really exhausted.' She smiled again, showing even more of her teeth. 'Does it show?'

'I'm afraid it does, Rebecca. What about you, Tom? Feeling tired?'

Tom wanted to tell him to mind his own business and to get on with telling them what they needed to know, but somehow this didn't seem the moment for a fight. This man was being friendly and mellow. Tom felt he should be friendly and mellow, too.

'You know what? I am really tired. Isn't that funny?' And Tom gave a smile that turned into a small chuckle.

'Do you want to get some fresh air? Would you like that, Rebecca?'

'Yes, Richard, I would. Thank you.'

'OK. Well, why don't you two drink up and we'll get some. That's it, finish off those coffees and we'll take a walk.'

Both Tom and Rebecca did as they were told, taking sips, more or less in silence, until there was no coffee left.

'All righty, then,' Richard said. 'About that walk.'

They got to their feet, Tom giving Rebecca a quizzical look: *This is odd, isn't it?* She gave him a semi-shrug back that said, *Let's just go with the flow.*

'Pick up your handbag, Rebecca.' Richard's wording—direct, as if he were giving an order—surprised Tom. But Rebecca didn't object to being bossed about by this strange man, this 'Richard'. Tom wanted to complain or at least make a sarcastic remark, but he didn't have the energy.

They were outside now, stepping into an immediate and fast-moving stream of pedestrians, rushing in such haste that Tom felt his head spin.

'Tell you what,' said Richard, his voice still calm and smooth. 'Since we all want fresh air, maybe we need to drive somewhere.'

'Drive?' Rebecca said.

'Yes, drive. And guess what, here's my car.'

Tom had noticed it already: a silver Mercedes saloon, hugging the kerb. He also noticed that the windows were blacked out.

At that very moment, just as Richard stopped speaking, Tom felt a firm and sudden push to his lower back. A second or two later, he found himself on the back seat of the Mercedes. Rebecca was on the other side and Richard was in between them.

He wasn't sure if it was real, or just his woozy imagination, but the car seemed to be gliding forward. There was no outside noise at all. Was it especially dark in this car? Tom tried rubbing his eyes. No, it made no difference. His vision still seemed soft, as if he were looking through a gauze.

'By the way, Tom, I'm sorry I had to drug your coffee.'

Tom had a vague sense that something was wrong, but he couldn't rouse himself to feel that strongly about it.

'Not nice to have tainted two perfectly good cappuccinos,' the man continued. 'Or was one a latte? Anyway, sorry about that.'

Richard's voice was getting more remote, as if he were speaking on a cellphone and had just gone into a tunnel. And that was how Tom felt. There was a tunnel of darkness, enveloping him, covering him. What harm would it do to surrender and allow himself some rest? He would tell this man, this Richard, that that was what he was going to do, that he was going to sleep. If only he could find the energy, he would tell him. He would tell him . . .

THE JOURNEY WEST took more than two hours, with the crawl out of London accounting for most of that time. Once they were on the M3, the traffic moved along pretty briskly and Richard could relax.

Richard. It wasn't a bad name; he'd had worse. And it had done the trick, hadn't it? Rebecca Merton had not challenged him to say more; he hadn't given her the chance. He'd been more worried about this UN lawyer she was with. True, he was more used to taking out men than women, but they tended to be intense, bearded young men who'd spent too long watching beheadings on the al-Qaeda version of YouTube. So this had been an extra challenge. And the level of resources was unusual, too; he'd been told he could spend whatever he liked, just so long as he got the subjects out. No one had said anything explicit, but the way his controller had spoken suggested that this was a job authorised from the top. Or close to it.

The driver's satnav announced they were less than a mile away from the rendezvous point. Richard checked his watch. They were on time.

THE BOMBARDIER CHALLENGER 604 was waiting for them on the tarmac, the jet engines looking massive on the plane's short torpedo body. The retractable seven-step staircase was already down, suggesting that the work of internal transformation had already been done. Most of the armchairs and tables would have been stripped out and replaced by flat-bed mattresses and banks of flickering, beeping medical equipment—everything, indeed, that you'd expect from a mobile intensive care unit.

Only now, in the dark, did Richard spot the two staff, one uniformed, nervously waiting at the foot of the staircase. Richard got out of the car, ID round his neck like a pendant, and strode confidently towards them.

The civilian, a woman, stretched her hand out. 'Welcome to Farnborough, Dr Brookes. I'm Barbara Clark, head of corporate liaison.'

'Thank you.'

'I appreciate the hurry you're in, Doctor. We'll make this as quick as possible. I take it you packed these bags yourself?' She proceeded with the usual questions, checked the bags by hand, then cursorily waved a wand over him and his colleagues. 'I need to have a quick look at the patients, I'm afraid.'

Richard turned back to the ambulance and gave a nod. The two 'paramedics' wheeled the trolleys to the foot of the plane. Clark looked down at the sleeping patients and moved her wand over each one. Halfway down the man's body there was a loud beep. Richard shot a look at his contact.

'Would you mind?' Clark said, pulling the sheet back.

Richard held his breath. It was the buckle of the belt strapping Byrne into place. The sound was repeated when she checked the woman.

'Well, all seems to be in order, Dr Brookes. I just need to ask you a little about their condition. Is there any more you can tell me about this trip beyond'—she glanced down at some paperwork—' "medical need"?'

'I'm afraid I can't, Ms Clark. Doctor–patient confidentiality.' He smiled apologetically, but in a way that conveyed there was no room for negotiation.

'Of course. A quick word with my colleague here from immigration and you'll be free to fly.'

Richard presented the passport of Dr Rick Brookes, then showed the ones belonging to Byrne and Merton. The official checked the photos against the people lying in front of him, then gave a nod. Richard gestured to his colleagues, who released the stretchers from their chassis and carried them, the man first, up the steps into the aeroplane.

'My thanks again, Ms Clark, to you and your team here,' said Richard, when the final checks were done. 'We'll be on our way.'

Richard nodded farewell to his driver, who headed back to the ambulance. He then climbed inside the plane, followed by his contact. They watched as the staircase retracted in a stately, electronic movement. He strapped himself in, and settled back into his soft leather chair.

A voice crackled on to the PA system. 'Good evening, gentlemen, this is your captain speaking.' The voice seemed amused by the absurdity of the situation. 'Welcome aboard this Challenger 604. Flying conditions are smooth tonight. We should be at our destination in about seven hours.'

JAY SHERRILL PLACED a protective hand on the laptop, covering the Apple logo. For the NYPD numskulls it would be one more confirmation that he was a white-wine-sipping college boy who should have been a graphic designer.

'The Commissioner will see you now.'

He gathered up his things and went straight through.

'Good to see you, Mr Sherrill. Take a seat. My office said you needed to see me urgently. That sounds like good news.'

'I hope so, sir.' *Calm. Breathe.*

'Why'd you bring that thing in here? You got something to show me?'

'Yes, I have.' He flipped open his computer, clicked open the iMovie program and selected the most recent project. Only then did he get up and move round to Riley's side of the desk. 'May I, sir?'

'What's this gonna be, *Debbie Does Dallas*?'

'Not quite, sir, no. But still pretty interesting.'

A small video screen opened up. Sherrill leaned down to expand it, then pressed play. Instantly an image appeared of a seated man, silhouetted against a window, clearly to preserve the subject's anonymity. There was a voice on the film, Sherrill's own, asking, *Please identify yourself.*

Then a reply: *I am an agent of the New York Police Department, Intelligence Division.*

That was enough to have Chuck Riley spin round in his chair and look up at the man over his shoulder. The excitement visible in his expression was what Sherrill had been hoping for. He heard his own voice again.

Can you verify that, without revealing your name?

Yes. I can reveal operational details that would be known only to an officer in Intel. I will do that only to an investigating authority.

I appreciate that, but perhaps you could say something now that might establish your credentials?

The silhouetted figure paused. *I could tell you about our operation during the Republican convention when it was in the city, monitoring protesters.*

The voice proceeded to give details of how he and his fellow agents had travelled beyond New York, to New Mexico and Illinois, snooping on political activists who were planning to demonstrate outside the convention.

Everyone thinks we were just watching foreign terrorists, but we were spying on people who had no intention of doing violence to anybody. I even infiltrated some church groups. And these people were US citizens.

The Commissioner was listening closely, turning his face from the screen so that his ear could be nearer to the computer's speaker.

We all had different code names. My unit was Tenzing. Another was called Simpson. And there was Hillary. All famous climbers, apparently. They say the boss is some mountain freak.

At this, Riley sat back and exhaled. That much was true: Stephen Lake, head of the NYPD's Intelligence Division, was a fanatic, challenging himself by climbing ever more improbable peaks. But that was not public knowledge. Besides, the Commissioner had heard about the unit called Hillary. He'd never have made the link to mountains, though; he'd just thought the units had girls' names. Like ships.

He signalled for Sherrill to stop the machine. 'OK. I believe him.'

'I'm glad, sir. Because I think what this man goes on to say explains who was responsible for the shooting of Gerald Merton.'

'That's very good, Sherrill. That's very good indeed.'

TOM'S EYES SNAPPED OPEN. He squinted, trying to focus on the wall ahead. It seemed to be plain white. There was no window, just a cross-hatched square in the door on the left. He swivelled his head round to the table at his side. A small wooden cabinet, with a plastic jug of water. Where the hell was he?

He tried to get out of bed, but his legs were leaden. He pulled away the tight, starched sheets covering him and saw that he was wearing green surgical scrubs. His mind raced. Had he had a traffic accident? Was this the intensive care unit of a hospital? What had happened? And then, halting this torrent of thoughts with a thud: *Rebecca.*

He had to think back. What was the last thing he could remember? They had been in Starbucks. He had been buying the drinks; he had turned to her. There was a man there, the man they had arranged to meet . . .

Tom tried again to get out of bed. This time he picked up his legs with his hands, grabbing his own thighs as if they were someone else's. Once his feet were on the ground, he buckled, and had to grab the bed to steady himself. His jaw clenched in determination, he headed for the wall and shuffled his way along it to the door. Through the rectangle of glass he saw an empty corridor and, opposite, what he guessed was a nurses' station.

He reached for the door handle, but it would not turn. He tried again and came up against the hard metal stop of a lock. Too exhausted to risk the trek back to the bed, he leaned against the door, then slid wearily to the floor.

Starbucks, Rebecca and him at the counter. He could see the woman who had taken their drinks order. The man who had greeted them. Rebecca's smiling face, warm and friendly towards the newcomer. Richard.

Tom had not noticed the small cameras in two corners of the room. Nor did he know about the motion sensors under the mattress, which sounded an alarm as soon as the normal ups and downs of breathing ceased for more than thirty seconds—and which were, of course, triggered when the patient left the bed entirely. So he wasn't to know that he had set off an alarm at the nurses' station. He couldn't hear it because his room was thoroughly soundproofed. Such were the demands necessitated by this ward's usual patients.

He reached up for the metal door handle, using it to haul himself up. Then he heaved himself round so his eyes were level with the glass window. It was filled entirely with a face.

Tom rocked back with shock. The face had been just a inch from his. And now he could hear the sound of the door unlocking, an electronic release.

Two men walked in, accompanied by a nurse. 'Thank you,' said the less bulky of the two men. 'We can take it from here.' He waited for the nurse to close the door behind her before he spoke again. 'I hope you slept well. In fact, I know you slept well because I've been watching you.'

Now that he heard his voice, Tom remembered him. It was Richard, the man they had met in the café.

'What happened? Where am I?' he said.

'It's a long story, Tom. Put it this way. We were in London; we needed you to take a little trip; and so we took it.'

The smugness of this man and his smooth, chatty manner sent the rage thudding through Tom's arterial network; the veins on his neck began to throb. Without planning it, and despite the sluggishness of his limbs, he brought back his right arm and curled his fingers into a fist.

He got within six inches of Richard's face but no closer. The bodyguard, or whoever the other man was, simply lifted up a hand and caught Tom's arm, pushing it back, twisting it in its socket. Tom let out a yelp of pain.

'No need for any of that, Tom. Now as it happens, we—'

'What have you done with Rebecca? Where's Rebecca?'

'Let me finish.' The bodyguard still had Tom's arm in a half nelson. 'As it happens, I was going to come and wake you anyway.'

'Where's *Rebecca*?'

'She's here. In this same city.'

Tom gasped his relief. Then, 'What city? Where am I?'

'I'd have thought you'd have worked it out. You're in New York, Tom.'

New York? It made no sense. He didn't remember flying anywhere.

'Who are you?'

Richard ignored the question. 'I'm sorry we had to do it this way, Tom. But the boss will explain everything soon enough. And look.' He lifted the travel bag he had been holding at his side. 'I even have your clothes.'

A few minutes later, Tom was in a wheelchair, watching as nurses and orderlies busied past him. Any risk of him crying out was tempered by the presence at the wheelchair's handlebars of the bodyguard; Tom did not doubt that, were he to cry out, he would be silenced.

He was wheeled into an elevator, which took them to an underground car park. They went into a side bay, one marked by a disabled badge. There was the electronic squawk of car doors opened by remote control.

The meat-head pushing the chair tucked his hands into Tom's armpits now and lifted him. In a single movement that was more efficient than brutal, Tom was loaded onto the back seat of a car.

He looked to his right and felt his heart squeeze.

In the dull twilight of an underground car park, it was almost impossible to discern anything but an outline. To make sure she was really there, he ran his fingers gently over her skin, her cheekbones, her chin.

'Are you OK? Did they hurt you?'

'I'm fine,' Rebecca said. 'Woozy, bit nauseous, exhausted. Like being a junior doctor, really.' She smiled weakly, sending a stab of pain through him that felt very close to love.

Richard stepped into the passenger seat, the bodyguard took the wheel, and the car took off, emerging up an exit ramp and into the daylight. Their captors had not been lying. They were in New York. It took him a while to realise it, but Tom was back on the very street he had driven down hours before he had left for London, though heading in the opposite direction.

A sensation that was part bafflement, part dread began to rise inside him. They were travelling towards the United Nations.

A picture of Henning Munchau floated into Tom's head. Could this really be his handiwork? What terrible secret could he, or those he served, harbour that he would do this—and to one of his oldest friends? Tom looked over at Rebecca, absorbing the sight of her in profile. *Unless it was not Tom that Henning had needed to get to New York . . .*

They were descending again, down another slope into an underground car park. Damn. He hadn't been paying attention at the crucial moment; he didn't know precisely where they were.

Once more they parked, and the bodyguard guided Tom and Rebecca into the lift. No wheelchairs this time. Saying nothing, Richard pressed the button. The top floor, Tom noticed.

The lift doors opened and now he understood: they were in a hotel, on the penthouse level, he guessed. They walked down a corridor to a door where two young men in dark blue suits, curled wires in their ears, stood as sentries on either side. Richard gave each of them a nod and the door was opened.

Inside was the sitting room of a suite, clearly one of the best in the building. Another young man was in the room. He darted a quick glance in their direction, then exchanged a few whispered words with Richard.

Finally, Richard led them through a connecting door into a larger sitting area. Tom could see the figure of a suited man, his back to them, standing at the large picture window, apparently taking in the view of Manhattan and the East River in the morning light.

At last he turned round. 'Welcome to the Presidential Suite,' he said.

Tom took in that voice, and the face, and felt his veins turn to ice.

Chapter Ten

He knew the smart thing to do, the precise course of action he needed to follow if he was to advance his own career. He simply needed to end his presentation, close the lid of his laptop, shake Commissioner Riley's hand and be on his way. But something nagged at Jay Sherrill. It would have been pompous to call it a pang of conscience. And wrong, too. It wasn't his conscience that was speaking so much as an irritating personality trait: this anal desire of his for neatness and completeness.

'There are a couple more elements to the story, Commissioner,' he said.

'Always are, Detective. Lots of chaff in any investigation. Our job's to put aside the chaff so all we got left is wheat.'

'I know that, sir. But I thought you ought to know—'

'Sure. You can speak to Donna outside and arrange another appoint—'

'This won't take long, sir. It's simply that identifying the dead man, Gerald Merton, as a terrorist may not wholly have been a mistake.'

'Well, that's a mighty interestin' theory, I'm sure.'

'It's not only a theory. There's the weapon—the hitman's friend, you called it—hidden in his hotel room. And the UN's man, who's been in London, says there may be a history of vigilante killings.'

The Commissioner's expression changed. 'What UN man?'

'Tom Byrne. He's the lawyer the UN put on the case.'

'Yes—to *oversee* your investigation. What's he doing investigating?'

'He's not. Not officially, of course. But the UN sent him to London to mend fences with the family, to head off any compensation—'

'Never mind that. You say he's uncovered what?'

'He's given me very few details, but he believes the weapon in the hotel room might be explained by—'

'*He* knows about the gun?'

'Yes, sir.'

Riley now sat upright and straightened the papers on his desk. 'I see,' he said, in a voice now drained of all southern bonhomie. Sherrill instantly understood what it meant: the Commissioner had concluded that his little game—blaming the Intelligence Division for the death of an innocent old man—was over now that the circle of knowledge had widened.

'Detective, a thought has just struck me. This killing took place inside the environs of the United Nations, correct?'

Sherrill could feel his throat turn arid. 'Yes, sir.'

'Is that inside the jurisdiction of the United States of America?'

'I suppose, technically speaking, it doesn't count as—'

'Nothin' technical about it. It's not. Yes, a shooting took place, but not on US soil. So there is no crime under US law and nothing here to trouble any US law-enforcement agency—such as the New York Police Department.'

'But you said this was a high-priority case; you said I should report directly to you.'

The Commissioner adopted a faux-official voice. 'In the post-9/11 environment, I didn't want to take any chances. In case this might have had implications for the rest of the city.' Then he leaned forward, fixing Sherrill with a stare. 'But the basic point still stands, as a quick call to the DA's office would instantly confirm. No crime here, Detective. You're off the case—because there is no case. This meetin' is over.'

TOM LOOKED OVER at Rebecca. She was as shell-shocked as he was.

'I'm sorry about the way this meeting has been arranged. Not my usual style. Not my usual style at all.'

Tom was too stunned to speak. To see this man, in this context, talking like this—it was dizzying.

'I never actually met your father, Rebecca, though our paths crossed. I wonder if he knew that. I'm not sure. But we're getting ahead of ourselves. We need to set some ground rules, talk about the terms of this meeting.'

Tom felt the ire boil inside him. This man was talking as if Rebecca and Tom were taking part in a routine New York business appointment. Tom wanted to scream about abduction, about involuntary sedation, about the thousand violations of basic human rights that this 'meeting' represented, but all he could manage was to squeeze out the words, 'This will destroy you.'

And at that the man gave a slight nod, the same rueful, thoughtful gesture Tom had seen him give on TV interviews going back—what?—forty years. It was the expression of the man who had, at different times, served as education minister, foreign minister and even prime minister of his country. And even though he was now well over eighty years old, the career of this veteran politician was not over.

Now Tom was facing him across this room, just a few yards apart. He was staring at the President of the State of Israel.

'I admit, I am taking an enormous risk here. Some think I'm being reckless.' He gestured in the direction of the connecting door, which Tom took to indicate the young aides in the other room. 'People say that I have been cautious throughout my career. "Cautious" is the kind word. One of my biographers preferred "cowardly".'

Tom remembered the list he had asked Munchau to compile of all visitors to this week's General Assembly over seventy. When Henning mentioned the President of the State of Israel, Tom had not given it a second thought.

Henning. A flush of shame passed through him. He had succumbed to the crudest of stereotypes in concluding that his old friend was doing the work of the Nazis. Tom would never be able to look him in the eye again.

The President had come forward now, away from the picture window. He stepped past the couch and sat on a plain, straight-backed wooden chair.

'But people misjudge me. I was always cautious in that I always made a *calculation* before every move I made. Sometimes the calculation called for boldness, even recklessness. This meeting comes into that category.'

'You keep calling this a meeting.' It was, to Tom's delight and relief, his own voice. The fury that had been coursing through his bloodstream had finally burst out. 'But you abducted us to bring us here. You drugged us and restrained us with force. This is not a *meeting*. This is a crime.'

'As I said, Mr Byrne, it is high risk. But like a lot of actions taken by my country, and misunderstood by the rest of the world, this is a case where we have performed one regrettable deed to avoid having to do much worse.'

'Regrettable? *Regrettable?* What you've done—'

'Mr Byrne,' the President said, 'there is something I need to know. To be more precise, there's something I need to know if *you* know. The simplest method would have been to send in men who could have asked you in a fashion designed to make you tell them. Do I make myself clear?' He did not wait for an answer. 'But I wouldn't do that. Not to a daughter of the Shoah.' And for the first time he looked properly at Rebecca.

Tom could see that she was meeting his gaze and holding it.

'You did this to be kind? Is that what you're saying?' she said. 'You *killed* a man. One of my father's friends is dead because of you.'

The President dipped his head. 'I apologise, Dr Merton. It was a terrible accident. He had a weak heart and he suffered a great fright. But he was not meant to die. He too, remember, was a child of the Shoah.'

Tom wondered if this was just political theatrics, but in the President's eyes he believed he saw something different: an old man's sadness.

'It was after Henry Goldman's death that I decided enough was enough. No more games. We would have to meet face to face.'

Tom's blood began to bubble again. 'So you thought you'd drug us—'

The President raised his voice. 'There was no way to make contact without exposing myself. You'll soon understand the calculation I made.'

'But we'll go straight out of this room and tell any reporter who'll listen what you've done. You'll be finished.'

'Of course I weighed up that risk. I concluded that it was not as great as you suggest. For a start, what evidence would you have?'

'But we're in New York!' Tom said, his voice rising. 'And there'll be no record of how we got here!'

'That has been taken care of. When you leave here, your passports will be returned to you, stamped in the right places. Dr Merton, you'll see from your bank statement that you withdrew the right amount of cash to pay for two tickets to New York. There are two boarding-pass stubs as well.' He smiled. 'Technology makes so much possible these days.'

'But we just have to tell the world what you've already confessed to us!'

'And who would believe *you*?' The emphasis was on the last word.

Tom was startled. 'What the hell do you mean?'

'I mean, who would believe a Mafia hack like you? The paid servant of organised crime, the hired help of the Fantoni family of Newark, New Jersey. Who, in case you've forgotten, have been charged with racketeering, money-laundering, drug-trafficking and, of course, prostitution—need I go on?'

Tom swallowed, hard and visibly. He could feel Rebecca's eyes on him. He could not bear to see her; his face was hot.

'Oh, I'm sorry. Perhaps this is something you've not yet shared with Dr Merton. The point is, no one will believe a word you say. A lawyer who freaked out, then sold his soul to Don Corleone.'

Rebecca spoke, her voice low but wavering with anger. 'Your thugs obviously injected us with something. There'll be traces of it in our bloodstream. There'll be puncture marks on our skin.'

'Are you sure this is a point you want to make, Dr Merton?'

Tom saw Rebecca whiten. 'What are you talking about?'

'I mean that your skin has probably quite a few marks on it.'

'That was ten years ago. How could you possibly—?'

'You can find out anything about anyone, if you really want to. You once had an intravenous drug habit, which means—'

'I didn't have a habit! It was a mistake. I was at a low—'

'I'm a liberal on these issues, but it could make your position—as a doctor, I mean—*complicated*. Let's put it no more strongly than that.'

Tom fell back into his chair. Rebecca, of all people. He would never have guessed. He contemplated the unhappiness that would have driven her to it. Remembering what she had said about growing up in a house of permanent darkness, he stretched a hand across the space between them and found hers. He could see that they had been comprehensively outmanoeuvred.

It was Rebecca who spoke, softer than before. 'I don't understand. You used to be the leader of Israel. Why would you be my father's enemy?'

The old man sighed and got slowly to his feet. It was the first time he had showed his age. He walked in deliberate steps over to the window. The city seemed to glitter in the morning sunlight.

'You're right,' he said quietly. 'It's time to get to the heart of the matter.' He paused to turn round and face them. 'My aides—the team out there— believe only what I have told them: that you hold information that compromises the security of our country. The problem is, I don't know if that's true or not.' He cocked his head to one side, a gesture designed to show he was about to correct himself. 'Of course, I know that you know nothing that directly threatens Israeli security. But I don't know if you know something that threatens me. And therefore threatens my country.'

A wave of exhaustion came over Tom. 'What are you talking about?'

'I knew Gershon Matzkin was still alive. I had people keeping an eye on him for me. I waited for the day I'd hear he had been hospitalised, or had fallen ill, but that day never came. Aron, the DIN leader, died long ago. Such a strong man, such a hero. Steiner lost his mind years ago. I knew he couldn't hurt me. But Gershon was still fit. He still had everything up here.' He tapped the side of his head. 'I would not be free while Gershon was alive. And then Monday happened. I was here, in New York, for the General Assembly. And I heard that name, on the local cable news. "A British man has been killed on the steps of the UN. He has been identified as Gerald Merton." Can you imagine what was going through my mind? I wondered who would want Gershon dead. They were saying it was an accident, but I didn't believe it. Gershon always took care of himself. He was the best.

'But then I began to get queasy. Why was he in New York? Could he have started'—he paused, unsure which word to use—'work again? Had he come to New York to kill me?'

Tom wanted to interrupt, to ask what motive Gershon Matzkin would possibly have had to murder the President of the State of Israel, a fellow

Jew, a comrade, it seemed, from the secret crusade that was DIN. But he bit his lip; the old man would eventually explain everything.

'You see—' He was about to speak but stopped himself, giving a smile as brief as a wince. 'But this is to take the greatest risk of all. Having worked so hard to ensure you don't have a certain item of information, I'm about to give it to you. But I can see no other way.'

'No other way of doing what?' Tom asked.

'Of being sure there's no other evidence. Now that Gershon is gone, I want this thing to be over. I want to sleep for more than three hours at night.'

'So you need to ask us what we know.'

The old man nodded.

'OK,' Rebecca said. 'Ask.'

The President examined his fingernails, which Tom couldn't help but notice were in perfect condition. Then at last he spoke, the reluctance making the slightest downward twist to his lips.

'What do you know about *Tochnit Aleph*?'

TOM TRIED TO MAKE a calculation, to work through his options, but his brain felt soupy, still thick from sleep and sedative. The word *Tochnit* had thrown him. But *Aleph* was now familiar enough and he had guessed that if there was a Hebrew expression for Plan A, this had to be it. So this was the aspect of DIN's work that had given this man sixty years of sleepless nights.

He knew that to tell him what they knew was to give away whatever leverage they held. The President needed something from them; once he had it, what protection would they have? Somehow he had to make the old man believe that he and Rebecca were saying all they knew, and yet supply him with an incentive for keeping both of them alive.

'We've seen the papers,' Tom said. 'The blueprints of the city waterworks. Of Munich, Weimar, Hamburg, Nuremberg and Wannsee.'

'So you know.'

'We know.'

'And you know about me?'

Tom stared hard. He didn't want to go for an outright bluff, but he wanted at least to keep the old man guessing.

'Do the papers point to me in any way?'

'I think that if someone knew what they were looking for, they could work it out.' He had crossed the border into the dangerous land of the lie.

'That's what I supposed. And where are these papers now?'

'I think you can understand why we'd be reluctant to tell you that.'

The President assessed the faces of the two people before him. He lingered over Rebecca and then directed his next sentence to her. 'I think you need to hear what happened. Then perhaps you'll see this differently.'

Tom exhaled silently. This is what he had wanted: for the President to start spilling.

'I was not a member of DIN. I was not even in Europe during . . . during those times. I left Russia in 1936. I went to Palestine to be a pioneer. Our aim was to create the *Ivri*, the Hebrew. A wholly new Jew. Strong, a worker, a soldier: no more cowering, no more passivity in the face of our enemies. We used to say that all that awaited the Jews of Europe was death.' He dipped his head. 'We had no idea how right we were.

'So I arrived in Palestine as a teenager. I went to university there: I studied chemistry. And, of course, I joined the youth movements, and before I knew it I was elected to this and then that. I was a politician even then. But I learned from the best. I showed them only humility and respect. Which is why they trusted me. Including him.'

Tom raised a quizzical eyebrow, a gesture he immediately regretted. He should have pretended to know.

But the President was not about to stop the flow now. 'The professor at Rehovot: the man who had led the Jewish movement for a homeland. He had returned to his laboratory and I was one of his students. So what do you think I said when he asked me to make up this mixture? I was a child, in my early twenties. Of course I said yes.'

The fog was beginning to clear. Tom could see that Rebecca was sitting stiff and upright. 'Did you know what it was for?' he asked.

The President smiled. 'It would be nice to say I didn't. But the note from the professor was clear. "Give this man a toxin that has no colour and no smell, yet will not lose its power in water." And the volume! Only an idiot would not have realised that this was designed for a mass water supply.'

'But you did it.'

'I did it.'

'And this is your great secret.'

The old man took a sip from the glass of water that sat on the table between them. 'Not just my secret. There are many in the world who hate my country, who believe that the very existence of the State of Israel is a crime. Imagine what they would do with this information. Would we ever recover?

'But I do not deny there are personal considerations here. Imagine what happens to my reputation as an advocate of peace and reconciliation if the world finds out that I was an accomplice to an attempt at mass murder. Death at the turn of a tap. To a million people. Not just Nazis, but children and women, too. Random, senseless killing.'

Rebecca leaned forward. 'Why didn't it happen?'

'In the end, cooler heads prevailed. The leadership in Palestine realised that *Tochnit Aleph* would be a disaster for the Jewish people; we would no longer be the victims of the greatest crime in human history. We would be guilty of mass murder. It would have destroyed our moral advantage.'

'Then did the leadership order DIN to call off the operation?'

The old man stretched, his first sign of fatigue. 'It wasn't that simple. DIN was a movement that had the highest righteousness on its side: it spoke for the six million. What were a few politicians in Tel Aviv next to that?'

'So how did they stop it?'

'Aron was on a boat leaving Palestine, on his way back to Europe with the poison. British military police boarded the ship and arrested him.'

'Somebody had tipped off the British authorities?'

'That's right.'

'Do you know who that was?'

'Of course I know.' He took another sip of water. Then he looked back at Tom and Rebecca with an expression of mock puzzlement. 'It was me.'

'Why? Why on earth would you have done that?' Rebecca's face was ashen. Tom could see she was struggling to make sense of what they were hearing.

The President fixed her with a steady gaze. 'The leaders were desperate to stop Aron. But they didn't know how to get to him. No one did. Then he contacted me, at the last minute. He had a question about storage of the poison. We met, and he let slip that he was leaving the next day. We knew he was going by British transport ship. So the British had to watch the port only for that single day. It was easy.'

'I still don't understand why.'

The old man let out a deep sigh. 'Ambition. I knew that the very highest echelons were determined to stop Aron and they couldn't do it. And then, thanks to me, they could. Within a few weeks, I was out of that laboratory, appointed as a personal adviser to the old man, the man who became my country's first leader, and I've been at the top ever since.'

Tom was struck by the man's honesty. Self-criticism was not usually politicians' strength and this went much further.

'Why don't you tell the world what you've told us?' Tom said. 'You're the man who stopped *Tochnit Aleph*. That should win you a few more prizes.'

'Oh, the world would be delighted, I agree. But in Israel, Aron of the Ghetto is a hero, and a hero on a Biblical scale. Against him, I am an ant. A politician, cutting deals. And that's before they know that I betrayed him.'

'So what are you going to do?'

'The question is, what are *we* going to do? We all need an exit strategy.'

'What the hell is that supposed to mean?' It was Rebecca.

'It means, my dear, that we need a way out. You need to leave here with a guarantee that you will not be troubled by any of this again.' He let the words hang in the air a while, until Tom and Rebecca could appreciate the threat. 'And I need a guarantee that what you know, what we have discussed here, will never be made public. That you will take this secret to your grave.'

At last, thought Tom: a negotiation. He sat up stiffly, an attempt to establish some authority in the room. His mind was revving. He had planned for this moment, but only over the past few minutes. He would have to improvise. 'OK. We each know what we want and what we have. You will give Rebecca safe passage back to London. Once there, she'll arrange to give you the papers you want. Once you have them, you'll know that there's no more hard evidence of your role in what happened.'

'Except what's in your heads.'

'Yes. But why, realistically, would we want to cause trouble? Now that we know what you can do to us.' This was the first move.

The President rubbed his chin. 'And in return?'

'You let us have our lives back.'

'And you will give me back those papers.'

'They will be yours. So long as nothing happens to us, no one will ever see them.' This was the second move, the one Tom hoped would be decisive.

'What does that mean?'

'It means that I have already made electronic copies of those papers and uploaded them to a website. A dormant website, programmed to stay dormant so long as I log in, with my password, every seven days. If for some reason I don't log in, the site goes live. And sends an email alert to a few chosen recipients: the *New York Times*, the *Jerusalem Post*. Oh, and we wouldn't want to leave out the BBC or CNN.' Tom glanced at Rebecca. She looked startled.

The President spoke again, his pitch now rising. 'You've done this?'

Tom nodded, a bead of sweat forming on his upper lip. 'We spent a lot of time at that Internet café, as I'm sure your friends have told you.'

'What if something goes wrong with this website, what if it acci—?'

'Don't worry, it's secure. Just so long as nothing happens to us.'

The President was pale, unsure. Rebecca leaned forward, as if keen to exploit this moment of weakness. 'I have one more condition.'

Tom swivelled round and glared at her: *Don't ruin this.*

She ignored him. 'In return for keeping what you have told us safe and secret, I want you to use your influence to get me a meeting. With the Secretary-General of the United Nations.'

'Oh, for God's sake, Rebecca—' Tom couldn't help himself. What the hell was she playing at?

With a half-smile that Tom interpreted as sheer disbelief at her cheek, the President held up a hand to silence him. 'Tell me again. What is it you want?'

'What I want is for you to get me a meeting with the Secretary-General,' Rebecca said. 'I want him to look me in the eye and admit what the UN did to my father. Then this nightmare can be over.'

'I understand,' the President said quietly. 'Dr Merton, I truly understand.'

Suddenly, as if snapping out of a trance, he turned to Tom and shook his hand, giving him no chance to refuse the gesture. 'I am prepared to accept these terms. And so long as you come to no harm, this Internet site of yours will remain locked, even after my death. Yes?'

'Yes.'

'Good. And now I would like to have a private word of remembrance with Dr Merton.'

He headed for the doorway. Tom wondered if he was about to usher Rebecca into the outer suite, but he gestured for her to stay behind, leaving Tom and Rebecca alone. Neither spoke. The old man was gone for no more than twenty seconds, no doubt preparing his aides for their departure.

When the President came back, he immediately placed an arm over Rebecca's shoulder, guiding her towards the window. Tom could see only their backs, but he could hear the old man muttering something in a language he guessed was Hebrew. Judging by Rebecca's low nod of response, it was probably a word of condolence for her father, perhaps even a memorial prayer. The President then removed his arm so that he could face Rebecca directly, clasping her hands in a double handshake, the kind of showy gesture politicians saved for special occasions. There were more inaudible words of farewell; then the door opened and Tom and Rebecca were shown out—leaving the President of the State of Israel gazing out of the window, quite alone.

THEY WERE IN HIS OLD OFFICE. It had been Henning's idea; the new occupant was away, in Slovenia on some EU-related business, and the room was empty. Tom was gazing out of the window, enjoying the generous and direct view of the Chrysler Building, easily his favourite New York landmark.

Rebecca was behind the desk, sitting in a graphite chair far grander than the creaking, fake-leather contraption he remembered.

'All that time,' Tom said at last, 'we were looking in the wrong place. Once I'd read your father's journal, I was certain that the only people who'd be doing this—smashing up the house, stalking us around London—would be some bunch of old Nazi war criminals. I never thought of . . . his own side.'

'Why would you have thought of it?' She gave him a smile, one that warmed the room. 'Anyway, even if you're not much of a detective, you're a helluva negotiator. That was quite a move you made.'

'He gave us time to think. All that talking. We just had to give him a reason not to get rid of us once he got the papers.'

'Oh, the papers.' She was still smiling. 'What *are* these mystery papers?'

'Well, we can choose. It could be the blueprints of the waterworks—'

'But those have no link to him.'

'Not now, they don't, but it wouldn't be difficult for you to add a few words to that card now, would it? Some clever little play on a Biblical verse that happens to name our old friend. There must be plenty of characters in the Bible with the same name as him.'

'I'm not convinced. What's the other option?'

'Your father's notebook. You could fake his writing, add a section about Plan A, explaining how the now-famous Mr X brewed up the potion. We hand that over with the blueprints. Enough to show we weren't bluffing.'

'Except we were—'

'Ssshh.' Tom placed a single finger across his lips. 'All that matters is that getting rid of us is now less attractive than it was. Or getting rid of me. He wouldn't lay a glove on you: you're a "daughter of the Shoah".'

They had gone to the Nations' Café straight after they had been escorted out of the presidential suite at the UN Millennium Plaza Hotel, from where Tom immediately phoned Henning to tell him that he and Rebecca had come on a hastily arranged trip to New York because the resourceful Dr Merton had deployed her own contacts to get her precious meeting with the Secretary-General.

'I know,' Henning had said. 'I just got a call from the SG's political office.' He sounded furious. 'I'd won the battle on this, Tom. The SG had some ludicrous idea about meeting your Dr Merton and I got it blocked. And now I'm undermined by an intervention from the bloody Israelis.'

Tom tried to placate his old friend. 'At least this way there'll be no publicity. By the time the media know about the meeting, it'll be over.'

Munchau told Tom that the only reason he wasn't resisting this insane idea more strenuously was that he had been notified the previous day that the NYPD were dropping their inquiry into the Merton killing. 'Since it falls outside their jurisdiction, the DA says no prosecutable crime was committed.'

'So the coast is clear?'

'I suppose so. But I still want her to sign a comprehensive end-of-claim agreement. Can't have her throwing a meeting with the SG back in our face in some future civil action, claiming it as admission of liability.'

'I'll draft something right away,' Tom said, confirmed in his view that Henning was one of the best men the UN had, protective of the institution and its reputation even when the boss was cavalier. Tom felt another sting of guilt at how quickly he had doubted him.

'I'm impressed,' Rebecca was saying now. 'You've got it all worked out.'

'Not quite everything. There's one thing I've never understood. The envelope that arrived at your flat. The list of names. I don't get who would have done it. It can't have been the Israelis—'

There was a knock on the door. Henning.

Rebecca leapt up from the chair, re-adopted the expression of grieving daughter, and extended her hand.

Tom did the introductions and Henning got straight to the point, too professional to show that his teeth were gritted. 'Dr Merton, the Secretary-General is so appreciative of the gesture you've made in coming here that he has asked if he can see you right away in his office, in accordance with the conditions I have discussed with Mr Byrne.' He looked towards Tom, who nodded. 'He has cleared his next two appointments.'

'Hold on,' Rebecca said. She took a deep breath, then exhaled. 'Can we just take a minute?'

'Of course.' Henning shot another look over at Tom.

Rebecca collected herself. 'Mr Munchau, I'm not used to this sort of thing. Meetings with world leaders. Would it be possible to meet somewhere, I don't know, less *grand*? Somewhere a bit quieter?'

'Of course.' Henning's diplomatic veneer was back in place. 'I can think of a place that will be ideal for an encounter of this gravity.'

'I really appreciate it.'

She stood up and visibly girded herself, like a candidate about to give a speech. Tom went to follow her, but Rebecca stopped him. 'Tom, you've helped me so much, but I need to do this on my own.'

He nodded. Henning gave him a brief smile, then ushered Rebecca out.

Tom watched them go, then sat back at the desk and switched on the computer. He needed to draft the agreement for Rebecca and Henning to sign. When prompted for a password, he used a 'system administrator' code that Henning had once taught him, and it let him in. He was about to open a Word document when he remembered another of Henning's lessons: anyone could access anything on the UN system. He would draft a text by hand.

He reached into his inside pocket, but there was no pen. Perhaps it had been left behind at the hospital. There were no loose pens on the desk and the drawers were locked. He saw Rebecca's bag; she had left it behind on a chair, along with her coat. He walked round to get it, opened it guiltily, saw a fountain pen and grabbed it. There was some paper in the laser printer: he took a couple of sheets and prepared to write.

Agreement between, he scratched without leaving a mark. He gave it a shake but still no ink would flow. He unscrewed the barrel and saw the explanation: there was no ink cartridge. Perhaps it had become detached and fallen back into the barrel. Tom held it up to the light and saw that there was indeed something inside—but he knew instantly it was no cartridge.

He tapped the pen on the surface of the desk and it popped out: a neatly rolled sheet—perhaps two sheets—of paper.

It took Tom no more than a second to understand what he was looking at. The handwriting was unmistakable. Tom scanned the words.

I received the list of names and worked my way through them methodically. I could not get to them all at once. Some of these men lived very far away; they had hidden themselves well. Each mission required papers, a fresh passport, money and a cover story . . .

Tom's head began to pound. So these were the missing pages torn from Gershon Matzkin's notebook. Rebecca had had them all the time. She had known all along the truth of her father's life.

A memory came to him. It was when they had argued, back in her flat, straight after the Goldman meeting. She complained that the old lawyer had been droning on, 'telling us what we already knew'. *What we already knew.*

Had the whole thing been one long act? She must have decided it from the start, tearing the key pages from her father's notebook before Tom had shoved it in his bag, perhaps the instant she heard her father had died.

But he had discovered the truth anyway; he had learned about DIN and their work of vengeance, seeing the evidence for himself, in the box at Julian Goldman's office. They had gone there straight after the envelope arrived.

Of course. No wonder he had not been able to work out who had sent that list of names. It must have been Rebecca herself. She had clearly wanted to put Tom on the path towards DIN—without revealing how much she knew. But why? Why lead them both on such a pointless charade?

He thought back to the last visit to her father's flat. The secret papers hidden in the *Aleph* painting had apparently been as much of a revelation to her as they had been to him. Perhaps Rebecca had known part of the strange, murderous life story of Gershon Matzkin—but not all of it.

Tom looked back at the handwritten pages in front of him. Sure enough, at least on the basis of this skim-read, Gershon seemed to be recounting only his work as an unofficial executioner of individuals. There was no sign of the Israeli's name, nor any mention of Plan A or Plan B.

The ink on the last sheet was thicker and fresher, and it was obvious that these lines had been added long after the rest of the journal had been completed. Gershon now wrote in the unsteady hand of an old man.

Rebecca, I promised myself—for your sake—that I would stop the work of DIN. And I kept my promise. For all these years, I have only been a normal, loving father to you. I have certainly tried.

But a long time ago, I made another promise, a promise to a young woman just as full of life and of beauty as you are today. I never thought I would have the chance to honour my word to her.

Now I have that chance and I cannot let it pass. This is why I am going to New York. If you want to understand, you must do as I say—and remember Kadish.

A new wave of electricity flooded into Tom's brain; he tried to process this latest surge of information. It meant that Rebecca had known not only that her father had been an assassin for DIN, but that this had been his purpose in New York. No wonder she had barely mentioned pressing a full legal case for compensation against the United Nations. She didn't want anyone probing too deeply into a story she knew only too well.

Now Tom was convinced: Rebecca Merton knew whom her father had come here to kill. But who was it?

Could it have been the Israeli President? It made no sense. Gershon

Matzkin was a first-class hitman. If he had wanted to get his revenge for the betrayal of Aron, he would have had countless chances years before.

Besides, the passage spoke of a promise to 'another young woman'. Was it Rosa, his benighted first love and early comrade in DIN?

Tom looked down at the torn page, lingering on the last sentence: *If you want to understand, you must do as I say—and remember Kadish.*

He now saw that there was another word, written in brackets and in pencil so that Tom had missed it the first time: (*March*). Perhaps that was when Gershon had made the note, a few months back.

Looking again at the final, inked phrase, Tom realised that he had seen it before, on a note pinned to Rebecca's notice board, written in her father's hand. It referred to the Jewish memorial prayer for the dead, she had said.

Tom looked through the two pages again. He found an account of the killing of Joschka Dorfman in his hotel room in San Sebastián, who, Tom now realised, had been using the assumed name of 'Herr Schroeder':

> *After the Dorfman job I went to the seashore, picked up a single stone and said Kaddish for all the Jews of Treblinka. It was the first time I had said Kaddish since I had been a child in Kovno, where I learned to say Kaddish for my father. I had not forgotten the prayer.*

So that confirmed it: Kaddish was precisely what Rebecca had said it was, a memorial prayer. Tom fell back into his chair, closed his eyes and grabbed his head. What on earth had Gershon meant: *If you want to understand, you must do as I say—and remember Kadish*?

And then it struck him. It was probably just an error of old age, but when referring to the prayer, Gershon had used two ds: *Kaddish*. Here in this final message, and in the note on the pinboard, there was just one: *Kadish*.

He turned back to the computer keyboard, opened an Internet browser and typed those six letters into the search window. Instantly Google made the same assumption that he had: Did you mean Kaddish?

Tom ignored that, and examined the list of entries for 'Kadish'. They seemed barren: a professor of electrochemistry in Indiana, a guitar teacher in Texas, a federal government official in Washington. Then halfway down the screen, he saw an entry from Wikipedia, the free encyclopedia.

George **Kadish** was a Lithuanian Jewish photographer who documented life in the Kovno ghetto during the Holocaust, the period of the Nazi German genocide . . .

Tom began to click frantically, hopping from one website to another, learning that Kadish had kept a homemade camera under his coat, secretly photographing his fellow Jewish inmates of the ghetto. Now the screen was filling up with photographs Kadish had taken. A young couple with yellow stars sewn to their clothes. Jews pushing wagons in the snow, their possessions loaded up in bundles, all of them yellow-starred as well. The caption: *Moving into the Kovno Ghetto. Credit: George Kadish, photographer.*

Now Tom was in a section of a website on Kovno entitled: Ninth Fort. There was a Kadish photo of Jews gathering in a square, a 'final muster', the caption explained, before they were taken to the Fort. Another showed a clump of men and women inside the Fort 'prior to their execution'. He clicked again and again until one image stopped him. The caption read: *The March: Lithuanian militiamen leading Jews to their death at the Ninth Fort.*

Tom's pulse was galloping. There was no date on this photograph either. But it had a title: *The March.* Surely this was the picture Gershon had had in mind, the one that he was urging his daughter to remember. It showed the Jews marching in a ragged column. At the head and at the sides of this human herd, wearing black jackets and armbands marked with some kind of insignia, were the Lithuanian militiamen. Most were smiling.

Tom's eye was drawn to the left of the picture. There were two men there, one taller than the other, the first beaming with what seemed to be pride. He was watching the man next to him, who, on closer inspection, was a tall, rangy teenager. This younger man was brandishing a truncheon. It was raised into the air, held at the same height as his ear, and he was about to bring it down onto the head of one of the Jews marching towards his death.

There was a strange delay in how Tom absorbed what he was seeing. His brain seemed to know what it was about to take in even before his eye had glimpsed it. When Tom's gaze, at last, moved away from the truncheon and towards the young assailant's face, it was as if it was merely to confirm what some sixth sense of Tom's already understood. There was no mistaking it. The features were sharp, unambiguous. It did not matter how many years had passed; this was the same face. It was the same person.

Tom felt a shudder ripple through him. He kept staring at the picture, as if hoping that somehow the very act of his observation would change what he had seen. But it did not change. He was gazing at the boy who had become the man, even if the two appeared to be from two different historical eras. There could be no doubt: they were the same person.

And then he remembered: *Rebecca.*

Chapter Eleven

Tom hurtled out of the office, heading first for the lifts, then thinking better of it and shouldering his way into the fire escape: taking the stairs reduced the risk of a collision with someone he knew.

He ran down the stairs as fast as he could, clutching the banister so he could vault the final three or four steps, leaping into the air and pounding onto successive landings. He emerged from the fire escape on the third floor, and disappeared into the throng, walking at his briskest pace. He took the stairs down another couple of flights, and there he was at last, by the huge stained-glass Chagall window known as the Peace Window, with its pale moons, eerie blues and desperate mothers clinging to their swaddled babies.

Tom stopped, breathing heavily. Only a hunch had brought him here. Rebecca had asked Henning if the meeting could be somewhere quiet, somewhere that was not 'grand'. If he knew Henning, and he did, the German would have brought her to this place.

They called it the meditation chapel. It was a plain, dark room, with no religious symbols, no holy texts, no artworks. It was meant to be 'multi-faith'. Tom had come here once or twice, late at night, after a particularly terrible session wading through eyewitness testimonies. But most UN staff could work in the place for twenty years and not know it was there.

Not Henning, though. He had been one of those adamant that the entrance to the area should become a memorial for those who had fallen serving the UN. There was a plaque for Count Bernadotte, the diplomat assassinated in Jerusalem, as well as the torn flag of the United Nations mission, bombed in Baghdad in 2003. To Henning, the meditation chapel meant something.

Tom tried to steady himself. He wanted to think, to work out what he would say or do, but there was no time. He walked through the partitioned walls—there was no door—and he knew he had been right.

They were both there, Rebecca and him. No aides, no advisers, just as Henning had promised. Just the two of them alone, facing each other.

The change in the light meant that they both turned round as Tom walked forward. Rebecca seemed aghast—with surprise, with confusion, Tom couldn't tell—but it was not her he wanted to examine.

Instead he peered hard at the features of the man. He had never worked with him; his appointment had come long after Tom had fled for the corporate hills. But his face had become familiar in the past few weeks, had been in the papers, on TV. The high forehead, the combed-back silver-grey hair, the wide mouth and firm, sharp nose. He was tall, too, and elegant in a dark, tailored suit and perfectly knotted tie.

But it was not the similarity of the real man to his TV likeness that Tom was trying to make out. Rather, he was comparing the face before him with the image he had seen just five minutes earlier on the computer screen. Was there room for doubt? No, Tom would have been ready to swear under oath that the man he was looking at and the teenage Fascist thug of Kovno's Ninth Fort were one and the same man. He knew that the eager participant in the massacre of the Jews of that town, a minor but murderous accomplice in the greatest crime of the twentieth century, was standing before him now as the Secretary-General of the United Nations.

'TOM, GET AWAY. This has nothing to do with you.' Rebecca's tone was harder than he had ever heard before. Yet there was anxiety in her voice, too.

'Rebecca, just talk to me. What are you doing?'

'I mean it, Tom. Just turn round and go away.'

Tom looked over at Paavo Viren, and saw that his face, usually a model of statesmanlike composure, was drawn, ashen.

'Rebecca, I've seen the photographs. *Remember Kadish.*'

'I'm sorry, Tom. I'm really sorry.'

'Why are you apolog—?' And then he stopped himself. 'Oh, I see. Now I see very well, Rebecca.'

'It's not like that, Tom.'

'Is that what this whole thing was about? Is that what I was to you: a ticket into this place?'

'Don't, Tom.'

His brain seemed to overflow with a whole new set of understandings, arriving in waves. She had wanted to be rid of him at first, but then suddenly she had softened. Now he realised she had seen his potential: with Tom at her side, she had a chance of penetrating the heart of the United Nations and completing her father's unfinished business.

He remembered their kiss; it had come once he told her that he not only understood what her father and DIN had done, but that he agreed with it. *They were right: they weren't going to get justice any other way.* Perhaps that was when she'd let down her guard, seeing Tom as a kindred spirit. Or maybe she had concluded that to rely absolutely on Tom to get her inside UN Plaza, she would first have to cloud his judgment . . .

When had her deception begun? Was it the moment he confronted her with evidence of Gerald Merton's meeting with the Russian and the discovery of an assassin's weapon? That was when she had thrust the notebook in his hand, telling him to read it in full. But she had torn out the crucial pages; she was playing a game even then.

'How many others know about this wild story of yours?' Paavo Viren raised himself to his full height, trying to take command of the room.

'I've not told anybody,' Rebecca said. 'Tom worked it out for himself. Like I said, this is between you and me.' And she turned to glare at Tom, her eyes imploring him to back off.

Viren spoke again. 'Since Mr Byrne is here, perhaps you can explain to him what it is exactly that you want. Because I am still unclear.'

Rebecca leaned closer to him. 'I want you to tell me the truth. That's all you have to do. After all these years, it's too late for anything else. But the victims deserve that. They deserve at least that.'

'You want me to start confessing to you, in this chapel?' He gave a snort of mockery. 'Are you some kind of priest?'

'I've told you, we have the evidence. There is a photograph of you, herding Jews to their deaths in the Ninth Fort.'

'I know this photograph.' He let his mouth widen into a joyless smile. 'That surprises you, yes? Of course, I have seen it. Perhaps there is a vague resemblance, but nothing more. The idea that this would count as evidence is laughable. You don't have "evidence". You have a baseless accusation.'

'So why don't you walk out?' It was Tom, standing in the shadows.

'What?'

'If this were all baseless nonsense, you'd have walked out by now. You'd have summoned your aides. You'd have called Security. But I'm looking round and I don't see anybody here. Now why would that be?'

Viren lifted his chin, as if making a more thorough assessment of Tom Byrne. 'I'm trying to be humane. Ms Merton is clearly in some dist—'

'Really? Or is it because you don't want anybody else, not even a security guard, to hear what she has to say?'

The SG began to pace, half turning his back on Rebecca. The movement made her flinch. Tom wondered then whether the man was armed in some way—an absurd thought, he realised, as soon as he had formulated it. Even so, Rebecca had been brave confronting him alone like this.

'Do you know how old I am?'

The question hung in the air. The longer it lingered, the more it made Tom feel unsteady. The physical resemblance in the photograph had been so striking, he had not even considered basic matters like age and chronology. But perhaps he had made an elementary error, succumbed to a universal human failing: perhaps he had seen what he had wanted to see.

Rebecca broke the silence. 'Your biography says you're sixty-eight.'

'Good, Ms Merton. You have done your homework. My biography says I am sixty-eight because I *am* sixty-eight. And how's your mental arithmetic? Because mine is quite good and it says that I was five years old when the war ended. We can agree that the man in your photograph was more than five years old, yes?' The smile again, this time with more enthusiasm.

'You lied about your age.'

'What, for all these years? Do I look seventy-eight to you?'

'My father didn't look his age either,' Rebecca shot back. 'He was fit and strong. He could have passed for sixty-eight, too.'

Tom felt his knees weakening. What if Rebecca was wrong?

But she did not budge. Instead she was standing even closer to Viren, examining him as if he were one of her patients. 'Oh, there's no hiding that, though, is there, Mr Secretary-General? That line around the ear gives it away. You've had some work done, I can tell.'

'So what? A little cosmetic surgery is nothing to be ashamed of in this day and age. Human vanity is no crime.' Then, as if he could sense Tom wavering, Viren continued, 'Besides, I am Finnish, for heaven's sake. I served as the foreign minister of that country. I am the wrong age and the wrong nationality—which means you have the wrong man.'

Tom looked down at his feet. He would need all his lawyerly skills to resolve this situation. He would have to offer an apology, explaining that Rebecca Merton had been under extreme stress, and that she withdrew her accusation, undertaking never to repeat it. And she would waive any claims for compensation for the death of her father.

He stepped towards Rebecca, aiming to place a gentle hand on her arm and guide her out of the chapel, hoping she wouldn't make a scene.

Rebecca wheeled round. 'Don't disappoint me, Tom.'

'What do you mean?'

'Do you really think my father would have come here, ready the way he was ready, if he wasn't certain that this man is exactly who he thought he was? Do you think I would be here now if *I* wasn't certain?'

'But it's just one photograph.'

'Oh, no, Tom. There are many more photographs of this man. He was one of the stars of the ghetto, weren't you, Mr Secretary-General?'

Tom looked at the SG—who had the same pitying expression fixed on his face—then back at Rebecca. 'There are more photos?'

'Yes, and they weren't all taken by Kadish. Lots were taken by the Nazis themselves. Half a dozen at least, some quite formal, some casual, the boys joshing around. Like a team photo. And young Paavo Viren, or whatever his name was then, always in the middle: the team mascot.'

'But he's just sixty-eight.'

'He lied about his age. Plenty of the young ones did. They got new papers, adding ten years to their date of birth. Once they were in their late twenties, it all sounded plausible enough.'

'He's from Finland.'

'He *went* to Finland, Tom. Not the same thing. Some went to Canada, some even went to Germany, for Christ's sake. They started over—new lives, new names. Finland was a good choice: hardly any Jews there, and certainly no survivors of Kovno. No one who would remember.'

Tom looked at her. 'Where is all this evidence, Rebecca?' He hated how his voice sounded: so sceptical, prosecutorial.

'It was all there, in London, in a file. But they took it.'

'So you've known this all along.'

'I knew about DIN. And my father told me what he was doing before he went to New York. But I knew nothing about the rest, I swear. The break-in made no sense to me. The bakery, *Tochnit Aleph*—I never knew about that.'

'It makes no sense, Rebecca. Why would your father tell you about DIN and keep the rest secret?'

'I've tried to work that out, Tom, really I have. All I can think of is that my father was ashamed. Plan A was *random*, indiscriminate. The DIN I knew of only went after the guilty. But if I knew about Plan B, I'd find out about Plan A. And then I think my father believed I'd stop loving him.'

Viren cleared his throat, as if he were politely requesting a hearing. 'You say this so-called "evidence" has vanished? It has been stolen?'

Rebecca did not answer. Tom said nothing.

'So we are back where we started, correct? Back with a wild claim?'

Tom was struck again by the simple fact that Viren was still here. Rebecca had no physical leverage over him, no gun pointing at him. Yet here he still was. Why? What was he frightened of?

Rebecca now stepped back a couple of paces, and raised her voice a notch. 'I'll leave you alone. I'll drop these claims. On one condition.'

'What? What condition?'

'That you let me examine your left arm.'

The features of Viren's face remade themselves, from initial confusion to horrified indignation. 'How dare you? Do you know who you are addressing? I am the elected representative of the entire world community!'

But still he didn't leave. Then a new thought struck. The SG was waiting for *him*, for Tom. If he, a former senior lawyer at the UN, agreed that Rebecca was just a traumatised, grieving daughter, her claims would be discarded. But if he lent her any credence, then the charges would gain some currency. Tom had been forced into the role of referee.

'I think you should let her see your arm,' he said softly. 'Then this thing can be over.' And he stepped forward and took hold of Viren's left wrist.

The Secretary-General desperately tried to remove his arm from Tom's grasp, but he did not shout or scream.

'OK, Rebecca,' Tom said. 'Take a look at his arm.'

She stepped closer, her nervousness clear. Slowly, she pushed up the sleeve of his jacket, then began to unbutton the cuff of his shirt.

'What are you looking for?' Tom said, the words squeezed out between short breaths as he struggled to keep the older man restrained.

'I'm looking for a scar,' Rebecca said, her voice steady. She looked up, and fixed the writhing Viren in her gaze. 'I'm looking for the scar my father's sister left on the arm of a young man who raped her, a young man who terrorised the children of the Kovno ghetto—a young man they called the Wolf.'

Tom wasn't sure that he felt Paavo Viren's muscles go rigid at the mention of that word. It could have been another trick of the mind. But now Rebecca had the old man's sleeve rolled up to his elbow and she was staring hard.

The Wolf. It had taken Tom a beat, no more, to remember that name. It had been one of the most chilling details in Gershon Matzkin's journal. So this was why Gershon had ended his retirement from the work of DIN. The Wolf was a special case, a personal score to settle. He must have promised his older sister that he would avenge her, that he would, one day, make the Wolf pay for what he had done.

Rebecca was peering intensely at Viren's forearm. Finally she spoke, uttering words that seemed to suck the air out of the room.

'There is no scar.'

JAY SHERRILL didn't like going over Tom Byrne's head, but he had no choice. He hadn't been able to get hold of Byrne since yesterday lunchtime, so he had contacted Henning Munchau late last night, asking to see him urgently.

Munchau had seemed reluctant to take his call. Maybe he wanted arm's-length deniability on the whole Gerald Merton business. Doubtless that was why he had contracted out the case to a lawyer who had left the UN more than a year ago. 'I'll see what I can do,' was the most Munchau had promised. Sherrill endured another anguished, unending night as a result.

And then a call from Munchau twenty minutes ago, saying that a window in his schedule had suddenly opened up. If Jay could be in UN Plaza in the next fifteen minutes, they could have coffee in the delegates' lounge.

'Sorry to spring this on you like that,' Munchau said, 'but the SG just asked me to clear an hour of his schedule, which suddenly gave me an hour I didn't have before. He's meeting Rebecca Merton, as it happens. One on one.'

'She's in New York?'

'They flew in together, she and Byrne. Didn't he tell you?'

Sherrill shook his head. 'I've had no word from him in twenty-four hours.'

'That's Tom for you. So, what can I do for you?'

'This conversation is strictly confidential, yes?'

'If you want it to be.'

'Well, my career—which is probably over—might depend on it.'

'What's on your mind, Detective?'

'Two days ago, I had a meeting with the head of the NYPD Intelligence Division, Stephen Lake. He said something then that I barely noticed at the time, but that I can't quite figure out.'

'What was it?'

'He said,' Sherrill read from his notebook, '"We may have had our eye on the UN for a while, with evidence of a ticking time bomb over there."'

'Are you saying that the Intel Division knew that there was a terror threat to the UN and didn't pass it on?'

'No, sir, I'm not. That's what I thought it meant, too. But Lake didn't say, "a time bomb *on its way* to the UN" or "aimed at the UN". He said, "a ticking time bomb *over there*". And he was using the phrase metaphorically.'

'So Intel knows something about this place that counts as a time bomb.'

'Something that could destroy the UN, yes, sir. That's what I suspect.'

The look of recognition and then alarm that spread across Henning Munchau's face meant that when he silently got to his feet, Jay Sherrill knew he had no option but to follow.

'WHAT DO YOU MEAN there's no scar?' Tom instinctively loosened his grip.

Now Viren spoke. 'At last this farce is over. I should report you—'

Rebecca cut him off. 'Or rather there is not the obvious scar.'

The Secretary-General tried to shake himself free. 'What the hell are you talking about?'

Rebecca pointed at the pale skin of his forearm. 'Unluckily for you, plastic surgery was not able to do then what it can do now. Back then, when they did skin grafts like this one, to cover up a scar, they couldn't help but leave a mark round the edges, like the outline of a patch sewn on a suit. See it? Right here.' She was being unnervingly calm.

'So what if I did have a skin graft? It was for a burn I had twenty years ago. It was an . . . an accident. At home. With a stove.'

'Well, that's very odd. Because, in fact, the marks you have on your skin in this area are clear signs of stretching. And the only way you could have got those is if you had a skin graft when your skin was still growing. And you weren't growing twenty years ago, Mr Viren, were you?'

At that, Viren finally shook Tom off. He raised his hand high, so that it was level with his ear, and it was about to come down on Rebecca when Tom grabbed him round the middle in a crude wrestling move that left the older man's fist flailing in the air.

And then Viren let out a shriek.

Tom's view was obscured at first by Viren's body, but now he could see the source of his alarm. Rebecca was holding a hypodermic syringe, which she was raising into the air, at eye level, to test it against the light.

Tom gasped. 'Rebecca, what the hell are you doing?'

She ignored him, addressing only the Secretary-General. 'Your great misfortune is that I'm a doctor. I know about scar tissue and skin grafts—and I also know about poisons. This one, for example, is odourless, clear and instantly effective.'

'Rebecca, where did you get that?'

'Let's say it was a gift from someone we just met.'

In an instant, Tom pictured the lingering farewell he had witnessed between Rebecca and the Israeli President: how he had muttered to her in Hebrew; how he had held her hands in a double-grip, one that could have concealed the handover of, say, a needle and a measure of deadly fluid.

If Gerald Merton had been able to work out the truth of Paavo Viren's past, it would not have eluded Israeli intelligence. Once the President was reassured that Merton had not been after him, that Viren had been DIN's last target, what better way to assuage his guilt over Aron than to give DIN what it needed from him once again—a vial of deadly poison?

Viren was making a half-hearted effort at writhing out of Tom's grip, but his eyes were on Rebecca. 'There must be a way we can resolve this. We could have an independent review, to examine the claims you've—'

'Oh, no, I'm far too unreasonable for that. You see, your second great misfortune is that you picked the wrong people to murder and maim. You raped and nearly killed my aunt, Hannah Matzkin, who, thanks to you, I never met.' She squeezed the syringe, holding it still as it squirted a brief jet of fluid. 'And you took part, an eager part from what I hear, in the massacres at the Ninth Fort. My aunts were among the thousands of people you and your friends shot into those pits.'

Tom was still holding the old man, but now out of sheer paralysis.

'You killed the wrong people, Mr Viren. You killed the family of Gershon Matzkin and he was not the kind of Jew you bargained for. He was an avenger, Mr Viren—and I am his daughter.'

With that, Rebecca leaned forward and placed the tip of the needle on Viren's neck, expertly finding the jugular vein.

The certainty of that action, the finality of it, seemed to snap Tom out of his state of disconnection. Rebecca intuited this immediately.

'If you make any sudden movements now, Tom, the needle will go in. Really, even a slight jerk and Viren will be dead.'

Tom could see that she was right. His job now was to hold the SG stock-still—for his own sake.

Viren managed to squeeze out a few words. 'What do you want from me? If you want to kill me, just kill me. Get it over with.'

'Oh, but that wasn't your way of doing things, was it, Mr Viren? You and the men from the Lithuanian militia enjoyed the whole performance. Get the Jews to come to the collection point, packing all their bags as if they were off on a journey. Then a long truck ride. Then a march to the pits. Then watching the women undress, lining them up by pits you'd made the Jews dig for themselves. And then only a single bullet, so that—what, one in ten, one in five?—did not even die straight away, but were suffocated, buried alive under a pile of corpses. So don't start bleating about "getting it over with". If this is trying your patience, Mr Viren, then I don't apologise.'

Tom was wincing, watching Rebecca standing so close to the SG, her finger capping the plunger of the syringe as if it were a detonator.

'Rebecca, listen to me. This can't work. You'll be caught. Even if people sympathise with you, you'll spend years in jail. Is that what your father would have wanted, to see his beloved daughter behind bars?'

'I could get away.'

'Come off it, Rebecca. Henning knows you're here. He'll be here soon. If he finds the Secretary-General dead, you'll be blamed.'

'We'll say he had a heart attack.'

'There'll be a needle mark, bruises on his arms where I've held him. Please, Rebecca.' Tom's arms were tiring from keeping his captive dead still. 'Your father never got caught, Rebecca. None of them ever did. I bet that was important to them: that a Jew would not suffer again because of the Nazis, not even for one more day.'

'There needs to be a reckoning, Tom.' She was staring at him, hard.

'I understand.' His voice softened. 'But this is not the way.'

'But I heard you in Goldman's office, saying that DIN was right, that the law had always failed the victims. "The bigger the crime, the less convenient it is"— that's what you said. Remember?'

Tom found it unbalancing, to be reminded of his own words. Yet theory was one thing; the physical deed was quite another. This was not justice. It was everything the law was meant to stop: the descent into barbarism.

'Rebecca, it can't be like this. DIN killed people because there was no other way. But you have evidence. You can take this to a court.'

She made a snort, her head tilting back in mockery. 'You think they would ever put this man on trial?' she said. 'They would come up with the same bullshit they always come up with: "He's too old. The evidence is cold. The witnesses are dead. The statute of limitations has passed. It didn't take place on our soil." I've heard every argument in the book.'

'Even so, the alternative is to sink to their level.' He sighed. 'The law is all we've got, Rebecca. It's not perfect, but it's all we've got.'

'I need to end this.' She was trembling now, her whole body shaking. 'I've lived with this my whole life, Tom. Can you imagine that, knowing your own life is trivial compared to everything that happened? Can you imagine that? Of course you can't. No one can.'

In a brief change in the light, Tom could see there were tears slipping slowly down her cheeks. 'Your life is not trivial. It matters,' he said.

She said nothing.

'It mattered to your father, Rebecca. He named you after his mother for a reason. I think you were meant to be her second chance.'

She reeled back, her clenched hand finally coming away from Viren's neck. The old man now seized his opportunity, using all his strength to shake Tom off. As Tom fell backwards, he stumbled, hitting his head on the edge of one of the benches. He was stunned.

In that same instant, Viren lunged at Rebecca and grasped her wrist. She was still clasping the syringe, now terrified that the old man was about to turn the needle back on her. She screamed as he tugged at her arm.

The light in the room suddenly changed. Two men had come into the doorway, casting new shadows. Viren looked up to see Henning Munchau staring at him, his face aghast. The Secretary-General seemed frozen.

That moment of delay, of paralysis, was all Tom needed. He hauled himself up and surged forward into the space between Viren and Rebecca, pushing the pair apart. Rebecca staggered backwards, at last out of the old man's reach. But the needle was no longer in her hand.

Tom turned, only to find Viren coming at him, his eyes wild, clutching the syringe and aiming it directly at Tom's heart. Tom reached for Viren's wrist, but the old man had remarkable strength. Even in Tom's grip, he was pressing forward, the tip of the needle getting closer and closer until it was no more than an inch from Tom's chest.

With an almighty surge, Tom shoved Paavo Viren's wrist backwards— listening to the roar of horror as the Secretary-General realised that he had plunged the needle deep into the jugular vein of his own neck.

Epilogue: one year later

'And how many displaced people are we talking about?'
'Maybe a million.'
'Mainly in Chad, or elsewhere?'
'Chad mostly.'
'Conditions in the camps?'
'Very overcrowded. Shortages of food. Disease. The biggest problem is panic. Everyone is terrified. Many of the NGOs have withdrawn.'

Tom pushed back into his chair, chewing the top of his pen. His concentration was total. But once this meeting was over, he would allow himself the same thought that kept occurring these days: it was good to be back, absorbed once more in the work he was born to do.

'I need to look at all the documents you have, all the paperwork. So we can assemble a cast-iron case. First we need to establish the general circumstances, paint a picture of the overall humanitarian situation. Then we move on to the specifics of each individual. OK?'

It was the fifth Darfur-related meeting Tom had had in the last month. He held up his hand to request patience, and called to his assistant. 'Lequasia!'

The secretary emerged from the back corridor, where Tom had added a decent coffee maker to the battered old kettle that used to sit there.

'Lequasia, thanks for gracing us with your presence. Let me introduce you to Ismael Yahya Abdullah.'

She reached over to shake Ismael's hand.

'He's here on behalf of himself and five other people seeking asylum in this country from Darfur,' Tom went on. 'He's studying at UCL. Since he's been here the longest and has the best English, he'll be the point of contact for the group. Could you give him six copies of the basic asylum form?'

Tom said goodbye, leaving Lequasia and Ismael in the waiting area, and retreated to the back corridor. As he waited for the kettle to boil, he smiled at the absurdity of it all. Little more than two years ago, he had been a top international lawyer, in the inner circle of the Legal Counsel of the United Nations. Now he was here, in a Hackney legal-aid practice where the client base consisted of the dispossessed and the unhinged, 'the migrated and the medicated', as Julian, his partner at the Kingsland Law Centre, put it.

When he first met Goldman Junior, Tom had assumed he was a naive young man who would soon learn the ways of the world, but it had been Julian who had taught Tom a lesson: that even if Justice with a capital J was elusive, you could still remedy a thousand little injustices every day—one asylum applicant, or one plastic-bag-carrying mutterer, at a time.

It felt much longer than a year; so much had happened. These days Tom struggled even to remember those few, crazed hours in New York; his memory of the scene in the meditation chapel was particularly murky.

But he remembered that by the time Henning Munchau and Jay Sherrill were at the Secretary-General's side, the old man was dead.

Henning proved himself all over again that day, not only as a good friend but as a first-class lawyer. He methodically ingested all that Tom told him about what had happened, visibly organising the information he was hearing, even its wildest elements, without losing his steady focus.

As Legal Counsel, he insisted there would be no cover-up. The Deputy Secretary-General held a press conference, announcing that Paavo Viren had been killed by former UN lawyer Tom Byrne, the latter acting in self-defence. Viren had lashed out at Byrne and his female companion after they had confronted him with evidence of a grave secret, one that an internal investigation had now confirmed. Legal Counsel Dr Henning Munchau and NYPD Detective Jay Sherrill had witnessed the killing.

The New York police held Tom and Rebecca for a day, before releasing them under caution. Tom testified that even though the poison was Rebecca's, she had not intended to kill Viren; she had merely been threatening him, in a bid to elicit the truth. The District Attorney rapidly concluded there was little mileage in prosecuting the daughter of a Holocaust survivor for the death of a man who, posthumously and overnight, and thanks to archive photographs reproduced on newspaper front pages, on the Internet and screened endlessly on twenty-four-hour TV news, had become the world's number-one hate figure. Besides, since the killing had taken place on UN soil, no crime had been committed under either New York or US law.

In Finland, there was a call for a national day of atonement, so great was their shame in having allowed a war criminal to have sullied their collective good name. In Lithuania, a few thousand ultranationalists marched in Vilnius with banners displaying Viren's face, including—incredibly—pictures of him as a young man, in his black blazer in Kovno.

In Israel, there was a brief flurry of controversy when it emerged that the country's aged president had used his influence to broker the fateful meeting between Rebecca Merton and the Secretary-General. The President said he had simply responded to a request for help from the daughter of a brave survivor of the Holocaust. He was as shocked by the turn of events as everyone else. Truly shocked.

Tom had imagined the Israeli President nodding with satisfaction as he watched the TV news in his Manhattan hotel room. At last the old man had had a chance to expiate the guilt he had carried for more than six decades. A chance he had seized with both hands.

Accordingly, Tom detected more than a hint of embarrassment in 'Richard', the man who had drugged and dragged them to New York, when he relieved Tom and Rebecca of the papers they had prepared for him the following week. The package included an extra postcard that featured a cryptic sentence, pencilled in Yiddish. If the President studied it, he would find the Biblical verse that alluded to his own name. That should be enough, they reasoned, to persuade the aged politician that what could damage him was now in his own hands.

Tom felt a vibration in his pocket. It took him a second or two to snap out of his reverie and realise it was his phone. He looked at the display: *Rebecca*.

She had been back in London for only a month, after spending most of the last year travelling around Europe and Latin America, volunteering as a doctor in many places. She had needed to clear her head, she said.

'Tom? It's me.'

He didn't know how to reply. Her voice could still send a charge through him, but now it made him feel wary rather than excited.

Without waiting for him, she spoke. 'I've just had some sad news. Do you remember Sid Steiner? The man in the retirement home?'

'Of course.'

'He died last night. In his sleep.'

'Oh, I'm sorry to hear that.' He remembered the old boy, playing the piano, his hands fluttering along the keyboard as if he were a teenager.

'He was the last one, Tom.' He could hear her voice wavering. 'There are none left now. I want to do what my father did, to continue what he started.'

Tom felt his chest seize up. What was she saying? 'Look, Rebecca, I'm sorry Sid's gone, but DIN has to end. It's not up to you to carry—'

'No, I don't mean that. DIN is over, Tom. I don't expect you to forgive me for how it ended in New York, but I need you to know that DIN is over. And to know that I will never lie to you again.'

'I want to believe that, Rebecca.'

The silence held between them. Eventually she spoke again. 'This is something different I need to do, for Sid's sake. Something my father always did when this happened. I've never done it before. I'm not even sure I know how. But I'd like you to be with me, at my side. Because you're the only one who knows everything that happened.'

'What is it you need to do?'

'I want to remember them, Tom. Sid, my father, Hannah, Rivvy, Leah, all of them. I want to remember them. I want to say Kaddish.'

SAM BOURNE

Born: February 25, 1967
Degree: PPE, Oxford University
Profession: journalist and presenter

When he's not writing fiction—*The Righteous Men*; *The Last Testament*, and most recently *The Final Reckoning*—or acclaimed nonfiction books such as *Bring Home the Revolution*, which made a case for a British Republic, Sam Bourne works as a journalist under his real name, Jonathan Freedland. He is a regular columnist for *The Guardian* and the *Jewish Chronicle*, as well as other newspapers, and has done stints as a reporter for the *Washington Post* and the BBC. He is also the presenter of BBC Radio 4's contemporary history series, *The Long View*.

After so many years as a reporter dealing with facts, what was it like turning to novel-writing? 'Journalists don't have anything so grand as a working method,' Freedland said in an interview recently. 'You have to be able to write anywhere, as quickly as possible and despite infinite distractions, whether in a war zone or a newsroom. I looked forward to novel-writing as a chance to sample the opposite: all quiet contemplation and unhurried creativity.' The reality, however, turned out to be different. Freedland's natural preference is to work during the hours of darkness, until around 2 a.m., but that's been disrupted by having a family, and now he has to stick to a regular working day. 'When I'm in book mode, that means getting to the desk by nine thirty. The biggest difference is the absence of an immediate deadline; hacks are like adrenaline junkies and without that pressure they can't get motivated. When writing a book, I resort to setting artificial deadlines, little goals to keep me at it.'

Freedland's great-great-uncle and great-uncle were Jewish, as was his own mother, Sara Hocherman, and he's written about their legacy in a memoir called *Jacob's Gift* (2005), exploring the tensions of identity that being Jewish can create, especially alongside other allegiances of nationality or political affiliation. His novels, too, all have Jewish themes, and *The Final Reckoning* touches on a subject of Jewish history that must surely be very emotionally charged for Freedland: the extermination of millions of Jews during the Second World War. Amazingly, Gershon Matzkin's diary in *The Final Reckoning*, in which he remembers joining a group of avengers who plotted to carry out death sentences on their Nazi tormentors who escaped trial, is rooted in fact. In an article he wrote earlier this year, Freedland talked about the 'Nokmim' (Hebrew for 'avengers'); a group that was probably formed in Budapest at a Passover gathering in the spring of 1945. Here, it seems, it was decided that if the international courts of justice would not mete out justice to the perpetrators of the Holocaust, the Jews should do it themselves.

Several books, notably *The Avengers* by Rick Cohen and *Forged In Fury* by Michael Elkins, have been written about what followed. Yet it is an aspect of the Holocaust that has barely registered on the world's consciousness; a shocking fact that triggered a stunning, true story of heroism and violence and a burning quest for justice and revenge.

TORMENTORS ON TRIAL

In November 1945, an international military tribunal began the Major War Criminals Trial at the Palace of Justice in Nuremberg, Germany. Of the 21 Nazi leaders in the trial (pictured above, seated in two rows and flanked by guards), three were acquitted, seven imprisoned and 11 received the death penalty and were hanged in 1946.

A large number of people who were involved in the slaughter of six million Jews across Europe were not brought to trial. *The Final Reckoning* focuses on the true story of how a handful of Holocaust survivors, known as the Avengers, sought to settle scores with their tormentors. Nazi war crimes campaigner Simon Wiesenthal, himself a concentration camp survivor who died in 2005 aged 96, dedicated his life to bringing war criminals to trial. His abiding motto was 'justice, not vengeance'.

DICK FRANCIS
AND
FELIX FRANCIS

SILKS

As an amateur jockey, Geoffrey 'Perry' Mason
is used to fierce competition when attempting
to stay ahead of the field in a big race. He's
also no stranger to pressure in his professional
life as a barrister at the Old Bailey. But when
he finds himself under a personal attack from
an anonymous enemy who orders him to
deliberately lose his next case, the heat
is really on . . .

PROLOGUE
March 2008

'Guilty.'

G I watched the foreman of the jury as he gave the verdicts. He was wearing a light-coloured tweed jacket over a blue and white striped shirt. At the start of the trial he had also regularly sported a sober striped tie but perhaps as time had dragged on the ultra-casual dress of the other eleven had made him feel uncomfortably formal and his shirt was now open at the neck. Unlike most of them, he was grey-haired and upright in his stance. I imagined that he was a retired schoolmaster, well used to taking charge.

'Guilty,' he said again rather nervously, but with a strong deep voice. He kept his eyes firmly on the bewigged judge sitting slightly above him to his left. Not once did he look at the young man in the dock to his right. We were in number 3 court at the Old Bailey, one of the older, Victorian courtrooms of the Central Criminal Court, designed at a time when the process of the law was intended to be intimidating and a deterrent. However, for all its formality, the courtroom was no larger than a reasonably sized drawing room. The judge, sitting up high behind his long bench, dominated the space, and defendant, counsel and jury were so close together that they could have leaned forward and touched one another, had they wanted to.

In all, the schoolmasterly foreman repeated the same word eight times before sitting back down with, I sensed, a small sigh of relief.

The jury had found the young man guilty on all eight counts, four of them for assault occasioning actual bodily harm, three of inflicting grievous bodily harm and one of attempted murder.

I wasn't really surprised. I too was certain that the young man was guilty, and I was his defence counsel.

Why, I asked myself, had I wasted my favourite days of the whole year sitting in the Old Bailey trying to save such an undeserving character from a lengthy stretch in the slammer? I would much rather have been at Cheltenham for the racing festival. Especially as, this afternoon, I had been expecting to ride my own twelve-year-old bay gelding in the Foxhunter Chase, also known as the Gold Cup for amateur riders.

Almost before the foreman settled again in his seat, the prosecution counsel rose to inform the court of the previous convictions of the offender. And previous there were. Four times before he had been convicted of violent offences including two of malicious wounding. On two occasions the young man had been detained for periods in a young-offenders' institution.

I watched the members of the jury as they absorbed the information. They had spent nearly a week in deliberations before delivering their verdicts. Now some of them were visibly shocked to discover the true character of the smartly dressed twenty-three-year-old man in the dock who looked as if butter wouldn't melt in his mouth.

So why had I taken on such a hopeless case? Because I had been urged to do so by a friend of a friend of the young man's parents. They had pleaded with me to take him on, promising that the charges were the result of mistaken identity. And, of course, because they were paying me handsomely.

However, I had soon discovered that the only thing mistaken in this case was his parents' unshakable belief that their little angel couldn't possibly have done such a nasty thing as to attack a family with a baseball bat. The only motive for the attack was that the father of the family had complained to the police about the young man using the road outside their house as a drag-racing strip each night until two or three in the morning.

The more I had learned about my client, the more I had realised my error in accepting the brief. So clear was it to me that he was guilty as charged that I thought the trial would be over nice and quickly and I would be able to go to the Cheltenham races with a light heart and a heavy wallet. That the jury had inexplicably taken so long to reach a conclusion of the bleeding obvious was just one of those things.

I had thought about bunking off to the races, claiming sickness, but the judge was a racing man and had only the previous evening commiserated with me that I would be unable to ride in the Foxhunters. To have feigned sickness and then ridden in the race would likely have put me up before him on contempt charges, and then I could kiss goodbye to any aspirations I might have of promotion to Queen's Counsel—a silk.

Every barrister wanted to be a QC, but only ten per cent or so made it. Becoming a QC was reserved for only the very best of the profession.

One didn't just enter a horse in the Foxhunters, one had to qualify by winning other races, and this was the first time I had managed to do so. Next year both horse and rider would be another year older and neither of us was in the first flush of youth. There might never be another chance for us together.

I looked at my watch. The race was due off in half an hour. My horse would still run, but there would be another jockey on board, and I hated the thought of it. I should be in the Cheltenham changing room right now, pulling on lightweight racing breeches and brightly coloured silks, not sitting here in pinstripe suit, gown and wig.

'Mr Mason,' repeated the judge, bringing me back from my daydreaming. 'I asked you if the defence wishes to say anything before sentence.'

'No, Your Honour,' I said. As far as I could see there were no mitigating circumstances. I couldn't claim the young man was the product of a deprived background. His parents were loving, both of him and of each other, and he had been educated at one of the country's leading private schools, or at least he had until he was seventeen, when he had been expelled for bullying.

'The prisoner will stand,' announced the court clerk.

The young man rose to his feet slowly, almost smugly. I stood up too.

'Julian Trent,' the judge addressed him, 'you have been found guilty by this court of perpetrating a violent and unprovoked attack on an innocent family including a charge of attempted murder. You have previous convictions for violence and you seem unable or unwilling to learn the errors of your ways. Therefore, you will go to prison for eight years. Take him down.'

Julian Trent simply shrugged his shoulders and was ushered down the stairs from the dock to the cells beneath by two burly prison officers. Mrs Trent in the public gallery burst into tears and was comforted by her ever-present husband. I wondered if a week of listening to the damning evidence in the case had made any changes to their rosy opinion of their little boy.

I had quietly hoped that the judge would lock young Julian up for life. I knew that in spite of the eight-year prison sentence it would be, in fact, only half of that before he was back on the streets, arrogantly using his baseball bat to threaten and beat some other poor soul who crossed his path.

Little did I realise at the time that it would be a good deal sooner than four years, and that it would be me on the receiving end.

'Hi, Perry. How're you doing?'

'Fine, thanks,' I replied, waving a hand. My name isn't actually Perry, it's Geoffrey, but I have long since given up expecting the other jockeys in the changing room to use it. When one is a lawyer, a barrister even, with the surname Mason, one has to expect it.

I was secretly quite pleased that I was addressed at all by the professionals with whom I occasionally shared a moment's contact. They worked together day in, day out at the many racecourses around the country, while I averaged only a dozen or so rides a year. An 'amateur rider', as I was officially defined, was tolerated, just, as long as he knew his place, which was next to the door of the changing room, where it was always coldest.

'Any juicy cases, Perry?' asked a voice from up the far end.

I looked up. Steve Mitchell was one of the elite, constantly vying over the past few seasons with two others for the steeplechase champion jockey's crown. He was currently the reigning champion.

'Just the usual,' I said. 'Kidnap, rape and murder.'

'Don't know how you do it,' he said, pulling a white roll-neck sweater over his head.

'It's a job,' I said. 'And it's safer than yours.'

'Yeah, suppose so. But some guy's life depends on you.' He pulled on his breeches. 'If you mess up, someone might go to jail for years.'

'They may go to jail because they deserve to, no matter what I do,' I said.

'Does that make you a failure?' he said, buttoning up his blue and white hooped jacket.

'Ha,' I laughed. 'When I win I take some of the credit. When I lose I say that justice takes its course.'

'Not me,' he laughed back, throwing his arms open wide. 'When I win I take all the credit, and when I lose I blame the horse.'

Everyone laughed. Changing-room banter was the antidote to danger. Five or six times a day, every day, these guys put their lives on the line, riding more than half a ton of horse over five-foot fences at thirty miles an hour with no seat belt, no air bag and precious little protection.

'Unless you stopped it.'

The voice had a distinctive Scottish accent. The laughter died instantly. Scot Barlow, it was safe to say, was not the most popular regular in the jockeys' room. That comment from anyone else would have been the cause for renewed mirth, but from Scot Barlow it had menace.

Like Steve Mitchell, Barlow was one of the big three and he currently led the title race by the odd winner or two. But the reason Scot Barlow was unpopular was not because he was successful but because he had a reputation of bleating to the authorities about his fellow jockeys if they transgressed the rules. As one of them had once said to me, 'Barlow is a snitch, so keep your betting slips out of his reach.' Professional jockeys were not allowed to bet on horses. It expressly said so in the terms of their riding licences. Some of them did, of course, and Scot Barlow was renowned for going through his fellow jockeys' pockets to find the illicit betting slips, which he then gave to the stewards.

We were in the jockeys' changing room at Sandown Park racecourse, in Surrey, and I was riding in the fifth race, a three-mile chase reserved for amateur riders. It was a treat for me to be part of a big-race Saturday. Races for amateurs were rare these days, especially at weekends, and I usually had to confine myself to such races as they tended to have higher weights than those in which I would compete with pros. My weight had inexorably risen to what was considered natural for someone nearing his thirty-sixth birthday and standing five foot ten in his socks. I tried my best to keep it down and regularly starved myself through the winter months in order to ride at the amateur riders' days in the spring.

The jockeys were called for the third race, the main event of the afternoon, and there was the usual lack of a mad rush for the door. Jockeys are generally very superstitious and many of them like to be the last one to leave the changing room, for luck. Some even hang around polishing their already clean goggles until the get-mounted bell has been rung and the officials are having palpitations trying to get them out. As the last of the tardy bunch exited, I put my tweed jacket over my silks and went out to watch the contest on the weighing-room televisions.

After Steve Mitchell's blue and white hooped colours had flashed past the post to win by a head, I went back into the jockeys' inner sanctum to get myself into the right frame of mind for the fifth race. I knew that if I wasn't properly prepared, the whole thing would seemingly be over before I was even ready for it to start.

I sat on the bench that ran all round the room, and went through again in my head where I wanted to be as the tapes went up, where I would be as we approached the first fence and where I hoped to be as we approached the last. Of course, in my mind's eye we would win the race. And that wouldn't be all that unexpected. My bay gelding and I would start as favourite. His win at the Cheltenham Festival in March would make sure of that.

Steve Mitchell came waltzing back into the changing room with a grin on his face wider than the eight-lane motorway down the road.

'What about that, then, Perry?' he said, slapping me on the back, bringing me out of my trance. 'Bloody marvellous. And I beat that bastard Barlow. You should have seen his face. Furious, he was.' He laughed expansively. 'Serves him bloody well right.'

'What for?' I asked innocently.

He stood still for a moment and looked at me inquisitively. 'For being a bastard,' he said, and turned away towards his peg.

'Well done anyway,' I said to him, but the moment had passed and he just waved a dismissive hand and turned his back on me.

'JOCKEYS!' AN OFFICIAL put his head round the changing-room door and called the group of nineteen of us amateurs to the parade ring.

Adrenaline pumped through my veins and I positively jumped up and dived through the doorway. No superstitious last one out of the changing room for me. I wanted to savour every moment.

I adored this feeling. This was my fix, my drug. It was a need in me, a compulsion, an addiction. Thoughts of heavy falls, broken bones and bruised bodies were banished simply by the thrill and the anticipation of the coming race.

I made it to the parade ring and stood, excited, on the tightly mowed grass with my trainer, Paul Newington.

When I acquired my first horse some fifteen years ago, Paul had been thought of as the 'bright young up-and-coming trainer' in the sport. Now he was considered to be the man who never quite fulfilled his potential. Far from being up-and-coming, he was now in danger of becoming down-and-going, struggling to fill his expansive training establishment in Great Milton, just to the east of Oxford. But I liked him, and my own experience of his skills had been nothing but positive. Over the years he had bought for me a succession of sound hunter-chasers that had carried me safely over hundreds of miles and thousands of fences.

'I think you should beat this lot,' Paul said, loosely waving a hand at the other groups in the parade ring. 'Fairly jumping out of his skin, he is.'

'Hope so,' I replied. My apprehension grew as an official rang the bell and called for the jockeys to get mounted.

Paul gave me a leg-up onto my current pride and joy. Sandeman was the best horse I had ever owned by a long way. Paul had bought him for me as an eight-year-old with a mixed history in hurdle races. He had reckoned that Sandeman was too big to run over hurdles and would be much better as a chaser, and he had been right. So far we had won eight races together and he had won five others without me in the saddle.

This was his first run since the summer layoff. He would be thirteen on January 1 and, consequently, he was close to the twilight of his career. Paul and I had planned that he would race just twice before what we hoped would be a repeat victory in the Cheltenham Foxhunters.

I had been introduced to steeplechase racing by my uncle Bill when I was twelve. He had been delegated to take me out for the day and keep me out of mischief. I had clambered eagerly into the passenger seat of his beloved open-topped MG Midget and we had set out for the south coast and the planned day at Worthing in West Sussex.

Uncle Bill had no intention of spending the day dragging his young nephew across Worthing's steep pebble beach. Instead he drove us about fifteen miles further to the west to Fontwell Park racecourse, and my abiding passion for jump racing was born.

At almost every British racecourse it is possible for the spectators to stand next to a fence, to experience the thrill of being close up as half-ton horses soar over and through the tightly bound birch, to hear the horses' hoofs thumping the turf, to feel the earth tremble and to sense the excitement of being part of the race. At Fontwell the steeplechase course is a figure of eight and one can run between the jumps that are near the crossover point and be close to the action twice on each circuit. By the end of the day I knew for certain that I wanted to be one of those brave young men in their bright coloured silks fearlessly kicking and urging the thoroughbred beneath him into the air at thirty miles an hour with hope in his heart.

Such was my conviction that I could think of nothing else for weeks and I begged my uncle to take me with him to the races whenever I could get away from more mundane things like school and studying.

I enrolled at a local riding stables, where my teacher tried in vain to get me to sit upright in the saddle with my heels down. I was determined to stand in the stirrups crouching over the animal's withers and riding at speed over jumps just as I had seen the jockeys do.

Sadly, by the time I was seventeen I had come to terms with the fact that I was never going to earn my living from race riding. For a start, I had grown too tall and was already showing signs of becoming too heavy to be a professional jockey. Coupled with that was an apparent gift for academic success, and the fact that my father had decided that I would follow him into the same firm of high-street solicitors that he himself had joined some thirty years previously. I would spend my life, like his, conveyancing property, drawing up last wills and testaments, and untying the knots of failed marriages. The promised boredom of it all filled me with horror.

I had been twenty-one and in my third year of a law degree at London University when my darling mother finally lost her long battle against leukaemia. Her death brought home to me the transitory nature of the human state. She died on her forty-ninth birthday. The experience made me resolve to do what I really wanted and not what everyone else expected of me. Life was too short to waste.

I duly completed my degree, as it somehow seemed a mistake to give it all up at such a late stage, but then much to my remaining parent's horror, I arranged to go to Lambourn as unpaid assistant and amateur jockey with a mid-ranking racehorse trainer.

'But how will you afford to live?' my father demanded.

'I will use the legacy that Mum left me,' I replied, sending him into a tirade about how the young these days had no sense of responsibility.

So I had gone to Lambourn in July, and used my mother's legacy not only to pay my living expenses but also to acquire a seven-year-old bay gelding. August had mostly been spent getting fit. Each morning I would ride my horse in the stable string to the gallops on the hills above the village and then each afternoon I would run the same route. By mid-September both horse and jockey were showing signs of being ready for the racecourse.

Quite by chance, my first ride in a proper race was at Fontwell in early October. We finished eleventh out of thirteen, and the trainer had seemed relatively satisfied. 'At least you didn't fall off,' he said on our way home in his car.

My horse and I raced together five more times that year and on each occasion we fared slightly better than the time before, finishing a close second at a steeplechase at Towcester races the week before Christmas. By the following March I had ridden over fences a total of nine times.

Even though I had not yet ridden a winner, I still loved the excitement of the actual races. But in the time between them I had begun to miss the intellectual stimulation that I had enjoyed at university. And my mother's legacy had started to show signs of exhaustion. It was time to put my fantasy back in its box and earn myself a living. I remained steadfast in my aversion to being a solicitor, so what else could I do with my law degree?

Not all lawyers are solicitors, I remembered one of my tutors saying during my first weeks at university. *There are barristers as well*. While solicitors generally do the legal paperwork in the background, alone in quiet offices, barristers are advocates, standing up and arguing across courtrooms.

All of a sudden the prospect of becoming a stand-up-and-argue barrister excited me hugely and I eagerly applied for a return to legal matters.

So here I was, some fourteen years later, well established in the world of horsehair wigs, silk gowns and courtroom protocol, but still trying to master this racing lark.

'Jockeys! Walk in.' The starter's call brought me back to the matter in hand. How careless, I thought, to be daydreaming at such a time. Concentrate! I told myself sharply.

The nineteen of us walked up slowly in a straggly line; the starter pushed the lever; the tape flew up and we were off. The pack went slowly from walk to trot, and then to canter as the race began in almost sedentary style. Three miles is a long way, especially in November mud after a wet autumn, and none of us was making the mistake of going too fast too early.

At Sandown the horses have to complete almost two full circuits, jumping a total of twenty-two fences. The first, which comes up very soon after the start, looks fairly innocuous but has caught out many a rider in its time. The landing side is some way below the takeoff point and the drop tends to pitch horses forward onto their noses. But all nineteen runners were still standing as the pace picked up and we turned right-handed into the back straight to face the most famous seven-fence combination in steeplechasing. Two plain fences and an open ditch fairly close together, then a slight gap to the water jump, then the famous Railway fences—three plain fences closer together than any others in British racing. It is always said that if you jump the first one well then all will be fine, but make a hash of the first and horse and rider will be lucky to get to the far end intact.

All nineteen runners were still standing and fairly closely bunched as we swung out of the back straight and round the long curve to the Pond fence and then up in front of the watching crowds for the first time.

The thing that struck me most when I started riding in races was the apparent isolation in which the participants find themselves. There may be thousands of eager gamblers in the grandstands, each shouting on their choices, but for all the jockeys can tell the stands may as well be empty. The sound of horses' hoofs striking the turf is the main noise that fills the senses. There are other sounds too: the slap of the reins or whip, the clicking together of hoofs, the shouts of the jockeys and the clatter of hoof or horseflesh on birch and wood as the animals brush through the top few inches of each fence. Together these make the race a noisy place to be, and they exclude any utterances from outside this bubble. No word of encouragement, not a single phrase of commentary, can enter. Quite often, afterwards, the jockeys are the least informed about the triumphs and disasters of others.

The pace quickened noticeably as we turned away from the stands and went downhill past our starting point. The race was suddenly on in earnest.

Sandeman and I had been hugging the inside rail, following the leading trio by a couple of lengths or so. Now, the horse immediately ahead of me began to tire slightly and I was concerned that I would be forced to slow with him as, with others alongside me, I had nowhere to go.

'Give me some damn room!' I shouted at the jockey ahead, more in hope than expectation. Racing was all about winning and one didn't win very often by being too courteous to the opposition.

Amazingly, he pulled slightly away from the rail and I sailed up on his inside. 'Thanks!' I called to him as I drew alongside him on his right. A fresh-faced, big-eyed young amateur grimaced back at me.

At the next fence two horses fell. Both animals pitched forward on landing, sending their riders sprawling onto the grass. One of the jockeys was the young man who had given me room up his inside. Phew, I thought, that was close. Thank goodness he hadn't fallen right in front of me. Being 'brought down' by tripping over a prostrate horse was one of the worst ways of losing.

The remaining seventeen of us were well spread out as we turned into the back straight for the second and last time. Sandeman was still going well beneath me and I kicked on hard into the first of the seven fences. He flew across the birch and gained at least a length on the two still in front.

'Come on, boy!' I shouted at him.

We swung into the final long sweeping turn with just four of us having a realistic chance. I was still on the inside rail. Kick, push, kick, push, my hands and heels were working overtime as we straightened for the Pond fence. Sandeman was just in front and another great leap from him took the others briefly out of sight behind me.

'Come on, boy,' I shouted at him again, this time with diminished breath.

We were tiring but so were the others. Three miles in bottomless going is a huge test of stamina. I could barely summon up the energy to provide the necessary kicks to Sandeman's belly.

We still had our nose just in front as we took off at the second last, but Sandeman hit the top of the fence and landed almost stationary on all four feet at once. Bugger. Two other horses came past us and I thought all was lost. But Sandeman had other ideas and set off in pursuit. By the last fence we were back alongside the others and the three of us jumped it line abreast.

Even though the three horses landed over the last together, both the others made it to the winning post ahead of us, their jockeys riding determined finishes while I was so tired that hanging on was about as much as I could do. We finished third, which was more to do with my lack of stamina than Sandeman's. I had clearly been spending too much of my time sitting on my backside in courtrooms.

In the unsaddling enclosure I slithered off Sandeman's back and nearly sat down on the grass, so jelly-like were my legs.

'Are you all right?' Paul, the trainer, asked, concerned.

'Fine,' I said, trying to undo the girths. 'Just a little out of puff.'

'I need to get you up on the gallops too,' he said. 'No good having a fit horse if the damn jockey sits there like a sack of potatoes.' It was a harsh assessment but probably fair.

'Sorry,' I mumbled. It was a good job I was paying the training fees.

Somehow I made it to the scales to be weighed in, and then back into the jockeys' changing room, where I sat down heavily on the bench and wondered if it was time to call it a day. If I were to continue for another year, I would have to become fitter than this or I might come to serious harm. I leaned back wearily against the cream-painted wall and closed my eyes.

ONLY WHEN THE VALETS began to pack up the equipment into their large wicker baskets did I realise that the last race had been run and I was almost alone in the changing room, and still I was not changed.

I stood up slowly and peeled off my lightweight riding strip, picked up my towel and went into the showers.

Scot Barlow was half sitting, half lying on the tiled floor, leaning up against the wall. He had blood trickling from his right nostril and his eyes were puffy.

'Are you all right?' I asked, going over to him and touching his shoulder.

He looked up at me but with no warmth in his expression. 'Sod off,' he said. 'Bloody amateurs. People like you take away my livelihood. I should be paid to let the likes of you ride races.'

Charming, I thought. I considered telling him that I had ridden in a race reserved for amateurs and he wouldn't have been allowed to ride in it anyway, but he clearly wasn't in the mood for serious debate.

'Do you need any help?' I asked. I assumed he must have had a fall and that his face was sore from using it on the ground as a brake.

'Sod off,' he said again. 'I don't need your help. You're as bad as your bloody friend.'

'What friend?' I asked him.

'Steve bloody Mitchell, of course,' he said. 'Who else do you think did this?' He held a hand up to his face.

'What?' I said, astounded. 'Steve Mitchell did this to you? But why?'

'You'd better ask him that,' he said. 'And not the first time, either. Now you piss off home like a good little amateur. And keep your bloody mouth shut.' He turned away from me and wiped a hand over his face.

I wondered what I should do. Should I go and fetch one of the ambulance staff, or should I find a policeman to report an assault?

In the end I did nothing, except collect my gear and go home.

'I DON'T FUCKING believe it,' someone said loudly in the clerks' room as I walked in on Monday morning.

Such language in chambers was rare, and rarer still from Sir James Horley, QC, the head of chambers.

The position of head of chambers was mostly an honorary title often held by the most senior member, the QC of longest standing. All of the forty-five or so barristers in these chambers were self-employed. The main purpose of us coming together in chambers was to allow us to pool services we all needed: the clerks, the offices, the library and so on. Each of us remained responsible for acquiring our own work.

Sir James was standing in front of the clerks' desks reading a piece of paper, looking irritated.

'What don't you believe?' I asked him.

'This,' he said, waving the paper towards me.

I walked over and took the sheet from him. It was a print-out of an email, headed CASE COLLAPSES AGAINST JULIAN TRENT.

I didn't believe it either.

'You defended him the first time round,' Sir James said. It was a statement rather than a question.

'Yes,' I said. I remembered it all too well. 'Open-and-shut case. Guilty as sin. How he got a retrial on appeal I'll never know.'

'That damn solicitor,' said Sir James. 'And now he's got off completely. Case dismissed for lack of evidence, it says.'

More like for lack of witnesses prepared to give their evidence, I thought. They were afraid of getting beaten up.

I had taken a special interest in the appeal against Julian Trent's conviction, in spite of no longer acting for the little thug. 'That damn solicitor' as Sir James had called him, was one of the Crown Prosecution team who had admitted cajoling members of the original trial jury to produce a guilty verdict. Three members of the jury had been to the police to report the incident, and all three had subsequently given evidence at the appeal hearing, stating that they had been approached independently by the same solicitor. Why he'd done it, I couldn't understand, as the evidence in the case had been overwhelming. But the Appeal Court judges had had little choice but to order a retrial.

Now, it seemed, young Julian would be walking free.

I recalled the last thing he had said to me in the cells under the Old Bailey courtroom last March after the verdict. It was not a happy memory.

'I'll get even with you, you spineless bastard,' he'd shouted at me with venom as I entered the cell.

I presumed he thought that his conviction was my fault because I had refused to threaten the witnesses with violence as he had wanted me to do.

'You'd better watch your back,' he'd gone on menacingly. 'One day soon I'll creep up on you and you'll never see it coming.'

The hairs on the back of my neck now rose and I instinctively turned round as if to find him right here in chambers. Over the years I had been threatened by other clients, but there was something about Julian Trent that frightened me very badly indeed. At the time of his conviction I had been exceedingly thankful to leave him in custody and I deeply wished he still was.

'Are you all right?' Sir James was looking at me with his head slightly inclined. 'You look like you've just seen a ghost,' he said.

'Fine,' I replied with a slightly creaky voice. 'Just remembering the original trial.'

'The whole thing is fishy if you ask me,' he said in his rather pompous manner.

As head of chambers, Sir James had his finger on all that was going on within these walls. He knew about every case in which barristers from 'his' chambers were acting, whether on the prosecution side or the defence. But equally, he knew nothing, nor cared, about cases where 'his' team were not involved.

'I didn't realise that anyone from these chambers was acting,' I said. 'Why the interest in this case?'

'Do I need a reason?' he asked, somewhat defensively.

'No,' I said. 'But my question remains, why the interest?'

'Don't you cross-examine me,' he retorted. Sir James had a bit of a reputation among the junior barristers for enjoying throwing his superior status around.

'It doesn't matter,' I said as a way of finishing the discussion. He would tell me if he wanted to, or not if that was his choice. My questioning would not sway the matter one way or another. Sir James was like the most unhelpful courtroom witness who has his own agenda about what evidence he will give and the direction of counsel's questioning will make no difference. Perhaps it takes an obdurate man to break down another of similar character, which was why Sir James Horley was one of the greatest advocates in the land.

'I was advising the judge in the case,' he said. So he did want to tell me after all. He was now showing off, I thought ungraciously.

'Oh,' I said noncommittally. I, too, could play his little game. I turned to collect some letters from an array of wooden boxes lining one wall of the clerks' room.

'The case hung on the question of intimidation,' Sir James continued. 'The problem with the new trial was that the prosecution witnesses now either refused to give evidence at all or said something completely opposite to what they had said before. It was clear that they had been intimidated.'

I stood patiently and waited through a silence as Sir James appeared to decide if he would continue or not. Then he went on, 'So the judge wanted some advice as to whether the initial statements from witnesses taken by the police at the time of the incident could be read out in court as evidence.'

'And what advice did you give him?' I asked him.

'Her, actually,' he said. 'Dorothy McGee. I advised her that such evidence could be admissible provided the witness was called, even if the witness was now declared as being hostile to the Crown's case. It seemed that all the witnesses in the case had changed their tune, including the victim of the beating and his family, who now claimed that the event didn't happen in the first place and that the injuries were due to him falling down some stairs. Do they really think we are stupid or something?' He was getting quite cross. 'I advised her to press on with the case. I told her that it is essential to justice that such intimidation cannot be seen to succeed and I was sure the jury would agree and convict.'

'Trent probably intimidated the jury as well,' I said. I wondered if he had intimidated the three jurors who had come forward at the appeal.

'We'll never know.' Sir James sighed. 'This note says the case has collapsed. I suspect that in the face of no witnesses to the event, except those denying that it ever occurred, they just gave up. What an absolute disgrace.'

Suddenly, he turned on his heel and walked away towards his room. My audience was over.

''Morning, Mr Mason,' said the chief clerk suddenly, making me jump. He had been sitting impassive and silent at his desk during my exchange with Sir James and I had not noticed him behind the computer monitors.

''Morning, Arthur,' I replied, moving to see him more clearly. He was a smallish man but only in stature, not in personality. I presumed he was now in his sixties as he claimed to have worked in these chambers for more than forty years. He had already been a well-established chief clerk when I first arrived twelve years earlier and he didn't seem to have changed one bit in the interim, apart from the appearance of a little grey in a full head of thick, black, curly hair.

'Bit late this morning, sir?'

I glanced up at the clock on the wall above his head. Half past eleven. I had to agree that it was not a particularly prompt start to the working week.

'I've been busy elsewhere,' I said to him. Busy in bed, asleep.

'Are you misleading the court?' he asked accusingly, but with a smile. Misleading the court was the most heinous of crimes for a barrister.

A chief clerk was supposed to work for the members of chambers, but Arthur clearly presumed that the reverse was true. If a junior misdemeanoured in some way, either through bad behaviour or poor work, it was usually the chief clerk rather than the head of chambers who dealt out the admonishment. Each member of chambers gave a proportion of their fees to pay for the team of clerks who were our secretariat, our minders and our chaperones. It was rumoured that in some chambers, with many high-earning barristers, the chief clerk was earning more than any of the masters he served. As a junior who had aspirations of becoming a silk, I would be a fool to cross Arthur.

'Sorry, Arthur,' I said, trying to look as apologetic as possible.

Fortunately for me, his telephone rang at this point and I scampered for the safety of my desk while he answered it. Why, I mused, did I always feel like a naughty schoolboy when in Arthur's company? Maybe it was because he instinctively knew that when I was not where I should be I was on a race-course somewhere having more fun. Fortunately for me, though, in spite of taking days away to ride in races, my fee base was strong. No one would be carried as a passenger if their fees were below par.

I sat at my desk and looked out of the window at the Gray's Inn Gardens, an oasis of calm in the centre of the great bustling metropolis of London. The lines of plane trees, which in summer gave shade to the hundreds of office workers who came here to eat their lunchtime sandwiches, were now bare of their leaves and stood forlornly pointing skywards. They reflected my mood. If our legal system couldn't lock away dangerous brutes like Julian Trent because they frightened people away from telling the truth, then we were all in trouble.

I leaned back in my chair and yawned. Contrary to what Arthur might think, the reason I had arrived late was not that I was lazy, but because at five in the morning I had still been reading the case notes for a trial in which I was currently leading for the prosecution.

I spent the rest of the day with my nose in leather-bound volumes of trial records and then in front of my computer screen searching on the Internet. Not all the work of a barrister is as exciting as that depicted on TV trial dramas. By seven thirty I'd had enough. I packed everything I needed into a box ready for the morning and slipped out into the night.

I LIVED IN BARNES, south of the Thames in west London, where my wife, Angela, and I had bought half of an early Edwardian detached house in Ranelagh Avenue overlooking Barnes Common. We had acquired the upper two floors with views over the treetops from the dormer windows of the bedrooms. Our neighbours below occupied the original ground floor of the property with its grand rooms, together with the old servants' area below.

Angela and I had loved it. It had been the first home that we had owned together and we had lavished time and money decorating the place and getting everything ready for the birth of our first child, a son, due six months after we had moved in. That had been seven years ago.

As usual, I walked home across the common from Barnes station. It was almost completely dark, with just a few beams of light filtering through the leafless trees from distant streetlights, but I knew every step of the route. The bottom half of the house was lit up. The upper floors were in darkness where I'd turned off the lights as I had left that morning.

I let myself in through my front door and went upstairs into the dark.

Angela wasn't there, but I knew she wouldn't be. Angela was dead.

I WONDERED IF I would ever get used to coming home to an empty house. Perhaps I should have moved long ago, but those first few months here had been the happiest of my life and somehow I hadn't wanted to abandon the memories.

Angela had died suddenly of a massive pulmonary embolism just four weeks before our baby was due. She had kissed me goodbye on that fateful Monday morning as happy as I had ever known her. It had been the first day of her maternity leave and she had still been in her dressing gown and slippers as I had left for work. All her life she had longed to have a child and now she was so close to fulfilling her dream. I had tried to call her several times during the day without any success but I had not thought anything was amiss until I had arrived home to find the place in darkness.

I had found her lying on the sitting-room floor, slightly curled as if she were asleep. But she had been cold, and had obviously been dead for hours. Our son was dead too, inside her.

There had been no warning and no pre-existing condition, no hypertension, no pre-eclampsia. She had gone from healthy and happy to dead in the space of a few moments. So sad, the doctors had said, but it was the most common cause of sudden death during pregnancy. They also told me it would have been very quick and that she was likely unaware, losing consciousness almost instantaneously.

Everyone had been so kind. Friends had rallied round, my father had come to stay so I wouldn't be alone, and even the judge in the trial I had been prosecuting had adjourned the proceedings until after Angela's funeral. There had been much rushing around by others, while I had sat still and alone in my grief as the hours and days had dragged by.

Gradually, over the next few months, my life had sorted itself out. My father had returned home. Friends had come round less often with ready-cooked meals; invitations again began to arrive. People started to say things to each other like, 'He's still young enough to find somebody else.'

Now it was seven years later and I had not found somebody else. I didn't really want to because I was still in love with Angela. I wasn't ready to find anybody else. Not yet. Maybe not ever.

I turned on the lights in the kitchen and looked in the fridge for something to eat. I decided on salmon with pasta and pesto sauce. Since Angela died I had become quite a dab hand at cooking for one.

I had just sat down in front of the television news when the phone rang. I picked up the receiver. 'Hello,' I said.

'Perry?' said a voice.

'Yes,' I replied slowly. After all, I'm not really Perry. I'm Geoffrey.

'Thank God you're there,' said the voice. 'This is Steve Mitchell.'

I thought back to our strange conversation in the Sandown jockeys' changing room two days before.

'Look, Perry,' he went on in a rush, 'I'm in a bit of trouble and I need your help.'

'What bit of trouble?' I asked him.

'Well, it could be a lot of trouble,' he said. 'That bastard Scot Barlow has got himself murdered and the police have arrested me for doing it.'

'And did you murder Scot Barlow?' I asked.

'No,' he said. 'Of course I bloody didn't.'

'Have the police interviewed you?' I asked him.

'Not yet,' he said. 'But I think they plan to. I asked to call my lawyer. So I called you. You're the only lawyer I know.'

'You need a solicitor, not a barrister,' I said.

'Solicitors, barristers, what's the difference? You are a bloody lawyer, aren't you? Will you help me or not?' He was beginning to sound a little desperate.

'Calm down,' I said, trying to sound reassuring. 'Where are you exactly?'

'Newbury,' he said. 'Newbury police station.'

I looked at my watch. It was 10.10. Which solicitors did I know in Newbury that could be roused at such an hour? None.

'Steve,' I said, 'I will see what I can do to get you a solicitor I know, but it won't be for a few hours at least.'

'Oh God,' he almost cried. 'Can't you come?'

'No,' I said. 'It would be like asking a brain surgeon to remove your teeth. Much better for you if you get a dentist.'

'The police have told me that I can talk to the duty solicitor,' Steve said.

'Well, you can,' I replied. 'But at this time of night he's likely to be a recently qualified young solicitor and you are facing a serious charge. I'd wait for someone with more experience if I were you.'

'OK, I'll wait,' he said.

'Fine,' I replied. 'I'll get someone there as soon as possible. And, Steve, don't answer any questions until he arrives. Do you understand?'

'Yes,' he said with a yawn in his voice.

'What time did you get up this morning?' I asked him.

'Usual time,' he said. 'Ten to six. I was riding out at seven.'

'Tell the police that you have been awake for nearly seventeen hours and you are entitled to have a sleep before being interviewed. And when the solicitor does arrive, take his advice absolutely.'

'OK,' he said rather flatly. 'I will.'

Did he, I wondered, sound like a guilty man resigned to his fate?

I called a solicitor I knew in Oxford and asked him. 'Sorry, mate,' he replied in his Australian accent. He was too busy teaching some gorgeous young university student the joys of sleeping with an older man. However, he did rouse himself sufficiently to give me the name of a firm in Newbury together with one of their partners' mobile phone number.

Sure, said the partner when I called, he would go. Steve Mitchell was famous in those parts, and representing a celebrity client accused of murder was every local solicitor's dream. To say nothing of the potential fee.

I put the phone down and thought again about last Saturday at Sandown. Particularly I recalled the strange encounter with the battered Scot Barlow in the showers.

It was not unknown for barristers to represent friends. To me, friendships were too important to place in jeopardy by having to lay bare all one's secrets and emotions, and a friend would far more resent being asked by me a question he didn't want to answer than if a stranger had done it. So I usually invented some little ruse to avoid the situation. I would say that so-and-so in my chambers was much better qualified to accept the brief, or that I was too busy with other cases.

However, this time I didn't need to invent an excuse. I couldn't act for Steve Mitchell because I was privy to some material evidence and was likely to be called to testify for the prosecution.

CHAPTER 2

The murder of top jump jockey Scot Barlow was the number-one item on the eight o'clock television news bulletin the following morning. A reporter, standing outside the property, claimed that Barlow had been found lying in a pool of blood in the kitchen of his home with a five-foot-long, two-pronged pitchfork embedded in his chest.

My mobile phone rang as I was buttering a slice of toast.

'Hello,' I said, picking it up.

'Is that Geoffrey Mason?' asked a well-spoken male voice in a whisper.

'Yes,' I replied.

'Do as you are told,' said the voice, very quietly, but very distinctly.

'What did you say?' I asked, surprised.

'Do as you are told,' the voice repeated in the same manner.

'Who is this?' I demanded, but, in response, the caller simply hung up.

I looked at the phone as if it would tell me. How very odd, I thought. I checked through calls received, but, as I expected, the caller had withheld his number.

The phone in my hand rang again suddenly, making me jump and drop it onto the kitchen counter. I grabbed it and pushed the button.

'Hello?' I said rather tentatively.

'Is that Geoffrey Mason?' asked a male voice, a different male voice.

'Yes,' I replied cautiously. 'Who is this?'

'Bruce Lygon,' said the voice.

'Oh,' I said, relieved. Bruce Lygon was the solicitor from Newbury I had called the night before.

'Your friend seems to be in a bit of a hole here,' he said. 'The cops think there's not much doubt he did it. That's clear from their questions. We've been at it since six this morning.'

'What's the evidence?' I asked him.

'I gather that the victim was stabbed with some sort of fork that appears to belong to Mr Mitchell. As well as Mr Barlow, there were some betting slips impaled on the fork. They had Mr Mitchell's name on them.'

'Oh,' I said.

'And,' he went on, 'there was a text message received yesterday on

Barlow's mobile from Mitchell saying that he was going to, and I quote, "come round and sort you out properly, you sneaking little bastard".'

'And what does Mitchell have to say?' I asked.

'He mumbled something about being framed,' Bruce replied, but I could tell from his tone that he didn't believe it. 'Do you want me to stay here?'

'It's not my decision,' I said. 'Steve Mitchell is your client. Ask him.'

'I have,' he said. 'He told me to call you and to do whatever you said.'

Bugger, I thought. I just could not get involved with this case. I knew too much about it, for a start.

'You had better stay, then,' I said, 'but remind Mr Mitchell that it's you and not me who's acting for him and I can't make these decisions. When's their time up?' The police had a maximum of thirty-six hours from when Steve first arrived at the police station before they charged him, brought him before a magistrate to ask for more time or released him.

'According to the record, he arrived at the police station at nine fifty-seven,' he said. 'So far they haven't asked for more time and I think it's unlikely they will. Their body language says that they have enough to charge without them.'

'So you'll stay until he's charged?' I asked.

'Only if they charge him before six,' he said. 'After that I'm taking my wife out to dinner for her birthday, and I'd rather face the Law Society than fail to do that.' There was laughter in his voice. 'But don't worry, there'll be someone here from my firm if I'm not.'

'Great,' I said. 'Please keep me informed.' I was not actually representing Steve, but, like everybody else, I was curious about murder.

STEVE MITCHELL'S ARREST was the front-page story on the midday edition of the *Evening Standard*. I grabbed a copy as I dodged the rain outside Blackfriars Crown Court on my way to a local café for some lunch. 'Top Jock Held for Murder' shouted the headline alongside a library picture of a smiling Scot Barlow. The report gave little more detail than I already knew, but speculated that the murder had been in revenge for Barlow giving the racing authorities details of Mitchell's illegal gambling activities.

I turned on my mobile phone. There was one voicemail message but it wasn't from Bruce Lygon. It was from the quiet, well-spoken male whisperer. 'Remember,' he said menacingly, 'do exactly as you are told.'

I sat in the window of the café eating a cheese and pickle sandwich, trying to work out what on earth it was all about. No one had told me to do anything, so how could I do it? I would have dismissed it as mistaken identity except that the caller this morning had asked if I was Geoffrey Mason.

Deciding to concentrate on the matter in hand, I called Bruce Lygon.

'Any news?' I asked him.

'No.' He sounded bored. 'They are apparently searching his place.'

'How is he?' I said.

'Pretty fed up,' he said. 'Keeps saying he should be riding at Huntingdon races. I don't think he fully realises the extent of the mess he's in.'

'So you think he will definitely be charged?' I asked.

'Oh, yeah, no doubt about it. They haven't even bothered to question him for the past four hours. They're sure he did it.'

'Well, for your sake, I hope they charge him by six,' I said, thinking of his wife's birthday dinner. 'Will it be you that goes with him to the magistrate's court in the morning?'

'Are you kidding?' he said. 'It's not every day I get a case that leads on the lunchtime news. Even the wife says to stay here all night if I have to.'

AFTER AN AFTERNOON in court I took a taxi back to chambers with a box of papers and my laptop. It was a miserably wet November day. I paid off the cabbie on Theobald's Road near the entrance to Raymond Buildings.

Julian Trent was waiting for me between two rows of parked cars. Why would he want revenge from me when he had got off? But here he was, with his trusted baseball bat, oozing menace and danger.

I didn't actually see him until I had walked beyond his hiding place. My peripheral vision detected a movement to my right and I turned in time to glimpse his face just before he hit me. He was smiling.

The baseball bat caught me across the back of both legs about halfway up my thighs. The blow caused my knees to buckle and I was sent sprawling to the ground, my papers spilling out in front of me. The suddenness of the strike left me gasping for breath. My legs felt numb and somehow detached from the rest of my body. I used my arms to roll myself over onto my back. I was determined that he wouldn't be able to knock my brains out without me seeing it coming.

He stood above me, swinging the bat from side to side. There was no one else about in the private road. He was clearly enjoying himself.

'Hello, Mr Clever-Dick Lawyer,' he said with a curl to his upper lip. 'Not so clever now, are we?'

I couldn't think of anything to say.

He raised the bat to have another swing and I put my arms up around my head to protect myself, closed my eyes and waited for the crunch. I wondered if Angela would be waiting for me on the other side.

The bat landed with a sickening thud but not on my head. Trent hit my unprotected laptop computer with all his might and it disintegrated into several parts that scattered noisily across the road.

I opened my eyes and looked at him.

'Next time,' he said, 'I'll smash your head.'

He then stepped forward and trod hard on my genitals, putting all his weight on his right foot and crushing my manhood between his boot and the road. This time there was pain, a shooting, stabbing, excruciating pain. I moaned and rolled away sideways and thankfully he released the pressure.

'And next time,' he said, 'I'll cut your balls right off. Do you fucking understand?'

I nodded ever so slightly.

'Good,' he said. 'Now you be a good little lawyer.'

Then he suddenly turned and walked away, leaving me lying in a puddle, curled up like a baby to lessen the ongoing agony between my legs.

I was shaking and I didn't know whether it was from fear, shock or the cold. I had been frightened more than at any time in my life. Only a few minutes had elapsed since I had stepped out of the taxi but my life had changed from one of discipline and order to one of chaos and fear.

In my line of work one encountered fear and intimidation on an almost daily basis. How condescending I must have been to potential witnesses too fearful to give evidence. 'We will protect you from the bullies,' I would promise, 'but you must do what is right.' Only now did I appreciate their predicament. I should have told Julian Trent to go to hell, but, in fact, I would have licked his boots if he had so asked, and I hated myself for it.

Eventually the intensity of the pain in my groin diminished, and I was able to roll over onto my knees. My computer was beyond repair and court papers were blowing along the road in the rain. My gown and wig, which had also been in the box, were soaking up the water from another puddle. But I didn't really care. It was as much as I could manage to stand approximately upright and stagger the few yards to the door of my chambers.

I leaned against the board with all the barristers' names painted on it and looked at the blue front door. I couldn't remember the code for the security lock so I pushed the bell and was rewarded with Arthur's friendly voice from a small speaker.

'Yes,' he said. 'Who is it?'

'Geoffrey,' I croaked, 'Geoffrey Mason. Can you come and help?'

'Mr Mason?' Arthur asked back through the speaker. 'Are you all right?'

'No,' I said.

Almost immediately the door opened and Arthur came to my rescue, half carrying me through the hallway into the clerks' room. He pulled up a desk chair and I gratefully but carefully sat down.

I must have been quite a sight. I was soaked through and the knees of my pinstripe suit were torn where I had landed on the rough tarmac. My hair dripped rainwater down my forehead.

'Goodness gracious,' said Arthur. 'What on earth happened to you?'

'I was mugged,' I said.

'Where?' he asked.

'Outside,' I said. 'My stuff is still on the road.'

Arthur rushed outside and returned with my gown in one hand and my wig in the other, both dripping onto the light green carpet. He had just a few of my sopping papers stuck under his arm.

'Is that your computer?' he asked, nodding his head towards the door.

'What's left of it,' I agreed.

'Funny,' he said. 'Muggers normally steal things, not break them. Is anything missing?'

'No, I don't think so,' I said, patting myself down. I could feel both my wallet and my mobile in the pockets of my jacket.

'I'm calling the police,' said Arthur, lifting the phone. 'Do you need an ambulance?'

'No,' I said. 'But a change of clothes would be good.'

The police promised to send someone round as soon as possible. While we waited I changed out of my sodden clothes into a track suit that Arthur found in one of my colleagues' rooms, and then I tried to make some sort of order from the saturated papers. I couldn't reprint them as nearly all the files had been on my computer only.

Two uniformed constables arrived about forty minutes after the call and they took a statement from me with Arthur hovering close by.

'Did you see the mugger?' one of them asked me.

'Not at first,' I said. 'He hit me from behind with a baseball bat.'

'How do you know it was a baseball bat?' he asked.

'I saw it later,' I said. 'I assumed it was what he hit me with.'

'Whereabouts did he hit you?'

'On the back of my legs,' I said.

They insisted that I show them. Embarrassed, I lowered the track-suit trousers to reveal two rapidly bruising red marks on the backs of my thighs.

'Funny place to hit someone,' said the other policeman. 'Most muggers would have hit you on the head. Did you get a look at his face?'

'Not really,' I said. 'It was dark.' Why, I thought, had I not told them that it had been Julian Trent who had attacked me? What was I doing? Did I not stand up for justice and right? Tell them, I told myself, tell them the truth.

'Would you know him again?' the policeman asked.

'I doubt it,' I heard myself say. *Next time, I'll smash your head*, Trent had said. *Next time, I'll cut your balls right off.* 'It was all a bit of a blur.'

'But you were sure it was a man?' he asked.

'I think so,' I said.

'Black or white?' he asked.

'I couldn't say.' Even to my ears, it sounded pathetic.

The two policemen clearly thought that I was not a helpful witness.

'Well, at least you didn't have anything stolen,' said one, bringing the interview to a close. He snapped shut his notebook. 'If you call Charing Cross station later they'll give you a crime number for any insurance claim.'

And with that, they were gone.

'You weren't much help,' said Arthur, rather accusingly. 'Are you sure you didn't see who it was?'

'I'd have told them if I had,' I said quite sharply, but I wasn't sure he believed me. I hated myself again for deceiving him. But I really didn't want a 'next time', and I had been very frightened by my confrontation with Julian Trent. I was alive and not badly damaged. And I intended to keep it that way.

I SAT AT MY DESK for a while, trying to recover some of my confidence. 'Be a good little lawyer,' Trent had said. What had that meant? I wondered. If I really had been a good little lawyer I would have told the police who had attacked me. Even now, he would be under arrest and locked up. And was he anything to do with the 'Do as you are told' whispered phone message? Something very strange was going on.

Arthur knocked on my open door and came in, closing it behind him.

'Mr Mason,' he said, 'may I say something?'

'Of course, Arthur,' I replied, not actually wanting him to say anything just at the moment.

'I think it is most unlike you to be so vague as you were with those policemen,' he said, standing full-square in front of my paper-covered desk. 'You are the brightest junior we have in these chambers and you miss nothing, nothing at all. Do I make myself clear?'

I was flattered by his comments and I was trying to think what to say to him when he went on.

'Are you in any trouble?' he asked.

'No, of course not,' I said. 'What sort of trouble do you mean?'

'Any sort of trouble,' he said. 'Maybe some woman trouble?'

Did he think I'd been attacked by a jealous husband?

'No, Arthur, no trouble at all. I promise.'

'You could always come to me if you were,' he said. 'I like to think I look after my barristers.'

'Thank you, Arthur,' I said. 'I would most definitely tell you if I was in any sort of trouble.' I looked him straight in the eye.

He nodded, turned on his heel and walked to the door. As he opened it he turned round. 'Oh, yes,' he said, 'this came for you earlier.' He walked back to the desk and handed me an A5-sized white envelope with my name printed on the front of it, with *By Hand* written on the top right-hand corner. Then he went out.

The envelope contained a single piece of white paper folded over and a photograph. It left me in no doubt at all that the whispered telephone calls and Julian Trent's visit had been connected.

Four lines of printed bold capitals ran across the centre of the paper.

BE A GOOD LITTLE LAWYER
TAKE THE STEVE MITCHELL CASE—AND LOSE IT
DO AS YOU ARE TOLD
NEXT TIME, SOMEONE WILL GET BADLY HURT

The photograph was of my seventy-eight-year-old father standing outside his home in Northamptonshire.

AN ENGLISHMAN'S HOUSE is his castle, they say. I sat in my castle with the drawbridge pulled up and thought about what was happening to me.

I had ordered a taxi to collect me and then deliver me safe and sound to Ranelagh Avenue, to my home, my castle. Now I sat on a bar stool at my kitchen counter and looked again and again at the sheet of white paper. *Take the Steve Mitchell case—and lose it*. From what I had heard from

Bruce Lygon there wouldn't be much trouble in losing the case. All the evidence seemed to point that way. But why was someone so keen to be sure that it was lost?

Do as you are told. Did that just mean that I must take the case and lose it, or were there other things as well that I would be told to do? And how was the attack by Julian Trent connected?

I called my father.

'Hello,' he said in his usual rather formal tone. I could imagine him sitting in front of the television in his bungalow watching the news. He had moved to the village of Kings Sutton, near Banbury, from his native urban Surrey after my mother had died.

'Hello, Dad,' I said.

'Ah, Geoff,' he said. 'How are things in the Smoke?'

'Fine, thanks. How are things with you?' It was a ritual. We spoke on the telephone about once a week and, every time, we exchanged these pleasantries. We had never been particularly close and sadly, these days we had little else to say to one another.

'Much the same,' he said.

'Dad,' I said, 'I know this is a strange question, but what have you been wearing today?'

'Why do you need to know?' he demanded suspiciously. We both knew that I was apt to criticise my father's ageing wardrobe.

'I just do,' I said. 'Please.'

'Fawn trousers and a yellow shirt under a green pullover,' he said.

'Does the pullover have any holes in it?' I asked.

'None of your business,' he said sharply.

'Does it have a hole in the left elbow?' I persisted.

'Only a small one,' he said defensively. 'What is this all about?'

'Nothing,' I said lightly. 'Forget I asked. I'll call you on Sunday.'

'Right. Bye for now.' He put down the receiver at his end. He'd never liked talking on the phone and today we had been briefer than usual.

I sat and stared at the photograph that had accompanied the note. It showed my father outside the front door of his bungalow wearing fawn-coloured trousers, a yellow shirt and a green pullover with a small hole clearly visible on the left elbow. The photo had to have been taken today.

But Julian Trent had been released from custody only on Friday, and Scot Barlow murdered only yesterday. I wondered if the one had been dependent on the other.

Bruce Lygon still hadn't called me, so I didn't even know if Steve Mitchell had yet been charged with murder, but here I was, already being told to make sure he was convicted.

As if on cue, my telephone rang.

'Hello,' I said, picking it up.

'Geoffrey?' said a now familiar voice.

'Bruce,' I replied. 'What news?'

'They charged Mitchell with murder at six this evening,' he said. 'He'll be in court tomorrow at ten.'

'Which court?' I asked.

'Newbury Magistrate's,' he said. 'He's sure to be remanded. No provincial magistrate would ever give bail on a murder charge. It will have to go before a judge for there to be any chance. I'll apply, of course, but I think it's most unlikely, considering the cause of death.'

'Yes,' I replied. 'I agree.' Under English law the granting of bail was a basic right for all accused and there had to be a good reason for refusing it. In this case the reason might be the ferociousness of the attack.

'Mr Mitchell is very insistent that you should defend him,' Bruce Lygon went on.

How ironic, I thought.

'I'm only a junior,' I said. 'The trial judge would expect a QC to lead.'

'He seems determined that it should be you,' he replied.

Even if I had wanted to lead the defence, the best I might expect was to be appointed as a silk's junior in the case. But what was I even thinking about? I told myself. I could not act in this case. The law wouldn't let me.

Do as you are told.

Someone will get badly hurt.

Oh hell. What do I do?

'Are you still there?' Bruce asked.

'Sorry,' I said. 'I was thinking.'

'I'll contact your clerk in due course, then. I've got the number,' he said.

'Fine,' I replied.

Was I mad?

AS EXPECTED, Steve Mitchell was remanded in custody at the brief hearing at Newbury Magistrate's Court at ten the following morning. According to the lunchtime news, he had been remanded to Bullingdon Prison, near Bicester, to appear again at Oxford Crown Court in seven days' time.

I called Bruce Lygon. He had left a message after the magistrates' hearing, but I needed him to do more.

'Bruce,' I said when he answered, 'I want to visit the crime scene. Can you fix it with the police?' The lawyers for the accused were entitled to have access to the scene but not prior to the collection of forensic evidence.

'With or without me?' he asked.

'As you like,' I said. 'But as soon as possible, please.'

'Does this mean you will act for him?' he asked.

'No, it doesn't,' I said. 'Not yet. It might help me make up my mind.'

'But only his representatives have access,' he said.

I knew. 'If you don't tell the police,' I said, 'then they will never know.'

'Right,' he said slowly. I could feel that he was confused. He was not the only one.

'And can you arrange an interview for me with Mitchell at Bullingdon tomorrow if possible?'

'Right,' he said again. 'I'll get back to you, then.'

Bruce had been a lucky choice. He was so keen to be representing his celebrity client that he seemed happy to overlook a few departures from proper procedure, to bend the rules just a little.

STEVE MITCHELL was very agitated when I met him at noon the following day at Bullingdon Prison.

'God, Perry,' he said as he came into the stark prison interview room. 'When can you get me out of this bloody place?'

'I really don't know, Steve,' I'd said. 'I think you had better prepare yourself for quite a lengthy stretch in here. The trial date will likely not be set for at least six months and it could be as long as a year away.'

'A year!' he exclaimed, turning white. 'I'll go mad.' He marched round the room. 'I didn't bloody do it. I swear to you I never did it.'

'Just sit down,' I said. Reluctantly, he ceased his pacing and sat on a grey steel stool beside the grey steel table and I sat on a similar stool opposite him. The room was about eight foot square with sickly cream walls. The only light came from a large fluorescent bulb in the centre of the white ceiling, surrounded by a wire cage.

'I didn't do it,' he said again. 'I tell you, I'm being framed.'

As it happened, I had reasons for believing him.

'Who's framing you?' I asked him.

'I've got no bloody idea,' he said. 'That's for you to find out.'

'Who is Julian Trent?' I asked him calmly.

'Never heard of him,' Steve said. Not a flicker in his eyes, not a fraction of hesitation in his voice. Either Steve was being straight with me or he was fairly good at lying. 'Who is he?' he asked.

'No one important,' I said. 'I just wondered if you knew him.'

'Should I?' he asked.

'No reason you should.' I decided to change the subject. 'So why do the police think you killed Scot Barlow?'

'Because it seems that it was my bloody pitchfork stuck into the little bastard.' I could imagine that Steve referring to Barlow as 'the little bastard' hadn't gone down too well with the police. 'And would I be so stupid to have killed the little bastard with my own pitchfork? At least I would have then taken the bloody thing home again.'

'What else do they have?' I asked him.

'Something about spots of his blood and some of his hairs being found in my car, and his blood being on my boots. It's all complete nonsense. I was never in his house.'

'So where exactly were you when he was killed?' I asked him.

'I don't know,' he said. 'They haven't told me when he actually died. But they did ask me what I was doing between one and six on Monday afternoon. I told them I was riding at Ludlow races. But I wasn't. The meeting was abandoned due to the bloody course being waterlogged.'

That was really stupid, I thought. It was so easy for them to check.

'So where were you?' I asked him again.

He seemed reluctant to tell me, so I sat and waited in silence.

'At home,' he said eventually.

'On your own?' I pressed him.

'Yes,' he said. 'I was alone reading all afternoon.'

Now he was lying. I was sure of it. 'That's a shame,' I said. 'If someone was with you, they would be able to give you an alibi.'

He sat silently.

'Do you know what the word "alibi" means?' I asked him. He shook his head. 'It's Latin. It means "somewhere else". An alibi is proof of innocence. Are you sure you were alone all afternoon?'

'Are you saying I'm a liar?'

'No, of course not,' I said. 'I'm just trying to make sure you remembered correctly.'

'I'll tell you what I do remember,' he said. 'I remember that I've never been in Scot Barlow's house. Not on Monday. Not ever. I didn't even know where the little bastard lived.'

'What about the text message?' I said. 'The one saying you were coming round to sort him out.'

'I didn't send any bloody text message,' he replied.

Surely, I thought, the police must have the phone records.

'I didn't do it, you know.' He looked at me. 'Not that I'm sorry he's dead.'

'What was there between you two?' I asked. 'Why did you hate him so much?' I thought that I wouldn't ask him about the incident in the showers at Sandown. Not yet. Much better, at the moment, if absolutely no one knew I had seen Barlow lying in the shower, and what he had said to me. There had been no witness to the exchange.

'I hated him because he was a sneaky little bastard,' Steve said. 'He would sneak to the stewards if anyone did anything wrong.'

'How do you know?' I asked. 'Did he ever sneak on you?'

'Well, no,' he said. 'Not on me, but he was a bastard nevertheless.'

'But why?' I said, imploring. 'If you want me to help you, you will have to tell me everything.'

He stood up and turned away from me. 'Because,' he said in a rush, 'he told my bloody wife I was having an affair.'

Ah, I thought. That would account for the hatred. Steve went on without turning round, 'Then she left me and took my kids away.'

'How did Barlow know you were having an affair?' I asked.

'I was having it with his sister,' he said.

'When did all this happen?' I asked him.

'Years ago,' he said.

'Are you still having the affair with Barlow's sister?' I asked.

'Nah, it was just a fling,' he said. 'But Natalie, that's my ex-wife, she wouldn't come home. Went and married some bloody Australian and they now live in Sydney. With my kids. It's all that bastard Barlow's fault.'

I thought that a jury would not necessarily agree with his assessment.

'And what about the betting slips found on the prongs of the fork?' I said. 'They had your name on them.'

'Yeah, and would I be so stupid as to leave them stuck on the bloody fork if I had planted it in Barlow's chest? Don't be bloody daft. It's obviously a sodding stitch-up. Surely you can see that?'

It did seem to me that the police must think Steve to be very stupid indeed if they were so certain he had done it based on that.

'Were they, in fact, your betting slips?' I asked him. We both knew that gambling on horses was against the terms of his riding licence.

Steve shrugged. 'If they were, do you think I would have had my name on them. I'm not that bloody stupid.'

'Is it true that Barlow used to go through other jocks' pockets looking for betting slips?' I said.

'I don't know,' he said. 'I doubt it. It was probably me that started that rumour.' He grinned at me. 'I'd have said anything to get at him.'

'I hope it wasn't that rumour that got him killed,' I said.

Steve looked at me. 'Bloody hell,' he said.

ON THURSDAY NIGHT I stayed with my trainer, Paul Newington, at his stable at Great Milton.

It was always an escape from my work to go to Paul's place. He was so different from the people I dealt with on a day-to-day basis. For a start, I don't think I had ever seen him in a tie. When he was at home he habitually wore blue denim jeans with frayed legs. He used to say that the horses didn't care if he was in his dressing gown so why should their owners. But it was one of the reasons why he had never quite broken into the big time. Rich owners want to be afforded due reverence by their trainers. And rich owners buy the best horses. I liked the relaxed atmosphere of his stable, but Paul's richest owners had continually been wooed away by other trainers more willing to bow and scrape to their whims.

Paul and I walked round the stables as his staff were busy mucking out and giving their charges food and water for the night. Sandeman looked wonderful in his box, with his shining golden tan coat.

I walked over and slapped his neck.

'Good boy,' I said to him calmly. 'Who's a good boy?'

He blew through his nostrils and shifted his bulk, turning his head to see if I had a titbit for him. I never came to Paul's without some apples in my pocket. Sandeman gratefully munched his way noisily through a Granny Smith, dripping saliva and apple bits into his bedding.

'See you in the morning, my boy,' I called to him as I left his box. I often wondered if our equine partners had any notion of the depth of our devotion for them.

Laura, Paul's wife, cooked us supper and we sat round the kitchen table eating her best macaroni cheese with onions. It wasn't long before the conversation turned to the hot topic in racing circles.

'So, do you think Steve Mitchell did it?' said Paul between mouthfuls.

'The evidence seems to suggest it,' I said. 'But he would have to have been incredibly stupid to have left all those clues,' I said.

'But who else would have done it?' asked Paul. 'Everyone knew that Mitchell hated Barlow's guts. You could cut the atmosphere between them with a knife.'

'Do you know why Barlow and Mitchell hated each other so much?' I asked.

'Wasn't it something to do with Barlow's sister?' Paul said. 'Mitchell had an affair with her or something.'

'Such a shame about Scot's sister,' Laura interjected.

'What about her?' I said.

'Don't you know?' she said. 'She killed herself in June.'

'How?' I asked.

'At a party,' Laura said. 'Apparently she was depressed and injected herself with a huge dose of anaesthetic.'

'How did she get anaesthetic?' I asked.

'She was a vet,' said Paul. 'Specialised in horses.'

'Where?' I asked.

'Lambourn,' Paul replied. 'She worked in the equine hospital there. Most of the local trainers used her practice.'

'You must remember,' said Laura. 'The papers were full of it.'

'I was away for the first half of June,' I said. 'I must have missed it. Whose party was it?'

'Simon Dacey's,' said Paul. 'He threw the party after winning the Derby. You know, with Peninsula.'

Peninsula was the hottest horseflesh property in the world. Horse of the Year as a two-year-old and, this season, winner of the Two Thousand Guineas at Newmarket in May, the Derby at Epsom in June, and the Breeders' Cup the previous month in California, and now on his way to some lucrative earnings at stud. Dacey was his trainer.

'That must have gone down well with the guests,' I said rather flippantly.

'It certainly didn't,' said Laura seriously. 'We were there. Massive marquee in the garden with live bands and everything. It was great fun. At least it was until someone found Millie Barlow upstairs in one of the bedrooms.'

'Who found her?' I said.

'No idea,' said Paul. 'The police arrived and stopped the party about nine at night. Took our names and addresses and sent us home,' he said. 'Most of us hadn't even been in the house.'

'And were they sure it was suicide?'

'That's what everyone thought,' he said.

'What was she depressed about?'

'You seem very interested all of a sudden,' said Paul.

'Just my suspicious mind,' I said with a laugh. 'One violent death in a family is unfortunate; two within five months may be more than coinciden- tal.' I wondered what the inquest had found and made a mental note to look it up on the Internet. 'So, how's my horse?' I said, changing the subject.

'Slow and fat,' said Paul, laughing, 'like his owner.'

I toasted our slowness and fatness with good red wine, and added a few more ounces with a second helping of macaroni.

I ADORED RIDING OUT on cold, crisp mornings with my breath showing in the air and the frost white on the ground, glistening in the brightness of the sun- light. Sadly, this Friday was not one of those. Rain fell steadily, the plop, plop of the large drops clearly audible as they struck my helmet.

Sandeman and I were number six in Paul's string of ten horses as we walked to the training gallops beyond the village, the horses' metal shoes clicking on the hard roads. Both horses and riders were soaked even before we had left the stable yard at dawn, but I didn't care and neither did Sandeman. I could feel his muscles rippling beneath me. He knew exactly where we were going. We were both clearly excited in anticipation of the gallop we would soon share.

The wind tore at my jacket and the raindrops stung my face, but nothing could wipe the grin from my face as we tore up the gallop with me trying hard to stop Sandeman going any faster. Paul sat on horseback at the top of the gallop, watching as we moved smoothly up towards him. A steady three-quarter-speed gallop, he had instructed. He had implored me not to over-tire my horse. I was doing my best to do what he had asked, but Sandeman seemed determined to race, keen as always to put his nose in front of the other horse. I took a tight hold of the reins and steadied him. In spite of Paul's casual manner with his owners, he was still a great trainer of racehorses and I never questioned his judgment in that department.

I pulled Sandeman up into a trot and then a walk, laughing as I did so. What a magnificent way to blow the courtroom cobwebs out of my hair. I walked him round and round in circles while he cooled and the other horses completed their work up the gallop. Then the string wound its way down the hill and back through the village to Paul's yard.

Laura came out of the house as I was sliding off Sandeman's back.

'A Mr Lygon called for you about ten minutes ago,' she said as I led Sandeman into his stable. 'He seemed very insistent that you should call him as soon as you got back.'

'Thanks,' I said, wondering how he knew where I was.

I removed the bridle and saddle from Sandeman and replaced them with his head-collar and a dry rug.

'Sorry, old boy,' I said to him. 'I'll be back to finish you in a while.'

I went inside, dripping water all over Laura's kitchen floor.

'Bruce,' I said when he answered. 'How did you know where I was?'

'Your clerk told me that you weren't due in court today, so you were probably riding your nag.' I could almost hear Arthur saying it. 'I looked up who trained your nag on the *Racing Post* website.'

'So how can I help you?' I asked him.

'I've managed to get us a visit to the crime scene,' he replied. 'The police say we can go there at two this afternoon. But they say it will be an accompanied visit only.'

'That's fine,' I said. 'Where is it?'

'Great Shefford,' he said. 'Small village between Lambourn and Newbury. Place called Honeysuckle Cottage.'

'Is there a pub?' I asked him.

'Yes,' he said. 'I think there's one on the main road.'

'Shall we meet there at one o'clock?' I said. 'For some lunch?'

'OK,' he said. 'See you later.'

CHAPTER 3

There were only three people in the bar when I walked into the Swan Inn at one o'clock sharp and two of them were clearly a couple, heads close together and holding hands. The third person was a man who looked to be in his mid- to late forties and who was wearing a light grey suit with white shirt and blue striped tie. He looked at me briefly, then his gaze slid back to the door as if expecting somebody else.

'Bruce?' I asked him, walking up close.

'Yes?' he said as a question, returning his gaze to my face.

'I'm Geoffrey,' I said. 'Geoffrey Mason.'

'Oh,' he said. 'I was expecting someone . . . you know, a bit older.'

'Older and wiser?' I said.

He laughed. Ironically, he was slightly older than I had thought from hearing him on the telephone.

'What are you drinking?' I asked him.

'I'm fine,' he said, pointing at a pint mug on the bar. 'My round.'

'Diet Coke, then, please,' I said.

We ordered some food and took our drinks over to a table in the corner.

'Did you see Mitchell yesterday?' asked Bruce.

'Yes,' I said. 'Says he's being framed.'

'Do you believe him?' said Bruce.

I didn't answer. 'Did you know Scot Barlow had a sister?' I asked him.

'No,' he said. 'Should I?'

'Seems she killed herself last June,' I said. He didn't look any the wiser. 'During a big party in Lambourn.'

'What? Not that girl vet?' he said.

'One and the same,' I said. 'Millie Barlow.'

'Blimey,' he said. 'That was big news in these parts. All those celebrities at that party being held by the police. Lots of cocaine-sniffing, apparently. It was initially thought the vet had died of an overdose of it, but it turned out to be horse anaesthetic and it seems she did it on purpose.'

'A strange place to do it. Ruining a party seems a bit . . .' I tailed off.

'Suicides do strange things,' he said. 'I once had a client whose ex-wife killed herself outside the registry office as he was getting remarried inside. Walked out under a lorry. Just like that. The poor driver had no chance.'

'Bet that went down well with the wedding guests,' I said.

'I actually think my client was delighted,' he said, grinning. 'Saved him a fortune in alimony.'

We both laughed. I was growing to like Bruce.

'So tell me, what are we looking for at Barlow's place?' he said.

'I'm not sure,' I said. 'I always try to visit scenes of crime if I'm acting in a case. It helps me when it comes to questions in court. Also, it often gives some insight into the victim.'

'So are you now acting in this case?' he asked me.

'Temporarily,' I said, smiling at him.

WE FINISHED OUR LUNCH and drove the few hundred yards to Church Street. Honeysuckle Cottage was a beautiful old stone building set back from the road among a copse of tall horse-chestnut trees, their branches now bare of the leaves that lay deep and uncollected on the driveway.

There were already two cars parked in front of a modern concrete-block garage that had been built alongside the cottage. The driver's door of one of the cars opened and a young man got out as we pulled up behind him.

'Mr Lygon?' he asked, approaching.

'That's me,' said Bruce, advancing and holding out his hand.

'Detective Constable Hillier,' said the young man, shaking it.

'This is Geoffrey Mason,' said Bruce, indicating me. 'Barrister in the case.' We shook hands.

'This will have to be quick, I'm afraid. I can give you no more than half an hour,' said the policeman. 'And we are not alone. Barlow's parents took a coach down from Glasgow. They're inside.' He nodded towards the house.

Oh bugger, I thought.

DC Hillier introduced us to Mr and Mrs Barlow in the hallway of the cottage. 'They are lawyers in the case,' he said. 'They are acting for Steve Mitchell.'

Mr Barlow looked at us in disgust. 'May you all burn in hell for eternity,' he said with venom. He had a broad Scottish accent and the word 'burn' sounded like it could be spelt 'berrrrn'. 'Why are ye givin' that man any assistance? He is sent from the devil, that one.'

'Now, now, dear,' said Mrs Barlow, laying a hand on her husband's arm. 'Remember what the doctor said. Do not stress yourself.'

Barlow relaxed a fraction. He was a big tall man with heavy jowls and bushy eyebrows, and he was wearing an ill-fitting dark suit with no tie. Mrs Barlow, in contrast, had a slight frame, was a good eight inches shorter than her husband and wore an inappropriately cheerful flowery dress that hung on her like a sack.

'Mitchell hasn't actually been convicted yet,' I said. It was a mistake.

'I tell you,' Mr Barlow almost shouted, jabbing his right index finger towards me. 'That man is guilty and he shall have to answer to Our Lord. And it's not just Hamish that he killed, but both of our bairns.'

'Who's Hamish?' I said. Another mistake.

'Hamish, man,' bellowed Barlow in a full rage. 'My son.'

Bruce spoke quickly into my ear. 'Scot Barlow's real name was Hamish.' On the racecourse, Barlow was always referred to as Scot, but, I now realised, that must have been only because he was one.

'What did you mean about Mitchell killing both your children?' I asked him.

'He killed our Millie,' said Mrs Barlow quickly in a quiet, mellow tone.

'I thought she killed herself,' I said as gently as possible.

'Aye, but that man was still responsible,' said Mr Barlow, his voice rising in both tone and volume. 'He was fornicating with my daughter.'

'How does that make him responsible for her death?' I asked.

'Because,' said Mrs Barlow in her gentle tone, 'he dumped her for someone else on the day she died.'

I wondered why Steve Mitchell hadn't thought it was important enough to tell me that. And what was more, if what the Barlows said was true, he had lied to me more than I thought.

MR AND MRS BARLOW hovered around us as Bruce and I inspected their son's house. Everywhere we went they followed and watched.

The police forensic team had covered every shiny surface with a fine silvery powder, fingerprint powder, hoping, no doubt, to display some of Steve Mitchell's dabs. According to the television reports Scot, or Hamish, had been found lying on his kitchen floor in a pool of blood with the pitchfork stuck in his chest. If there actually had been a pool of blood, someone must have since cleaned it up. However, the floor and the cupboard doors were covered with little yellow labels to show positions where blood spots had been discovered.

Lying on the kitchen table was a broken photo frame, its glass badly cracked but still held in place by the silver surround. But there was no photograph in the frame and the back of it was hanging off.

'I wonder what was in here,' I said to Bruce, holding up the frame.

'It was a picture of our Millie,' said Mrs Barlow from the doorway. 'He must have taken it.'

The emphasis she placed on the word 'he' left me in no doubt that she meant Steve Mitchell. But why would he take it?

'Was it a portrait?' I asked her.

'No,' she said. 'It was taken when she was at work in the equine hospital. It showed her with a horse. It used to be hers but Hamish had it when . . .' She couldn't finish. Tears began to well up in her eyes.

'I'm so sorry, Mrs Barlow,' I said. I knew only too well the despair that grief can engender.

'Thank you,' she said, dabbing her face with a white handkerchief.

'It must have been a fairly significant photograph to have been in a silver frame,' I said. 'Do you remember which horse Millie was with?' I looked at Mrs Barlow.

'I'm afraid I don't,' she said. 'But I recall seeing the picture in her room after she died. Hamish said he wanted it. To remember her by.'

'Where did she live?' I asked.

'What? When she wasn't living with that man?' she said with unexpected anger. 'She shared a flat at the equine hospital with another female vet.'

'Do you know who?'

'I'm sorry, I can't remember her name,' she replied.

DC Hillier had listened to most of the exchanges between the Barlows and me but he seemed unconcerned and disinterested.

'Have you seen all you want?' he asked. 'I've got to go now.'

Bruce held the Barlows at bay in the hallway while I had a quick peep at the bedrooms and bathrooms upstairs. Overall there was not much to see. Hamish Barlow had been a tidy man with a wardrobe of smart designer clothes and two cupboards on his landing full of racing-related memorabilia like race cards, copies of the *Racing Post* and numerous horse-related magazines and books. But there were no skeletons with them for me to find.

The policeman ushered us all out of the house, padlocked the clasp on the front dor and invited us to leave the premises.

'Do you have a telephone number where my solicitor could contact you?' I asked the Barlows. 'In case he has any more questions for you.'

Mr Barlow, who had been quiet after his earlier outburst, suddenly turned to me and said, 'I don't want to answer any more of your questions.'

'Look,' I said, 'I am as interested as you are in finding out who killed your son.'

'Mitchell killed him,' said Mr Barlow emphatically.

'How can you be so sure?' I asked him.

'Because Hamish used to say that, one day, Mitchell would kill him as sure as he killed his sister. And now he has. I hope he rots in hell.'

There was no answer to that.

BRUCE DROPPED ME BACK at the Swan Inn to collect my car, before rushing off for a meeting. It was almost five o'clock and I decided, as I was near there, to take the opportunity to visit the equine hospital at Lambourn.

I explained to the young receptionist that I was looking for someone who had shared a room with Millie Barlow before last June.

'Sorry,' she said. 'I'm new here. You'll have to ask one of the vets. But we've got a bit of an emergency at the moment and they're all in the operating theatre.'

'How long are they going to be?' I asked.

'Oh, I don't know,' she said. 'They've been in there for some time already. But you're welcome to wait. Through there.' She pointed at a door opposite.

'Thank you,' I said.

I went through the door into the waiting room. It reminded me of going to the dentist. A dozen pink upholstered armchairs with pale wooden legs and arms were arranged around the walls with a few occasional tables between some of them. The hard floor was covered with a thin blue carpet. It was functional rather than comfortable.

A man sat on one of the chairs on the right-hand side and he looked up as I entered. We nodded at each other in informal greeting and he went back to reading some papers. I sat down opposite him and glanced through a copy of *Country Life* that someone had left on a chair.

I had looked at all the estate agents' adverts and was beginning to read the book reviews when someone came through the far door. It was a woman wearing a green scrub tunic and trousers with short green Wellington boots. A vet, I surmised, fresh from the operating theatre.

The other man stood up as she entered. 'How's it going?' he said eagerly.

'Fine,' she replied. 'I think we have managed to save most of the muscle mass in the shoulder. It shouldn't greatly impair him after proper healing.'

The man let out a sigh of relief. 'Mr Radcliffe will be relieved to hear it.'

'I have to get back in there now,' said the vet. 'To finish off. We will keep him here overnight and see how he's doing in the morning.'

'Fine,' said the man. 'Thank you. I'll call you around nine.'

'OK,' she said. The man began to collect together his papers. The vet turned to me. 'Are you being looked after?' she said.

'No, not really,' I said. 'I was hoping to talk to someone who knew one of the vets who used to work here.'

'Which vet?' she asked.

'Millie Barlow,' I said.

The reaction from the man was dramatic. 'Right little bitch,' he said almost under his breath, but quite audibly in the quiet of the waiting room.

'I beg your pardon?' I said to him.

'I said, she was a right little bitch,' he repeated, looking at me.

'I'm sorry,' the vet said to me, 'but I have to go and close up the wound on the horse we have been operating on. If you'd like to wait, I'll talk to you when I'm finished.'

'I'll wait,' I said, and she disappeared through the door.

'I know you,' the man said. 'You have horses with Paul Newington.'

'I'm Geoffrey Mason. I'm a barrister,' I said.

'Simon Dacey,' he said holding out his hand.

Ah, I thought, no wonder he thinks Millie Barlow was a little bitch. She ruined his party by killing herself in one of his bedrooms.

'Do you have a problem?' I asked him, nodding towards the door through which the vet had disappeared.

'One of my yearlings got loose,' he said. 'Gashed himself on a parked car.'

'Will he be all right?' I asked.

'I sincerely hope so,' he said. 'He cost almost half a million at the sales.'

'But surely all racehorses are insured?' I said. I knew mine was.

'Mr Radcliffe, that's the owner, he says that the premiums are too high. He has about a dozen with me and he says he would rather spend the money he saves on another horse. But I know he insured Peninsula against being infertile or being injured so he couldn't perform at stud.'

Oh, I thought, Mr Radcliffe owned Peninsula. He wouldn't be short of a bob or two.

'So tell me why Millie Barlow was a right little bitch,' I said, bringing the subject back to what really interested me.

'She ruined my party,' he said.

'That's a bit ungracious,' I said. 'The poor girl was so troubled that she killed herself. She probably didn't ruin your party on purpose.'

'But she did ruin it, nevertheless,' he said. 'Why didn't she go and do it somewhere else? That party for winning the Derby was the best day of my life until she spoilt it. How would you like it?'

I could see his point of view. 'Do you know why she killed herself?' I asked him.

'No idea,' he said. 'I hardly knew her.'

'Did you know she was having an affair with Steve Mitchell?' I asked.

'God, yes,' he said. 'Worst-kept secret in Lambourn. Look, I really have to go now. Evening stables are already well under way.'

'OK,' I said. 'Thanks. Can I call you again if I need any more answers?

I'm representing Steve Mitchell,' I said, handing him one of my cards.

'Oh, are you?' He smiled, looking at it. 'Seems you may have your work cut out there.'

'Why does everyone think he did it?' I asked him.

'Because everyone in Lambourn would have heard them arguing at one time or another. And word is that either of them would have thought nothing of putting the other through the wings.' Putting someone through the wings of a fence by squeezing them for room was one of the worst crimes one jump jockey could do to another, and one of the most dangerous. 'And no one much cares for either of them,' he went on. 'Barlow was slightly weird, and Mitchell is arrogant.'

'But do you really think he's a murderer?' I asked.

'I don't know,' he said. 'I have to say I was surprised when I heard he'd been arrested. But people do funny things when they're angry. They lose control.'

'So can I call you if I need to ask you anything else?' I asked.

'I suppose so,' he said. 'But I can't think I would know anything. I didn't have much to do with either of them. I really must go.'

'Fine,' I said. 'Nice to have met you. Good luck with the yearling.'

'Thanks.'

He departed and I sat down again. The clock on the wall read 6.15.

What was I doing? I asked myself. I had now told far too many people that I was the barrister acting for the defence in Steve Mitchell's case, but I knew that I shouldn't act. I couldn't act. I was a potential witness in the case. All my training told me to go and make my exchange with Scot Barlow at Sandown known to the police. All my instincts as a barrister were to have nothing to do with this case and let justice take its course.

But what was justice? I had been emphatically told by someone to take the case and then to lose it. Was that justice? If I walked away, would someone else be frightened into ensuring that Steve Mitchell was convicted? Did the very fact that someone was so keen to see him sent down for the murder prove that he didn't do it?

But even if I could successfully defend him, where would that leave me? *Next time, I'll smash your head*, Trent had said. *Next time, I'll cut your balls right off.*

'Angela, my darling,' I said quietly into the empty waiting room, 'tell me what to do.'

She didn't reply. Once again, I longed for her presence and her wisdom.

She had always instinctively known what was right. Without warning my eyes began to fill with tears.

The lady vet in the green scrubs chose this moment to reappear. I quickly wiped my eyes on my sleeve and hoped she hadn't noticed.

'Now, how can I help you?' she asked wearily.

'Busy day?' It was more of a statement than a question.

'You bet,' she said, smiling. 'It could have stopped him racing if we hadn't been careful. But I think we saved Mr Radcliffe his money. He's young. He should heal as good as new.'

'Yes,' I said. 'Simon Dacey told me.'

She raised her eyebrows in slight surprise. 'And who are you exactly?'

'Geoffrey Mason,' I said, pulling out another card from my pocket and handing it over. 'I'm after some information. I'm a barrister and I'm representing Steve Mitchell.' There I go again, I thought.

'Arrogant little shit,' she said, somewhat surprisingly.

'Is he?' I said. 'Why?'

'Thinks he's God's gift to women,' she said. 'Expects every female round here to drop her knickers on demand.'

'And do they?' I asked.

She looked at me and smiled. 'Remind me never to be in the witness box when you're asking the questions.'

'I'll try.' I smiled back. 'But at least tell me your name so I can be sure.'

'Eleanor Clarke,' she said, reaching out a hand, which I shook. 'I thought you said you wanted to ask about Millie Barlow?'

'I do,' I said. 'Did you know her?'

'Certainly did,' said Eleanor. 'She lived in the house out the back here with three others of us until . . .' She tailed off.

'Until she killed herself?' I asked, finishing her sentence.

'Yes,' she said. 'But she didn't sleep there every night.'

'Because she was with Steve Mitchell?' I said it as a question.

'Yes,' she replied rather hesitantly.

'Was she sleeping with anyone else?' I asked.

'God, you're sharp,' she said. 'Our Millie was a sweet girl, but I'm afraid she would sleep with anyone who asked nicely.'

'Why do you think she killed herself?' I asked.

'I don't know,' she said. 'Lots of people said afterwards that she had been depressed, but I didn't think so. She was always so happy. She always had a plan to get rich quick.'

'Was she selling sex?' I asked.

'No,' she said with some emphasis. 'Perhaps I exaggerated a bit. She didn't sleep with everyone. She had her favourites. And she would say no occasionally, especially to some of the married ones.'

I wondered how strict Millie's upbringing had been. Maybe as soon as she was free of her father's control she went a little mad, sampling life's pleasures to excess.

'How did she get the anaesthetic?' I asked.

'Well, we have it here, of course, but it's funny.' She paused. 'The toxicology report on Millie indicated that she had injected herself with thiopental. We don't use thiopental in the hospital. We use ketamine, usually mixed with either xylazine or detomidine.'

'Isn't that a bit odd?' I asked.

'A vet can get medicines from any drug supplier just by filling in a form,' she said. 'And anaesthetics are used by vets all the time.'

'But it does mean she didn't kill herself on the spur of the moment,' I said. 'Not if she had to order the stuff especially.'

'She may have already had it,' Eleanor suggested. 'I have a few things in my bag that didn't come from the hospital drug store. And barbiturate anaesthetics are used a lot. Thiopental is used in most vets' practices to put dogs and cats to sleep.'

'Where does the hospital get its drugs?' I asked her.

'We have a specialist veterinary pharmacist in Reading.'

'She must have ordered it separately from them,' I said.

'No,' she replied quickly. 'They had to check their records for the police and there was nothing. Look, I've got to go. We aren't normally open after six and there's someone waiting to lock up.'

'How about the horse you operated on?' I asked.

'He's in the stables at the back now for the night. He has a monitor on him and CCTV to the duty vet's room.'

'But I would really like to ask you some more questions about Millie,' I said imploringly.

'Let me get changed first,' she said. 'I fancy a drink. Are you buying?'

'How about supper?' I said.

'Don't push your luck, Mr . . .' She looked again at my card. '. . . Mason.'

'No. Sorry,' I mumbled. 'I didn't mean it like that.'

'Oh, thanks,' she said. 'Just when I thought I was being asked out on a date, he says he didn't mean it.' She laughed. 'Story of my life.'

WE WENT IN SEPARATE CARS to the Queen's Arms in East Garston, a village a few miles away. I was there well ahead of her. I ordered myself a Diet Coke and perched on a bar stool, thinking about what questions I needed to ask.

I did not immediately recognise Eleanor Clarke when she walked into the dimly lit bar. She had changed out of her scrubs and was now wearing a white rib-pattern roll-neck sweater over blue jeans. However, the main reason I didn't know her at first was because her blonde hair was no longer tied in a ponytail but hung down close to each side of her face. My first instinct was that the change of hairstyle was a mistake as it hid her beautiful cheekbones and somewhat reduced the sparkle from her stunning blue eyes.

I was suddenly quite shocked by these thoughts. I had hardly given a woman's face a second glance since the day I had first met and fallen instantly in love with Angela.

'There you are,' said Eleanor, coming over and sitting on the bar stool next to mine.

'What are you drinking?' I asked her.

'G and T, please.'

I ordered her drink and we sat in silence as the barman poured the tonic over the gin.

'Lovely,' she said, taking a large gulp. 'It's been a long day.'

'I'd better order you another,' I said.

'I'm driving,' she said. 'I'll just have the one.'

'You could stay for dinner,' I said.

'I thought you didn't really mean it.' She looked at me with the sparkly blue eyes. They smiled at me.

'I meant that,' I said. 'I just didn't mean . . .' I was getting lost for words. 'Will you stay to dinner?'

'Yes,' she replied without hesitation.

'Good.' I smiled.

'Are you married?' she asked suddenly.

'I was,' I said slowly.

'Divorced?'

'Widowed.'

'Oh.' She was embarrassed. 'I'm sorry. I shouldn't have asked.'

'It was a long time ago,' I said. But it felt like only yesterday.

'Still painful?' she asked.

I nodded.

'Sorry,' she said again. Some of the sparkle had gone out of her eyes.

We sat in silence for a while.

'Let's go and eat,' I said eventually.

We opted for a table in the bar rather than in the restaurant—no tablecloth, less formal, but the same menu. I chose a fillet steak, while Eleanor decided on the pan-fried sea bream.

'How well did you know Millie?' I asked when our food arrived.

'Pretty well,' she said. 'We worked together at the hospital for three years and lived in the house together for most of that time.'

'Did she have money worries?' I asked.

'No,' Eleanor replied emphatically. 'In fact she always seemed rather well off. She bought a brand-new red Mazda sports car the year before she died and she always had lots of nice clothes. I think her father still sent her an allowance, even though we all earn pretty good money at the hospital.'

I thought back to my encounter with the Barlow parents in their ill-fitting clothes. Did they seem the sort of people who could afford to send their high-earning daughter an allowance?

'Was she pregnant?' I said. It was only a wild thought.

'Highly unlikely,' said Eleanor. 'She used to boast that she had a good supply of the morning-after pill. She was medically trained, remember.'

'And medics have a higher suicide rate than almost every other profession,' I said. I had researched the rates for a case.

'Do they?' She seemed surprised. 'I suppose medics know how to take their own lives. They also have easy access to the necessary drugs.'

'Did Millie get on with her brother?' I asked.

'Well enough, I think,' she said. 'But I don't think he was too happy with her reputation for being the easiest ride in the village.'

'No,' I said. 'Not really a reputation to cherish. How many casual lovers would you say she had?'

'At least half a dozen on the go at once,' she said. 'She wasn't particularly discreet. Suffice to say she liked jockeys.'

'Didn't you see them in the house?' I said.

'We have a sort of unwritten rule,' she said. 'Long-term relationships are OK, but no casual partners to stay over. Needless to say, Millie broke it all the time. It was the only thing we argued about.'

'How about Steve Mitchell?' I asked. 'Did he stay over?'

'No, never,' she said. 'Millie was always keen to go to his place. She was forever telling us about his hot tub.' She lifted her eyebrows in disapproval.

'Why exactly do you dislike Mitchell?' I asked her.

'Is it that obvious?'

'Yes,' I said.

'When I first came to Lambourn about ten years ago, he was just starting as a jockey and we went out for a while. I thought he was serious but he wasn't. He was two-timing me with some stable hand and, when the silly bitch got pregnant, he dumped me and married her.' She paused. 'I suppose she did me a favour really.'

'How long did his marriage last?' I asked.

'About six years. They had two children. When Natalie, his ex-wife, finally saw some sense and left him, he came back to my door and wanted to carry on as if nothing had happened. I told him to piss off and Steve didn't like that. I actually think he then made a fuss over Millie to get back at me.'

So Steve's affair with Millie Barlow hadn't just been a fling as he had claimed, but had continued long after his wife had found out and left him. He had indeed lied to me about it.

'Didn't Steve mind that she had other partners as well as him?' I asked.

'Mind? Are you kidding? According to Millie, Steve loved a threesome.'

'Do you remember a photo of her and a horse in a silver frame?' I asked.

She nodded. 'Her prized possession.'

'Why?' I asked.

'It was a picture of her with a newborn foal,' she said. 'It was the first foal she had ever delivered on her own, just after she'd arrived in Lambourn. Bit of an emergency in the middle of the night. She was the only vet on duty. But she did OK, apparently. I was away.'

I was disappointed. I thought it would be more significant than that.

'Why are you interested in the photo?' she asked me.

'Because someone took it from Scot Barlow's house,' I said.

'Perhaps it was for the silver frame,' she said.

'No. Whoever took the photo left the frame.'

'Well, I can tell you that it was of Millie and a foal that was lying in the straw, with the mare and a stud groom behind.'

'Do you know who the stud groom was?' I asked.

'No idea,' she said. 'But I know which foal it was. That's why it was Millie's prize possession.'

'Go on,' I encouraged her as she paused.

'Peninsula,' Eleanor said with a flourish.

Was that the reason why Millie Barlow was at Simon Dacey's party?

CHAPTER 4
March 2009

By the time of the Steeplechase Festival at Cheltenham in March, Steve Mitchell had been in prison for four months and his name had all but been erased from the racing pages of the newspapers.

Bruce Lygon had done his best at Oxford Crown Court in November to get Steve Mitchell bail, but, unsurprisingly, the judge had listened to him with courtesy and then declined his application. Letting murder suspects out on bail was never going to endear a judge to the general public. I had sat beside Bruce in court, but I hadn't really helped him much.

I hadn't actually planned to attend the bail hearing, but I had received another little reminder from God-knows-who two days before it was due to take place. It had been a slim white envelope delivered as before to my chambers by hand. No one had seen who had left it. Again, in the envelope there had been a single sheet of folded white paper and a photograph. As before, there had been four lines of print across the centre of the paper.

GOOD LITTLE LAWYER
I WILL BE WATCHING YOU IN OXFORD ON WEDNESDAY
DON'T GET MITCHELL BAIL
REMEMBER, LOSE THE CASE OR SOMEONE GETS HURT

The photograph had been of my dead wife, Angela. In fact, to be accurate, it had been a photograph of a photograph of Angela in a silver frame that I had placed on her dressing table in our bedroom soon after she died. I said, 'Good morning, my darling,' to that photograph every day. Someone had been into my house to take that shot. It made me very angry. Just who were these people?

I SAT AT MY DESK in chambers twiddling my thumbs and thinking. It was Monday morning and I was having a few easy days. I had recently finished acting in a large case, which my client had won. In order to prevent a repeat of last year, when I had been stuck in court instead of jumping my way round Cheltenham in the Foxhunter Chase, I had instructed Arthur to schedule absolutely nothing for the whole week.

Sandeman had qualified for the Foxhunters partly by virtue of winning the race last year and Paul had assured me at the end of January that the horse was fitter this time, implying that failure to win again this year would not be Sandeman's fault. It had been a direct warning to me not to be the weak link in the partnership, an explicit instruction to get myself fit.

For weeks now I had been running every day, mostly at lunchtime. In addition, in mid-February I had been skiing in Meribel in France. I had risen early each morning and spent the whole day on the slopes, catching the very last lift of the day to the highest point and arriving back at the chalet exhausted, just as the daylight faded. Then I would spend hours in the sauna, sweating off the pounds, before a high-protein dinner and an early bed. By the second week in March I was toned like I hadn't been since my time in Lambourn fifteen years before.

Arthur came into my room. In spite of an excellent internal telephone system, Arthur was of the old school and liked to talk face to face when making arrangements.

'Sir James wishes to have a conference about the Steve Mitchell case,' he said. 'I have scheduled it for nine thirty tomorrow. Is that all right with you?'

'I asked you not to schedule anything at all for this week,' I said to him.

'But you're not going to the races until Thursday,' he said. I looked at him. How did Arthur know I wasn't planning to go to Cheltenham until Thursday? It would be no good asking him. He would reply as he always did. 'It's my job to know everything about my barristers,' he would say.

'Nine thirty tomorrow will be fine,' I said.

He smiled. 'I thought it might,' he said. 'I'll tell Sir James.'

Sir James Horley, QC, was now the lead in Steve Mitchell's defence. When Bruce Lygon had called Arthur to engage counsel for the case, Sir James had jumped at it. He could never be accused of not being eager to take on a celebrity client. Sir James loved the limelight. He adored the television cameras waiting each day outside court so that they could show him on the six o'clock news.

I still had not yet told anyone of my encounter with the murder victim in the showers at Sandown. It had been so long since I should have said something that I couldn't really do so now without placing myself in a very compromising position. I would be damned if I did, and damned if I didn't, but, in the latter case, only if anyone else knew about it from Barlow.

Within just a few hours of the appointment of Sir James Horley as defence QC being posted on the courts' website, I had received a call on my mobile.

'I told you to take the Mitchell case,' the quiet, well-spoken whisperer had said. 'Why are you not listed as the defence barrister?'

I had tried to explain that a QC would always have to lead in such a high-profile case and I wasn't one. I had told him that I would be assisting.

'You are to ensure Mitchell loses,' he had said.

'Why?' I had asked him.

'Just do it,' he had said, and then he'd hung up.

As before, he had withheld his number.

Why, indeed, did they, whoever 'they' were, want Mitchell to lose? Was it to have someone else convicted of their crime, or were they simply making sure he got his just deserts? How would they know he was guilty unless they were there with him at the time?

No, I still believed that Steve was being set up.

Although all the disclosed prosecution evidence put together would be very convincing to a jury, any part of it on its own could be described as circumstantial. No one questioned that the pitchfork, the murder weapon, had belonged to Steve Mitchell, but his pitchforks had not been kept locked away and anyone could have taken one of them. Blood and hairs from the victim had been found on a pair of Mitchell's Wellington boots as well as in his car, but the boots had been kept in the same feed store as the pitchfork. The Defence Case Statement stated that Mr Mitchell was being framed for the crime that someone else, unknown, had committed. And that the crime had been planned meticulously so as to appear to have been perpetrated by our client.

The prosecution had been unable to establish definitively that Mitchell had sent the threatening text message to Barlow. It could only be determined by the police that it had been sent by a free texting service accessible from any computer, anywhere in the world.

The betting receipts, however, did belong to Steve Mitchell and he had been stupid enough to have his own name on them. Steve denied that they were his but even I knew he wasn't telling the truth. I had told to him firmly that the time for lying about betting was now over, he had more serious allegations to deal with, but he was so used to denying that he gambled that it came naturally to him to continue to do so.

I had explained to Steve that if he had an alibi he must declare it prior to the trial. To suddenly produce one in court would not assist his case.

However, he had remained adamant that he had been on his own at home reading all afternoon on that Monday.

'Steve,' I had implored, 'I don't believe you. If you were with someone, perhaps someone you shouldn't have been with, you must tell me now.'

'I tell you, I was on my own,' he had said. 'That's the truth. What do you want me to do? Lie?'

I had thought that it would be counterproductive to say that I knew he had lied to me before about the ending of his affair with Millie Barlow.

'Don't you realise the mess you are in?' I'd shouted at him, banging on the grey metal table with my fist. 'You're facing a long stretch in prison for this. It's not some game in the park, you know.'

'I can't,' he had said finally.

'Is she married?' I had asked, guessing the reason.

'Yes,' he'd said. 'And I don't even think I was with her when that bastard Barlow got himself killed. It was a last-minute lunchtime bonk, arranged when the racing at Ludlow was called off. I'm not embroiling her in this mess when it wouldn't even give me an alibi for the right time.'

The prosecution case was that Barlow had died sometime between two and four in the afternoon. His body had been discovered around six by a policeman responding to an anonymous call to Newbury police station about an intruder at Honeysuckle Cottage.

'The fact that you were not alone all of the time from one o'clock until six might help to plant some doubt in the minds of the jury,' I had told him.

'She was gone by two thirty at the latest,' he'd said. 'So what difference would it make? Barlow's bloody house is only ten minutes' drive from mine. I could easily have been there well before three, so it's not a bloody alibi. No. I won't get her involved.'

'Tell me who it was,' I had said to him. 'Then I can ask her if she would be prepared to give a statement to the police.'

'No,' he had said. And he had been silent on the matter ever since.

I had also asked him about Millie Barlow and why he hadn't told me about her death at our first meeting.

'I didn't think that it was that important,' he'd said.

'Of course it was important,' I had shouted at him. 'You tell me absolutely everything and I'll decide whether it's important or not.'

He had looked at me with big eyes, like a scolded puppy. 'I didn't do it, you know,' he'd said mournfully.

'So did Barlow blame you for his sister's suicide?' I had asked him.

'All the bloody time,' he'd replied. 'Called me a bloody murderer. I told him to shut up or I'd bloody murder him.' Steve had suddenly stopped and looked up at my face. 'But I didn't, I promise you I didn't.' He had then buried his head in his hands and begun to sob.

'It's all right, Steve,' I'd said, trying to reassure him. 'I know you didn't do it.'

He had looked back at my face. 'Convince the bloody jury, then.'

Maybe that is what I should do, I thought, sitting here at my desk. Perhaps I should tell the jury that I had been threatened to make sure I lost in court. Then I could become a witness in the case and tell the jury all about baseball bats and Julian Trent. Would that be enough to help Steve? It might just support our belief that Steve was being framed.

But where would that leave me? I wondered. Did I just sit and wait to have my head smashed in and my balls cut off? And how about my elderly father? What danger would I be putting him in? It seemed to me that the only solution to my multiple dilemmas was to discover who was intimidating me and then show that they were the true murderers of Scot Barlow.

Simple, I thought. But where do I start?

Julian Trent. He must be the key.

THE FOLLOWING MORNING Sir James Horley, QC, and I sat on one side of the table in the small conference room on the lower ground floor in chambers. Bruce Lygon sat opposite us. For two hours we had been once again going through every aspect of the prosecution case.

The prosecution was required to disclose to the defence anything that they, or the police, had discovered that would assist us based on our Defence Case Statement. The response had been that they had no information other than that already disclosed in their primary disclosure and Statement of Case. We hadn't really expected anything.

'Are you sure that Mitchell shouldn't plead guilty?' said Sir James. 'The case against him is very strong.' I wondered, ungraciously, if Sir James liked the idea of a guilty plea to save him a courtroom loss.

'He's adamant that he will not plead guilty to something he didn't do,' I said firmly. 'Our defence is that our client is being framed.'

'Then we had better find out who's framing him,' said Sir James. 'Otherwise we shall have egg on our faces. Trial date is set for the second week in May at Oxford. That's eight weeks from now. I suggest we meet again in two weeks to see if we are any further on.'

I went back to my room. I had ordered a transcript of the Julian Trent appeal hearing from last November and now I sat at my desk and scanned its close-typed pages looking for a certain name.

Josef Hughes of 845 Finchley Road, Golders Green, north London, was the rogue solicitor who had forced the appeal. It was his supposed intervention with the jury that had got Trent off. If, as I suspected, he had been coerced into giving evidence to the Court of Appeal, he might be prepared to help me find out how Julian Trent was connected to Scot Barlow's murder.

I WENT TO GOLDERS GREEN first thing on Wednesday morning.

Josef Hughes went white and his knees buckled as soon as I mentioned Julian Trent. I thought he was going to pass out completely in the doorway of his bedsit. He might have collapsed to the floor if I hadn't helped him through the door and into the room. He sat down heavily on the side of the double bed that took up most of the available floor space.

We were not alone. A young woman sat on an upright wooden chair nursing a young baby. She stared at me silently with big brown, frightened eyes.

I looked around. Apart from the green blanket-covered bed and the chair, there was a small square table under the window, another upright chair and a tiny kitchenette in the corner.

I went over to the kitchen sink to fetch Josef a glass of water. There was a chipped coffee mug upturned on the drainer. I splashed some water into it and held it out to him. He drank some of the water and the colour in his face improved fractionally.

'It's all right,' I said in as comforting a manner as I could muster. 'I haven't been sent here by Julian Trent.'

At the sound of the name, the young woman gave out a slight moan and curled her body round the child as protection.

What had Julian Trent done to these people to make them so afraid?

I looked around the room again. Everything was very basic, with threadbare carpets, paper-thin curtains and bare cream-painted walls.

'We used to have the big flat on the top floor,' said the young woman, watching me look. 'With our own bathroom. Then Joe lost his job and we had to move down here. Now, we share a bathroom with three other rooms.'

'How old is the baby?' I asked her.

'Eight months on Friday,' she said. I thought she was close to tears.

'What's your name?' I asked her, smiling.

'Bridget,' she said.

'What do you want?' Josef said.

'Tell me what happened,' I said quietly.

Josef shivered next to me.

'It was a man,' said Bridget. 'He came here, to our flat upstairs.'

'No,' said Josef suddenly and forcefully.

'Yes,' said Bridget back to him. 'We need to tell someone. I can't go on living like this.' She started to cry.

'I promise you,' I said, 'I'm here to try to help you.' And to help myself.

'He broke my arm,' said Bridget quietly. 'I was six months pregnant with Rory and he came into our flat, hit me in the face and punched me in my stomach. Then he broke my arm by slamming it in the door.'

'Who did?' I asked her. Surely, I thought, Julian Trent had been in prison.

'Julian Trent's father.'

IN THE END, between them, they told me everything. It was a horror show.

The man who had said he was Julian Trent's father had arrived wearing a smart suit and tie one evening soon after Josef had arrived home from his work at the Crown Prosecution Service. Josef had qualified as a solicitor only the year before and had loved his job with the CPS. He and Bridget had married while he was at the College of Law and they had moved into their first family home together in preparation for the birth of their first child. Everything was fine and they had been blissfully happy. That is, until the shadow of Julian Trent had been cast over their lives.

Initially the man had been nice and even offered Josef money to get some information for him.

'What information?' I asked him.

'Names and addresses of jurors,' he said.

'In the Julian Trent trial?' I asked, but I already knew the answer.

He nodded. 'The jurors' names are in the transcript,' he said. The jurors' names may have been in the public domain, but their addresses wouldn't have been.

'And we really needed the money,' said Bridget. 'What with the baby coming, there were things we had to buy.'

'But you knew it was wrong,' I said to him. It was against the Law Society rules, and would quite likely have been in contempt of court.

He nodded again.

'So when did he come back?' I asked them.

'The following day,' Josef said. 'He was meant to be bringing the money for the information I had ready for him.' Tears welled up in his eyes. 'I couldn't believe it. He just walked straight into the flat and hit Bridget. He knocked her down; then he dragged her over to the door and broke her arm while she was lying on the floor.' The tears began to flow and he swallowed hard. 'I felt so helpless.' Bridget placed a hand on his arm.

'Then what happened?' I said.

'He said to give him the information immediately or he'd break Bridget's other arm.' He sobbed again. 'I had to get an ambulance,' he said when his sobs had diminished a little. 'We were so afraid we would lose the baby. Bridget was in hospital for nearly a week.'

'Did you call the police?' I asked him.

'No.' He cried again. 'The man said he would come back and make Bridget lose the baby if we told anyone.'

'But he came back?' I asked him.

'No,' he said. 'He sent me a letter after the trial was over.'

'Saying what?' I asked, but I suspected I already knew that, too.

'He told me to go to Julian Trent's lawyer and tell him that I had talked to some of the jury to try and ensure that Julian Trent was convicted,' he said in a rush. 'But I hadn't, I swear it.'

'What was the name of the lawyer?' I asked.

'Some solicitor in Weybridge,' he said. 'I can't remember the name.'

'Please try to remember who it was,' I said to him. The solicitor who had engaged me to act for Trent had not been from Weybridge.

'I can't,' he said. 'I had it on the letter, but the lawyer took that. I know it was in Weybridge High Street, above some shops.'

'Was there anything else with the letter?' I asked.

'There was a photograph.' He gulped. 'It showed Bridget and me coming out of her antenatal class. Someone had drawn an arrow on it with a red marker pen. The arrow was sticking into her stomach.'

ALTOGETHER I SPENT more than an hour with Josef and Bridget Hughes. Their lives had been totally destroyed by the man offering money for information. Josef had been stripped of his professional qualifications and avoided prosecution only by a whisker. He had to do casual work stacking supermarket shelves at night. He would come home in the mornings with out-of-date food as part of his wages.

'Please help us,' Josef pleaded as he came downstairs to the main door of the property. 'I only keep going for Bee and Rory.'

'How can I contact you?' I asked him.

'There's a payphone here.' He pointed at it just inside the front door and I took down the number.

I also gave him one of my cards. 'Call me if you need anything,' I said.

He nodded slightly, but I doubted that he would. His life may have been in tatters but he had kept his pride.

We shook hands inside the hallway and Josef peered cautiously round the door as he opened it to the street. I pressed some banknotes into his hand.

'Buy some food for the baby,' I said.

'Thank you,' he mumbled. Things were so bad that he couldn't refuse the cash, even though he clearly hated not doing so.

NEXT I WENT TO HENDON, in north London, to see one of the three jurors from the original trial who had testified at the appeal.

George Barnett tried to slam the door in my face. He was the school-masterly gentleman who had been the jury foreman, but he seemed a shadow of his former self. Gone were the upright posture and the air of self-assurance. In their place there was an old-age stoop, and fear. Lots of fear.

'Go away,' he shouted through the crack in the door that my foot was preventing from closing. 'I did what you asked. Now leave me alone.'

'Mr Barnett,' I called to him, 'I've come here to try to help you. I have not been sent by Mr Trent.'

There was a muffled 'Oh God' from inside and he pushed harder on the door. 'Go away,' he shouted again.

'Mr Barnett,' I called again, not moving my foot out of the door. 'I was also beaten up by Julian Trent. I want to find out why. I need your help.'

'Please go away,' he said again, pleading.

'All right,' I said. I lifted my foot and he slammed the door shut.

'Mr Barnett,' I called through the door, 'do you want to spend the rest of your life in fear, or do you want to help me stop these people?' I pushed one of my cards through his letterbox. 'Call me if you change your mind. I promise I'm on your side.'

He hadn't told me anything useful but he had at least confirmed what I had suspected: Julian Trent, together with his friends and relations, had left a trail of broken lives wherever they went, intimidating good people into doing what they wouldn't normally contemplate and perverting the course of justice for their own ends.

It was time to take a stand.

CHAPTER 5

On Thursday I left my troubles behind and went to Cheltenham. The Foxhunter Chase, my ambition, was the following afternoon, directly after the Gold Cup. Thursday was World Hurdle day, the long-distance hurdle race for the best 'stayers' in the country.

Today I was a guest of a Lambourn horse-transport company that had hired a private box. I had acted for them the previous year when I had successfully defended a charge of careless driving against one of their drivers.

The private box was on the top level of the huge grandstand that would later hold tens of thousands of cheering race fans. This was the meeting that all owners, trainers and jockeys worked towards for the preceding twelve months. The Grand National may be the most famous English steeplechase, but the Cheltenham Festival is where most would love to win.

'Ah, Geoffrey.' Edward Cartwright, the transport-company owner, extended a large plump hand as he came to meet me at the door. I shook it warmly. 'Welcome to Cheltenham,' he said. 'Let's hope for a great day.'

The box was about four metres square, and the centre was taken up with a large cloth-covered table set for lunch. I gratefully accepted a glass of champagne that a waitress offered and then went out to join some of the other guests on the viewing balcony.

'Hello,' said one of them. 'Remember me?'

'Of course,' I said, shaking his hand. I had last seen him at the equine hospital in November. 'How's the yearling?'

'Two-year-old now,' Simon Dacey said. 'No apparent ill effects. Almost ready for the racecourse. Can I introduce you to my wife, Francesca?'

I shook the offered petite hand. Francesca Dacey was blonde, tall, slim and wearing a yellow suit that touched her in all the right places. We smiled at each other. Simon waved towards the other two people on the balcony, a middle-aged couple, he in a pinstripe suit and she in an elegant long brown open jacket over a cream top and brown slacks. 'And Roger and Deborah Radcliffe.' Ah, I realised, they were the Peninsula connections.

'Congratulations last June,' I said. 'With the Derby.'

'Thank you,' said Deborah Radcliffe. 'Greatest day of our lives.'

I could imagine. To win the Epsom Derby must be anyone's life ambition.

'I'm so sorry,' said Simon Dacey. 'I remember you have horses with Paul Newington, but I'm afraid I have forgotten your name.'

'Geoffrey Mason,' I said.

'Ah, yes, Geoffrey Mason. Lawyer, I think you said?'

'Yes, that's right,' I replied. 'But I'm here as an amateur jockey.' I smiled. 'I have a ride in the Foxhunters tomorrow.'

'Best of luck,' said Deborah Radcliffe, rather dismissively. 'We don't have any jumpers.' She gave the impression that she believed jumpers weren't real racehorses, and not like proper racing on the flat. More fool her, I thought.

Roger Radcliffe, who obviously agreed with her, moved back inside the box to replenish his champagne. Why, I wondered, did they bother to come if they weren't excited by the racing? Francesca Dacey and Deborah Radcliffe moved to the far end of the balcony for, I imagined, some girlie talk. It left Simon and me standing alone. There was an awkward silence for a few moments.

'Didn't you say you were acting for Steve Mitchell?' Simon Dacey finally asked, almost with relief.

'That's right,' I said, relaxing. 'I'm one of his barristers.'

'Do you really think he's innocent?' he asked me.

'That's not relevant,' I said. 'I don't have to prove his innocence, just create a reasonable doubt in the jury's mind about his guilt.'

He shook his head. 'It's a funny old system,' he said.

'I agree,' I said. 'But it has worked pretty well for hundreds of years.' The jury system had its origins in Roman times, when huge juries would vote on the guilt or innocence of the accused. The right to be judged by a jury of one's peers for all but very minor offences was established under law in England as far back as the thirteenth century. 'Have you ever heard of anyone called Julian Trent?'

'No,' he said. 'Should I? Is he in racing?'

'No, I don't think so,' I said. 'I asked just on the offchance.' If he was lying, he was good at it.

The waitress popped her head round the door and informed us that lunch was about to be served, so would we please take our seats.

I FOUND MYSELF SITTING between Francesca Dacey and Joanna, wife of Nicholas Osbourne, the trainer I had gone to in Lambourn all those years ago. Nicholas and I had nodded cordially to each other as we had sat down.

'So tell me what you're up to,' Joanna said, as we ate the starter of steamed asparagus with hollandaise sauce.

'I'm representing Steve Mitchell,' I said.

Francesca Dacey, on my other side, jumped a little in her seat.

'How exciting,' said Joanna with relish. 'Is he guilty?'

'That's for the jury to decide,' I said.

'Don't be so boring,' Joanna said. 'Tell me, did he do it?'

'What do you think?' I asked her. Francesca was trying not to show that she was listening.

'He must have,' she said. 'They wouldn't have arrested him if he didn't do it. And everyone knows Barlow and Mitchell hated each other's guts.'

'That doesn't make him a murderer,' I said. 'In fact, if everyone knew that he hated Barlow, then he was the obvious person to frame for his murder.'

Our empty starter plates were removed and replaced with the main course of chicken breast in a mustard sauce.

Joanna turned to talk to the man on her left, another trainer. I, meanwhile, turned to Francesca. She was giving a good impression of a health inspector, so keen was she to keep her eyes firmly fixed on her food.

'So how long have you known Steve Mitchell?' I asked her quietly.

'I don't,' she said. But both of us knew she was lying.

'Were you with him the day Scot Barlow died?' I asked her, so quietly that no one else would have been able to hear.

'No,' she replied in the same manner. 'I don't know what you mean.'

'Were you really gone from Steve's house by two thirty?' I said, keeping my eyes firmly on my chicken.

'Oh God,' she said. I thought for a moment that she was going to get up and leave, but she took a couple of deep breaths. 'Yes,' she said. 'I had to be home by two thirty to meet the plumber. He came to fix the dishwasher.'

So, just as Steve had told me, getting her involved wouldn't actually give him an alibi for Barlow's murder.

'Steve didn't tell me,' I said, turning towards her and keeping my voice low so that others wouldn't hear. 'He refused to say who it was he was with.'

She gulped. 'Please don't tell my husband,' she pleaded in a whisper.

'No,' I said. 'No need to.'

She half coughed, half sobbed and then suddenly stood up. 'Sorry,' she croaked to our host. 'Something went down the wrong way.' She rushed out, holding a white linen napkin to her face.

CHELTENHAM DURING THE FESTIVAL is like no other day at the races anywhere in the world. After lunch I wandered around absorbing the atmosphere. I walked down to the Guinness Village, now an institution at the track and transient home to thousands of Irish whose annual pilgrimage to Gloucestershire does much to make this event unique. Irish folk bands and English rock bands vied for favour in the huge marquee behind a temporary grandstand, entertaining the crowd prior to the main attraction of the afternoon, the racing.

I leaned on the white rail next to the horse walk to watch a quartet of happy punters from across the Irish Sea. Aided and abetted by a continuous flow of Guinness, they had linked arms in a line and were trying to perform an Irish jig.

'Hello, stranger,' said a familiar voice behind me. I smiled broadly and turned round.

'Hello, Eleanor,' I said, and gave her a kiss on the cheek. 'How lovely to see you. Are you here for work or pleasure?'

'Both really,' she said. 'I am technically on call but that means I can do pretty much what I want. I just have to carry a bleep.'

'Fancy a drink?' I asked.

'Yes, but not here,' she said, indicating the Guinness bar.

'No,' I agreed. 'Come on, let's go up to the boxes.'

I was sure that Edward Cartwright, my host, wouldn't mind me bringing Eleanor into his box and so it turned out. In fact, he rather monopolised her and left me wishing we had stayed in the crush downstairs.

I had seen Eleanor twice since November. The first time had been in London, when I had asked her to a black-tie dinner in the hall at Gray's Inn. It hadn't been a particularly successful evening. The seating plan had us sitting opposite each other and conversation between us had been difficult because of the noise of three hundred people talking, and because the centre of the table was full of flowers and candelabras. We had hardly spoken to each other the whole evening and I think she had been bored by the lawyers' speeches. At the end of the dinner she had rushed off to Paddington for the last train home.

Why I had asked her to that dinner, I could not imagine. If I had wanted a romantic evening à deux, I couldn't have chosen anything less appropriate. Maybe I was scared to embark on a new amorous adventure. It also made me feel guilty that I was somehow deserting Angela.

The second time we had met, we had both been guests at a Christmas ball thrown by a big racing sponsor at Newbury racecourse. I had been delighted to see her again and immediately asked her to dance, but she had been with someone else and he'd been determined that I wouldn't get a look-in with 'his' girl. I had felt wretched all evening.

'Penny for your thoughts,' Eleanor said, coming up behind me again. I had been leaning on the balcony rail watching the crowds below and I hadn't noticed her escape Edward's clutches and come outside to join me.

'You,' I said, turning and looking into her blue eyes.

She blushed, crimson spreading up from her neck and over her face.

'Did you know,' I said, 'that if you are naked you blush all over your body.'

'Bastard,' she said. She turned away and laughed.

'What are you doing tonight?' I asked her.

'I'm not coming to another of your awful dining-in nights, that's for sure.'

We laughed together.

'I have to admit that it was a bit of a disaster,' I agreed.

'I had always thought lawyers were boring, and now I know they are.'

'You just haven't met the right lawyers,' I said.

She paused and smiled at me. 'Oh yes I have,' she said.

SADLY, I DIDN'T SPEND the evening with Eleanor. Her bleep went off as we were still on the balcony. She had to go back to Lambourn for an emergency at the hospital, something about a prize stallion and a twisted gut.

'Will you be here tomorrow?' I shouted after her rather forlornly as she rushed away.

'Hope so,' she called back. 'Call me on the mobile in the morning.'

Suddenly she was gone. I was surprised at how disappointed I felt. Was I really ready after seven and a half years? Don't rush things, I told myself.

The World Hurdle, the big race of the day, was a three-mile hurdle race for horses with stamina for the long distance, especially the uphill finish in the March mud. And stamina they had. Four horses crossed the last obstacle abreast and each was driven hard for the line, the crowd cheering them on, the result to be determined only by the race judge and his photographs.

There was a buzz in the crowd after the horses swept past the winning post, such had been the effect of the closest of finishes. These moments were what brought the crowds to Cheltenham. The best horses, ridden by the best jockeys, stretching to reach the line first. Winning was everything.

'First, number seven,' said the announcer to a huge cheer from some and a groan from others. The jockey on horse number seven stood up in his stirrups and punched the air. How I longed for it to be me doing that the following afternoon.

Most of the guests rushed off to watch the winner come back to the unsaddling enclosure. I, however, decided to stay put.

The lunch table was now heaving under trays of sandwiches and cakes ready for tea. I looked longingly at a chocolate éclair.

'I hear you are a lawyer,' said a female voice on my right.

I turned to find Deborah Radcliffe next to me. Why did I think she didn't like lawyers? Maybe it was the way she looked down her nose at me.

'That's right,' I said, smiling at her. 'I'm a barrister.'

'Do you wear a wig?'

'Only in court,' I replied. 'Lots of my work is not done in courts.'

'Oh,' she said, as if bored. 'And do you represent jockeys at inquiries?'

'I have done,' I said. 'But not very often. How is Peninsula?'

'Fine, as far as I know,' she said, showing more interest. 'He's now at Rushmore Stud in Ireland. In his first season.'

Retired at the age of three to spend the rest of his life being treated like royalty, passing his days eating, sleeping and covering mares. Horse paradise.

'But he wasn't born at Rushmore?' I said.

'Oh, no,' she replied. 'We bred him at home.'

'Where's home?'

'Near Uffington,' she said. 'In south Oxfordshire.'

'Do you remember Millie Barlow being there when Peninsula was born?' I asked. 'She was the vet who was present.'

'Not really,' she said. 'We have foals being born all the time. Why do you ask?'

'It's just that she killed herself last June and I wondered if you remembered her,' I replied.

'Not that vet who killed herself during the party?'

I nodded.

'I remember her doing that, of course,' she said. 'But I didn't know it was the same vet who had been there to foal Peninsula.'

'So you didn't see a photo of her with Peninsula after the birth?'

'No,' she said emphatically. 'Why? Should I have done?'

'It seems to have gone missing,' I said.

'Sorry,' she said, losing interest again. 'I can't help you.'

I WOKE EARLY the following morning with butterflies in my stomach. The Foxhunter Chase at Cheltenham is known as the amateur riders' Gold Cup. It is run over the same course and distance as its big brother, although, while the Gold Cup had the highest prize money at the Festival, the Foxhunter Chase had the lowest. But it wasn't the prize money that mattered. For me, winning the Foxhunters would be like winning the Gold Cup, the Grand National and the Derby all rolled into one.

I called Eleanor.

'Hello,' she said, sounding sleepy.

'Late night?' I asked.

'I was in theatre until nearly four,' she told me.

My heart sank. I had so hoped she would be there to see me ride.

'Are you coming today?' I asked without any real hope.

'Probably not,' she said. 'I'm still technically on call. I must get some sleep. I'll try and be there, but if I don't make it, I'll make sure I watch it on the telly.' She yawned. 'Call me after. From the winner's circle.'

'I hope so,' I replied, with more of a smile in my voice.

By the time of the first race at two o'clock my guts were twisted tighter than those of Eleanor's equine patient. I sat on the bench round the changing room and made myself calm down. I even managed to force down a cheese and pickle sandwich. I spent much of the afternoon running the race over and over in my head. Sandeman was fit and so was I. Today both horse and jockey would have the stamina to come up the Cheltenham hill after three and a quarter miles.

I stood on the scales in my riding clothes holding my saddle. The digital read-out settled on twelve stone, the required mark, and the clerk of the scales ticked me off on his list. All that running and skiing had done the trick.

Having successfully cleared the scales, I handed my saddle and the rest of the tack to Paul Newington, who was standing by waiting to receive it.

'See you in the parade ring,' he said, and he hurried away to get Sandeman ready in the saddling boxes. I could tell that he too was nervous.

I went back into the changing room and paced around. With the Gold Cup now over, the Foxhunter Chase was less than half an hour away and the butterflies in my stomach had turned into full-size eagles. I made all my last-minute adjustments, making sure that my back protector was correctly fitted, checking that my silks were on properly with rubber bands round the wrists to stop the wind rushing up the sleeves, retying the cords on my cap to ensure it didn't fly off my helmet during the race. It was like waiting outside the exam room before my law finals at university.

Eventually, the call was made for the jockeys to go out to the parade ring. As always, I felt a burst of adrenaline course through my body, but this time, I wasn't sure I was enjoying it. Riding last year's winner and this year's favourite was taking much of the fun out of it.

Paul and Laura stood on the grass in the paddock and both seemed to hop from foot to foot with nervousness.

'Good luck,' said Laura breathlessly, giving me a kiss on the cheek.

Paul gave me a leg-up onto Sandeman's back and slapped a hand on his neck. 'Go get 'em, cowboy,' he said in a mock-American accent.

'Do my best, pardner,' I said back to him.

We were led out towards the course by two huntsmen in scarlet jackets. Sandeman beneath me was eager to get going and he didn't like being crammed in on all sides by the massive crowd five deep against the horse-walk rail.

'Good luck, Geoffrey,' called a voice to my left.

I looked down from my vantage point atop a seventeen-hand horse and there was Eleanor, waving madly. She had made it after all. How wonderful.

'Thanks,' I shouted at her inadequately above the bustle of the crowd.

I turned to take one last look at her before Sandeman and I went out onto the course. She was smiling broadly, still waving, but someone else caught my eye.

Standing just behind her was Julian Trent, and he was smiling at me too.

Oh shit. I tried to shout to Eleanor but she didn't hear me. I wanted to jump off, to run back, to protect her, but Sandeman and I were now on the course, walking up in front of the expectant crowd. Surely, I told myself, Eleanor would be safe among all those people. Perhaps Trent had not seen the exchange between us and would think of her as another eager spectator.

The horses were to be led up in front of the grandstand and then we would turn and canter back to the start of the race. So distracted was I that I almost fell off when the stable lad turned Sandeman and let him go with a reminding slap on his rump. Instinct made me gather the reins tight in my hands and set off in a gentle canter to the start while I searched the faces in the crowd, desperate for a glimpse of Eleanor.

I felt sick.

All my pre-race planning of where I wanted to be at the start went out of the window. When the tapes flew up, Sandeman was caught flat-footed owing to my negligence and I instantly gave the rest of the field ten lengths' start. I could imagine Paul swearing on the trainers' stand, but somehow I didn't care. I was more concerned about Eleanor's safety.

Sandeman set off in pursuit of the others and made a magnificent leap at the first with me hardly participating at all. Come on, I said to myself, Eleanor will be fine, concentrate on the matter in hand.

I eased Sandeman back from his headlong gallop to a steadier pace and we gradually closed the gap. This was a three-and-a-quarter-mile chase with twenty-two jumps, twice round the course. Fortunately the first circuit was not being run too fast as everyone realised there was a long way to go in fairly heavy ground.

At the top of the hill for the first time, I pulled Sandeman slightly wider and we overtook eight other horses easily in the run down to the point where we had started. As we began the second circuit, we were in the middle of the pack, lying about tenth, but with those ahead tightly bunched.

By the time we reached the water jump halfway down the back straight the race was really on in earnest. Sandeman flattened his back and sailed over the water like a hurdler. We passed three horses in midair and landed running fast. But two other horses had got away at the front of the pack and a three-length gap had opened up behind them.

I kicked Sandeman hard in the ribs. 'Come on, boy,' I shouted in his ear. 'Now is the time.'

It was as if he changed gear. We were eating up the ground and two great leaps at the open ditches found us lying third, turning left and starting down the hill for the last time.

I was exhilarated. I looked ahead. The two horses in front seemed also to be going well and they were about four lengths away, running side by side.

I gave Sandeman a bit of a breather for a few paces, sitting easily on his back rather than pushing hard at his neck. There were two fences down the hill. I adjusted Sandeman's stride and asked him for a big leap. He responded immediately and flew through the top of the first fence, gaining half the distance on his rivals ahead.

I now kicked him and asked for his final effort. We needed to be ahead at the last with the momentum to carry us up the hill to the finish in front.

'Come on, boy,' I shouted again in his ear. 'Now, now, now.'

Both the horses in front wavered slightly as they approached the fence and I knew, I suddenly knew, that we were going to win.

I gave a slight pull on the reins, setting Sandeman right for another great leap. I was watching the ground, looking at our takeoff point, and only peripherally did I see one of the horses ahead hit the top of the fence hard. I pulled Sandeman slightly wider, but it was the wrong way. The horse in front overbalanced badly on landing, and rolled sharply to its right onto the ground, straight into our path. Sandeman and I were in midair before I realised that we had nowhere to land.

Sandeman tripped over the bulk of prostrate horseflesh in front of him and somersaulted through the air. My last memory of the day was of the green grass rushing up to meet me, just before the blackness came.

CHAPTER 6
May 2009

I sat at my desk in chambers reading through the paperwork for an upcoming disciplinary hearing.

The phone on my desk rang. It was Arthur.

'Mr Mason,' he said, 'there's someone here to see you.'

'Who is it?' I asked.

'He won't say,' said Arthur, clearly disapproving. 'He just insists on talking to you, and only you. Shall I bring him along?'

'Yes, please,' I said. 'But will you stay here until I ask you to leave?'

'All right,' he said. 'But why?'

'Just in case I need a witness,' I said. But I hoped I wouldn't. Surely Julian Trent wouldn't show up and demand to see me in my room.

I put the phone down. It was a general rule that members of chambers met visitors only in one of the conference rooms on the lower ground floor, but, since I had returned to work after Cheltenham, Arthur had been kind enough to grant me special dispensation to meet people in my room. Climbing up and down even just a few stairs on crutches wasn't easy.

There was a knock on the door and Arthur entered, followed by a nervous-looking man with white hair, wearing the same light-coloured tweed jacket and blue and white striped shirt that I had seen before in court number 3 at the Old Bailey. It was the schoolmasterly foreman of the jury whom I had last glimpsed when I'd had my foot in his front door in Hendon.

'Hello, Mr Barnett. Good to see you,' I said. 'Come on in. Thank you, Arthur, that will be all.'

Arthur looked at me with a questioning expression. I smiled back at him and he turned on his heel and left. I stood up clumsily and held out my hand. George Barnett approached cautiously and briefly shook it.

'Please sit down,' I said to him, indicating the chair in front of my desk.

'Did Trent do that?' he asked, pointing at the cast that stretched from my left foot to my upper thigh.

'No,' I replied. 'I had a fall from a horse. Smashed my knee.'

'Oh,' he said. We sat for a moment in silence while he looked around at the mass of papers and boxes that filled my room.

'Mr Barnett,' I said, 'how can I help you?'

'I thought it was me who needed to help you,' he said.

'Yes, indeed,' I said, slightly surprised. 'Would you like some coffee or tea?'

'Tea would be lovely,' he said. 'Milk and one sugar.'

I lifted the phone on my desk and asked one of the junior clerks if he would be kind enough to fix it.

'Now, Mr Barnett,' I said, 'tell me everything.'

He was reluctant at first but he relaxed when the tea arrived, and the whole sorry story spilled out.

'I was pleased when I received the summons for jury service,' he said. 'I had been retired for four years and I thought it would be interesting.'

'What had you retired from?' I asked him.

'I was in the civil service,' he said. I had been wrong about him having been a schoolmaster.

'So tell me what happened,' I encouraged.

He looked around him as if about to tell a big secret that he didn't want anyone else to overhear. 'I turned up at the Old Bailey and was selected for a trial. I remember being so excited.'

'The Trent trial?' I said.

He nodded. 'It was all right for a while,' he said. 'Then during the first weekend a man came to see me at home.'

'Did he give a name?' I asked him.

'He said he was Julian Trent's father,' George Barnett replied, 'but I don't think he actually was. I called him Mr Trent a couple of times and I didn't think he realised I was talking to him. Well, I immediately told him to leave. I knew that we shouldn't talk to anyone about the case, especially not the defendant's family. But he wouldn't go away. Instead, he offered me money to vote not guilty.'

I sat quietly, waiting for him to continue.

'I told him to go to hell,' he said. 'But he just sat there in my living room and looked around him. He said that I had a nice place and it would be a shame if I lost it all, or if my wife was injured in an accident.' He stopped again. 'I asked him what he meant. He just smiled and said to work it out.'

'So did you vote not guilty?' I asked.

'My wife has Parkinson's disease,' he said. 'And a bad heart.' I assumed that meant yes, he had. 'I knew that you only need ten of the twelve people on the jury to vote guilty to convict, so my vote wouldn't really matter.' I suppose he was trying to justify himself, but he must surely have realised that the man would approach other jurors too.

'So what happened in the jury room?' I asked him. It was against the law for him to tell me and I could quite likely get disbarred for even asking him, but what difference did one more misdemeanour make? I thought.

'Nine of them said straight away that they thought he was guilty as hell. There were three of us who didn't.' He stopped. 'I think now that the man must have been to see all three of us. None of us could give any reason for saying he was not guilty. We just did. The others thought we were mad. One or two of them got really angry as the time dragged on and on.'

'But you did return a guilty verdict in the end,' I said.

'And it was me who had to say it in court as they had made me foreman right at the start. It was terrible.'

I remembered the nervousness with which he had delivered the verdicts.

'Who cracked?' I said.

'One of the other two,' he said. 'A woman. I was so relieved. I had often so nearly changed my vote, but every morning the man had called me and reminded me that my wife would have an accident if I didn't stay firm.'

I remembered the judge had kept calling the jury back into court to ask them to try again to reach a verdict on which at least ten of them agreed. It had taken more than six days.

'So what happened afterwards?' I asked him.

'Nothing for ages, at least a month,' he said. 'Then the man turned up at my door and pushed me over when I tried to shut him out. He simply walked into the house and kicked me twice in the stomach. I could hardly breathe. Then he went over to my wife and tipped her out of her wheelchair onto the floor.' His eyes filled with tears. 'It was absolutely horrid.'

I could see that it was.

'And he told you,' I said, 'to go to the police and say that you had been approached by a solicitor who had asked you to make sure you found Trent guilty?' It was a question but, as all barristers know, one should never ask a question to which you don't already know the answer.

He nodded and looked down into his lap. 'It was dreadful, lying like that in the court,' he said. 'The appeal judges kept asking me if I was telling the truth or saying it because I had been told to do so by someone else. I was sure they knew I was lying. I felt so ashamed.' He said the last part in little more than a whisper. 'That's why I'm here,' he said more strongly. 'When you came to my house, I was afraid of you. I've been afraid of nearly every-one for the past year. I've hardly been out of the house since the trial. I've been looking at your card for weeks and trying to pluck up the courage to come here.'

'I'm so glad you did,' I said. He smiled a little. 'And how is your wife?'

'They took her into a nursing home yesterday, poor thing. The Parkinson's is becoming too much for me to manage on my own. She's safe now. The security at the nursing home is pretty good.'

'And what would you like me to do about what you have told me?' I asked. 'Do you want to go to the police?'

'No,' he said quite firmly. He paused. 'I don't think so.'

'Are you still frightened of this man?' I asked.

'Damn right I am,' he said. 'But you can't live your life being too fright-ened to step out of your own house.'

'So what do we do?' I said.

'I don't know,' he said. 'Perhaps I shouldn't have come here. I'm sorry. I think I should go now.' He stood up.

'Mr Barnett,' I said, 'I won't tell anyone what you have told me, I promise. But if I try to stop this man and put him behind bars, will you help me?'

'How?' he asked.

'I don't know yet,' I said. 'Would you recognise the man again?'

'I certainly would,' he said. 'I'll never forget him.'

AFTER A SANDWICH LUNCH at my desk, I took a taxi to University College Hospital to see an orthopaedic surgeon, with my left leg resting straight across the back seat. Seven whole weeks had now passed since I had woken up in Cheltenham General Hospital with a pile-driver of a headache that had made my skull feel as if it were bursting. With a return to con-sciousness had also come the discovery that I had to remain flat on my back, my left leg in traction, with a myriad of tubes running from an impressive collection of clear plastic bags above my left shoulder to an intravenous needle contraption in my left arm.

'You are lucky to be alive,' a smiling nurse had cheerfully informed me. 'You've been in a coma for three days.'

'What happened?' I had croaked at her from inside a plastic oxygen mask.

'You fell off your horse.'

I had suddenly remembered everything up to the point of the fall.

'I didn't fall off,' I had croaked back at her. 'The horse fell.' An important distinction for every jockey. 'How is my horse?'

She had looked at me in amazement. 'I have no idea,' she had said.

Over the next few hours my headache had finally succumbed to increasing doses of intravenous morphine. Sometime after dark, a doctor had arrived and informed me of the full catalogue of injuries that I had sustained by hitting the ground at thirty miles an hour and then having more than half a ton of horse land on me.

My back was broken, he had said, with three vertebrae cracked right through, but, fortunately, my spinal cord was intact, thanks probably to the back protector that I had been wearing. Four of my ribs had been cracked and one of those had punctured a lung. My brain had been badly bruised. My left knee had been broken, and the doctor himself had operated to fix it as best he could but only time would tell how successful he had been.

'So will I live?' I had asked him flippantly.

'It was a bit touch and go for a while,' he had replied seriously. 'But I think you'll be fine in time.'

'And will I ride again?' I'd asked him more seriously.

'Again, time will tell,' he'd replied. 'It will depend on how mad you are. I personally think that all you jump jockeys are completely bonkers.'

It had only been when Paul and Laura Newington had come to see me later that evening that I had heard the full story of the disaster.

They had just been getting excited about the prospect of another win when Sandeman and I had spectacularly disappeared in a flurry of legs. Paul had run the half-mile from the grandstands down the course to where, lying unmoving on the turf, we had both been hidden from the sight of the thousands of spectators behind hastily erected canvas screens.

Sandeman, it appeared, had been badly winded and had damaged his back. He had taken fifteen minutes to get gingerly to his feet and only Paul's intervention had prevented the racecourse vet from putting him down. Fortunately for me, no questions had been asked about whether or not to shoot the jockey. I had been attended to by the racecourse doctor for nearly an hour before being lifted ever so carefully into an ambulance and driven away at a snail's pace.

'There was someone else down there as well,' he had said. 'A girl. Ran all the way down the course in high-heeled shoes. Nice looker. Called herself Eleanor. Do you know her?'

I'd nodded.

'She seemed a bit cut up about you,' he'd said, almost surprised.

'What happened to her?' I'd asked him.

'I don't know. I was so busy trying to get Sandeman sorted out.'

'How is he?' I'd asked him.

'Not great,' he'd said. 'He was taken straight to the equine hospital in Lambourn. They are treating him for a badly strained back.'

I'd laughed. 'Eleanor is a vet at that hospital.'

'I THINK THAT CAST can come off your leg,' said the orthopaedic surgeon. 'The X-rays show the knee mending well. But you will need to keep using the crutches and only put a little weight on it for a while.'

'What about my back?' I asked him.

'The scans show that the bones are mending slowly but you still need to keep that straitjacket on for another six weeks at least.'

He was referring to the hard white plastic shell that I wore to prevent me bending my back. It was in two halves that had been heat moulded to fit my torso exactly, the two parts being held together by half a dozen Velcro-covered nylon straps. The damned thing reached from just below my neck almost to my groin in the front and from my shoulder blades to the top of my buttocks behind. It made sitting near impossible, but wearing it had at least allowed me to walk around.

'Six weeks?' I said in exasperation. 'It's damned uncomfortable, you know. It makes me itch all the time.'

'Better than being paralysed,' he replied.

And there was no answer to that. I would just have to put up with the discomfort for another six weeks.

'When can I start riding again?' I asked him.

He stopped making notes and looked up. 'Are you serious?'

'Absolutely,' I said.

He put his pen down and looked at me. 'Well, I suppose from my point of view, all your bones will heal in a few months, but I would be worried about your head. The brain can only take so many knocks like that.'

'But I don't intend to ever land on my head again,' I said.

'No one intended there to be a second world war after the first one. But there was.'

WHEN I RETURNED to chambers later that afternoon, I felt I was walking on air, albeit with only one leg. The full-length cast had been heavy and annoyingly restrictive. It was such a joy to once again scratch an itch in my thigh, or to rub away an ache in my kneecap.

Arthur looked up at me from his desk as I hopped my way through the clerks' room. 'On the mend, I see,' he said.

'Slowly,' I agreed, smiling.

'There's another one of those hand-delivered envelopes in your box,' he said, wiping the smile from my face. 'It came while you were out.'

'Right,' I said. 'Thanks.'

Arthur looked me in the eye and I thought for a moment that he was going to ask me straight out what was in the envelope, but he didn't, instead returning his attention to something on his desk.

I went over to the boxes and stuffed the envelope into my trouser pocket before negotiating the corridor on my crutches to the privacy of my room.

I sat in my chair and carefully opened the envelope. As before there was a single sheet of folded paper, and a photograph. On the sheet of paper there were just two short lines, again in black capital letters.

JUST REMEMBER, LOSE THE CASE
MITCHELL GETS CONVICTED

The photograph showed Eleanor in her green scrubs walking along the path between the house she lived in and the equine hospital in Lambourn.

Why was it, I wondered, that I felt like I was being dangled on a string by an unknown hand, being made to dance a jig by some puppet master hidden from the light? Sometimes I even began to wonder if my fall at Cheltenham had been his doing, but I knew that was ridiculous.

I sat at my desk and turned the photo of Eleanor over and over in my hands. Even if Julian Trent had seen her call and wave to me at Cheltenham, how did he know where she worked?

I was pondering this question when my phone rang.

I picked it up with some trepidation but then heard a familiar voice.

'What did the doctor say?' Eleanor was asking.

'He told me I can go on living,' I replied with a smile.

'Good,' she said. 'So he must have told you that you were quite well enough to take me out to Maximillian's tonight whether you like it or not?'

I liked it.

'How's the conference?' I asked her. She was attending a two-day international equine-medicine symposium at the London Veterinary School.

'Boring,' she said. 'Look, I must dash. They're about to start a lecture about the caecum and its role in colic.'

'Sounds like fun,' I said.

'Anything but,' she said. 'See you at the restaurant at seven thirty.' She disconnected before I had time to say goodbye.

I had seen her four or five times since my fall at Cheltenham.

'Typical,' she had said when she first came to see me in hospital after I had woken up. 'I sit here beside him trying to wake him up for nearly three whole days and nights and then, when I have to go to work, hey presto, he opens his eyes.'

I had smiled at her. 'You didn't have to do that,' I'd said.

'I didn't have to,' she'd said. 'But I wanted to.'

That was nice, I'd thought.

She had been back to see me a couple more times and then helped me on the day I went back home. She had stayed that first night sleeping in the room that, seven and a half years before, Angela and I had so gleefully decorated with teddy bears' picnic wallpaper as a nursery for our unborn son, and which I hadn't yet bothered to change. But I think Eleanor had felt uneasy sleeping at my place, as uneasy as I had at her being there. She had stayed only one night in Barnes before returning to Lambourn, although we had spoken often on the telephone.

I liked her. I liked her a lot. But I still wasn't sure if I was ready for a serious relationship. However, I was greatly looking forward to seeing her for dinner, and I had a spring in my one-footed step as I finally left chambers at seven o'clock.

Julian Trent was standing next to the gate on to Theobald's Road, leaning on the gatepost, and I saw him immediately when I walked out of chambers.

There was no point in trying to run away. At the best speed I could manage on one leg and two crutches I would have hardly outrun a toddler, let alone a fit and healthy young man of twenty-four. I turned towards him and he watched me as I slowly covered the sixty or so yards between us. As I approached he took a few steps forward and I began to regret that I hadn't simply gone back inside my chambers as soon as I had seen him. However, I did gratefully note that he wasn't accompanied today by his sidekick, the baseball bat. He seemed about to say something to me but I beat him to it.

'What the hell do you want?' I shouted at him.

He seemed a little taken aback and looked around to see if anyone had heard me. Theobald's Road is a busy place at seven o'clock on a sunny May evening, and a continuous stream of pedestrians flowed past the gate. A few heads had turned as I'd shouted but no one had actually stopped.

'Didn't you hear me?' I shouted again. 'I asked what the hell you want.'

Trent was definitely unnerved by a reaction he hadn't been expecting.

'Did you get the message?' he said.

'Do you mean this?' I shouted at him, pulling the paper out of my trouser pocket and ripping it into several pieces. I threw the bits of paper into the air and they fluttered to the ground at his feet. 'Now sod off.'

'Stop shouting,' he hissed at me. 'Shut up.'

I stood my ground and raised one of my crutches as a potential weapon. 'I'll shut up,' I shouted, 'when you go away and leave me in peace.'

'Do as you're told,' he said menacingly, again almost under his breath.

'Why?' I shouted. 'Who wants me to? Who are you working for, you little creep? Get out of my life, do you hear? And stay out.'

One or two heads out on Theobald's Road turned our way and one man stopped and stared at us. Julian Trent seemed to be losing his nerve.

'You'll bloody regret this,' he said quietly through gritted teeth.

And with that, he was gone, dodging out via the gateway and off down Theobald's Road towards Clerkenwell.

I stood there for a moment breathing deeply and wondered if I had made a big mistake. Perhaps, as Trent had said, I would regret it. But simply rolling over was not an option.

I was aware that over the past few months I had become fairly ambivalent about the outcome of the Steve Mitchell trial. If he was convicted, then I would have nothing to fear from Julian Trent, or whoever was behind him. If he was acquitted, then I could hold my head up for justice.

Now, suddenly, the result became incredibly important to me.

ELEANOR WAS AT THE RESTAURANT before me. She was seated on a stool at the bar facing away from me. I had been looking forward to this evening all day, so why, all of a sudden, did I now experience the urge to run away?

She turned round on the stool, saw me at the door, smiled and waved. I waved back. What, I asked myself, was I really afraid of here? It was a question I couldn't even begin to answer.

Over dinner, Eleanor and I discussed everything except ourselves, and specifically our relationship. I asked her about the equine symposium.

'I've learned a lot,' she said over our starters. 'Several of the new treatments have potential for us in Lambourn. There are some wonderful things being done with artificial replacements.'

'Bionic horses,' I said flippantly. 'The six-million-dollar horse.'

'No. Much, much more than that,' she said, laughing. 'Peninsula was syndicated to stud for ten times that.'

'Wow,' I said. 'And to think he was foaled by a first-time vet.'

'Quite a responsibility,' she agreed. 'But, of course, they didn't know then how good he'd turn out to be.'

'I wish I had a copy of that photograph of Millie with Peninsula as a foal,' I said.

'You really think it's important?' Eleanor asked.

'I don't know,' I said. 'But whoever took it must have thought it was important to remove it from its frame and to wipe the frame clean. There were no fingerprints on it.'

'I remember that photograph so well,' Eleanor said. 'Millie kept it on the mantelpiece in her room and she was always polishing the frame.'

'Describe it,' I said.

'It was just a photo,' she said. 'Millie was kneeling on the straw with the foal's head in her lap. The stud groom was standing behind her. I think he was cleaning the mare after foaling, you know.'

'And you don't know who took the picture?' I asked her.

'No idea,' she said.

Our main courses arrived and we ate in silence for a few minutes.

'Tell me what the doctor told you,' Eleanor said between mouthfuls.

'I've got to wear this damned body shell for another six weeks at least,' I said, 'and it's very uncomfortable.'

The restaurant had kindly given us a booth and I was able to sit half sideways and lean back against the wall whenever it began to hurt too much.

'But at least that cast is off your leg,' she said.

'Thank goodness,' I said.

Main course finally gave way to coffee, with a Baileys on the rocks for Eleanor and a glass of port for me.

'I asked the surgeon when I could ride again,' I said.

'And?'

'He said that my bones would be fully healed and as good as new in a few months, but he wasn't so sure about my brain.'

'What about your brain?' she asked.

'He said it couldn't take too many bangs like that.'

'Seems all right to me,' she said, smiling broadly. The sparkle in her lovely blue eyes was there again; the same sparkle I had noticed at the equine hospital at our first meeting.

I smiled back. Then suddenly I looked away, almost in embarrassment.

'Tell me about her,' she said.

'About who?' I asked, but I knew who she meant before she replied.

'Angela,' she said softly. 'I need to know what I'm up against.'

I looked down at the table and cupped my mouth and nose in my hands. I breathed out heavily once or twice, feeling the hot air on my skin. Eleanor just sat quietly, an expectant expression on her face.

'She was a second-year student at King's reading clinical psychology,' I said. 'We were guests at the same party and we just clicked. Right there and then. We got married six months after that first meeting. We were blissfully happy together for five years. She wanted to have a baby as soon as we were married but I talked her into waiting until she had qualified. Then we discovered that having a child was not as straightforward as we thought. We tried *in vitro*—you know, test-tube baby and all that—and that worked straight away. We were both so pleased that she was carrying a boy.'

I stopped. Tears welled in my eyes for Angela and our unborn son.

'She was eight months pregnant when she died.' I had to stop again.

Eleanor reached across the table and took my hand.

'It was a pulmonary embolism,' I said. 'I found her lying on the floor. The doctors said it would have been very sudden.' I sighed loudly. 'That was more than seven years ago now. Sometimes it seems like yesterday.'

We sat there together in silence for what felt like ages until a waiter came over and asked us if we wanted some more coffee.

'Thanks,' I said, back in control. He poured the hot black liquid into our cups and then left us alone again.

'So,' said Eleanor with a sigh, 'not much chance for me, then.'

We laughed, a short embarrassed laugh.

'Give me some more time,' I said. But I'd had seven years. How much longer did I need? How could I dispel the feeling that making a fresh start would somehow be disloyal to Angela's memory?

'How much more time?' she said.

'I don't know,' I said in exasperation.

'But I need to,' she said in all seriousness. 'I like you a lot, Mr Barrister Man, but I do need some response if I'm going to invest my time and my emotions. I'm thirty-three years old and, as they say, my body clock is ticking. I want . . .' She tailed off and dropped her eyes.

'What?' I said.

'A house and kids and . . . family life,' she said, looking back up. 'When I started out as a vet, I only cared about my job and my career. I loved it, and I still do. But now I find I need more than just that.' She took my hand again in hers. 'And I think I want it with you.'

CHAPTER 7

In the morning a car from a private hire company came to collect me from my home. Eleanor had gone back to her hotel near Tower Bridge for the night. It wasn't that we took a conscious decision to go in opposite directions, it was just sensible logistically, as the equine symposium would start again at nine.

Bob, the driver, stepped out of the silver Mercedes to hold the door for me as I clambered awkwardly into the back seat. Then he carefully placed the crutches in the boot. I could get quite used to this, I thought, as I gave him directions to our first stop.

Sandeman was eating from his manger when I went in to see him. He looked casually in my direction, blew hard down his nostrils and then went back to his oats. I hobbled over to him and slapped his neck with the palm of my hand.

'Hello, old boy,' I said to him as I fondled his ears and rubbed his neck. He put his head down against me and pushed me playfully.

'Whoa,' I said, amused. 'Careful, my old boy, I'm not yet able to play.' I slapped him again a couple of times and left him in peace.

'He's doing well,' said Paul Newington at the door, from where he'd watched the exchange. 'We've started walking him every morning, and he has even trotted a bit round the paddock on a lunge. Still too early to put any weight on that back, but he doesn't seem to be in pain.'

'Good,' I said. 'Will he ever be able to race again?'

'I suspect he could,' he said. 'But he's thirteen now and he would quite likely not be fit enough to run before he becomes fourteen.' All horses in the northern hemisphere become a year older on January 1, irrespective of the actual day on which they were born.

'Are you saying he'd be too old?' I asked.

'Racehorses can race at that age,' he said. 'I'm just not sure it would be fair on the old boy.'

We stood there looking at my dear old horse.

'You think it's time to retire him?' I was miserable. Retiring Sandeman from the racecourse would be tantamount to retiring myself from race riding. I knew that I was too old to start again with a new horse.

'I do,' he said bluntly. 'And I do realise that it would quite likely mean that you wouldn't have a horse with me again.'

'But what would we do with him?' I asked forlornly.

'Now don't take this the wrong way,' he said, 'but I am in need of a new hack.'

'But what about old Debenture?' I said.

Debenture had been Paul's hack for almost as long as I could remember.

'He's too old now,' said Paul. 'It's time to put him out to grass.'

'Can Sandeman go on living in this stable?' I said.

'Geoffrey, you are far too sentimental,' he said, laughing. 'No way. He'll have to live in the dog kennel. Of course he can stay here.'

'Can I still ride him?' I asked.

'Geoffrey,' he said laying a hand on my shoulder, 'you don't want to ride him as a hack. If you really want to ride out, you can ride one of the others.'

'Do you mean that?' I asked, surprised.

'Of course I do,' he said. 'Come any time you like, as long as you stay reasonably fit, and light. I won't let you if you go over twelve stone.'

'I have absolutely no intention of doing that,' I said.

'That's what all those fat ex-jockeys said.' He laughed.

Sandeman finished his lunch and came over to the stable door for an apple from my pocket. I rubbed his ears and massaged his neck.

'Well, old boy,' I said to him, 'seems like you and I have run our last race.'

Somehow this felt like a defining moment in my life. Gone, abruptly and unexpectedly, were the days of excitement and adrenaline that I had coveted for so long. Suddenly, I was no longer an injured jockey on the road to recovery and my next ride. I had become an ex-jockey, and I was very aware of having lost something. There was an emptiness in me, as if a part of my soul had been surgically excised.

'Are you OK?' said Paul, as if he, too, was aware of the significance of the moment.

'Fine,' I said to him with a smile. But inside I was hurting.

'You'll just have to get a new hobby,' Paul said.

But riding races had never felt like a hobby to me. It had been what I had lived for, especially these past seven years. It really was time to get a new life, and now I didn't have any choice in the matter.

I STAYED FOR a leisurely lunch with Paul and Laura, and then Bob drove me further west to Uffington and the Radcliffe Foaling Centre. I had called ahead and spoken to the manager, Larry Clayton, who seemed bored with his job and quite keen to show a visitor around the place.

The tyres of the Mercedes crunched over the gravel as we drove slowly up the driveway and parked in front of a new-looking red-brick single-storey building to the side of the main house. VISITORS REPORT HERE ordered a smartly painted notice stuck into the grass verge. So I did.

'It's very quiet at this time of the year,' said Larry Clayton as we sat in his office. 'Most of the mares and foals are gone by now, back to their owners for the summer.'

'So when's your busy time?' I asked.

'January to April,' he said. 'That's when most of them are born. Absolutely crazy here in February and March. Foals dropping every five minutes.'

'How many?' I asked.

'Too many,' he said with a wry smile. 'About a hundred, and the Radcliffes want to double that next year.'

I looked at his feet on the desk. He was wearing badly scuffed cowboy boots under tight blue jeans with a check-pattern open-necked shirt. I wondered if the Radcliffes knew that their manager was so casual with their guests. I had picked up some of their marketing material stacked in a rack in the reception area on my way in. It was a glossy brochure with impressive facts and figures about the equine care provided for the expectant mothers, and a smiling picture on the front of Roger and Deborah Radcliffe standing together next to some mares and foals in a paddock.

'Are they at home?' I asked Larry.

'Nope,' he said. 'They are in Kentucky for the sales and the Derby.'

'Can I have a look round?' I asked.

'Sure,' he said, lifting his feet off the desk. 'Not much to see.'

We walked around a new complex of foaling boxes and other stalls, each angle covered by a closed-circuit television camera.

'How many staff do you have?' I asked.

'About a dozen in the high season but only a couple now,' he said. 'We have an onsite delivery team when we're foaling. But they've gone now.'

We walked past the rows of deserted stables and looked into the new foaling boxes.

'Where was Peninsula foaled?' I asked.

'No idea,' he said. 'This is my first year here. Lots has changed.'

'Do you know if the stud groom still works here?' I asked. 'The one who helped with Peninsula.'

'No idea,' he said again. 'Do you know who it was? Stud grooms come and go round here like wet Sundays.'

'Have you ever heard of anyone called Julian Trent?' I asked him.

'Nope,' he said. 'Should I?'

I decided that it really hadn't been a very helpful excursion.

BOB DROPPED ME BACK at Ranelagh Avenue around a quarter to eight.

I was about halfway up the stairs to my flat when I heard the sound of running water where there shouldn't have been. I realised that something was very wrong.

It was running through the light fitting in the ceiling of my sitting room onto the floor below. It wasn't just a trickle, more of a torrent. And that wasn't the only problem. My home had been well and truly trashed.

I made my way as quickly as possible up to the top floor to turn off the water, only to discover that the washbasin in the second bathroom had been torn completely away from its fittings and the water was jetting out of a hole in the wall left by a broken pipe. The stream was adding to the inch depth that already existed on the bathroom floor and was spreading across the landing and down the top few steps like a waterfall.

Where, I wondered, was the stopcock?

I carefully descended the wet stairs again and telephoned my downstairs neighbours to ask for help. There was no answer.

I sat on the torn arm of my sofa and looked about me. Everything that could have been broken had been. My brand-new, large flat-screen plasma television would show no pictures ever again. Angela's collection of Royal Worcester figurines was no more, and the kitchen floor was littered deep with broken crockery and glass.

At least the phone was working, so I used it to dial 999 and asked the emergency operator for the police. They promised to send someone as soon as possible but no one was hurt or dying, they said, so I would have to wait. I thumbed through a sopping copy of Yellow Pages to find an emergency plumbing service and I was still speaking to them when the ceiling around the light fitting, which had been bulging alarmingly, collapsed with a crash. A huge mass of water fell into the centre of my sitting room and spread out towards my kitchen area like a mini tidal wave. I lifted my feet as it passed me by. The plumbing company promised that someone was on the way.

I hobbled around my house inspecting the damage. There was almost nothing left that was usable. Everything had been broken or sliced through with what must have been a box cutter or a Stanley knife. Cuts through the hide of my leather sofa showed white from the stuffing beneath. A mirror that had hung on my sitting-room wall now lay smashed among the remains of a glass-and-brass coffee table, and an oil painting was impaled over the back of a dining chair. Surprisingly the electrical system seemed to have suffered no ill effects.

Upstairs in my bedroom, the mattress had also received the box-cutter treatment and so had most of the clothes in my wardrobe. Worst of all was that the perpetrator, and I had little doubt who was responsible, had smashed the glass and twisted to destruction the silver frame that had stood on the dressing table, and had torn the photograph of Angela into tiny pieces.

I stood there looking at these confetti remains and felt not grief for my dead wife but raging anger that her image had been so violated.

The phone rang. How was it, I wondered, that he hadn't broken that too?

I found out. 'I told you that you'd regret it,' Julian Trent said down the wire, his voice full of menace.

'Fuck off, you little creep,' I said, and slammed down the receiver.

The phone rang again almost immediately and I snatched it up.

'I said to fuck off,' I shouted into the mouthpiece.

There was a pause. 'Geoffrey, is that you?' Eleanor sounded hesitant.

'Oh God, I'm so sorry,' I said. 'I thought you were someone else.'

'I should hope so,' she said. 'I called because I have some good news for you. I've found a copy of the photo of Millie with the foal.'

IT TOOK THE EMERGENCY PLUMBERS forty-five minutes to arrive at Ranelagh Avenue, by which time not only had the ceiling in my sitting room collapsed but also two ceilings below. I knew because I heard about it at full volume from my neighbours when they arrived home at 9.05.

Two uniformed police officers showed up at least an hour after the plumbers had successfully capped off the broken pipe and departed. They wandered through the mess, shaking their heads.

'Do you have any idea who may have done this?' they asked me.

I shrugged my shoulders. Somehow not actually speaking seemed to reduce the lie. Why didn't I just tell them that I knew exactly who had done it? Julian Trent could get himself off an attempted-murder rap. I had no doubts that he would easily escape a charge of malicious damage to property. To have told the police the truth would simply have given him an additional reason to come back for another dose of destruction.

The police officers spent some time going all round my house both outside and in.

'Whoever did this probably got in through that window,' one of them said, pointing at the now-broken glass in my utility room. 'He must have climbed the drainpipe. Is there anything missing?'

'I have no idea,' I said. 'It doesn't seem so. It's just all broken or slashed.'

'Mindless vandalism,' said the policeman. 'Happens all the time, sadly. You should be grateful that the whole place isn't also smeared with shit.'

'Oh thanks,' I said rather sarcastically. 'So what happens now?'

'If nothing's been stolen, then CID won't really be interested.' He sounded bored himself. 'If you call Richmond police station in the morning, they will give you a crime number for your insurers.'

And with that, they left.

No photos, no tests, no search for fingerprints, nothing. They had no expectation of ever catching the person responsible, and, to be fair, I hadn't exactly been very helpful with their inquiries.

Eleanor arrived at just before ten. She had been so distressed to hear me on the telephone describing the shambles that was now my home that she had driven up from Lambourn as soon as she could. She had only been back there an hour, having caught the train from London to Newbury at the end of the veterinary symposium.

I hobbled down the stairs to the front door to let her in and we stood in the hallway and hugged. I kissed her briefly with closed lips. It was a start.

She was absolutely horrified at the damage and I was pleased that she cared. I had grown somehow accustomed to the mess over the couple of hours since I had first discovered it. It wasn't that I didn't care about my stuff—I cared a lot. It was just that the loss of everything fitted in quite well with the feeling I had of moving on, of starting again.

'Have you called the police?' she asked.

'They've just left,' I said. 'They didn't hold out much hope of catching whoever did this.'

'But, Geoffrey,' she said seriously, 'this isn't just some random attack. This was targeted directly at you personally. You must have some idea who did it.'

I said nothing. It was answer enough.

'Tell me,' she said.

WE SAT AMID the wreckage of my home for two hours while I told her about Julian Trent and his apparent connection with the murder of Scot Barlow. I told her how I shouldn't be acting in this case and how I had withheld information from the police. I told her about Josef Hughes and George Barnett. And I showed her the photograph of her walking down the path near the hospital in Lambourn. I had kept it in my jacket pocket and it had consequently survived the demolition.

She held the photograph in slightly shaking hands and went quite pale.

I dug around in the kitchen and finally found a pair of unbroken plastic mugs and a bottle of mineral water from the fridge.

'I'd rather have some wine,' Eleanor said.

My wine rack, along with its dozen bottles of claret, lay smashed, a red stain spreading inexorably across the mushroom-coloured rug in my hall. I went back to the fridge and discovered an unbroken bottle of champagne in a door rack.

So we sat on my ruined sofa among the carnage and drank Veuve Clicquot out of plastic mugs. How romantic was that?

'But why didn't you tell me about this photo sooner?' she asked accusingly. 'I might have been in danger.'

'I don't believe you are in real danger as long as Trent, or whoever is behind him, still thinks I will do as they say.'

'Darling,' she said, using the term for the first time, 'you absolutely have to go to the authorities and explain everything to them.'

'It isn't that simple,' I said to her. 'For a start, coming clean to the authorities might cost me my career. I have told outright lies to the police, and the law is pretty unforgiving of lies. I have certainly misled the court and that alone is enough to get disbarred.'

'But you have a good reason,' she said.

'Yes, indeed I have,' I said. 'I was scared. And I still am. But all that will have little bearing for the court. I know. I've seen witnesses sent to prison for the night because they refuse to tell the judge something they know but are too afraid to say.'

'So what are you going to do?' she asked finally.

'I am going to defeat him by getting Steve Mitchell acquitted,' I said. 'The only problem is that I'm not quite sure how I'm going to manage it.'

'But then what?' she said. 'He won't just go away.'

'I'll cross that bridge when I get to it,' I said with a laugh. But it wasn't really a laughing matter.

'Does the picture of Millie help?' she asked.

'It might,' I said. 'Where is it?'

'Here,' she said, pulling out a digital camera from her handbag. 'The photo frame was in the background of some pictures I took in Millie's room when we had a drinks party there for her birthday. After what you said last night I checked when I got home and there it was.' She smiled in triumph.

She scrolled through the pictures until she arrived at one of three young women standing with glasses in their hands in front of a mantelpiece. And there between the heads of two of them could be clearly seen the frame and the missing photo. Eleanor zoomed in on the image.

'Amazing things, these cameras,' she said. 'Over eight million pixels, whatever that means.'

It meant that she could zoom right in and fill the whole screen with the picture of Millie Barlow with Peninsula's head in her lap and the mare standing behind with the stud groom.

'Well?' she said as I studied the image.

'I don't know,' I said. 'It surely has to be important, otherwise why was it stolen from Barlow's house? But I just can't see why. It must be something to do with the stud groom, but I don't recognise him. It's not Julian Trent, that's for sure.' Somehow I had suspected that it might have been.

ELEANOR SPENT her second night in my house and, this time, she slept alone in my bed, or what was left of it, while I dozed fully clothed on the torn-up sofa downstairs. Neither of us felt that it had been the right circumstance to make any further moves towards each other.

I woke early with the daylight, and what it revealed was no better than it had been the night before. It wasn't that I couldn't replace what Julian Trent had destroyed, but he had made my life so much more complicated and annoying. Where did one start to get rid of all this mess?

I looked in the drawers of my desk for my insurance policy. Clearly not all the wine was soaking into the rug. Trent had saved a couple of bottles to pour into my paperwork, which was now red and still dripping.

Eleanor padded barefoot down the stairs wearing my dressing gown.

'Careful,' I said. 'There's broken glass all over the floor.'

She stopped on the bottom stair and looked around. 'Must have been quite a party,' she said with a smile.

'The best,' I said, smiling back. She retreated back to my bedroom and soon reappeared, dressed and with her shoes on.

'I'd better be going,' she said, more serious now. 'It's well gone six and I need to be at work at eight. Will you be all right?'

'I'll be fine,' I said. 'I have a car picking me up at eight.'

'You'd better have this,' she said, handing me her camera.

'Right,' I said. 'Thanks. I may use it to take some shots for the insurance company.'

'Good idea,' she said, standing still in the middle of the hallway.

It was as if she didn't really want to go.

'What are you doing tonight?' I asked.

'I'm on call,' she said miserably. 'I have to stay in Lambourn.'

'Then can I come down there and return your camera to you this evening?' I asked.

'Oh, yes, please,' she said with a wide grin.

I used the rest of the free memory in Eleanor's camera to take shots of every aspect of Julian Trent's handiwork. I found a clean shirt lurking in the tumble drier that young Mr Trent had missed and, even though there was no water in the bathrooms with which to wash, I managed to shave with an unbroken electric razor. I felt quite respectable as I hobbled down the steps and into Bob's waiting Mercedes at eight o'clock sharp.

While Bob drove, I set to work finding someone to fix the utility-room window and called my insurance company. Bob took me first to chambers, where he went in to collect my mail. He reappeared with Arthur in tow.

'Mr Mason,' said Arthur through the window, formal as always.

''Morning, Arthur,' I said. 'What's the problem?'

'Sir James is very keen to see you,' he said. 'He needs to speak to you about Monday.' Monday was the first day of Steve Mitchell's trial in Oxford. 'He thinks it may be impossible for him to attend as the case he is on at the moment is overrunning.'

What a surprise, I thought. I bet it's overrunning because Sir James keeps asking for delays. I suspected that he would find a good reason not to go to Oxford at all. I had the distinct impression that, rather than face a court-room loss, he was going to be happy to let me conduct the case. And that would suit me just fine.

'Tell Sir James that I will be perfectly all right on my own,' I said. 'Ask him to call me over the weekend on my mobile if he wants me to request an adjournment for a day.' I wouldn't hold my breath for the call, I thought.

'Right,' said Arthur. 'I will.'

Both he and I were plainly aware of what was going on, but protocol and good manners had won the day. I asked him to arrange for all my boxes, papers, files, gown, wig and so on for the trial to be sent direct to the hotel I had booked in Oxford, where I would be spending the weekend in prepara-tion for Monday.

'Back to Barnes?' Bob asked after Arthur had left.

'No, Bob,' I said. 'Could you take me to Lambourn?'

'Be delighted to,' he said with a big smile. He was being paid by the mile. 'Round trip or one way?' he asked.

'One way, I think,' I said. 'I need to make a call. And, Bob, can we find a photo shop where you can stop outside to drop me off?'

He found one in Victoria Street and I spent about half an hour at a self-service digital photo machine printing out the pictures I had taken that morning with Eleanor's camera. I also printed out ten six-by-four-inch copies of the blown-up image of the Millie and foal picture. They looked a little more blurred than on the camera, but they would have to do.

I phoned ahead to the Queen's Arms Hotel, where Eleanor and I had met for our first drink and meal back in November.

'Yes,' they said. 'We have rooms available for tonight. For how many?'

'For one,' I said. 'But I would like a double-bedded room, please.' Well, you never knew.

Bob took me straight to the hotel, where the receptionist was surprised that I had no luggage. It was too complicated to explain, so I didn't. She kindly allocated me a room on the ground floor in a modern extension, and I went and lay down on the bed to rest my aching back and to wait for Eleanor to arrive.

WE HAD DINNER at the same table as before, but on this occasion our evening was interrupted by an emergency call on her pager.

'I don't believe it,' said Eleanor, disconnecting from her mobile phone.

'Do you want me to save your dinner?' I said.

'No, I'll be longer than that,' she said. 'I'll call you.'

I was disappointed. And, for the first time, I realised that I didn't feel guilty about being out with someone other than Angela.

She rushed off to her car and I finished my dinner alone, drank my wine alone and, in time, went along the corridor to my bed alone.

CHAPTER 8

On Friday morning I went shopping in Newbury. A taxi picked me up from the hotel and I spent a couple of hours buying myself maybe not a complete new wardrobe, but enough to see me through the next few weeks at Oxford Crown Court.

Back at the Queen's Arms, I eased myself gingerly out of the white plastic shell and, standing in the shower, let a stream of cool water wash away the grime and bring relief to my itching body. I washed my hair with new shampoo, brushed my teeth with a new toothbrush and shaved my chin with a new razor. I then reluctantly put myself back in the plastic straight jacket before dressing in a crisp, clean new shirt and trousers. I felt like a new man.

After lunch I took a taxi to Uffington, back to the Radcliffes' place. I had called Larry Clayton to say I was coming and he was sitting in his office when I arrived at about two thirty, the same scuffed cowboy boots resting on his desk.

'How can I help?' he said, not getting up.

I handed him a copy of the Millie and foal photo.

'Do you recognise anyone in this picture?' I asked him.

He studied it quite closely. 'Nope,' he said finally.

'The foal is Peninsula,' I said.

He looked again at the picture. 'Sorry,' he said. 'Still can't help you.'

'When did you say you arrived here?' I asked him.

'Is there anyone working here now who was here when Peninsula was born?' I asked.

'Doubt it,' he said unhelpfully.

'Well, keep the photo anyway,' I said. 'If anyone recognises the man, will you ask them to give me a call?' I handed him one of my cards. 'When did you say the Radcliffes will be back?'

'The Kentucky Derby is at Louisville tomorrow,' he said, leaning further back in his chair. 'They'll be back sometime after that.'

'Right,' I said. 'Would you ask them to look at the picture as well, please?'

'Maybe,' he said.

The taxi had waited for me and I asked the driver to take me back to the Queen's Arms. That had all been a waste of time, I thought.

I called Eleanor and asked her if I should stay for a second night or go on to Oxford. Arthur had booked my hotel from the Friday, and I had already called to check that all my boxes had arrived there safely.

'I'm on call again,' she said. She seemed strangely reticent for someone who had previously been so forthcoming, almost eager.

'Would you like to have dinner together?' I asked. There was a pause from the other end of the line. 'But we can leave it if you like,' I went on quickly. Was I being too pushy?

'Geoffrey,' she said seriously, 'I'd love to have dinner with you, but . . .'

'Yes?' I said.

'I'll have to come back here afterwards.'

'That's fine,' I said, upbeat. 'Why don't we have dinner at the Fox and Hounds in Uffington, and then I'll get a taxi to take me on to Oxford?'

'Great,' she said, sounding a little relieved.

'Are you sure everything's all right?' I asked her.

'Yes,' she said. 'I promise. Everything is fine.'

We disconnected and I was left wondering whether men could ever fully understand women.

THE FOX AND HOUNDS was a yellow plastered building in Uffington High Street. Eleanor and I had arranged to meet at eight and I arrived early at 7.10, in a taxi with my two suitcases.

'I'm sorry,' said the publican as I struggled in through the door with two cases and my crutches. 'We don't have any accommodation, we're a pub.'

I explained to him that another taxi was picking me up later and he kindly allowed me to store my bags in his office in the interim.

'Now,' he said as I half sat myself on one of the Windsor-style bar stools. 'What can I get you?'

'Glass of red, please,' I said. 'Merlot, if you have it.'

He poured a generous measure and set the glass down on the bar top. I looked around the bar. I was his only customer.

'Quiet tonight,' I said to him.

'It'll be much busier later,' he said. 'All my regulars will be in soon.'

I pulled a copy of the Millie and foal photograph from my jacket and placed it on the bar. 'Do you recognise either of the people in this picture?'

He had a good look. 'I don't know the woman,' he said, 'but I think the man is Jack Rensburg.'

I could hardly control my excitement. 'Does he live round here?' I said.

'He used to,' the publican replied. 'He worked at the stables on the Woolstone road. He's been gone for three or four years, at least.'

'How well did you know him?' I asked.

'He's a nice enough chap,' he said. 'South African. He played for the village team here and they come into the pub after matches in the summer.'

'Do you know why he left?' I asked.

'No idea,' he said. 'I think he went away on holiday and never came back. Somewhere exotic it was. Far East or something.'

'And you don't know when exactly?' I asked him.

He thought for a moment but shook his head. 'Sorry.'

Some more customers arrived and he went off to serve them.

Eleanor arrived promptly at eight and I was still half standing, half sitting on the bar stool enjoying a second glass of Merlot. She gave me a peck on the cheek, sat on the stool next to me and ordered a glass of white.

'Had a good day?' she asked rather gloomily, tasting her wine.

'Yes, actually, I have. I've bought up most of the menswear in Newbury, washed, shaved and preened my body, and,' I said with a flourish, 'I've discovered the name of the man in the picture.'

'Wow,' she said, mocking. 'You have been a busy boy.' She smiled and it felt like the sun had come out.

'That's better,' I said, smiling back. 'And what have you been up to?'

'I've spent most of the day monitoring a two-year-old from last night and discussing his future with the owner.'

The publican came over and asked us if we were ready to eat, so we moved to a table in the corner of the bar.

'Tell me about the man in the picture,' Eleanor said as we sat down.

'Not really much to tell,' I said. 'His name is Jack Rensburg, and he's a South African who used to work for the Radcliffes but has now gone away.'

'Where to?' she said.

'I don't know. He's been gone for three years or more.'

'Bit of a dead end, then?' she said.

'Yeah,' I agreed. 'But I'll set Arthur on to it on Monday.'

'Arthur?' she asked.

'Chief clerk at my chambers,' I said. 'Knows everything, walks on water.'

'Useful,' she said, smiling broadly, but the smile faded.

'Horse walks into a bar,' I said. 'Barman says, "Why the long face?"'

She laughed. 'The old ones are always the best.'

'So, why the long face?' I said to her again.

She stopped laughing. 'It's nothing,' she said.

'Have I done something wrong?' I said.

'No, of course not,' she said. 'Forget it.'

'I can't,' I said. 'For the first time in seven years I don't feel guilty about being out with another woman and, suddenly, there's something wrong.'

'Geoffrey,' she said laying a hand on my arm, 'it's nothing like that.' She laughed, throwing her head back.

'Well, what is it, then?' I asked determinedly.

She leaned closer to me. 'Wrong time of the month,' she said. 'And I was so afraid you would ask me to sleep with you.'

'Oh,' I said, embarrassed. 'I'm so sorry.'

'It's not a disease, you know,' she said with a laugh, the sparkle back in her eyes. 'It'll be gone by Monday or Tuesday. And I'm not on call on either night.'

I didn't know whether to feel embarrassed, excited or just plain foolish.

The evening flew by and I wasn't at all ready to go when the taxi arrived at 10.15 sharp.

Eleanor and I kissed each other good night, with open mouths. It was a revelation to me after such a long time. Something stirred inside me and I reluctantly struggled into the back seat of the taxi to be borne away to the City of Dreaming Spires, dreaming of the future, and especially Monday.

I SPENT SATURDAY MORNING going through, yet again, the papers for the case. As a matter of course, we had received copies of Scot Barlow's bank statements, with the rest of the prosecution disclosure, but I had also asked the bank for those of his sister, Millie. I spent quite a while examining them. They showed that Millie had a regular payment into her account over and above her salary from the equine hospital veterinary practice. And Scot's statements showed that the money didn't come from him, or at least not from his bank account.

The amounts weren't that big, just a few hundred every month, and they had been paid to her for at least a year and a half before she died. I didn't have any information for before that.

I thought back to when I had met her parents at Scot Barlow's house. Were they likely to have been sending their daughter money, even though she was working? One never knew. Their ill-fitting clothes and simple ways didn't necessarily mean they had no spare cash. It might just mean they were careful with their money.

Scot, meanwhile, had been doing very well indeed. Almost all his deposits were from Weatherbys, the racing administrators, who paid all the riding fees and win bonuses to owners, trainers and jockeys. Scot had been at the top of his profession and earning accordingly, but there was nothing unusual in any of his transactions.

I met Bruce Lygon on Saturday afternoon and we fairly gloomily went through the prosecution case once again. At first glance the evidence seemed overwhelming, but the more I looked at it, the more I began to believe that we had a chance to argue that Mitchell had no case to answer. There was no proof anywhere. Everything was circumstantial.

'But what would you think if you were on the jury?' Bruce said. 'Especially when you add in the fact that everyone knew Mitchell hated Barlow.'

'That's why we have to argue that there's no case to answer,' I said. 'If it goes to the jury, we are in deep trouble.'

ON SUNDAY I went by train to have lunch with my father in his bungalow at the edge of the village of Kings Sutton. He came down to the station to collect me in his vintage Morris Minor. He had always loved this old car and there was nothing he adored more than tinkering for hours with the engine.

My father and I had never been really affectionate towards each other, even when I had been a small child, although I suppose we loved each other in the way that parents and children must. However, that Sunday, I had a lovely time with him, sitting at his dining-room table eating a roast-beef lunch with Yorkshire pudding.

'I'm very impressed,' I said, laying down my knife and fork. 'I never realised you could cook so well.'

'You should come more often,' he said in response, smiling.

We moved with our coffees into his sitting room.

'Would you do me a favour?' I asked him. 'Would you contemplate going away for a couple of weeks?'

'What on earth for?' he said.

How could I explain to him that it might be for his own protection?

'I'd like to give you a holiday,' I said.

'But why?' he said. 'And where would I go?'

'Wherever you like,' I said.

'But I don't want to go anywhere,' he said. 'If you really want to give me something, then give me the money to have my windows painted.'

'It might be safer for you to go away,' I said.

'Safer?' he said. 'How would it be safer?'

I explained a little about how some people were trying to influence the outcome of a trial by getting me to do things I didn't want to do.

'You ought to go and tell the police,' he said.

'I know,' I replied. 'I will. But for the time being it might be best if the people concerned didn't know where you were.'

'Don't be ridiculous, boy,' he said, putting on his most authoritative voice. 'Why on earth would anyone care where I live?'

I took a photograph out of my pocket and passed it to him. It was the one of him standing outside his front door.

He studied it carefully. 'Are you saying that someone took this?' he said.

I nodded. 'Last November,' I said. 'Do you remember me calling you about that hole in your jumper?'

'Vaguely,' he said, still staring at the picture.

'Well,' I said, 'I just don't want these people coming here again, that's all.'

'But why would they want to?' he persisted.

'Because,' I said with a forced laugh, 'I have no intention of doing what they want me to do.'

STEVE MITCHELL'S TRIAL started at ten thirty sharp on Monday morning in court number 1 at Oxford Crown Court with a red-robed High Court judge parachuted in from London for the purpose. This was a murder trial with a celebrity, albeit a minor one, in the dock and nothing was to go wrong.

As expected, I had received no call over the weekend from Sir James Horley, QC, asking me to request an adjournment and had, in fact, been advised by Arthur in an email that Sir James was now doubtful of making it to Oxford before Thursday at the earliest.

The defence consisted solely of Bruce Lygon, his secretary and me. I had asked him to bring his secretary to court so that we didn't, as a line-up, appear too thin on the ground. To be fair, we also had Nikki Payne at our disposal. Nikki was an eager young solicitor's clerk from Bruce's firm, but she wasn't in court because she was busy in London trying to discover the answers to some questions I had set her the previous evening.

The prosecution, meanwhile, had seven players in situ. A top QC was leading, with a local barrister as his junior. These two sat in the front row, to our right. Two CPS solicitors sat behind them, with two legal assistants in the row behind that, plus a cross between a secretary and a gofer in row four. If they were trying to impress and intimidate the defence by weight of numbers, it seemed to be succeeding.

The press were represented in force, filling all of the green upholstered seats in the press box. This trial was going to be big news, and the thirty or so seats reserved for the public were mostly full as well. Mr and Mrs Barlow, Scot's parents, were seated in the front row.

Steve Mitchell was brought into court from the cells by a prison officer. Both the prison officer and Steve sat in the glass-fronted dock at the back of the court, behind the barristers' benches. I turned round and gave Steve an encouraging smile. He looked pale and very nervous but was dressed, as I had suggested, in a blazer, white shirt and tie that I had bought for him in Newbury on Saturday.

'All rise,' announced the clerk. Everyone stood and the judge entered the court. He bowed. We bowed back. Then everyone sat down again.

The court clerk stood up. 'The defendant will rise,' she said. Steve stood up.

'Are you Stephen Miles Mitchell?' said the clerk.

'Yes, I am,' Steve replied in a strong voice.

'You may sit down,' said the clerk, so he did.

'Are you leading for the defence, Mr Mason?' the judge asked.

I struggled to my feet. 'Yes, My Lord,' I said.

'Do you not think that your team needs strengthening?' he asked. It was his way of asking whether I thought that a QC might be more appropriate.

'My Lord,' I replied, 'Sir James Horley is nominally leading for the defence in this case but is unable to be here today. Sir James and I have made the preparations for the case, and my client is content for the case to proceed today with me acting for him.' I couldn't exactly tell the judge that my client had been ecstatic when I'd told him earlier in the cells beneath the court.

'I need to make it clear to you, and to your client, that this will not be grounds for an appeal if the case goes against you.'

'I understand that, My Lord,' I said. 'And so does my client.'

Steve Mitchell nodded his agreement to the judge from the dock.

'Very well,' said the judge.

The prosecution team were all looking at me and smiling, confidence oozing out of their every pore. I simply smiled back.

'The defendant will rise,' the clerk said again.

Steve stood up in the dock.

'You are charged,' the clerk said to him, 'that on the 17th of November, 2008, you did murder Hamish Jamie Barlow, also known as Scot Barlow. Do you understand the indictment?'

'Yes,' Steve replied.

'How do you plead?' the clerk asked him.

'Not guilty,' Steve said strongly.

Next came the selection and swearing in of the jury.

Everyone watched as a mixed bag of individuals entered the court and sat on more green-covered seats on the other side. There were eighteen of them in total, drawn randomly from the electoral roll and summoned to attend the court, whether they wanted to or not. Twelve of the eighteen had their names drawn from a box by the court clerk and each one, in turn, seven women and five men, took their places in the jury box.

And now we were ready to begin. The judge called on the prosecution to start proceedings proper by outlining the case for the Crown.

'Ladies and gentlemen of the jury,' the prosecution QC began, 'you will hear, in this case, of a bitter feud in the world of horse racing that was so acrimonious that it led to the gruesome killing of one jockey at the hands of another.' He paused briefly to draw breath. 'You will hear how the defendant did premeditatively murder the victim by driving a pitchfork into his heart, and how the defendant now claims that he is innocent and is being framed by person or persons unknown. But the evidence presented to you will convince you, beyond reasonable doubt, that the defendant is, in fact, culpable of the murder, and that his claims of being framed are unfounded and nothing more than the last refuge of a guilty soul.'

He was good, I thought. Too damned good.

In all, it took him more than an hour to outline, in considerable detail, the case for the prosecution, by which time I could see some of the jury members glancing at the dock with distaste.

When the judge adjourned proceedings for lunch, I went straight down to the cells to see Steve.

'My God,' he said, 'did you see the way the jury was looking at me? I've got no bloody chance.'

THE AFTERNOON proved to be as frustrating as the morning had been, with Detective Inspector McNeile, the investigating police officer, in the witness box for the whole two and a half hours. Only once did the judge briefly adjourn things for a few minutes for us all to stretch our legs, and to give me some relief from the damn body shell cutting into my groin.

The policeman, consulting his notebooks, went through the whole affair from the moment that the police had first arrived at Barlow's house to discover the body until they had arrested Steve Mitchell that evening. He also went on to describe the investigation after the arrest.

'Inspector,' said the prosecution QC, 'what model of car did the defendant own at the time of the murder?'

'An Audi A4,' he said. 'Silver.'

'Yes,' went on the QC, 'and in the course of your inquiries did you determine if this car was fitted with a security alarm and immobiliser system?'

'Yes,' he said. 'It was.'

'So would it be accurate to say that the car could only be unlocked and then driven if the correct key had been used for the purpose?'

'That is my understanding, yes,' said the inspector.

'Did you find any keys for the vehicle?' the QC asked him.

'Yes,' he said. 'One on the defendant, in his trouser pocket, and another one in the top drawer of Mr Mitchell's desk in his study.'

'And did you approach an Audi dealer and ask them about keys for their cars?'

'Yes,' he said again. 'They informed me that it was normal for two keys to be issued with a new car and also that replacement or additional keys are only provided after strict security checks.'

'And had any additional keys been requested for Mr Mitchell's car?'

'No,' he said. 'They had not.'

'One last thing, Inspector,' the QC said with a flourish. 'Was Mr Mitchell's car locked when you went to his home to arrest him?'

'Yes,' he said. 'It was.'

'Your witness,' the prosecution QC said, turning to me.

I looked at the clock on the courtroom wall. It read 4.20.

'Would you like to start your cross-examination in the morning, Mr Mason?' asked the judge expectantly.

'If it pleases My Lord,' I said, 'I would like to ask a few questions now.'

The judge looked at the clock. 'Ten minutes, then,' he said.

'Thank you, My Lord.' I turned to the witness. 'Inspector McNeile, can you please tell the court how the police first became aware that Mr Barlow had been murdered?' He had left that bit out of his evidence.

'I believe it was a call to the police station reporting an intruder at Mr Barlow's residence,' he said.

'Who was this call from?' I asked him.

'I'm sorry, I don't have that information.'

'But surely, Inspector, all emergency calls to the police are logged with the time they are made, and who they are from?'

'That is the usual practice, yes,' he said.

'So how is it that you have no record of who it was that called the police?'

He looked slightly uncomfortable. 'The call was taken by the telephone on the desk of a civilian worker in the front office of the police station.'

'And was the number of that telephone widely available to the public?' I asked him.

'Not that I'm aware of,' he said.

'Do you not think it is strange that the call was taken on a telephone where the number was not widely known, where no log was taken of incoming calls and to which no recording equipment was attached?'

'Mr Mason,' the judge interjected, 'that's three questions in one.'

'I'm sorry, My Lord,' I said. 'Inspector McNeile, would you agree with me that, until the police arrived at Mr Barlow's house to discover his body, it is likely that the only person or persons who knew that Mr Barlow was dead would be those responsible for his murder?'

'I suppose so, yes,' he said.

'Inspector, how many years in total have you been a detective?' I asked.

'Fifteen,' he said.

'And how often in those fifteen years,' I asked him, 'have you been telephoned anonymously, on an unrecorded line, to report an intruder in a property so that the police would turn up there and discover a murder victim surrounded by a mass of incriminating evidence?'

'That's enough, Mr Mason,' said the judge.

'My Lord,' I said respectfully, and sat down. It had been a minor victory only, in a day of unremitting bad news.

ELEANOR DIDN'T COME to Oxford on Monday night. In one way I was relieved, in another disappointed. When I arrived back at the hotel from court my head was aching from all the concentration. It was the first such headache I had suffered for some time after the fall at Cheltenham and I had begun to forget the ferocity of the pain. I knew that relaxing horizontally on a bed for a couple of hours was the best and only remedy.

At some point I drifted off to sleep and I was woken by the phone ringing beside the bed.

'Yes?' I said into it, struggling to sit up because of the body shell.

'Mr Mason?' a female voice said.

'Yes,' I replied.

'This is Nikki Payne here,' she said. 'I've been to the Home Office and the South African embassy as you asked and neither of them had any record of a Jack Rensburg, but they did of someone called Jacques van Rensburg. Apparently van Rensburg is quite a common name in South Africa. In fact there are three of them who live in England. Two are at university here on student visas, one at Durham and the other at Cambridge, and both have been here for the past two years.'

'What about the third one?' I asked.

'His visa has expired, but it seems he's still here although his right to work has expired too. Apparently, that's not unusual. A nice chap at the embassy is searching for him back in South Africa just in case he went home without telling the Home Office. There aren't any proper records kept when people leave the UK, only when they arrive.'

'But you did show them the photo?' I asked her.

'Of course I did,' she said. 'My friend at the embassy is trying to get me a copy of this Jacques van Rensburg's passport snap sent from the South African Department of Home Affairs so I can see if it is actually him.'

'Good,' I said. 'Call me tomorrow if you get anywhere.'

She hung up and I rested my head back on the pillow.

The phone on the bedside cabinet rang once more, waking me again.

Damn it, I thought, can't a man have any peace?

'Hello,' I said, irritated.

'Just make sure you lose the case,' said a whispering voice.

I was suddenly wide awake. 'Who are you?' I demanded loudly.

'Never mind who,' said the whisperer. 'Just do it.' The line went dead.

CHAPTER 9

Detective Inspector McNeile was back in the witness box on Tuesday morning for further cross-examination. 'I remind you that you are still under oath,' the judge said to him.

'Yes, My Lord,' he replied.

I levered myself to my feet, pulling on the lectern in front of me.

'Inspector McNeile,' I said, 'I believe that the police discovered that Mr Barlow had received a text message on his mobile telephone on the day of his death. Is that correct?'

'Yes,' he replied.

'And did this text message say, and I quote'—I picked up a sheet of paper and read from it—'"I'm going to come round and sort you out properly you sneaking little bastard"?' I paused for effect. 'And then sign off with Mr Mitchell's name?'

'I haven't got access to the actual text,' he said.

'No,' I said. 'But does that sound about right to you?'

'Yes,' he said. 'I believe it said something like that.'

'Thank you,' I said. 'And were the police able to establish that this text message had indeed been sent to Mr Barlow by Mr Mitchell?'

'No,' he said. 'We were not.'

'Am I correct in saying that you discovered that the message had been sent anonymously by a free text-messaging service available to anyone with access to any computer and the Internet anywhere in the world?'

'Yes,' he said. 'That is correct.'

'So, in addition to an anonymous, unrecorded telephone call to the police directing them to a murder scene to discover incriminating evidence against the defendant'—I glanced at the judge, who was looking at me intently—'there was an anonymous text message sent to Mr Barlow's telephone that was made to appear as if it had come from the defendant?'

'I didn't say that it hadn't come from the defendant,' said the inspector. 'I only said that we were unable to establish that it had.'

'Thank you,' I said to him. 'No further questions.'

I sat down feeling rather pleased with myself. Bruce Lygon patted me gently on the shoulder. 'Well done,' he whispered.

I turned round to thank him and caught sight of young Julian Trent sitting right next to Mr and Mrs Barlow in the seats reserved for the public. He was watching me. I went quite cold.

The next witness for the prosecution had been called and there was a lull in proceedings as the court usher went to find the right person. Julian Trent watched me watching him and clearly decided it was time to leave. He stood up and made his way to the exit.

MY CROSS-EXAMINATION of Detective Inspector McNeile proved to be the high point of the day for the defence. The three further witnesses called by the prosecution gave us little respite from the damning evidence that implied that the murder had been carried out by the man in the dock.

A forensic expert explained to the jury, in monotonous detail, the method of extracting DNA from blood and hair, and then went on to show beyond any doubt that drops of blood and two hairs from Scot Barlow had been found in the driver's footwell of Steve Mitchell's car and also that more of Barlow's blood and four more of his hairs had been found adhering to the underside of both of Steve Mitchell's Wellington boots, subsequently discovered at the Mitchell premises. He was further able to show that fresh bloody footprints at the scene matched both of Mr Mitchell's Wellingtons.

I did manage to get the expert to concede that none of Mr Mitchell's DNA had been discovered on the murder weapon or on the deceased's body. Furthermore, I got him to agree that, even though Barlow's DNA had been found on Mr Mitchell's boots and in his car, this did not prove that Mr Mitchell had been wearing his boots at the time, nor driving his car at any point during that afternoon.

The final witness of the day was the pathologist who had done the post-mortem examination of Scot Barlow's body. The prongs of the five-foot-long pitchfork had not, as I had imagined, passed through the rib cage and then into the heart, but had been thrust upwards underneath the ribs, through the diaphragm, one of them entering the heart from below. A single strike had been sufficient to cause death within just a few minutes.

The pathologist conceded that considerable force would have been needed to cause the fatal injury. The prosecution counsel then established without difficulty that a fit man of thirty-three, especially a professional sportsman, would have easily had the strength required to deliver the fatal blow, even if he did only stand five foot six inches tall.

The murder weapon was produced as an exhibit. In the stillness of the courtroom it looked huge and menacing with its ten-inch-long, thin, curved and very sharp metal prongs. The pathologist was invited by the prosecution counsel to demonstrate, on the floor of the court, the upward thrusting action that would have been needed to cause the injuries sustained by Barlow's body. It was a moment of high drama and I noticed some members of the jury shuddering with revulsion.

ELEANOR DIDN'T COME to Oxford on Tuesday night either. She left a message on my mobile explaining that one of her colleagues was ill and she had to stay in Lambourn to cover for her. Again, strangely, I was somewhat relieved. Perhaps it was the expectation, her expectation, that worried me most. It had been a long time since I had slept with anyone, and suddenly the prospect of someone new between my sheets filled me with apprehension.

There were, in fact, two messages on my phone.

The other one was from the whisperer. 'Lose the case,' he said. 'Or else.'

The message had been left at noon that day. No doubt shortly after Julian Trent had reported back to him on the court proceedings and my determined efforts to undermine the police inspector. How long would it take the whisperer to work out, I wondered, that every time he told me to lose I became more and more determined to win?

DETECTIVE CONSTABLE HILLIER, the young policeman I had first met at Barlow's house, was the next witness for the prosecution when the court reconvened at 10.30 on Wednesday morning.

DC Hillier proved to be a model witness for the Crown, stating clearly and persuasively to the jury how the murder weapon was identical to two other pitchforks found at Mitchell's property, and how further investigations had discovered a receipt from a Newbury supplier showing that Mitchell had purchased three of the forks the previous year.

He went on to describe how he had ascertained that the debit-card receipts found impaled on the prongs of the fork were from a Maestro debit card issued by Lloyds Bank in the name of Mr Stephen Mitchell.

Furthermore, the said debit-card receipts were from payments made by Mr Mitchell to a licensed bookmaker based in Hungerford.

'Detective Constable Hillier,' I said, starting my cross-examination, 'do you not think it is strange that a murderer would leave incriminating debit-card receipts with his name on them at the scene of the crime?'

'Not particularly,' he said. 'Many criminals do strange things.'

'But did you not suspect that the receipts had been left on the fork by someone who simply wanted the police to believe that Mr Mitchell had been responsible for the crime?'

'Not really,' he said. 'Perhaps Mitchell put them on the fork to goad Barlow and hadn't really intended leaving them behind. Maybe he couldn't get the murder weapon out of the body to remove them.'

'This is conjecture,' interrupted the judge. 'The witness will confine himself to the facts he knows, rather than those he can merely speculate about.'

'Sorry, Your Honour,' said DC Hillier. But the damage had been done.

I thought of further pointing out that the murderer could surely have ripped the receipts from the fork without removing it from Barlow's body if he'd wanted to, but this whole line of questioning clearly wasn't helping our case so I let it go.

'YOU HAVE ONE NEW MESSAGE,' said my voicemail when I turned my phone on at lunchtime. It was from Nikki Payne.

'Mr Mason,' her disembodied voice said in some excitement, 'I've found your Jacques van Rensburg. Call me back when you get this message.'

I called her immediately.

'He was the third one,' she said in a rush. 'They sent his passport photo over from South Africa and there was no mistake.'

'So he's still somewhere here with an expired visa?' I asked.

'Well, no,' she said. 'Not exactly.' She then went on to give me some very interesting information about Mr Jacques van Rensburg, information that explained why the photograph of Millie and the foal had been so important that someone had taken it from Scot Barlow's house. Maybe so important, indeed, that Barlow had been murdered to get it.

THE AFTERNOON SITTING of the court was taken up almost exclusively by witnesses called by the prosecution to testify about the well-known hatred that had existed between the defendant and the victim for some time.

Any hopes that we, the defence, had of keeping quiet about Barlow's sister, Millie, were dispelled by the very first on the list, Charles Pickering, a racehorse trainer from Lambourn.

'Mr Pickering,' said the prosecution QC, 'how well did you know Mr Barlow?'

'Very well,' he replied. 'Scot had ridden for me as number-one jockey ever since he came down south from Scotland eight years ago.'

'And how well do you know the defendant, Mr Mitchell?'

'Reasonably well,' he said. 'He's ridden my horses a few times, when Scot was unavailable or injured.'

'Did you ever hear Mr Mitchell and Mr Barlow arguing, Mr Pickering?'

'All the time,' he said. 'Like cat and dog, they were.'

'Do you know what they argued about?' the QC went on.

'Scot's sister, mostly,' said Charles Pickering.

'Scot Barlow's sister?' the QC said for effect, turning towards the jury.

'Yes,' Pickering said. 'Scot accused Mitchell of as good as killing his sister. Scot's sister had killed herself and he believed that Mitchell's treatment of her had driven her to it. Mitchell used to tell him to shut up or he'd kill him too. It was the same argument every time.'

'Were Barlow and Mitchell on reasonable terms before Barlow's sister killed herself?' the QC asked.

'Oh, no,' said Pickering. 'They've hated each other for years. Scot didn't like Mitchell seeing his sister at all, right from the start.'

'And when was the start?' the QC asked.

'About three or four years ago, after Barlow's sister came down from Scotland to live in Lambourn.'

'Thank you, Mr Pickering,' said the QC. 'Your witness.' He smiled at me.

'No questions, My Lord,' I said. I didn't want to inadvertently lead him to reveal more damning details such as Barlow's disclosure of the affair to Mitchell's wife.

But my hopes of keeping that a secret only lasted as long as it took for the next witness to be sworn in. He was Remo Clemens, now the leading jockey.

'Mr Clemens,' said the QC, 'I believe you are a successful steeplechase jockey. Is that correct?'

'Yes, sir, I am,' Reno Clemens said in an Irish accent. 'I am leading the jockeys' table at the moment.'

'Do you know the defendant well?'

'Yes, sir.' He glanced briefly at Steve in the dock.

'And you knew Mr Barlow well?'

'Yes, sir, I did.'

'Did you ever hear Mr Mitchell and Mr Barlow arguing?' the QC asked.

'Were they ever not?' said Reno. 'Sometimes they would even argue all the way round during a race. The rest of us got fed up listening to them.'

'And what did they argue about?' asked the QC.

'Anything and everything,' said Reno. 'But mostly about Barlow's sister and Mitchell having had an affair with her.'

'And was Mitchell married at the time of the affair?' asked the QC.

Oh, no, I thought, here we go.

'He was at the beginning,' said Reno, 'but not at the end.'

'Do you know if Mitchell's wife was aware of his affair with Scot Barlow's sister?' the QC asked almost smugly.

'She was after Barlow told her,' Reno said.

'Is that something you know, Mr Clemens, or just something you have heard from others?'

'I heard it from Mitchell himself,' Reno said. 'He would often shout at Barlow in the jocks' changing room and accuse him of being a Judas for snitching to his wife.'

'You bloody lying bastard.' Steve Mitchell stood up and shouted at him from the dock, hammering on the glass partition with his fists.

The judge had his gavel banging down almost before the echo in the courtroom had died away.

'Silence,' he ordered. 'Silence in court. Mr Mitchell, another outburst like that and I will have you taken down to the cells. Do you understand?'

'Yes, My Lord,' said Steve sheepishly. 'I'm sorry.'

Steve sat down again. But more damage had been done to our side.

'Now, Mr Clemens,' the prosecution QC said, greatly enjoying himself, 'are you telling the court that you had often heard the defendant shouting at Mr Barlow that he, Barlow, had been a Judas for telling Mitchell's wife that Mitchell was having an affair with Barlow's sister?'

'Yes, sir,' said Reno Clemens very distinctly, 'I am.'

A motive for Barlow's murder had just been clearly established.

THE NEXT WITNESS for the prosecution was Fred Pleat, who worked as a groom at Mitchell's stables.

'Now, Mr Pleat,' said the prosecution QC, 'were you present at Mr Mitchell's property the day three new pitchforks were delivered?'

'Yes, I was,' he replied.

'And can you recall the actions of Mr Mitchell when he saw that they had been delivered?'

'Yes,' he said again. 'He picked one of them up and thrust it forward and said something about sticking that bastard Scot Barlow with it.'

There was a moment of silence in the court.

'Thank you, Mr Pleat,' said the QC. 'Your witness.'

I rose to my foot. 'Mr Pleat,' I said to him, 'were you frightened by this action you say Mr Mitchell performed?'

'No,' he said.

'Why not?' I asked him.

'I figured Steve was only joking, like,' he said. 'He was laughing. We were both laughing.'

'Thank you, Mr Pleat,' I said. 'No more questions.'

Fred Pleat left the court and, as a bonus to our side, he gave Steve a slight wave as he passed the dock. I hoped the jury had been watching.

'My Lord, that concludes the case for the prosecution,' said their QC.

The judge looked at the clock on the courtroom wall. It showed 4.10. Then he turned towards the jury. 'Ladies and gentlemen of the jury,' he said. 'You are free to go now until tomorrow morning at ten o'clock. May I remind you not to discuss the case among yourselves, nor with anybody else, not even your families.'

The jury was then ushered out of court.

'Mr Mason,' the judge said when the jury door had been closed. Members of the jury were never present in court during legal argument and I had earlier informed the judge that I wished to make a submission at the conclusion of the prosecution's case.

'Yes, My Lord,' I said, struggling upright. 'Thank you.' I collected together some papers in front of me. 'My Lord, the defence wishes to make a submission to the court that the defendant has no case to answer. The prosecution have presented nothing more than circumstantial evidence. There is nothing to show that my client was ever in Mr Barlow's house, let alone there at the time of the murder.'

I took my time going over each of the witnesses' evidence in some detail.

'In conclusion,' I said, 'while the defence readily accepts that our client and Mr Barlow held a deep-seated antagonism towards each other, this is not evidence of murder. If it were, then half the nation would be so tainted. The defence further accepts that our client does not have an alibi for the time of the murder, but failure to have an alibi is not evidence of guilt. It is our contention that the prosecution has failed to present prima facie evidence of Mr Mitchell's guilt. My Lord, we submit that you should direct the jury to return a not-guilty verdict because there is no case for Mr Mitchell to answer.'

'Thank you, Mr Mason,' said the judge. 'I will consider your submission overnight and make a ruling in the morning. Court adjourned until ten o'clock tomorrow.'

ELEANOR FINALLY DID COME to Oxford on Wednesday night. She was waiting for me in the dimly lit hotel lobby when I returned from court. I hadn't expected her to be so early, so I was caught unawares as I struggled with both my box of papers and the crutches. She came up behind me and took the box just before it dropped to the floor.

'Oh, thank you,' I said, thinking it had been one of the hotel staff.

Eleanor peeped at me round the side of the box.

'Hello,' I said with a grin from ear to ear. 'How absolutely wonderful.'

'I thought I'd surprise you,' she said. 'I've been here more than an hour.'

'Blimey,' I said. 'If I'd known that, I would have been here more than an hour ago.'

'Why weren't you?' she said in mock annoyance.

'I was busy telling my client what a complete fool he'd been,' I said.

'Why?' she said.

'He shouted at one of the witnesses,' I said. 'What an idiot!'

I had indeed spent the last hour giving Steve a roasting in the holding cells beneath the court.

'I couldn't help it,' Steve had whined at me. 'I was so mad. That bloody Clemens has been riding all my horses. He'd be delighted if I got convicted. Be laughing all the way to the winner's circle.'

'But you still mustn't do it,' I had urged him. 'You showed the judge your temper. He might think that your temper has something to do with the murder.'

'I'm sorry,' he had said.

If the trial were to continue, I needed him to remain sitting calmly in the dock, no matter what the provocation.

Eleanor now leaned forward and gave me a brief kiss on the lips.

'Do you want to go for a drink?' I asked her. 'It's nearly six.'

'No,' she said emphatically. 'I want to go to bed.'

In the end we did both.

I ordered a bottle of champagne and two glasses from the bar to take up to my room.

All my apprehension about this encounter came flooding back with a vengeance and I was shaking like a leaf by the time we had negotiated the long hall to my room, so much so that I couldn't even get the cork out of the champagne bottle.

'Here,' said Eleanor taking it from my trembling hands. 'Let me do that.' She poured the golden bubbling liquid into the two tall flutes.

'I'm sorry,' I said.

'Don't be,' she said. 'I'm pretty nervous too.'

I sat on the edge of the bed, kicked off my shoes and lay down. I tapped the hard plastic shell beneath my shirt.

'This damn thing doesn't help either,' I said.

'Let me look after you,' she said, coming over and lying down beside me. And she did.

MY APPREHENSION drifted away to nothing and all my fears were unfounded. Making love with a broken back is, by necessity, a gentle and tender process, but we discovered it could also be a sensual and passionate one.

Afterwards, we lay entwined together for a while, drifting in and out of light sleep. I would have been so happy to stay like that all night but I needed to do some reading, ready for the morning.

Eleanor stirred as I tried to remove my arm from beneath her waist.

'Hello,' she said, smiling up at me. 'Going somewhere already?'

'Yup,' I said, smiling back. 'I really do need to get back to my work to be prepared for tomorrow. And, what's more, I'm hungry.'

'I'm hungry for you,' Eleanor said, seductively fluttering her eyelashes.

'Later, dear. Later,' I said. 'Man cannot live by sex alone.'

'But we could try,' she said. Then she sighed and rolled off my arm, releasing me.

'Let's have some room service,' I said. 'Then I can work and eat.'

Eleanor called down for the food while I set about looking through the papers that I would need in the event that the judge did not rule in our favour over the defence submission. To be honest, I didn't really expect him to. Even though much of it was circumstantial, there was probably enough evidence to leave the question to the jury.

Over our room-service dinner, eaten in our bathrobes, I told Eleanor about the news I had heard from Nikki at lunchtime.

'What are you going to do about it?' she asked.

'If the judge doesn't rule in our favour in the morning over the defence submission, and I don't think he will,' I said, 'I intend calling a witness to explore what Nikki found out. I asked my solicitor, Bruce Lygon, to contact my new witness this afternoon,' I said. 'I am still waiting to hear what he says but I fully expect that the witness won't want to come to court.'

'What happens then?' Eleanor asked.

'I can apply to the court for a witness summons to be served.'

'But surely that doesn't mean they also have to answer your questions.'

'No,' I agreed. 'But if they don't, they have to give a reason not to answer, and the only reason here would be that in doing so they might incriminate themselves. And that should, at least, put some doubt into the minds of the jury as to Steve's guilt.' I took another mouthful. 'But what I really need is time. Time for more investigating.'

CHAPTER 10

As I had expected, on the Thursday morning the trial judge rejected the defence submission that there was no case to answer.

'If it then please My Lord,' I said, standing up, 'the defence would like to submit the name of a witness we wish to be summonsed.'

I passed a sheet of paper to the court usher, who delivered it to the judge. He looked down at its brief contents.

'Why has this name not been previously submitted to the court, so that summonses might have been issued in good time?' he asked rather sternly.

'My Lord, information came to our knowledge only yesterday which indicates that the witness is essential to our case that the defendant is innocent of the charges and is being framed for a crime he did not commit. Mr Mitchell's solicitor attempted to contact this potential witness, who indicated that they had no intention of attending court to assist the defence in this matter. Consequently, I would like to apply to the court for a witness summons.'

'Mr Mason,' said the judge after a brief silence, 'have you shown the name to the prosecution?'

'I have, My Lord,' I said. 'I gave a copy to my learned friend just prior to the court sitting this morning.'

The judge invited the prosecution to respond to the request.

'My Lord,' said the smarmy prosecution QC, 'the prosecution has no objection to the summonsing of this witness if it is likely to aid justice. However, the defence has had ample time to prepare for this case and further procrastination should not be tolerated.'

Or in other words, I thought, we don't object but oh, yes, we do after all. Anything to sound reasonable, while not actually being so.

'Very well,' the judge said. 'I will allow a witness summons to be issued. But be warned, Mr Mason, I will take a firm line if I consider that the defence is in any way wasting the court's time. Will this witness be ready to be examined this afternoon?'

'My Lord,' said the prosecution QC, 'the prosecution requests more time to prepare for cross-examination of this witness.'

It was exactly as I had hoped.

'Would you be ready by tomorrow?' asked the judge.

'We would prefer Monday, My Lord,' said the QC.

'Any objection, Mr Mason?' asked the judge.

'No, My Lord,' I said, trying hard to keep a grin off my face.

'Very well,' said the judge. He was probably looking forward to a day on the golf course. 'Court is adjourned until ten o'clock on Monday morning.'

Excellent, I thought. Just what I had wanted, and just what I needed.

I ORDERED A TAXI to take all my papers back to the hotel. As I waited inside the court building lobby, I called Nikki.

'I have the documentation,' she said excitedly. 'It all came through this morning.'

'Great,' I said. 'Now I need you to go to Newbury to ask some more questions.' I explained what I wanted her to find out, and where to find it.

'Right,' she said. 'Call you later.'

She hung up as my taxi arrived.

The taxi took me to the hotel and then waited as I packed a few clothes into one of my new suitcases. Then the taxi took me and my suitcase to Oxford station, where we caught a fast train to London.

'WHAT ARE YOU DOING HERE?' asked Arthur as I walked into chambers some time after noon.

'The case has been adjourned until Monday,' I said. 'Perhaps Sir James will be ready to take over from me by then.'

'Er,' said Arthur, floundering, 'I believe that his case is still running on.'

'Arthur,' I said sarcastically, 'I pay you to lie for me, not to me.'

'Sir James pays me more than you do,' he said with a smile.

I had no intention of telling Sir James Horley anything about my new witness. The last thing I wanted was for him to feel that the case wasn't such a lost cause after all, and for him to step back in and hog all the limelight.

I went through to my room and telephoned Bob, the driver.

'I'll be there in about half an hour,' he said.

'Fine,' I said. 'I have some more calls to make anyway.'

I called Weatherbys, the company that administered British horse racing. I needed some information from them and they were most helpful in giving me the answers.

I also called Eleanor and left a message. She had left the Oxford hotel early in the morning to get back to work in Lambourn, but not so early that we hadn't had time for a repeat of the previous evening's lovemaking.

She called me back on my mobile as Bob drove me away from chambers.

'I'm in London,' I said to her. 'The judge adjourned until Monday. I'm on my way to Barnes to face the mess. And I'll probably stay there tonight.'

'I won't plan to go to Oxford, then,' she said, laughing.

'No,' I said. 'I won't be back there until Sunday night.'

'Sunday night!' she said. 'Don't I get to see you before then?'

'I have plans for during the day tomorrow,' I said. 'And then I thought I'd come down to you for the night, if that's OK.'

'Great by me,' she said.

THE STATE OF MY HOME was worse than I had remembered. The stuff from the fridge that Trent had poured all over the kitchen had started to smell badly. It had been a warm May week and plenty of sunshine had streamed through the large windows into the airless space. I opened all the windows and let some fresh air in. Next I found a cleaning company in the Yellow Pages and promised them a huge bonus if they would come round instantly to do a clear-up job. No problem, they said.

When the team of four arrived from the cleaning company they didn't seem to be fazed one bit by the mess that, to my eyes, was still appalling.

'Had a teenager's party?' one of them asked in all seriousness.

'No,' I said. 'It was malicious vandalism.'

'Same thing,' he said, laughing. 'Now, is there anything here you want to keep from this lot?' He waved a hand around.

'Don't throw out anything that looks unbroken,' I said. 'And keep all the paperwork, whatever condition it's in.'

'Right,' he said. He gave directions to his team and they set to work with mops, cloths and brooms. They removed the torn and broken furniture and stacked it on the back of their vehicle outside. I was amazed at how quickly things began to improve. Within just a few hours most of the furniture was out, and the carpets and rugs had been pulled up. The kitchen had been transformed from a major health hazard into gleaming chrome and a sparkling floor.

'Right, then,' said the team leader finally. 'That wasn't too bad. No rats or anything.'

I shivered. 'What a job,' I said.

'Pays well,' he said.

'Ah, yes,' I said. 'Didn't find my chequebook, did you?'

'All your paperwork's over there,' he said, pointing at a couple of large cardboard boxes sitting alone on the floor. Amazingly, my chequebook had survived, and was only slightly stained by the red wine.

I wrote him out a cheque and then they departed, taking with them most of my worldly goods to be delivered to the council dump.

I decided not to spend the night at Ranelagh Avenue as there was nothing left for me to sleep on. At about six o'clock I ordered a taxi and booked myself into the Novotel in Hammersmith.

The trip back to Barnes had been worthwhile. Not only had I managed to bring some order to my remaining belongings, but my hatred and contempt for Julian Trent had been rekindled too. There was fire in my belly and I aimed to consume him with it.

BOB COLLECTED ME in the Mercedes at 8.30 on Friday morning, and we set off northwards from Hammersmith to Golders Green.

Josef Hughes was waiting for us when we arrived at 845 Finchley Road. I hadn't been very confident that he would be there because I'd had to leave a message for him with someone else in the house using the payphone in the hallway, but, thankfully, my fears were unfounded. He came quickly across the pavement and climbed into the back seat of the car.

''Morning, Josef,' I said to him, turning round as best I could and smiling.

''Morning,' he said. He had the frightened look that I had come to know so well. He turned to glance a few times through the rear window and then finally settled into his seat.

'This is Bob,' I said, pointing at our driver. 'Bob is most definitely on our side.' Bob looked at me somewhat strangely but I ignored him.

'Where to now?' he asked me.

'Hendon,' I said.

We picked up George Barnett from outside Hendon bus station, as he'd requested. He didn't want me going near his home, he'd said, in case anyone was watching.

I introduced him to Bob, and also to Josef.

'Where now?' asked Bob. I purposely hadn't told either of them where we were going.

'Weybridge,' I said to him.

Josef visibly tensed. He didn't like it, and the closer we came to Weybridge, the more agitated he became.

'Josef,' I said calmly, 'all I want is for you to point out where you were told to go and tell the solicitor about approaching the members of the jury in the first Trent trial. We will just drive past.'

He mumbled something about wishing he hadn't come. The long finger of fear extended by Julian Trent and his allies was difficult to overcome.

As we went slowly along the High Street Josef sank lower and lower in the seat until he was almost kneeling on the floor of the car.

'There,' he said breathlessly, pointing above a Chinese takeaway.

COULSTON AND BLACK, SOLICITORS AT LAW was painted on the glass across three of the windows on the first floor.

Bob stopped the car in a side street and then helped me out with the crutches. I asked him to try to ensure that neither of his remaining passengers lost their nerve and ran off while I was away. I also asked him to get Josef out of the car in precisely three minutes and walk him to the corner and stay there until I waved from the window. Then I walked back to the High Street and slowly climbed the stairs to the offices of Coulston and Black.

A middle-aged woman in a grey skirt and tight maroon jumper was seated at a desk in the small reception office.

'Can I help you?' she said, looking up as I opened the door.

'Is Mr Coulston or Mr Black in, please?' I asked her.

'I'm afraid they're both dead,' she said with a smile. This was obviously a regular turn of hers that clearly amused her. 'Mr Hamilton is the only solicitor in the firm now. I am his secretary. Would you like to see him?'

'Yes, please,' I said. 'I would.'

'Personal injury case, is it?' she said, indicating towards the crutches.

'Something like that,' I replied.

'What name shall I say?' she asked, standing up and moving as if to go through the door behind her.

'Trent,' I said boldly. 'Julian Trent.'

The effect on her was startling. She went into near collapse and lunged at the door, which opened wide and sent her sprawling onto the floor inside the other room. There I could see a smartly dressed man sitting behind a desk.

'Patrick,' the woman managed to say, 'this man says he's Julian Trent.'

There was a tightening around the eyes but Patrick Hamilton was more in control.

'It's all right, Audrey,' said Mr Hamilton. 'This isn't Julian Trent.' He looked at me. 'Who are you?' he said. 'And what do you want from me?'

'Tell me what you know about Julian Trent,' I said to him, walking across to his desk and sitting down on the chair in front of it.

'Why should I?' he said.

'Because otherwise,' I said, 'I might go straight to the Law Society and tell them about your role in getting Julian Trent off an attempted murder conviction.'

'You can't,' he said. 'You don't have the evidence.'

'Ah,' I said. 'There you might be wrong. I assume you've heard of Josef Hughes?'

He went a little pale. I stood up and went to the window. Bob and Josef were standing on the corner opposite.

'Would you like him to come up and identify you?' I said to Hamilton.

He stood up and looked out of the window. Then he sat down again, heavily, in his chair. I waved at Bob.

'Now, Mr Hamilton,' I said, 'what do you know of Julian Trent?'

In all I spent forty-five minutes in Patrick Hamilton's office listening to another sorry tale of petty greed gone wrong. As before, a small thing had been asked for, to start with. Just to collect a statement from someone who would deliver it with no questions asked and to notarise it as a sworn affidavit. Then had come the further demands to attend at the High Court and, if necessary, commit perjury in order to convince the appeal judges the truth of the statement. There was no risk, he'd been told by his persuasive visitor. Josef Hughes would never tell anyone, the visitor had guaranteed it.

I showed him a photo and he seemed to visibly shrink. I didn't need to ask him if the photo was of the visitor. I could tell it was.

I stood up to go. 'Just one last question,' I said. 'Why you?'

I didn't really expect an answer, but what he said was very revealing.

'I've been the Trent family solicitor for years,' he said. 'Michael and Barbara Trent have now moved, but they lived in Weybridge for a long time.'

'But your visitor wasn't Julian Trent's father?' I said to him.

'No, it was his godfather.'

I TOOK JOSEF HUGHES and George Barnett to lunch at the Runnymede Hotel, in the restaurant there overlooking the Thames. Nikki Payne came to join us. I had chosen the venue with care. I wanted somewhere peaceful and quiet. I wanted somewhere to tell Josef and George what I had discovered and what I needed them to do to help me.

The four of us sat at a table in the window, with Nikki next to me and Josef and George opposite us. For a while we made small talk and chatted about the weather as we watched the pleasure boats moving up and down through the lock. Everyone relaxed a little over a glass of cool Chablis.

Finally, after we had eaten lunch, we sat over our coffee while I told them about the murder of Scot Barlow and how Steve Mitchell was currently on trial for it at Oxford Crown Court.

'I've seen reports in the papers,' George said, nodding.

'I have no doubt whatsoever that Steve Mitchell is being framed,' I said seriously. 'And I believe he's being framed by this man.' I placed a copy of the photograph I had shown Patrick Hamilton on the table in front of them.

The effect was immediate. Both Josef and George shied away from the image as if it could somehow jump up and hit them. Josef began to take fast, shallow breaths, while George just sat there grinding his teeth.

'It's all right, guys,' I said, trying to lighten the moment. 'He doesn't know we're here, or even that I know either of you. And with your help I can put this man behind bars where he can't get at you.'

They went on looking scared and uncertain.

'Julian Trent was behind bars,' said Josef quickly. 'Who says he can't still get at us from there? Where's the guarantee?'

'I agree with Josef,' said George with a furrowed brow. 'Julian Trent would simply repay the favour and get him out.'

I felt that I was losing them.

'Let me first explain to you what I want to do,' I said, 'and then you can decide if you'll help. But, I'll tell you, I'm going to try to get this man whether you help me or not. And it will be easier with your backing.'

Between us, Nikki and I told them everything we had discovered.

'But why do you need us?' said Josef. 'Why don't you just take all this to the police and let them deal with it?'

'I could,' I said. 'But the police would take ages to do their investigating and in the meantime, Steve Mitchell would be convicted of murder.'

'So what do you intend to do?' asked George.

I told them.

I had to trust them all, including Nikki, not to tell anyone of my plans, so I didn't tell them quite everything. That would have meant telling Nikki the inconvenient truth that I was being intimidated to influence the outcome of a trial, and that might put her under an obligation to tell the court, or, at least, to tell Bruce, who was her immediate superior.

When I had finished, the three of them sat silently for quite a while. Eventually it was George who broke the spell.

'Do you really think it will work?' he said.

'It's worth a try,' I said. 'And I think it might if you two play your part.'

'I don't know,' said Josef. 'I've got to think of Bridget and Rory.'

'Well, I'm game,' said George, smiling. 'If only to see his face.'

'Good,' I said, standing up. 'Come on, let's go. There's something I want to show you.'

Bob drove us the half a mile or so to the far end of Runnymede Meadow and then waited in the car while the rest of us made our way across the grass to a small, round classical-temple-style structure on the south side of the meadow.

It had been no accident that we had come to lunch at Runnymede. This was where King John had been forced to sign the Magna Carta, the Great Charter of June 15, 1215. The Magna Carta remained the basis of much of our common law, including the right to be tried by a panel of one's peers.

The Magna Carta Memorial had been built in 1957 by members of the American Bar Association, in recognition of the importance of the ancient document in shaping laws throughout Western civilisation. Eight slim pillars supported an unfussy, flattish, two-step dome, and in the centre of the memorial stood a seven-foot-high granite pillar with the inscription TO COMMEMORATE MAGNA CARTA, SYMBOL OF FREEDOM UNDER LAW.

Every lawyer knew that most of the clauses were now either obsolete or had been repealed or replaced by new legislation. However, four crucial clauses of the original charter were still valid in English courts, nearly eight hundred years later. Two of them were about the freedom of the individual.

As translated from the original Latin, with the 'we' meaning 'the Crown', these ran:

No freeman shall be seized, or imprisoned, or dispossessed, or outlawed, or in any way destroyed: nor will we condemn him, nor will we commit him to prison, excepting by the legal judgment of his peers, or by the laws of the land.

and

To none will we sell, to none will we deny, to none will we delay right or justice.

These clauses provided for freedoms that most of us took for granted. Only when the likes of Julian Trent or his godfather came along did we understand what it meant to have our rights and justice denied.

I had spent the time we had been walking telling the others about the great meeting that had taken place so long ago on this very spot between King John and the English barons, and how the King had been forced to sign away his autocratic powers, and how, in return, the barons, together with the King, had agreed to provide basic freedoms to their subjects.

Now, I leaned against the granite pillar and its succinct inscription.

'So will you help me?' I said to Josef. 'Will you help me get justice and allow us freedom under law?'

'Yes,' he said, looking me straight in the eye. 'I will.'

BOB TOOK JOSEF AND GEORGE back to their respective homes in north London, while Nikki drove me to Slough and dropped me at the station.

As I waited on the platform my phone rang in my pocket.

'Hello,' I said.

'What does it take to get you to do as you're told?' said the whispering voice.

'More than you could ever know,' I said, and hung up.

What he probably didn't realise was how frightened I had been at what he might do. In fact, I still was.

I called my father on the new mobile phone I had bought him.

'Having a nice time?' I asked him. I had sent him to the seaside, to stay in the Victoria Hotel in Sidmouth, Devon, where he could get plenty of healthy fresh air, and where, I hoped, Julian Trent wouldn't think of looking for him.

'I suppose so,' he said. 'But everyone else here is so old. When can I go home?'

'Soon,' I said. 'I'll let you know when.'

'Why?' he said. 'Why do I have to stay here?'

'I'll tell you everything next week,' I said. 'In the meantime please stay there for a bit longer.'

'You're a strange boy,' he said. It was his usual answer for everything.

'Maybe,' I said. 'But please, Dad, stay there. Please just do as I ask.'

'All right,' he said reluctantly.

Next I called Eleanor. 'Are you free from now on for the night?' I asked.

'All weekend,' she said happily.

'Good,' I said. 'Please will you pack a bag now, go to Newbury station and wait for me there.'

'Geoffrey'—she sounded worried—'you're frightening me.'

'Eleanor, please,' I said. 'Do it now and quickly. Get away from the hospital and the house and then call me.'

'Right,' she said. 'I'm on my way.' The urgency of my voice had clearly cut through her reservations.

'I'll be at Newbury in forty-five minutes,' I said. 'Try to keep on the move until then and don't take lonely lanes. Main roads only.'

'OK,' she said. 'I get the message.'

I sat restlessly on the train until Eleanor called to say she was safely away from Lambourn and was now on the M4.

'Is anyone following you?' I asked her.

'Not that I can see,' she said.

'Good,' I said. 'I'll see you at Newbury station.'

ELEANOR PULLED UP outside the red-brick station building as I struggled through the narrow doorway with my suitcase and crutches. I tossed the suitcase onto the back seat of her car and climbed into the passenger seat. She leaned over and gave me a kiss.

'Where to?' she said, driving away.

'Oxford,' I said.

I made Eleanor drive twice round the roundabout where the A34 crosses the M4, but if there was someone tailing us, I couldn't see them.

'Do you really think that someone would have come to Lambourn looking for me?' asked Eleanor.

'Yes,' I said, 'I do. I think these people will stop at nothing. It's no longer about Steve Mitchell any more, it's to do with them not getting convicted for the murder of Scot Barlow.'

For the rest of the journey Eleanor spent almost as much time looking in the rearview mirror as she did watching the road in front, but we made it to the hotel safely.

As we pulled up at the hotel entrance, Eleanor's phone rang.

'Hello,' she said, pushing the button. She listened for a few moments. 'Suzie, hold on a minute.' She turned to me. 'It's Suzie, one of the other vets at the hospital. Seems a young man has turned up there asking for me, says he's my younger brother.'

'And is he?' I asked her.

'I'm an only child,' she said. 'The young man has talked his way up into my room and is waiting there. Suzie is downstairs.'

'Let me talk to her,' I said.

Eleanor handed the phone to me. I tossed my own phone at Eleanor. 'Call the police,' I said to her. 'Tell them there's an intruder in the house there with a girl on her own. Suzie,' I said into Eleanor's phone, 'this is Geoffrey Mason. I'm a friend of Eleanor's.'

'I know,' she said, laughing. 'She's talked of nothing else for weeks.'

'Are you there on your own?' I asked her, cutting off her laughter.

'Yes,' she said. 'Except for him upstairs. The others have gone down the pub, but I didn't feel up to it.'

'Suzie, I don't want to alarm you too much, but the young man is not Eleanor's younger brother,' I said. 'And I fear he could be dangerous.'

There was silence from the other end of the line.

I went on, 'Eleanor is talking to the police now.'

'Oh God!' she said shakily.

'Suzie,' I said urgently, not wanting her to go into a complete panic, 'if you can leave the house without him seeing you, then go straight away. Go round to the pub and stay there with the others.'

'OK,' she said rapidly. 'I'm going now.'

'Good,' I said. 'Are you talking on a mobile phone?'

'Yes,' she said.

'Then keep talking to me as you leave the house. Do it now.'

I could hear her breathing and also the squeak of a door being opened.

'Quietly,' I hissed into the phone, but I don't think she heard me.

There was the sound of her feet crunching on the gravel as she ran down the path.

'He's coming after me,' she screamed.

'Run,' I said.

I didn't need to say it. I could hear Suzie running. Then the running stopped. I heard a car door slam and the central locking click.

'I'm in my car,' she said breathlessly. 'Oh my God,' she said, her voice rising in panic. 'He's walking down the path.'

'Where's Eleanor Clarke?' I could hear Julian Trent shouting, his voice muffled by the car doors and windows.

'Go away,' screamed Suzie. 'Leave me alone. I've called the police.'

'Where's Eleanor?' Trent shouted again, banging on the car windows.

'With her boyfriend,' shouted Suzie back at him. 'In London.'

Well done her, I thought. It went quiet, save for the sound of Suzie's rapid shallow breathing.

'Suzie?' I asked. 'What's happening?'

'He's run off,' she said. 'He's disappeared round the back of the hospital.'

'The police are on their way,' I said. 'Stay in the car until they come.' I hoped that Trent hadn't disappeared simply to get his trusty baseball bat, so he could smash his way into Suzie's car.

'Who the hell was it?' she asked me.

'I don't know,' I lied. 'But he definitely wasn't Eleanor's brother. I think he may have been someone on the lookout for women.'

'Oh my God,' she said again. 'He might have raped me.'

'Suzie,' I said as calmly as possible, 'be happy he didn't. You're fine.'

'The police are here.' She sounded relieved.

'Good,' I said. 'Give Eleanor a call later, after you've spoken to them.'

'OK,' she said. 'I will.' By now she sounded quite normal. Vets were obviously made of stern stuff.

I hung up and passed the phone back to Eleanor.

'Why didn't you tell her it was Julian Trent?' she said, almost accusingly.

'We don't absolutely know for certain that it was him, even if we are pretty sure that it was. The police are bound to be in touch with us. They'll have the phone number. If we want, we can give them Trent's name then as a possible suspect,' I said.

She nodded. 'But why do you suddenly think that I am now in danger from Julian Trent when I wasn't before?'

'Because since the witness summons was delivered, he now knows for sure that I won't do what he wants. I think he would try to use you as a lever rather than as just an implied threat.'

'And it seems you are right,' she said. 'So now what?'

'Eleanor,' I said, turning to look at her face, 'no one, not even you, has really understood what sort of people we are dealing with here. This is a story of blackmail and murder, where seriously nasty people would as easily kill you as they would a fly.' She stared at me with wide eyes. 'But I don't intend to let them do either.'

WITH THE KNOWLEDGE that Julian Trent had been in Lambourn only fifteen minutes previously, Eleanor and I felt quite relaxed as we made our way into the hotel with the stuff from her car.

I locked the door with us securely on the inside, and felt safe for the first time in hours. Then I called down to the front desk, asked the receptionist to ensure that I wasn't disturbed and ordered a bottle of red wine and some glasses. Eleanor and I may have needed to be locked up for the weekend, but it didn't mean we couldn't have a few of life's little pleasures to while away the time.

CHAPTER 11

'All rise,' called the court clerk. The judge entered and took his seat behind the bench. Everyone else then sat down. The court was now in session.

'Mr Mason,' said the judge.

'Yes, My Lord,' I said, rising.

'Is your witness present?' he asked.

'As far as I am aware, My Lord,' I replied. I hadn't actually been outside into the waiting area, but Bruce Lygon seemed happy the witness was ready. In fact, I hadn't been outside at all since last Friday.

At 10.30 on Friday evening the telephone in the hotel room had rung.

'Mr Mason, we are sorry to disturb you,' the hotel operator had said, 'but we have your nephew on the telephone, and he's frantic to get in touch with you. I'm sorry, but he tells me your elderly father has had a fall and he's been taken to hospital.'

'Did you confirm to my nephew that I was here?' I'd asked her.

'Of course,' she'd said. 'Shall I put him through?'

'Thank you,' I'd said. There had been a click or two, but no one had been on the line. Trent had already gained the information he had wanted.

Thereafter Eleanor and I had not left the room for the whole weekend. We had ordered room service for every meal and told the staff to ensure that they were alone when it was delivered. They had probably thought we were totally mad, but they had been too polite to say so, to us at least.

I had called Bruce to discuss how to get safely to court on Monday morning. Without telling him exactly why I was concerned, I explained that I didn't want to run into my witness before the hearing and I needed some secure transport from the hotel to the court buildings. He had come up with the ingenious idea of getting a private security company to collect me in a prison transfer van. The van had then delivered us right into the court complex through the security gates round the back, just as it would have done if we had been defendants on remand. Eleanor, who had called the equine hospital to say she wasn't coming in to work, now sat behind me in court, next to Bruce.

'Very well,' said the judge. He nodded at the court usher, who went to fetch the jury. As we waited, I looked around the courtroom. The press box was busy but not quite so full as it had been at the start of the trial the week before. Only about half of the thirty or so of the public seats were occupied, with Mr and Mrs Barlow sitting together in the front row, as ever.

The five men and seven women of the jury filed into the court and took their seats to my left in the jury box. Mothers and fathers, brothers and sisters, professional people and manual workers, all thrown together into a panel by chance. There was nothing extraordinary about any one of them, but collectively they had to perform the extraordinary task of determining the facts and deciding if the defendant was guilty or not. They'd had no training for the task. Our whole legal system was reliant on such groups of people, who had never met one another prior to the trial, doing the 'right' thing and together making exceptional decisions on questions far beyond their regular daily experiences. I hoped they had been well rested by four days away from the court. They might need to be on the ball to follow what would happen here today, and to understand its significance.

'Mr Mason,' said the judge, looking down at me from the bench.

It was now time.

'Thank you, My Lord,' I said, rising. 'The defence calls . . .' Suddenly my mouth was dry and my tongue felt enormous. I took a sip from my glass of water. 'The defence calls Mr Roger Radcliffe.'

ROGER RADCLIFFE was shown into court by the usher, who directed him to the witness box. He was asked to give his full name. 'Roger Kimble Radcliffe,' he said confidently. He was then given a New Testament to hold and asked to read out loud from a card. 'I swear by Almighty God that the evidence I shall give shall be the truth, the whole truth and nothing but the truth.'

One could but hope, I thought.

Before I had a chance to say anything, Radcliffe turned to the judge.

'Your Honour,' he said, 'I have no idea why I have been asked to come here today. I knew Scot Barlow only by reputation. He has never ridden any of my horses. I'm a very busy man running my own company and I resent having to waste my time coming to court.'

He stood bolt upright in the witness box looking at the judge with an air of someone who had been greatly inconvenienced for no good reason.

'Mr Radcliffe,' the judge replied, 'the defence have every right to call whomsoever they wish, provided that their evidence is relevant to the trial. If I consider that your presence is a waste of your time, or of the court's time, then I shall say so. But that decision shall be mine, not yours. Do you understand?'

'Yes, Your Honour,' Radcliffe said.

'Mr Mason,' invited the judge.

'Thank you, My Lord,' I said.

The silence in the courtroom was almost tangible and every eye was on me, waiting for me to begin. I took another sip of water.

'Mr Radcliffe,' I said, 'could you please tell the jury what your company does?'

It was not what he had expected and he seemed to relax a little.

'My main business,' he said, 'is the Radcliffe Foaling Centre.'

'And could you please explain to the jury what that involves?' I asked.

'It involves exactly what the name implies.'

I waited in silence.

He finally continued without further prompting, 'We have about one hundred mares come to us each year. The foals are delivered with proper veterinary care on hand and a team of specially trained grooms.'

'And how long has your business been in operation?' I asked him.

'About seven or eight years,' he said, 'but it has expanded recently.'

'And are there specific reasons for that expansion?' I asked.

'We are doing well,' he said, 'and over the last twelve months I have been able to inject a substantial investment into the business.'

'Would that investment be due to the success of your horse Peninsula?' I asked.

'Yes,' he said. 'Exactly so.'

'Mr Radcliffe,' I said, 'some members of the jury may not be familiar with horse racing so perhaps you could tell them about Peninsula.'

Roger Radcliffe looked imploringly at the bench.

'Please answer the question, Mr Radcliffe,' said the judge.

Roger Radcliffe blew down his nose with irritation. 'Technically, Peninsula is no longer my horse,' he said. 'He was syndicated for stud last year and is now owned by a number of individuals or organisations. I have retained only two shares out of sixty.'

'But you did own him throughout his racing career?' I asked.

'Yes, I did.' He smiled at the memory. 'And I bred him. I owned his mare and he was foaled at my place.'

'And he was a success on the racecourse?' I asked.

'Yes, indeed he was,' said Radcliffe. 'He was the champion two-year-old and he was named Horse of the Year in 2007.' Radcliffe was enjoying himself now. 'He won the Two Thousand Guineas at Newmarket in May, the Derby at Epsom in June and the Breeders' Cup Classic in California last October. It was quite a year.' He smiled at the jury and many of them smiled back at him.

Nikki came into the courtroom and sat down next to Eleanor. 'All set,' she said quietly to my back.

I turned round and leaned down to her. 'Good,' I whispered. 'Keep watch from the door. I'll give you the signal.'

She stood up, bowed slightly to the bench and departed.

'Mr Mason,' said the judge, 'I am sure the jury and I have enjoyed our little lesson in racing, but could you please show us the relevance of your questions, or else I shall release Mr Radcliffe back to his busy business schedule.'

'Yes, My Lord,' I said rather sheepishly.

Roger Radcliffe was enjoying my discomfort. Now, I thought, it was time to rub that smirk off his face.

'Mr Radcliffe,' I said to him, 'how well do you know the defendant, Steve Mitchell?'

'Mitchell has been champion jockey over the jumps,' he said. 'I personally don't have jump horses, but I know him by reputation. We may have met a few times at events. I really can't remember.'

'And how about Millie Barlow, Scot Barlow's sister? Did you know her?'
I noticed a very slight tightening of the skin around his eyes.
'I don't believe I did,' he said calmly.
It was his first lie.
'She was an equine veterinary surgeon,' I said. 'Sadly, she died last June.
Does that jog your memory?'
'I know that a vet died during a party last year,' he said. 'Was that her?'
'Yes,' I said, 'it was. An inquest jury concluded that she had taken her
own life by injecting herself with the anaesthetic thiopental.'
'Very sad,' he said, condescendingly. 'But I can't see the relevance.'
'Mr Radcliffe,' I said, 'were you having an affair with Millie Barlow?'
'No, I was not,' he almost shouted. 'How dare you suggest such a thing?'
He glanced across at his wife, Deborah. She had come into the court
with him when he had been called and was sitting in the public seats.
'Mr Radcliffe, did you attend the party where Millie Barlow died?'
'Yes,' he said, 'as a matter of fact, I did.'
'And can you recall if there was a reason for the party?'
'Yes, there was,' he said. 'It was a party given jointly by me and Simon
Dacey, at Simon's house, to celebrate Peninsula winning the Derby.'
'Simon Dacey being the trainer of the horse?' I said.
'Yes,' Radcliffe replied.
'Can you recall why Millie Barlow was a guest at this party?'
The judge was looking at me intently. 'Mr Mason, are these questions
really relevant to the case before this court?'
'My Lord,' I said, 'the prosecution has previously made it clear that the
relationship that existed between the defendant and Miss Barlow was a
major cause of the antagonism between the defendant and the victim, and
hence, they claim, it ultimately provided the motive for murder. It is my
intention to explore this relationship further.'
'Very well,' he said. 'You may continue.'
'Thank you, My Lord.' I turned back to the witness box. 'Now, Mr
Radcliffe,' I said, 'I was asking you if you knew why Millie Barlow was
invited to the party.'
'I have no idea,' he said. 'I told you I didn't know her.'
'Then why,' I said, picking up a piece of paper from the table, 'did you
purchase a brand-new sports car and give it to her?'
He was initially flustered, but he recovered fast. 'I have no idea what you
are talking about.'

'I'm talking about a bright red Mazda MX-5 Roadster purchased in September 2007 from the Mazda dealership in Newbury'—I referred to the piece of paper that Nikki had obtained from the dealership the previous Friday—'at a cost of fifteen thousand, seven hundred and fifty pounds.'

He stood silently in the witness box staring at me.

'Mr Radcliffe,' I said, 'last Friday my solicitor's clerk visited the dealership and they told her they remembered this car being paid for, in full, with a banker's draft, which is most unusual. The draft did not have the name of the purchaser on it. However, the sales representative remembered the purchaser, and he was able to identify you from this photograph.' I held up the glossy brochure that I had taken from the foaling centre on my first visit there, the brochure with the photograph on the front of a smiling Roger and Deborah Radcliffe, the same brochure I had showed to Patrick Hamilton, and then to Josef Hughes and George Barnett.

'I can call the Mazda sales representative as a witness if you want me to.' I paused. He said nothing. 'Now, Mr Radcliffe, please can you tell the jury why you gave Millie Barlow a brand-new car?'

'It's none of your business,' said Radcliffe defiantly.

'Mr Radcliffe,' the judge intervened, 'you will answer the question, unless you wish to claim that, in doing so, you might incriminate yourself. And if that is the case, the question may be of interest to the police.'

Radcliffe stood silent for a moment and then he smiled. 'It was a gift to her for doing a fine job when Peninsula was foaled. She was the attending vet. I didn't want to give my name when I purchased the car as I didn't want the Inland Revenue to consider it a payment for services and require her to pay income tax on its value.' He smiled at the jury. 'I am sorry I tried to avoid a little tax,' he said with a laugh. 'We all try it occasionally, don't we? I will pay back the tax right away.'

He had done well, I thought. Quick thinking, in the circumstances.

'Was it not payment to her because she was blackmailing you?' I asked him.

The smile disappeared from his face. 'Blackmail?' he said. 'That's nonsense,' he said with an air of confidence.

I turned and waved at Nikki, who was watching me through the glass panel in the courtroom door. She entered the court followed by two other people. All three new arrivals bowed slightly to the bench and then came and sat behind Eleanor and Bruce.

I watched the colour drain out of Roger Radcliffe's face as he stared at the newcomers. He gripped the sides of the witness box as if to prevent himself from falling.

Josef Hughes and George Barnett sat quite still and stared back at him.

'Mr Radcliffe,' I said, 'do you know someone called Julian Trent?'

Roger Radcliffe was more than flustered this time. I could tell from the way the skin had tightened over his face and there was a slight tic in the corner of his left eye. He stood quite still in the witness box, but I was sure that, behind those steely eyes, his brain was working fast.

'Julian Trent is your godson, isn't he?' I asked him.

'Yes,' he said quietly.

'I'm sorry, Mr Radcliffe,' I said. 'Would you please speak up? The jury can't hear you if you whisper.'

The irony of the comment was not lost on him. He glared at me.

I noticed that the press box had filled considerably since the start of the day. Word had clearly been passed outside that something was afoot. Detective Inspector McNeile sat in a row of seats in front of the press box, and he too was taking a keen interest in the proceedings.

'Now, Mr Radcliffe,' I said, 'can we return to the question of blackmail?'

'I don't know what you mean,' he replied, but the confidence had gone out of his performance.

'We have heard that you bought a new car and then gave it to Millie Barlow,' I told him. 'Is that correct?'

'Yes,' he said.

'I repeat my question.' I paused. 'Was that car given by you to Millie Barlow as a payment for blackmail?'

'No, that's utter rubbish,' he said.

I collected some more papers together in my hands.

'These are bank statements. Millie Barlow's bank statements. They show that she received regular payments over and above her salary from the equine hospital,' I said. 'Can you explain these payments?'

'Of course not,' Radcliffe said.

'Were these also blackmail payments, Mr Radcliffe, from you?'

'No,' he answered. But some of the jury looked sceptical.

'Mr Radcliffe,' I said, changing direction, 'do you ever have need for anaesthetics at your equine maternity unit?'

'No,' he said firmly. 'Why should we?'

'Perhaps for a Caesarean birth if a foal cannot be born naturally?' I asked him.

'No,' he said, suddenly back on surer ground. 'The mare would be transferred to one of the local equine hospitals and anaesthetised there.'

'And what would happen if a foal was born grossly deformed, or blind?'

'That is very rare,' he said.

'But it must have happened at least once or twice in your experience. Would the foal be immediately put down?'

He could see where I was going, and he didn't like it.

'I suppose so,' he said.

'And isn't a very large dose of a barbiturate anaesthetic used for that purpose, a barbiturate anaesthetic like thiopental for example?' I asked.

'I wouldn't know,' he said.

'Mr Radcliffe,' I said, changing tack again, 'do you know of someone called Jacques van Rensburg?'

'I don't think so,' he said, but he started to sweat.

'You may have known of him simply as Jack Rensburg,' I said. 'He used to work for you as a groom.'

'We have lots of grooms during the foaling season,' he said, 'and they come and go regularly. We've had quite a few Jacks.'

'Perhaps I can help you,' I said. 'I have a photograph of him.'

I took a stack of the Millie and foal pictures out of one of my boxes and passed them to the court usher, who passed one to the judge, one to the prosecution, six to the jury and, finally, one to Radcliffe in the witness box.

Some of the colour had returned to his face, but now it drained away again.

'Members of the jury,' I said, 'you will see that the photograph is of a newborn foal. The woman in the picture is Millie Barlow, the veterinary surgeon who had been present at the birth, and the man standing behind her is Jacques van Rensburg. Isn't that right, Mr Radcliffe?'

'If you say so,' he said.

'I do. And the foal is Peninsula, the horse that went on to be such a champion,' I said. 'Isn't that right?'

'It might be,' he said. 'I can't tell. Many foals look alike.'

'Of course,' I said. 'But I assure you that the foal in this picture is Peninsula. He was the very first foal that Millie Barlow delivered on her own. She was so proud of that horse and her part in his life that she kept a copy of that picture in a silver frame. Isn't that right, Mr Radcliffe?'

'I have no idea,' he said.

'After his sister's death, Scot Barlow asked for the picture in the silver frame to keep in his home as a lasting reminder of her, but the photo was removed from its frame and taken away from Scot Barlow's house on the night he was killed. Why do you think that was?'

'I have no idea,' he said again.

'I put it to you, Mr Radcliffe, that the picture was removed because it was being used by Scot Barlow to blackmail you in the same way that his sister had done previously. Isn't that right?'

'No,' he said. 'That's nonsense. I don't know what you're talking about.'

'Does Jacques van Rensburg still work for you?' I asked him.

'No,' he said. 'I don't believe he does.'

'No,' I said. 'He couldn't, could he? Because he's dead. Isn't that right, Mr Radcliffe?'

'I have no idea,' he said yet again.

'Oh, yes, I think you do,' I said. 'Jacques van Rensburg went on holiday to Thailand, didn't he?'

'If you say so,' Radcliffe replied.

'Not if I say so, Mr Radcliffe,' I said, taking yet another sheet of paper from my stack. 'The South African Department of Home Affairs in Pretoria says so. He went to Thailand on holiday and he never came back. Do you know why he didn't come back, Mr Radcliffe?'

Roger Radcliffe stood silently in the witness box.

'He didn't come back because, as the South African government records show, he was drowned on Phuket beach by the Great Asian Tsunami. And, Mr Radcliffe, do you know when the Great Asian Tsunami occurred?'

Radcliffe shook his head and looked down.

'It is sometimes known as the Boxing Day Tsunami, is it not, Mr Radcliffe?' I said. 'Because it took place on December the 26th. Isn't that right?'

He made no move to answer.

I continued. 'Which means that, as Jacques van Rensburg was drowned in Thailand on the 26th of December, 2004, this picture had to have been taken before Christmas that year. Which also means, does it not, Mr Radcliffe, that, even though the record of the birth submitted by you to Weatherbys shows otherwise, Peninsula had to have been foaled prior to January the 1st, 2005 and was therefore, in fact, officially a four-year-old horse when he won the Two Thousand Guineas and the Derby last year and not a three-year-old as demanded by the rules of racing?'

For what seemed like an age, the silence in the court was broken only by the sound of fast-moving pencils on notebooks in the press box, and by a slight sob from Deborah Radcliffe in the public seats.

The judge looked intently at Roger Radcliffe, who was standing silently in the witness box with his head down.

'Well?' said the judge to him. 'The witness will please answer the question. Was Peninsula a four-year-old horse when he ran in the Derby?'

Radcliffe lifted his head a fraction. 'I refuse to answer on the grounds that I might incriminate myself.'

It was as close to a confession as we were likely to get.

But I hadn't finished with him yet. 'Mr Radcliffe,' I said, 'did you murder Millie Barlow because she made further blackmail demands on you after Peninsula had won the Derby?'

His head came up sharply and he looked at me. 'No,' he said.

'And did you then murder Scot Barlow when he took over the blackmail demands from his dead sister?'

'No,' he said once more.

'Or was it your godson, Julian Trent, who actually carried out that second murder, on your instructions, after you had used intimidation of these innocent people in order to secure his release from prison for that very purpose?' I waved my right hand towards Josef Hughes and George Barnett behind me.

Radcliffe's demeanour finally broke completely. 'You bastard,' he shouted at me. 'You fucking bastard. I'll kill you too.'

He tried to leave the witness box, but he had made just two steps towards me when he was surrounded by court security guards and the police.

The judge banged his gavel and silence was briefly restored.

'The defence rests, My Lord,' I said, and sat down.

Perry Mason himself would have been proud of me.

THE JUDGE ADJOURNED the case for lunch while Roger Radcliffe was arrested by Detective Inspector McNeile. The man I had come to know as 'the whisperer' was led away, still spouting obscenities in my direction.

The smarmy prosecution QC came across and firmly shook my hand. 'Well done,' he said with obvious warmth. 'We don't often get to see the likes of that in an English court.'

'Thank you,' I said. 'I intend to request an acquittal.'

'Up to the judge, old boy,' he said. 'I'll seek instruction from the CPS, but I don't think there will be any objection from our side.'

Eleanor, behind me, rubbed my shoulders.

'You were brilliant,' she said. 'Absolutely brilliant.'

I turned and smiled at her. Josef Hughes and George Barnett sat behind her, beaming away as if smiles could go out of fashion.

'You two can have your self-respect back,' I said. 'Without you here I think he might have bluffed his way out.'

If it was possible, they smiled even wider, and then shook me and each other by the hand.

'How about a coffee?' I said to them.

As we made our way out of court I bumped into Scot Barlow's parents. Mr Barlow was a big man and he stood looking down at me, blocking my path to the door. I waited in front of him, staring back. I wondered if he was pleased or not. He had just discovered the truth about who had killed his children and why, but he had also discovered that they had both been black-mailers. Eventually he nodded just once, then turned aside to let me pass.

Eleanor, Josef, George, Bruce, Nikki and I sat at one of the tables in the self-service cafeteria area in the main court corridor, drinking vending-machine coffee from thin brown plastic cups, toasting our success.

'But why was the horse's age so important?' asked Bruce. 'So what if the horse was a year older than it was supposed to be when it ran in the Derby? I know that it was cheating, but was it really worth murdering someone over? It was only a race.'

'It may have been "only a race",' I said, 'but horse racing is very big business indeed. Peninsula was sold to stud for sixty million US dollars. And it was mainly because he won that race as a three-year-old running against other three-year-olds that he was worth all that money. Only horses of that age are allowed to run in the "classic" races held in England.'

'I never realised,' said Bruce.

'Peninsula was syndicated into sixty shares,' I said. 'Radcliffe says that he kept two for himself, so there are fifty-eight other shareholders who each paid Radcliffe a million dollars for their share. I suspect that most of those will soon be wanting their money back. It will all get very nasty.'

'But why didn't Radcliffe just register the horse with the right age and run him the year before?' Josef asked.

'Most racehorse foals are born between February the 1st and the end of April,' I said. 'The trick is to mate mares at the right time so that the foals arrive as soon as possible after the turn of the year, meaning they are as old as possible without being officially a year older. Peninsula was probably due to be a very early foal and was born prematurely. Radcliffe must have decided to keep his birth secret until January. If he had registered it correctly in December, Peninsula would have been officially a yearling when he was biologically less than a month old. He would have been at a great disadvantage against horses classified as the same age but born nearly a whole year before him. He would most likely still have been a good horse, but not a great one. Not sixty million dollars great. To say nothing of the prize money that Radcliffe will now have to give back for all of those races.'

'But Millie knew the truth because she'd been there when Peninsula was foaled,' said Eleanor.

'Exactly,' I said. 'Radcliffe had probably paid her off. But maybe she was greedy, and that cost her her life. It was our good fortune that you were able to find that picture of Millie and Peninsula as a foal. The silly thing is that if Radcliffe hadn't taken that photo from the frame in Scot Barlow's house, I would never have realised that it was important.'

'How did you know about Millie's car?' Eleanor said.

'I became suspicious when I couldn't find regular payments to any car-finance companies on Millie's bank statements,' I said. 'And there was no one-off large payment around the date you told me she had bought it. So I sent Nikki to the dealer in Newbury to ask some questions. I only found out that Radcliffe was connected to Julian Trent when I showed the picture of him to Josef and George on Friday and saw their reaction.'

'How about Trent?' asked George. 'What will happen to him?'

'I hope the police are looking for him in connection with Barlow's murder,' I said. 'In the meantime I intend to keep well clear of him.'

'So do we all,' said George. He was clearly still frightened by the prospect of coming face to face with young Mr Trent. And with good reason.

CHAPTER 12

When the court resumed at two o'clock, I hardly had to make my submission. The judge asked the prosecution for the Crown's position and their QC indicated that he had been instructed not to oppose the application. The judge then instructed the jury to return a not-guilty verdict and Steve Mitchell was allowed to walk free from the dock.

The story had travelled fast and there was a mass of reporters and television cameras outside the court building when Bruce and I emerged with Steve Mitchell at about three o'clock, into a wall of flash photography. As we were engulfed by the sea of reporters, Eleanor shouted that she would go and fetch her car. There would be no chance of finding a taxi with all this lot about.

'Be careful,' I shouted back at her, thinking of Julian Trent, but she was already gone.

Steve and Bruce answered questions until they were nearly hoarse from having to talk over the traffic noise and the general hubbub, and even I was cajoled by some of the reporters into a comment or two. I was careful not to say things that might be pertinent to the future trial. Finally, with deadlines approaching, the reporters began to drift away and leave us in peace.

'Bloody marvellous, Perry,' Steve said to me, pumping my hand up and down. 'Almost as good as winning the National. Thank you so much.'

I decided not to mention my fee—not just yet, anyway.

Bruce and Steve departed together on foot, while I stepped back inside the court building to wait for Eleanor and the car.

I decided to call my father.

'Hello, Dad,' I said when he answered. 'How are things?'

'It's good to be home,' he said.

Alarm bells suddenly started ringing in my head.

'What do you mean, it's good to be home?' I said.

'Got back here about ten minutes ago,' he said. 'I left the hotel as soon as I got your message.'

'But I didn't give anyone a message,' I said.

'Yes you did,' he said with certainty. 'On this phone. One of those text things. Hold on.' I could hear him pushing the buttons. 'Here it is. "Hi, Dad. Everything fine. Please go home as quickly as possible. Love, Geoffrey".'

'What time did you get it?' I asked him.

'About half past ten this morning,' he said. 'My old Morris is quite slow on the motorway these days.'

Radcliffe had already been in the witness box at half past ten. The message had to have been sent by Julian Trent.

'I thought I told you not to tell anyone where you were.'

'I didn't,' he said, sounding pained. 'No one knew other than you.'

'But who else knew the number of that phone?' I asked.

'Oh, I called and gave it to Beryl and Tony on Saturday,' he said. 'They're my neighbours. Just in case anything happened to the house.'

I could just imagine Julian Trent turning up to find the place deserted and asking the neighbours, in his most charming manner, if they knew where Mr Mason had gone.

'Dad,' I said quite urgently, 'please go back out and get in the car and drive anywhere. Just get away from your house.'

'What on earth for?' he said, annoyed. 'I've only just got back.'

'Dad, please just do it, and do it right now.'

'Oh, all right,' he said. 'I'll just make my cup of tea.'

'Please, Dad,' I said more urgently. 'Leave the tea. Go now.'

'All right,' he said, his annoyance showing again. 'You're a strange boy.'

'Dad, take the phone with you. I'll call you back in a few minutes.'

Eleanor pulled up in the car outside the court buildings, and I hobbled out to her as quickly as I could.

'Drive,' I said urgently as I struggled in. 'Straight on. My father's gone home and I think Julian Trent is somewhere around his bungalow. Trent sent him a text message this morning as if from me, telling him to go back home as soon as possible.'

'Oh my God,' she said, putting her foot down on the accelerator.

'I'm calling the police,' I said.

I dialled 999 and the emergency operator answered almost immediately.

Eleanor dodged a few bollards and drove down Cornmarket Street, which was usually reserved for pedestrians but was the best short cut through the city. We were soon racing down St Giles and away from the city centre.

I heard the police come on the line and the telephone operator gave them my phone number. 'Yes,' said a policeman finally. 'How can we help?'

I tried to explain that my father was in danger from a potential intruder.

'So there isn't actually an intruder in the house at the moment?' the policeman said.

'No,' I replied. 'But I think that he might be outside.'

'We can't send emergency police cars just because people think they may be troubled at some time in the future, now can we, sir?'

'Look,' I said, 'I am a barrister and I have been acting at the Crown Court in Oxford and I'm telling you that I have very good reason to believe that my father may be in great danger. I am on my way to his house right now, but I will be at least another twenty minutes getting there. Will you please send a patrol car immediately?'

'I'll do what I can, sir,' he said. 'I'll record the incident as a priority, but it will take some time to get a car to that part of Northamptonshire.'

'Hopeless,' I said to Eleanor, hanging up. I dialled my father's number again. 'Are you out of the house?' I said when he answered.

'Nearly,' he said.

'What have you been doing?' I asked him in exasperation. It had been at least ten minutes since I had first called him.

'I've been looking for the little present I bought Beryl and Tony in Sidmouth,' he said. 'I know it's in my suitcase somewhere.'

'Dad, please,' I almost shouted at him, 'get yourself out of the house right now.'

'Ah,' he said triumphantly. 'I've found it.'

'Good,' I said. 'Now get out of the house and stay out.'

'Hold on a minute,' he said. 'There's someone at the door.'

'Don't answer it,' I shouted into the phone, but he obviously didn't hear me.

The phone was still connected in his hand and I could faintly hear the exchange taking place on my father's front doorstep. 'What do you want?' I heard my father say. There was something that I didn't catch from his visitor, and then I could hear my father again, his voice now full of concern. 'I don't want any,' he said. 'Please go away.'

Suddenly there was a crash and the phone line went dead.

I quickly called the house land-line number, but it simply rang and rang until, eventually, someone picked it up, then it went dead. I tried it again, but this time there was nothing but the engaged tone.

'Oh my God,' I said. 'I think Julian Trent has just arrived.'

Eleanor floored the accelerator as we swept onto the A34 dual carriageway northwards. Fortunately, the rush hour had yet to get into full swing and we hurtled up to the motorway junction and onto the M40 at breakneck speed.

'Call the police again,' said Eleanor.

This time I was connected to a different policeman and he promised to dispatch a patrol car immediately.

'How long will it take?' I said.

'About twenty minutes,' he said. 'At best. Maybe longer. The patrol car has to come from Towcester.'

'Twenty minutes!' I said incredulously. 'I don't believe it. Just get someone there as soon as you can.'

Eleanor had been driving like a woman possessed, overtaking a lorry on the outside of a roundabout when turning right, and then causing a group of mothers and toddlers crossing the road to leap for their lives. But we made it safely to Kings Sutton in record time and she pulled up where I told her, round the corner and just out of sight of my father's bungalow.

'Wait here,' I said, struggling out of the car with the crutches. 'Show the police which is the right house when they arrive.'

'Why don't you wait for the police?' she said. She came round the car and took my hand. 'Please will you wait?'

'Eleanor, my darling, my father's in there on his own with Julian Trent,' I said.

Eleanor grabbed me and hugged me hard. 'Be careful, then, Mr Barrister Man,' she said. 'I love you.'

'I love you more,' I said, but then I pushed her away. I had things to do.

I made my way gingerly through an herbaceous border and along the side of the bungalow to my father's front door. It was standing wide open. I could see nothing unusual, save for the mobile phone that lay on the floor with its back off, the battery lying close by.

I stepped through the doorway into the hall, rather wishing that the crutches didn't make so much of a clink when I put them down on the hard wood-block floor. But I needn't have worried. As I moved across the hallway I could hear Julian Trent and his baseball bat in the bedrooms systematically doing to my father's home what he had done to mine.

I looked into the sitting room. My father lay face down on the carpet, blood oozing from his head. I quickly went over to him and bent down, using one end of the sofa for support. I turned him over slightly and saw that he had been struck severely across his face, and that there was a nasty wound behind his right ear. I couldn't tell if he was breathing or not, and I tried unsuccessfully to find a pulse in his neck. However, the cuts on his head were still bleeding slightly, which gave me some hope.

Where were those damn police? I thought.

The noise of destruction in the bedrooms suddenly ceased and I could hear Trent's footsteps coming back along the corridor. I struggled up and hid behind the open sitting-room door.

My father groaned.

Trent heard him and he stopped in the doorway.

I looked down at my father on the floor and realised with horror that I'd left one of my crutches lying right next to him on the carpet.

It was too late to retrieve it now.

Trent came into the sitting room. I pressed myself back tight against the wall behind the door. I could see the end of the baseball bat as he held it out in front of him.

'OK,' he said loudly into the silence, making me jump. 'I know you're here. Show yourself.'

The door was pulled away from me, exposing my hiding place. And there he was, swinging his baseball bat back and forth and smiling.

'Time to complete some unfinished business,' he said with relish.

'It won't do you any good,' I said defiantly. 'Your godfather was arrested in court this morning and the police are on their way here to arrest you.'

He hardly seemed to care. 'I'd better make it quick, then,' he said nonchalantly. 'That's a shame. I was planning to enjoy taking my time killing you.' He swung the baseball bat at my head so fast that he almost caught me unawares.

At the last moment I ducked and the wooden bat thumped the wall, right where my head had been only a fraction of a second before. I dived away from him, hopping madly on one leg. I would just have to put the other foot down, I thought, and hope my knee would carry my weight. I tried it as I made my way across the room but I was too slow, and Trent had time to turn and swing the bat again, landing a glancing blow on my left bicep, just above the elbow. It wasn't a direct hit, but it was enough to cause my arm to go dead, numb and useless.

I leaned up against the wall by the window, breathing heavily. Two months of inactivity since the races at Cheltenham had left me hopelessly unfit. This battle was going to be over much too soon for my liking.

Trent advanced towards me, grinning broadly, and he raised the bat for another strike. I stood stock still and stared at him. If he was going to kill me, he would have to do it with me watching him. I wasn't going to cower and let him hit me over the back of the head.

I dived down to my left at the last instant and again the bat thumped the wall above my right shoulder. I grabbed it with my good right hand, and also with my nearly useless left. I clung on to the bat for dear life.

With both hands above my shoulders, my body was completely unprotected. Trent took his right hand off the bat and punched me as hard as he could in the stomach.

It was a fatal error on his part. He clearly didn't know about the hard plastic body shell that I still wore beneath my starched white shirt.

He screamed. A long, loud, agonising scream.

It must have been like punching a brick wall. The bones in his hand would have cracked and splintered from the impact. He dropped the baseball bat from his other hand and went down on his knees in obvious pain, clutching his right wrist.

But I wasn't going to let him get off that easily. I picked up the bat and hit him with it, audibly breaking his jaw and sending him sprawling onto the floor, seemingly unconscious.

I sat down on the arm of the sofa and looked out of the window. There was still no sign of the boys in blue, but now I wasn't so worried. I picked up the phone and called for an ambulance. Then I went across to my father. His breathing was perceptible but shallow, and there was a faint pulse in his wrist. I moved him into the recovery position and he groaned obligingly. I stroked his hair.

Julian Trent moaned a little, so I went back and sat on the arm of the sofa and looked down at him lying on the carpet in front of me, the young man who had brought so much misery to so many innocent people.

He began to stir, pulling his knees up under him so he was kneeling on the floor facing away from me, his head bowed down. As I watched him, his head came up a fraction and he tried to reach out slowly with his left hand towards the baseball bat that I had put down on the sofa beside him.

Would he ever give up? I asked myself.

I leaned down quickly and picked up the bat before he could reach it. Instead, he used his left hand to push down on the upholstery, as if he were about to try to stand.

No, I suddenly realised. He would never give up, not ever.

Eleanor and I might make our life together but there would always be the spectre of Julian Trent hovering nearby, forever waiting for the chance to settle the score. Even if he were to be convicted of Scot Barlow's murder, he would simply spend the time planning the completion of his 'unfinished business'. Just like Josef Hughes and George Barnett, we would never be free of the fear. Not for as long as Julian Trent was alive.

In common law, self-defence is called an 'absolute defence'; that is, it doesn't just mitigate a crime, it means that no crime exists in the first place. But in order for a justification of self-defence to succeed, two conditions needed to apply. First, did the accused genuinely believe that force was necessary to protect himself? And, secondly, if he did have that belief, then was the degree of force reasonable to meet the threat as he saw it?

The degree of force used was the key. The force used should not have been excessive or, if it had been, then the perpetrator had only done what he honestly and instinctively thought was necessary to uphold the law rather than taking the law into his own hands for the purposes of retribution.

I glanced briefly out of the window. There was still no sign of the police, nor of the arrival of an ambulance.

Julian Trent drew his left leg forward and slowly began to rise.

It had to be now or never.

I stood up, lifted my arms high over my head and hit him again, bringing the bat down hard and catching him at the base of the skull. There was a terrible crunching noise and he went flat down onto the carpet and lay still.

I wasn't certain whether it had been a lethal blow or not, but it would have to be enough. I felt sick.

All the frustration and fear of the past six months had gone into that strike, together with the anger at losing my possessions, the rage I had for him having torn to shreds the photograph of my Angela, and the fury at what he had done to my father.

I sat down again calmly on the arm of the sofa. It was finally over. I had done only what I honestly and instinctively thought had been necessary to meet the threat as I saw it, and I would have to take my chances in court.

I glanced out of the window once more.

At long last I could see two policemen coming down the driveway.

But now I needed help of a different kind.

I picked up the telephone and called Arthur.

DICK FRANCIS AND FELIX FRANCIS

Dick Francis is known to millions of fans as a best-selling writer, and to many more as the jockey who won a place in the affections of the late Queen Mother. It was in 1956 that he famously rode one of her horses, Devon Loch, in the Grand National Steeplechase, but suffered a shattering blow when the horse, then in a commanding lead, collapsed forty yards from the finish. It was 'both the high point and low point of my career as a jockey,' Francis says. Shortly afterwards he decided to retire as a jockey and to embark on what would become a hugely successful career as a writer.

Born to ride

Richard Stanley Francis was born in Lawrenny, South Wales in 1920. From an early age, he and his brother Doug rode on donkeys, horses and ponies at their grandparents' farm and Dick Francis says he cannot remember a time when he didn't dream of becoming a jockey. The boys' father had been a steeplechase jockey before the First World War and had since become a successful horse dealer. As a teenager, Dick Francis spent his time breaking in and teaching horses to be ridden. He also rode in the show ring at all the major UK horse shows, where he won many 'best boy rider' awards.

For king and country

The outbreak of the Second World War saw the end of the budding young horseman's aspirations when, in 1940, Dick Francis joined the RAF. For two years, he was stationed in North Africa. Then he undertook pilot training in Spitfires, graduating in the summer of 1944, and piloted Lancaster bombers until the war ended. He is pictured (right) at one of the annual Battle of Britain Memorial Flight days.

A national celebrity

Following the war, Dick Francis soon became a celebrity in the world of British National Hunt racing. He won more than 350 races, becoming Champion Jockey in both 1953 and 1954. He was retained as jockey to Her Majesty Queen Elizabeth the Queen Mother for four years, from 1953 to 1957. He is seen here with one of his mounts, and (below) jumping 'the Chair' on the winning horse, Finnure, wearing No 2, in the Champion Chase at Cheltenham, 1950.

A glittering new career

In 1957, when he was con-templating the end of his days as a jockey following a serious fall, Dick Francis was advised by a lit-erary agent that he should work on his autobiography. That same year, he was invited to write six features for the *Sunday Express*—he would remain that paper's racing correspondent for sixteen years. *The Sport of Queens* was

published to warm reviews, and was followed by forty-one chart-topping thrillers, commencing with *Dead Cert* (1962), the biography of Lester Piggot, and a collection of short stories. Dick Francis would be the first to say that his beloved wife, Mary, who died in 2000—the year in which Francis was awarded the CBE—was an integral part of his success, researching storylines and polishing his words.

Father and son

Felix Francis, the younger of Dick and Mary's two sons, has also played a vital part in his father's writing career. He assisted with research for over forty years, and in 1991 he gave up teaching A-Level Physics to manage his father's affairs. After Mary's death, which ended a happy marriage of fifty-three years, a heartbroken Dick Francis said that without her his writing days were over. Then, in 2005, on a visit to Virginia, he met sixty-year-old Dagmar Cosby. 'We had a wonderful weekend, in spite of incessant rain, and, for the first time in sixty years, I fell in love,' he says. It was the spur he needed to pick up his pen again. Felix did the research for *Under Orders* (2006) and took on a more significant role in the writing of *Dead Heat* (2007). *Silks* is the second father-and-son collaboration and a sure-fire winner from the Francis family stable.

LOST & FOUND

JACQUELINE SHEEHAN

Roxanne Pelligrino has a great life: a happy marriage, a fulfilling career and good friends . . . and then, tragically, her husband dies.

Tormented by grief she cuts all her ties and heads off to a tiny island off the coast of Maine. As she seeks comfort in solitude, Roxanne stumbles across a badly injured black Labrador. And so begins a remarkable friendship, in which the young widow and the loyal stray find a new beginning.

Chapter 1

Bob had left the food carton on the counter the night before and it now smelt of grease and fish. Roxanne picked up the box and a puddle of oil pooled beneath it. Her husband ate deep-fried food when salted fat was the only way to soothe the layers of accumulated sadness after a day telling pet owners, 'Your dog has had a good long life and this cancer won't be cured by surgery or chemo. What would you like me to do?' Looking at the contents of the carton, Roxanne knew that yesterday had gone badly for Bob and that his mumbled response to her as he had got into bed was a result of self-medication with the worst sort of fast food.

She tossed the white container into the garbage. She was on her way to the university, but then remembered her promise to order new socks for them to wear as they scuffed about the house. She felt annoyed that Bob had been so insistent that *she* call Lands' End. Why couldn't he make the call?

She picked up the cordless phone and had just punched in the number for Lands' End, when she heard a thick sound from the upstairs bathroom. She pictured Bob brushing his teeth or shaving his face, but neither of those predictable morning rituals accounted for the sound.

'Good morning. This is Priscilla. Let's start with your catalogue number,' said the voice on the phone. Roxanne hit the OFF button and climbed the stairs, head cocked to one side, listening for another sound to explain the first one. She held onto the phone with her right hand as she went through the doorway into their bedroom.

She called to her husband and the hollowness of the house hit her beneath her ribs. 'Bob, are you OK in there? Did you drop something?' She tried to open the bathroom door but something was wedged against it, letting her open it only an inch. There was nothing else in the bathroom other than Bob that could provide such resistance. Had he fainted? She shoved the door open, inching his body back and wondering if she should call 911. When the door was open wide enough to stick her head in, she saw his open-eyed stare and punched the number into the phone. Then she heaved all her weight against the door and entered the bathroom with such velocity that the latch caught at her trousers, ripping them at her thigh.

She dropped to the floor and put two fingers of her left hand on Bob's neck. She had been a lifeguard since high school, through college and grad school. Someone answered the phone and Roxanne put the receiver near Bob's head so that she could shout her replies. 'No, he's not breathing . . . Yes, I know CPR . . . No, I'm not going to keep listening to you. I'm doing the CPR now. Just get someone here fast! Please!'

She breathed into him, first tilting back his head and closing off his nose, then sealing his lips with hers and blowing air into his mouth, keeping her left eye open to see if his chest rose. Her brain stopped working except to think things like, The front door is open because I let the cat out. The ambulance guys can get in, so I won't have to stop breathing for Bob. Her body took over. She pressed the heel of her hand slightly to the left of his breastbone and met with surprising resistance. Bob's chest was unyielding. Five compressions, another breath—was this right? Roxanne looked at her watch. How long had he not been breathing? His wonderful brain needed blood. Where the hell was the ambulance? She did not want to be the one compressing his heart and breathing into his lungs; someone more experienced, more medical, should be doing this.

A young cop with closely cropped hair was the first one in.

'Good, good form,' he said. 'I'll take over the compressions.' He knelt by Bob and pressed the heel of his hand shockingly hard into Bob's chest. 'How long have you been doing CPR?' He placed his hat on the bath mat. His hair was buzz cut so severely that his white scalp beckoned through.

'I don't know. Maybe ten minutes. Don't break his ribs. He's a vet and he has to go to work today.'

The young cop glanced at her for a moment and the morning light reflected oddly, as if she could see a tidal wave coming in his iris.

The ambulance crew arrived, and only moments later applied the paddles that shocked him into a rag-doll dance. When they loaded him into the ambulance, Roxanne ran to her car and followed it to the hospital, going through every red light that the ambulance did. When the ER crew gave him further care, she waited for someone to say, 'We got him, here he comes!' And she could live her life again, just as she had before starting to order socks from Lands' End.

She watched from outside the hospital room as they tried again and again to electronically goad his heart into starting. Bob's refusal to come back into his body left Roxanne stunned, frightened—and worried, that he was lost, just beyond her reach. The instinct to try to find him was overwhelming. They ventilated him and Roxanne felt the rasp of the tube in her own throat, forcing air into her lungs.

A nurse came out and said, 'He's had a major heart attack. Does he take any medication? Has he been ill recently?'

'No.'

'How old is he?'

'Forty-two.'

Both the nurse and Roxanne looked up as a man dressed in blue cotton scrubs came out of the room where Bob lay stubbornly stiff.

'Are you his wife?'

Roxanne was unsteady. She looked past the man's head at a wall clock and saw that two hours had passed since Bob had collapsed. It occurred to her just then that they had been working on him too long.

'Yes, I'm his wife.'

'Would you like to sit down?' He had an earnest face, clear eyes.

'I don't want to go far away from him,' Roxanne said. She realised her voice was shaking and pressed her lips together to stop the vibration that ran all through her body. She wished the doctor would offer her a blanket, but this doctor was not going to offer her anything warm.

They sat in two chairs in the hallway under bright lights. The doctor told her everything about Bob's heart. He explained the blown-out lower left ventricle and the length of time since any brain activity had been recorded.

'He's dead, isn't he?'

The doctor didn't blink. 'Yes. If we take him off the ventilator now, his heart will cease to beat. There are no further messages coming from his brain to any part of his body.'

The doctor waited for Roxanne to respond. It was her turn and she wanted to blast out the fluorescent lighting and hide. She waited out the doctor.

'The cop told me you were doing CPR when he came to the scene. He said you were great, that you were doing everything that you could for Bob.'

'Then why is he dead if I was so great? CPR is supposed to work!'

The doctor tried not to flinch, but he looked worried about the direction that this sort of questioning could go.

'There is a sad little secret about CPR. It doesn't work most of the time. It saves lives, that's true. It's great for children who have just fallen in the pool. But with heart attacks, even when you kick-start a heart with CPR, eighty per cent of the time the patient will die anyhow.'

Roxanne wondered why she hadn't known this. When was the last time she had taken a review class in CPR? Would it have mattered to her if she had known this?

'This is where I tell you to take him off the ventilator, isn't it?'

The doctor nodded.

A hospital chaplain slipped quietly into a chair on the other side of Roxanne. She asked Roxanne if she wanted to call anyone. She did not.

'But there is something that I want you to do. Will you just stay outside the door so that no one else comes in? I want to be alone with him.' She stayed with Bob while the ventilator was shut down, and for half an hour after that, standing by him as his skin began to cool. She wanted to get on the gurney with him and press her body against his, but he was exactly in the middle and there was not enough room.

The cop, who had waited in the hallway, attempted to comfort her. 'You did a good job with the CPR; that's not why he died. I'm zero for five.'

'What do you mean?'

'I've done CPR five times and no one has lived to tell about it,' he said with great seriousness. Under other circumstances, his attempt at consoling her would have been funny, but now she just felt tricked.

'I thought this always worked,' she said, in a dazed, dry-mouthed way.

She walked out of the hospital into brilliant sunlight and felt the stab of every pebble beneath her feet as she walked through the parking lot. It was as if the day had torn apart and left her bleeding. When she found her car, she got in the back seat and locked the door. She pulled into a foetal position, covered her head and cried with a violence that shook the car.

THEIR FRIENDS and Bob's office staff rallied round Roxanne and planned the memorial service. She followed Bob's wishes and had his body cremated.

'I just don't want him to be afraid or sad. What if he doesn't know where he is?' Roxanne whispered to her mother at the service. Her mother, who had flown in from California, put her hands on either side of Roxanne's face. 'He knows where he is, sweetheart. It's the rest of us who are confused.'

The doctor had told Roxanne that her husband's heart was etched with a poor combination of defective genetics and the aftermath of a shotgun approach to radiation treatment for cancer when he was in his teens, long before Roxanne had met him. Bob was the miracle, cured of the worst thing they could think of, and all the rest of his time was supposed to be easier. He had been forty-two, getting soft in all the right places, a countable number of white hairs on his chest, and Roxanne would have been content to watch these glacial changes for another thirty or forty years.

When she finally dreamt of Bob, when she slept long enough to actually have a dream, she was neither sad nor afraid. In the dream, he was asleep in a field and Roxanne was so close to him that she could see a sleepy crease along the edge of his nose. He looked like he was in a special death rehab unit, slowly recuperating into formless intentions.

'This is what it's like after death, I've seen it,' Roxanne told her mother later on the phone. She was sure she had been given a private showing of the place where people go after death. When she woke, she pulled his pillow over her face and breathed in the scent of him, and the terror of being left behind came back in torrents.

OVER FOUR MONTHS had passed. The new fall semester had started and this was the time of the year that Roxanne had always loved. But all she could think of was preserving Bob's scent on his pillowcase. When he had died, the brushed cotton sheets had been on their bed for one week. Only one week of precious scents left on their bed, one week of his head pressing deeply into his pillow. The sheets had not been the same because her scent and hair were mixed in with Bob's. Reluctantly, she had changed them after a month, but his pillowcase remained unwashed. Every morning she covered it, dreading the day that it would be empty of his smell.

She kept three of his flannel shirts and one grey cashmere sweater. The rest of the clothing was stuffed into black plastic sacks and taken across the state line into New York. She didn't want to see any local people suddenly dressed as her dead husband. Dead husband. Not like the live one.

The clerk at the Salvation Army store said, 'Do you want a receipt?'

Roxanne looked at the four black plastic sacks, lumpy with Bob's clothes. She wanted the clerk to know that they weren't just clothes that someone got tired of, or grew too fat to wear. 'These are my husband's things. He died. His heart was bad.'

'Do you want a receipt?' the clerk asked again, with a hint of impatience.

'Yes, I do. I want a receipt.' Roxanne felt the crush of the clerk's coldness start at her brain and descend like a thick poison throughout her body. After she got home, she did not leave the house again for three days.

EVENTUALLY, ROXANNE RETURNED to her job as a psychologist at the counselling centre at the university in western Massachusetts. She lasted two weeks before the director asked her to come to his office. He told her that several clients had reported that she had stood up in a therapy session and just stared out of the window. He asked her if she needed more time off. Roxanne told him about the clerk at the Salvation Army.

'The strange thing about you is that you expect store clerks to understand your grief instead of opening up to people who care about you,' said Ray Velasquez. He was older than Roxanne, closing in on fifty. 'Did you really expect a clerk at the Salvation Army to be an empathetic angel? She was probably tired, horribly paid, and afraid of your grief.'

Roxanne rubbed a hunk of her long dark hair between her thumb and forefinger. 'I thought just getting in my car and coming to work was such an accomplishment. But now I can't remember why any of this matters.'

They agreed that the university would give her a year's leave of absence, and she would be guaranteed her job when she returned. 'Are you sure about this?' Velasquez asked her. 'Work can sometimes be the best friend after a death. It can give you structure.'

'I'm not sure about anything, but I know that I can't possibly help anyone right now,' Roxanne replied. She did not add that she was still awake every night until 2 a.m. and then awake again an hour later.

CUTTING HER HAIR was Roxanne's last project before closing the house in the foothills of the Berkshire Hills and heading east to the coast. She had left it long, partly in defiance of the more professional, crisper look, and partly because Bob had loved it. But without him her hair grew sad.

Roxanne turned on the light in the bathroom and peered at her reflection. Some Native American cultures cut their hair whenever there is a death; a year's worth of hair, about six inches. She decided that Bob's death deserved more than one year's worth of grief. She pulled some dark, tightly curled hair with one hand, cut it at jaw level, and saw the equivalent of four years' worth of grief hanging from her other hand.

She cut it all off at jaw length and her hair stuck out expectantly, so she cut more. Then she swept up the fallen hair, put it in a bag and released it over her September garden. The weeds in the garden did not tempt her as they had before. She saw them differently this year.

'I want the weeds to grow from beginning to end, uninterrupted,' she said when her brother, Caleb, came by for her door key. The deal was that Roxanne would call Caleb when she got her own place. He was two years younger than her and he had hovered around her since Bob's death.

'Let me drive you out to Peaks Island in my truck and you'll be able to take more stuff,' he said as he watched Roxanne tossing her hair onto the garden. He had the same thick curls as Roxanne, but his hair was lighter.

'No. Everything I need fits in my car.' The Honda was packed mostly with winter clothing, her own bedding and Bob's pillow. For all their years as foster pet owners, they had had only one full-time pet and that was Gremlin, the cat. After Bob died, Gremlin, who was a stout twelve years old, grew restless and spent longer and longer periods of time outdoors. He had finally disappeared altogether. Roxanne suspected that marauding coyotes had killed him. She wondered who would oblige her. She envied Gremlin.

Caleb bent down awkwardly and yanked a clump of crabgrass that threatened to choke out a thin group of chrysanthemums. 'Look, I promised Mom that I'd drive out with you. She's worried about you.'

He sounded uncomfortable with the switch in roles with his sister. She had been the one to comfort him and urge him on through the special-ed classes where all the kids with learning disabilities got tossed. She had defended him from schoolyard bullies. In more ways than one, he had inspired her to learn about the brain, how memory works, why trauma takes some people by the throat and others churn through it. Now, in the warm months, he painted houses; in the winter he worked in his pottery studio.

Roxanne put a hand on Caleb's sleeve and squeezed his arm. 'I'll call you when I get a place. I'm going to stay at a motel on the island until Columbus Day, when the season ends.'

She avoided the big roads and instead took the side roads, driving east and north to Portland. She had called ahead and made a reservation on the Casco Bay ferry. Driving the car onto the ferry, she knew she appeared to be one of the more purposeful people, clearly not just a day-tripper. In reality she had no reason to stay, no reason to go.

She had been to Peaks Island only once, long before she met Bob. She had been ten when her family had driven to Nova Scotia for a vacation. Roxanne vividly recalled an afternoon stop in Portland and an impulsive ferry trip to Peaks Island. They stayed long enough for Roxanne and Caleb to climb on the rocks along the shore and eat hot dogs before heading back.

Roxanne didn't know if the others in the family remembered that day the way she did; the island had stood bathed in sunlight, full of hope. It was not much to hang onto, but Roxanne drove straight off the ferry and into the flicker of memory.

THE FEW WEEKS Roxanne spent in the motel overlooking the ferry dock disappeared into mist. She walked the beaches and the inland trails and noticed that, as the days went by, the crowds of tourists thinned until, after Columbus Day, a quietness settled on the island. The air, as if on command, turned cool and the mornings required her to put on a jacket. She read the local paper at Stan's Seafood Diner, and one morning saw a job announcement after she had heard a waitress pointing it out to another customer.

'Animal control warden,' said the waitress. 'We haven't had one of those all year. Budgets must be looking up.'

Roxanne folded the paper in half and asked her what she knew about it.

'You need to talk to Isaiah Wilson; everybody knows him. Tell him you heard about the job from Jill at Stan's. He and my father are old friends.'

Isaiah was the director of public works on the island. He was also a former Methodist minister and currently a substitute schoolteacher over in Portland, when they were desperate, Jill told her.

Roxanne went to his office to fill out an application. She paused after writing in her name, Roxanne Pelligrino, and held the pen still. To apply for the position, she had to give a reference and a job history. She finally wrote the truth—psychologist—and gave Ray Velasquez as a reference.

Isaiah looked at the application and his forehead wrinkled.

Roxanne explained. 'Before you say anything, I want you to know that my husband was a veterinarian. I learned how to handle sick animals and I can tell which ones will bite and which ones won't. But if you hire me, I want my personal life to be private. I need to start over.'

Isaiah had a full head of grey hair and his reading glasses sat low on his nose. His skin was dark, and from the slight cadence in his voice, Roxanne thought he might be from Haiti.

'Divorce?' he asked, looking up at her over his glasses.

'My husband is dead. Heart attack. He was young and we didn't know anything was wrong.' Roxanne had practised these facts and this was her trial run.

Isaiah took off his glasses. 'I'm sorry.' Roxanne saw the minister settle in and the public works director recede. 'When did he pass away?'

'This spring, the end of the spring.' She suddenly felt like she was in the chaplain's office and she shifted in the chair.

'"After the first death there is no other." Do you know who wrote that? Elizabeth Barrett Browning? I'm not sure. I remember the first time I heard it and I knew it was true. The first death changes everything, and all deaths afterwards bring us back to the first death. I'm sorry; I lost both my parents last year and even at my ripe age, I feel like an orphan.'

Roxanne brushed an escaping tear from one eye. 'If you hire me, I'll do a good job. If I don't know how to do something, I'll ask. Just keep all this private, OK? I'm not ready to be a widow yet. I have a year's leave of absence from my job. I can work right through next year's tourist season.'

'I'm a professional secret-keeper. I was a minister for fifteen years and that's part of what I did. I held secrets. The same as you.' Isaiah stood up and held out his large paw of a hand to Roxanne. 'Let me tell you about your new job and all the fancy extras that go along with it.' She let him take her hand. 'You get a truck that can't pass emission control standards on the mainland and the key to the storage shed. When can you start?'

'Now. I can start right now,' she said.

He nodded. 'Do you need a place to live?'

'I was waiting for the off-season rates before I looked around,' she said.

'I can help you with that. I have a rental house, nothing fancy. In fact, very far from fancy. And the off-season rates just started this minute.'

THE COTTAGE WAS THE LAST on the dirt road. Beach grass, stiff and breeze-worthy, surrounded it. Isaiah opened the door and a whiff of dead fish hit them. 'Damn! The last renters left their garbage under the sink. Whatever's there has been building steam for a week. Don't take this as an omen. Just look at it as the best introduction you could have to summer people. Stay here while I go grab that garbage and open the window.'

Roxanne stood on the small deck, which was bleached silver by the salt and sun. The front of the house faced southeast and stared directly out to the expanse of the Atlantic Ocean. Between the house and the ocean was a quarter of a mile of thick vegetation, held together by a crosshatching of vines that looked like honeysuckle. A hobbit-sized path wound through it to the rock-covered coast.

Roxanne pulled her eyes from the ocean and headed into the house to give Isaiah a hand. He stood in the midst of a kitchen covered with crumpled papers, cups half filled with butter that had once been melted for lobster, bowls with the hard unpopped kernels of corn on the bottom and paper bags filled with slightly crushed beer cans. 'At times like this, I think the whole human race is going to hell,' said Isaiah.

It was a mess, all right. 'I hope you got a huge deposit from these people,' Roxanne said. 'Who were they anyhow?'

'You wouldn't believe it. They drove a new Volvo and said they were teachers. But they won't ever rent on this island again.'

They opened all the remaining windows, hauled out the trash and set the dishes to soak. Roxanne ran a vacuum cleaner over the floor. She shook the few scatter rugs outside and made a mental note to take them to the Laundromat. Isaiah left with his truck brimming with black plastic sacks.

Later, his wife, Charlotte, delivered a box of cleaning supplies complete with rubber gloves. She was darker than Isaiah, with a sprinkling of white hairs on her temples. She wore sweatpants and a jacket. 'Sorry about my scruffy appearance, but I was in the garden when my husband came home sputtering about low-life trash who drive Volvos. Can you handle the rest of this? We won't charge you for the full month of October.'

After Charlotte left, Roxanne examined every inch of the cottage. The living room/dining room had the best view over the top of the shrubbery, out to the ocean. The two bedrooms were small, each with room enough for a bed, chest of drawers and chair. Roxanne picked the room that had two windows instead of one, which made up for it facing north.

When the cottage was as clean as she could get it, and all signs of the former tenants were removed, she began to unload her car. By dusk, her sheets were on the bed and her winter clothes were folded in the chest of drawers. She'd brought two electrical appliances from her old life: a radio-cassette and a hair dryer.

Dusk changed too quickly into night and the completion of her unpacking left her with the sudden despair that comes with darkness when no other footsteps are expected. This was the worst part of the day and getting through it was an exercise in endurance. She prepared for what she knew would be a night of grief and self-accusation while she replayed the morning of Bob's death.

How many times had she helped clients with the lightning-bolt arrival of grief that kidnapped people from their daily lives? Hundreds. But what her clients had not told her was that the chemistry of her body would alter until she would no longer know who she was when she looked in the mirror; that food would taste like cardboard, and that two months after her husband was dead she would wake up with a full-blown panic attack at 3 a.m. and drive herself to the emergency room. She had been convinced that her heart was exploding and had been embarrassed to learn that she was having her first-ever panic attack.Or had her clients told her, and she had listened with only part of her brain—thinking that this was temporary, this was part of grieving—without fully grasping the horrible landscape of the present? There was something essential and awful that she had missed: she had failed to save her husband, and she had failed to see the true terror of the land where mourners travelled.

Suddenly, Roxanne heard a clear, penetrating peal, like a light that pierces the fog. She looked at the sliding glass door and a striped feline face stared in at her from its base. A tabby, eyes wide and insistent, white chest and calico body, had come calling. Roxanne slid the door open and the cat dashed past her and leapt onto the couch, purring with urgency. The creature paced the couch with familiarity, then bounced to the floor and headed for the exact place on the kitchen floor where two saucers had been sitting hours before.

'Oh no, they left you behind,' said Roxanne, crouching beside the cat, which pushed her spine into Roxanne's palm, offering her a generous view of her back end. A female, although she had already guessed that by her head size. Bob had always said, 'Male cats generally have a bigger skull.'

The cat moved in with a level of confidence that Roxanne wished she could have patented and injected into several of her former clients. The animal did not appear to know her pitifulness, did not know the fate that awaited her if she was returned to her negligent owners or to the abyss of an animal shelter. Roxanne saw the irony of the situation; both of them had been left behind and both were pitiful.

She did not want the world to treat her like this abandoned cat, in need of food and sympathy. She pictured the cat's owners driving away in their Volvo. Being filthy and irresponsible with a rental was one thing, but she could not fathom the decision to leave the cat. Thus she began her career as animal control warden by not looking for them. She judged them harshly and, she believed, correctly. The cat slept on the couch the first night, but Roxanne imagined that she heard her purring all night and padding round the small house. For the first time in months, she woke not at 3 a.m. but at 4 a.m., and she decided that was reason enough to keep the cat.

THE FIRST TWO WEEKS of Roxanne's new job offered a sampling of life in the post-tourist season. The island slumped with relief after an exhausting summer when it had exploded with a population ten times that of the winter. Several places closed immediately. The kayak company put away most of the sleek kayaks for the season, leaving just two on the porch for the owner to use on days when the ocean was quiet.

Isaiah and Charlotte invited Roxanne to lunch one Sunday. Roxanne wondered if Isaiah's promise not to say anything about her past had extended to his wife. She pictured someone telling Bob a secret and asking him not to tell Roxanne. What would he have done? But Isaiah was a minister, or he had been. And ministers were bound by confidentiality.

Charlotte had fixed them huevos rancheros with a robust salsa made from the last of her tomatoes. At the end of the meal, she brought out a fresh pot of coffee. 'Isaiah tells me that your husband died this past year. I'm sorry. This must be a terrible time for you.'

Roxanne threw an accusatory stare at Isaiah.

He grimaced. 'I apologise. It's not Charlotte's fault. She caught me talking to myself when I didn't even know I was doing it. I'll have to watch myself as I get older and start blathering all the secrets that people have told me. I could be a national security risk.' Clearly, he was horrified that he had spilled the beans to a person who knew the absolute importance of maintaining secrets. Tiny beads of sweat popped out on his forehead.

Charlotte ignored him and sipped her coffee. 'You're not ready to say the words yet, are you? Not long after my grandfather's funeral, I was with my grandmother at the beauty parlour and she had a new girl working on her hair who kept asking her questions to be polite. She finally asked her some questions about her husband. My grandmother said, "I'm a widow." And she hadn't been ready to say it. Her face collapsed and she looked sadder than the day of the funeral. You don't have to say the words until you're ready. And I'll try to keep my husband from talking to himself in public.'

Roxanne felt the outrage melt down her tight neck muscles. Charlotte understood. 'Thank you,' she said.

ROXANNE CALLED HER BROTHER as she had promised she would.

'I'm fine. I've got a job, a very part-time job, probably not more than ten hours per week. It's on an as-needed basis. And I've rented a little cottage,' she said, in what she hoped was her most convincing voice.

'Where are you again?'

'I'm on Peaks Island. People fish and they sell stuff to tourists. Oh, I'm the new dog warden. Except they call it animal control warden.'

'What the hell do you know about being a dog warden? Because Bob was a vet, do you think you picked up special dog-warden skills? You hardly put foot into the clinic the last few years.'

Roxanne was jolted by the mention of Bob. She felt like she had suddenly swallowed wood chips.

'We're talking lost cats and dogs,' she said.

'Just get a tetanus shot right now, Roxanne, and if you see a raccoon that's foaming at the mouth and walking in circles, shoot it.'

'Shoot it? They didn't give me a gun.' Sparring usually felt good with Caleb, but she had not been able to spar with him since Bob died. 'Is everything working out with the renters?' While she had been at the motel, Caleb had written to say he had found people to rent her house.

'They're harmless. He's an English professor, he told me. He asked me about the oil burner like it was a rocket or something. I'm going over there again to give him another lesson in how to run it.'

'Thanks. If Mom calls you to check up on me, tell her that you talked to me and I'm OK. Will you do that?'

'I should tell her that you sound like shit and you took a job that you know nothing about. Would you at least go get a book that tells you how to recover animals?' said Caleb before he signed off.

ROXANNE MET TESS in the only bookstore on the island, in the nonfiction section, where Tess turned to her and said, 'During the winter, people on the island either drink too much or read too much. Which are you?'

Roxanne wasn't sure she'd do either and wondered if those were her only choices. She had come to the bookstore to get a book on wildlife of the eastern shores, and ended up getting Peterson Field Guides' *Mammals of North America*, a broader selection.

She wondered why this woman would ask her such a thing. Had she let slip her secret somehow? Could this woman know that Roxanne hadn't been able to save her own husband when she'd had the chance? That she couldn't make him breathe again as he lay on the bathroom floor?

'Oh, you're the new arrival. Maybe you've thought of something else to do over the winter?' She put her hand on Roxanne's arm and squeezed it for a second. No one had touched her since she had arrived, other than Isaiah, who had shaken her hand. Roxanne pulled her arm away.

'Welcome to the island. I'm a caretaker for some of the houses over the winter and manage a couple of rental properties in the summer. Let me know if I can help you get acquainted,' she said. She wrote her name and number on a sales receipt.

Roxanne took her book home and began to study the only animal that she had thus far encountered, a cat. *Felis catus*. The coat is shed and regrown every spring and fall, gestation is fifty-eight days (that part she had known because Bob lamented the reproductive capability of cats) and that cats will refuse to learn something that is not to their advantage. Her own adopted cat demonstrated this by refusing to stay indoors during the day. She arrived at the sliding glass door each evening demanding to be let in and campaigned as heavily each morning to be let out. Roxanne obliged.

THE FIRST OFFICIAL CALL that she got came from Tess. 'Some fool from the summer left a cat on the north side of the island. It won't come to me and it looks like it's starving or sick. Can you come and get it?'

Roxanne called Isaiah to check on Tess, to see if she might be some weird old woman who was left here by her family to haunt the islanders.

Isaiah laughed when she asked him. 'You mean Tess? Good God, they don't come more solid than her. She's been out here for years, since she retired. Well, she's mostly retired. If she tells you that a cat has been abandoned, then that's the truth.' He told her the best way to get the cat.

Roxanne thought she would wait until early morning. She didn't want to keep the cat overnight. If she caught it early, she'd still have time to get it over to Portland to the pound. As she lay in bed with her own newly found cat purring on the chest of drawers, she considered her options. She would generously bait the Havahart trap with wet cat food and hope for the best.

The next morning she pulled up at the house, several miles north of the dock. The snare was an ugly contraption. She hoped the cat wasn't peeking from the bushes so she could set the trap unobserved. She pulled the tab on the can and hoped that the rich smell wouldn't attract every cat in the neighbourhood. A black Saab pulled up as Roxanne was finishing her job, and Tess stepped out.

'Let's go for a walk while the cat meets its destiny. I'll show you some of my favourite spots along the shore.'

They walked on the dirt road that ran along the north coast, both of them slapped by the wind, and then headed for the beach. It was surprisingly easy for Roxanne and Tess to fall in step with each other. When they returned several hours later, a tattered cat sat howling in the trap.

'There's your first customer,' said Tess.

Roxanne delivered the cat to the Portland animal shelter still in the trap, not wanting to tangle with the very sick-looking creature. Tess went along for the ride because she said she needed to buy some fish at the docks. She was about thirty years older than Roxanne, a trim woman whose movements were swift and light. She reminded Roxanne of the image of a wood sprite: a nymph who blended in easily among a pine-needle forest floor or the firm grasses that grew on sand.

'I'm no wood nymph,' said Tess. 'I'm just a retired physical therapist. There's a difference.'

Tess had painted a Buddha on her blue bathroom door, and had a Christmas tree of dried deciduous branches festooned with seashells and dried seaweed, which stayed up twelve months of the year. 'Well, this certainly looks more like the house of a wood sprite than a former physical therapist,' said Roxanne.

They went walking several times a week and, before long, Roxanne had accompanied Tess on her job of house-sitting for the summer people who didn't want the hassle of draining their pipes for the winter. Tess made periodic checks, opening doors and letting in fresh air.

Roxanne's second call was a skunk emergency. Mrs Todd called to say that a skunk was in her garage and that she was unable to leave her house.

Roxanne looked up skunks in the Peterson guide: *Mephitis mephitis*. She read that the creatures were trash hounds and when tourists left behind their abundance of overflowing trash bins, skunks became particularly brash until the cold weather set in, which would slow them into a drowsy trance. Skunks would spray only as a last resort; they would first stomp their feet, growl, spit, or clack their impressively sharp teeth. This should be warning enough for anyone, except dogs, who often blundered in and misread all those signals.

Roxanne thought her chances of remaining scent-free, while relocating the skunk with the Havahart trap and a hamburger patty, were good.

She called Mrs Todd. 'Don't go out to the garage and don't let your dog out of the house. What kind of dog do you have? . . . Oh, a terrier . . . Don't even open the door when you see me drive up because your little terrier thinks the skunk is a big rat and he wants to grab it by the neck. You don't want that to happen. I'll be there shortly.'

She drove to the grocery store, where she picked up the cheapest grade of beef available, then drove on to Mrs Todd's house. When she arrived there was no sign of the skunk, but there was evidence of trash that was not tightly sealed. Roxanne offered to pick up a new garbage can the next time she was in Portland. Solutions were easy in this job.

THE NEXT MORNING Roxanne met Tess for breakfast before she was due to meet Isaiah to talk about additional duties. 'He wants me to start documenting any change in erosion along the south beach. I'm not sure how I'm supposed to do that. I mean erosion is change, and that is probably best done over a number of years.'

'You sound like a scientist. What did you say that you did before?'

'I worked with young kids, in a day-care centre,' Roxanne said. The lie felt partial and thus tolerable.

Tess sipped tea. Roxanne had picked up a cup of coffee. She bent over to gather up a dropped napkin and whacked her elbow on the metal strip along the edge of the table. She grimaced and let out a yelp.

'That must be pure orange. I can feel it from here,' said Tess.

'What?' said Roxanne, cradling her elbow.

'When I hit a nerve like that I see orange for as long as it throbs.'

'What do you mean?'

'I have synaesthesia. Two places in my brain go off at once. When I stub my toe, I holler orange, because that's what I see and feel at the same time.'

Roxanne recalled having read about this in a neuropsych journal.

'I didn't know the name for it until about ten years ago when I heard a guy talking on National Public Radio. He'd written a book about us. I broke down and cried. I didn't know I was a member of a club.'

'Do you see colours only when you hurt yourself?'

'No. Everything has a colour. Like letters: B is light green with a dark base; T is grey and shiny. The days of the week each have their colour and shape. Tuesday is a blue cube and Wednesday is a muted red globe. Sunday is light yellow and sort of floppy.'

'You are a multimedia event,' said Roxanne as she sipped her coffee.

'That's just the half of it. Now that I've learned more about synaesthesia, I know just how plain and unfortunate your poor world is, I'm sorry to say.'

'I've never thought of my world as plain.'

'That's because you don't know any better. Your name is green because R is green. How old are you?'

'I'm thirty-eight.'

'OK. Numbers one through ten go up a gradual slope, then eleven through twenty are on a plateau, twenty-one through thirty turn right and the thirties zigzag back the other way. So now, when I think of you, I'll see a green R zigzagging backwards.'

'Jeez,' said Roxanne.

'Exactly. Now, doesn't that make your number system seem plain? I'm sorry, it's just that I'm a synaesthete out of the closet. There's nothing as annoying as the newly converted.'

Tess did not regret for one minute the uniqueness of synaesthesia, only that it had taken her so long to know its name. There were a few kindred spirits out in the world who were touched by the crossfiring of senses, the same tweak in genetics as Tess, and finding them had changed her life.

As a child, she had been driven to silence when she had discovered that none of the other children saw numbers as colours, and that her teacher and her classmates lived in a monochrome world. Piano notes did not brush against their cheeks and smell like cinnamon and, most odd of all, when they fell and scraped their knees, they did not shout, 'It's too orange, now red!' They cried of course, as she did, but they could not see the pulse of the pain in great orange splats with a deep red core.

Tess found she had a huge capacity for memorising anything and she graduated top of her small Nebraska high school. When numbers and letters each have their own colour, shape and size, subjects like history and maths fitted into neat packets that Tess was able to pull out at will; she had constant access to a colour-coded filing system in her brain.

At teachers' college, Tess studied maths then moved on to biology. When she took a class in anatomy, she was in heaven, picturing the heart, the blood vessels and all the interiors of the body. For her, the nerves that ran down the arms and spread out across the hands were sky-blue and smelt like lilacs. Her professor told her: 'If you were a young man, I'd say you had the makings of a fine doctor. But you'll be married before graduation.'

Tess, for all her fine multi-sensed brainwork, had not noticed what her professor had seen from the first day of class: Len, a sandy-haired boy in the back of the room who stared at Tess every day. By finals, they were spending evenings in nearby cornfields, gazing at the stars from their entwined position on a sturdy wool blanket. By their final semester of college, Tess was pregnant and uncomfortable in her simple wedding dress. Len had promised the most exciting thing of her life; they would marry and go to Boston where he would start medical school in the fall.

Tess had often told people that alcoholism is a thief. After Len's drinking had resulted in two car accidents and become a serious threat to his job security at the hospital, Tess took their two children and divorced the man who no longer resembled the sandy-haired boy she'd met in college. She then applied to a college to study physical therapy, and excelled.

She had been almost sixty when she'd heard the programme about synaesthesia on NPR. That had been ten years ago and she counted most of her years before that as painful and ill-spent. She made friends with her ex-husband again. He had remarried, but then discovered that he had married someone far more addicted to alcohol than even he had been. After losing his medical licence, Len had attended AA five times a week. When he sobered up, his second wife left him.

Tess 'came out' to her grown children. Her two little grandchildren were growing up knowing that Granny heard motorcycles as jagged brown, streaked with battleship grey. If they spotted motorcycles, they cried, 'Granny cover your ears, the brown and silver are coming by!'

She knew that synaesthesia had skipped her own children, but her grandchildren had a filtered-down version and Tess gloried in it.

And now the new woman on the island, the animal control warden, was keeping Tess busy. Tess was drawn to things that didn't fit and people who didn't fit, either in their own skins or because they were in the wrong place at the wrong time. She didn't know if synaesthesia accounted for it—she'd seen no evidence of that in online chatter from the synaesthetes—but she was sure that Roxanne didn't fit.

Chapter 2

Someone had phoned in a complaint about a black Labrador that had been scrounging the south beach for several days and was acting strange, drooling and limping, bobbing his head. The dog had last been seen beside the Dumpster at the back of Stan's Seafood Diner.

'He could be sick. Eighty per cent of all raccoons have rabies and he could have been bitten by one,' said Phil, who washed dishes at the diner.

Roxanne stopped at the grocery store and bought a small package of low-grade ground beef. She drove the old truck up to the diner, hoping that the dog had not left. She pierced the plastic wrap round the meat with her truck keys and walked to the back of the building. She felt a sharp tingle in the early November air. Tonight would be hard on a sick dog.

She saw him scrunched next to a pile of wood covered by a bright blue tarp. She announced her arrival. 'There you are; good dog.'

He lifted his head with a cloudy-eyed weariness.

She crouched down about eight feet away. 'Come get some breakfast, buddy.' Roxanne held out the meat. The Labrador's deep brown eyes focused on her and she thought she saw the look of great despair that she had seen in the eyes of people who were in mourning or depression.

The dog tried to stand, and yelped when he put his weight on his front legs.

'OK, big boy. I'll come to you. I'll deliver breakfast.'

The Lab lowered himself back down and accepted the meat that she placed right in front of his nose. He sniffed it and gave it a lick. He looked too sick to eat. After letting him smell her hand Roxanne rubbed his head, then reached over to the front leg that he was protecting and gingerly felt around. Her hand stopped on something jutting out of his shoulder. She leaned over cautiously. He had a shaft sticking out of the front of his chest and Roxanne could feel the heat of the infection.

She untied the blue tarpaulin covering the woodpile, then went inside to get Phil. Together they slid the dog onto the folded tarp and lifted him into the back of the truck. Roxanne closed the camper shell and headed straight for the ferry landing.

The first ferry of the day was getting ready to go to Portland and she knew that Sam Reynolds, a vet with a practice in South Portland, would be on it. She had already taken a series of sick cats to him on the one morning per week that he had office hours on the island. She had discovered that Sam and his wife kept one car parked at a friend's house off-island and one car exclusively on the island.

Roxanne reached the ferry as the crew was starting to latch the closing chain across the landing. 'Wait!' she yelled, jumping out of her truck. 'You've got to let me on. I've got a dog that's been hurt.' She scanned the deck for Sam and saw him, hugging a coffee mug. She waved her arms at him and he lowered his mug and headed down the metal staircase.

Roxanne drove onto the ferry and pulled in beside the other pick-up trucks. Sam opened up the back of the truck as she described the dog's injury. He felt the Lab's shoulder and chest area. 'This is an arrow. He probably broke it off while trying to get it out.' He unzipped his green jacket and draped it round the injured animal.

When they landed in Portland, Sam got into the truck and Roxanne drove him to his office, then backed the truck up to the front door. Within thirty minutes, Sam and his technician had the dog inside and hooked up to an intravenous drip.

'He's being prepped for surgery. Nothing left for you to do here, Roxanne. I can get a ride to my car in Portland. Why don't you go back home? I'll give you a call tonight.'

Roxanne knew that Sam would save the dog if he could, but instead of taking the next ferry back, she drove to Portland and parked the truck in a parking lot. She had breakfast, then went to the library and used the Internet to check her email.

She returned to Sam's office in the middle of the afternoon. He handed her the tag that had hung round the dog's neck. It was a piece of octagonal aluminium, painted with yellow reflective paint.

'This would have been a lot more helpful if it had had all the rabies information and the local vet on it. But it probably helped the owner to see this guy at night. We went ahead and gave the dog a rabies shot along with enough antibiotics to clean out Boston Bay.'

Roxanne tossed the dog tag in her hand. 'How's he doing?'

'Thought you'd never ask. Come on back. Be careful. He probably won't remember you.'

Roxanne knew that if she were a dog she would run like crazy to get out of a vet's office. The smells were awful. Even her inadequate human nose could smell fear and pain, and loneliness. Sam pushed open the new metal door to the recovery room—and it smelt like Bob.

The Lab was in the largest cage that they had and he was on his left side. The white bandage round his right front leg made Roxanne wince. He lifted his head when Roxanne knelt down. Sam opened the door wide and the dog thumped his tail once when Roxanne put her hand near his nose, then tried to stand up. When his right leg hit the floor he yelped, but he stood up anyhow, dizzy from the anaesthetic, keeping most of his weight on three legs.

'They heal faster than we do, you know,' Sam said. 'He's a young, strong dog, probably four or five. In a couple of days, we'll start looking for a foster home for him until we can locate the owner.'

The dog turned his head and looked straight at Roxanne.

'Be careful, Roxanne; he has just given you the look. When Labs give someone the look, it is a powerful, mind-altering drug that makes you think you have been personally locked into a soul contract.'

'I'm not an easy mark. I just don't like to see a good dog suffering,' Roxanne replied. 'If you haven't contacted the owners by the time he's ready to be released, I'll provide the foster home until we find them.' She stood up. 'Or maybe I shouldn't. I just remembered, he'll be alone while I'm working.'

'While you're out, he'll be sleeping. Dogs would hate this secret to get out, but they're a lot like cats. They look for a good place to curl up and sleep.'

Roxanne took a breath and shook away the memory of past foster dogs. 'Yeah, yeah. Show me his meds. Or will he be done with meds by then?'

The conversation was making Roxanne's head go woozy. This was the longest time that she had spent in the back room of a vet clinic since Bob had died. She put her hands on the edge of the table and leaned into it.

'Are you feeling OK? This dog is going to be fine, I'm not trying to stick you with a dying dog.' Sam sounded like he was trying to reassure her. 'You really are new at this, aren't you?'

For a moment Roxanne wanted to tell him that nothing was new, everything was new.

She pushed off from the table. 'You're right. I'm new at this.'

IN TWO DAYS, Roxanne got the call that the dog was ready to be released.

'I've been out of town for a day. When you come to get the Lab, I want you to take a look at the arrow that I pulled out of him,' said Sam. 'We close at noon today. Stop over then. You'll need to bring your truck.'

Reserving a place for vehicles on the ferry was difficult for visitors to the island, especially during the season, but Roxanne discovered she had the power to make last-minute requests if she was on emergency business.

Sam Reynolds's clinic had a cat door and a dog door. Roxanne paused a moment and went in through the dog door.

Sam showed her the shaft and point of the arrow that he had removed from the black dog. 'Did you notice anything about this arrow?' he asked her.

'I only saw the shaft and, to be honest, I was thinking a lot more about the dog. But you want to tell me something, so let's jump to that part.'

He rolled the shaft around in his palm. 'The entire arrow is handmade.' He pointed at the string round the arrow head. 'This is made from tendons of a deer, wrapped round the shaft to attach the point. If you include the time it takes to cut and dry the wood, it takes about three months to make one of these. I know that if you go to that amount of trouble, you don't shoot it at a dog; you want to shoot a deer, a turkey, a pheasant. Something is very wrong here.' He dropped the arrow shaft into her hands.

'Does anyone on the island have this as a winter hobby, like rug braiding or bookbinding?' asked Roxanne.

'I have never heard anyone brag about making a bow and arrow the good old-fashioned way. And it's the kind of thing someone *would* brag about.'

Roxanne leapt through the obvious possibilities in her brain. 'So this probably wasn't the work of a child. This was an adult hobby. Have you ever seen a dog shot by an arrow before?'

'Not on the island. On the Web I found several places that specialise in this type of arrow; there's one in Minnesota and one in Nebraska.' He shrugged. 'The good news is that this is a strong animal and he will heal. I had to remove some necrotic tissue, which unfortunately was muscle. I'd say he walked around with that arrow sticking out of him for maybe three days.'

'May I keep this?' she asked, holding up the remains of the arrow.

'It's yours.'

Sam rode in the back of the pick-up with the Lab while Roxanne drove. The ferry was not crowded; a late afternoon in November brought in only a third of the usual number of passengers.

As Roxanne approached her rental house, she wondered how Sam would see her situation. He and his wife Michelle had just remodelled their house on the south side of the island. Here she was, a single woman in her late thirties, living on the part-time salary of animal control warden and staying in one of the holiday cottages that was barely suitable for winter.

Sam's khaki trousers picked up dirt from the back of her truck as he slid out. 'Let's lift him down and see if he can make it into the house,' he said. He wrapped his arms round the dog's rib cage and Roxanne lent support to the rear end. When they set him on the ground, the Lab limped five feet away and squatted slightly as he let loose with a stream of urine.

'He's not ready to stand on three legs yet,' Sam said.

The three of them made it up the wooden steps that led to her deck. Roxanne unlocked the door and urged the dog inside.

Sam looked round with the quick eye of a professional medic. 'I used to live in a place like this in college, except there were four of us, and one guy never washed his own dishes and finally the rest of us wouldn't wash his dishes either, so we all used paper plates. It looks like you're a lot neater.'

No one else had been in the house, just the cat, and she stayed only part of the time. Roxanne had begun to call her Peterson, after the guidebook.

Roxanne listened to Sam's voice, and although she didn't hear his words as such, she was measuring the level of her rapid breathing. She noted that since her breathing was not increasing in pace, a panic attack was unlikely. She hadn't had another attack after the first one, two months after Bob had died. And although her horror at the sound of another person breathing in her house was now reaching tolerable levels, the thought of Sam and Michelle, who was going to drive over to collect him, seeing inside her house made her want to throw up.

'Do you have a water dish for the dog?' Sam was asking her. 'If you are going to be the nursemaid for this guy, you might consider a way to feed him.'

Taking a breath, Roxanne said, 'There's a pan under the stove. Did you bring in the amoxicillin? Seven more days with the meds, right?'

The dog, limping and exhausted from his ordeal at the clinic, the ferry ride, and the ride in the back of the truck, now slid to the floor and panted.

Sam called Michelle. 'Yeah, it's Isaiah's rental, off Bracken Road. OK. See ya.' He leaned against the chipped Formica counter. 'She'll be here in about twenty minutes; then we have to pick up the kids at day care.'

Roxanne retrieved the rectangular pan from beneath the stove. She tore open the top of a bag of kibbles, scooped out a handful and let them chink into place. By the time Michelle pulled up, Roxanne had put the cap back on the adrenaline. She had not had a panic attack, but the effort of averting one had drained her. When the couple left, she was exhausted.

She looked at the dog. 'I'm no bargain, but I'm all you've got until we can find your owner. I'll try to be a good host.'

Peterson had kicked up a royal fuss when Roxanne let her inside, hissing and pushing her spine into a curve of hysteria, then fleeing for Roxanne's bedroom. Both Roxanne and the dog ignored the behaviour.

The Lab looked at Roxanne. She took the throw rug from the bedroom and bunched it up near him. He was her first save and she didn't want this to go wrong. He slept in the kitchen on the first night, near the front door, like a shy house guest not wanting to intrude.

THE LAB HAD all the signs of depression: listlessness, lack of enjoyment in the things normally enjoyed; he even turned his black nose up at food. And his sleep was fitful. Being a dog, he couldn't say things like, 'It wouldn't matter if I was gone; no one would notice,' but Roxanne wondered if that was exactly what the Lab would say if he could.

She did what she could for him in the first days of his foster care, postoperative life. She was assured that infection would be annihilated by the broad-spectrum antibiotics and his recovery would not be complicated.

She let him figure her out slowly, smell her as much as he needed to, always offering her open hand slowly, letting him sniff. She crouched to stroke his head, to find out what he liked. Was it under the chin, behind the ears? 'Take your time, big guy,' she said to him as she refreshed his water and made sure that the few kibbles he had taken were replaced.

Fussing over him would only wear him out. She settled into a chair to read one of the mainland newspapers, but was instantly distracted by the thought of a person shooting a dog with a bow and arrow. She knew little about this sort of weaponry.

'Who in the world would do this to a dog?' asked Tess, who had been called in to help with the dog when Roxanne went to work. The sight of the wound on his shoulder made Tess wince and imagine the blasts of red and orange that he had endured.

Later, Roxanne found the older woman and the dog sitting together on the floor, Tess with her back against the wall, her legs stuck out like a young girl. The dog, like all good dogs, kept himself between Tess and the door. Roxanne cringed when she saw him try to stand.

'Did you give Black Dog the antibiotics?'

'Of course, an hour ago. He gets one more before you go to bed.'

'Can you stay until I take him outside to pee? If he falls, it will be easier if there are two people to carry him inside.'

Tess put on her coat and the two women coaxed the Lab outside. The wind came in surges, just like the surf of the ocean. The dog peed, wisely not trying to lift a hind leg, but squatting like a puppy.

'You can't call him Black Dog,' said Tess, when they were back in the kitchen. 'That's like calling someone Furrowed Brow or Capped Tooth.'

Roxanne reached over and patted the dog. 'Somewhere the dog has an owner and he has a name. I can't just change his name. I've got calls in to the animal shelters and wardens on the mainland, and I put an ad in the newspaper. I know that he doesn't belong to anyone on the island. And he has no computer chip on the back of his neck.'

'Good for you,' said Tess to the dog. 'I don't plan on getting a chip either.' She turned back to Roxanne. 'He needs a strong name, one with deep, mellow tones to match his voice. He's a most dignified dog.' She squatted down by the dog and looked into his dark eyes. 'Lloyd. Lloyd!' she said.

The dog lifted an ear. As a temporary name, they decided it would do.

Roxanne's work was nothing like her work as a psychologist: relocate the raccoons, the skunks; capture dogs abandoned by the summer people and the new litters of kittens destined to become feral; pick up dead seagulls. Monitor beach erosion: this was in addition to her job description, but she filed weekly reports for Isaiah and left them in his mailbox.

She had been slow to get to know people other than her boss and Tess, but she had a neighbour, Elaine, a teacher at the island school. They had often passed each other on the dirt road, their cars kicking up dust.

One day, when she saw Elaine at the grocery store, her arms filled with bags, struggling to get out of the door, Roxanne had an impulse to turn her head and pretend she didn't recognise the woman, but it was too late.

'Hello, neighbour. Can you get the door for me? I feel like a pack mule with all this stuff,' Elaine said with a broad smile.

Roxanne accepted an invitation to dinner because she was out of practice at declining. How had she and Bob said no before? 'Let me get back to you after I check at home.' That's right, that's what it had been like. Having a partner was a buffer, an excuse to contemplate, and a reason to say no.

Elaine had a 1950s ranch-style house, to which someone had attached a second storey. Roxanne arrived with a bottle of wine, even though Elaine had said, 'No, this is my welcome to you. I'm already guilty of bad manners for letting you be here for months before I invited you in.'

The smell of fresh tomato sauce filled the house and Roxanne suddenly remembered that she liked pasta, but she couldn't remember the last time that she had prepared it. She handed over her offering to Elaine.

Elaine turned her head to the door leading into the living room and Roxanne remembered what her college room-mate had once said about the fundamental difference in facial features. Some were destined to be finely chiselled in marble, others were best described in soft clay. Elaine was in the clay category, with soft round cheeks and a furrow between her eyebrows.

'Honey, it's dinner,' Elaine said to the open doorway. Roxanne had not seen anyone else with Elaine on the occasions they had passed each other on the dirt road. She waited to see who Honey was.

A young girl appeared, with her hair pulled back tight, her ears sticking out like a mouse. She wore bulky sweatpants, running shoes and a T-shirt with a partially zipped-up sweatshirt.

'Melissa, this is our neighbour, Roxanne. This is my daughter.'

Roxanne felt the hit first in her solar plexus, where she always felt it. She put her hand out to Melissa and got back not a solid athlete's grasp but a cold, dry, reluctant hand. Even as the two hands touched, Melissa offered a profound determination to pull away. The skin on her face was tight, but because she was young, no one was yet alarmed. Before Roxanne could stop herself, she said, 'Track or cross-country? Let me guess; you do both.'

Elaine, who was taking the cork out of the wine bottle, stopped in mid-pull. 'How did you know?'

Roxanne flicked a glance at the girl. 'I've known a few cross-country people. It was the shoes. You wear them only if you really mean business.'

Over dinner, Elaine asked Roxanne the sort of questions that she dreaded: Where did she come from? What did she do before being an animal control warden? She had settled on a stock answer: 'No children, used to work in child care, not married, just coming out of a relationship and trying out the island.' She was surprised at how easy it was to change who she was.

'I haven't seen you with your mother before,' said Roxanne, turning to Melissa.

'I stay at my dad's in Portland some of the time. Every other weekend. Sometimes more if I have school stuff.'

Elaine's mouth tightened up. 'We've done things this way for so long, I forget that it must sound strange. Melissa's father and I were divorced when Melissa was eight.'

Roxanne didn't have to watch long to see what Melissa was doing with her dinner. The girl patted her stomach and said, 'I'm so full from eating after I ran, I don't know how much I can eat.' She put a hard-boiled egg, some lettuce, sprouts and cucumber slices on her plate, followed by a golfball-sized portion of spaghetti with a tablespoon of sauce. Then she elaborately sliced the cucumber into eight pieces like a pie. The spaghetti was pushed around and rearranged without one strand going into her mouth. She ate a mushroom from the sauce and suddenly stopped.

'Did you put oil in the sauce, Mom?'

'Oil? Well, I had to use a tiny bit of oil when I sautéed the mushrooms.' Elaine shrugged her shoulders. She looked down and tucked her highlighted hair behind her ears. Roxanne knew this was not the first time that the girl had questioned her mother about ingredients.

Melissa was the kind of kid that Roxanne had not wanted to work with at the counselling centre. None of her training had truly prepared her for the tenacity of anorexia or the pure malevolence of the voice of an eating disorder that wrapped round the girls like a smirking python. Her mantra as a therapist had been, 'I don't specialise in eating disorders,' and because another therapist at the clinic did, she had sent all the determinedly starving young women to her.

Ellen was the perfect therapist for girls with eating disorders. She was round, unembarrassed by her own girth, and no threat to girls who were in competition for deprivation. The unhappy army of girls, defined by skin, bones and grit, found solace with Ellen. Roxanne had watched them arrive for their weekly meetings, pulling their osteoporotic spines straight. From her office, she could spot their skin, desperate with goose flesh and extra hair, trying to warm the bodies that insisted on living without fat.

And then, last winter, Ellen had married a dentist and moved to Albany. The clinic director said to Roxanne, 'We have to talk about our clients with eating disorders now that Ellen is gone.' She knew what this meant, and a solid sense of dread lodged in the back of her throat. She tried everything to escape the big-eyed skinny girls with their hair pulled back tight and their baggy pants and big sweatshirts worn to hide the clatter of their bones.

'It's not ethical to offer services that are beyond our scope of expertise. We can refer out. Let's put this in the job description: "Must have experience in eating disorders",' said Roxanne. She said anything except the truth, which was that the tiny young women who refused to eat, but who thought of nothing else all day except food, terrified her, outwitted her, showed that all of her training was for naught. Here, on the island, no one expected cures from Roxanne.

She watched Melissa rearrange the lettuce and the now yolkless, hard-boiled egg and wondered if Elaine realised. As the mother, she would be blamed, no matter what she did. If Elaine didn't know, she'd be blamed for being in denial. If she did know, she would still be the culprit for colluding with her daughter who refused the egg yolk.

Roxanne shifted her attention to the girl and a suddenly liberated mean streak ran through her. 'Hey, can I have a slice of that egg white? It looks delicious.' She reached across the table with her fork as if to stab the egg white. The mother and daughter drew in tight. Roxanne had broken through the perimeter of their rules. She put her fork back on her plate and scooped up more pasta. Roxanne revelled in the freedom of being non-therapeutic.

When all the food was mercifully taken off the table, Melissa slid her chair back and said she had some chemistry to do. Roxanne tried to salvage the rest of the evening by talking about Lloyd, but the tone of the earlier welcome had cooled, and she made an early, nine o'clock, departure. She knew that the evening had gone badly.

Sleep had always been a comfort to her, but, since Bob had died, it had become an unpredictable landscape. In the first months after his death, she had dreamt endless versions of the cardiac resuscitation she had attempted. In one dream she tried to plug his heart into the hair dryer to shock him back to life. He had sat up and said, 'Stop it! You're burning us.'

But now, try as she might, her dreams flitted away before she could grab them and she woke each morning blinded by the complete darkness of sleep. If she couldn't remember her dreams, would she forget Bob?

She tested herself: What did his face look like? She closed her eyes and the image of him was distressingly impressionistic. Her breath caught and then quickened. Adrenaline fed in a fury throughout her body, quickening her heart. Could she still smell him?

She pulled Bob's pillow into her face and flared her nostrils to catch his scent. But the pillow, after six months of such work, was giving up the last memory of Bob; of his oily skin and heavy aroma, which used to make Roxanne put her face on his chest and close her eyes.

Her heart beat too fast and she noticed that her hands were trembling. *Is this what a heart attack is like? If she died of a respectable, early heart attack, would she find Bob?*

The well-meaning say that the dead are not really gone; they live on in our hearts. Roxanne wondered if she had ever said that to anyone. If so, she wanted to find the client and say, 'I'm so sorry. The dead are gone. I can't find my husband in my heart. The dead leave us. Death is unbearable.'

The wind shook the tightly woven nest of vines and trees outside. These trees, shrubs and vines had adapted to the savage winds off the ocean. Their roots were deep and determined.

If Bob were here, she would have wanted him to make love. He would have pulled her to him, letting her straddle his body. He would have put his warm hands on her hips . . .

But he was gone. The memory of him had slowed her heart again, numbing it back into sadness, and the dog, who had been in the room the entire time, began to pace as if even he had had enough of this reverie.

Roxanne got up, washed and dressed, then walked the dog briefly before getting into the car and driving down to the small grocery store. It was Saturday and she was out of tampons.

She was in the aisle of feminine hygiene products, deliberating over nondeodorant or regular tampons, when she spotted Melissa. 'Hey!' said Roxanne, before the girl could duck round the corner. She put the two boxes behind her back. 'Do me a favour, Melissa, and pick left or right. I can't make up my mind.'

Melissa looked mortified.

'Go on, pick one; I can't stand the indecision.' Roxanne knew she was once again going down the wrong path with the girl, but she couldn't stop.

Melissa pointed a bluish hand to the right.

'Ah, the variety pack. Thanks, track star,' said Roxanne.

Melissa remained in a state of frozen stupor, and Roxanne stared first at the blue tint of her hands, then at her face. She saw the evil sneer of the girl's eating disorder peering at her behind Melissa's thin shoulders.

'Oh. Your periods have stopped, haven't they? How long?'

The girl's eyes opened wide in savage exposure. 'You're nuts! There's something wrong with you. You don't belong here,' Melissa said. She turned and ran out of the store, abandoning what she had come for.

Roxanne felt guilt descending on her for slamming the girl with the weapons that the food-deprived child was not prepared to deflect. She had a big, blossoming eating disorder and Roxanne knew it. And the kid thought she was fooling everyone. But it was unfair of Roxanne to take a swipe at her if the kid couldn't fight back.

Roxanne had to do something to even the score on her bad behaviour in the store. She called Melissa when she got home and said, 'Hey, I think I was too blunt with you the other day. And I'm sorry about today at the store. I can be that way . . . I have to go to the mainland for a couple of days at the end of the week and I was wondering if you could take care of Lloyd, the dog that I'm fostering? . . . Yeah? . . . I'll bring him over with his mountain of food. Could you stop by and bring in my mail? Oh, and put some cat food out for Peterson? . . . I'm leaving on Friday and I'll be back on Sunday . . . Yeah, I'll give you the key.'

Roxanne felt better, as if the cruel stab at the girl had been partially erased. She wrote a paragraph in her journal about how she didn't wish every day that she'd die in an accident, or in her sleep, or like Bob did, suddenly, brutally, and without a moment's thought for those left behind.

She had told clients who were grieving that doing anything helped: writing in journals, talking, walking or painting their house. Was everything that she told them worthless? After a few days, she had given up on writing every day in her journal and had left it sitting on her chest of drawers. If Bob had been alive, she would have slipped it into a drawer. Without knowing it, she had made an adaptation to living alone.

THE VISIT TO HER BROTHER'S HOUSE was compulsory. Both her mother and Caleb had said that if she didn't come, they were coming out to the island to see her and she didn't want this ascetic life disturbed by their caring.

Later in the week, when Roxanne took Lloyd to Melissa's house, she explained again about the food, about the mail. 'Here you go, kid, front-door key.' She handed the key to Melissa, who was doing homework.

'You do homework on Friday morning?' asked Roxanne. It was 6.30 a.m.

'I can't finish it all at night.' Melissa had her game face on; the good-girl look that probably worked so well with her coach.

'OK. Well, Lloyd will park himself somewhere between you and the door. He's still gimpy in the leg so don't take him running with you no matter how much he tries to convince you. Dogs will force themselves to keep up with you even if they can't. Know what I mean?'

'I know how to take care of a dog.'

'Right, sorry. You'll do fine. Here is Tess's number in case you need anything. Do you know Tess?'

'I guess so. The old lady with the hair?'

Roxanne paused. She hadn't really thought of Tess in that way, but yes, Melissa apparently did know her. 'That's the one.'

Roxanne left after bidding goodbye to Elaine, who stepped into the kitchen, with coffee cup in hand, dressed for work and with a softer look in her eyes than the last time Roxanne had blundered into their lives.

Chapter 3

The first place Melissa went when she got home from school was Roxanne's house. Lloyd came with her, happy to pee on everything that required his urine-soaked messages to other dogs. He could now balance on his two front legs well enough to once again raise his rear leg. The cat greeted them at the door and dashed out, between Melissa's legs.

On Saturday, Melissa took in the mail. It was thrilling to be in someone else's house alone. She opened the cabinets over the sink; two coffee cups and a couple of glasses. All the cabinets revealed the same sparseness.

Melissa opened the refrigerator. 'Let's see what she eats.' One quart of milk, a loaf of bread, peanut butter, margarine, a jar of salad dressing.

'She's one to talk,' said Melissa to Lloyd, who raised a questioning ear.

She closed the refrigerator and moved on to the bathroom. She thought of the girls she knew at high school who threw up. Everybody knew who they were. She didn't throw up, because she ran. The girls who threw up didn't get that part: that if you run and do 300 sit-ups at night in your room, quietly so no one hears you, who needs to throw up? She opened the mirrored cabinet and inspected each item . . . boring stuff, no make-up.

Then she went into the bedroom and walked over to the chest of drawers. She put her hands on the black journal and opened it.

'Oh, this is good, this is very good,' she said to Lloyd, reading the first page. She ran her fingers along the lightly embossed cover as she read the entries that started last spring, and saw the laboured handwriting, erratic spiking and pages that had been destroyed by a pen dragged fiercely across the page. 'I hate you . . . I want to die,' was the message in jagged lines.

July 16. There is no one here to give me caution and I am glad of that. I do not need to close the cover of this book to protect someone else's sensibilities. I leave it open at night and in the morning. No hand has disturbed it, no eyes have scanned my thoughts. What would it take to join you, my love? Of all the ways, carbon monoxide seems the best and the surest, the least likely to alert the outside world. You would be furious, shocked, disgusted if you saw me plotting my death. But I am not worried about your disapproval; I am terrified about the unknown, about not finding you if I kill myself.

Melissa closed the book. She had been sitting on Roxanne's bed and stood up, startled. She hurriedly smoothed the blankets on the bed. Where exactly had the journal been on the chest of drawers? Which direction had it faced? She would be more careful when she came back tomorrow to read more.

On the way out of the bedroom, Lloyd looked at her from the doorway. She knelt down beside him and ran her hand over the ridge of the dog's neck. She felt him press his head into her hand.

Roxanne could spoil everything for Melissa. No one had said a word to her about not eating enough until Roxanne came to dinner and blew her cover. That wasn't entirely true; her mother had begun to make everything that Melissa had ever said she loved to eat.

At home, Melissa logged on to the websites for girls with eating disorders. She knew her mother would never think to track where she had been on the Web and this gave her the freedom of a world traveller, disguised as a high-school girl and track star, but really she was a terrorist. Her camouflage gear included sweatpants, pristine running shoes, two layers of shirts. When she heard her mother go to sleep, the click of the bedroom light, the outer gear came off and bone girl appeared, skin stretched smooth over bone, enough toned flesh to keep her running.

On to the websites: her favourite was www.annierexia.com. The sites of resistance, the guerrilla fighters of world food. How to do without, to exist on defiance with an apple for lunch, to live on the razor's edge between perfect brevity of body and the hospital. At all cost, said the Web-page star, do not let them put you in the hospital. As a prisoner of war, they can do anything to you, restrain you, and take away privileges. At the very worst, they will slide a feeding tube down your throat and defile you with a disgusting mixture of blended drinks.

Melissa shuddered. She was ashamed for not being as brave, as strong, as perfectly beyond her body as Annie was. Melissa's friend Krystal had been her starving partner last year, but now Krystal had a boyfriend and she had lost her edge.

As if by magic, Melissa spotted a new flag on the site that said, *Going Solo*. She clicked on it and the text sprang up: *If everyone has left you and gone back to food it's because you have something that they don't. You are ready to cross over. I'm not stopping. Are you?*

Her breath stopped, and then she clicked off, suddenly fearful. She had a cooked egg white waiting for her downstairs that she would have to eat by tomorrow morning, but the whole day could stay under 700 calories. She could easily move down to 600. She padded silently downstairs and into the kitchen, where she pushed the hard-boiled egg across a plate, separating the yoke from the white, and cut the egg white into tiny cubes.

The cubes of egg white looked like granite blocks on her plate. She lined them up in grids, a small pile for each direction, north, south, east and west. After she finished her calculus, she could eat the northern pile.

When it was done, she let one pile of cubes plunk dangerously into her belly. She waited an hour before eating the next pile, and by then she had finished her chemistry and was well into rewriting her history notes. She loved the way her schoolwork looked in the late hours of the night, each pile of work lined up perfectly straight. When she wrote, she used a precisely sharpened pencil, so that errors could be erased and rubbed clean. By the time she was done with her homework, the books were set out on the Formica counter, ready to be stuffed in her book bag on Monday morning.

Two piles of egg cubes were left. She pierced the rest with one tine of the fork and put it in her mouth, careful not to touch her teeth. This last group of creamy cubes had to wait on her tongue, pressing them to the roof of her mouth. The cubes had to compress into flat compliance, then dissolve, travelling the long journey over the rough backside of the tongue, down where throat muscles must squeeze and push and escort the flecks of egg to the unwelcoming cavern of the stomach. She knew she had to wait, uneasy, and that she had to count to 100 several times to allow the cubes to stay in her body. The dog, who had laboured determinedly to come down the stairs to be with her, positioned his black body at her feet. His body glowed with warmth and she placed her feet under the blanket of his belly.

'THERE IS SOMETHING oddly perverse about you wanting to learn about bows and arrows after this dog was nearly killed by a fool shooting him.'

Lloyd stood up and, with the barest limp, positioned himself between the women and the door. Tess winced, as she always did, when she saw him limp.

'I know,' said Roxanne. 'You would imagine that I would be repulsed by the idea of archery, but I'm not. I don't want the dog to know. I mean I won't do it around him. I won't even keep the stuff here. I'll go over to the mainland. I looked up some places.'

'Why don't you take up tai chi or qigong?'

Tess was helping Roxanne winterise her cottage. They were hanging plastic at the windows in the living room and her bedroom. Roxanne plugged in her hair dryer and aimed it at the plastic that was attached to the window frame. All the fold marks from the packaging remained. She aimed the hair dryer slowly up and down the marks.

'Oh, that noise!' said Tess, putting her hands over her ears. 'It's bright green and disagreeable. I'll be outside until you finish.'

Roxanne kept shrink-wrapping her windows and wondered what it would be like to be Tess and have sharp noises be green, see the days of the week as big coloured cubes that each hold their own niche in space. When Tess learned that Roxanne was interested in synaethesia, she had let her know more and more of her synaesthete world. Tess didn't hide it from people, but she didn't elaborate unless she knew someone was truly interested.

Roxanne turned off the hair dryer. She saw the strong wave of Tess's white hair as she walked past the deck, inspecting something along the ground. The dog sat sentinel at the door, knowing that his pack was divided, one outside and one inside. His look of distress suddenly lodged in

Roxanne. This was now her world, a dog who could not tell her his secret and a woman who held her ears to keep out the bright green noise of a hair dryer. And she had a palpable yearning to put her hands on a bow and pull back the string.

Despite Tess's warning about archery, she looked in the Yellow Pages for sporting goods stores in Portland and called while Tess was outside. She phoned the very first one listed, Sporting Equipment Store, and asked if they had archery supplies. Ron Wilcox, the owner, said, 'We got all the compound bows. What we ain't got, you can order.'

When Tess returned to the house, and the dog relaxed with a sigh, Roxanne explained that she had found the store that she was looking for. 'But I didn't understand something that he told me,' Roxanne said. 'What's a compound bow?'

Tess shrugged. 'How should I know? I'm a retired physical therapist, not a sportswoman.'

THE MAINLAND SEEMED foreign to Roxanne. The smell of the ocean was still present as she drove along the streets of Portland, but less dense. Lloyd had seemed well enough for a car trip, so she'd brought him along for the ride.

When she pushed open the door at the Sporting Equipment Store, a bell clattered overhead. A large-bellied man, who Roxanne assumed must be the owner, looked up from behind the desk. Behind him was an arsenal of guns, riflescopes in cases and pistols resting like reptiles under the glass countertops. She smelt oil and metal.

'Ron Wilcox? I called yesterday about archery equipment?'

'Yeah, over here,' Ron said. 'What draw weight are you looking for?'

Roxanne was amazed at how quickly she could be stripped naked in places like garages, timber yards, or, now, sports supply stores.

'I've never used a bow before. What do you mean, how much weight?'

She followed Ron to the back where the archery supplies were lined up.

'I'm gonna expand this section next year. We've got a growing number of people looking into archery. What do you plan to hunt?'

'Nothing. A target, I guess. I just want to learn how to shoot.'

Roxanne looked at the bows. They were complicated devices with pulleys that looked like a combination of technology and medieval utility. This was not what she was expecting.

'Are these the only kind you have?'

'These are the only kind I have in stock,' Ron said. 'These compound bows are all anyone ever asks for now. The pulley system means that the archer doesn't have to exert so much power.'

Roxanne had brought along the remains of the arrow that had nearly killed Lloyd. She took it from her bag. 'I want a bow for this sort of arrow.'

'Oh, now that's a different thing altogether. You're looking for someone who's into traditional archery. I don't do that here.' Ron folded his arms.

'Who does?' asked Roxanne.

She followed him back to the counter. The wall behind it was covered with business cards. Ron removed one and handed it to Roxanne. 'This guy, Hill Johnson, hunts with traditional bows. He used to give lessons. I don't know if he still does. He's up in Brunswick. You need a pencil to write down his number?'

She thanked him and left. Lloyd jumped into the passenger seat. Even though it was early December, Roxanne cracked open the passenger window several inches and, as she drove, Lloyd turned his snout to a tendril of scent going by a restaurant. And then he leaned his upper body towards the window and tilted his nose skywards. Finally he closed his eyes.

Farther on, Roxanne pulled into a Dairy Mart to get a Coke. As she got out of the car, Lloyd assumed a more proprietary posture, staring ahead. Roxanne looked back with encouragement at the dog.

'I'll be right back.'

A green and black SUV pulled in right next to her, too close, and she said under her breath, 'Big asshole.' She would have to get in on Lloyd's side.

She went round to the front door of the SUV and, with studied sarcasm, held the door open for the tight-jawed young man who leapt from the vehicle. Roxanne wanted to let loose with a tirade about his behemoth guzzling eighty per cent of the world's resources, but both of them stopped dead as the black Lab went off like a bomb in Roxanne's car. The hair on Lloyd's back stood up straight and the car rocked as he thrashed his body.

'Jesus, Lloyd. Cut it out. What's got into you?'

The man did a double take when he saw Lloyd and then he looked hard at Roxanne. 'Is that your dog?' he asked.

'Yeah. I don't think he likes you,' said Roxanne.

He offered her a contemptuous look, but since Lloyd did not let up his show of force, the look was brief. Roxanne noticed that the man had short brown hair. He seemed to forget whatever he had needed at the store and stumbled back to his vehicle, finally making a tyre-squealing exit.

Roxanne got into her car. Lloyd stopped as quickly as he had begun, yet the fur on his back was still raised. Roxanne ran her hand over his head to settle him and imagined the danger button in his body switching off. 'So you're not Mr Nice Guy all the time,' she said. She wondered if Lloyd knew that guy and if he did, why did he want to rip off the man's head?

Back home, she called Hill Johnson to set up an initial lesson.

'The best thing to do is to come out in a couple of days' time and try it, then decide if you want lessons,' Hill said.

LATER THAT WEEK, they stood in Hill Johnson's back yard in Brunswick. They hadn't gone into his house; instead they had skirted round his garage to the back. His archery shop took up half of his garage, right on the end of a cul-de-sac. Hill looked younger than she was by more than a few years, and was taller than she had expected. Roxanne guessed that he was late twenties, early thirties. Something about him said military. Maybe back from Iraq. What was it that looked so military about him? No, not military. He was a hunter. She was startled by his features, the combination of rich, dark eyebrows highlighting his face in contrast to an adolescent rosiness in his cheeks. And one eye was blue-green and the other was green-blue.

Roxanne asked him about his name. 'Hill? You mean Hillary? That must have been a tough one in junior high.'

'Nothing tough about it. It's a family name. Only my grandmother called me Hillary and she's no longer with us,' he said.

Roxanne assumed the lessons would begin immediately. His back yard extended at least an acre and bumped up against a railroad track. Two paper targets were tacked to hay bales. He handed Roxanne a bow. 'My wife started on this one,' he said. 'This is a good size for you.'

She was relieved there was a wife. Now they could be all business without an undercurrent of sexual tension. She hefted the bow in her hands. 'I don't even know where to start and I'm not sure what I'll do with this.'

'Today, you'll start with breathing and flexing your knees. If you can become still enough, you'll move up to pulling the bowstring.'

'I notice you didn't include arrows. No arrows?'

'No. Too breezy anyhow.' There had not been one hint of breeze until that moment and suddenly the treetops began to dance.

'Good call,' she said.

'I just watched the weather channel.' He let her have a loose, slightly crooked smile. 'I'm one-eighth Lakota, but I don't think one-eighth of anything counts for much. I'm half-Irish, and then some Austrians got into the mix. Then there's the English part. That's where Hillary came from. I bet even the Indians watch the weather channel.'

Roxanne noted that the only people who said 'Indian' any more usually were Native Americans.

'OK, stand sideways with your left side closest to the target. Turn your head to face the target. No, just your head, not your shoulders; they're like the arrow. Your arms and shoulders are going to become part of the whole arrow. You're holding a lot of energy between your shoulder blades; let it drop down until you can feel your feet touching the earth.'

The wind picked up, carrying messages from the south. Roxanne's tightly curled hair flipped up, exposing her forehead, making her feel naked. She shook her head to get the hair to come back down. They practised soft knees, turning heads, shoulders going still. They practised finding her centre, dropping energy down, pulling energy up, breathing from the belly, letting all the breath out, and then the deeper stillness.

'Everyone wants to pull the arrow back and let her rip. That's like saying to a mathematician, "What's the final answer?" The arrow is the least of it. What did you eat before you came? Your energy is too high in your body.'

'Let's see. I had a juice and coffee. I haven't had lunch yet.'

'That's part of it,' he said, shrugging off his jacket and getting into the stance himself. 'Watch me. Tell me what you see.'

He closed his eyes for a few seconds and turned to the side. His thick eyelashes rested on his cheeks. His chest and belly filled up with air. He opened his eyes. On the release of breath, he turned his head with hydraulic fluidity. His shoulders were back and down. He looked like a tree trunk swaying with imperceptible movement. And then he entered stillness. He mimed pulling back an arrow with his right hand, which glided smoothly from a spot an arm's length in front of him back to his ear. Finally he released the imaginary arrow. Roxanne thought she could hear the thwack of it hitting the target. Her eyes darted to the target despite what her brain knew. She looked back at Hill, who remained in his still posture. She knew he had noticed that she looked at the target. Tiny muscles round his lips struggled to keep from smiling.

'In this posture, nothing should be able to knock me over. It's like being anchored to the ground, but the upper body can stay flexible. Push me,' he said. 'Hard.'

'This demonstration is not going to be very effective, if you're trying to show how powerful you are against equal strength. I don't have a lot of brute strength these days. I must have left it somewhere else,' said Roxanne.

'Well, give a really big push, then.'

What was the point of this? That a woman would ricochet off him in an attempt to tackle him? She was suddenly irritated at the predictability of the exercise. She impulsively put her head down and dived into him with her shoulder, the way she had seen American football players do. She imagined the man as firmly planted as a tree, so the point of this demonstration was to show what little impact she could have on him, and she simply did not care. She wanted to hit someone hard. She knocked him over. Or more exactly, he seemed to collapse like a bridge that had rusted out.

'Damn,' he said from the ground. 'I never know when that knee will go out. All this from playing football at a state college.' He rubbed his knee from his flat-back position. 'You sure you want to learn archery? You have potential in the more aggressive sports, like hockey.'

Without waiting for an answer, Hill stood up, rubbed his knee some more and said, 'Practise breathing, practise everything you did today, except the part where you tackled me. I've got space for a student. I lost one a few months ago. Oh wait; I'm assuming you want the lessons. Do you?'

Roxanne had not tackled anyone with such satisfaction since sixth grade when she could still overpower Caleb. And she had not touched another man, other than griever's hugs, since Bob had died.

'Yeah, I want to sign up for lessons. I'm not a hunter, but there's something about archery . . . I want to learn how to do this.'

Hill grabbed his jacket and put it on. 'Lots of people will start something like archery, but when it gets hard they quit. How about you? What do you do when things get hard?'

She shoved her hands into her pockets. 'I don't quit,' she said.

They scheduled lesson two for the following Wednesday afternoon at three. Hill taught English at Brunswick High School and Wednesday was the only day he didn't stay late. Roxanne tried to picture an English teacher grading papers after a day of shooting deer.

LESSON TWO WAS HARDER. 'The first thing we have to do is test for eye dominance. That will tell us which hand will hold the bow and which will pull the bowstring,' said Hill.

'I'm right-handed,' said Roxanne.

'That may be, but we don't know if you're right-eyed or left-eyed. Hold both hands out at arm's length, put your hands loosely together like this so there's a hole to look through. Keep both eyes open and look at the centre of the target. Keep it in focus and slowly move your hands towards your face.'

She just wanted to shoot the arrow. Aim and shoot. This felt like going to the doctor. She pulled her hands towards her slowly.

'Your hands are pulling over to the left eye. Centre the hole over your left eye and focus on the target. Now do the same thing over the right eye. Which one is it?'

Hill stood with his legs spread wide; his arms rested lightly at his sides. He waited for Roxanne to figure out what he already saw.

'It's my left eye. How can that be?'

Hill shrugged. 'Happens all the time. People think that their eyes work the same way on each side. We are not symmetrical. Let's see how strong your left arm is. We have to balance out strength with accuracy.'

He put a bow in Roxanne's hands. 'This is the longbow, the only kind of traditional bow that I use. Take a wide stance, right side to the target. Hold the bow with your right hand and pull the bowstring with your left. Point your elbow higher, pull your hand right up near your jawline.'

Roxanne struggled to pull back the bowstring, her arm shaking with the effort. Soon the entire bow was wobbling as she finally managed to pull back the string. Then she did the same on the opposite side; left side facing the target, left hand holding the bow, right arm pulling the bowstring. Her arm pulled the string back in a nearly steady effort.

'There's our answer. Your right-handed dominance is going to be more important than your left-eyed dominance. You pulled the bowstring back in a smooth line with your right hand. That's the good news. The bad news for you is, that's a child's bow. You've got a lot of work to do.'

Roxanne's shoulders slumped. 'That's a kid's bow? What the hell does a real one feel like?'

'You're about to find out.' Hill flipped the tarp off a wooden table and an array of bows appeared.

IT SEEMED to Roxanne that Hill had found her lacking in the archery department and the competitive spirit in her flamed to life. When had she last really wanted to get better at something? She was horrified when he gave her a child's bow after her quivering inability to pull back a bowstring with even a thirty-pound draw weight. And the final insult left her reeling.

'You don't have enough mass, and what you have is not muscle mass,' Hill told her. 'Let me say this in another way: you don't have enough weight in the right places in the right density. Your ability to knock me over had to do with a combination of my bad knee and lucky physics, and I think you were also pissed off at something . . . but that's your business. Plainly speaking, you just don't have enough muscle mass.'

Roxanne pondered this on the drive back to the ferry. She put her hand to her thigh and wondered if this leg was hers. Wasn't hers bigger, ready to spring? Standing at the dock, waiting for the ferry, she opened her coat and put her hand on her waist, inched upwards and connected with a set of newly exposed ribs that had not been there six months ago. She put her thumbs into her waistband and pulled out. Trousers that had once been snug now gapped by inches. Roxanne carried the child's bow, zipped into its canvas bag, under her arm. Like everyone else, she headed for the enclosed room on the ferry. The wind was too cold for even the hardiest passenger to stay outside.

Bob would have noticed right away if she had lost this much weight. He would have said, 'Don't go skinny on me. I need something to hang on to.'

But Bob was seven months dead.

The NEXT DAY was shrill with sunshine and cold wind. Roxanne had no place that she had to be; no animal calls had come in, and even Isaiah was gone today so that an impromptu visit to his office was not possible. Then she remembered her body.

She stepped out of her clothes and they fell round her like petals. The rental house had a long mirror, but she had taken it down when she first moved in and had slid it behind the couch. She pulled it out again and hung it back in its place in the living room. She stared at her face, torso and legs. The cat and dog watched her from a pool of sunlit floor. Peterson had recently agreed to sit in the same room with Lloyd.

Maybe she had lost weight; so what? It wasn't unusual after a death. What truly astounded Roxanne was that she hadn't noticed. Hadn't she always had broad shoulders? Now they just looked angular. The swimmer's build, Bob had called it. When they were newly married, he had introduced her as 'the one with the shoulders'. Somehow, he had made her more real.

She had thought she was real enough before they met, before she had seen him swimming in the town pool, paddling like a large poodle, straining to keep his head above water. Surely she had been the one to be in the physical realm. She had been the one with the whistle round her neck, pausing to ask him, 'Do you need assistance?' And he, barely able to ask one more thing of his body, such as turning his head, had eyed her with one eye, the way a whale might, and with the same effect. If a whale ever looks right at you, with its one-sided watery vision, you are never the same.

With much sputtering, Bob had dog-paddled his ultra-dense bones to the side of the pool and said, 'I've been working on this all summer. If you think this is bad, you should have seen me in June.'

She didn't know where he'd been practising his torturous swimming programme, but it had not been here at the town pool because she had been lifeguarding all summer each afternoon.

He had attempted to pull himself out of the pool with all the grace of an unfortunate elk that had fallen in. He grappled and slipped and finally pulled himself to a seated position. Roxanne was fascinated by his determination.

She squatted down and extended a muscled arm and said, 'That was a most extraordinary pool exit.'

Maybe that was it, that first touch, culminating in the combination of her well-defined body and his determined body, coming together in a way she had not imagined.

'I can show you how to make more efficient use of your strokes,' she offered.

He later told her that was the best line he had ever heard. He had just graduated from veterinary school. She had one more year of grad school before completing her doctoral degree in psychology.

They started swimming lessons and dating simultaneously; a one-hour lesson after Roxanne was off duty, followed by sandwiches at the bagel place across from the university. Each lesson was more fascinating to Roxanne than the one before. Bob's body was unlike anyone else's she had ever encountered. He was a stone, filled with granite instead of blood and bone marrow.

'What happens if you just try to float, or even lightly tread water?' she asked him on the third swimming lesson.

'I'll show you,' he said, as he stopped his vigorous stroking and kicking. He became horizontal in the water for a moment, languidly moving his arms, and, as if his feet were extra dense, he began to sink feet first. Roxanne watched him slowly drop to the bottom of the twelve-foot depth, landing lightly on his toes. She expected him to spring back up, pushing off with his knees bent. But instead he sank even more, sat crosslegged on the bottom of the pool and placed his palms on his legs.

Roxanne waited a moment, treading water above him, then she jack-knifed straight down to him, her head coming even with his, her feet kicking about her. She looked at him sternly and gave him a thumbs-up sign for him to get going. His cheeks were puffed up and he stared directly into her eyes and slowly began releasing the air out of his lungs.

Roxanne's body went into the automatic response that had been ingrained into her brain and into every cell since she had first been trained as a lifeguard in high school. She gave a huge kick that brought her body down until her feet touched the bottom of the pool, wrapped one arm round his neck and torso, and at the same time that she kicked off, she heaved him up and got her hip under him. She aimed up and diagonally for the side of the pool. As they broke the surface, her fury gave an extra bolt of strength and she nearly threw him onto the poolside.

'What the hell is wrong with you?' she spat.

Bob had swallowed a bit of water and coughed it out of his lungs. The lifeguard on duty came over and said, 'Do you need help here, Roxanne?'

'I was just giving lessons to an idiot who decided to sit on the bottom of the pool and exhale.' She glared at Bob, checked to see that he was pulling himself up on the ladder, then strong-armed herself onto the side of the pool. 'Don't you ever pull that stunt again,' she said.

'Look, I wanted to see what it would be like to be saved, to be really saved by an incredibly beautiful woman.' Bob reached for her hand. 'I'm sorry.'

When he touched her she felt the jolt of energy going through her all over again. He smiled his big smile. 'If you had to, would you save me again?'

His penance was to be the official victim for the water-safety class. After they made love for the first time, he whispered to her, 'I'm in love with a woman who won't let me drown. What an incredible extra.'

SHE WAS GOING back for another archery lesson in seven days. She would pull back the damn child's bow and move up five pounds. She set up a practice target at the back of Tess's house. She had already decided that Lloyd shouldn't see her in the act of archery. She didn't know what kind of post-traumatic stress disorder dogs could muster up, but it seemed cruel to expose him to a reminder of his nearly fatal encounter. And she was going to have to build her body back up again.

She spent the next day in Portland searching for an athletics club, signed up at the YMCA and got a trainer to work with her for an hour. The trainer was young and eager. He advised her to go for a full-body, free-weights fitness regime, and not just upper-body work, as she had requested.

'It doesn't matter if you used to be fit; you're starting from scratch,' he said as he wrote down the number of the free weight that Roxanne pushed above her head. Roxanne stopped, and the two plastic-coated, six-pound weights paused overhead like heavy birds. She slowly lowered them.

'You're right, I'm starting from scratch, aren't I?' She knew that this happened sometimes; that strangers could speak as sages, pulling truths from the air so deep that it seemed like they were momentarily inhabited by wisdom completely beyond them. And there is always the choice of whether to listen or not, whether to act or not.

'That's what I'll do, then. Start from the beginning.'

Chapter 4

Roxanne expected to see improvement; this was the third lesson. She had worked out a deal with Tess to use the old car that her friend kept on the mainland. Often, if people could find a spot in Portland to leave another car they did, rather than paying for the more expensive car ferry. Roxanne knew she was ready to move up to a heavier bow and part of her was eager to hear Hill say, 'Good pull and release. This is the day to move up to a twenty-five-pound bow.'

She had practised for two hours each day behind Tess's house. At first, the arrows had flown wildly over, under and to the side of the target, which was the size of a garbage-can lid. The first time that the arrow actually hit the target, Roxanne was amazed at the thrill she felt.

She was anxious for Hill to see the improvement. She had eaten breakfast and lunch and, the last time she checked, her energy was right where it was supposed to be, dropped down low in her body.

She parked Tess's car on the street in front of his house and walked to the back yard after not finding him in his shop garage. He was already pulling back on his sixty-five-pound bow as if it were no harder than the rubber band that secured the Sunday paper. Thwack! He hit as close to the centre as an arrow could get.

There was no question of startling him, she knew that. He was a hunter and he listened to sounds. Roxanne pictured him noting the noise of her car door closing, the knock on the shop door, and the way she had let the gate slap shut when she came into the back yard. For the first time, she saw that Hill moved his body in a way that was graceful. His shoulders swivelled in perfect opposition to his hips.

She greeted him with sudden shyness, and tried to pull back hard into a sisterly approach with him. After the general greetings, she unzipped the canvas bag and took out the borrowed bow. She took her stance and began to slow her breathing. She prepared to pull back.

'Are you married?' asked Hill from his perch on a wooden picnic table.

She crumbled inside and let her arms drop. She was baffled. Why did people have to ask this? Wasn't she enough as she was? Finally, she said, 'Not any more. I'm not married any more.'

He picked up his bow again and walked towards Roxanne. 'Tough answer. Simple question,' he said. 'I've thrown you off. Sorry. Let me take a couple of shots while you recuperate.'

He turned his left side to the target. 'Here's where archery is like fencing. Remember, these are weapons of battle and in battle you want to expose the least amount of body surface to the enemy. No full-frontal attacks. Your side can take an arrow, and it's better if you're a lefty so your right side faces the enemy. Keeps your heart farthest away and protected.'

'I'm right-handed and left-eyed,' said Roxanne.

'I know. You'll have to watch your heart.'

She wondered if she heard everything as a double entendre; was everything a sign? Why would she have to watch her heart? All she had wanted this morning was to hear the validating words from Hill that she had got stronger, that he could tell she had been practising. She suddenly hated that she cared what he thought.

The wind started to pick up from the east and tossed Roxanne's hair forward. Long hair had been easier: braid it, tie it up, clip it. But this was different. She had armed herself with a pocketful of clips to pull her chin-length hair out of her eyes. On the island, she had taken to wearing a baseball cap for just that reason.

'What did you say you did out on the island?'

'Animal control warden.'

He leaned his upper body slightly forward and with one motion he pulled the bowstring back with his right arm and extended the bow with his left.

'I'm sighting the target with one eye. The thing that takes a while to get is to stop your breath. But you've been practising, right? Your footsteps sounded eager when you came in, not dragging reluctantly like the kid who hasn't done her piano lessons. Right there, that's the stillness. Now the winds will want to carry it to the left. Account for that, use it, use all the information that you have, and release.'

His arrow went true to the centre of the target. Roxanne saw the flawlessness of his movements, the sparseness of motion that comes with practice, where every muscle knows its job perfectly and springs to service. She had a feeling that even if his brain was absent for the moment, his body would remember the pull and release, the pause between breaths.

'What do you hunt?'

'Do you mean what do I kill? Deer mostly.'

'Have you ever heard of a dog being shot by an arrow?' she asked.

He turned to face her. 'A dog? Most people don't take dogs bow-hunting because they keep the game away. But I have seen them hit, mostly by accident when a dog is in the wrong place. Why do you ask?'

She raised her bow and notched an arrow. 'Because I found a dog a few weeks ago that had been shot. That's how I found you, indirectly, when asking about traditional bows. Then I got curious about shooting.' She took her stand, and although she wished that she could erase his presence so that she could concentrate better, she could not. But she did pull smoothly. And the arrow did hit a good mid-zone on the target.

'Do it again,' he said, without comment about the shot. 'There's no bow season on the island. A special deer season was declared a few years back to bring down the deer population, but it wasn't a bow season. So who shot the dog?'

'Nobody knows, or nobody is saying. Isaiah thinks it might have been a tourist.'

'Who's Isaiah?'

'My boss, long-time resident, public works director, minister. Older black man. There's probably more that he does but I don't know everything. He's a little sour on tourists these days. The last renters trashed his house.'

Hill's jaw muscles tightened and his eyes narrowed. 'Anyone who is a skilled archer is not going to mistake a dog for a deer. There's no excuse for idiots who forget that they are working with a major weapon. Or worse yet, someone doing it on purpose. If someone was trying to shoot a dog on purpose and the dog lived, then they were a lousy archer to begin with.'

'The dog is recovering. I've taken him in until his owners can be found, but that is looking less likely as time goes on. Usually, owners are either frantically searching for a dog or they don't want to be bothered. There's not much in between.' Roxanne paused, suddenly noticing the lack of something at Hill's house. No dog sounds, no dog barking inside. Wouldn't a guy like Hill have a dog? And his wife was never here, or, if she was here, she was the quietest woman on earth.

'Do you have a dog?' asked Roxanne.

Hill picked up the next weight bow with the twenty-five-pound draw, and handed it to Roxanne. 'Used to. My wife and I are separated and the dog went with her. Julie said I'm not home enough to have a dog. Let's see you try that bow,' he said, without pause.

She was less accurate with the next size bow, but not bad, and she knew she'd be better by the next lesson. She knew she'd do even better if she could get more sleep, which still eluded her.

LLOYD'S RECOVERY was remarkable: flesh grew back with flesh, muscle accommodated, bones meshed. His limp grew less noticeable, his large black body tweaking less to the left. But Roxanne noted that his early-morning restlessness continued. She woke every day around four thirty, pulling herself reluctantly from her dreams, where she searched for Bob, scoured the land where souls of the dead live, to catch a glimpse of him. When she woke, exhausted, the dog was always there, standing near her bed, his ears up in alarm and with a whine coming from his throat.

As soon as she peeled back the covers, he appeared to relax, his ears settled down and he put his nose into her hand.

'You too, big guy? Looks like neither of us can sleep.'

They went outside to walk along the beach. Walking brought Roxanne back into her body and she knew the dog needed to keep moving to get stronger. She added a few more minutes to their walk every day.

In mid-December she left the island for one night, to meet up with her brother. They needed to discuss details of her house, which had been rented out for the year. She knew Melissa would be staying at her father's house so she asked Tess to keep Lloyd for the night. She forgot to warn Tess about the dog's restlessness.

When she came back Roxanne said, 'You're probably never going to take him again, are you, Tess? I'm sorry that I forgot to tell you he's a restless guy at four thirty in the morning.'

'What do you mean?' said Tess. 'This guy didn't budge until I got up at seven. I'm not one of those old farts who gets up at dawn.'

'No way! This dog is wide awake every morning at four thirty when I get up,' said Roxanne.

Tess handed the bag of dog food to Roxanne. 'That's the hour of the distressed. Why are you waking up then?'

The truth of the situation hit Roxanne. The dog woke up because she did. *She* was the one disturbing *his* sleep.

Maybe Lloyd smelt her sadness in a way that humans couldn't sense. Bob used to tell her about the neurotic behaviour of dogs who belonged to anxious people. Or of dogs who were overly protective of people who were afraid of everything, who were sure that criminals lurked in every corner. 'There's not much about us that they don't know,' he had said.

Roxanne knelt by the black Lab. She gave him her hand to sniff. 'Lloyd, I think I'm keeping you awake at night. Sorry, buddy.'

THE DOG STILL CAUGHT old wisps of the First One's scent, once at the food store, again on a beach chair stacked near a restaurant, and when he did, the pain of first loss rose up in him. The smell of death was given to all dogs and it was carried back throughout time from the very first death when dogs came in from the bush to join humans.

It was a primordial scent that announced the end of one human, a different smell to the death of another dog. Once dogs joined the packs of humans, this smell was unlike all others. He knew she no longer lived; the one he had joined with, slept near, awaited, greeted, licked, cajoled into play, soothed through bad times. And she in turn had loved him, remembered him, delighted him with food, thrilled him with car trips where he hung his great black head out of the car window.

She was gone. He had failed to protect her and save her. His powerful nose tortured him in moments when a thread of her scent caught him off guard and made him halt in his tracks.

The New One who had saved him—and he knew that without her he would have perished—needed extra watching at night. By day he kept a leisurely vigil between her and the door, between her and unknown people. When she slept, her terror began. He smelt it the first night, even groggy from his own surgery, his own disaster. He sensed the alarm, the hunt. Her body, restless in sleep, sent off waves of scented pain to him.

Once she was awake, he urged her outside. The fresh air was a relief to him, blowing all her dream horrors away. They made their way to the beach and each day he urged her to walk further than the day before.

MELISSA COULD NOT AFFORD to trust Roxanne. The woman seemed to peer directly through her skin, into the abandoned quarry of her stomach. Yet when she asked if Melissa wanted a job walking Lloyd after school, she thought only of the chance to be with the black dog. Cross-country season was over and she could skip some of her workouts until Lloyd was fully recovered or Roxanne located his real owner. They had agreed that Melissa would take Lloyd for a walk every day.

After school she hopped on the ferry back to the island and walked the mile from the dock to Roxanne's house. She knocked to make sure that Roxanne was out, even though the truck was gone. She found the key under the mat and let herself in, calling to Lloyd as she entered.

'Hey, Lloyd, it's me, just me.' He greeted her with the unabashed joy that only a full-sized black Lab can offer. *Touch me, touch me!* signalled the dog as he offered his head, the scruff of his neck and the favourite spot above his tail. *I have missed you more than anything, and now you have returned and I adore you*, his body and dark brown eyes intoned to her.

Melissa let Lloyd out for a quick pee. She stood in the doorway, her thin hands rubbing the painted edges of the frame. He bounded back into the house, knowing that Melissa was, on this day, the bearer of food. She closed the door and it was just the two of them, which was how Melissa liked it. She sighed and, for the first time that day, relaxed the barest fraction.

She opened the closet and scooped three cups from a bag of dog food. Roxanne had insisted that dry food was enough, but several times a week Melissa brought a can of wet food and Lloyd was guaranteed to do an appreciative dance at those times, bounding from one side to another.

'Not tonight, sorry,' she said.

He was a lay-down eater. That's what Roxanne called him. He lay down with the dish between his front paws and dipped his head into the dish, eating his food in a surprisingly delicate manner, one kibble at a time. Melissa liked this part best. She sat down near him, pressing her back against the wall as he ate with sureness and innocence.

'You are so good, Lloyd. Everything about you is good.'

He paused and lifted his ears as he listened to her, thumping his black tail twice at the sound of one of his favourite words.

ROXANNE'S WEEKLY REPORTS accounted for dead animals removed from roadways, animals taken to the mainland, calls about lost cats and calls requesting her help with troublesome animals. She also added, although

Isaiah had said her level of detail was not necessary, an accounting of her walks along the shore: of seagull carcasses and of unusual high tides that ate new inches out of the cove.

'You're not responsible for the work of the ocean,' he said, when he had read one of her first reports. 'I know I mentioned that you could keep track of beach erosion, but I forgot that you would be such a scientist.'

'I think there should be an accounting of all changes,' Roxanne replied.

Isaiah had reached into a box beneath his desk, extracted a folder and put the report in it. On the folder he wrote: *Life as recorded by the animal control warden.* 'Agreed. Write down everything happening on our fair island,' he told her.

So she did. After Lloyd came along, she added in his recovery and his rehabilitation. She also added brief notes about her archery practice. One week she wrote: *Five hours' archery, no change.* The next week she recorded: *Moved up to the twenty-five-pound bow. Now it is hard again.*

Roxanne had just stopped by with her latest report, which Isaiah was reading approvingly. 'I haven't asked you because you told me not to back in October,' he said. 'But is this helping you in any way, pretending to be who you are not? Is this all constructed so you don't have to talk about your husband? People handle death in all sorts of ways.'

He had both of his hands wrapped round a blue coffee mug. Roxanne still had her coat on and her nose stung from the cold wind that pummelled the island. She weighed her choices. There was something about the hiss of the woodstove and the way a jet of steam rose out of the dented aluminium pot of water on the stove and the way the black dog suddenly gave one deep-throated bark from her truck.

'Let me get Lloyd, if we're going to talk awhile. He gets worried that I'll get into trouble if I'm gone too long.'

Since the dog had come into her life, Roxanne had been thinking about how everyone might live in bodies but only like costumes in a play. She had watched Lloyd struggle with his injury, fight to survive, endure the worst loneliness and despair, just to keep living in his black-furred body that had healed miraculously. But his body had changed. His limp was integrated into a slightly altered body. Lloyd had a new life and a modified body.

Her body had changed too. After Bob's death, she had stopped caring about it. But somewhere between the dog and archery she had slid back into her arms and legs, wrapped her torso round her heart and lungs, and started making, and eating, grilled cheese sandwiches.

Roxanne and Isaiah talked for hours, until his wife called and said where in the world are you at this hour, and he told her. Then they talked more and Roxanne told Isaiah everything about Bob, about the way he could put his hand on the small of her back and warm her entire spine, and how he had had two free spay-and-neuter clinics every year that just about killed him, and how they talked about having kids and had not ruled out the idea.

Lloyd was asleep by her feet. Sometimes his feet danced in dream-running, and she saw the muscles contract in his haunches.

'So now you're here and you've just about worn out the usefulness of pretending that you're someone else, someone who you must have thought would be less touched by life. Someone who should have been able to save her husband. How's it working?'

'You sound like a talk-show therapist,' Roxanne said, pulling her head back in surprise.

'Maybe I should try that career. Me by the woodstove, or better yet, on the porch in my rocker, giving out advice. Let's make it a call-in show. So how is it working, Roxanne?'

They were in the hours of early morning where most pretences fall away. Dawn was still several hours down the road. The wind had picked up and rattled ill-fitting windows in Isaiah's office.

'I liked being someone else, or thinking I was someone else. But I never was anyone else. I was still essentially me in a different costume. Do you think that's what being dead is like? Do you think we shed the body and the essential us continues?'

She prayed that he would say yes, that in fact Bob might just be sitting there with them, listening in on the whole discussion, that he would always be with her. And she would believe anything that Isaiah would say, because this moment was filled with truth and they both knew it. If he told her that Bob was an angel, she would buy it. Anything; just say it.

'I think you've gone a long way into the land of the dead. Let the dead ones answer some of their own questions. What is it like to be alive? That's the question,' Isaiah said.

THE THROB HAD STARTED prematurely, because grieving was supposed to take a year and she wanted to believe that. Bob hadn't been dead even eight months and she still searched for him in her dreams.

Hill had said, 'Pull your hand back even with your jaw, make it one line,' and he had lightly grazed her skin. Roxanne was not prepared for the flutter that she felt. They had started holding their lessons twice a week in the old Grange building. He had set up two targets on hay bales. It had been just the two of them in the large cavern of a room. And ever since he had touched her the last time, she felt her inner circuitry begin to power up.

This can't be right, she argued with herself. She endured all the signs, the quickened pulse, the sudden fit of energy, and the 3 a.m. wide-awake restlessness that felt remarkably unlike despair. She even walked the dog at that hour, although she discovered that it is hard to keep track of a black dog at that blackest of hours. He kept disappearing every time the moon dipped behind a cloud. One night they walked until dawn, came back and went to bed and when she did, finally, sleep, she dreamed of Bob. She had found him quite by accident; he was dressed in a crisp, white uniform, selling ice creams in a wooden shack on an ocean boardwalk.

'Eat it before it melts,' he said, handing Roxanne an ice cream that had already begun to ooze over her fingers. That was all she remembered.

She sat up in bed and said to Lloyd, 'He's selling ice cream, big guy. I think he's going to be OK.'

She had found him, and it had not been as she had imagined. She did not try to pull him from the land of death and he did not yearn to come back with her. And she had not pleaded to stay with him.

ROXANNE AND HILL had agreed to continue archery lessons until Christmas, when Hill had family to go and see. Roxanne was going to tough it out in her island home even though her brother threatened to haul her out of there.

Most days in early December, she fed Lloyd and waited until a respectable time to go to Tess's house where she could practise archery. She left the dog at home and practised with the twenty-five-pound bow for two hours until her muscles were tired and she started hitting only the outer ring.

Although retired, Tess took a few patients privately. One afternoon, when Roxanne tumbled into Tess's house, her friend put her hands on her hips and said, 'At least let me do a little acupressure to keep you from seizing up.'

Roxanne climbed gratefully onto the treatment table and lay down on her front. Tess talked as she pressed her thumbs and knuckles into key places along Roxanne's back.

'It was a waste of time for me not to come clean with my synaesthesia when I was working full-time. I should have offered "synaesthesia-assisted techniques". Do you want to know how I see your body?'

'Sure, what do you see?' said Roxanne.

'Most bodyworkers see through their hands. They send them a picture of what's out of place and the therapist works out how to get it back in place. Others see or feel a certain tick, a rhythm that each person has. By tuning into it, they can tell if it's too erratic, too fast. The therapist sort of joins with it and changes the beat. I don't know how to do that. It's not my style.'

Tess's hands paused over Roxanne's shoulder blades, then, with one hand at the back of her neck, and with surprising gentleness, she placed a knuckle above her tailbone. Roxanne felt a clear buzz run up her spine.

'When I close my eyes, I see a picture of your body, colour and texture.' Tess placed one hand on the front of Roxanne's left shoulder and guided the shoulder in a small circular motion.

'I see some burnt umber here. Not screaming orange, but tiny muscles that have been overtaxed and need time to repair. The body is amazing; you let these muscles rest for two days and they'll be ready to go again.'

Tess placed a shockingly hot palm on the small of Roxanne's back.

'Oh. Now this is interesting. I feel a swarm of pollen-filled bumblebees. Not really, but that's the sort of buzz I get. This area is about sex and creativity. Generativity.'

Abruptly, Roxanne pushed her body up with both hands. 'Thanks, Tess. That's all the healthy intervention my body can stand.' She swung her legs round and leapt off the table. She grabbed her parka and left. When she got into the yellow truck outside, she felt the drone of honeybees, drunk with nectar, between her hipbones.

Chapter 5

It was well into December when Isaiah called Roxanne and told her to meet him for coffee. 'I think I've got some news about the dog.'

Roxanne was well into her second cup when Isaiah came to the diner. At this time of year, the counter seats were filled with builders. Isaiah gave them all a nod and ordered a cup of decaf.

'Charlotte says I'm too old for anything but decaf. Fortunately, I can't tell the difference.' He slid an Orono newspaper, several days old, towards Roxanne. It was folded to a second-page article. 'Take a look,' he said.

Roxanne read the article. A woman's body had been found in a house in

Orono. Although the body was badly decomposed, and thought to have been there for a month or more, the police did not suspect foul play. The body had been identified as Elizabeth Townsend, aged twenty-eight. An autopsy was being conducted. The mother, who lived in Providence, said that her daughter had a history of mental instability and they had been estranged for over a year.

Roxanne pushed the newspaper away. She shrugged her shoulders. 'I don't get it. You think this woman was the dog's owner? That's quite a leap.'

'She had just bought a house here. The old Hamilton place. It was a rental for years; fifteen years easy. The original owners were island people, came here every summer. But when they died, the kids couldn't be bothered with it and rented it through a management company in Portland. The sale was done by a real-estate agent off-island, which is not all that unusual these days. We never even saw a FOR SALE sign on the island. This Elizabeth purchased the house in October, just about the time you got here.'

'Did you ever see her?'

'No. She probably only owned the place for a few weeks before she died. Unofficially the cops are saying it's a suicide. They said she left a note, most of which was incomprehensible, but clearly the intent was suicide. She had owned the house in Orono, sold it, and was just renting from the new owners until the end of the year.'

Roxanne switched back to diagnostic thinking. Her first stopping place was manic depression: a blast of manic purchasing that induced Elizabeth to buy a house on an island, followed by a bottomless depression. It sounded like she had burned bridges with her family, which meant that she might have had severe episodes without medication, severe enough for her mother, or Elizabeth, to rupture their relationship.

'I can't say I recall seeing her,' continued Isaiah. 'The only person who can say for sure is one of the kids working the ferry in October. He says he remembers her because of the dog.'

Roxanne had seen people bring dogs on the ferry. If they had their cars, they usually kept the dog in the car. But if they were on foot, she noticed a variety of dogs. Almost all of them baulked at the grated walkway from ferry to dock.

'So what did he recall about the dog?' asked Roxanne.

'The kid said the dog was a big black Lab. He was waiting for him to dig in his heels at the walkway. But this Lab never looked down. He just walked across the grating. He thought at first he might be a guide dog. That's when he noticed the woman, expecting her to be blind. Fits the description of Elizabeth Townsend. Young, dark hair, short with lots of blonde streaks. Nose stud. He said she looked like a tourist.'

The Portland police, who came once a day to the island, had told Isaiah some details that the newspapers didn't have. They said that the death had all the hallmarks of a suicide, even without the note. The doors were both dead-bolted from the inside and empty prescription bottles were found near the body. In the old Hamilton place they had found only a sleeping-bag, plastic bowls on the floor with dog-food remains, and some canned soda.

'The place was going to need a lot of work before someone could move in. She might have just come over for a day or so to look it over, see what needed fixing. You know what a place can look like after fifteen years of renters,' said Isaiah. 'Roxanne, it could be that your dog, I mean Lloyd, might have been her dog.'

Roxanne felt an ill wind blow past her.

'There's one more thing,' Isaiah continued. 'Charlotte looked up the obituary from a Providence newspaper on the Web. They said Elizabeth was an accomplished archer. A competitive archer.'

'She shot her own dog? Is that what you're thinking?' Roxanne asked him. 'Surely she wouldn't try to kill a creature that provided her with the adoration that only a dog can generate?' But she knew it could happen, if delusions were severe enough.

'If the dog did belong to Elizabeth, the mother needs to know. The dog was the deceased's property and should be handed over to the family.'

Was Lloyd 'property'? He seemed more like a companion.

'I think you should ask Sam to check with the Orono vets. He must have some swift way to email particular areas. It shouldn't be hard to figure out if the dog belonged to the deceased woman. If you find out it was hers, you could contact the mother.'

Roxanne recoiled. She didn't want to call a mother who was wrestling with the death of a daughter from whom she had been estranged for a year. She didn't want to call her about a dog, as if the death of her daughter wasn't the most horrible thing that had ever happened to this woman.

'You'd be better at it, Isaiah. You must have been called on hundreds of times to talk with people after a death. We count on you ministers for this. We want you at hospitals and funerals. This is what you used to do, right?'

Roxanne rushed home, driving the yellow truck as fast as she dared. If Isaiah was right, his owner, Elizabeth Townsend, had shot him. What kind of woman would shoot her own dog? A Lab is loyal beyond all reason, and attaches primarily to one person. It might be fond of other people, but it would lay down its life for that one human.

She pulled up to her rental house and Tess was there, just opening her car door. She waved. 'I wanted to give Lloyd a walk. He needs to keep that shoulder moving—' She stopped in midsentence when she saw Roxanne's face. 'What's wrong?'

Roxanne didn't pause; she jumped onto the deck and pushed open the green front door. Lloyd was waiting. He had heard the truck and was ready to greet her. She dropped to one knee and wrapped both arms round him, and then she started to cry with one hand over her face. Lloyd squirmed, backed up and sat down as Tess came into the house.

Roxanne eased back into a squat. 'Isaiah told me he thinks he found Lloyd's owner. A woman who killed herself. *Probably* killed herself,' Roxanne told Tess. 'She was an archer. I think she shot Lloyd.'

'Oh, no. Now you don't know that. Tell me what you really do know,' said Tess as she reached an arm down to pull Roxanne up. She brushed the hair out of Roxanne's face.

Roxanne repeated what Isaiah had told her at the diner.

'I wondered what had happened to the Hamilton place,' Tess said. 'It had a different look to it this fall. Sort of broken, cracked. I should have known the place had been sold. But I think you're wrong about this woman shooting Lloyd, and I can't even tell you why.'

As soon as Tess said that, Roxanne remembered the man at the Dairy Mart in Portland and the way Lloyd had nearly blown the top off her car when he saw the guy. And how right after that she had called Hill and set up archery lessons and hadn't thought of the incident again.

'There was this guy at the Dairy Mart in Portland who Lloyd recognised. The dog went nuts in the car. At least I think Lloyd recognised him; he definitely didn't like him. And the guy looked startled to see Lloyd.'

'What was the guy doing?'

'He had just parked up too close to my car. I went round to his door before he got out of the SUV.'

'So Lloyd saw him getting out of the truck and he was stuck in your car.' Tess looked down at the dog. 'Sounds like he was trying to protect you. Has he done this again?'

'No. I'm going to call Sam's office to see if they can give me a list of all the vets over in Orono. I'm going to start calling them to see if they know about the dog. Hopefully we can find out what Lloyd's real name is.'

After Tess left, Roxanne called Sam and then went to the island library and picked up the list of vets that Sam's assistant had faxed there. Each time she called, she said the same thing. 'This is the animal control warden on Peaks Island. I have a dog that I think may have been one of your patients. Was Elizabeth Townsend the owner of a black Lab?'

She called six offices before she got the direct hit. She knew it right away when the receptionist said, 'Hold on, please. I'm going to have you speak with Dr Harris.' Two minutes of local radio music followed.

'This is Ann Harris. You called about a black Lab.'

'Yeah, I have an injured black Lab that I've been fostering for about a month while he's been healing. I'm trying to locate the owner. We just learned that Elizabeth Townsend was found dead in Orono. She bought a summer house here in October. Did she use your services?'

'I read the obituary. Liz had a Lab that we took care of since he was a puppy. She'd been coming here for about five years. We were hoping that nothing bad had happened to the dog. Didn't he have his tags on?'

'No, just a reflector tag, nothing else. He's a big guy, probably around ninety pounds, although he was thin and dehydrated when I found him.'

'That could be him but it could also be a lot of black Labs. I offered to install a locator chip in Cooper, but Liz didn't like that idea.'

'Cooper? The dog's name is Cooper? Lloyd will be very pleased to know that we've finally figured out his name.'

The dog had been lying on his side in the afternoon sunshine on the kitchen linoleum. At the sound of his name, his head came up and his legs contracted, bringing his body to standing, as if he had heard a bugle call.

The vet continued, 'We had heard nothing about the dog being found in Liz's house. She would have been found a lot quicker if the dog had been there. He would have alerted someone. I've seen that happen before.'

'If this is Lloyd . . . Cooper . . . there's something I need to know. He was injured when I found him. Shot with an arrow.'

Roxanne heard the controlled silence on the other end of the line. 'During bow season, I see about one dog every other week that's been shot. It's not uncommon,' said the vet.

'But the dog was shot on the island. We don't have a bow season here. I know Elizabeth was an archer. I can't help but put some of this together. Her death was probably a suicide; there is no reason to think otherwise, according to the police report. I'm asking you to speculate about something. Did you ever see anything that would make you wonder if the dog was mistreated?'

'Cooper is a great dog because he's got great genes and because he had an owner who trained him and took good care of him. If you are asking whether I think Liz tried to kill her dog? Absolutely not. Not unless she lost her mind.'

Roxanne didn't say it, but she thought, Don't you have to do just that to be twenty-eight years old and kill yourself?

'The other thing about bow hunters is that if they mean to kill a dog, they will. A dog won't bolt and run like a wild animal. They're an easy target. Any dog that I've ever seen that was shot by an arrow had been in the wrong place at the wrong time. It was always an accident.'

Roxanne thanked the vet and hung up. She pulled on a jacket and the dog skittered to his feet and headed for the door. She wanted to clear her head with sharp air; an accommodating blast from the northwest welcomed her into icy arms. She pulled up her hood and walked with Cooper through the dried beachgrass, crisscrossing every trail along the beach. They sat together in the twilight; Roxanne uncomfortable on a damp log and the dog peacefully gnawing a stick, until the chill in her bones forced Roxanne up.

In the middle of the night, Roxanne continued to feel the steady caffeine-driven thump of her heart. She had not been asleep since she turned out her light three hours earlier. With each turn from her back to her side, to her stomach, to the other side, the dog rustled on the floor, his sharp leg joints rearranging, claws clattering, sighing impatiently.

Roxanne's thoughts reached for the woman who had stayed long enough on the island to leave a wounded and loved dog, and then died in Orono. Roxanne sat up and flicked on the light. This woman, Liz, had been twenty-eight. She had just purchased a house. How did everything go wrong?

The first hint of daylight was still hours away. Roxanne got up and pulled on a sweater and her jeans. There was something wrong; this dog had not been mistreated, he did not display overly passive or aggressive behaviour; he had not been afraid in his life with Liz. She looked at Cooper, who had risen stiffly. 'I know what it's like to lose someone,' she said to him.

PROPERTY. THAT WAS THE QUESTION. If the dog had been discarded, abused or shot, couldn't he then come under the protection of the dog warden?

'Hang on, Lloyd . . . I mean Cooper.' Roxanne scooped three cups of dry food into his bowl. She put the bowl down and the dog looked up in what appeared to be gratitude, a slight tilt to his head, a three-wagged thanks.

The sky ignited with a blood-red sun peeping over the horizon. She watched for what she knew would be brief moments of red before the sun settled into its daily dress of yellow. The shortest day of the year, December 21, had just passed, and by midafternoon, the sun would begin to depart.

Roxanne had welcomed this time of year with Bob, the turning inwards, staying indoors, abandoning all hope of yard work in the dark evenings. She loved driving up to their house when it was just dark, and seeing the golden glow of lights in the house welcoming her, meaning that Bob was home. If she was very lucky and it was his turn to get dinner, the house would be filled with smells of food and the promise of comfort.

Food. Right, she needed to eat. She made coffee and shook cereal into a bowl, doused it with milk, then set the bowl on the table. While she ate, she thought about the right thing to do with the dog. First she'd call Isaiah and tell him to hold off on calling the woman's family in Providence. There was no rush. Everyone needed to slow down and think. She put her bowl of almost finished cereal on the floor and Cooper licked the remainder.

'Need to go out? You go first; I'll be right there.' She opened the door for the dog, then picked up the phone and punched in Isaiah's number.

'Morning, Charlotte. Is this too early to call?'

'Hi, Roxanne. He was just getting ready to call you. Before he gets on, I wanted to ask you about the holidays. Will you be staying over Christmas?'

Roxanne had tried hard not to think of Christmas, but it loomed with unbearable weight. She was determined to stay on the island, barricade the door and wait until it passed. 'I'll be here. You two off to see the family?'

'Our son in North Carolina wants to have the big family gathering at his place. Would you stop in and feed our cat? Isaiah is too shy to ask you.'

'Give me the lowdown on the cat, when and what to feed her. She's an indoor/outdoor model, right? Let me know if there's anything else I can do while you're gone,' said Roxanne.

'You're a lifesaver. Here's the man about town.'

Roxanne was startled by the term 'lifesaver'. A deep, sickening jolt ran through her legs as if her bones were dislodging. She wanted to tell Charlotte that she was no lifesaver.

''Morning, Roxanne,' Isaiah said.

'Isaiah, hold off on calling the woman in Providence about the dog.'

'I already called the mother last night. They can't believe that you found the dog. And you know, she said the dog's name is Cooper.'

'I know about his name. You already called them last night? I need more time to check a few things. I can't turn him over to just anyone after what he's been through. I think I found the vet in Orono who has taken care of him since he was a puppy. I want to take him up there just to make sure we're all talking about the same dog.'

Even as she spoke, Roxanne felt she was sounding like an idiot.

'Things are happening quicker than I expected,' said Isaiah. 'The parents, Jan and Ed Townsend, wanted to come today to get the dog. I hedged and said that we needed to finish up some paperwork. I talked them into coming tomorrow. I figured you'd want one more day with the dog.'

'Tomorrow? They're coming tomorrow?'

'They're coming over on the first ferry,' Isaiah replied. 'I know this is hard for you, but let's not forget what they're going through. This dog is their last connection to their daughter. You understand that, don't you, Roxanne? I'll bring them by your place.'

'You're bringing them to my place? I think we're making a mistake. Just because Cooper was Liz's dog, that doesn't mean this is the best solution. Why can't we try to do what's best for the dog?'

'Or do you mean what's best for you? Does it help to have someone tell you the best way to remember a daughter who has died . . . or a husband? This is not our call, Roxanne. I'm sorry. I know you've got attached to the dog.' Isaiah's voice softened. 'We'll come by after the first ferry.'

Roxanne put the phone down and turned to look out of the open door at Cooper. Her chest tightened as she pictured strangers coming to get him. She pictured a life for him with people who didn't care about him. They lived right in Providence, in the city, and he would become a city dog.

She grabbed her jacket and joined the dog. 'Come on, big guy. This is going to be a short walk.' They headed down the trail to the beach. When they returned twenty minutes later, Roxanne loaded water and food for the dog into the truck, along with Cooper, and drove to Tess's house.

Tess lived a full five minutes away by car. Nothing was far away on the island, except maybe the newer houses on the interior of the island, where developers had cleared trees and built new homes in mosquito-ridden areas. Roxanne and Cooper jumped out of the truck. Roxanne knocked on the kitchen door and, seeing Tess inside, she pushed it open.

'We've got trouble. How long does it take to drive to Orono? Elizabeth Townsend's people are coming up from Providence because they think Lloyd, I mean Cooper, is Liz's dog. They're coming to get him tomorrow.'

Tess had not been awake long. She ran her hands through her hair. 'His name is Cooper? Green and blue letters. Probably fitted him better when he was a puppy. Why are you going to Orono?'

'I found a vet who thinks Liz was one of her clients. She says she'd remember Liz's dog,' said Roxanne.

'And do you want to find out about the dog or about Liz?'

'I told you, this is about the dog. How long does it take to drive to Orono?' Roxanne asked again.

'It takes about two and a half to three hours. When are you going?'

'Now,' said Roxanne. 'We need to go now. I want you to come with me, Tess. They're coming for the dog tomorrow morning and I don't want to let him go without checking out his identity. He doesn't have to belong to this woman who killed herself.'

Roxanne thought she saw sympathy flicker across the older woman's face and the sight of it made her step back. 'What? Don't you want to go? I just thought you—'

'I like this dog too. But you're on a life-and-death mission. I can smell it all over you, Roxanne. If you're going to ask me to join your rescue mission, you must tell me what you're leaving out,' said Tess.

Roxanne had planned on slowing life down, holding on to every shred of Bob, and now someone had just put a lead foot on the accelerator. Talking to Isaiah about Bob had not been as frightening as she had imagined. Something had loosened in her. Of course she should talk to Tess. Why hadn't she thought of that before? 'Let's talk while we drive,' she said.

THEY DECIDED TO TAKE Tess's car instead of the truck, because Tess refused to ride for three hours with Cooper wedged under her feet, and neither one of them wanted him to ride in the back of the truck.

They pulled up to the dock in the ten-year-old Saab in time for the 9.30 ferry to Portland. Once across, they pointed the car inland for an hour, then headed north. Cooper stretched out on the back seat.

Roxanne drove the first leg. 'Please don't look at me while I'm telling you this, Tess. I don't want us driving off the road,' she said.

It took longer than she imagined to tell Tess about Bob, about the day she was downstairs ordering socks and he was upstairs shaving and his heart seized up, and how she tried to force him back to life. Then she told her about how finding each other had seemed like the perfect turn of the universe.

'You're a psychologist? Please tell me you don't work with little children,' said Tess after a bathroom stop at a McDonald's.

'No. Why do you ask?'

'When you told me that you worked with young kids in a daycare centre, I thought, Pity those poor kids. Some people just don't have the knack to be with young people, and I dare say you're one.'

Roxanne thought about being offended, but Tess was right. Little children confused her.

Tess took her turn at the wheel. 'Can I ask you something?' said Tess. They were back in the car on Route 95 and Bangor was forty miles away.

Roxanne sighed and adjusted her seat so that it tilted back without infringing on the dog's space. 'Go ahead. I think I've told you everything.'

'What was the point in telling me you were something that you weren't? I thought we were getting on pretty well as friends. I never thought to tell you a lie about me.' Tess rubbed her lower abdomen as if she had a belly-ache. 'I feel tricked and I don't deserve it.'

Roxanne knew Tess was right. 'I am willing to accept my new status as a defective friend, the inferior model, but will you give me another chance?'

'You are on probation. Your penance is to be nicer to your neighbour's girl. Melissa likes you,' said Tess as she checked her rearview mirror before pulling out to pass a logging truck. 'I hate to drive behind these.'

Roxanne told Tess her strategy for going to the vet clinic in Orono. 'If this vet took care of Cooper since he was a puppy, she's got to be able to identify him. And she might be able to tell us about Liz.'

Dr Harris's clinic was on the north side of Orono. No cute names here, just Orono Animal Clinic. A sign said: ALL DOGS MUST BE LEASHED.

'OK, Mr Cooper-Lloyd, time to leash up,' said Roxanne. She had a nylon lead for him, but she had discovered that he generally didn't need it.

It was colder in Orono and there were the remains of several snowstorms piled up on either side of the path to the clinic. Cooper climbed out of the car, pushed his snout into the snow, then headed for the door.

'He knows where he is,' said Tess. When she opened the front door, the young woman behind Reception stared at the dog, then at Roxanne and Tess, then pushed herself up to standing. 'Cooper, is that you?'

TESS'S FIRST INKLING of danger came in the rich moments before waking when she was filled with light and dark, warm under the duvet and cool on her face. The dark green rectangle was a bad shape to have in the abdomen, and the shade of green was not forest green, but necrotic. Lower right pelvic bowl. She couldn't stop seeing it.

Tess's memory for anatomy could not be called a photographic memory, since it was not based on photos of the interior world of the body. What she learned about the body was not just to be found in textbooks. Her vision of it looked more like Michelangelo's sketches, someone she suspected of being a synaesthete. That would account for a lot.

In Tess's world, the kidneys and liver were orange brick factories with reliable workers who continually brought in boxes and bags of goods to be sorted. Some were used for fuel, some were trouble, and some were stored. A big recycling effort with a continually turning water wheel.

Or take the heart. It was ruby red and midnight blue, a creature from the sea, a sightless fish that heard everything, vibrated to sad movies and disappointed lovers, and sent its messages in flowing movement, undulating from its core. And the uterus, Fallopian tubes and ovaries were one continent with a long string of islands on either side, book-ended by volcanoes that erupted with a glistening egg each month in an unerringly egalitarian manner, one volcano never taking two turns in a row.

Tess knew the inside of her body, or anyone's body, but hers in particular. The green rectangle had set up shop, had slipped in under cover of darkness. She was sixty-eight. Was this going to be all she had?

She would wait before going to see a doctor, before the long series of tests that would no doubt be run to tell them what she already knew. She wondered how long it had been lodged in her body and what damage it had already done. She felt the pain again in her lower abdomen, saw the hard edges. She was driving to Orono with Roxanne and she could smell the panic coming off the younger woman's skin, a scent like cider vinegar and mangoes that had gone too far past ripe. Tess shifted in the driver's seat and put her left hand on the wheel and placed her right hand on the crease between torso and thigh. Roxanne was absorbed in her own cold fear and wouldn't notice a little tummy-prodding. With her thumb, she pressed with curiosity to see if the dark, angular shape could be felt from the outside, and somewhere deep inside responded with a honeycomb of orange pain.

Tess put her right hand back on the steering wheel but part of her brain fell through her body, tumbled down into her lungs, slid past a kidney and liver, made its way around a maze of intestines large and small, and settled in the neighbourhood of the unwelcome intruder.

No, you don't. Not now. I'm not ready.

Then she left the intruder as she listened to Roxanne telling her who she was and how death had robbed her. The irritation she felt at Roxanne for not trusting her felt good, felt like life compared to the destruction going on in her body. She revelled in the chance to give her a suitable lashing.

'I feel tricked and I don't deserve it,' said Tess. *Was this for Roxanne or her own body?*

They drove to the edge of Orono, to the town where Liz Townsend had lived. Tess pulled up to the clinic and Roxanne leashed the dog. Once they were inside, a receptionist called him by name. The young woman behind the desk looked stunned. Tess could see a healthy sceptic, a scientist disguised as an office manager. She moved away from the counter and walked slowly to the dog. She slid a hand into her pocket. 'Cooper, I have a biscuit for you.' As soon as she said this, the dog walked up to her, sat down and then lay down. This must have been her test and with the success of her experiment, she crumbled.

'Oh, Cooper. I was so worried that we wouldn't see you again!'

Chapter 6

Dr Harris clinched the dog's identity.

'I had forgotten this when you called yesterday. Liz's dog had a dewclaw missing on his right front leg. He had snagged it badly in some tough underbrush and I had to remove it.'

The doctor knelt by the dog and ran her hand along the back of his leg.

'Yup, no dewclaw, but I would have known him anyway. This is Cooper. Liz didn't want him to have a chip installed, no matter how much I tried to convince her. Cooper was pretty popular here. He always acted like he knew we were doing the best that we could.'

The doctor checked the shoulder area where the Lab had been injured over a month ago.

'This is what you were talking about, right? Dogs heal so quickly. Once they begin to mend, you might never be able to tell they had surgery. But I can see he lost some muscle and he might keep the limp.' She explored the area with fingers that read his body like Braille' then she stood up.

'So now you've identified the dog, what are you going to do with him?'

'Liz's parents are coming to the island tomorrow to get him. Right now he's under my custody,' said Roxanne. She was startled by her use of the word custody, as if this were a divorce case involving children. 'Do you have any idea what Liz's wishes would have been?'

'She was a good pet owner, one of the best. She seemed like she might be sort of impulsive in other parts of her life. But not about taking care of Cooper. They were devoted to each other. Sometimes you see that with a dog like this; they become companions. So I guess she would want him to have a home where people cared about him. What about the boyfriend? The last time I saw her, back in May, Liz had a boyfriend living with her. I only know this because she said he had tried to make Cooper sleep outside the bedroom, but the dog made such a fuss that he gave in.'

At the mention of a boyfriend, Roxanne looked at Tess and they both factored in one more person.

'Did he get along with the dog? I mean, was he jealous?' asked Tess.

The doctor took the moment to check the dog's ears. 'No. Liz said he wanted the dog to like him more, but Cooper politely ignored him. Wouldn't do one thing he asked him to do. Are we done here?'

Roxanne remembered what she'd brought, what she had thrown in her daypack at the last moment.

'I brought the arrow that was surgically removed,' she said. 'The one someone used to shoot him.' Roxanne took the small black pack off her shoulder, put it on the examining table and unzipped it. She pulled out the arrow. About four inches remained of the shaft.

Dr Harris picked it up. 'Traditional bow hunter. I have to say that I admire this more than the other type. If you can be accurate with a traditional bow, you are part of an elite group. But you don't have the power of a compound bow, which is what may have saved our friend here.' She nodded her head at Cooper, who had decided to sit on Roxanne's feet. 'If you're wondering if I knew anything about Liz's archery, I didn't. When people come here, they only talk about their animals. She was a good, responsible pet owner.' Dr Harris looked down at the dog. 'He's taken you on, hasn't he?'

Roxanne noticed the weight of Cooper's rump on her feet. 'Yeah, and that's why I want to find out if Liz would want him to go to her parents. Wasn't she out of touch with her family?'

Dr Harris put her hands in the pockets of her coat. 'You're an animal control officer? You've got a couple who want this dog and you drove three hours to make sure it was truly Liz's dog. You are either the most dedicated dog warden I've ever seen, or something else is bothering you.'

Tess and Dr Harris faced Roxanne. The dog, sensing a change in the atmosphere, tilted his head up and also looked at Roxanne.

'I needed to hear you say that Liz wouldn't have hurt him. I thought that would have been enough. But something is wrong here and we're all missing what it is. There's a certain order to things.' Roxanne paused. 'A leads to B, causality of certain events, but something is out of order here.'

Dr Harris looked puzzled.

Tess said, 'She's a dog warden, recently removed from her life as a psychologist. Some sort of career move.'

'Can you tell me where Liz lived?' Roxanne asked.

The vet thought for a minute. 'Well, there's no standard of confidentiality about to be breached. I guess there's no reason not to,' she said. She opened up Cooper's file. 'Liz lived over in Old Town, near the college. It's still Orono, but they like to have their own name.'

Roxanne wrote down the address and suddenly something shifted. She realised that she was in a veterinarian clinic, really in it, and her first thought, and second, and third had not been about Bob. But her reprieve was over. The different smells thundered in on her, all joining forces to drag her back to the empty well of Bob's death.

Her heart began to pound and drum blood through her ears. Her breath turned shallow, as if she didn't want anyone to hear her, and she could no longer hear the words that Dr Harris was saying.

'I need some air . . . must have been the drive,' she said as she headed with determination for the door of the examining room. She heard Cooper's claws scuttle to standing as she touched the doorknob.

'I'll be outside,' she said in a small, dry voice. She walked past the receptionist and pushed open the front door. Cooper followed with his leash dragging on the floor. Outside, she leaned on Tess's car and gulped in fistfuls of cold, biting air, filling herself back up.

Tess joined her. 'I said our goodbyes in there. And here's the arrow.' She handed it back to Roxanne. 'You don't look so good. You are exactly the colour of wet ash.'

'It's just being in a vet clinic again. It took me by surprise, that's all.'

'Smells. Happens to me all the time. The olfactory sense goes to a part of our brain that lights up memory. Being in a vet clinic must be like standing in your husband's pyjamas.' Tess extracted gloves from her pocket and pulled them on. It was early afternoon and a storm front from the northwest was steadily approaching. 'This would be a good time for us to head home. I don't want to drive in a blizzard,' she said.

Roxanne straightened up. 'Not yet. We've got Liz's address. I want to drive past her house. Look, I don't know—'

The clinic door opened and the receptionist waved an arm at them. 'Hey, wait up a second.' The young woman did a little jog to the car, then wrapped her arms tightly round her torso. She had on a T-shirt and a green lab coat over that. 'Whatever you do, don't let Peter talk you into giving the dog to him. Liz was done with him.'

Tess and Roxanne exchanged glances.

'I didn't catch your name,' Roxanne said.

'Sorry. I'm Shelly. I was a friend of Liz's. Or we were just starting to be friends again. Nobody could be friends with her when Peter was around.'

'Was that her boyfriend?' asked Tess.

'He had been, unfortunately, for about six months. And then she spent the next three months trying to get rid of him. She never really understood the effect that she had on men. They got addicted to her,' said Shelly.

'Was he an archer too?' asked Roxanne.

'No. And he tried to get Liz to quit spending so much time with archery. He didn't like that she competed with men. He didn't even like that Cooper was so close to Liz. I told her that Peter was pure trouble. She told me later that she wished she had listened to me.' Shelly's chin quivered and she tried not to cry. 'I went to the memorial service. That asshole slithered in like the snake that he is. Didn't speak to anyone.'

'I'm sorry you lost your friend,' Roxanne said. She waited until Shelly could talk again. 'Did Dr Harris tell you how I found Cooper? Someone used a traditional bow and arrow to shoot him. Is that what Liz used?'

'That's what I wanted to tell you. Liz would never, no matter how whacked out she could get with her bipolar disorder, hurt Cooper. Did you know she was bipolar?'

'I wondered,' said Roxanne.

'Until she met Peter, she had her meds figured out and it was like she finally got it, how to manage meds with sleep and diet. She hadn't had a manic episode for ages until he convinced her to go off her meds and let him take care of her. He was against all medication. And yeah, she was way into the traditional bow-and-arrow stuff. She got her equipment from some guy out in Nebraska who made everything by hand.'

Two cars pulled into the parking lot to the side of the clinic. An agitated Doberman wearing a plastic cone collar jumped out of one car, accompanied by a woman with a wool plaid jacket. From the second car, a silver-haired man lifted an animal carrier from which the howls of one cat, possibly two, could be heard.

'Look, I've got to go. Just don't let Peter have Cooper,' said Shelly. She turned to go back inside.

'Wait. What about Liz's parents? They're coming to Peaks Island tomorrow to get Cooper,' Roxanne told her.

Shelly stopped. 'I don't know them. Only heard her talk about them. But let me ask you something. Would you want your dog to go to someone who hadn't talked to you in almost two years? It wasn't Liz who cut off the relationship. It was her mother. Sorry, I've got to go.'

Tess, Roxanne and the dog got into the car.

Roxanne unfolded the map of Maine. 'We're in the neighbourhood. How long could it take?' she asked Tess.

THE FIRST THING they noticed was the green skip in the driveway. The supersized kind, the ones that people use when they are going to gut an entire house. Two pick-up trucks were parked in the street, both with ladders sticking out at the back.

'What should we do with Cooper? He already knows we're back in his hometown and apparently in front of his former house. We can't do this to him; it would be too upsetting,' said Tess.

Cooper stood up in the back seat and began to pant.

'Don't stop. Drive a couple of blocks away and let me out. I'm going to talk to the builders,' said Roxanne.

Tess pulled to the kerb a short while later and Roxanne slipped out. Cooper made a dive for the front seat and Tess grabbed his collar.

'I'll be back at this corner in thirty minutes,' said Tess.

Roxanne jogged back to the house. It was a solid, white house from the 1940s, with an inviting porch and two dormers on the first floor. The shrill whine of a saw was coming from inside. As she passed the Dumpster, Roxanne noticed a couch sticking up and old panelling and kitchen linoleum that had been ripped out. She knocked at the open door, then stepped inside and headed for the source of the noise.

A blond-haired man hollered to someone, 'All these cabinets got to come out. That Dumpster is leaving in two days.'

'Excuse me,' said Roxanne.

The builder whirled round. 'Hey, I didn't know anyone was here. I don't suppose you brought us hot coffee and a late lunch?' he asked.

'Sorry. I'm not the lunch lady. I'm the animal control warden from Peaks Island. Elizabeth Townsend used to own this house and I am in possession of her dog. I need to place him in the best possible home. Elizabeth's parents are meeting me tomorrow to collect the dog, but I don't have a really great feeling about them. Did you find anything, I don't know, that stands out to you?' Roxanne knew this sounded too vague.

'All I can tell you is that the young woman killed herself and she wasn't found for close on a month,' the builder said. 'After the police left, a crew that specialises in that kind of thing had to come in. The parents came up here and took a couple of items—pictures, I think; that's what the present owners said—then we were hired to gut this place. They're thinking of selling it. No one wants to live in a house where someone committed suicide.'

'Did you know her?' asked Roxanne.

'No. I heard she was a university type. Hung out there, taking classes. We have to finish emptying out this place. You got anything in particular that you're looking for? I can't see how I can help you.'

'Could I just look round the house?'

'For what? We're down to the walls and floors upstairs. What did you say you did?'

'Animal control warden. When you were throwing stuff out, did you find anything that had to do with a dog?' Roxanne asked him.

'Nothing about a dog. I did save something, though. She had sawed right through a bow-and-arrow rig. Didn't know what it was at first, then I started putting it together. She sawed it into pieces about three inches long and stacked it in neat piles on the kitchen table. But I already gave that to her boyfriend. He came round the other day and I figured it meant something to him. He looked pretty broken up.'

Roxanne remembered the man at the Dairy Mart parking lot in Portland.

'Did he say anything else?' she asked.

'No, just that he had lived here for a while during the summer.'

'What was he driving?'

'Some kind of dark rig. It was almost quitting time when he got here. Too dark to really see what it was,' the builder said.

Roxanne asked if she could look through the downstairs rooms. He had already told her that everything had been stripped upstairs.

'Don't fall down and hurt yourself,' he said.

She went into the small dining room, the living room and the cloakroom, and felt the brakes go on in her head. She went back into the dining room, with its tall casement windows. Out in the back yard were bales of hay stacked with an archer's target. Of course there was a target; no secret there. But something was familiar, something pulled at her and she used the edge of her jacket to wipe the windowpane. Sawdust and explosions of dust had been created by days of demolition. She peered through the window, trying to understand what it was she saw.

'Jesus Christ!' yelled the builder. Over his voice a clatter of claws burst from the kitchen. Roxanne tore her face from the dining-room window. She heard the man scuffle more and curse as she headed for the commotion.

'Hey, hold up there! Is this your dog?' he asked.

Cooper careered into the dining room and when he saw Roxanne he lowered his head slightly and wagged his entire back end furiously.

'Cooper! How did you find me?'

The dog whined in discomfort, as if his bad leg had suddenly got worse. But Roxanne knew it was the house filled with smells of Liz and the terrible smell of death that would be exploding in his nostrils like fireworks. More footsteps, heavy breathing, and another blast of cold air. Tess entered, breathless from running. She quickly put her hands on her knees and bent over to take in as much air as she could.

'I'm too old for this,' she said, as she nodded to the builder. 'I took him over to the park at the college and as soon as I let him out, he bolted. I knew where he was heading.'

'I'm sorry to interrupt, but we now have a small crowd, which is never a good thing with demolition work,' the man said. He looked at Roxanne. 'Are you done?'

'Done,' she said. 'Come on, Cooper.'

When the three of them reached the sidewalk, the dog stopped and did an about-face. Before Roxanne could grab his collar, he ran to the back yard and quickly rounded the corner, barking an alarm. Tess put her hand on Roxanne's arm. He circled again.

'Let him go. He's getting something out of his system.'

After his third time circling the house, Cooper stopped at the cross of the sidewalk and the path to the house. He looked at the two women.

'We're coming,' said Tess.

Cooper led them back to Tess's car. When he settled in the back seat, he put his head on his paws and closed his eyes.

By the time they arrived back in Portland, Roxanne had driven for six hours through a blizzard, which had turned to icy rain as they neared the coast. They caught the 8.30 ferry to the island. When Roxanne collapsed into bed, the last thing she heard was the deep sigh of Cooper.

ISAIAH'S TRUCK PULLED UP to the cottage midmorning. It was closely followed by a beige sedan. Roxanne watched from her kitchen window. A man and a woman, both fiftyish, climbed out of their car. They were heavy, solidly shaped, and moved badly. The threesome climbed the few steps to the deck. Before they could knock, Roxanne opened the door. She had told Tess to stay home and sleep; the older woman had looked unusually exhausted when they had returned, and later in the day she was leaving to spend the holidays with her family.

Roxanne locked eyes with Isaiah in desperation, but he gave her a stern, resolved look and held open the door for the Townsends.

'There he is; there's the good boy,' said the man.

Cooper rose and sniffed the man's hand.

'You remember me, boy, don't you?' he said.

'Roxanne, this is Ed and Jan Townsend. This is our animal control warden who saved Cooper and has been taking care of him since.'

'I'm sorry about your daughter,' said Roxanne. She saw the familiar signs of grief in the man's eyes. Jan looked more complicated; her lips were pressed together in ancient anger and Roxanne suspected that the strong aroma of cigarette smoke came from her. Her husky voice confirmed it.

'Thank you for taking care of the dog. It hasn't been easy closing Liz's estate. We've had to take care of many things she tried to destroy,' Jan said.

Roxanne knew that the relationship between mother and daughter had been ruptured by Liz's disorder, but she had expected death to soften her mother. Roxanne was jolted by the anger that washed over the woman.

'Do you mean Cooper's injury? No, no. I'm sure that Liz didn't harm him, if that's what you mean. I was in Orono yesterday and spoke to a friend and the vet who took care of him. Liz loved this dog—' said Roxanne.

'You don't understand,' said Jan. 'Our daughter was very sick. She had bipolar disorder. Manic depressive. You don't know what we have gone through with her since she was first diagnosed when she was nineteen years old.' Neither of the Townsends moved to take off their coats.

'When was the last time you spoke with your daughter?' asked Roxanne.

Jan had not made one move towards Cooper, even when the dog had sniffed her shoes.

'I don't see the point in this, but we hadn't talked with her in nearly two years. We offered to let her live at home so we could monitor her medication and make sure that she attended therapy. Once Ed's father died and left the house in Orono to her, we didn't have as much leverage. We had to set boundaries with her to keep our own sanity. She refused to abide by our rules and we had no choice,' she said.

Ed cleared his throat. 'We're going back on the next ferry, so if you could hand over the dog, we'll be on our way. We can manage from here.'

Cooper sat down with his haunches wedged against Roxanne's feet. Her shoes still held the sand and salt from that morning's walk. Her hand went automatically to his head and she rubbed the loose skin of his scalp.

'I suppose there are vet bills. How much do we owe you?' asked Jan.

'That bill was taken care of. I paid it, well most of it. We got a deal from the vet. He lives on the island,' said Roxanne. 'I've got sort of attached to this guy and I want to let you know that I would be willing to keep him, if you two don't really want a dog.'

'We take care of our own. We're cleaning up after our daughter and this is part of what she left,' said Jan. Had Liz's illness washed all the life out of this woman? Or had Jan always been this way?

'Cooper is not part of a mess. He's a dog who loved your daughter and was loyal to her. If you think that you're not going to have time for him, I'll take him. He likes it here. He likes me,' said Roxanne.

Ed unzipped his jacket several inches. 'This might not be a bad idea, honey. He did overpower the house the last time he was there.'

'No. I just hired someone to put a run in the back yard and we have a new barricade fence. He'll do fine out there,' said Jan.

Isaiah moved towards the door. 'We've got twenty minutes to the next ferry. The Townsends have made up their minds, Roxanne. The dog is leaving with them. Let's not make this any harder on them than it already is.'

Ed took the leash off the kitchen counter and snapped it onto Cooper's collar. The dog's ears dropped and the centre of his eyebrows rose. Everybody, including the dog, looked at Roxanne for the next move.

'Come on, Coop,' said Roxanne. She followed the couple and the dog to their car, where Ed opened the back door. Cooper looked back at Roxanne as if she were coming with him. She bent down and put her arms round his neck and kissed the top of his head. 'Get in, Cooper,' she said.

The dog hesitated, then leapt with surprising ease into the back seat. The Townsends got in, then Ed backed up, turned round and drove off. As they left, Cooper turned his head to look back towards Roxanne. She stared at the departing car, frozen to the spot.

'You did the right thing,' said Isaiah.

Roxanne spun round. 'This is not the right thing and you know it! This stinks! A dog run! He's not that kind of dog. He's a people dog and he has to be with his person. That's me!'

Roxanne felt the last two words settle into her as the shocking truth. She turned and walked back into the house and felt the unstoppable convulsions of sorrow howl out of her as she leaned against the door. Isaiah knocked.

'Go away!'

He was quiet outside the door, then slowly scuffed off the deck. She heard his truck pull out.

After her sobs emptied out, she went to the bathroom and splashed cold water on her face. It wasn't fair that she had to keep losing everyone and everything she loved.

This time, though, she had a choice. As the animal control warden she had some authority. She could stop this disaster from happening. Her Honda was out of gas, but she grabbed her keys and ran to the truck. The battery, which had been acting peevish, gave its death rattle, the reluctant sound of a battery that would like to oblige, but has lost its juice. She pounded the steering wheel with her fist. 'No, no, no!'

The dock was one mile away. She had five minutes before the ferry left, but sometimes, in the winter, their schedule was less than exact. She could make it and she would stop the Townsends from leaving.

She got out of the truck and started to run. The sandy gravel tried to drag her down, but she pushed off with each step, pumping her arms as she ran. She heard the blast of the departure horn as she skidded round the corner to the dock. The ferry was already churning up water and was fifty yards out. There was only one car on its deck, and she could still see the top of Cooper's black head through its back window.

Roxanne reached the end of the dock and, without wanting to, she yelled, 'Cooper!' She thought she heard his deep, resonant bark over the wind and the engine as she collapsed to her knees and the ferry carried him away.

MELISSA KNEW SOMETHING was wrong when she saw Roxanne running, really running, not jogging for exercise. It was not normal for adults to run unless they had on running gear: slick running pants, matching shirts and windbreakers. But she was quickly diverted from anything that might be happening in Roxanne's life. This weekend her father was going to be away, so she could stay home. She would like to stay home more often, but she didn't want to hurt her father's feelings.

Her room, and all her stuff, was here, in the house where she was born. After the divorce, when she'd been eight, her father hadn't really known how to set up a house so that it felt like a home, although he had tried.

Later that morning, she noticed Roxanne walking back, looking pissed off and oddly shrunken, like she was caving in on herself. Melissa didn't dare approach her when she looked that mad. She waited until late in the afternoon of the next day and knocked on Roxanne's door. Lloyd loved to go with her for jogs on the beach and she needed a break from studying.

Roxanne answered the door in what looked like the clothes she had slept in. Melissa thought that the woman might be sick. She peered round her to look for the inevitable rush of appreciation from Lloyd.

'I'm going for a run, a slow run,' said the girl. 'Where's Lloyd? Can he go with me?'

Melissa didn't like speaking to adults and her words came out in a rush. Then she remembered Roxanne's journal and the rambling entries and wondered if the woman was still suicidal, because she didn't look right and she was taking too long to answer. She wondered if Roxanne was crazy. If she was, that somehow made it easier to be around her.

'His name isn't Lloyd, Melissa. I found out that his name is Cooper. And he left the island yesterday,' said Roxanne.

'He left? You mean he's gone? With who?'

'His owner died; that's why no one was looking for him. She had died over in Orono. Her parents came to collect Lloyd . . . Cooper, yesterday.'

Melissa put her hand on the door frame to steady herself. She had been caught off-guard. She was assaulted by the news, struck hard in her midsection and it felt like her ribs were going to break.

'You let him go? *I* would have taken him, if you didn't care about him!'

'Do you want to come in? I can tell you the whole story. I didn't want Cooper to go, but he was part of the dead woman's estate,' said Roxanne.

Melissa didn't make a move to come in. Her eyes filled with hot tears.

'You have ruined everything! I wish you'd never come here!' she cried and ran off the deck and down the dirt road. She took the path to the ocean. She knew all the paths that twisted and turned. Melissa did not want to remember her life before the dog; she did not want to remember who she had been before he had come to the island. Why had Roxanne done this?

Even Roxanne, stupid Roxanne, had loved the dog. How could she have let him be taken away?

If Melissa had known, she would have broken into Roxanne's house and taken the dog and hidden him away. Or she could have taken the ferry to Portland and gone to her father's house. Would he have understood? She wondered if he was friend or foe. She didn't know if he could be trusted.

When she got in from running along the labyrinth of trails, her mother was on the phone in the kitchen and looked up at Melissa with dark eyes. 'That was Roxanne. She told me about the dog. I'm sorry he's gone.'

And for the first time in nearly a year, Melissa let her mother wrap her arms round her.

COOPER WAS STUNNED by his exile. There had not been one minute with the New One, the one who had saved him, when he had doubted her. And then she had sent him away. The First One was gone. Liz, Liz. He knew the sound of her name. She was the one he had known since leaving the litter, the one who had urged him on, trusted him, loved him. She had been tremulous at times, speeding up like a storm, and he had learned to sniff the change before it came and would refuse to leave her side. He had known of her death, felt it, but the waves of death scent in the old house where they had lived together confirmed it. The First One was gone.

He had run round the house three times in the ancient way of saying goodbye that he had not known before that moment, but which came to him out of the merging with all the canines before him who had come in from the wild to be with humans. Three times round the site of death, barking a heralding cry to let the other side hear of their coming. She was no more.

A good life, a very good life, is finding one person who knows you, who shares the joy in chest rubbing, the pleasure of eating, of running damp and happy in the heavy dew of morning. He had found two such humans.

The New One had been another miracle; she had found him when he was broken. She also needed watching and, as soon as he had been able, he had taken up his post with her. But now the New One had changed course. She had let two people, the man and the woman, take him. She had hesitated, her scent had turned to fear and sadness, yet he'd heard her say, 'Get in, Cooper,' when the man and the woman opened their car, and he had obeyed.

These two are Liz's parents. Their house held ghostly scents of memories for him, when there had been rage and frustration between his Liz and her parents. They had not known how to soothe Liz as he had.

When the long car trip ended, he was led through the house to the kitchen, where he was taken into the yard through sliding glass doors. It was surrounded by a wooden fence, higher than he could ever jump, and he could see nothing of the surrounding area. Here he was tied to a lead that ran along a high wire. He had never been tied before and he was ashamed. They brought food and placed it in a bowl; then they brought water.

The man and the woman left the house the next day and did not return until the light began to fade. When they returned they came to look at him and brought him more food. More time passed, darkness settled, and they allowed him into the kitchen. He made the mistake of trying to follow them as he thought he should, down the hallway to their bedroom. But the woman scolded him, smacking a newspaper with her hand to make a sharp noise, and put up a barrier to let him know to stay in the kitchen.

The next night, after the man brought him food and left him in the yard, he saw the glow of the woman's cigarette in the kitchen. She sat in the dark smoking. If allowed, he could help her. He would permit her to weep and to drain the anger and sadness from her blood by stroking him. He could urge her outside and drag her senses to stick throwing and the thrill of physical exhaustion. But she would not permit it.

He knew this was it; there would be nothing else. In this life he had had two people who were beyond what he could have hoped. He had seen other dogs who had not fared as well, and he was grateful. But the New One had sent him away to this place and he could not understand why. He stopped eating on the second day and no longer hoped for her to come for him.

Chapter 7

Isaiah had replaced the battery on the truck for Roxanne the day after the Townsends had driven away with Cooper. Roxanne had watched him from the house. She had refused to speak to him, and he knew better than to come to the door. She called Charlotte and said, 'I'm not mad at you, and I probably won't be able to stay mad at Isaiah much longer, but I think we made a huge mistake. Tell him thanks for fixing the truck. And I'll feed your cat while you're gone.'

She had not been able to go to sleep the first night until dawn, and the second night was not much better. She missed Cooper's breathing, his scent, his demand to go outside, to draw her out, his soft eyes and his need of her. She missed the sprawl of his body, his satisfaction after his meal, his enthusiastic tail-wagging when she walked in the door, or watching him gnaw on a stout stick until some artistic culmination caused him to stop and add it to a pile of similar sticks on the deck. She kept picturing him running three times round Liz's old house in Orono. Had he really done that? He'd come and stood by her when he was done.

She'd spent days picturing his ritual and in an early-morning bout of insomnia, she had suddenly realised what had happened. He had completed what he needed to do with Liz and had signed on with Roxanne completely.

This was a miserable job and she regretted taking it. When Isaiah returned after Christmas, she would tell him that she was resigning before she did any more harm. She had hurt Cooper by getting too close to him and letting him get too close to her. He couldn't understand about property laws and estates.

The island was muffled in the silence of empty houses. Christmas came and went. She drove the truck round the island twice each day. No stray animals were reported, no lost animals needed finding and no dead animals needed removal. Isaiah and Charlotte were in North Carolina, Tess was on the mainland with her ex-husband and their two children and grandchildren, and even Hill had disappeared to points unknown. He had called to tell her that their lessons would not resume until after New Year. She hoped her disappointment had not shown, but that, if it had, he would think it meant she was dedicated to archery, not that she would in any way miss him.

Roxanne went to Tess's house and practised for hours each day, letting her thumb slide along the edge of her jaw as Hill had demonstrated. She wore long, silk underwear under her jeans so that she could stay outside as long as possible to shoot again and again at the target. Fewer and fewer arrows strayed to the outer edges.

One afternoon, as the light was fading, she sighted the target and saw, before she released the arrow, exactly where it would pierce it. She took a breath and released the air in a slow and perfect stream. And she suddenly found it, the deeper stillness that Hill had talked about. What he had not told her was that it was as real as a spot on a map and that she could step into it. She released the arrow and followed it to its certain home, dead centre. Roxanne felt a tingle of exquisite light run up her spine. She shot for several more minutes before the strange, new sensation left her.

When she returned home, she called Information for the Townsends' phone number in Providence. They were unlisted. Then she remembered that she had the obituary from the newspaper. She'd send a note, care of the funeral home, and they would forward it to the Townsends. She tore a sheet of paper from her black journal:

Dear Mr and Mrs Townsend,

If love is the reason that you want Cooper, then I am glad and I wish you well. But if you took Cooper in order to repair something that was broken between you and your daughter, then I ask you to look into your hearts and think about what Liz would want and what the dog wants. I think you know. I think he belongs with me. I will take him back any time. I will come and get him and I will take care of him for the rest of his life.

She took the letter to the grocery store and dropped it into the mailbox outside. That evening, she telephoned Hill's number and got his answering machine. She left a message: 'Hill, this is Roxanne. We don't have another lesson fixed until next week, but if you're back home, could you meet me in Portland, um, for coffee? Or could you meet me on a street corner? What I mean is, that dog that I told you about, well, he's gone—' *Beep.*

Hill had his message machine on a timer to keep messages short. Why didn't he say so up-front? As in, 'Leave a message and make it short. You have thirty seconds starting now.'

Roxanne called back.

'It's Roxanne again and I think you should warn people about the time limit. Most people will just get to hello when they are beeped out. But here's the thing: everyone I know on the island is gone, and I'm going to resign my job, and I wanted to talk it out with someone—' *Beep.*

If he put those two messages together, he would get something, but she wasn't sure what. She did not want to seem needy.

'Hi. It's me again. I hope you hear this message before the other two that I've left you. If so, don't listen to the next two messages from me. It's not that it was hard being Christmas and all and this was the first Christmas since my husband died, which I hadn't told you up until this moment, but it's that I had to give the dog to people who won't understand him. Some people shouldn't have dogs; they shouldn't have gerbils. And I thought I could stop this one bad thing from happening—' *Beep.*

She would not leave him another message.

ROXANNE HEARD the solid sound of a truck door closing. Everyone was gone until the end of the week, except the girl, Melissa, and her mother. The girl had started to be a regular visitor, but Roxanne was sure that if it had not been for Cooper, Melissa would have ignored her. She had seen that the girl was shattered when she learned that the dog was gone.

Roxanne looked out of the small kitchen window and saw Hill hefting his bow and arrows, running his fingers through his hair, squaring off his shoulders, and looking at her house as if he had already decided something.

She had on the same jeans that she had worn for three days, her hair was unwashed, and there was an empty, unrinsed tuna can in the sink. She heard his boots on the deck and, without hesitation, the knock.

When she opened the door, he was framed in cold air. His eyes blinked and she thought she saw alarm in his face. Could he see that she was coming undone?

She ran her fingers through her hair and said, 'This is my new camouflage outfit. It's what all the hunters are wearing this year.'

'When did you become a hunter?' he said, the right side of his mouth lifting before the other side caught up.

She took in a larger breath. 'I haven't yet. Just checking out the clothing options. I was wondering what it would take to be a hunter.' She took one step backwards.

'We can start by practising.' He scanned the area from left to right. 'Where do you practise?' he asked.

'At a friend's house. I set up a target behind her house.' It was early afternoon and they might have an hour or two of strong daylight left.

'Let's go there,' he suggested.

'Come in. It'll take me a few minutes to get ready.'

He came in and stood in her kitchen with its faded yellow and orange linoleum and chipped Formica countertops. She retreated to the bedroom, aware that every sound that she made clattered in naked disclosure through the house. When she came out, she found Hill standing in the sitting room.

He turned towards her. 'I didn't learn to hunt from men. I learned first from my grandmother, then later, when she was gone, my father took over.'

Roxanne sat on the arm of the couch. 'Tell me,' she said.

'I learned to hunt early on. My grandmother refused to use a compound bow. She said it was unfair to the animals. She told me that if I learned to use a traditional bow, I'd understand the prey better. And I'd understand myself better.' Hill put the archery equipment on the table. 'She taught me to find deer skat, dried in neat little piles of pellets, and to put that on a flat stone and grind it with another stone until she had a fine powder that she put on our boots, jackets and hats. It masked our scent. She taught me to construct a hunting stand.'

'What exactly is a hunting stand?' asked Roxanne.

'They differ, depending on what you're hunting and what weapon you're using. My grandmother was a bow hunter, so hers was a small platform of roughly bound branches about fifteen feet up in the lower branches of a tree, a place to wait for deer traffic. She taught me to wait in complete silence when I was ten years old. She claimed that she had never wounded a deer; all of her kills had dropped to the floor of the forest within seconds.'

Roxanne stood up and tucked her hair under a fleece hat. 'Let's catch the last of the light. I set up a target behind Tess's house because I never wanted the dog to see me shooting. I didn't want to scare him,' she said.

They climbed into Hill's truck and he turned to Roxanne. 'I came as soon as I heard your message,' he said. 'There's a pile of unopened mail sitting in my kitchen and a refrigerator with bad milk. I got in my truck and came straight here. I'm sorry about your husband. What happened?'

Roxanne clicked her seat belt into place and her hands trembled. 'His heart. I thought I could save him. I tried to. I did CPR as soon as I could get my hands on him. He had this thing that he said, that he married a woman who could save him.'

Hill backed up the truck. 'What was that supposed to mean?'

'It was a joke about me being a lifeguard when we met. He wasn't the kind of guy who needed saving, not like a wreck of a person, you know? That wasn't it. Only it wasn't a joke and I really did need to save him and I couldn't. A couple of months after he died, I came here and then the dog came here and I let him go without a fight, and I want to get him back because he needs me, or I need him. Can we talk about this after we practise? I hate to say this, but I need to shoot something.'

They drove the short distance to Tess's house, then Hill reached over to grab his quiver of arrows and his bow from the back of the truck. Roxanne could smell the man scent on Hill's jacket. Each round molecule of it rolled with urgent desire up her nose and took the express to her brain. Her body responded in a jet stream of warmth cascading between her eyes and spiralling with alarming speed through ribs, pooling between her hip bones, gaining speed down the insides of her thighs. She reached for the door handle and pulled it open with a click.

Hill opened the gate to the back yard and Roxanne passed through, holding her breath, avoiding the chance to inhale more of him. She pointed to the ringed target fifty yards away, attached to a stack of three hay bales.

'Let's start fresh,' Hill said, as he covered the old target with a fresh paper one, tacking it with the pins that held the old one in place. 'You've been practising,' he said. 'I can tell. There's a turning point with students, when they stop carrying the bow as if it will take a bite out of them.'

In fact she had passed over a threshold, faster than she thought she should have, when the arrow, her arm, the bow and the target had all flowed together. She told Hill about it.

He listened as he paced out a distance.

'I don't know why that happened for you so soon. I've had students practise for a year before they step into a space where all the parts work. Did it just happen that one time?'

'Yeah; this week. So I shouldn't count on it happening again soon?'

He put his bow on a section of stone wall. 'I can't predict how it will go for you. For most of us, those moments are hard-earned, inch by inch with a lot of outright humiliation, followed by nagging self-doubt. Then it starts to change. First the arrows hit the outer rings, then a few strays dive towards the centre. And suddenly the eye of the target reaches out to you and the archer only has to let go. I have never told anyone that before.'

He had stepped closer to her with each word and now he reached out and removed her hat and dropped it on the ground; then he put his hands on the edges of her jaw and into her hair. Roxanne grabbed both of his hands.

'I want to tell you about why I'm here and about the dog and about this woman who was an archer, who used to own him, and how she killed herself after something terrible happened to the dog, and now the dog is gone. Her parents came to get him and this is such a terrible mistake . . .'

A look of bewilderment followed by horror came over his face. He dropped his hands and stepped back. 'I can't believe this. Why didn't I put it all together?' He sank down on the stone wall, then looked back at the shocked Roxanne. 'I need to tell you something.' He swallowed hard and pressed his lips together. 'The world of archery competition in Maine is a small community and the number of women archers is an even smaller piece of the pie,' he said.

Oh, no, thought Roxanne, already skipping ahead to a likely conclusion. I am such an idiot.

'The reason my wife and I are separated is because I went to a competition about a year and a half ago in Orono and stayed the night. I met a woman there. I'd never seen her before at any of the competitions and she was good, really good. I couldn't help but notice her. She really had something. That flow that we were just talking about? She could step into it like no one I've ever seen. Anyone could see she loved everything about archery. I stayed with her for one night at my motel. After that I dragged myself home and Julie knew it the first minute I walked in the door.'

A gust of wind found them and Roxanne's hair blew into her face. She reached down to pick up her hat and rammed it back on her head. 'You knew Liz Townsend? Does everyone but me know this woman? Am I suddenly her receptacle for dogs and old lovers? Why didn't you tell me?'

'Tell you what? That I cheated on my wife? I'm not proud of what I did. And I didn't want my wife to leave me.'

'No. I mean, yes, you should have said something. But you should have put two and two together about the dog. I told you I had a dog that had been shot. You knew, didn't you?'

Everything that had opened in Roxanne was closing down. How could she have been so wrong about him?

Hill stood up. 'How could I have known anything about her dog? Roxanne, this was a one-night stand. I told her the next morning that we couldn't see each other again.'

'This whole thing just got too weird for me. Forget that I left you a message, forget about lessons, forget that you ever drove out here,' said Roxanne. She wrapped her arms round her torso.

Hill took a step towards her and she wondered how much of a mistake she had made. There was no one else around within shouting distance. He stopped and opened both his palms towards her as if she were a stray animal needing reassurance. 'OK, Roxanne. I'm not exactly sure what happened here, but try not to blame me for something that happened before you even met me. I did read about Liz's death, but I never put it together with your wounded dog.'

'You should go,' Roxanne said.

'Let me give you a ride home,' he said.

'No. I'm going to stay here.'

He nodded and seemed like he was going to say something else, but then he gathered up his gear and walked away, pulling open the gate. She waited until the sound of his truck faded before she pulled out some arrows, set one in the notch, pulled her hand along her jawline and released. Nothing was right. The arrows stuck round the outside perimeter of the target as if the centre were covered in a glass dome. She tossed her bow on the ground and went to collect her arrows. As she approached the target, her eye was drawn to the mark that Hill made on all his targets on the bottom-left corner; a stamp of a hunter with a fully drawn bow.

'Oh Jesus,' she said. That was what she had seen at Liz's old place. That's what had caught her eye when she'd looked out of the window. The target with the stamp on the bottom-left corner.

Chapter 8

In Providence, Rhode Island, Liz's mother smoked the last cigarette in her pack and smashed the stub in an overflowing ashtray. Her daughter was dead and she was raging day and night, smoking two packets of cigarettes per day, coating her lungs with an anaesthetic of tar.

With every breath that she had taken during the two-year strain of not speaking to her daughter, she had imagined Liz and what she'd be doing at any point in the day. Would she take her medication? Did she know how angry Jan was? That her mother was right? She had pictured a future when Liz would ask for forgiveness, when the time of punishment would be over and Jan would have her daughter back. But the side effect of shunning her daughter, not taking her calls, not reading her imploring letters, was that her world had grown dark and small.

She had busied herself with the logistics of death: arranging for the cremation, writing the brief obituary, discovering that the house in Orono had been sold and Liz was only renting it, and suffering the tangle of paperwork that comes with death.

Jan pulled a cigarette from a new pack and clicked on the plastic lighter. The dog was still outside, tied to the zip line that allowed him what Jan thought was a perfectly fine run of thirty feet. He had stopped eating his food. He was stubborn like Liz. She'd let him inside when it was time for her to go to bed. The weather report predicted freezing temperatures. She was not impervious to the suffering of others.

Outside in the yard, the dog sat up, tilted his head back and howled as if a fire truck was splitting the night with its siren.

ROXANNE HIT the redial button. She had already left a message at the funeral home ten minutes earlier, but she wanted to speak to a *person*, not a recording. She'd heard nothing in response to the letter she had written to Liz's parents, care of the funeral home, and now she wanted their phone number. This place, listed in the obituary, was her only hope. She'd searched for them on the Web at Tess's house. Nothing. Isaiah had been the only one to talk to them on the phone and he was still away.

As a last-ditch effort, she'd tried the vet clinic in Orono, but they were closed for two days. 'In case of emergency, leave a message for the doctor on call and he'll get back to you.' Roxanne had tried the doctor on call, who said he couldn't give her information from another vet's practice.

Cooper had been gone for days and Roxanne was frantic. She hit the redial button for the funeral home in Providence seventeen more times in the next hour. Then on the eighteenth, a voice said, 'Harsdale Mortuary.'

Roxanne swallowed hard and spoke. 'I'd like to call the Townsends in Providence to offer my condolences. I believe you handled the arrangements for their daughter, Elizabeth. Do you have their phone number?'

'Who's calling, please?'

'This is an old friend of Liz's from Maine. I just found out about her death,' said Roxanne. Why had she fabricated this lie? Why didn't she just tell the man that she was the dog warden and that she needed to get in touch with the Townsends about the dog?

'We can't give out phone numbers of our clients. But you can send your condolence card to us and we'll be sure to get it to them.'

'I've already done that. Now I want to call them. Calling is better. I mean I used to have their phone number, but I've changed address books and that was back when Liz lived with her parents. I just don't have the address now, it's not like I never had the address and phone number. So could you just give me the street address? I'd like to send flowers too,' said Roxanne.

'We can handle the flower arrangements also. What would you like to send? Do you have a price range?' he asked.

Roxanne hung up.

DESPERATE FOR ANY connection to Liz and Cooper, Roxanne decided to drive over to the old Hamilton place where Liz had so briefly lived, possibly for only a few days. Tess had described it as one of the few old properties that had been built towards the centre of the island.

It was the last house on a sandy road that plunged inwards, crossing a small bridge over a marsh, edged on both sides of the lane by impenetrable undergrowth. The road ended in the yard of a weathered house that was tucked behind a façade of screened-in porch. There were newer additions on either side of the house and an outbuilding stood to the left. Roxanne opened the door of the truck, grabbed her gloves from behind the front seat and jumped out.

Had this been Liz's dream, to come here with her dog? And do what? It might have been the impulsiveness of youth, the result of manic buying, or the simple desire to live within an easy commute of Portland. Roxanne zipped her jacket and walked to the outbuilding, a large barn that was rapidly rotting into the ground. With a forceful heave, she slid open one of the doors. Air that was even colder than the outside temperature escaped and ran over her, chilling her to the core. She stepped inside and waited for her eyes to adjust to the grey light. Late-afternoon sunlight came in through two dust-covered windows.

Someone had shot Cooper out here. He had to have been shot on the island. And by all accounts, no matter how difficult Liz's life had been at times, she loved Cooper more than anything or anyone else. The two of them must have had just a few days of their new life on the island before things went terribly wrong. Roxanne scratched the heel of her shoe along the dirt floor and the low rays of sun caught the disturbed dust.

Her heart double-timed as she heard a truck pull up. She was terrified that it was Hill, because if he knew about the Hamilton place, then he had lied about everything. She went to a window and peered out.

Roxanne knew it was Peter, the boyfriend of the dead woman, the minute he stepped out of his green and black SUV. She walked out of the barn, mustering her best body language to appear confident and official.

How was it that his neediness and obsession were translated into the way he held his shoulders in so tight that she could see it through his jacket? And in the way he walked towards her, smiling with the bottom half of his face while his eyes hooked into her?

'I saw your truck. Are you the animal control lady? Someone at the dock said you drove a yellow truck. I think you have a dog that I'm looking for.'

He stopped four feet from Roxanne. She didn't know if he would remember running into her in the parking lot of the Dairy Mart in Portland, when Cooper had gone off like a grenade in her car.

'Hey, that was you, wasn't it?' The man drew in closer and pointed a finger at her chest. 'In the parking lot about a month ago, over in Portland.'

Roxanne felt one of her fingernails pierce her palm. 'Yes, and I recall the dog didn't seem to take to you. He went ballistic, didn't he?'

'That dog belonged to my girlfriend. I know how to handle him. A dog like that, you have to be firm, show him who's the alpha. She'd want me to have him. She's dead.'

Roxanne willed herself into being a therapist again and not a woman alone with the crazed ex-boyfriend of a dead woman. Peter was stalking the dog because that was all he had left.

'I'm sorry,' she said. 'It's so hard to lose someone.'

She saw his eyes flicker, revealing a brief glimpse of who he had been before he had turned into the bad boyfriend who couldn't let go.

'I took the dog to the shelter in Portland. Why don't you check with them tomorrow? And I'd like to send the family a sympathy note. What's the street in Providence?' said Roxanne.

The address and phone number slid off his lips so easily. Roxanne knew instantly that he had prowled the neighbourhood in Providence. She thanked him like she meant it and walked past him to her truck.

Once inside she locked both doors and pressed her palms against the steering wheel, afraid that he would have caught her lie that the dog was being held at the shelter in Portland. But he made no move. She knew that the phone line at the shelter would be unstaffed at night. She had until tomorrow morning, when he might call and find out that Cooper had never been there. With shaking hands she turned the key in the ignition and drove away from the house.

IT WAS DARK as she pulled up to her cottage. A light was on inside. Oh yeah, she thought, I asked Melissa to look after the place when I was away. She prayed that the girl wasn't waiting inside to hear news of Cooper.

As she approached the steps, she turned her head slightly to one side as she tried to discern a familiar sound. She turned the knob and pushed open the door, to be met by the great black shape of Cooper wagging and twisting towards her with his lips pulled into the biggest retriever smile. Tess and Melissa stood on the far side of the island counter with jubilant faces, eyebrows high, eyes glowing, their cheeks spread wide and high from smiling. Cooper took one huge lunge and put his front paws on her chest and flattened her against the wall. He made a high sound like singing.

'Oh, Cooper! Oh my God, Cooper-Lloyd!' Roxanne slid to the floor and dug her fingers into the thick winter fur round his neck. 'What are you doing here?' she asked him. Getting no answer, she looked at her two guests. 'How did he get here? What's going on?'

Roxanne had never seen Melissa excited before. The girl spoke rapidly.

'I was here bringing in the mail, leaving some cat food out, and this car pulled up. I realised it was those people who took Cooper. They brought him back. I couldn't believe it!' Melissa said. Her face lit up, and for one second Roxanne got a glimpse of how Melissa would look as a grown-up, when she was first in love, or standing at the rim of the Grand Canyon.

'You mean the Townsends? Jan and Ed? What did they say?' The dog whirled his way to Melissa and wrapped his body round her thighs. The girl crouched down to get the full effect of his affection.

'The guy said they changed their minds, that's all. But the woman said they couldn't do right by Cooper and she wanted to make it right with her daughter. Do you know what she was talking about? Look, they brought all this food and a new water dish.'

Roxanne took her eyes off the dog long enough to see that the Townsends had delivered a fifty-pound sack of food. A blue nylon leash sat abandoned near the couch.

'Did the Townsends wonder where I was?' asked Roxanne.

'I told them you were off on business. My father said never give people who you don't know more information than they absolutely need.'

Tess raised an eyebrow. 'Let me guess . . . your father is a lawyer?'

'Yeah, he is. Did I say the right thing?'

Roxanne sighed with relief. 'You did great, Melissa. I don't know why they returned Cooper, but I'm not going to argue with the best thing that has happened since I got to this island.'

Tess slid her jacket on. 'I leave this place for a few days and the world gets turned upside-down. I want to hear about everything that happened, but right now I have to check on a handful of summer houses. Melissa filled me in on Cooper's odyssey, but I have a feeling that you have been through hell and back.'

Roxanne hugged the older woman as she left. 'I need to talk to you, but I'm ready to drop. Will you come by tomorrow?'

'Tomorrow, late afternoon. I need to make a trip into Portland first thing.'

Melissa stayed longer than she ever had at Roxanne's. The exhausted, well-fed dog dozed on his side and fell into a dream. He whimpered in dream talk, his feet jerking as if he were trotting. Roxanne and the girl stopped talking and watched him.

Melissa said, 'I think animals dream like we do, but they can't tell us their dreams, so we'll never know.'

Roxanne looked, really looked at Melissa. This was the first time that the girl had offered something that she had pondered. The fragility of the moment was not lost on Roxanne. She tried to remember her old life, when she knew the right words to say to people to enable them to open up all the dark places on the inside. She stopped trying to think and just asked, 'What do you think Cooper is dreaming?'

On the far corner of the couch, Melissa tucked one leg beneath her. 'Maybe he's dreaming about running before he got hurt. I heard that people who get their legs amputated always dream with their legs on.'

'I never would have guessed that,' said Roxanne. 'I would have said food or catching a stick. You're more complicated than I thought . . .' She stopped, not wanting Melissa to retreat again into her thinning bones.

MELISSA WAS BACK at school for a week before she realised that she hadn't gone running even once after school. Instead, she took the first ferry home and stopped to get Cooper for a walk. A winter storm had dumped six inches of snow and the dog rolled in it like a displaced polar bear.

Roxanne had taken to calling her Lissa and she let her. Nobody called her that except her old friend, Chris. She thought that Roxanne was ready to drop on the floor. She had dark circles under her eyes and looked like she was straight out of chemotherapy treatment. Melissa had checked out Roxanne's kitchen before the big dog reunion. Roxanne had no food in the house. OK—two cans of tuna, a greenish loaf of bread, a jar of dill pickles and milk that said it was best if consumed six days ago. Roxanne had terrible eating habits. Didn't she know anything about nutrition? It had been weeks since Melissa had logged on to the pro-Anna websites, but she remembered the calorie of every food she had ever encountered.

Melissa rattled through the kitchen at home and found a brownie mix, read the directions, and produced a tray of brownies.

Her mother returned home after dark. When she walked into the kitchen, she said, 'Did you make something, Melissa?' She looked at the brownies.

'Most of these are for Roxanne,' Melissa said before her mother could say more. 'I don't think she knows how to cook. I'm worried about her.'

Her mother sat down without taking off her coat. She slowly pulled off her fleece hat. 'I can't tell you how good this smells. It's like our house is beautiful again,' she said quietly.

ROXANNE KNEW she had been wrong about Isaiah's intentions concerning Cooper and she left a phone message for him to call her on his return.

Isaiah phoned her that night, explaining that their flight from North Carolina had been delayed. 'Does this mean you're speaking to me again?' he asked.

'Yes, and it means a lot more than that. It means I'm not going to quit my job, which I was going to do. Can we be friends again? I'm sorry,' she said. They agreed to meet at his office the next morning.

She told him everything, or mostly everything. She didn't tell him how confused she had been when Hill had told her he had slept with Liz, that he had known her. She did say that she was done with her archery lessons.

'There's one more thing. Liz's old boyfriend, Peter, has probably figured out that I have Cooper by now. He sounded determined to get him and I sent him on a false trail. The guy has no right to Cooper, but he still sounds obsessed with Liz, and now that Liz is dead, Cooper has become his focus.'

Roxanne saw Isaiah's eyebrows moving together in a mountain of worry.

'What's his last name?' he asked.

'I don't know, but I might be able to find out.'

'Once you get his name, I can call the Portland police.' The older man paused. 'Did he threaten you?'

'No. It was like he was still after Liz, or anything that belonged to her. I've worked with a few men who were obsessed with ex-girlfriends, and their ability to stay focused on one person was staggering,' said Roxanne.

'I've known some too. They give men a bad name and we're skating on thin ice as it is.'

PETER'S LAST NAME came from a surprising source. The Townsends called Roxanne to say that Peter had called them right after they'd got back to Providence. 'The nerve of that guy. He called us to see if we had Cooper. I told him he was one sorry son of a bitch and if he came anywhere near here, we'd call the police.' Jan's voice got softer. 'How is the dog?'

'He hasn't left my side except when his fan club is around,' said Roxanne. 'He's pretty popular in these parts. Thank you for bringing him back.'

'I think Liz would have liked that. I've never been good with animals. That's probably a sign of me being a defective human being, but I've got to be honest with you; dogs give me the creeps. Got bitten by one when I was a kid. Eighteen stitches on my thigh. Liz wanted a dog from the time she could speak, but I was terrified of them.'

Roxanne pictured Liz longing for the thing that most terrified her mother and she saw how mismatched the mother and daughter had been. And then she remembered that Jan had ostracised her own daughter and she wondered how she would live with that.

'What made you decide to bring him back?' asked Roxanne.

'I made mistakes with Liz and I have to live with that. But you were right; she never would have hurt her dog. And he would have protected her at all costs. I can at least let Cooper live with someone who loves him. He deserves that.' Jan's voice shook. 'There's something missing from the picture about Liz's death and I wish I knew what it was.'

Roxanne said, 'I know what you mean. I haven't been able to stop thinking about it. Jan, did Peter say his last name?'

'I think he did. What the hell did he say? . . . Ellis; yeah, like Ellis Island.'

'Thanks,' said Roxanne.

Roxanne waited for Peter to turn up. She had never seen obsession dissipate quickly. She locked her door at night and she never left Cooper alone. If she had to go places without him, she left him with Tess or Melissa.

And then there was the matter of Hill. She purchased her own archery equipment to replace what he had loaned her. She took Hill's equipment back to him. She went to his house midmorning when she knew he'd be teaching. At the last minute, she left him a note: *My dog is back.*

THE FIRST THING Tess noticed about the young man was his shimmering jaw muscle. The two of them were the only people standing outside on the ferry, headed for Portland. January had chased all the other passengers inside. Those bringing cars simply sat in them, hanging onto the warmth.

Tess wore a large shearling hat, leather mittens lined with thick polyester, a sweater and a jerkin beneath her coat, and boots with woollen socks inside. Winter was a fine time for her; it was the unfortunate people who didn't know how to dress for the cold who whined in misery until spring.

She guessed the man was past a turning point, early thirties, where he imagined he would know something with certainty, and he looked angry that his life was not unfolding in a way befitting him. She glanced at his hands. They were red and sore from the cold.

She felt a tug, a draw to the young man, and took a few steps closer to him. 'At this time of year you can almost see my favourite building in Portland,' she told him. 'Too overgrown in the summer.' She pointed in the direction of a Victorian house that had emerged unscathed from the days of urban renewal. She knew her small size and her age would prevent him from being alarmed. Age especially gave her a stealth covering. Who knew that getting older was going to be this much fun?

She scanned his posture. His head thrust forward as if his brain needed to arrive before his body. Oh, the anxious ones. In her practice, she could help people align their bodies into less torturous postures, but she was frequently daunted by the toll that anxiety took on a person.

'Cold day to visit the island,' she said. 'Were you there for the day?' She hadn't seen him before, but it was not uncommon to see strangers. The fifteen-minute ferry ride from Portland opened the island to the world.

'The cold doesn't bother me,' he said, pulling his head back. He wore a charcoal Puffa jacket, zipped to the centre of his chest. The filling of the jacket exaggerated his size, giving him larger shoulders and arms.

'Not much open on the island in the winter. I sometimes wonder what visitors do,' she said. As she got one step closer, she thought she caught the scent of something metallic coming off him. She stepped back.

'Business,' he said. 'I had business to take care of.' She could see his muscles tightening, starting at his jaw and spreading through his body. She glanced down and saw that both his hands had formed into dry, chapped fists. 'I'm working on one of the new houses in town.'

Tess relaxed a bit. Of course, there was a dreadful amount of construction going on. She hated being the old woman who groused about people moving in, but soon all of Boston would move here and clog up the tiny roads with their oversized cars. She shuddered. 'With every new house, something precious gets sacrificed,' she said.

The man smiled, his lips spreading like a wet opening to a cave. 'That's right. Sometimes a sacrifice must be made.'

The ferry jolted as it made first contact with the tyre-lined pier and the man turned and walked quickly to the gangway. When the attendants opened the sturdy chain-link barrier, he slipped off the ferry and just disappeared. Tess had wanted to ask him: when is a sacrifice needed?

Tess was walking to a restaurant to meet her ex-husband for dinner. She was worried he might notice that she carried herself differently. He was long retired from medical practice, but his diagnostic skill had been brilliant when he was young and sober, and he was sober now. He had told her once that he could spot someone with cancer when he looked at them. 'It's the skin,' he'd said. 'And something about the eyes.'

During her visit to the family at Christmas, she'd moisturised her skin and put eyedrops into her eyes until the sclera were parchment white. Only her granddaughter, who she suspected had received the thread of synaesthesia through little knotted bunches of DNA, had noticed. She had taken Tess's hand and whispered in her ear, 'Granny, your colour has a dent in it. Why is that?' The child was six and Tess did not want to lie to her.

'What you're seeing is a tummy ache. Thanks for noticing. I'll fix it when I go back home. Would you mind not telling the others? We're having a party and no one wants to hear about bellyaches.'

Tess did not want to make the child a silent co-conspirator. That was wrong. She would make it right later, somehow. If it was as bad as she imagined, she would tell the child, 'You were the first to notice and you helped me.' The child had to know that what she'd seen was real.

Tess pulled the flaps of her enormous hat over her ears and walked up the dark hill to the restaurant. She'd agree only to surgery, not chemo and not radiation. She would not sacrifice the end of her life to a drugged and hairless stupor.

Chapter 9

Roxanne had purchased a bow with a thirty-pound draw. In the five weeks since Cooper's return, she had practised almost daily. Now it was February, and on the few days that were both without wind and above freezing, she practised behind Tess's house. On all the other days, she went to the storage house at the boat club. On Isaiah's advice, she'd asked if she could practise there. It was surprisingly spacious, with plenty of room down the centre, between the boats. She'd brought in some hay bales and set them between the rows of boats that sat stacked in neat formation. The cement floor drove the cold through her shoes after an hour. That was long enough for her. Once or twice Isaiah showed up, just to sit and watch, he said, but Roxanne didn't like it when he was there. After two arrows skittered off a hull, she said, 'This is like having someone watch you practise the piano or take a bath. I shoot lots worse when you're here.'

Isaiah wore a leather bombardier hat with flaps over his ears.

'Well, if you're not going to bring your dog with you, I thought you would like to have some company. I won't watch. I'll do some old man thing like whittle, which I'll have to learn to do eventually.'

Since they'd had a fight and made up, Isaiah had grown more important in her life.

'You don't need to look out for me, Isaiah,' Roxanne said. 'I think Liz's stalker ex-boyfriend has gone. It's been over five weeks.' She set an arrow, drew back, and released. Thwack. Outer ring. She sighed.

Isaiah stood and zipped his jacket. 'I can see your game is off when I'm here. Either that or you're just plain terrible all the time and you're trying to blame it on me.'

Roxanne had her sights set on the forty-pound bow by spring. She was swimming again at the YMCA in Portland and could feel her arm and back muscles firming. Last night she had eaten a pile of spaghetti and meatballs.

She guided Isaiah to the sliding metal door. 'You're right, in a way. I'm not confident enough yet to let people watch me. If I was really focused in the way that I should be, I wouldn't even notice you sitting there,' she said.

'Get yourself a tune-up with that archery teacher,' Isaiah said, as he walked up the gravel path. 'That's what you need.'

Roxanne pulled the door shut. No, she did not want a tune-up from Hill. She wasn't sure if she trusted him about anything.

TODAY WAS ONE of the days when Melissa had come directly to Roxanne's home after school and taken Cooper for a walk. Roxanne had started leaving the dog alone for an hour or two; she couldn't be with him constantly.

Melissa. Didn't she have any friends on the island? Roxanne thought as she drove back towards home in her truck. She had never seen her with another kid. Could she broach the subject? Was it any of her business? She remembered how alarmed Melissa had looked when she'd told her that she was a psychologist and that her husband had died on their bathroom floor.

'Why did you make up a big story?' Melissa had asked.

'Because I couldn't stand the truth. I couldn't stand the idea that people would expect me to know what I was doing because I was a therapist. When Bob died, it was like I was handed a whole new set of skin that was sad and miserable and I didn't want to be that person. Now I've got a couple of minutes each day when I don't think of death at the same moment that I'm thinking of my husband. I think of him the way he was, not him dying.'

Melissa hadn't said anything, but late that afternoon she had brought round the brownies she had made and a card from her mother: *We are sad that your husband died and that it made you hide from us when you first came here. It is good to get to know you.*

Roxanne turned her thoughts to Cooper. A few days ago, she had taken him to see Sam Reynolds, the vet, who had confirmed that Cooper's leg was now as good as it was going to get.

'He's a strong dog,' Sam had told her. 'Given the extent of his injuries, it's amazing that the only remaining result is a slight limp.'

'You saved him,' Roxanne had said. 'You're a good vet, Sam.'

Roxanne parked the truck and walked into the house. She'd only been inside for a few minutes when she caught sight of Melissa and Cooper coming up the road and was startled at the transformation. They both walked with abandon; the girl had dropped her tight control of every bone, muscle and capillary in her thin body. Once, when Cooper stopped abruptly, the girl didn't have time to catch herself and she tumbled over him. Roxanne could swear they were old friends or playmates, apologising to each other. Then the black Lab bounded round Melissa's legs and dived off the side of the road to roll in the last pile of snow in a shaded spot, kicking his legs into the air. Melissa squatted next to him, staying clear of his paws that punched the air.

Roxanne watched with longing, wishing to ingest whatever it was that they had. They were happy. If anything were to happen to her, Cooper would be fine. He'd spend the rest of his life with Melissa. Everybody loved him. Tess and Isaiah treated him like a good brother. She couldn't stay here on this island for ever; her leave from the college would be over at the end of the coming summer.

Roxanne shook her head. It was the first time she'd thought about the next step, about going home and living her life without Bob, about her lonely bed, about wearing the mantle of widow . . .

Melissa and Cooper burst through the door. 'He knew you were home,' the girl said. 'He can tell. How do dogs do that? How do dogs know when you're driving home even if it's a different time each day?' She didn't wait for Roxanne to answer, but carried on: 'Their noses are like one hundred times better than ours and their eyes reflect more light than ours do, so they can see better at night, and they hear stuff at frequencies that we don't notice.'

Roxanne gave Cooper several hearty thumps on his haunches that sent him into curls of delight. 'You've been reading up on dogs.'

Melissa stuck her hands in the front pouch of her sweatshirt. 'I've been reading about animal behaviour on the Internet. It's like they have a different language, like dolphins or whales, and we only want them to know our language but we never try to speak theirs.'

The phone rang. Roxanne had been mesmerised. Not because Melissa's musings were so extraordinary, but that she was sharing them; she was thinking about something aside from calorie intake and sit-ups.

Roxanne picked up the phone. It was the post office. 'You've got a box here, from a sporting goods place.'

Roxanne tilted her head to one side. 'I didn't order anything. Must be a mistake.'

'Well, it's got your name on it. You need to come and get it.'

She hung up, frowning. Who would send her something from a sporting goods store?

Melissa headed for the door. 'I have calculus to do,' she said. Roxanne walked the girl to the deck. The girl leapt off, spread her arms wide and yelled, 'I do calculus, therefore I am.'

It was the first completely frivolous thing she had seen Melissa do. The leap was crooked and she landed awkwardly, yet she had a lightness that was untouched by the forces of gravity.

Roxanne said, 'See you later.'

Melissa turned and smiled for two seconds, then sprang off home on her young stick legs.

Roxanne took the dog and walked the mile to the post office. The package was not from the sporting goods store in Portland, but from an archery company in Nebraska. Roxanne checked the name, and, yes, it was addressed to her. The return address was unfamiliar. Hansen Bow Company, Traditional and Primitive Archery, Allen, Nebraska.

Roxanne gave the package back to the postal clerk. 'What should I do? I didn't order anything from them,' she said.

'You can send it back as long as you don't open it,' the clerk suggested.

Roxanne kept the package. She carried it under one arm and walked slowly back to the house. It was about three foot long and light for its size. She pulled the cardboard apart and unrolled a Styrofoam blanket. Within its protection was a group of arrows, the shafts deep amber, the feathers notched tight. A flier said, *These arrows are made of Osage orange and dried slowly in the open air of Nebraska.*

The arrows clattered to the table, the tips eyeing her with a husky glare.

Nebraska. What had Sam said back when he first saw the arrow in the dog? He had told her that there was a place in Minnesota and one in Nebraska where they made something like these. Liz had bought her supplies from a man in Nebraska. Someone was sending her the same arrows that Liz had used, the same type of arrow that someone had used to shoot Cooper.

Cooper. She looked over at him. He had carried his favourite stick into the house. It was about two feet long and dotted with tooth marks. He dropped it with a clatter. She immediately thought of Peter. And in the next breath another name came up.

ROXANNE PULLED IN to Hill's driveway and as soon as she turned off the ignition, her throat grew dry and her hands went cold. Her heart pounded and she could hear her pulse thundering in her left ear. If she could slow down her breathing and take deep breaths, she could regain enough control to get out of the car. She took in a large gulp of air.

Beside her was the box with arrows from Hansen's in Nebraska. She scooped up the box in one arm, opened the truck door, and walked up to Hill's house. She had never been in his house; all the lessons had taken place in his back yard.

She hadn't seen him since the day he came out to Peaks Island. He had called once and left a message but she had not returned his call. She had not erased his message either. 'Roxanne, what happened with Liz was long before you. You can't control the past, especially my past. I'd like to see what we've got here. Give me a call.'

She hesitated at the fence then stepped through the gate into the back yard. She paused a moment, then headed for the side door. And there was Hill. He stood in the doorway looking at her. 'Nothing's easy with you, is it?' he said, standing aside to let her in.

He was just home from work. He wore khaki trousers and a navy-blue sweater. It had never occurred to her that he might wear different clothes to those that he wore when he taught archery. Of course, archery was just one part of his life, and his livelihood was teaching high-school kids.

She held out the box to him. 'Did you send this to me?' Her hands shook as she passed the box to him and she knew that he noticed.

'What? Send you what? I got the clear message from you that you weren't interested. I don't need a duplicate copy of the memo. I get it.'

Roxanne wanted very much to believe him, but she could not afford to be lied to. She watched his eyes and they met her straight on. She pulled an arrow out of the cardboard box. 'These arrows are exactly the same as the one used to shoot Cooper. There are only two people who I can think of who would send these to me: you and Liz's boyfriend, and I'm not feeling too great about either option.'

Hill took the arrow from her and ran it between his thumb and forefinger. 'Before we speculate on the sender, do you mind if I admire these for about thirty seconds? These are beautiful. See that binding around the point? Deer gut. I bet this wood was cut by the same guy who made this arrow. But I didn't send these to you. Stay and tell me what's going on before you decide to bolt out of here.' He pulled out a chair and she took off her coat and sat down.

'You swear that you didn't order these and have them sent to me?'

Hill leaned against the sink and placed both palms on the edge. 'I didn't send you this,' he said, and for the first time she really believed him. 'I'd like an excuse not to read sixty essays. Why don't you stay and tell me what's happening,' he said. He pulled two Mexican beers from the fridge and set one in front of Roxanne. He slipped a knife from a drawer and cut a lime in half. Hill squeezed one lime into his beer and handed Roxanne the other half. 'Vitamin C. It's been a long winter,' he said.

'Here's what's happening. I saw one of your paper targets at Liz's old house. I didn't know it was yours until you came out to the island and tacked up one of your targets.'

She saw the flicker of surprise on his face, then he met her gaze. 'You're wondering if I'm not telling you something. If I'm lying. If I kept seeing her after that one time. If I'm a psychopathic killer.'

'Yes, and in that order. If you're the psycho guy, save that part until last.'

She clubbed down the part of her that wanted to touch the perfect half spiral of his eyebrow near the middle and follow the dark hairs up and out to the edges where they ended with soft down.

Roxanne told him about the house in Orono, and the meticulously sawn arrows that had been set aside by the carpenter and given to someone who sounded like Peter.

Then she told him about Peter finding her at the old Hamilton place, about the way she lied to him about the dog to get the address of Liz's parents. He pushed his beer away and she watched him turn into the hunter.

'You've got what he wants,' said Hill. 'He could just be waiting for the right moment. Let me help you. A guy like this is bad news.'

Roxanne stood up and drew the box of arrows towards her. She wanted to stay. She wanted to put the box down and take off her shoes and toss the keys to the truck on the table.

'When I went to Liz's house in Orono, she had one of your targets up in her back yard. That means that she hadn't forgotten you.'

Hill rubbed one hand across his face in a way that far older men do. 'I am not going to lie about this. Liz was an amazing woman, sort of like a bolt of lightning. I wish I could have known her better, but I was married and it was just not going to happen. I tossed a roll of my targets into her car when I left. Stupid, huh?'

'You wanted her to remember you, and I guess she did,' said Roxanne. 'Look, I'm glad I talked to you again.' She tucked the box under her arm. Hill might be separated, but he was still married, and Roxanne suddenly felt foolish in his kitchen.

'You don't have to go. We don't have to keep skimming the surface,' he said when he saw her grab her coat.

'Sometimes the surface is the safest place to be,' she said as she left.

ROXANNE SPENT the next week practising at the boathouse. Late on Friday afternoon she was deep into the rhythm of releasing the breath and the arrow when she heard a screech of metal against the door. Her first thought was that a tree had fallen. Had she been so engrossed with her archery practice that she hadn't noticed the wind? She went to the door and pulled on the handle, then tried to slide open the massive door. The door held fast. The last rays of daylight were filtering through the window up in the loft and she climbed the ladder and peered out. There was no sign of anyone.

This was the hour of homecoming, a time to have a hot drink, have a beer, come in from the cold time of day. Cooper was with Tess. Roxanne had dropped him off with her earlier that afternoon. Tess had looked a bit drawn and off-colour. Roxanne had said, 'You look like you're sick, Tess. Are you sure it's OK to leave Cooper with you?'

Tess kept one hand on her belly and said, 'Must have been something I ate, an out-of-season crab cake. Cooper will keep me company while I nap on the couch.'

So Tess was in no shape to come looking for her. Roxanne would have to find a way out. The window in the loft opened about four inches. She would not be able to get her head or her butt through. She went back down to search for something to prise it open a few more inches.

The building was remarkably devoid of anything but boats. She climbed the ladder again and found a kayak paddle, which she separated into two halves. She placed the fat end against the bottom edge of the window and pushed hard. She felt the window open one more inch. Encouraged, she pushed harder. The paddle slipped and met the glass full force, shattering it into tiny pieces.

'Jesus Christ!' she shouted, as she tumbled forward with the momentum of the paddle. She cleared the glass out of the sill with her boot, put on her leather gloves and hung on to the window frame, facing the building, edging her legs outside. She dropped the two floors to the ground and crunched down onto the broken glass. She straightened up and brushed the edges of her boots against a nearby tree, hoping to dislodge any glass fragments.

She rounded the corner of the building and stopped with icy awareness. Someone had wedged a piece of two-by-four against the door, effectively locking it in place. The plank was wedged so tightly that she finally had to kick it out with her foot. Roxanne ran inside the boathouse and grabbed her equipment, tossing her arrows into the quiver. Slinging the bow over her arm, she ran to the truck.

It was Peter, she was sure of it. He'd come back after weeks of silence. If she'd had any doubts, when she opened her truck door she saw a pile of neatly sawn arrow pieces stacked on her dashboard. Roxanne felt like the top of her head had opened, and the icy Atlantic water had filled her spine.

How long had it taken her to get out of the building? Night was closing in, but the sky was clear and she could still see the nearby dock.

He was bold, and somehow he knew everything. He knew where she lived and he knew that she'd gone to Liz's house in Orono and talked to the builder working there. She should have listened to Hill; Peter was not going to go away without Cooper.

She had spent about thirty minutes getting out of the boathouse. That meant Peter had a thirty-minute lead on her. He must think that he had plenty of time to get Cooper. Thankfully, though, the dog was with Tess at her house. Roxanne got in the truck and slammed the door. She fishtailed out of the gravel drive and headed to Tess's house. Once she got there she'd call Isaiah and let him know that Peter was on the island and that he had tried to trap her in the boathouse. He'd never make it off the island; they'd stop him at the ferry.

In five minutes Roxanne was in front of Tess's house. She jumped out and even before she got to the door, she saw the piece of paper attached to a clip. *Roxanne, I'm taking the big guy to your house. Feeling sick, heading to Portland.* If Tess was already gone and had left the dog, then Roxanne might be too late.

She got back in the truck and drove the two miles to her house. She passed Melissa's house and a warm, yellow light spilled from the windows. She drove on and pulled the truck as close to her house as she ever had, and was out of it before it came to a stop. She heard Cooper barking. He was still in the house, but his bark was different. Roxanne had only heard him bark with this explosive, split-open-the-sky sound on one other occasion.

'Cooper, Cooper, it's me,' she cried, as soon as her feet hit the deck. She pushed open the door. Cooper stopped barking long enough to greet her, but he was clearly alarmed. His black ruff was raised along his back and he turned his head as if he heard a sound on the ocean side of the house. He boiled up a growl that raised the fine hairs on Roxanne's arms.

What was the other sound? Roxanne turned, followed the soft noise, and pushed open the bathroom door with the tip of her shoe. Cooper faced the kitchen windows, pulling his lips up, revealing the full danger of his teeth.

Roxanne saw the small boots first, the legs folded on the floor, then she saw Tess's body up against the bathtub.

'Tess!'

She put her hand on Tess and the woman stirred immediately.

'Something's wrong,' Tess whispered. 'My stomach . . . I can't stand up, can't walk.' She squeezed out the words as if the effort would kill her.

Roxanne knelt on the linoleum floor and put one hand under the stricken woman. 'I'm going to pull you up, Tess, and get you out of the bathroom.' As soon as she put an arm round Tess's ribs, the woman shrieked, and Roxanne knew a hot orange bolt of pain had shot through the older woman. 'I'm sorry, I'm sorry, but you are not dying in the bathroom. We're going to get you out of here. I'll call Isaiah and he'll get the water ambulance.' She dragged Tess to the hardwood floor in front of the couch.

Roxanne punched in Isaiah's number as Cooper continued to bark.

'Cooper, stop. I won't be able to hear.'

After six rings, the answering machine came on and Roxanne said, 'Tess is sick and needs to get to the hospital. I'm calling nine-one-one right now.'

She hoped that the volunteer squad was home. 'We need the water ambulance immediately. Isaiah's rental house.' She hung up without offering details. She wanted to be ready for Peter if he tried to get in.

More than anything she wanted a weapon, and, despite the dog's unrelenting barking, she slipped out of the front door, did not turn on the outside light, and pulled her bow and arrows from the truck. She left the terror of the unseen behind; this fear was about Tess and the dog and losing what she had left. She wanted to see Peter, and she was convinced that he was there in the darkness. She wanted to run over him and flatten him like a can.

Back in the house, Cooper had barked so hard that foam pooled at the corners of his black mouth and his body exploded with electricity. He emitted a musky scent and his challenge of attack filled the house.

Roxanne grabbed her bow and notched an arrow. She held the bow in her left hand with the arrow pointing to the floor. The dog stopped barking for a moment and she watched him. He tilted his head to one side and listened with heightened awareness, then he growled and faced the door. Headlights bounced into the windows.

'Take it easy. It must be the fire crew. We're going to get Tess out of here.'

She pulled aside the curtains of the front door and saw a familiar outline. It was Hill, getting out of his truck. She felt a twinge of relief. At the same moment, Cooper went ballistic. Hill had parked at the far side of the drive fifty yards from the house. The dog threw himself at the door, claws digging at the wood. Yes, it was Hill. She recognised the outline of his thick hair, his coat. What was he doing here?

'Down, boy, it's a friend,' she said.

She opened the door a few inches with her right hand, blocking the opening with her body so Cooper couldn't get out. Then she grabbed him by the collar and opened the door the rest of the way. The bow in her other hand clattered awkwardly against the door frame as she stepped onto the deck.

Hill stopped when he saw Roxanne and the dog. And at the same moment Roxanne realised that Cooper had never seen Hill before. So why was the dog acting like this? Then the torrent of facts hit her. Hill was the one who knew everything because she had told him. He knew about the dog being saved, about the house in Orono, about her friend Isaiah . . . Oh God . . . Isaiah . . . he hadn't answered his phone.

'Stay there or I'll let him go!' she shouted, as Cooper strained against her.

Hill took another step and said, 'Roxanne, get inside; don't let the dog go!'

She didn't have time to pause. If he got closer, and if he had a weapon, neither of them could take Hill down. Everything was at stake. She had to do it quickly. She turned off all extraneous power routes in her body and nothing was left except the path from her brain to her arms, connected with a fibre-optic line to her eyes.

In one elongated moment she let the dog loose with her right hand, pulled the bow up with her left and pulled back with her right. She saw Hill jog to the right and her eye followed him like a missile. Breath exhaled and released. Hill dropped to the ground with a howl.

Cooper spent one moment barking on the deck, then burst off the planks. He was nearly even with Hill when the man fell to the ground. But the dog didn't stop. His muscled body lowered several inches as he ran. Roxanne had seen other dogs run like this when they were in competition, streamlining themselves like jaguars or leopards in the final moments of running down prey. But Hill wasn't the prey. Cooper ran past Hill as if he were a tree stump and straight through the thicket of brush.

Roxanne leapt off the deck, bow in hand, and came closer to Hill, keeping her legs flexed, not getting close enough to him that he could reach her. He lay in the dim light that ribboned out from the house. An arrow was embedded in his thigh and he grabbed his leg with both hands.

'Peter is out there,' he said with a grimace. 'I found out where he's been watching you. Get the hell in the house. You don't know what you're dealing with.'

Roxanne turned and looked at the place where Cooper had entered the brush. She still heard him.

She cupped her hands round her mouth. 'Cooper!'

She knew what she had to do. She took one step closer to Hill. 'I was wrong. I'm sorry and I do know what I'm dealing with.' She reached into Hill's truck and saw what she had prayed was there, his quiver of arrows. Thank God this man travelled with arrows. She hooked the bag round her left shoulder and ran into the brush, following the sound of the dog.

The darkness in the trail hummed with Cooper's musky scent. Roxanne reached for the primitive part of her brain that operated on smell. She ran as if she could see in the tangle of dark and branches. Her lungs opened wide with the call of urgency from her legs to pound faster.

Two high shrieks, and a dog's scream cracked open the blackness. Then silence. Peter had hurt Cooper! He might have killed him. The sound came from the part of the trail closest to the ocean. Roxanne stopped, notched an arrow and let her body lead the way to the last sound that Cooper had made. She no longer thundered through the brush; now she walked with soft steps, right hand on the string, arrow pulled halfway back, crouching, deadly. The wind was above her, unable to dip down into the dense tangle. She would not have to contend with the wind when she took her shot. There was nothing else but her heightened senses; she was no longer woman, but eyes, ears, nose . . . hunter.

The scent of Cooper hit her first, and now a new scent carried to her by a tendril of moist air. Peter. He was close.

A voice from her right side said, 'Drop what you're carrying or I'll give him a blast of this. And I don't think this Taser gun will mix well with the tranquilliser dart.'

Roxanne spun round and, to her horror, saw the dark outline of Cooper on the ground and Peter holding a Taser inches from the dog.

'I told you this dog was mine,' he said.

Roxanne considered her options, with Cooper's ability to withstand an assault from the Taser being her primary concern. She lowered the bow.

'Drop your little bow and arrow on the ground,' he said, and Roxanne heard a hint of pleasure in his voice, a sort of satisfaction. The bow dropped to the ground and she measured its distance from her. She could see the satisfaction that he got from bagging his prey. He would want to be noticed.

'How did you know I had him?' she started. She didn't care what the answer was; she only wanted him to talk.

'Are you kidding? I knew the day I talked with you. You were just like Liz. You thought I was stupid, didn't you? You were going to say anything to get rid of me. Didn't turn out so well for Liz either.'

He stepped closer to her and kicked the bow to the edge of the trail. Roxanne chanced a look at the dog. He was still. She prayed that Peter had not overdosed Cooper.

'He's alive. I want him alive. You and Liz aren't the only ones with silent weapons; a Taser gun is such a nice weapon. Do you know how it works? It shoots two little darts that deliver a wonderful bolt of electricity. I think it will work nicely on Cooper. This is one dog that needs to be trained. Liz wouldn't let me train him. If it wasn't for him, I'd still be with Liz.'

Roxanne willed her body to relax; she and Cooper could not afford for her to freeze into fear. 'She loved you. What happened?' she asked. Come on, she thought, I know you can't think of anything else but Liz; talk to me.

'I had got her off that medicine she was taking. I was taking care of her. She was off all that junk for six months.'

Roxanne pictured Liz without her medication for six months: moods skyrocketing and plummeting. Angry bile rose in her throat. She saw

Cooper's front feet begin to twitch. She didn't have as much time as she had hoped. 'But she died from an overdose of meds. I thought you took all her medication away,' she said.

Peter grabbed her arm securely and pulled her to the far edge of the small clearing. She judged his strength from the sharp points of pain where his fingers pressed flesh against bone. He tossed her a roll of duct tape.

'Here, bind up his feet. Tight. I don't want any more trouble from him.'

'Where are you taking him?' Roxanne knew if she kept him talking long enough, the island fire truck would arrive and Hill would tell them that she was in trouble. Then what? What would a crew of volunteer medics do?

'You think I'm leaving here on the ferry? I told you, I'm way ahead of you. Start wrapping his legs.'

Roxanne took the tape and pulled out a strip for Peter to cut with the pocketknife that he took from his jacket. She wrapped Cooper's front legs together just above his feet and prayed for him to stay dazed a bit longer.

'But how did she overdose?' Roxanne asked again.

Peter snapped open what looked like a boat bag, the kind that kayakers use to keep their gear dry. He held the stun gun beneath one arm. 'I had saved all her medicine. I kept it locked up in my truck. After she went nuts on me, after I brought her back from this island . . . that's when I said, "Here, take all this shit. You want it, then take it!" And I dumped it at her house. We all make choices and Liz made hers.'

Roxanne wrapped Cooper's legs with as much care as she dared. Peter had not noticed the quiver that she carried. She let it fall quietly beside her. With one hand, she slipped out one of the arrows.

'She was in a manic phase and you gave her six months' worth of meds and then left her? Did you give up on her? No, wait, did she give up on you?' she asked.

Peter stood over her. 'I'm telling you, if she had done everything I told her to do, she'd be here right now. "Get rid of the damn dog," I told her. No, she keeps the dog, treats him better than she treats me. When I found her on this island, she was crazy; she thought I was the devil. She ran from me. Me! I ran after her and she had her archery stuff, pointing at me. I told her, "Liz, it's me for Christ's sake!" Then the dog leaps at me. She shoots and hits the dog instead of me. Suppose I should be grateful to the dog.'

Roxanne slid the arrow partway up her jacket sleeve. She knew Peter hadn't told this saga to anyone, and it had been fermenting since the fall. Now he let his aggressive posture fall rapidly away while he talked.

'Here's what you're going to help me do. We're going to drag this dog down to the beach where I've got a boat,' he said. 'I've been slipping in and out of this island for weeks.'

No, thought Roxanne. This is all wrong; I needed someone to see us trying to leave on the ferry. I needed someone to help me. I can't do this alone. That's when she remembered Bob, sitting serenely at the bottom of the pool, waiting to be saved by her, trusting her with his life.

Peter pulled the tranquilliser dart out of the dog's back leg and slipped the bag under Cooper's hindquarters. 'Here, grab one side of this bag. We don't want our doggy to get wet on the crossing, do we? And you're coming with me, at least part way. Look like a good night for a swim?'

He crouched down and set the Taser beside him to stuff the dog into the bag. Roxanne suddenly lay back on the ground and punched hard with both legs, hitting him in the chest. He fell sideways with a shout.

She fumbled with the arrow and pulled it out of her sleeve, rolling onto her side. Peter reached for the stun gun; it was so close to him. Roxanne rose up on her knees and drew her arm back, holding the arrow inches from the point and bringing it down on Peter's hand with the full weight of her body. He screamed in shock and Roxanne grabbed the stun gun and stood up. She pointed what she hoped was the front end of the gun at him.

'I will shoot you. I've already had a very bad day, and you are not the first person I've shot today. So don't move.' She had no idea if the gun had a lock, or how it worked, but she had her fingers at what felt like a trigger.

Peter grabbed the protruding arrow with his free hand, and with a curdled howl he broke it in half. He rose up on one knee and stood up like a wrestler ready to lunge. Roxanne knew that he was coming at her and this was her last chance. And it was Cooper's last chance. She squeezed the trigger and the force of the charge from the two wires dropped him, convulsing, to the ground. With her free hand, she grabbed the bag that half-contained Cooper and dragged him onto the trail, far away from Peter.

Cooper whimpered as a light bounced round the corner of the trail. It filled Roxanne's eyes and she put her hands up to cover her face.

Melissa shouted, 'I've found them! Isaiah, I've found them! Over here!'

The sudden presence of the girl both heartened and dismayed Roxanne. She did not want her harmed if Peter recovered quickly. 'Lissa, toss me that roll of tape and then get that stuff off Cooper's legs.'

Roxanne saw Peter trying to get up and she pulled the trigger again, praying that the gun still held a charge. It did, and Peter's body jerked into spasm. She ripped an arm's length of duct tape, placed one foot on his back, grabbed one arm, then the other, and circled his wrists with the steel-grey tape. Finally, she stood up, panting and shaking, just as the sound of Isaiah's voice, calling her name, boomed along the trail.

Chapter 10

The ride to the mainland in the water ambulance was harrowing but brief. Tess and Hill were wrapped in thermal blankets and strapped to stretchers. Two volunteer fire-fighters sat on Peter, while Isaiah kept his arm round Roxanne, who could not stop shivering. She was keenly aware of how small the boat was compared to the rumbling ferry. Every time it hit the top of a wave, she felt a jolt from her tailbone to her head. There was at least some comfort in the fact that Melissa and her mother were back at Roxanne's house with Cooper, and they had promised to call Sam Reynolds to see if the dog would need medical attention after his ordeal.

As they pulled into the Portland dock, two police cars waited to take Peter away and an ambulance waited with the rear doors open to take Hill and Tess to the hospital. As it pulled away, Roxanne impatiently answered the police officer's questions, with Isaiah urging her to report every detail about Peter.

'We'll get to the hospital, but let's make sure Peter's stalking days are over first,' he said.

By the time they arrived at the hospital, Tess was being prepped and sedated for emergency surgery. Pre-op medication appeared to have relieved Tess of the intensity of her pain. She grabbed Roxanne's sleeve.

'I might as well tell you, Roxanne; I've got cancer. I've known for months. It's been setting up shop in my abdomen. You'd better call Len; he understands hospitals and their language. His phone number is in the address book in my bag. He'll call the children.' Tess's eyes were dreamy with medication.

'What! What do you mean, cancer? You're not dying, are you?' cried Roxanne, as she collapsed in tears. Tess disappeared behind the automatic doors leading to the surgery unit.

Len did not live far from the hospital and was there in fifteen minutes.

Isaiah had checked in on Hill, who was asking for Roxanne. 'He can wait,' she insisted. 'He's not dying, and I can only attend to one disaster at a time.'

Roxanne had never met Len before. She did not expect the tall, handsome man with the searing blue eyes. He moved easily in the hospital and was able to get a report from an obliging nurse. Tess had a ruptured appendix. Len shook his head. 'The doctor said that she must have suffered with an inflamed appendix for weeks, even months. If she had just come in to be examined, they could have figured this out in fifteen minutes. Instead, her appendix ruptured.'

Roxanne said, 'So she doesn't have cancer? She's going to live?'

'Cancer? Where did she get that idea? Did she think she was dying? And she wasn't going to tell me?' Len's eyes registered anger, but Roxanne knew that the emotion was layered thick with years and that anger was just the surface.

Roxanne reached for his hand. 'Maybe it was one of those synaesthesia things; maybe she thought she saw something. Maybe it was green or shaped funny or made a sound that the rest of us couldn't hear. But is she going to be OK?'

He squeezed her hand in return and sighed, relief pouring off him. 'Yes. There's the infection to deal with, and the surgery, but she'll recover.'

'I've got one more emergency to handle. Will you excuse me?' asked Roxanne. She located Hill's room as he waited for surgery. An IV bag hung by his side and, just as Roxanne walked in, a man in blue scrubs injected something into the line. 'This should relax you. We'll come and get you in fifteen minutes, as soon as the last surgery is cleared out.'

Hill looked up at her and said, 'You're not going to shoot me again, are you?' He held out his hand to Roxanne as she came closer to him. 'This is going to score so many points with my students in B period English. We're studying *Beowulf*, and I brought a few bows to school for them to try. They're going to love this.'

'What in the world were you doing on the island?' asked Roxanne. She sat next to the gurney and took his hand in hers.

'You had a very bad guy out there. I was hunting the bad guy.' He smiled his crooked smile. 'But the bad guy didn't know who he was up against. I'm not sure you needed me.'

Roxanne lifted his hand to her mouth and pressed her lips to his palm. 'Not true; not true at all,' she whispered.

TESS DID NOT RETURN to the island until March, after spending weeks recuperating at her daughter's home.

Roxanne was thrilled to have Tess back again, as if everyone was finally settled in the right place. It was an unseasonably warm day and Roxanne followed Tess's instructions about uncovering her crocuses from the winter debris so they could emerge unfettered. Tess watched her from a chair placed next to the garden. Cooper assisted by digging his own spot in the garden, until Roxanne made him stop by throwing a stick for him.

'Come inside. I'm done with your garden work. I've got some of Melissa's photos to show you,' said Roxanne.

Melissa had joined the photography club and Cooper was her number-one subject. Whenever Roxanne noticed Melissa these days, a girl named Chris was with her. The two girls carried their cameras everywhere.

Roxanne spread the photos of Cooper on the coffee table for Tess to see, but no sooner had Tess curled in her overstuffed chair than she dozed off. Roxanne picked up one of the photos of Cooper. In this one he was looking noble, offering the camera his best senatorial profile. And here, in this one, Cooper and Tess were sitting on the deck and he had one mighty paw on her foot. And in this one, Melissa caught him in midflight, back legs extended, head driving forward, all for the glory of catching a tennis ball. There was not a hint of sadness in any of the photos. Where had it gone?

Roxanne had gone over the scene again and again, knowing only snippets from the police report, filling in the rest with conjectures: Liz's sleep-deprived psychosis, her full-out non-medicated mania, fleeing an obsessive boyfriend. Liz must have bought the old Hamilton place as a refuge, and for a brief moment in time it was, until the unexpected arrival of Peter.

Shouldn't Liz have known that Cooper would try to protect her? Liz would have faltered for a second, as she stood with her weapon, doubting her own perceptions, doubting the danger. The dog had leapt, following Peter's scent, had leapt as high as he dared, to pull the man down, and Liz, at that very moment, had pulled back on her bow and taken her shot. Liz had plucked her own dog from the air.

Peter would not tell the police exactly how he had dragged Liz from the island. He did say that he told her over and over again that she had killed her dog. Roxanne pictured the last days of Liz's life in Orono: the fragile structure of her mind unravelling when Peter had left her at her house after tossing her bottles of stored medication at her. It would not have taken Liz long to die by her own hand.

Roxanne nudged Cooper with her foot. 'Come on, you. Let's go home.' She slipped quietly out of Tess's house. Her job still called and she had an important delivery to make today. But Cooper needed to go home first and she needed lunch.

As soon as Roxanne and Cooper entered the house, Peterson began her new game of pouncing at the dog's tail and then dashing off. Cooper eyed her with the same level of interest as one might have for a fly. Yet, just last night, Roxanne noticed that Peterson had wedged herself behind Cooper as he lay gnawing on a stick. Cooper had peered over his backside, as the once-skittish cat curled against him, and eyed her with surprise.

Roxanne made a ham-and-cheese sandwich and considered two letters that sat on her counter. One was from her boss at the university, asking her to verify her return date in the fall. The other was from Jan Townsend, who said they were coming out to the island soon to look at the house that was part of Liz's estate. Did Roxanne know anyone on the island who might have an interest in buying the place? The letters jostled for her attention. Roxanne turned them face down on the counter and placed her used plate on top of them. Not yet; she didn't have to decide anything yet. Right now she was still an animal control warden.

Ten days ago, a tomcat had been discovered on the east side of the island, reported by a neighbour who had said, 'He's not exactly feral, but he's darn close. Guess you'd better come and get him before he starves to death.'

Roxanne had easily trapped the cat, which was black with three white paws and a white diamond on his face. He hissed at her each time she came near. She waited twenty-four hours in case anyone called about a lost cat, then took him to the animal shelter in Portland.

Yesterday, she had received a call. 'This is Mrs Hancock. My cat has been missing. He usually comes back after three days, but I'm afraid something has happened to him. He's black with white paws.'

Roxanne rang up the shelter, fearing that the unclaimed tom might have been put down.

The receptionist said, 'You're not going to believe this. We made a mistake and put him on the schedule for neutering. He's here. Do you hear that sound? He's not a happy boy. I'll send someone down to the pier with him tomorrow.'

The next morning, Roxanne took the ferry over and was met at the pier by one of the shelter volunteers with a cat carrier. She got back on the same ferry for the return trip and delivered the cat to Mrs Hancock.

Roxanne explained his shaved abdomen, with apologies. The women stroked him and the cat purred like an outboard motor.

'I know he's ugly. I'm not blind. But I don't know what I would do without him. There's no explanation for love. But it's all that matters, isn't it?'

Roxanne felt her body rearrange itself; her bones slid into their sockets in a slightly different way, and a chunk of asphalt lifted off her heart. In its place, a space opened up that had been reserved only for Bob.

She left the reunited cat and its owner and drove home to get Cooper. They were going to visit Hill.

AT LAST, A PACK OF HIS OWN. With the First One, Liz, they had been a majestic pair and he had steadied her wild course. But they were cut off from others, isolated. Who could say why he had not been able to save her?

He felt the formation of his pack grow daily. The cat pressing against his backside, the New One settling into this place muscle by muscle, the girl eating bits of food, the Old One healing from the injury within her. And the others who circle his pack with the watchful eyes of friends: the man with the limp who looks at the New One with longing, or the old dark man who stands sentinel over the island.

But in this life, he is dog. His life is ocean, stick, ball, sand, grass, ride in the truck, sleep by the bed, look deep into the eyes of humans, lure them outdoors, greet them with a burst of joy when they come home, love them. Fill this brief life with more. And more.

JACQUELINE SHEEHAN

Home: Massachusetts, USA
Profession: psychologist
Website: www.jacquelinesheehan.com

RD: What inspired you to write *Lost & Found*?
JS: *Lost & Found* is a profound departure from my first book, *Truth*, a novel about Sojourner Truth, the courageous nineteenth-century slave and abolitionist. It took five years to write *Truth* and during this time period, I periodically took breaks from my historical novel to give voice to the flawed and irreverent Roxanne and thus the character for *Lost & Found* was born.

RD: Is the book autobiographical?
JS: No and yes. No, because it's fictional, and, yes, because Roxanne is a psychologist and so am I. *Truth* required that I dive into another culture, another time. I wanted Roxanne to come primarily from my own experiences and from our contemporary world. Yes, I was once a lifeguard, but only for one summer and I wasn't a terribly good one. And, yes, I was called on to perform CPR and the victim did not survive. And, yes, I have known and loved two of the most extraordinary dogs, both of whom would have stood in front of a speeding train to save the ones they loved.

RD: Have you had experiences of death that influenced the way you wrote about the tragic loss in Roxanne's life?
JS: When I was nine years old, my father died from a massive heart attack. People didn't talk much about the impact of loss back then. He died in mid-June and I don't recall the summer at all except that the sky was constantly grey. Back at school, I selected to study Edgar Allan Poe and spent the year reading everything he ever wrote. He understood losing someone to the thief of death and he took grief to the furthest, most macabre level in his writing. His mother died when he was two years old and his father before that. He brooded over the mystery of death and I brooded with him.

RD: Do you feel you've since found other ways to deal with grief?
There are infinite ways of dealing with grief. My ex-husband was killed in a motor-cycle accident while I was writing *Lost & Found*. I knew immediately what I had to do. I took a dear friend to a bar and ordered shots of Jack Daniel's and a cigar. These were potent symbols of my former spouse and I felt connected to him as I rolled the smoke in my mouth and the Jack Daniel's scorched my throat and belly. Roxanne's

reaction to her husband's death tells us just how far off centre she has blown.

RD: Will you tell us about the two extraordinary dogs you have known?

JS: I met the first one when I was twenty-five and living in Chicago, working with street kids. Poncho was a golden retriever, and I could walk anywhere in Chicago, at any time of day or night, and feel safe if I had him with me. Once, in a deserted industrial area of the city, a man suddenly appeared out of the shadows. Poncho lunged at him, growling and displaying every impressive fang. The man fled and Poncho covered his fangs with his golden retriever smile. This dog never bit anyone, but I knew that if he had to, he would. Poncho was my companion in Chicago, my hiking partner in Oregon, and in his old age, my pal for exploring the high desert arroyos of New Mexico. The second exceptional dog belonged to my sister. He was a barrel-chested black Labrador named Spud and he played soccer amazingly well with my three nephews. As he matured, he exhibited what I could only call a heroic personality. He never fought with other dogs, he calmed them.

RD: Did you set out to make a dog into a major character in *Lost & Found*?

JS: In my stories, animals are a presence and a personality. They are a part of the plot. But did I imagine that the dog would take such a front and centre role? Absolutely not. Much as dogs do in real life, this dog walked brazenly into my novel and persistently revealed his personality until I paid attention.

TECHNICOLOUR SOUND AND VISION

The rare condition of synaesthesia occurs when a person perceives the world through an unusual union of the senses. He or she may taste a sound, or associate a letter of the alphabet with a certain colour, or experience an emotion as a colour. In *Lost & Found*, Tess sees numbers as colours, and she interprets pain in shades of red and orange.

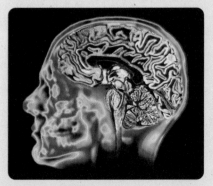

Synaesthetes are often creative thinkers and a number of creative people have admitted to being synaesthetics, among them artist David Hockney, composer Oliver Messaien and novelist Vladimir Nabokov.

Developments in neuroscience and MRI scans (pictured) have furthered psychologists' understanding of the condition and shed new light upon how the brain constructs our experience of the world around us.

JAMES HOLLAND

THE ODIN MISSION

Sergeant Jack Tanner of the King's Own
Yorkshire Regiment knows that he and
his men are ill-equipped for the icy
mountains above Lillehammer.
They have little ammunition or food, and
the Luftwaffe can easily spot their uniforms
against the snow. Yet the small patrol is
about to embark on a dangerous and vital
mission—one that's going to need all
Tanner's courage and ingenuity
if it is to succeed.

1

Thursday, April 18, 1940. The German invasion of Norway was nine days old, but in that time the small Norwegian village of Økset had seen little sign of the disaster that faced their peace-loving nation—a few aircraft overhead, that had been all. Indeed, Stig Andvard had listened to the unfolding news on his wireless with a feeling of mounting unreality. Swastikas now flew over the capital, Oslo. The King and Government had fled—God only knew where to, but His Majesty's voice could still be heard crackling over the airwaves. A number of lads from the village had responded to the general mobilisation and had hurried off to Elverum to join their army units. Where were they now? Still fighting, or prisoners of the Germans? Norwegian resistance in the south was crumbling, that much was obvious, but to the north, British troops had landed at Namsos and the Royal Navy had sunk a number of German warships.

These cataclysmic events all seemed so far away. On his farm, Stig still had his pigs to feed, his cows to milk and his sheep to watch. He had still drunk beer in the bar the past two Wednesdays, just as before. During the nine days since the lads had left, life had continued with the same unwavering regularity that Stig had always known.

In the valley, patches of grey grass were beginning to emerge through the snow, but the landscape was still monochrome, as it often was in April. Spring: a curious time of year, when the days were long and light, with barely more than three hours of darkness, but the ground remained stuck in winter, as though it had yet to catch up with the sun.

That morning, however, as Stig dropped in the slops to the pigs, he heard a distant, dull thud from the south, followed by further muffled crumps. He stomped inside to find his wife. 'Guns,' he said to her. 'From Elverum.'

Agnes put her hands to her mouth. 'My God,' she said. 'Do you think they'll come here? What are we going to do?'

Stig shrugged. 'It's only a little village. What do the Germans want with a place like this? Try to keep calm.'

In truth he had no idea what they should do. He wondered whether he ought to walk into the village to see what everyone else was planning, then dismissed the idea. What would anyone else know? He glanced briefly at Agnes and could see that she was looking to him for guidance. The sound of detonations and explosions from the south was becoming louder and more persistent.

What to do for the best? Stay, or pack up the truck and head north? He went over to the shed and opened the bonnet, checked the oil and fuel levels, and that the plugs and points were clean. Slamming the bonnet down, he sighed and strode back across the yard to the farmhouse, into the kitchen. He sat down at the table and drummed his fingers on the ageing pine.

'I'm going to fetch Anton,' said Agnes, after a few moments' silence.

Stig nodded. Their second son was still at school in the village. As she was taking off her apron, he said, 'We'll stay put. Stick together. They won't want anything with us.' Agnes looked at him and then left.

Stig tried to pretend that all would be well, but he had read reports of the fighting in Poland. The newspapers had printed pictures of burning villages. Polish resistance had been brushed aside and he hated to think what had happened to the people. Agnes returned with Anton, and Nils, their elder son, came back from the wood, where he had been sawing pine into logs. 'I want all of you to stay near the house,' Stig told them.

At lunch, they sat round the kitchen table, saying and eating little. Stig toyed with his soup and eventually pushed the bowl away. He went out into the barn where he hoped the banging of his hammer would deafen the sound of battle nine kilometres to the south.

Anton fetched him early in the afternoon. 'Henrik's here, Papa,' he said, 'with some men.'

They were standing in the kitchen when Stig entered—five of them.

'Forgive the intrusion,' his cousin, Henrik Larsen, said, clasping Stig's hand firmly, 'but I'm afraid we need your help.'

'Of course.' Stig looked at the other men. All wore the grey-blue serge greatcoats of the Norwegian Army. Their large green canvas haversacks were piled in the corner, along with their rifles. One of the men stepped forward. There was a gold band round the kepi he clutched in his left hand.

'Forgive us,' he said. 'I am Colonel Peder Gulbrand of His Majesty the King's Guard. We urgently need to head north, but unfortunately our car broke down some kilometres to the south.' He was, Stig guessed, in his early forties. The colonel looked exhausted—they all did. Stig glanced at them again. A lieutenant of perhaps thirty, and another younger officer, like Henrik. The fifth man was older, with round spectacles and a dark moustache flecked with grey. Stig noticed he was not wearing a tunic under his greatcoat, like the others, but a rollneck sweater and woollen jacket. Colonel Gulbrand said hastily, 'Please believe me when I tell you our mission is a vital one and undertaken at the direct request of King Håkon.'

Stig nodded. 'You've come from Elverum?'

'Yes. The town will be in German hands by evening.' Colonel Gulbrand looked at Stig, then at his watch.

'I've a truck out the back,' Stig told him. 'You take it. I checked it this morning. The tank is full and I've some spare cans of petrol you can have.'

'I can't thank you enough,' replied the colonel.

'Have you time for some soup and bread?' Stig asked him.

'Thank you,' said Gulbrand. 'God knows we could do with something.'

Agnes had already put the soup and a coffee pot on the range.

'Nils, go and get the fuel from the shed and put it into the truck.'

Nils hurried out and Stig ushered the men to sit down. As they did so, Gulbrand said, 'I think you were intending to use the truck yourself.'

'I had thought about it,' said Stig. 'But I decided we must stay.'

The colonel smiled. 'Even so, I appreciate what you're doing.'

'We must all do what we can,' said Stig. He turned to his cousin. 'Where are Else and little Helena? Are they safe?'

Larsen nodded. 'In Oslo still. I hope so. It's been difficult . . .'

The soup had barely been set on the table when Nils rushed into the kitchen. 'The Germans are coming!' he exclaimed, pointing wildly towards the road.

The men stood up. 'How far?' Gulbrand asked him.

'Half a kilometre,' Nils replied. 'Two trucks full of men and a car out front.'

'Quick,' said Gulbrand, 'to the truck.' The men grabbed their packs and rifles, but Stig said, 'I don't think you'll make it. They're too close. Let me hide you. Perhaps they'll go on through the village. Then you can head back to the bridge.'

Gulbrand peered through the window and nodded. 'All right.'

Stig led them through the house and out of the back, then across a patch of packed snow to the barn, where the cows still sheltered. The animals shuffled nervously as the men made their way up a dusty ladder to the floor above. The upper deck of the barn was filled at one end with a stack of hay. 'Get under that,' Stig told them. The men did as they were bidden just as the sound of the trucks reached the barn from the road. As Stig covered the men, he heard muffled shouts in German and felt his heart quicken. He hurried down the ladder and stepped out into the yard once more. Not more than forty metres away, several German troops were clambering out of a grey-painted Opel truck and running over to an officer who stood a little way from his staff car. The remainder—some thirty in all, Stig guessed—waited in the two lorries, the tips of their rifles pointed skyward.

'You!' shouted the officer. 'Come here!'

Stig walked towards him, praying Agnes and the boys had cleared away any sign of the five men. The officer stared at him.

'Who lives here?' the German asked, in fluent Norwegian.

'Myself and my family.' Stig looked at the implacable face.

'Have you seen any Norwegian troops?'

Stig shook his head. He felt a bead of sweat run down his back.

'Show me around. If you're telling the truth you have nothing to fear.'

Stig led the way, his heart thumping, to the house, then opened the door. The officer ordered his men to start their search.

'Where are your family?' he asked.

'Probably in the kitchen. It's where I left them.'

'What do you mean?'

'After lunch,' Stig said quickly.

The officer studied him. 'You seem nervous.'

'We're not used to having troops here. All these weapons . . .'

The German's eyes bored into him. 'Continue the guided tour.'

Stig led him to the kitchen where Agnes and the two boys stood anxiously beyond the bare table. Stig walked over and stood beside his family. The officer found the door to the cellar. He shouted to his men, who were checking upstairs, the sound of heavy feet clonking loudly through the timber boards. Two appeared soon after and went down into the cellar. They found nothing.

'Outside now,' the officer said, and Stig followed.

'I've a couple of sheds and a barn,' said Stig. 'Nothing more.'

'You have a truck,' said the German. 'We might need that.'

Stig's heart sank, but the officer was now looking at the barn.

ABOVE, HENRIK LARSEN had his face pressed against the floorboards. Through the tiniest crack he could see Stig leading the German troops into the barn. He could feel his heart pounding.

'And what have you got up there?' the German officer was asking Stig.

'A few stores. The remnants of last year's hay,' Stig replied.

Larsen watched as the officer stared up at the floorboards above, so that it seemed to him that the German was staring straight at him from under his peaked field cap with its curious flower embroidered on the side. Larsen tensed as he watched the officer unfasten his holster and remove his pistol. By God he felt hot under the hay, in his thick tunic and greatcoat. He could feel the sweat running down either side of his face. Fighting off a desperate urge to wipe his brow, he remained still. Stig, he could see, was terrified: his eyes were darting from one man to another, and he swallowed repeatedly. Come on, Stig, he thought. Don't go and get yourself killed.

The other soldiers were also looking upwards, their rifles at the ready, as the officer began purposefully climbing the rungs on the ladder. Moments later, he heard the man clamber out onto the floorboards beside them. There was a clatter as he moved something out of his way, and then Larsen heard movement in the hay to his left. Closing his eyes, he heard the German cock his pistol. An earthshattering crack jolted him as a shot rang out. But instead of feeling any pain, he was aware of the officer laughing. 'You have one less rat in your barn,' he called out to Stig.

AFTER THAT THE GERMANS LEFT, but it was not until the trucks and the car had moved on and Stig had crept back up the ladder that any of them spoke.

'They're searching the village,' Stig told them, and one by one the men stood up and dusted themselves down. 'They won't be able to see you— there's a bend in the road between us, the church and the rest of the houses.'

Colonel Gulbrand clasped Stig's hand. 'Thank you,' he said. 'I shall make sure the King hears of what you have done for us.'

Stig smiled, his earlier terror receding. 'Head back a couple of hundred metres, then cross the bridge over the Glåma,' he told Gulbrand. 'The road along the valley leads northwest and it's clear of snow.'

The men hurried out of the barn to the truck. Throwing their packs into the back first, the younger guardsmen clambered in, while Gulbrand and the curious bespectacled man jumped into the cab. Stig looked up at Larsen. 'Good luck,' he said.

'Stig, thank you,' Larsen replied. 'Take good care of yourself.' He gripped the side of the truck as they turned out onto the road. As Stig had assured them, there was no sign of the Germans. Larsen glanced back to the farmhouse one last time and saw his cousin wave.

Gulbrand turned the truck across the bridge, then right onto the valley road. On the other side of the Glåma River the village drifted into view between the trees. Larsen could see the German trucks by the church, and a dull ache churned in his belly. Surely, he thought, they would be spotted.

A sickening feeling washed over him as it dawned on him that his cousin would be in trouble. The Germans would return to the farm, find the truck gone and put two and two together. Jesus, he thought. What have I done?

They had not driven more than a dozen metres when two Messerschmitt 110s were bearing down on them. Rows of bullets spat up lumps of soil behind them before catching up with the pick-up truck, smashing one of the headlights from the front wings and puncturing the bonnet. They watched the two fighters roar onwards, then bank and turn.

Gulbrand pulled over into the side of the road. 'Out! Quick!' he shouted.

Grabbing their rucksacks, they leapt out and ran into the dense pine forest that rose high above the valley. This time Larsen heard the clatter of machine-gun bullets before the roar of the aircrafts' twin engines. Pressing his head into the snow, he felt an explosion as the truck exploded in a ball of flame. Shards of glass and metal rained through the trees. Larsen glanced at the colonel and saw him almost smothering the civilian, Hening Sandvold.

'Anyone hurt?' called Gulbrand. No one was. 'Good.' He pulled out a map. 'We'll climb into the mountains, then cut across and join a road here.' He pointed.

Larsen hauled himself up beside the colonel. 'You knew they'd come back for Stig.'

'It was inevitable,' he said. 'He's a strong man, though. I'm sure he'll come through.'

Larsen smiled weakly, then continued scrambling up into the mountains.

But Stig Andvard was already dead. The Germans had seen the pick-up speeding along the far side of the valley. When they returned to the farm and found the truck had gone, Hauptmann Wolf Zellner, in his fury at being duped by a mere farmer, had taken out his pistol and shot Stig in the head.

MORE THAN 250 miles away, a British Royal Navy light cruiser steamed across the North Sea towards the Norwegian coast. There was a moderate swell, enough to ensure that HMS *Pericles* pitched and rolled with gusto as she carved her way through the grey-green sea. Below decks, soldiers lay in their bunks, pallid and groaning. The stench of vomit was overwhelming.

It was why one soldier was on the main deck. An experienced sailor, he'd had no seasickness and had stepped out into the bracing North Sea air.

Sergeant Jack Tanner stood a little over six foot tall, with broad shoulders and dark skin from years of being baked in a hot sun. Dark brown hair and brows accentuated his pale blue eyes, from which spread the lines of crow's-feet. His nose was narrow but slightly askew, broken several times over the years. Otherwise his face was as yet largely unlined—although he was still only twenty-four, the overall impression he gave was of someone several years older.

Three cream chevrons on either arm marked his rank, while above, at the top of the sleeve, was a black tab with 'Yorks Rangers' written in green. It was a regimental marking idiosyncratic to all three battalions of the King's Own Yorkshire Rangers, and a distinction the sergeant still felt proud to wear after eight years. The Rangers had had a long history, having fought from Africa to Asia to the Americas in numerous campaigns, and Tanner was glad to be part of that. It gave him a sense of purpose and belonging.

He had assumed that once his leave was over, he would be returning to Palestine, where his regiment, the 2nd Battalion, was still based, but he had been told that the 5th Battalion needed experienced men and had been packed off to Leeds to join them. He had been distraught to leave behind many good friends but it was also a matter of pride. The 5th Battalion were Territorials, barely more than poorly trained part-timers.

In the six weeks he had been with them, he had not seen much to alter that view. Most of the men in his platoon were decent lads, but the majority were from impoverished families living in the industrial cities of Leeds and Bradford. They lacked the stamina and fitness he was used to with the regulars. Lieutenant Dingwall, his platoon commander, had been a solicitor in Ripon before the war and although harmless enough he could barely read a map, let alone fell a man from 500 yards. Tanner knew the subaltern inspired little confidence, yet now they were heading off to war, and it was Tanner's job to keep them alive and help to make them into an effective fighting unit.

He looked out at the ships of their small force steaming with *Pericles*. No more than 200 yards away the transport ship, *Sirius*, carried the battalion's artillery, motor transport and much of their ammunition and other equipment. He would have liked to know whose idea it had been to put so much of their equipment onto one ship. 'Bloody idiots,' he muttered.

In fact, he had begun to doubt whether anyone in the entire army, let alone 148th Brigade, had much idea about what they were doing. Since leaving Leeds, they had boarded three different ships, loading and unloading their equipment on each occasion. Chaos had ensued. Kit had been lost and mixed up with that of the Sherwood Foresters and Leicesters, who were also part of the brigade, while once they had even set sail before turning and heading back to port. Nobody seemed to know why. It had been universally agreed that the top brass needed their heads examining. This was no way to fight a war.

Even when they had finally set sail early the previous morning, the battalion had been horribly mixed up: two companies and HQ Company on *Pericles*, and one each on the other two cruisers, along with the Foresters and Leicesters. Worst of all, no attempt seemed to have been made to split up their heavy equipment. 'Bloody idiots,' he said again, shaking his head.

'You all right, Sarge?' Corporal Sykes was standing beside him, cupping his hands as he tried to light a cigarette.

'Yes, thanks, Stan. Not so much of a croaker now?'

'Think I'll pull through. The smell down there's bloody terrible.'

'Why do you think I'm standing out here?' Tanner grinned, just as the ship pitched again. Then, out of the corner of his eye, he spotted a trail of white rushing across the surface towards *Sirius*.

'Jesus!' he said, shaking Sykes's shoulder. 'That's a bloody torpedo!'

Across the 200-yard stretch of water, the men on board *Sirius* had also seen the missile, their frantic shouts carrying over the grey sea. Both Tanner and Sykes watched in silence as the torpedo reached the vessel. A split-second pause, then a deafening explosion. A huge tower of water erupted into the sky, followed moments later by a second detonation. Suddenly the ship was engulfed in flames and oily black smoke.

The *Pericles* began to turn away rapidly, tilting hard to avoid the U-boat that must still be lurking below. Tanner and Sykes lost their footing but grabbed the railings and watched as *Sirius* groaned in agony. She was now dead in the water. Men hurled themselves into the ice-cold sea. Then, with a haunting wail of tearing metal, *Sirius* split in two. The stern went under first, sliding beneath the waves, but the prow took longer, the bow pointing almost vertically into the sky before gently sinking out of view. It had taken a little under four minutes.

'How are we expected to fight the Jerries now, Sarge?' asked Sykes.

Tanner rubbed his brow. 'I don't know, Stan. I really don't know.'

A DORNIER ROARED overhead, so startlingly low that Tanner ducked involuntarily. It was unnerving to think that German aircrew were just 100 feet above him, and hurtling ever further behind Allied lines.

'Cocky bastards,' he said, turning to Private Hepworth.

'When are we going to get some aircraft, Sarge?' Hepworth asked. 'I don't think I've seen a single one of ours since we got here.'

'God knows,' replied Tanner. 'But these jokers seem to do what they like. They must be able to see our every move.' He opened the door of the truck and jumped into the cab, Hepworth following. 'Now,' he said, to himself as much as to Hepworth, 'let's try to get this thing started.' It was a dark blue Renault, standing in a yard behind a butcher's shop in Lillehammer. He found the choke and the ignition switch, turned the switch clockwise, then located a starter button in the footwell. Pressing it down with his boot, he was relieved to hear the engine wheeze into life. The dials on the dashboard flickered: a quarter of a tank of fuel. It was better than nothing.

Tanner ground the gear-stick into reverse, and was inching back when he became aware of a middle-aged man running towards him, waving angrily.

'Hey! That is my truck,' the man shouted in English. 'What do you think you are doing?'

'Sorry,' Tanner yelled back, 'but I'm requisitioning it. We need it to help defend your country.' He sped past the man, out into the street. 'Poor bastard. We should have our own damned trucks. It's bloody chaos here, Hep. Absolute bloody chaos.'

Not that it showed on the streets of Lillehammer that Monday morning, April 22. Barely a soul stirred as Tanner drove through the deserted town to a warehouse next to the railway station. Two platoons from B Company had been unloading stores since shortly after midnight. Piles were still strewn along the platform and in the yard, waiting to be taken away.

As Tanner came to a halt, the quartermaster, Captain Webb, strode over. 'Ah, there you are, Sergeant. Where the hell have you been?'

'We were as quick as we could be, sir. There're not many trucks about, though. We could start taking cars, perhaps.'

The quartermaster sighed. 'Let's get this loaded first. The sooner we can get it going, the sooner it can come back for another trip.'

Another German aircraft thundered over. 'Bastards!' shouted Captain Webb, shaking his fist.

Tanner called over some men and they began loading the truck with boxes of ammunition, grenades and two-inch mortars. When it was full,

Tanner took the opportunity to sit down on a wooden crate of grenades until another lorry returned. He rubbed his hands together. It was cold but not freezing in the town. He was exhausted. Neither he nor any of the men had slept more than a few hours since they'd landed nearly four days before.

Orders, counter-orders and confusion had dogged them every step of the way. He supposed that someone somewhere knew what the hell was going on, but if they did, it certainly hadn't percolated down the ranks.

Tanner lit a cigarette and rubbed his eyes. He was gripped by a sense of impending doom: that they had come to this cold, mountainous country, still white with snow, completely unprepared. What a disaster the sinking of *Sirius* had been. Trucks, armoured cars, ammunition, guns, mortars, rations—not to mention their kitbags—all now lay at the bottom of the North Sea. Three infantry battalions were fighting with nearly half their equipment gone. It wasn't a problem the enemy appeared to share.

Sykes was walking towards him. 'Here,' said Tanner, offering him a smoke, 'take a pew for a minute.'

'Cheers, Sarge,' said Sykes, sitting down beside him on a box of Bren magazines. 'Fiasco this, isn't it?'

'Too right.' It was now nearly thirty-six hours since they had reached Lillehammer Station. Tanner winced as he thought of their arrival. Exhausted men had stumbled off the train, and loaded with the kit of their full marching order they had begun banging into one another. For a while they had stood on the platform wearing dazed expressions, stamping their feet against the cold. What pained him most, though, was seeing Brigadier Morgan, commander of 148th Brigade, and the Norwegian commander, General Ruge, watching. With a stiff, high-collared, blue-green tunic, pantaloons and black cavalry boots, Ruge had looked like a relic from the Great War. His disappointment at seeing such a tired and poorly equipped bunch of troops had been obvious. It had been humiliating.

'I'm wondering what the hell we're playing at here,' Tanner muttered. 'I mean, the entire battalion's mixed up and no one knows what the hell is going on except that we're getting a pasting. Why on earth we ever bothered trying to help the Norwegians, I don't know. Did you see them last night?'

'Not exactly inspiring, Sarge.'

'That's an understatement. I saw one machine-gun team, but otherwise I didn't see a single man carrying anything bigger than a rifle.' And as the Norwegians had trudged back, so the Rangers' C Company had been sent forward to reinforce A Company to the south of Lillehammer. Tanner had watched them head off towards the fray. Aircraft, like black insects, had swirled over the lake to the south. Smoke had pitched into the sky. Explosions, some muffled, some sharp, had resounded up the valley. By the time dusk began to fall, the remains of A Company had been streaming back to Lillehammer too. Since then news had been scarce. With no radios, each company had been depending on civilian telephone lines; they had been cut.

As darkness had fallen, a sense of defeat had hung heavy over the town. Just after midnight, General Ruge had ordered withdrawal to a position a mile north of Lillehammer. The stores that Tanner and the rest of Four Platoon had spent an entire day unloading were to be moved to the new position with all urgency. That had been nine hours ago, and still boxes lay stacked in front of the warehouse and along the platform. Sykes flicked his cigarette clear of them, then said, 'Better see where the rest of the boys are.' He stood up and walked off.

Tanner rubbed his eyes again. Lillehammer lay perched on the lower slopes overlooking Lake Mjøsa. It was a grey day, but above the high, steep outcrop known as the Balberg, there was a patch of blue. Smoke still rose into the sky from the south and Tanner peered up at the town, prettily snug against the mountain, and wondered how long it would stay that way once the Luftwaffe were bombing the place. Stretching away above, the mountains were covered with snow-clad pines. The whole country, it seemed, was the same: deep U-shaped valleys, wide rivers and mountains. He had fought in mountains before, in the North-West Frontier between India and Afghanistan, but those had been jagged, dry and dusty.

Another German aircraft thundered over, then banked in a wide arc across the northern end of the lake. Tanner tried to remember his aircraft recognition chart—a Junkers 88, he was sure of it.

Hepworth brought over a mug of tea. 'There you go, Sarge,' he said. 'Feels like they're toying with us, don't it?'

'Recce planes,' said Tanner. 'Making sure they have a damn good look before they start up again.' He took a sip of tea. 'Great char, this, Hep.'

A car pulled into the yard and Lieutenant Dingwall stepped out. A thin-faced man in his mid-twenties, he strode over to Tanner, his face ashen.

'Grim news, I'm afraid. Looks like most of D Company's had it. The Norwegians had promised transport to get them out, but apparently it never showed up. We're hoping most are PoWs, but we've had no contact from Company HQ since the early hours and Jerry's only just south of the town. My God, you can hardly believe it, can you? We watched them march off last night, and they've gone—a whole bloody company, devoured . . .'

'Best not to think too much about it, sir,' said Tanner.

'No . . . no, you're quite right, Tanner.' He bit his lip and then his eyes were on Tanner's breast pocket.

Tanner realised the lieutenant was studying the tiny ribbon, blue, white and red stripes, of his Military Medal above the left breast pocket of his battle blouse. He quickly buttoned his leather jerkin.

Dingwall swallowed hard. 'Our turn to face the Germans soon.'

'You'll be fine, sir,' said Tanner. He wanted to give his platoon commander some reassurance but it was a difficult line to tread; it wasn't his place to undermine the man's authority. Yet he could see the fear in Mr Dingwall's eyes and it was important the lieutenant did not show it to the men. If Tanner was honest, the telltale nausea in his stomach and the constriction in his throat were troubling him now. He tried to remind himself it was the anticipation of battle that was the worst. Even so, the Germans had control of the skies and, he'd heard, had tanks, armoured cars and large amounts of artillery; 148th Brigade had none of those things, and neither, it seemed, did the Norwegians. So how the hell were they supposed to stop them?

Tanner looked to the south and sensed Lieutenant Dingwall do the same.

'When do you think the bastards will attack?' the subaltern asked.

'Shouldn't think it'll be long.'

'What about all these stores? We've not cleared half of them.'

'Might be worth mentioning to Captain Webb that we should think about blowing it up, sir. Don't want Jerry to get his mitts on it.'

'I'll do that right away, Sergeant, thank you.'

It was unfortunate, however, that just as the lieutenant was speaking with the quartermaster, two lorries arrived back for another load. 'Jerry's not here yet,' Captain Webb told him, 'and so, for the moment, we'll do no such thing. Let's load up these trucks pronto.'

Tanner, close by, groaned to himself. The bloody fool, he thought.

Half an hour later, with the trucks dispatched, he broached the matter with Lieutenant Dingwall again. 'Sir, I really think we need to get this place wired and move out. The Jerries could be here any moment.'

'Yes, all right, Sergeant,' Lieutenant Dingwall snapped and strode off.

He had not gone ten paces when there was a roar of aero-engines followed by a series of colossal explosions. Seconds later two more aircraft hurtled over, flying at no more than a few hundred feet off the ground.

Tanner fell flat on the ground but turned his face to see a stick of bombs falling wide of the yard but still terrifyingly close. As the bombs exploded, with an ear-shattering din, he felt the air around him sucked away before he was lifted clean off the ground by the blast and smacked back down again. He closed his eyes as stones, shards of wood and glass rained down around him. Choking dust and smoke shrouded the yard and warehouse. 'Number Four Platoon,' he shouted, 'to me!' Men stumbled towards him. 'Right, lads. Get your kit. Make sure that your rifles are loaded, then grab as much ammunition as you can easily carry. It's time we got the hell out of here.'

By the warehouse, Captain Webb was also barking orders for them to retreat. 'Everyone fall back!' he shouted. 'Leave everything!' Tanner saw him hurrying to the car the lieutenant had been driving earlier.

Tanner ran to Lieutenant Dingwall. 'Sir, I'll follow you out.' Spotting Hepworth, he grabbed him, and said, 'Not you. I need you to help me.'

More shells whistled overhead. Hepworth looked distraught. 'But, Sarge, the Jerries'll be here.'

'We won't be long. Follow me,' he snapped. Tanner was fuming—with Captain Webb for not thinking ahead and for cutting and running before the others, but also with Lieutenant Dingwall for not pressing the quartermaster hard enough. As a result, they were leaving a mass of weapons and ammunition that any advancing force would gladly use against them.

They ran to the side of the warehouse. There, out of sight of the yard, they saw a small shed.

'What's this place, Sarge?' asked Hepworth. 'Can't say I'd noticed it.'

'That'll teach you to have a proper scout round in future, won't it?'

The previous day Tanner had quietly moved half a dozen four-gallon tins of petrol to the shed. He had also discarded some of his kit and replaced it with a number of items carefully put aside during the day's unloading. His gas mask had been removed from its case and he had filled the respirator bag with a tin of detonators and two five-pound packs of Nobel's gelignite. He had taken his hairbrushes and canvas shoes out of his large backpack. Abandoning his greatcoat had been a harder decision. However, he had kept his thick, serge-lined leather jerkin, which would keep him warm and allow him to have his arms free. He filled the pack with a number of cartridges of Polar dynamite, a tin of safety fuse, half a dozen hand grenades, ten rounds of Bren-gun tracer bullets, and as many clips of rifle rounds as would fit.

'Leave your pack and rifle here for the moment,' he told Hepworth, 'and help me with these cans. Iggery.'

'Iggery, Sarge?'

'Yes, Private. Iggery. It means get a bloody move on.'

They ran back to the yard. Tanner pulled out his seventeen-inch sword bayonet and stabbed the top of the tins, while Hepworth returned to the shed for the remaining fuel. The sergeant then poured the petrol over the remaining stores. When Hepworth returned, they finished their task. Suddenly there was a clatter and squeaking to the south of the station yard.

'Tanks!' said Tanner. 'Quick! to the shed.' They sprinted back, Tanner putting on his jerkin, then heaving his respirator bag and pack onto his shoulders. Slinging his trusted Enfield on his back, he said, 'Let's go, Hep.'

As they ran round the front of the warehouse, a German tank swung into view. The two men sprinted on, until Tanner slid into a ditch by the far side of the yard.

'You'd better be quick, Sarge,' said Hep, his face taut with fear.

Tanner said nothing. Instead, his shaking hands struggled to pull out a single .303 tracer round and push it into the breech of his rifle. German troops were now moving up round the sides of the tank, half crouching in long, field-grey coats and their distinctive coal-scuttle helmets.

One of the enemy troops shouted and, with his rifle, pointed to the stacks of boxes. Tanner watched as a dozen or more Germans ran across. He pressed the wooden stock of the rifle against his cheek. *Just over 150 yards.* Closing one eye, he aimed at a box of gelignite that he had doused with petrol. Holding his breath, he squeezed the trigger.

The tracer round struck the wooden box. Immediately an explosion ripped the air, sheets of flame engulfed the largest stack of stores, followed in succession by a second, third and fourth explosion as the fireball engulfed the yard.

'Run, Hep!' shouted Tanner. Then the two were scrambling to their feet, minds closed to what was going on behind them, concentrating on sprinting northwards for all they were worth, away from the yard and the warehouse.

Above the din of further explosions, Tanner was aware of a cannon shell whooshing past him. A few seconds later, machine-gun bullets fizzed over their heads. He and Hepworth dropped to the ground a few yards short of the bridge over the Mesna River. Tanner rolled over, unslung his rifle and pulled it into his shoulder. *A little over 300 yards*, he reckoned. He could see the tank commander's head sticking out of the turret; he was now firing the machine gun towards them. Tanner pulled back the bolt and fired. The man's head jerked backwards and the gun was silent. He yelled at Hepworth to start running again. More soldiers were crouching by the tank. Tanner pulled back the bolt again and hit a second man. *Two. Pull back the bolt, fire. Three. Again. Four.* This time he only clipped a soldier. Back came the bolt. *Five. Six. Seven.* Three rounds left. *That'll do.*

He turned and ran over the bridge and away from the inferno. Ahead, the road curved out of sight of the yard. A bullet fizzed past his ear. He could see Hep had already made it. Another bullet zipped by, and another, and then he was safe, for the moment at any rate, out of sight of the enemy.

Hepworth was up ahead, slowing now, and Tanner paused, hands on his hips, gasping for breath, his pack cutting into his shoulders. Bending double to relieve the weight, he grimaced, then began running again, albeit more slowly. Behind him, clouds of pitch-black smoke rolled into the sky.

Tanner drew level with Hepworth, who grinned. 'Some explosion, that one.' He watched as Tanner pressed another clip of bullets into his magazine. 'Shoot a few of the buggers, did you, Sarge? Did you get that tank man?'

'Less of the chitchat, Hep,' said Tanner. 'Let's concentrate on catching up with the others and getting out of here in one piece.'

They were nearing the edge of the town. He had hoped to come across a car or even bicycles, but there had been nothing and no time in which to look more thoroughly. The houses thinned and then they were in the open, running along a road. Of the rest of the platoon there was no sign.

'How much further, Sarge?' gasped Hepworth.

'A mile. Not much more.' Tanner could see the mass of the Balberg strutting imperiously above them. German field guns continued booming behind them. They could see the dark shells as they hurtled across the sky and exploded among the Allied positions. 'Keep going, Hep,' urged Tanner. 'Soon be there.'

Then, behind them, they heard the sound of gears grinding and the chugging drone of vehicles. A column of trucks emerging from Lillehammer. Tanner's heart sank. Coming round a bend in the open road he could see at least half a dozen, filled with troops, each pulling an antitank gun.

'What are we going to do now, Sarge?' said Hepworth. 'We'll never be able to stop them.' Hepworth was a small lad, barely nineteen, his face pale and his brows knotted in despair. Tanner glanced around him. About fifty yards ahead there was a farmhouse.

'First we're going to head to that house where we can get a bit of cover.'

'And then what, Sarge?'

'If you asked a few less questions, Hep, I might be able to think a bit more clearly,' Tanner snapped. He was trying to weigh up a couple of options in his mind. 'What a mess,' he mumbled. No matter what he decided, the reality was that he and Hepworth were now caught between the new Allied lines and the vanguard of the German attack. He had a good mind to floor Captain Webb if and when he ever saw him again.

TANNER NOTICED that a large barn extended out at right angles from the house. Good, he thought, grateful for whatever cover he could get. He crouched beside the ramp that led up to the barn's first floor and opened the haversack slung behind his left hip. He pulled out an old piece of oily cloth and carefully unwrapped it.

'What's that, Sarge?' asked Hepworth, crouching beside him.

'It's a telescopic sight,' said Tanner. 'An Aldis.' It had once belonged to his father, and Tanner had carried it with him throughout his army career. Most gunsmiths could modify the Enfield rifle easily enough by milling and fitting two scope mounts and pads to the action body. Consequently, having joined the 5th Battalion in Leeds, he had wasted no time in having his newly issued rifle specially adapted and his scope sighted without his superiors noticing. It was a good scope and his father had sworn by it.

Screwing the scope into place, Tanner stood behind the ramp and, using it as a rest, peered through the sight. The column was now about 700 yards away, and his sight zeroed at 400. He had found that allowing a foot's drop for every fifty yards beyond the zero usually did the trick, but this was going to be a long shot; as it was, he could only just see the driver of the lead vehicle. He lowered his aim to the bottom of the truck, then lifted it again by, he guessed, about six foot. Half exhaling as he pulled back the bolt, he held his breath and squeezed the trigger.

The truck lurched and ploughed off the road, so that the vehicle immediately behind quickly emerged. This time Tanner aimed at the indistinct figure of the driver and fired again. The man was hit—Tanner could see him thrown backwards. The soldier next to him grabbed at the steering wheel, but it was too late and the truck hit the back of the first vehicle and came to a halt across the width of the road. Men were pouring out of the trucks now and taking cover. Tanner smiled to himself with satisfaction.

There were two bicycles in one of the sheds adjoining the house and the two infantrymen grabbed them. 'Right, let's go,' said Tanner.

German artillery shells were whistling overhead, bombarding the Allied positions just half a mile ahead. Tanner wove back and forth across the road, hoping to make himself a more elusive target should the Germans attempt to fire at them. Hepworth, making faster progress, repeatedly looked back until Tanner urged him to press on. Suddenly he became aware of an eerie silence. Then there came a faint whirr and Tanner yelled at Hepworth and leapt into the snow at the curb, just as a stream of bullets spat up a line along the road followed by four Messerschmitt 110s thundering over.

He stood up and saw them strafing the Allies ahead, then shouted to Hepworth. To his relief, the private got up, dusted off the snow, and waved.

Further on, they reached the Allied forward positions, waved in through the hastily prepared roadblock by a corporal from the Sherwood Foresters.

'Where're our lot?' Tanner asked.

'Two hundred yards, on the right of the road under the Balbergkamp.'

A subaltern approached Tanner. 'Anyone behind you, Sergeant?'

'Only a column of enemy infantry. I counted at least half a dozen trucks. They were all towing guns. And they've got tanks.'

'Good God,' muttered the lieutenant. 'You'd better report to HQ right away. It's the only brick building around, a few hundred yards behind by the road. It's a Joint HQ for all three battalions.'

Tanner thanked the officer and then, with Hepworth, hurried forward. Men were still trying frantically to dig holes in the thin soil, officers and NCOs were shouting orders, while others were building makeshift sangars. The afternoon air was still heavy with the smell of cordite and smoke.

They found Joint HQ easily enough. Outside, several civilian cars were parked haphazardly in the mud and slush. Tanner recognised one as the vehicle in which Captain Webb had made good his escape. In the yard beside the house there were a number of foldaway tables on which stood a row of field telephones, lines of cable extending across the snow.

'You stay out here, Hep,' said Tanner, pushing his way through the throng of clerks and other staff. His boots squelched on the mud. It was not cold, but the sky was grey and overcast and the snow was melting.

Inside HQ there was pandemonium. The house smelt musty, of coffee, sweat and damp clothes. Tanner spotted Lieutenant Wrightson, the battalion intelligence officer, sitting on the corner of a table in a room at the end of the hallway. Tanner knocked on the open door.

Wrightson looked up. 'Yes?'

'I've been told to report to Battalion CO, sir, regarding what I've seen of enemy troop movements.'

Wrightson disappeared to fetch Colonel Chisholm.

A few moments later the colonel appeared with Captain Webb. 'Tanner, what the bloody hell are you doing here?' asked Webb. 'Shouldn't you be with the rest of your platoon?'

'All right, Captain, that will do,' said Colonel Chisholm, a tall man in his mid-forties. A North Yorkshire landowner and Member of Parliament, he, too, was new to war. 'What have you got for me, Sergeant?'

'I think Private Hepworth and I were the last out of Lillehammer, sir. We saw a tank entering the station with a number of accompanying troops, then a long column of motorised infantry deploying out of the town. The lead trucks had antitank guns attached to the back.'

The colonel ran his hand through his hair as Tanner spoke. 'How many tanks do you think they've got?'

'Hard to say, sir. There was one entering the station yard and another not far behind, but I heard the tracks of others as we were heading out of town.'

'Good God,' muttered Chisholm. 'And now they'll have taken our stores. Damn it, Webb, why the hell didn't you blow them first?'

'There wasn't time, sir,' said Webb, defiantly.

Tanner shifted his feet. 'Excuse me, sir, but Private Hepworth and I poured petrol over the stores, sir, and blew them up.'

'And what were the enemy doing while this was happening, Sergeant?'

'Getting burnt and shot, sir.'

Colonel Chisholm smiled. 'Good man, Tanner. That's something at least.' He squinted at his watch. 'All right, Sergeant, you'd better hurry back to your position.' The colonel strode past him, but as Tanner was about to leave, Webb grabbed his arm.

'I don't appreciate being humiliated like that,' he hissed.

Tanner had a strong desire to hit Webb; instead he glowered at the man, yanked his arm free, then left the room. Outside, Hepworth was waiting. 'Come on,' growled Tanner. 'Let's go.'

They left the road to head through the trees and across the thinning snow. It was still in the woodland, and Tanner paused to light cigarettes for himself and Hepworth. He passed one to the private and breathed in the smell of tobacco mixed with burning pinewood. A brief release of tension spread through him. A moment later a Junkers roared over. A split second afterwards came the whistle of falling incendiaries, and once again Tanner and Hepworth flung themselves to the ground. A deafening ripple of explosions erupted a short distance behind them and the ground shuddered.

Lifting himself to his feet, Tanner saw his crumpled cigarette in the snow.

'I reckon it's dangerous being near you, Sarge,' said Hepworth.

'You're alive, aren't you?'

'Yes, but only just. Look, Sarge, my hands are shaking.' He held them out to show Tanner. 'I don't think I'm cut out for war.'

Tanner could not help smiling. 'Another beadie will sort you out,' he said, pulling out his packet of cigarettes again. A moment before he'd thought to save his last precious few, but his resolve was weakening. 'Just don't go telling the rest of the lads or they'll think I've gone soft.'

They found B Company soon after, strung out between the trees next to a company of Norwegian troops. Number Four Platoon held the end of the line. Each of the three sections was trying to make their own defences—a sangar of sorts for the Bren team and whatever holes in the ground they could manage. Tanner was in despair. Nothing he had seen since reaching their lines had convinced him they had the remotest chance of holding off the enemy, and the efforts of his own platoon were the worst of them all. What good were a few stones and a hole barely deep enough to lie flat in against tanks, guns and aircraft? He sighed, pushed his helmet to the back of his head and looked around for Lieutenant Dingwall.

The subaltern had seen him first, however. 'There you are, Tanner. You took your bloody time.'

'I'm sorry, Mr Dingwall,' said Tanner. 'We got a bit held up and then I was ordered to report to Joint HQ.'

'Well, all right, but we've got a lot to do on these defences. Get digging.'

'What about reinforcements, sir?'

'Some Norwegian troops have joined us.'

'I saw them, but with all respect, they're not going to manage much, are they? They have less equipment than us and most of them have only been in uniform a fortnight. Where's the heavy stuff? Have you heard anything, sir?'

Dingwall shook his head. 'Apparently there's another company of Leicesters on its way, but Captain Cartwright has heard that another supply ship has gone down. Rather you didn't spread that about, though.'

'My God, sir,' said Tanner, 'this is madness. What the hell are we going to achieve?'

'Keep your voice down, Sergeant,' said Dingwall, sharply. 'We're trying to keep the enemy at bay and help the Norwegians.'

'Then why not keep them at bay a hundred miles back towards Åndalsnes? We've got a one-hundred-and-fifty-mile supply line here, with no guns to speak of, no tanks, no trucks, and a railway line that Jerry will knock out in no time. And the men are exhausted. When did we last have proper grub?'

'We've got to do what we can, Sergeant,' said Dingwall. 'Captain Cartwright has been promised that hot food will be issued tonight.'

Tanner knew there was no chance of a hot meal—how would it reach them? Captain Cartwright had been fobbed off, but there was no point in saying more. He'd said his piece, only it hadn't made him feel any better.

'I'd like you to take over the end of the line and make sure our defences are up to scratch,' said Lieutenant Dingwall.

Tanner saluted, and wandered through the trees until he found Corporal Sykes and his section.

'Afternoon, Sarge,' said Sykes, cheerfully.

Tanner was pleased to see that Sykes had made the most of a large rock and a pine tree for positioning the Bren. The machine gun was almost entirely hidden from view. 'Good work, Stan,' he said, as he eased off his pack and haversack.

Sykes grinned. From his battle blouse he pulled out some chocolate and offered half to Tanner.

'Thanks. I'm starving. Where d'you get it?'

'From some Norwegian bloke in Lillehammer. Said he'd rather give it to us than have it stolen by Nazis.'

Tanner liked Sykes. Of slight build, he was far stronger than he looked. And Sykes was sharp too—always ready with a quick reply—and the only man other than himself in the company who hadn't come from Yorkshire. Tanner had sensed an unspoken affinity between them, in part because he regarded himself and Sykes as outsiders. Every time Tanner opened his mouth, he revealed a West Country burr. Sykes's south London accent was even more marked among the thick Yorkshire tones of the other rankers.

He took out his spade and was about to start helping Sykes and the other men in the section when a Messerschmitt 110 pounded overhead, strafing their positions. They all hurled themselves flat on the ground as bullets kicked up gouts of earth and snow. Tanner heard a bullet ricochet from the rock beside him and a tiny sliver of stone nicked the back of his hand.

It was over in a trice. Cursing, Tanner got to his feet. His hand was bleeding. 'This is a bloody joke!' he said. Angrily, he picked up his spade and hacked at the ground. The spade cut through a few inches of soil, then hit rock. Every time it was the same. Rock.

'Who gave us these poxy spades anyway?' he barked at Sykes. 'Bloody useless, they are. I wouldn't want one of these at the seaside, let alone in the middle of sodding Norway.' He dug in the spade and the wooden handle snapped. With a curse, he flung what was left of it behind him.

'Who threw that?' snapped a voice.

Tanner and Sykes swung round to see a platoon of strange troops approaching through the trees. Leading them was the man who had spoken. 'Who threw that spade handle?'

Ah, thought Tanner, catching the accent. French. 'I did,' he said.

The man walked up to him in silence. He was shorter than the sergeant by several inches, with a narrow, dark face and an aquiline nose. 'Isn't it customary to salute an officer, Sergeant?' Tanner slowly brought his hand to his brow. 'And stand to attention!' said the Frenchman, sharply. 'No wonder you British are making such hard work of this war. No discipline, no training.'

Tanner fumed.

'Well?' continued the Frenchman. 'What have you to say for yourself?'

Tanner said slowly, 'I apologise, sir. I hadn't appreciated there were French troops in the vicinity.'

'Well, there are—one company of the Sixième Bataillon Chasseurs Alpins. We have been sent here because you British have no elite forces capable of fighting in the mountains. So when *les Allemands* attack, you can take comfort from the fact that we shall be above you, watching guard.' He pointed up towards the Balbergkamp, then repeated the line in French to his men with a knowing smile. They laughed.

'Where are the rest of the company, sir?' Tanner asked.

'You don't need to know such things, Sergeant.'

'Only I'm not sure one platoon will be able to do much to save us. The mountain's a big place. Furthermore, you've only got rifles. Jerry's got machine guns and artillery and, even better, he's got aircraft. But I appreciate your help, sir.' It was now the turn of British troops to laugh.

The Frenchman bristled. 'I don't like insolence, Sergeant. Not from my men or any others. You've not heard the last of this.' Then, with a last glare at Tanner, he continued on his way.

IT WAS BY NOW nearly three o'clock on Monday, April 22. The shelling had intensified, as had the number of enemy aircraft overhead.

Tanner was soon ordered back to Platoon HQ to cover the absence of Lieutenant Dingwall, who had been summoned to see the B Company commander, Captain Cartwright. When Dingwall returned, his expression was grim. 'It looks like we might be outflanked,' he told Tanner. 'There have been reports of German mountain troops climbing round the Balbergkamp.

The CO wants me to send a fighting patrol to watch out for them and, if possible, hold them off.'

'What about the Frogs? There was a platoon of mountain troops heading that way.'

'Yes, but Captain Cartwright wants some of our own troops up there.' He paused. 'I say, you haven't got a cigarette, have you, Sergeant?'

Tanner handed over his Woodbines. 'I've three left, sir. Be my guest. Think I'll have one too.' The whine of a shell whooshed overhead. Dingwall flinched, but both men remained standing. The shell exploded some distance away. Tanner handed the lieutenant his matches and watched as Dingwall lit his cigarette, fingers shaking.

'I want you to take the fighting patrol, Sergeant. Fourteen men. One section and three others, not including yourself.'

Fourteen men, thought Tanner. It wasn't a lot. 'I'd like to take Sykes's section, sir, if I may. Shall I take the other three from Platoon HQ?'

'You can have Hepworth, Garraby and Kershaw. If you see anything up there, only open fire if you really think you can hold them up. I need you all back here . . . Look, I think we both know we won't be staying here very long. If for any reason we have to move out, it'll be along the valley. You might be able to make some ground across here, where the river loops westwards, then back towards Tretten.' He gave Tanner a hand-drawn map. 'It's the best I can do, I'm afraid. Another thing we're short of—decent maps.' Dingwall held out his hand. 'Good luck, Sergeant.'

'And you, sir.'

The lieutenant looked at the ribbon on Tanner's chest, visible beneath his jerkin. 'I've been meaning to ask. What you were given your MM for?'

Tanner shrugged bashfully. 'It was during the Loe Agra campaign a few years back. On the North-West Frontier. Those jokers weren't as well armed as the Germans, but they were vicious buggers. Had rifles but bloody great swords as well. Those *wazirs* would slice your belly open without a second thought, give them half a chance.'

'I envy you that experience. I'm sure it's the best training there is. I heard about what you did today,' he added. 'You want to watch it, Tanner. They'll be giving you another bit of ribbon if you're not careful.'

TEN MINUTES LATER, Tanner and his patrol were climbing through the snow and trees round the northwest side of the Balbergkamp. The slopes were steep and the men soon gasped for breath. Lack of sleep and food hardly helped. Nor did the weight of their equipment. Tanner had ordered them to discard any non-essentials and replace them with extra rounds of .303 and Bren ammunition. Most wore their greatcoats, pockets bulging, so that their large packs could be left behind, but Tanner carried his haversack, full of rounds and explosives, on his hip. He had with him about sixty pounds of kit.

The men grumbled as they forced their way up the mountainside, but Tanner knew it was not his job to be popular. His task was to lead by example and to inspire trust. Being a tough bastard was what mattered, not making friends. The ribbon on his tunic helped. Now, though, he was about to be properly tested. Battle was about to be joined. His mouth felt dry.

He wondered what they would find up on the slopes. It seemed rather pointless for the Germans to try to outflank their position from the mountains when they could attack head-on and achieve the same result; the Allies would not be standing firm for long, of that he was sure. But there were always rumours in war. He supposed it was the commander's job to decide which of them was worth taking seriously. Someone had considered the threat of an attack by enemy mountain troops to be real enough.

No matter, he and his thirteen men were now cut adrift from the rest of the platoon and, indeed, the entire company and battalion. His gut instinct was that they would not be rejoining them for some time. He had no radio link, only a hand-drawn map, and no easy route back to the valley. His only means of signalling Lieutenant Dingwall was a Very pistol and three flares, only to be fired if they spotted significant numbers of German troops. But the lieutenant had no way of contacting him: if the battalion was overrun, he could not let Tanner know. And if they fell back, there was no guarantee that Tanner would be able to get as far as Tretten before the Allies had passed through.

Two of the Bren group stopped, exhaustion written across their faces. 'Come on, you idle sods,' Tanner chided. 'Here, give me that.' He took the Bren off Corporal Saxby. The machine gun was heavy, but he knew they needed to reach the plateau at the top of the mountain as soon as possible.

Several Junkers thundered down the valley, and bombs dropped from the planes directly over B Company's positions. First the whistle of falling iron and explosives; then the spurts of flame and clouds of smoke mushrooming across the entire position. A moment later, the report, echoing off the mountainside.

'All right, let's move,' said Tanner. He almost wished he could meet some Germans now. It would take his mind off things.

2

In a large room on the top floor of the Bristol Hotel in Oslo, three men sat round a table. Although it was afternoon, the room was dark. In the far corner away from the window, a lamp cast a circle of amber light towards the ceiling, but it remained a room of shadows.

It was part of the largest suite in the hotel, requisitioned by the newly arrived Reichskommissar, Josef Terboven. Nothing about the room suggested it was inhabited by the most powerful German in Norway: there were no flags, no pictures of Hitler, no army of staff scurrying in and out.

Reichsamtsleiter Hans-Wilhelm Scheidt glanced at the new Reichskommissar, then turned to the person sitting next to him. As he did so, he felt mounting contempt. The Norwegian was a mess. Globules of sweat had broken out on his forehead and the man kept running his hand over it. His face was podgy, the nose rounded, but the lips were narrow and his eyes darted from side to side as he spoke. The suit he wore was ill-fitting and, Scheidt noticed, there was a stain on the sleeve near the left cuff.

And the drivel coming from his mouth! Scheidt had heard it over and over again during the past week: how he, Vidkun Quisling, had long been a true friend of Germany; that he was the head of the only Norwegian political party that could govern Norway effectively. Norway was a peace-loving nation; the fighting had to stop. He could help deliver peace and ensure Norway remained a fervent ally of Germany. As founder and leader of the National Party, he could govern Norway now and in the years to come.

That was the gist, at any rate, not that Quisling was a man to say something in one sentence when given the opportunity for a long-winded rant. What was the Reichskommissar making of him? Scheidt wondered, and glanced again at the compact, slimly built man sitting opposite.

The contrast could not have been greater. Terboven was immaculate. The fair hair was combed back perfectly from a pointed widow's peak. Gold-framed round spectacles sat neatly on his nose, while his narrow eyes watched the Norwegian with piercing intent. His double-breasted black suit was beautifully tailored, the shoes were polished to glass, the shirt cuffs starched white cotton. Terboven exuded confidence, command and control. It was a Party rule that Scheidt had learned well: look superior, feel superior.

Terboven raised a hand. 'Stop, please, Herr Quisling. For a moment.' He closed his eyes briefly, as though in deep thought. 'All you say may be true,' said the Reichskommissar, 'but what about the King—who, it must be said, has shown nothing but contempt for your political ambitions?'

Quisling shifted in his chair. 'The King fears his position,' he said. 'It is why he must be captured and brought back to Oslo. I'm sure with a little coercion he can be persuaded to cooperate for the greater good of Norway.'

'It probably won't surprise you, Herr Quisling, to know that I'm no admirer of the King. Neither, it should be said, is the Führer.'

'Once the King is publicly supporting the National Party, Norway will be the friend and partner Germany needs,' said Quisling. 'But so long as King Håkon remains at large, there will always be Norwegian resistance to Germany. You *must* find him. Not only that, Herr Reichskommissar, it is imperative you also find the nation's bullion and the crown jewels. The King and the former government took them when they fled the capital.'

'Well, thank you, Herr Quisling,' said Terboven. 'Now, I will bid you good night. There is much to be done, not least a battle to be won.'

He stood up, signalled Scheidt to remain, and led Quisling to the door. Scheidt watched him shake the Norwegian's hand. It had been a masterly performance: Terboven had been cool and authoritative, but gracious too. He was, Scheidt realised, a formidable opponent.

And right now he was, indeed, an opponent. Scheidt knew that he was hanging by a thread, but he had not crawled up the Party hierarchy without learning to keep something up his sleeve. Terboven was in Norway with far-ranging powers—powers that Scheidt could not hope to undermine. However, there was still a part for him to perform.

With Quisling gone, the Reichskommissar wandered over to the window. 'Not an impressive man,' said Terboven, 'and yet you pushed for him to remain as Prime Minister.'

Scheidt remained seated. 'I never viewed him as anything more than a malleable stooge,' he said. 'What one has to remember is that Quisling has unwavering loyalty to Germany, as the Führer clearly recognises.'

Terboven wandered back to his chair opposite Scheidt. 'And what about the King? Is Quisling right about him?'

'In my opinion,' said Scheidt, carefully, 'he is right.'

'And about the bullion and jewels?'

'Resistance needs funding. So yes.' Scheidt shifted in his seat. Was this the time to reveal his hand?

'There's something more, isn't there, Herr Scheidt? Please.'

By God he's good, thought Scheidt. 'The bullion and crown jewels are not with the King,' he said at length. 'There are more than fifty tons of gold. I'm afraid we've lost track of it—we were not quick enough off the mark when the Norwegian Government fled Oslo. I have no doubt that at some point an attempt will be made to smuggle it out of the country—but we will catch them. We have complete mastery of the skies and the Norwegians cannot hope to move fifty tons of gold without being spotted.'

'You sound very confident.'

'It's just a matter of time. And patience.' Terboven had not taken his eyes from his. 'Some of the important crown jewels, however, are with a small group of the King's Royal Guard led by a certain Colonel Peder Gulbrand, and we have been tracking them more closely.'

'And why are these men not accompanying the King?'

'They were. But they came back to Oslo to collect a man. Someone more valuable than gold.' Scheidt saw Terboven blink. A chink at last, he thought.

'Are you going to tell me who this man is?' said Terboven, slowly.

'We're not yet certain of his name,' Scheidt lied, 'but what he knows is literally worth liquid gold.'

Terboven said, 'Don't try to play games with me, Herr Scheidt.'

Scheidt took a deep breath. His heart thumped. Keep calm, he told himself. 'Herr Reichskommissar,' he said slowly, 'I ask you now to trust me to deliver this man, and to believe me when I say that when I do so, we will have the eternal thanks of the Führer.'

'And what measures are you taking to capture him?'

'It is in hand, Herr Reichskommissar.'

'I could have you arrested and tortured, you know.'

'Yes,' said Scheidt, 'and then you lose the source too.'

Terboven stood up. 'Very well. I shall give you a week, Herr Scheidt. And I hope very much for your sake that you can deliver on all counts—the man, the information and the jewels. A week, Herr Scheidt, that is all.'

Scheidt felt the tight grip of the Reichskommissar's hand, then he was out of the room. My God, he thought, a week. But I must be able to find him. How hard could it be? He prayed his hand was as good as he hoped.

SERGEANT JACK TANNER and his patrol had reached the mountain plateau some 2,000 feet above the valley. Here, the air was noticeably colder, but so long as the sun shone, Tanner knew they had nothing to fear from the temperature. More of a concern was the depth of the snow, which in places was waist deep. Then Sykes spotted what appeared to be a drover's track where the snow had been compacted quite recently so Tanner directed the men towards it. He guessed it ran over the Balbergkamp to the south.

Ordering Privates Bell and Kershaw to walk ahead as scouts, he directed the rest to move in staggered threes at either side of the track, so that the entire group was spread out over almost 100 yards.

The plateau now rose only gently; the summit of the Balbergkamp was less than a mile ahead, while to the east, the land fell away again only to climb gradually once more. Tanner paused to scan the landscape. It was so still. Nothing stirred. Just the occasional explosion down in the valley.

He could see no sign of the enemy. Lieutenant Dingwall had been unable to tell him whether German mountain troops would be wearing special snow uniforms, or even if they would be using skis. He was certainly conscious of how ill-suited their own uniforms were to snow-covered mountain warfare. Tanner sighed. Surely someone had thought about the conditions they were likely to face in Norway? And if so, why hadn't they organised white overalls and jackets?

The mountain seemed empty. He began to think the rumour of enemy mountain troops must have been just that. There were trees on the summit of the Balbergkamp, albeit sparsely spread, and he had it in mind to climb almost as far as the top. If any attack was coming, they would see it from there. They were only 100 yards from the summit when Tanner caught the faint hum of an aircraft. So, too, did the others.

A Messerschmitt appeared, thundering directly ahead of them as if from nowhere, and flying so low it seemed close enough to touch. The noise of the engines tore apart the stillness. Tanner yelled at his men to lie flat but it was too late. The twin-engined machine was spurting bullets and cannon shells from its nose. Tanner felt bullets ripping over his head. Something pinged off his helmet. Eyes closed, he pressed his body to the ground.

Two seconds, maybe three, that was all. The ugly machine was past. One of the men called out. Tanner got to his feet. It was Kershaw, one of the two men sent ahead as scouts.

'Christ, oh my God!' he shouted. He sat half upright in the snow staring down at something beside him.

'Calm down, Kershaw!' called Tanner. Now there was gunfire a short way to the north. The Messerschmitt was strafing something else.

'Gordon's down, Sarge,' shouted Private McAllister.

Tanner turned to Sykes. 'You go to Gordon, I'll deal with Kershaw.' He hurried ahead, keeping his eye on the Messerschmitt. He saw it turn and double back towards them. He was about to yell a warning when the aircraft banked and swept out in a wide arc over the valley and disappeared south.

As he approached Kershaw he saw a mess of dark red stark against the snow. A cannon shell had struck Keith Garraby in the midriff, tearing him in half. Kershaw sat rooted to the spot, ashen-faced.

Tanner closed Garraby's eyes, then offered Kershaw a hand. 'Come on,' he said. 'Up on your feet.' Kershaw did as he was told.

Private Bell was beside Tanner. 'Best hurry, Sarge,' he said. 'Gordo's in a bad way.' Tanner ran back. Sykes was crouched over Private Draper, desperately pressing field dressings over two wounds in his chest and arm.

'Give me some more dressings,' said Tanner, pulling out his own packs of bandages from his trouser pockets. He opened Draper's jerkin and slit open the battle blouse, shirt and vest with his sword bayonet.

Tears ran down the side of Draper's face and he was shivering. 'Help me,' he sputtered. 'I don't want to die.'

'You're going to be fine,' said Tanner, stuffing wadding into the bullet-hole in Draper's chest. 'Stan, press down here,' he said to Sykes. 'Quick— he can't feel a thing. He's in deep shock.' Draper's eyes were filled with fear and he was frothing at the mouth and kicking. 'Easy, Gordo, easy. You're all right,' said Tanner. But, of course, he was not. The kicking stopped and his head dropped limply to one side.

'Goddamn it!' cursed Tanner, slamming a fist into the ground. Standing up and scanning the mountains, he could still see no sign of any troops, enemy or otherwise. 'Stan, you and three of your lads bury Gordon and Keith.' Sykes nodded. 'Then we're going back to the battalion.'

IT WAS OFTEN HARD for a pilot to hit a human target on the ground. Travelling at high speeds there was little time to aim, and no time to respond should the targets suddenly fling themselves out of the line of fire. Nor was there much chance to see the fruits of such an attack.

Leutnant Franz Meidel was pleased with his efforts, though. He had not been expecting to see a patrol of British troops, but at just under 100 metres off the ground he had seen their distinctive wide-rimmed helmets clearly. A three-second burst of fire had certainly knocked them over.

Meidel had flown on, spotting five men. They looked like Norwegian troops. He had opened fire on them too. His rear-gunner told him he was certain at least one man had been hit. Meidel swooped back low to examine his handiwork and spied a trail of blood in the snow. Good, he thought. 'I think we can go home, Reike,' he said.

ALTHOUGH SERGEANT TANNER had heard the second attack, it had not been his intention to investigate further. His orders were to look for German mountain troops, not get caught up in somebody else's trouble.

So, with nothing to report from the summit of the Balbergkamp, he had told his shaken patrol they would head down to rejoin the rest of the company. They had retraced their steps so that they were looking down on the Rangers' positions, when Tanner realised something was wrong in the valley. Sykes had spotted it too.

'If the lads are still down there, Sarge,' Sykes said, 'why isn't there any gunfire? I reckon they've bloody scarpered.'

Tanner pulled the Aldis sight from his haversack. With one hand he held the leather lens cap as a shield to avoid any light reflecting into the valley, while with the other he put it to his eye. 'I can't see any sign of them. Jerry aircraft and Jerry shells have done for them, I think.'

'It was a bloody hopeless position in the first place,' said Sykes.

Tanner put the scope back into his haversack. 'Damn it,' he hissed. Lieutenant Dingwall had mentioned Tretten, some miles to the north, but in the snow, with almost no food and on the back of four days and nights of very little sleep, this would be tough on the men.

A chatter of small arms could be heard further up the valley—it was the indication Tanner needed. 'We head north,' he said. 'We'll rejoin that track.' The men looked glum. 'Unless you want to end up in some Jerry cooler, we've got to keep going. If you've any rations left, eat something now.'

Lack of food was his prime concern, and as they set off once more it played on his mind. The lads were not grumbling yet; rather, they were quiet, most still stunned by the loss of Garraby and Draper. Tanner had to remind himself that those deaths had probably been the first his men had witnessed. To lose good friends so violently was hard to take.

He wondered whether he should have told them that the first dead body was always the worst. That the brain becomes used to such sights and it was possible to put the death of even a close mate to one side. The moment for such words had passed, though. They would work it out soon enough.

From the valley below came the continued sounds of battle. He pulled out Dingwall's map. Tanner reckoned they were nearing a bend in the

Lågen River just south of a village the lieutenant had marked as Øyer. But although the patrol appeared to be making progress, he knew they must still be behind the front line. A breather in the fighting, that was what he needed. The chance to get ahead of the German advance, and then they could rejoin the battalion.

His thoughts returned to his stomach. By God, he was hungry. A raised hand from Sykes provided him with distraction. Tanner had sent the corporal and McAllister up ahead and the two were now squatting fifty yards in front. Warning the rest of the patrol to halt, Tanner moved in a crouch towards the two men. 'What is it?' he whispered.

'I thought I saw someone up ahead behind that rock,' said Sykes. He pointed to an outcrop some 100 yards ahead. Silently, Tanner signalled to the rest of the patrol to move forward. The three men of the Bren group were the first to reach them. 'Dan, get ready with the Bren,' he said, under his breath to Lance Corporal Erwood. 'Mac,' he said softly to McAllister, 'make a run for a tree, then cover me as I go to the next. Then I'll cover you. All right? Dan, you cover us with the Bren. The rest of you stay here.'

McAllister took a deep breath, then set off. Tanner followed. Whoever was behind the rock—if anyone—made no attempt to move. They pushed forward again until Tanner spotted blood and footprints in the snow. 'There's someone there, all right,' he whispered to McAllister. 'Wait here.'

Treading carefully, Tanner approached. Yards from the rock, he paused. From the other side he could hear voices, faint and indecipherable. Slinging his Enfield over his shoulder, he began to climb the rock. Having deftly scaled the southern side, he unslung his rifle, pulled back the bolt and peered over the edge.

There were three men, two soldiers in grey-blue Norwegian uniforms. On the right was a young officer with blond hair, on the left a much older man who, although clad in a Norwegian army greatcoat, wore civilian clothes. In the middle, clutching his side, was another officer.

'You look like you're in trouble,' said Tanner. The three men flinched and looked up, startled. 'Who are you?'

'I am Colonel Peder Gulbrand of His Majesty the King's Guard,' gasped the man in the middle.

Tanner noticed another set of footprints. 'Whose are those?' he asked.

'Lieutenant Larsen,' said the younger man, in heavily accented English. 'He has gone to find somewhere for us to hole up. Our colonel needs help.'

Tanner clambered down from the rock. 'Me and my men are from the

5th Battalion, the King's Own Yorkshire Rangers,' he told them. 'That makes us allies. I'm Sergeant Tanner.'

'And I am Lieutenant Nielssen,' replied the blond officer.

Tanner looked at the colonel. 'Is it bad?'

'A splinter in his side,' Nielssen told him. 'He's lost a lot of blood. The German missed us, but a shard of wood from a tree struck the colonel.'

'We saw the attack,' said Tanner, kneeling beside Gulbrand and pulling a pack of field dressings from his trouser pocket. 'He was more successful firing at us. Two dead.'

'I'm sorry,' said Nielssen. Tanner was conscious of a tapping sound and turned to see the civilian clicking together two small stones. The man looked exhausted, with dark hollows round his spectacled eyes.

'And who are you?' asked Tanner.

'Someone we are escorting,' said Gulbrand hoarsely before the other could answer.

Tanner nodded. *You don't want to tell me. Fine.* It wasn't his business. 'Is the shard still inside?' he asked.

'Yes.' Gulbrand grimaced, then opened his coat and tunic. Tanner inspected the wound. The tip of the shard protruded from the colonel's side.

'What do you think?' asked Gulbrand, his English near flawless.

'That it's embedded in your liver, Colonel,' said Tanner.

'I think you're right.' He took a sudden sharp breath and winced.

'I can't pull it out,' said Tanner, still peering at the wound. 'Do that and you'll bleed to death in about ten minutes. It's a bad wound. You need a hospital, Colonel.' He delved into his haversack and produced a small tube of gentian violet antiseptic ointment. 'This should help prevent infection.' He gingerly pasted the cream over the wound, then placed the dressings over it. 'Why can't your men take you to Lillehammer, sir?' he asked.

'They can't,' Gulbrand gasped. 'It's impossible.'

'Why?'

Gulbrand stared at him hard but did not answer. Instead he said, 'Sergeant, what are you doing up here?'

Tanner told him, then added, 'Now we need to get a move on. The front's fallen back this afternoon. I'm damned if we are going to get stranded here.'

'We're holding you up. I'm sorry.'

'But you're natives, sir. You can help us. We need a map, and someone who speaks Norwegian would be useful.' He noticed the sounds of battle from the valley had quietened. 'What about you, sir? Why are you up here?'

Gulbrand closed his eyes. 'It's a long story.'

Tanner was about to ask more when Lieutenant Larsen appeared. He had found a *seter*, a mountain hut used by herdsmen and shepherds during the summer, not far away. It would offer them shelter.

'We'll help get you there,' said Tanner, 'but then my men and I must push on.' He called back to Sykes. 'Stan, come here and give me a hand, will you?' They lifted Gulbrand. 'Can you walk?'

'With your help, I'm sure.'

The strange civilian got awkwardly to his feet with enormous effort, slung his pack onto his back, then staggered a pace or two. 'Does he speak English?' Tanner asked Gulbrand. He was conscious he had not heard the man utter a word.

'Yes. Almost everyone does in Oslo and the coastal cities.'

Tanner turned to the man. 'Carry the colonel's pack, will you?'

The man pulled it onto his shoulder, faltering as he did so.

SCHEIDT SAT AT HIS DESK in his rooms at the Continental Hotel, the telephone receiver to his ear. Anger surged through him as he listened to Sturmbannführer Paul Kurz's latest report. Terboven was not a man to mess with, and only a couple of hours after his meeting with the new Reichskommissar, Kurz was on the line telling him that the most important man in his life had just missed getting a cannon shell through his guts.

'For God's sake, Kurz, that's the second time one of those fly-boys has nearly killed him. We need him *alive*, not spread over some mountain.'

'Calm down,' said Kurz, from his newly requisitioned office in Lillehammer. 'We've just heard. They got the colonel, and seriously too. Even if he doesn't die of his wound he's out of the picture. Odin is as good as in our hands already.'

'Only if the Allies haven't got him before you reach him,' snarled Scheidt. 'Tell that idiot Geisler to stop his pilots attacking those men.'

'Don't try to tell me my job, Herr Scheidt,' Kurz told him flatly.

'Listen,' fumed Scheidt, 'if anything happens to Odin before we've had the chance to get the information from him, neither you nor I will have a career. Tell me what you're doing to find Odin. What troops have you got for the operation? Tell me they're already tracking him down. Tell me something that makes me believe you're actually trying to get to this man.'

'You politicians,' said Kurz, 'always the same. I'm sure it seems very straightforward from where you're sitting on your arse in Oslo, but up here

Engelbrecht's division are facing the British and Norwegians—there's been heavy fighting all day. You're forgetting that we only learned of Odin's whereabouts this morning, and that's pretty vague—and it was only earlier today that Lillehammer fell. As it happens, I've got a company of reconnaissance troops from Dietl's Gebirgsjäger Division, and I've had to pull a lot of strings to get them. They're attached to Engelbrecht's division and are setting off to hunt them now. They'll get Odin because those Norwegians aren't going to get far, up on that mountain. Tomorrow morning, Herr Reichsamtsleiter, we'll have an altogether more pleasant conversation.'

It was Scheidt's turn to sigh. 'Just get men up into those mountains, Kurz, find Odin and bring him to me in one piece.' He slammed down the receiver and slumped back in his chair. Perhaps Kurz was right. Perhaps he *was* just sitting on his arse. Was there really any need to remain in Oslo for the rest of the month? Quisling could do without him for a few days. He stood up, walked to the window and gazed out over the city. Yes, damn it, he would head to Lillehammer and oversee the operation to capture Odin. That would shake up that idler Kurz. Scheidt smiled. Already, his mood was lightening.

ANOTHER AIRCRAFT OVERHEAD, higher this time. No firing of guns, no bombs dropped; a reconnaissance aircraft, then. Had any of the crew spotted them? Tanner couldn't know, but he felt as though he was being watched. It unnerved him.

Sykes joined him as Tanner scanned all around with his scope.

'Got a spare beadie, Stan?' Tanner asked him.

Sykes tapped the packet out of his pocket. 'There's something funny going on with these Vikings,' he said, as he struck a match into his cupped hands. He passed a lit cigarette to Tanner. 'They look terrible and not just the colonel. Why are they up here? What's more, who's that civvy geezer? I tell you, Sarge, there's something they don't want to tell us.'

Tanner shrugged. 'Maybe. But I don't care what they're doing up here as long as they can help us get back to the battalion. I'm going to get one of those Norwegians and sort out a plan of action. We've wasted enough time.'

Tanner went back into the *seter,* where most of the men sat huddled together. He sighed. Christ, he was tired. Tired and starving. Several of his men were already asleep and they'd only been there five minutes. He stooped over Gulbrand. 'He's asleep,' said Larsen.

Tanner stood up again. 'We've got to get him out of here somehow.'

Larsen nodded. He had a pale, lean face, with several days' growth of gingery beard. Like the others, he was exhausted, his eyes grey and hollow.

'Who's the most senior of you lot after the colonel?'

'I am,' said Larsen. 'I've been two years a lieutenant.'

'Have you got a map?'

'Here.' He delved into his rucksack.

'Look, my corporal's outside. Do you mind if the three of us have a talk?' Larsen followed him out. 'It's after nine now,' said Tanner, blowing into his hands. He could see his breath on the chill evening air. 'It doesn't get dark until after eleven, so we've a couple more hours of daylight. But we've got two big problems. First, Colonel Gulbrand. We're not going to get far if we take him with us.' Larsen nodded. 'Second,' continued Tanner, 'we've got a lot of starving and exhausted men—and I include myself.'

'And me an' all,' said Sykes.

'Yes,' said Larsen, 'it is the same for us.'

Tanner eyed him. 'Are you going to tell us what you're doing up here?'

Larsen shook his head. 'But please believe me, it is of vital importance.'

'All right. And I'm assuming you want to reach the Allies too?'

'Yes. Very much.'

'So, first we need to know where we are and find out what's going on down in the valley. I want to see where Jerry's got to. How far down do we have to go before we get to some farmhouses?'

'Not so far. I think we are above Øyer.' Larsen opened the map. 'Look, this stream is just ahead—you can see the ground falling away. If so, there are bound to be farms high above the village.'

'And from the contours it looks as though the valley sides are not as steep here as they were around Lillehammer.' Tanner looked at them both. 'In that case we should take the colonel. We can leave him at one of the farms. I suggest you and I, sir, go on a recce. We'll take one of my lads and Lieutenant Nielssen. Between us we can carry the colonel. Stan, you stay here. Make sure there's a guard at all times, but that'll give the rest a chance to get some kip. If things are quiet, we'll head down into the valley tonight.'

'How will you carry the colonel?' asked Sykes.

'We find a couple of strong sticks and thread the arms of two greatcoats through them to make a stretcher.'

THE COLONEL, HOWEVER, woke as they tried to lift him onto the improvised stretcher. 'No,' he said, through gritted teeth. 'I will not be handed over to the Germans. Leave me here.'

Tanner did as he was ordered. Whatever their reason for such secrecy was their affair. In any case, he reasoned, their climb down the mountain would be easier without the colonel.

He took Private McAllister, one of the riflemen in Sykes's section—he seemed less affected by the afternoon's events than the others. At any rate, he appeared to have his wits about him. Nielssen accompanied Larsen, leaving the civilian with the colonel.

Overlooking the steep ravine cut by the stream, they found the outline of a rough track that wound its way off the slopes. The further they climbed down, the more the snow thinned until the stone of the track was revealed and they were able to walk freely. Spread beneath them was the snaking valley of the Lågen River. Above the water's edge was the village of Øyer, the valley and the single railway line clearly visible. Isolated farms dotted the lower slopes on both sides of the river, and around them, marking clear breaks in the thick pine forests, were small fields—which would soon be full of rich grass for haymaking and grazing. Now, though, in the third week of April, the valley was black and white and shades of grey. Only the water of the Lågen, icily blue, offered colour.

Almost directly below there was a farmstead and another beyond, 100 yards further down. Tanner admired the now-familiar design: the steep-pitched roof, the ornate wooden verandah, the barn with its stone ramp. A dog barked briefly, but otherwise it was eerily still.

'It seems quiet enough,' said Larsen.

Tanner pulled out his scope. 'There's movement,' he said. Several Heinkels flew along the valley, dropping their bombs a few miles northwest of the village. Clouds of smoke erupted on the lower slopes of the mountains and across the river. In the distance there were bursts of small arms.

'They're making some kind of stand up there,' said Tanner.

'What can you see,' asked Larsen.

'Hard to tell, even with this. There are a few vehicles on the road in front of us, though. What looks like several carts. I need to get closer.'

'Nielssen and I will try these farms,' said Larsen.

'All right,' said Tanner. 'McAllister and I will cover you. We'll be able to see if the coast is clear, then we'll head down a bit further.' Tanner looked at his watch. 'Meet back here in half an hour. If the front really is only a few miles up the valley, we've a good chance of catching up tonight.'

Larsen nodded. 'Good luck, Sergeant.'

Tanner and McAllister watched the two Norwegians approach the farm.

A pair of dogs barked and ran towards them. Nielssen held out his hands and they approached, tails wagging. Larsen knocked on the door, which opened. A middle-aged man, with a grey moustache. Talking—an explanation. Then the two men were inside.

'Good,' said Tanner. 'Looks like we might get some grub. Come on, Mac, let's get going.'

They moved back into the trees. Melting snow dripped round them, but they were able to move easily. Tanner stopped by a clearing in the trees from where they could see the road a few hundred yards ahead.

A column of men and horses pulling artillery pieces was working its way towards the village. Tanner peered through his scope. 'Damn it,' he hissed.

'Jerries?' whispered McAllister.

Tanner nodded, then turned towards the village. There were trucks, cars, and by the church, a tank. Emerging from the village was a line of men. From their helmets, he knew they were British. 'Jesus,' he murmured.

'What is it, Sarge?'

'You don't want to know.' Several German infantrymen were walking beside them, rifles in hand. As they tramped out on the valley road, Tanner saw the Germans jeering, then realised that none other than Captain Cartwright and Lieutenant Dingwall were leading the column. For the moment, though, he would keep it to himself. 'Come on, Mac, we've seen enough.'

THEY FOUND Nielssen and Larsen waiting for them by the track above the farm. Between them they had managed to get hold of some ham, hard-boiled eggs, cheese and several loaves of bread. Larsen cut Tanner and McAllister some ham now and passed it to them with some bread.

'Damn me, that's good.' Tanner grinned. His energy was returning.

After they had finished eating, the sky was darker. 'We should get going,' Tanner said. 'Those are dark clouds. We could be in for some snow.'

By the time they were nearing the *seter*, snowflakes were falling. Tanner was pleased to see that the guard outside the hut was awake and alert. Hepworth asked him whether they had managed to find food and if the front had fallen back. 'Yes to both,' Tanner replied. Inside, most of the men slept, although they soon stirred with the arrival of the recce party. The two Norwegian officers passed round the food with, Tanner noticed, considerable fairness. Nielssen produced a Primus stove and a mess tin, then put some water on to boil. The men eagerly crowded round.

Tanner crouched down beside Gulbrand, then looked at the gaunt-faced, middle-aged civilian sitting next to him. A politician or diplomat perhaps?

The man dabbed the colonel's brow. 'He's getting a fever,' he said.

'That probably means his blood's infected.' Tanner opened Gulbrand's greatcoat to peel back his clothing. The smell as he lifted the tunic was overpowering, meaning gangrene was setting in. Probably septicaemia too.

'It's all right,' said Gulbrand. 'I know I'm going to die.'

'I'm sorry, sir. If you'd let us take you down the mountain . . .'

'It would have made no difference.' He gripped Tanner's arm. 'Tell me, Sergeant, can I depend on you?'

'To get your men to safety? I don't know, sir. We've a few problems just at the minute. But you can depend on me to do my damnedest.'

Gulbrand turned to the civilian. 'Sandvold? Will you leave us alone a moment?' The man got up and walked to Nielssen. Gulbrand watched him, then said, 'We should be with the King. I have been in the King's Guard for twenty years. My loyalty is total. It's why the King chose me for this task.' He paused. 'April the 9th was a terrible day,' he said, his voice a whisper.

The Germans had attacked Oslo. It soon became clear that the capital would fall. Prime Minister Nygaardsvold was persuaded by his government that they should leave Oslo and head north. The King was informed of the decision and agreed that he and his son, Crown Prince Olav, should go with them. Shortly after, he called for Gulbrand. King Håkon wanted a dozen men to act as his bodyguard. Gulbrand was to remain with the King, who entrusted to him a number of documents and jewels for safekeeping.

The train for Hamar had left at seven that morning. 'It felt as though we were running away,' said Gulbrand. In truth, they had had little choice. Norway was a neutral country and her armed forces were ill-equipped. 'A mobilisation order was announced that same morning,' Gulbrand told him, 'but it was too late. Most of the men fighting in the valley here have had no training. They've been given a uniform and a rifle and sent off to fight. We've got no tanks, no antitank weapons, no mines. We don't even have any hand grenades. Our field guns are old. We've got some machine guns but few men have had any training on them. There haven't even been enough uniforms. So, you see, we had no choice but to leave Oslo.'

The train took them to Hamar, but by evening word reached them that German forces were on their way so they boarded another train for Elverum. Two days later a German delegation arrived, offering peace terms, which had been rejected. It was shortly after this that Gulbrand had been summoned by the King. Prince Olav had also been present. King Håkon

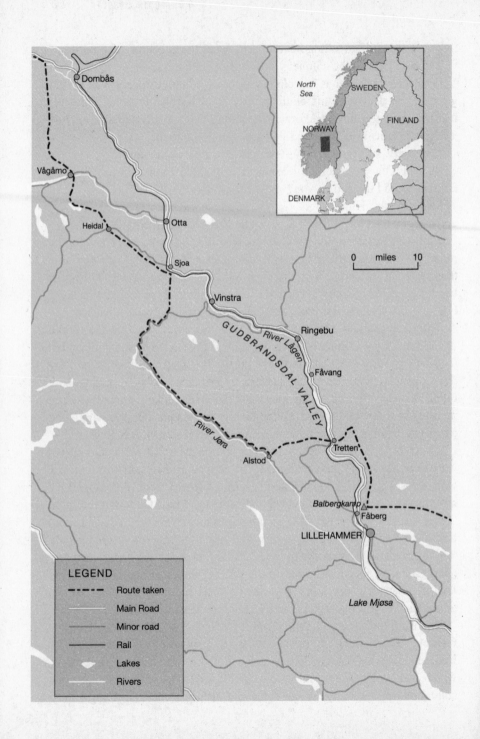

Dombås

Vågåmo

Heidal

Otta

Sjoa

Vinstra

River Lågen

GUDBRANDSDAL VALLEY

Ringebu

Fåvang

River Jøra

Alstod

Tretten

Balbergkamp

Fåberg

LILLEHAMMER

Lake Mjøsa

North Sea

SWEDEN

FINLAND

NORWAY

DENMARK

0   miles   10

LEGEND

▬ ▪ ▬ ▪   Route taken
▬▬▬▬   Main Road
▬▬▬▬   Minor road
▬▬▬▬   Rail
◣   Lakes
▬▬▬▬   Rivers

had a task for Gulbrand. In the chaos of their departure from Oslo, they had left behind a man named Hening Sandvold. The King wanted Gulbrand to go back to Oslo and fetch him. 'I still cannot tell why he is so important,' said Gulbrand. 'I made a solemn vow to the King and Prince Olav. But I will tell you this: if Sandvold fell into Nazi hands, it could have catastrophic consequences, not only for Norway but for Britain and all of the free world too.'

Tanner looked over at Sandvold, now standing by the door, then turned back to Gulbrand. 'How did you get him then, sir?'

'By keeping it simple,' the colonel replied. 'I decided to take just three others: Larsen, Nielssen and Lieutenant Stunde.' They had left their uniforms in Elverum and headed to Oslo. The city was calm and they were surprised by how few German troops were there. They found Sandvold easily enough. When they showed him the King's letter, he agreed to leave.

Getting back to Elverum had been more difficult. They had driven whenever they could, stealing cars and ditching them if they drew near roadblocks. They had walked many miles too. When they reached Elverum, the King had gone. The monarch's instructions had been to catch him up if they could, otherwise to find the British and get Sandvold to England.

They had headed north from Elverum, had nearly been caught hiding in a barn and soon after shot at by aircraft. They had abandoned their transport to cross the mountains. It had been a difficult four-day journey. On the second day, Lieutenant Stunde had broken his leg and they had been forced to leave him. 'It was,' said Gulbrand, weakly, 'the worst decision I have ever had to make. We found a *seter*, and hoped someone would find him, but we knew there was little chance of that. Poor Roald. It would have been kinder to put a bullet in his head. So, you see, Sergeant, I couldn't ask Nielssen or Larsen to make an exception for me. And I couldn't allow the enemy to catch me. What if I told them something when I was delirious?'

Gulbrand's teeth were chattering now. His skin looked sallow, his eyes hollow. 'I have entrusted Larsen and Nielssen with the jewels and papers, but what I ask of you now is of far greater importance. You must get Sandvold to safety. To the coast and then England.'

'All right,' said Tanner, 'you have my word that I'll try. But why aren't you saying this to Larsen or Nielssen?'

Gulbrand coughed, which caused him further agonies. Eventually he sank down again. 'I've watched you, Sergeant. You are in command of these men, not Henrik Larsen. And I think you have more experience than the rest of us.' He smiled weakly. 'Yes, Sergeant Tanner, I can see you are already a decorated soldier. This is a thankless task I have given you. But you will have the eternal thanks of my King and country if you succeed, and I suspect your own as well.' He closed his eyes. 'One last thing. Trust no one. Kill Sandvold rather than let him fall into enemy hands, and destroy any papers he may be carrying. If the others try to stop you, kill them too. Do you think you can do that?'

'Yes,' said Tanner. 'One thing, though, sir. Do the Germans know about him? Are you being followed?'

'I don't think so. Why would those planes have tried to kill us? Sandvold's no use to them dead.' He gripped Tanner's sleeve. 'They mustn't get him.'

Tanner left Gulbrand. What a mess, he thought. The whole bloody show. He thought of Captain Cartwright and Lieutenant Dingwall, prisoners now. He wondered if anything remained of the company. It was a damned stupid waste of lives. And now he had the extra burden of Hening Sandvold. What was so special about him? A scientist, he supposed. What those boffins knew was beyond him. He hoped that in Sandvold's case it would be worth it.

He stepped outside to find the snow falling heavily now. He prayed it was snowing in the valley too—then the front would be held up as they were.

'You were having a long chinwag with the colonel, Sarge.' It was Sykes, taking his turn as sentry.

'We've got to take the Norwegians with us,' said Tanner. 'That civvy—he's special. A boffin or something. We've got to get him to Britain.'

'Where's the front?'

'Not at Øyer.'

Sykes tutted. 'So where are our boys?'

In the hands of the Jerries, thought Tanner. 'Not so far. A few miles. And I just want to get going.'

'Well, we can't go anywhere in this,' said Sykes.

At that moment he heard something moving between the trees not forty yards ahead. Then Tanner heard it too. Footsteps. In the faint glow of the snow they saw the dark shape of troops approaching.

BRIGADIER HAROLD DE REIMER MORGAN, commander of the British 148th Brigade—or what was left of it—placed his index finger on the map at a point roughly three miles west of Øyer. 'Here is a composite force of Allied troops. Come the morning, they won't be able to hold on. The rest of our force is here,' he added, pointing to the narrow gorge south of Tretten, a couple of miles further back along the winding valley. 'I have to tell you,

General, that without support, I cannot guarantee that we'll be able to hold Tretten for long.'

General Ruge studied the map. 'Where is the extra company of Leicesters from Åndalsnes? Are they at Tretten?'

'Yes, but without much kit. The Tretten Gorge is a good natural defensive position, but I'm worried about our flanks. The enemy's mountain troops went round us successfully at the Balbergkamp and I'm concerned they'll do so again. I don't have enough men.'

'Very well, I take your point,' snapped Ruge. 'Beichmann,' he said to the staff officer seated next to the desk, in English so that Morgan could understand, 'find Colonel Jansen. Order him to place his Dragoons there, and tell him he is now under the direct command of Brigadier Morgan.'

'Sir.' Colonel Beichmann saluted and left the room.

General Ruge sighed wearily. 'What else can we do?'

'It would help the men greatly if they could have something to eat, sir.'

'All right, Morgan, I'll look into it. The problem, as you know, is transport.' He chuckled mirthlessly. 'Just one of many.'

Brigadier Morgan drove back towards Tretten in a requisitioned Peugeot, squashed into the back seat next to Major Dornley, his brigade-major. It was cold, and he pulled up the collar of his coat so that the coarse wool scraped against his cheeks. He was fifty-two, no great age to be a brigade commander during peacetime, but too old in a time of war. He felt the cold more than he had in his younger days, and right now he felt more exhausted than he had ever done as a young man in the trenches.

'Are you all right, sir?' asked his brigade-major.

'I suppose so, Dornley. It's difficult trying to command a brigade when you've got someone like General Ruge breathing down your neck.'

'I thought you were getting along all right, sir,' said Dornley.

'That's not what I meant. He's a decent fellow doing his best in difficult circumstances. But the fact is, General Ruge has only just been promoted from colonel, and is now ten days into the job of being commander in chief of a tiny tinpot army. A couple of weeks ago he was junior to me in rank, yet now we're subordinate to him. It's all rather absurd.'

'He's giving you a pretty free rein, though, isn't he, sir?'

'Now he's got us down here, you mean?' He sighed heavily. 'I'm beginning to think I made the wrong call. We should be at Trondheim now. Instead, the brigade's being chewed up in this damned deathtrap of a valley.'

'Sir, you had very little choice in the matter. We had no word from

London and, as commander of Norway's forces, every Allied officer had to come under his command. And his orders were to reinforce his troops here.'

'It's good of you to say so, Dornley, but I should have waited longer for a response from London. I had no idea what state Ruge's forces were in and it's clear he expected more from us. He must have been thinking that we'd be bristling with guns, aircraft and military transport.'

'But it's not your fault that we lost our supply ship.'

Morgan laughed with exasperation. 'It *is* my fault, Dornley, that I allowed myself to be persuaded by Ruge to move the brigade south. We haven't got a single bloody antiaircraft gun. Those Luftwaffe boys are laughing their heads off.' He glanced at Dornley, but this time his brigade-major was quiet. Perhaps I've said too much, he thought. He had begun to accept that in the Germans they were confronting a formidable enemy, both in tactics and strength. Overwhelming air support working hand in hand with the troops on the ground was a devastating combination—yet such tactics had barely been discussed back at Staff College.

His confidence in his country, and in the army he had served loyally for so long, had been shaken. They could never hope to defeat Germany like this. War could no longer be fought without support from the air and without modern equipment. Britain needed to catch up—and quickly.

Tretten. He wondered whether Colonel Jansen and his Dragoons would materialise. Even if they did he doubted that he could hold the position for more than a day. His only hope was the arrival of 15th Brigade, which was expected to reach Åndalsnes within forty-eight hours. And with 15th Brigade came Major General Paget, who was to take over command, thank God. Paget was an old friend. His own task was to complete a successful fighting retreat, holding the Germans at bay for as long as possible until he could hand over the reins to Paget.

Even that would be a considerable challenge.

THE FIGURES STUMBLING through the thick snow towards Tanner and Sykes were so close there was no time to warn the others. Tanner whispered to Sykes to move to the side of the *seter* and to have a hand grenade ready. He tensed as he unslung his rifle from his shoulder and pulled back the bolt.

Several shapes became clearer as they reached the hut.

'*Halt! Hände hoch!*' shouted Tanner. The men, shocked, swivelled towards him.

'*Vous tous, vite faites ce qu'il vous dit!*' one of the men shouted.

Relief surged through Tanner. They were French. He laughed to himself as he approached, rifle still pointed at them.

'You are British?' said one of the Frenchmen.

'Too bloody right,' said Sykes, emerging from the other side of the *seter*. At the same moment, a startled Larsen opened the door.

'A patrol of Frenchmen, sir,' Tanner told him.

'How many?' Larsen asked, pulling out a small torch.

'Seven. Myself and six men,' came the reply. The French commander stared at Tanner. 'You! The Tommy who likes to throw shovels at his allies.'

Tanner's heart sank. 'The Chasseurs Alpins,' he said. 'I appreciate that you're elite forces, but since you've surrendered to me, perhaps you'd like to tell me what your men are doing up here?'

'How dare you speak to a superior officer like that? And how dare you suggest that I have surrendered to you?'

'But you did, sir,' said Tanner. 'I said, "Halt, hands up," and you put your hands in the air.'

'Perhaps you could tell me your name,' Larsen suggested to the Frenchman. 'I am Fenrik Henrik Larsen of His Majesty the King's Guards.'

The Frenchman turned to Larsen, his face tense with anger. 'And I am Lieutenant Xavier Chevannes of the Deuxième Compagnie de Fusiliers Voltigeurs. We were on a reconnoitring patrol after the British ordered a withdrawal to Øyer. But it seems our allies have fallen back yet again so we were stranded. When the snowstorm came we went looking for shelter.'

As Chevannes and his six men followed Larsen into the *seter*, Tanner placed a hand on Sykes's shoulder. 'He's a pain in the ruddy arse.'

'Sarge, be careful. He could make life tricky.'

'He's a show-pony,' said Tanner, irritably. 'Anyway, we'll soon be shot of him and his patrol. Look up. What can you see?' He pointed to the sky.

'Stars, Sarge.'

'Exactly. It's barely snowing any more. So, let's kick everyone awake and get the hell out of here. Leave those Frogs to get some kip.'

Tanner and Sykes burst noisily into the *seter* and immediately began to shake awake the rest of their men.

'Just what do you think you're doing, Sergeant?' said Chevannes.

'We're off,' Tanner said tersely. 'Time to go.'

'You'll do no such thing, Sergeant.' In the dark half-light, Chevannes glared at him, almost daring Tanner to challenge him.

'You're not in command of my men, sir. I am. And, furthermore, Colonel

Gulbrand has ordered me to take Mr Sandvold here to the safety of the Allied lines. If I'm to do that, I need to get going.'

Chevannes laughed. 'The colonel ordered you, did he? Tell me, Sergeant, why on earth would a Norwegian colonel order a mere sergeant to carry out such a task when two of his fellow countrymen and officers senior in rank are infinitely better placed to undertake that role?'

'He ordered me not fifteen minutes ago. Ask him yourself.'

Chevannes' mouth curled into a barely suppressed smile. 'Yes, why don't we?' Crouching beside the colonel, he said, 'Colonel Gulbrand? Can you hear me?'

Gulbrand gibbered, his words inaudible.

'Colonel!' said Chevannes again, then stood. 'He's delirious with fever.'

Tanner knelt beside Gulbrand. 'Colonel!' Gulbrand's eyes locked on his. With one hand he clutched Tanner's shoulder and began speaking in Norwegian, gabbling frantically.

'He thinks he is talking to the King,' said Larsen, quietly.

Tanner felt Gulbrand's grip loosen. 'Colonel!' said Tanner again, searching desperately for life in Gulbrand's face. 'Come on, damn you!'

'Sarge.' It was Sykes, standing beside him. 'Sarge, he's gone.'

'So,' said Chevannes, 'I am in command.'

'We still need to get going—and now,' said Tanner, getting to his feet.

'We *need* rest.'

'Sir, half an hour before dark, the Germans were attacking a position only four or five miles west of here. My guess is that they're still there, and I'd put money on the rest of our forces being at Tretten. That's no more than six or seven miles. We can do that in three hours. The men can rest then.'

'Sergeant, it is still dark, the snow is deep, and although my men have mountain boots, yours do not. It is freezing cold and my men—yours too—are exhausted. If we stumble out there now, we are asking for trouble.'

'We'll be in worse trouble if we don't get to Tretten before the Germans.'

Chevannes smiled. 'You've obviously not been studying the German modus operandi, Sergeant. Let me enlighten you. Every morning at first light, reconnaissance planes are sent over. Later, their field guns start firing. At noon, the Luftwaffe arrives and bombs and strafes the position they are going to attack. In the afternoon, with our infantry nicely softened up, their infantry and armour attack. And he will do the same tomorrow. So we stay here now and leave in the morning. We will still be at Tretten before noon.'

Tanner appealed to the Norwegians. 'You're surely not going to listen to this?' But as he said it, Nielssen avoided his eye and Larsen was unmoved. His men were awake now, but no one spoke in his defence. They wouldn't: it wasn't the place of privates and lance corporals to argue with officers.

'Sergeant,' said Larsen, his voice placatory, 'we have been on the run for more than a week. Neither I nor Nielssen have had any sleep for two days. I believe Lieutenant Chevannes is right.' He nodded at Sandvold, huddled in the corner of the hut. 'He is still asleep. Leave him be a while longer.'

Tanner was defeated. 'Very well,' he muttered. He realised he was exhausted too. 'We need to bury the colonel,' he said.

Chevannes spoke to two of his men, who went over to Gulbrand's body, lifted it and took it outside. Tanner slumped against the far wall next to Sykes.

'We'll all be better for the rest,' whispered Sykes.

'I don't give a damn,' muttered Tanner. 'We're soldiers and we're at war. Our task is to get back to our lines as quickly as possible. If we fail because of that French bastard, I'll kill him.'

THEY WERE on their way by seven, their stomachs warmed with coffee. The sky above was blue and bright, the air cold and the snow deep. The landscape had changed. Three of Chevannes' men were scouting ahead of the column, followed by the French lieutenant and the Norwegians, Tanner and his men trudging silently behind. He felt better for the sleep, but his anger had not subsided. Neither was his mood improved when he realised the French and Norwegians were walking faster than his own men. He had promised himself he would keep Sandvold in sight at all times.

'Come on, lads,' he urged. 'Get a move on.'

'We're not so well dressed for a snowy stroll in the mountains as they are, Sarge,' said Sykes. 'Look at the clobber of those Froggies.'

It was true, and Tanner had eyed the Chasseurs Alpins' uniforms with envy. Each man had a thick sheepskin jacket. Underneath, they wore a waterproof khaki canvas anorak and a thick wool sweater. Stout studded mountain boots kept their feet warm and waterproof gaiters covered their ankles and shins. Again, Tanner cursed the brass who had planned this expedition. Already, his feet were painfully cold; the leather of his boots was not waterproof now that the polish had largely worn off, while the soles were slippery in the snow. No wonder his men were struggling to keep up.

And when, Tanner wondered, were they going to head back into the trees? 'Why the hell are we slogging through this?' he muttered to Sykes. 'I'm going to have a word with Chevannes.'

'Ah, Sergeant,' said Chevannes, as Tanner approached, 'your men seem to be struggling. I hate to think how many we would have lost in the dark.'

'Why aren't we pushing further down towards the tree line, sir? If we go along beneath the lip of the valley, the snow won't be so deep and the trees will give us greater cover. Up here we stand out like sore thumbs.'

'Are you questioning my decisions again, Sergeant? We are taking the most direct route. Get back to your men and tell them to hurry. I do not want to hear another word.'

Tanner heard the now-familiar sound of aero-engines and paused to scan the sky. A moment later he spotted the dark outline of a German aircraft moving in their direction from the south.

Chevannes saw it too. 'Quick! Lie down!'

The Junkers flew over, 1,000 feet or so above them, circled twice then flew west. Tanner, who had remained standing, watched Chevannes get to his feet and brush the snow off his jacket. 'You were right, sir. A recce plane,' he said. 'I wonder how long it will take them to get that information back.'

'Go to your men, Sergeant!' Chevannes hissed.

Soon after, the scouts changed direction, heading west towards the tree line. At last, thought Tanner. Perhaps now they'd make progress. The sooner they got back to the Allied lines the better. Then they could be shot of the Norwegians and, more especially, of Chevannes and his Chasseurs Alpins.

3

Reichsamtsleiter Scheidt reached Lillehammer shortly before noon, having driven the 100 miles without incident. Conscious that he would soon be among fighting men, he had been mindful to change out of his civilian suit and into the tan Party tunic instead. With his Amtsleiter tabs on the collar, Party badge on the right breast pocket and military belt, he felt more suitably attired. Black trousers, knee-length boots and a high-peaked cap completed the make-over.

He had managed to secure a brief audience with the Reichskommissar before leaving Oslo. Terboven had not been best pleased to have his breakfast interrupted but had given Scheidt the written authority to demand whatever assistance he required.

It was with this letter tucked into his tunic pocket that he strode past two SS policemen in Sturmbannführer Kurz's new headquarters, a comfortable town house that, until the day before, had been a lawyer's premises.

Kurz was on the telephone when Scheidt walked in. He was wearing the pale grey uniform of the Allgemeine-SS and his black boots were crossed on the desk in front of him while he gesticulated airily with one hand. Seeing Scheidt, he swung his boots off the desk and ended his conversation.

'Ah, Reichsamtsleiter Scheidt,' he said, beaming. 'Here in person!'

'Have you got him?' Scheidt asked.

'Alas, no.' He stretched forward, tapped a cigarette from a packet and offered it to Scheidt. 'Cigarette? Coffee? Or perhaps something stronger?'

Ignoring Kurz's small talk, Scheidt said, 'So, are your mountain troops closing in?'

'My dear Scheidt,' said Kurz, 'please, sit down.' He motioned to a chair in front of the desk. Scheidt did as he was told. How he disliked men like Kurz. Still young, and with the kind of arrogant insouciance Scheidt knew he had once perfected in himself but which he despised in others. 'There was a heavy snowstorm last night,' Kurz continued. 'A complete whiteout. Not even mountain troops can operate in such conditions. But then again, Odin and his friends would not have got far either.'

'And now?'

'We have reconnaissance aircraft looking for them.'

Someone knocked lightly on the door. 'Yes?' said Kurz.

'A Luftwaffe message just in, sir,' said a junior officer. Kurz read it, smiled, then passed it to Scheidt. 'They've been spotted. And they've got some followers now—what looks like a British patrol. Most considerate of them. Much easier to find twenty men than three.' Kurz unrolled a map. 'The fools are crossing this high open ground here.' He chuckled. 'No cover, just deep snow.'

Impatiently Scheidt grabbed the map. 'Where are the mountain troops now? They should be able to cut them off as they descend towards Tretten.'

'Exactly. You and I will go together to Engelbrecht's headquarters.' Smirking, he opened the door and, with a flourish, ushered Scheidt out.

They took Kurz's car and drove through Lillehammer. Piles of rubble were evidence of the conflict that had taken place the previous day. They passed the station where the structure of a large warehouse still smoked.

'A British supply dump,' Kurz told him. 'Unfortunately it was blown up by a couple of Tommies as our boys entered the yard.'

'I thought the enemy were rolling over?'

'Oh, they are. They've no guns and, it seems, no air force to speak of. The Tommies are beaten and so are the Norwegians. It's really not a question of *if* we catch Odin but *when*.'

As Kurz had promised, General Engelbrecht confirmed that he had a detachment of mountain troops ready for the task. They drove on to Øyer where they found soldiers preparing to attack the Allied lines at Tretten. Horses were pulling artillery pieces, howitzers and antitank guns. There were trucks and other vehicles—even one of the huge Panzer VI heavy tanks, the 'land battleships', that had been brought to Norway. As Kurz threaded his way through the milling troops and past the tank, it suddenly burst into life, a cloud of exhaust erupting from its rear. Scheidt started.

Kurz laughed. 'Don't worry, we'll soon be out of the battle zone.'

Scheidt ignored the comment. A little further on, they reached a farmstead. Kurz pulled into the yard. Some soldiers were playing cards, while others stood round a small fire where a mess tin of coffee was brewing.

'Come on,' said Kurz, leading him into the farmhouse. Several junior officers stood up as they entered. 'Where is Major von Poncets?' he asked.

A lieutenant showed them through to a room where clerks were tapping at typewriters. Major von Poncets, commander of the 4th Battalion, 138th Mountain Regiment, extended a hand. 'I was told you'd be coming.'

'You seem busy here, Major,' said Scheidt.

'My men are going to be attacking the enemy lines at Tretten later. Fortunately, outflanking the Tommies is proving easier than we'd hoped.'

'The men certainly seem in good heart,' said Scheidt.

'Of course,' von Poncets said. 'We're winning!' He clapped his hands together, then said, 'I've got some men for you from the Reconnaissance Battalion of the 6th Mountain Regiment.' He turned to one of his officers and asked him to fetch Hauptmann Zellner. 'He's commander of 1 Company.'

'And a company is how many?' Scheidt asked. 'A hundred?'

Von Poncets smiled. 'I take it you're not a military man, Herr Reichsamtsleiter.'

Scheidt noticed Kurz smirk. 'No,' he said. 'I've been fortunate enough to serve the Reich in other ways.'

'And, of course, we need people like you,' said von Poncets, slapping him convivially on the arm. He added, 'No, Zellner's company is nearer two hundred, although I'm afraid I've told the battalion commander I need most of his men for the fight here. But one platoon of fifty or so should be more than enough and you do have a company commander to lead them. Ah, here he is now.' A young officer entered and saluted crisply. Over his field tunic he had on a thick green-grey cotton wind-jacket, into which was tucked a wool scarf, and a mountain cap, with an embroidered *Edelweiss* on the left side. A pair of tinted round lenses rested on the peak. Hauptmann Wolf Zellner stared ahead implacably.

'Stand easy, Zellner,' said von Poncets. 'I've told these gentlemen that you are taking just one of your platoons.'

'Yes, sir.'

'And you're sure that will be enough men?' Scheidt asked.

Zellner glanced at von Poncets. 'Yes, sir. I don't wish to sound arrogant but one platoon of my men will be more than enough for a few fugitives.'

'I want to underline how important Odin is,' said Scheidt. 'He could be of vital importance to Germany. He must be captured alive. Whether you kill the others or take them prisoner is of no consequence to me. But Odin I must see in person. You have his photograph?'

'Yes, sir,' Zellner replied. 'You can depend on me and my men.'

'Good,' said von Poncets. 'Now, if you'll excuse me, I've a battle to win.'

Zellner saluted again, then left. He would have preferred to be taking part in the attack on Tretten, leading his company into battle, yet von Poncets had insisted. Well, he now knew where that had come from—the politician. At least this mission gave him a chance for revenge. These were the men he'd so nearly caught five days ago north of Elverum. This time he was not going to fail.

By NOON the mixed column of British, Norwegian and French was still some miles southeast of Tretten. The going had been tough. Even the Chasseurs Alpins had struggled, the men frequently losing their footing, or taking a stride forward only to find themselves buried to their waists in drifts. Tanner had been forced to admit to himself that his claim that they would cover six or seven miles in three hours had been over-optimistic. Still, if they had left the *seter* when he had suggested, they would have had more than six hours' start.

Shortly after noon the telltale sounds of battle had begun in the valley below. More aircraft had droned over, while the dull thud of artillery fire had resounded ominously. The unwavering German battle plan. Chevannes, it seemed, had judged that about right.

Four hours later, they were nearing Tretten, the valley sides steeper once more. Below them, the shelling had increased. A flight of bombers arrived, dropping their loads with a rip of detonations. Occasional small-arms chatter drifted to them on the afternoon breeze.

Chevannes and Larsen consulted the map. The Frenchman looked directly behind him to a peak marked as the Skjønsberg. 'We're no more than three kilometres from Tretten,' he said.

'Then we should start dropping into the valley,' said Tanner, who had walked over to join the impromptu conference.

'No,' said Chevannes. 'That's far too risky. We head due north, then cut down to the village. Two more minutes, then we get going.'

Tanner walked back to his men. 'One last effort, lads,' he said. 'Stan, keep an eye on Sandvold, will you? I'll catch you up.' He moved through the trees until he could see Tretten just up the valley and pulled out his scope. He squatted by a jutting rock and peered through the lens. Troops and vehicles were on the road, emerging round a bend in the gorge. Suddenly, movement caught his eye in the trees below to his left. Men moving. A mass of German troops, just a few hundred yards below and no more than a quarter of a mile to the south.

'Bloody hell,' he muttered. 'We're running out of time here.' He scrambled to his feet and caught up with Lieutenant Chevannes.

'German troops, sir, on the slopes below, not far behind.'

'Who would have caught us if we had done as you suggested.'

'No, sir. The moment we saw them we would have altered course.'

'You can't admit it when you are wrong, can you, Sergeant Tanner? Your insolence is wearing very thin. You are speaking to a senior officer.'

'I don't give a damn,' said Tanner. 'If we'd left last night when I said—'

'Please,' said Sandvold, speaking up for the first time. 'No more arguing. Let's just keep going.'

Chevannes glared at Tanner. 'We must push on beyond the village. There is little we can do to stop the Germans outflanking Tretten now.'

Tanner thought of the gelignite and TNT in his pack. There was quite a lot they could do with a sackload of explosives and the advantage of height and steep, rocky slopes. 'I'll tell my men, sir,' he said.

'What's going on, Sarge?' Sykes asked, as Tanner rejoined him.

'Jerries,' said Tanner. 'Down below.' He walked on. He needed to think. Gulbrand had said the Germans were not following them, but what if he had been wrong? The Norwegians had been nearly caught during a German search, strafed twice, and the reconnaissance plane must have spotted them that morning. Coincidence, perhaps. Maybe the enemy didn't know about Sandvold but were aware that they were carrying something important. He rubbed his eyes. Tiredness was putting ideas into his head.

'Sarge! Sarge!'

Tanner was startled from his thoughts.

'Looks like we're being followed,' Sykes gasped.

Adrenaline coursed through Tanner's blood and in an instant his mind cleared. He reached the end of their column where Private Riggs and Chambers were each crouched behind a pine, looking backwards.

'How far?' said Tanner, as he pulled out his scope once more.

'Couldn't say, Sarge,' said Riggs, 'but mebbe a third of a mile.'

Tanner peered through the scope. Yes, there they were, climbing in their direction. He passed the scope to Sykes.

'They're wearing caps and goggles,' said Sykes.

'Mountain troops,' said Tanner. 'Right. Let's get out of here.' He hurried his men forward, until they caught up with Chevannes.

'*Mon dieu*,' muttered Chevannes, when Tanner told him.

'We need to find out exactly how many men there are,' said Tanner. His mind was alert now, his heart thumping. 'I'll take Sykes here and two of my men and head back for a dekko. You keep going and we'll catch you up.'

Chevannes nodded, his face taut.

Tanner hurried over to Lance Corporal Erwood, the Bren leader. 'Dan, I want you to take charge of the rest of the lads. And see that Norwegian civvy up ahead with the Frog officer? Don't let him out of your sight.'

'Aye, Sarge. I won't.'

Tanner slapped him on the back. Then, collecting Chambers and Riggs, he looked around at the snow and trees covering the mountain. He spotted a small spur a short distance above and decided it would offer the view and cover they needed. 'Up there, quick, to that crest.'

They scrambled up and, as they crouched, Tanner was relieved to see they had a fine view down the undulating slopes of the valley sides.

'There they are,' hissed Sykes.

Tanner watched the enemy troops reach a clearing, pause, spy the tracks in the snow, then continue forward. 'Start counting them,' he said quietly, then screwed his scope onto his rifle.

'You going to start firing, Sarge?' asked Chambers.

'Keep counting, Punter,' said Tanner, 'and if you've got a full magazine, take it from your rifle and hold on to it until I ask you to pass it to me.' He raised the rifle. Through the scope he could clearly see the first section of men spread out in a loose single file and, Tanner was glad to see, their rifles were still slung over their backs. Behind the section leader was a machine-gunner, his weapon carried on his shoulder. A further section of ten followed, and another beyond that. Tanner led his aim along the column.

'Thirty-nine, sir,' said Riggs.

'That's what I make it,' agreed Sykes.

'Fine,' said Tanner. 'You ready with that magazine, Punter?'

'Yes, Sarge,' said Chambers.

Tanner reckoned the leading troops were now at about 400 yards. Remembering that distance was easily overestimated when you were looking downwards, he aimed just a fraction low at the lead trooper and fired.

The man dropped immediately, and Tanner fired his next three shots while the startled troops looked around wildly. Even once they were prostrate on the snow, there were some easy targets. Tanner reckoned he had hit seven men with his first magazine. The first German rifle shot cracked through the mountainside, way off, but was followed by many more, bullets zipping through the trees above and below them.

'Give me that magazine,' said Tanner. He unclicked the first, drove the replacement into its place and fired again. Five shots and by then the machine-gunner of the second section was firing. The aim was wild, but the bursts were well spread. Tanner fired twice more. Another burst from the machine gun, and this time bullets fizzed close by. Riggs screamed.

'Sarge, we need to get out of here!' Sykes had grabbed Riggs, who was clutching the side of his head.

Tanner pulled back the bolt one last time and hit a man square in the chest. 'Is it serious?' he said to Sykes as they scrambled down from the spur.

'I've been hit in the head!' Riggs shouted, but he was still upright.

Shots continued to ping through the trees, but most were fizzing harmlessly above their heads. 'Just keep going, lads,' Tanner urged.

Only once the shots died out did they pause. Tanner put an arm round Riggs's shoulders. 'Let's have a look at you.' Blood covered the side of Riggs's face and neck. 'Under all this red stuff you look pretty intact,' said Tanner. Then he spotted a gash and laughed. 'It's a nick! You've been grazed but you'll be fine.'

'It really hurts, though, Sarge.'

'Stop being such an old woman,' said Sykes, pulling out a dressing pack.

'Hang on a minute,' said Tanner. 'Blood in the snow could be useful.

Good thing about a cut on the head—lots of blood. That's it, drip there.'

'Hang on, Sarge, I'm draining away!' Riggs was indignant.

'King and country, Riggs, think of that,' said Tanner. 'Right, now let's get a move on back to the others.'

'How long do you reckon that'll hold them up?' Sykes asked.

'Not long. But it'll make them more cautious, and that'll slow them. And, of course, there's a few less for us to worry about.'

'That was good shooting back there, Sarge,' said Chambers, as they hurried onwards, following the tracks in the snow.

'Thanks, Punter. I reckon maybe ten won't be going any further today.'

Pausing often to glance behind them, they marched on, following the tracks of the rest of the column. Tanner conceded that Riggs now needed to staunch the flow of blood, so they stopped to wrap a bandage round his head. Despite the holdup, they caught up with the others half an hour later. Tanner reported to Chevannes. He told the Frenchman little, except to warn him that there were now about thirty men pursuing them.

It was just after six o'clock. Tanner guessed they must be level with Tretten. How much further was Chevannes going to take them before they cut down into the valley? They were so close. The sound of battle told him the Allies were still there. Another half-hour and they'd make it.

And then they all heard the increase in shelling, the intensity of small-arms fire, and through the trees they could see Stukas wheeling and diving, their manic sirens screaming through the din of battle.

No one said a word. What was there to say? The Allied positions in Tretten were about to be overrun. How could it be otherwise with that weight of fire? All too soon they'd be back where they'd started, high on a mountain, without food or rest, out of reach of safety once more. Only now the enemy was stalking them.

Tanner tried desperately to think. Despair engulfed him. Then ahead, through the trees, he saw something that gave him a glimmer of hope.

SCHEIDT HAD RETURNED to Lillehammer in a better mood than when he had walked into Kurz's office earlier that day. He had been right to leave Oslo. In Lillehammer he could chivvy Kurz and badger army men like Engelbrecht. Keeping control was essential—he simply couldn't afford to allow others to let Odin slip from his grasp.

Where was Sandvold? Perhaps already in the hands of the mountain troops. Scheidt had been impressed by von Poncets and Zellner. Both men had the kind of energy and determination that gave him confidence. The Wehrmacht might be rigid and narrow-minded, but they were straightforward to deal with—a damn sight more so than the Allgemeine-SS.

Scheidt lit a cigarette and looked out of the dormer window of his hotel room. In the streets below, Lillehammer was quiet but he could hear the reverberation of battle to the north. 'We're winning,' von Poncets had told him. Now Reichsamtsleiter Scheidt had to win his personal battle.

DESPITE SCHEIDT'S mounting confidence, Zellner had not yet caught Odin.

Less than an hour earlier, however, when the tracks of about twenty men had been spotted in the snow, he had been convinced that success was just round the corner. Footsore and weary, the Tommies would gladly surrender and Odin would be theirs. He had even played in his mind the scene at von Poncets' HQ, as he handed over the Norwegian. 'Odin, sir, as requested.'

But then they had been ambushed. Eleven men, he'd lost. Four dead, and another five soon would be if he didn't get them off the mountain. They had left one group from the platoon behind at the request of his Battalion CO, but he wished he had those extra ten men now. Common sense suggested he should return. He now had twenty-eight fully fit men, of which at least four would have to stay behind to carry the two most seriously wounded off the mountain. That gave him only a slight numerical advantage. To make matters worse, the enemy had proved they would not lie down.

Zellner had trained for years, waiting for the chance to test himself in battle, yet as far as he could make out, the war in Norway had been won so far by the Luftwaffe and the gunners. It bothered him, too, that the only time he had been given a specific task—namely the capture of the Norwegian King's men a few days before—he had failed. Duped by a peasant farmer. The man had made a fool of him so Zellner had killed him.

Nagging doubts entered his head again. That had been clever shooting by the enemy. Two or more of them must have had sniper rifles and that had surprised him. His men, once so confident, were now stunned, he could tell; good comrades were dead. It had stopped them in their tracks.

With sudden clarity Zellner cast aside the doubts. Instinct told him that his enemy was not well armed, despite the sniper rifles. Furthermore, if the streams of British and Norwegian prisoners he had seen earlier that day were anything to go by, the enemy up ahead would be ill-equipped and short of sleep and food. His men were fit and healthy. They would capture Odin. Then he would find the men with the sniper rifles and kill them.

SERGEANT TANNER regarded the *seter* ahead. It was much like the one they had sheltered in the previous evening, but further up the mountain and in a clearing. Beyond it, a mountain stream ran from a narrow ravine above it into a shallower one below.

'Do you see what I see, Stan?' Tanner said to Sykes.

'Another hut, Sarge,' said Sykes.

'Correct,' said Tanner. 'And a stream.' He rubbed his chin. 'Nice place to set up a juicy ambush, I reckon.'

Sykes looked at him doubtfully. He couldn't see how a run-down shack could be a good place for an ambush. In fact, he wasn't sure any kind of ambush was a good idea.

'Listen, Stan. Those buggers are going to catch us up soon enough, so we've got no choice but to stand and face them. I know they're Nazi bastards but they're not going to leave their wounded to die, are they? That means there'll probably be only twenty of them—maybe twenty-five at most.' Sykes still seemed doubtful. 'We all walk into the hut, then jump out the back and into the stream. No more footprints. By going up and down the stream we can get the men into position without Jerry seeing where we've gone. A few can clamber up onto that small cliff—it'll give a perfect line of fire. Others can go down the stream and hide behind trees and rocks.'

Sykes was smiling now.

'Jerry's going to see the tracks going into the hut and none coming out,' Tanner continued. 'And he'll see a bit of Riggs's blood. If he's got any sense he'll smell a rat. If it's Mr Sandvold he's after, he's not going to risk spraying the hut with machine-gun fire, is he? Which means he's got to send some men forward to investigate.'

'And we shoot them.'

'I reckon so. Then he's got even fewer men. First we've got to persuade Chevannes. Maybe you should suggest it. He'll take it from you.'

To Tanner's surprise, Chevannes was receptive to the idea, as explained by Sykes. 'Yes, I think there is something in what you say.' He turned to Tanner. 'You could learn something from your clever corporal, Sergeant.'

The French lieutenant ordered the men to walk quickly to the *seter*, while Sykes and Tanner unwrapped Riggs's head once more. With drops of blood from Riggs's cut spreading in the snow, they followed the rest of the men into the hut. There was a shuttered window at the back, leading straight to the stream. Chevannes divided the men, posting his Chasseurs Alpins on top of the shallow ravine above the *seter*, and ordering Tanner to disperse his men south of the hut. 'No one will fire until I do so, understand? *Vite*. We don't have much time.'

Chevannes' men clambered out first, followed by the Norwegians. As his own men were about to follow, Tanner stopped them. 'Listen, lads,' he said, 'make sure you position yourselves with decent cover, all right? Make sure your ammo's near to hand. And don't fire until Lieutenant Chevannes gives the order. Once he fires, you can fire at will.' They were frightened, but exhilarated, too, he knew. 'And don't worry about getting wet feet because when we've got these bastards beat, we can pinch their boots.'

He patted them on the back as they squeezed out of the window, one by one, then noticed Sykes pulling at the straps of his pack.

Sykes caught his eye and grinned. 'We could always give 'im an even bigger 'eadache, Sarge. I lifted a few bits of high explosive. No point leaving it all at that train depot.'

Tanner smiled. 'What do you think I'm carrying in these?' He pointed to his respirator satchel and pack.

Sykes chuckled. 'Bloody 'ell, Sarge, and there was me thinkin' I was the only sneaky bastard round 'ere.' He looked round conspiratorially. 'We could string something up to the door.'

'Have we got time?' Tanner peered through a slit in the timber wall.

Ignoring the sergeant's concerns, Sykes was already taking a length of safety fuse from his haversack. He cut a short strip with his clasp knife, tied one end round the latch on the door frame and threaded it through the handle. He took out a hand grenade, loosened the pin and tied the other end of the fuse, so that the grenade hung gently against the door.

'Now for an extra something.' He produced a packet of Nobel's gelignite and tied it to the door handle with more safety fuse. 'Let's get out of here.'

Jumping into the stream, they clambered along the rocks, praying they wouldn't be spotted. Tanner wanted to run but the splashing would be too noisy, yet if the enemy arrived now he and Sykes would be sitting ducks. Fifteen yards ahead he spotted a pine, leaning out over the stream. If we can just reach that, he thought. The trunk would hide his tracks on the far side. 'Stan!' he whispered, and pointed urgently to the tree. Sykes nodded.

Reaching the tree first, the corporal clambered up out of the stream bed, holding out a hand for Tanner. A short distance away there was a knoll offering good cover. The two men ran over to it. For a moment, Tanner lay on his back. In the valley below he could still hear the battle, but there was silence around them, save for water gurgling through the rocks.

Tanner rolled over, pulling his rifle to his chin. They were about sixty yards from the hut, well hidden from the enemy. Only a few yards away Erwood and the Bren crew had their machine gun ready.

A minute ticked by. Tanner wondered where the Germans were. 'Come on, damn you,' he muttered.

'There, Sarge!' whispered Sykes. 'Look! See that Jerry?'

The man was studying the tracks in the snow that led to the *seter*. Tanner gripped the barrel of his rifle. About bloody time, he thought.

HAUPTMANN ZELLNER saw the leading group stop. He hurried forward.

'Tracks, sir,' said the sergeant, 'leading to the hut. And there's blood on the ground. Looks like at least one is wounded.'

Zellner took out his pistol. He waved his arm in a circular motion, the signal for his men to deploy into an open skirmish line. Two machine-gun teams hurried through the trees sixty yards either side of him, while the third fell in beside him. At the same time, the rest of the men had taken up positions behind trees and on the ground. The *seter* was now covered. Zellner felt proud of his men.

'Do you think they're in there?' the sergeant asked.

Zellner was not sure. It seemed likely. These were the only tracks. He lifted his binoculars. He could see nothing out of the ordinary. But what if the hut was a trap? He bit at his thumbnail. He had to do something. His mission was to capture Odin. He must act decisively.

'I'm going to tell them to surrender,' Zellner told his sergeant, 'and if they don't come out, I'll send you forward. What can they do? We've got them covered.'

TANNER HAD SEEN the German officer lift his binoculars. Seconds ticked by. The enemy officer could not have seen them. Tanner sighed with relief.

'*Ergebt euch!*' he heard suddenly. '*Waffen neider!*'

'What's he goin' on about?' whispered Sykes.

'I think he wants us to show ourselves.'

'Come out with your hands up!' the German shouted in English.

Tanner lifted his head. The German officer was ordering his men across the open ground to the *seter*. Four stood at either side of the door, while two stood back a few yards, their rifles aimed at the hut's entrance.

'The moment of truth, Sarge,' whispered Sykes.

One man walked to the door, listened a moment, then kicked hard.

The door swung open. Then came a deafening crack and the hut erupted in a ball of angry orange flame. A shot rang out. Dan Erwood's Bren began to chatter. The Germans seemed frozen to the spot. Tanner began firing. He saw one man go down. *Where's that Jerry officer?* Already his view was clouded by smoke rolling across the clearing. Spurts of flame and tracer bullets glowed curiously through the haze, pinning down the rifle fire from beyond the stream.

'We've got to take out those MGs,' Tanner said to Sykes. 'Dan!' he called. 'Keep firing bursts, all right? I need you to cover me and Sykes.'

Tanner turned to Sykes and pointed behind them. 'On three we're going to head back twenty yards over there where the ground slopes away, then get underneath the line of fire and work round their flank. OK?'

Sykes nodded.

Tanner took a deep breath. 'One, two, *three!*'

Bullets followed them like a swarm of bees but it appeared luck was with them. Suddenly twenty yards had been crossed, the ground was falling away, and the bullets were zapping clear into the wood above him. To his relief he saw that Sykes was beside him.

'Bloody hell!' gasped the corporal. 'That was a bit hot, Sarge!'

'Pretty warm,' agreed Tanner. 'Where are the rest of them?' He spotted Hepworth, Kershaw and Bell. Then he saw McAllister, across the stream from Bell. Good, he thought. That'll do.

He picked up a lump of snow and hurled it at Hepworth, who saw him, and began to scurry over. Another snowball caught the attention of the other three. Short bursts of machine-gun fire still spat intermittently above their heads, while cracks of rifle fire rang out. 'We're going to take out those MGs,' said Tanner, to the five men. 'We cross the stream out of the line of fire, move on sixty yards, then come round the back of them.' The boys looked tense. 'You know the drill,' he said. 'We work in pairs. Two forward, two pairs covering. Let's go.'

They made it across the stream and pushed forward. He hoped the enemy would be too busy with the fire in front of them to have thought of an attack from behind. He was glad to see his guess had been correct. Signalling to the others to follow, he pulled McAllister by the shoulder, then ordered Hepworth to pair off with Sykes, Kershaw with Bell. 'Watch out for our own fire,' he warned.

He pulled out three grenades and briefly scanned ahead. They were behind the far left of the German skirmish line. One of the machine guns was just forty yards ahead, while the second was sixty yards to the right. He could hear bursts from a third further away. His intention was to get within twenty yards of the first two and lob grenades at them. The danger would come if the gunners saw them first.

'Stan, you and Hepworth run towards that first MG and hurl a couple of grenades,' he whispered. 'Mac, you and I'll get the other. Bell, follow Sykes and Hep and cover them. Kershaw, you cover me and Mac. On three.'

He gripped the first grenade in his hand, counted down visually with his fingers, then sprinted through the snow, praying the bullets would miss them once more. Thirty yards to go. Twenty. Pull the pin from the grenade. *One, two, throw*. A rifleman saw the grenade, looked round in horror, but it was too late. It detonated, spraying the machine-gunners with shards of searing iron. A second detonation came a split second later, just as Tanner brought his rifle to his shoulder, pulled back the bolt and fired, silencing the startled rifleman. Bullets fizzed above his head. Tanner ducked but, keeping his rifle tight into his chin, shouted, *'Hände hoch! Hände hoch!'*

To his amazement, several German troops dropped their rifles and slowly raised their arms. 'Where's the bloody officer?' shouted Tanner, then saw him, crouched by a tree, still clutching his pistol. *'Hände* bloody *hoch*, mate,' Tanner said to him, his rifle pointed at the enemy officer's heart.

Zellner dropped his pistol, his face flexing with anger.

'Cease firing!' yelled Tanner. A bullet pinged through the trees to his right. 'Bloody stop shooting. They've surrendered!' he shouted, as he stepped forward and picked up Zellner's pistol.

AS THE GUNS FELL SILENT on the mountain above Tretten, the battle continued to rage in the valley below. The day had been every bit as difficult and depressing as Brigadier Morgan had suspected. It was nearly eight o'clock in the evening when Major Dornley stepped into his office. 'Latest news?'

Dornley looked grave. 'Enemy mountain troops have overrun the village. Our men fighting there are presumed captured. All lines are dead.'

Morgan steadied himself against the doorway and put a hand to his brow. 'God almighty,' he muttered. 'We've got almost no brigade left.'

Suddenly there was a loud drone of aircraft. Dornley and Morgan looked up as the wailing siren of Stuka dive-bombers shrieked overhead.

Both men fell flat on the ground. The whistle of bombs was followed by an ear-splitting explosion. Morgan felt himself lifted up and pushed down on the ground again. With every boom and whoosh, the building shuddered.

Then the Stukas were gone, but as Morgan staggered to his feet, he could hear artillery and small-arms fire drawing closer. My brigade, he thought.

They could do no more. 'Dornley,' he said, 'order survivors to block the roads, get the remaining trucks and vehicles loaded up and tell everyone to fall back.'

Dornley nodded.

Morgan hurried back into his office to collect his papers. His brigade, as a fighting force, had ceased to exist. They would head for the village of Kvam, where General Ruge intended them to meet Major General Paget's freshly arrived 15th Brigade. It would take the Germans a while to get there, Morgan hoped. Kvam was some forty miles away.

4

Tanner put an arm to the nearest tree and rested his head against it. Now that the fight was over, the adrenaline surge that had kept him going evaporated as quickly as it had arrived.

'Sarge,' said a voice. Sykes was standing beside him. 'Three casualties. Gibson's dead, Saxby and Riggs wounded.'

'Riggs again?' asked Tanner.

'Bullet through the shoulder. The lads are patching him up now.'

'What about Saxby?'

'Shoulder as well. Should pull through. Neither'll be going far, though.'

'We'll have to think about what's best for the wounded. And Sandvold?'

'Not a scratch. One of the Froggies bought it and another was wounded. Lieutenants Larsen and Nielssen are still good.'

'And Chevannes?'

'Nothing wrong with him,' said Sykes, with a wry smile.

Tanner should have felt pleased. His plan had worked and the enemy threat was, for the moment, over. Yet despair overwhelmed him once more. It was half past eight in the evening and the sound of battle from the valley was receding into the distance by the minute, and with it their chance of freedom. They had been so close again—just a mile or two from the safety of their own lines. Now the finishing line had been moved far out of reach. It was Chevannes' fault. By God, Tanner hated the man.

'Sergeant Tanner!' *Chevannes*. 'A good victory,' said the Frenchman, 'although you should not have blown the shelter without my permission.'

Tanner took a deep breath. 'It gave us the chance to hit them hard.'

'Always answering back,' Chevannes snapped. 'We need to tie up these prisoners and bury the dead. See to it quickly, while I question their officer.'

Tanner walked away and called his men over. 'Well done, lads.' He looked into their faces. They had fought their first fight, had been touched by death and had survived. He knew they were better soldiers for the experience.

He ordered six to fetch the dead, instructing them to line the bodies up by the stream, then strip them of usable clothing and kit. They were to cover them with snow and stones from the brook. Burying the dead; a grim task.

He took McAllister and Hepworth to the prisoners, who were being guarded by two of Chevannes' Chasseurs Alpins not far from the blackened crater where the hut had once been. Thick smoke rose into the air from the still-burning logs, a beacon for any passing aircraft. They needed to get a move on. 'Iggery, lads,' Tanner said. 'Let's get into the woods.' He began pushing and shoving the prisoners and, with the help of McAllister and Hepworth and the two Frenchmen, walked them to the cover of the trees.

A hundred yards from the *seter*, he ordered them to stop. 'What's this?' Tanner asked a youth with dark hair, pointing to the flower embroidered on his sleeve. The same flower was on their field caps too.

'*Ein Edelweiss*,' the man replied. 'It is the symbol of all Gebirgsjäger troops.' His English was heavily accented. 'We are mountain troops.'

'And your kit? Good, is it?' Tanner asked.

'Yes. We have the best of any fighting soldier in Norway.'

'Good,' said Tanner. 'You tell the others that I want all of you stripped. I want your jackets, tunics, boots and caps. And your goggles.'

'Isn't that against the Geneva Convention, Sarge?' asked McAllister.

'Mac, do you want to survive this?' Tanner snapped.

'Yes, Sarge.'

'Then don't worry your head about things like that. And, no, I don't think it is against the Geneva Convention. I want them to empty their packs too.'

'You can't do this to us,' said the English speaker.

'I can and I will,' said Tanner. 'Now, give me your pack and get undressed.' The man slowly slipped off his rucksack. Tanner emptied it onto the ground. To his delight there was a chunk of bread and some sausage. The man had a flask of schnapps too. Tanner ate hungrily, took a swig from the flask and felt the burning liquid soothe his throat. He passed the food and the flask to Hepworth then exchanged his boots for the German's. 'Beautiful,' he said aloud. He threw his own boots to the prisoner whose boots he was now wearing. 'Here,' he said. 'Have these.'

He went to help Sykes and the others, and found them laying stones on Gibson's grave. 'Take it in turn to get yourselves some kit from the prisoners,' he told them. 'Kershaw, hop it.'

'What do we do now, Sarge?' Sykes asked.

'We're too late to get to Tretten.' Tanner sighed. 'We've got to find somewhere to rest. A farm or something.'

'Can't we just take our lads and scarper?' Sykes asked.

Tanner shook his head. 'If this Sandvold is as important as the colonel made out, we've got to get him out. I can't abandon him to Chevannes.'

THE BURIAL WAS COMPLETED, as was the reassignment of German kit. The prisoners, stripped to their shirts and trousers, huddled together, shivering.

Eventually Chevannes reappeared with the German officer.

'Captain Zellner,' said Chevannes.

'What have you got out of him?' said Tanner.

'The captain refuses to say anything.'

Tanner was about to speak when Lieutenant Larsen appeared. As he saw the German, his eyes widened. 'You! You were at the farm. At Økset. North of Elverum. What did you do to the farmer?'

Zellner glanced at Chevannes. 'Nothing,' he said. 'Nothing at all.'

'Liar!' said Larsen, punching Zellner hard in the stomach. The German doubled over and collapsed onto the ground.

'What do you think you are doing?' shouted Chevannes.

Larsen grabbed Zellner by the scruff of the neck, pulled him to his feet. 'I want to know what he did to my cousin!'

Chevannes turned to Zellner. '*Capitaine*,' he said, 'can you give me your word as an officer that you did not harm Lieutenant Larsen's cousin?'

Zellner ran his hand round his collar. 'Of course.'

Larsen glared at Zellner. 'You lie.'

Tanner put a hand on Larsen's shoulder. 'Leave it, sir.'

Shaking his head, Larsen walked away.

'Sir,' said Tanner now, 'do you really think his say-so counts for anything? He's a bloody Nazi.'

'He is still an officer,' the Frenchman replied. 'You may not understand what honour is, Sergeant Tanner, but I do.'

'I don't believe this.' Tanner spun round and went to his men.

The German caught sight of his troops huddled in the trees, and spoke angrily to Chevannes, who turned sharply.

'Sergeant! Come back! What have you done to the prisoners? They will die of cold if we leave them like that.'

'Then that's one less thing to worry about, isn't it, sir? Actually, sir,' Tanner continued, ignoring the lieutenant's barely disguised fury, 'I was wondering what you were thinking of doing with them. We can't take them with us and we can't let them loose. There is, of course, one way of getting them off our hands—'

'What are you saying, Sergeant? That we shoot them?'

'Of course not, sir. I was thinking we could try to find another hut and tie them up there. If they keep cosy they'll probably live. It's not that cold.'

'Or you could behave honourably and give them back their uniforms.'

Tanner's patience snapped. 'All you seem to care about is honour. This isn't knights-in-shining-armour, this is war. I don't give a toss about upsetting these Jerries. I care about making sure my men survive and that we get back to our lines. I made a solemn promise to get Mr Sandvold to safety and I'm going to bloody well do it. But we're in a whole load of trouble and we need every bit of help we can get our hands on. If you think that's wrong, then you're an even bigger fool than I thought. Sir.'

Chevannes' lips moved as though he was about to answer. Instead, he barked orders that they were to get going and take the prisoners with them.

They set off in a column, the prisoners carrying Riggs, Saxby and the wounded Frenchman on stretchers made from rifles and greatcoats. It was, Tanner guessed, still a few degrees above freezing. Although the light was fading, there was still a couple of hours' daylight ahead.

Every so often, Chevannes paused to scan the area with his binoculars. They had been going for almost half an hour when the French lieutenant told them to head up the mountain, out of the tree line and towards the open plateau. The men groaned, but even with his naked eye, Tanner could see the *seter* through the trees above. Perhaps Chevannes was starting to listen.

'Not another night in a bloody hut,' said Hepworth.

'I'm sure Mr Chevannes knows what he's doing,' said Tanner.

'You've changed your tune,' Sykes said, in a low voice.

'Only because it's what I told him we should do. We're going to ditch the prisoners in that basha up there.' He pointed through the trees to the *seter*.

On reaching the hut, Chevannes ordered the prisoners to be herded inside. Using fuse cable, they bound the men. Tanner noticed that Zellner still had his binoculars round his neck and his empty holster at his side.

'I'll take those,' said Tanner, lifting the binoculars over Zellner's head and removing the holster and bullet pouches from his belt.

Zellner stared at him, then at his rifle. 'A sniper rifle,' he said in English. 'I'll not forget this, Tanner. And next time I see you, I will kill you.'

'I'm sure you will.' Tanner smiled, drew his hand into a fist and rammed it into Zellner's temple. The German gasped and lost consciousness.

'Where d'you learn to do that?' asked Sykes.

'The army can teach you a lot,' Tanner replied, 'including how to box. I don't like knocking someone out like that but he's a filthy piece of work and he threatened to kill me.'

With the Germans tied and left in the *seter*, the men retraced their steps to the trees. Chevannes called a halt. 'We'll rest a while,' he said.

Larsen joined Tanner. 'I'm sorry. I behaved badly with that German.'

'No need to apologise, sir.'

'It was my fault,' he said. 'We stopped at my cousin's farm and took his truck. I didn't think at the time. It was obvious to me later that the Germans would come back and find it gone.'

'And you think they took your cousin?'

'I do not know. They might well have killed him.' He sighed. 'It has been preying on my mind, you see. Anyway, I just wanted to explain.'

Tanner nodded. 'Thank you, sir,' he said, then moved a few steps and leaned against a tree next to Sandvold. The Norwegian was as white as a ghost. 'Are you all right, sir?' Tanner asked him.

'I am tired,' he replied. 'I am forty-seven, after all. This has been a long trek for a man of my age.' He slumped against the tree. Tanner caught him and lowered him to the ground.

'My God, what has happened to him?' Larsen had hurried over.

Nielssen joined them. 'Is he all right?' he asked.

Tanner felt for a pulse. 'He's passed out.' He took out the flask of schnapps and tipped it into Sandvold's mouth. The Norwegian spluttered and opened his eyes. 'I am sorry,' he said. 'What must you think of me?'

Tanner gave Sandvold the flask. 'It's all right. Drink some more.' He stood up beside the two Norwegians. 'None of us can go much further tonight. We need to find somewhere to rest, something to eat.'

Larsen said, 'You are right, Sergeant. If we keep going like this, none of us will make it, let alone Professor Sandvold.'

Professor? Tanner looked at the man. Just what was his secret?

'There are farmsteads along this side of the valley,' said Nielssen.

'We must be careful,' said Tanner. 'With the Germans in the valley, it will be hard to know who to trust. But if that means we have to take our chance with some farmer, so be it.'

'Hot food.' Nielssen smiled. 'I would risk a lot for that right now.'

It began to snow, only lightly, but Tanner was pleased to see the flakes drifting down. There was, of course, every chance that Zellner and his men would free themselves and get off the mountain. And then what? It wouldn't take them long to get down to the valley, where they would fetch help and begin to search the mountain once more. He tilted his face to the sky and felt the flakes land and dissolve. At least the snow would hide their tracks.

He saw Sandvold lift himself to his feet, then reach back to the tree for support. 'Let me get you a stick, Professor.' He picked up a fallen pine branch and cut off the loose twigs with his sword bayonet.

'Thank you.' Sandvold straightened his back. 'You know, I never in my wildest dreams imagined tramping across a mountain at dawn, praying not be shot.' He shook his head. 'Do you have a family, Sergeant?'

'No,' Tanner replied. 'Only the army.'

'A bachelor like me,' Sandvold smiled, 'wedded to your work. But I do have a mother still alive. At least, I pray she is. I was told to leave Oslo the moment the invasion began, but my mother would not come with me. I felt I could not leave her. And then Colonel Gulbrand arrived with three men and suddenly the matter was no longer in my hands. And all because of my work and what I know.' He sighed again. 'Sergeant, I would be most grateful if you could get me to safety. I want to help my country. And I also want to live for the sake of my mother, if that is not too sentimental.'

'Why are you asking me this?' asked Tanner. 'Lieutenant Chevannes is in charge. And there are two of your countrymen.'

'I am saying this to you because I know what Colonel Gulbrand told you. I heard every word. And I agree with him. You are evidently a highly capable soldier, Sergeant. Even a pacifist like me can see that.'

'Thank you,' said Tanner. 'I'll do my best, Professor.'

CHEVANNES AGREED that they should find a farmstead in which to lie up. They were now a couple of miles north of Tretten, walking through dense forest. They emerged along the top of a mountain pasture. The snow had stopped. At the far end of the field there was a gate and beyond that a path.

Nielssen and Larsen led them along the track, which ended at an old farmstead. The two Norwegian officers approached cautiously while the rest waited. The promise of warmth and food was intoxicating. Tanner watched the men reach the front door and heard a dog bark.

Anxious minutes. Tanner could see the tension and exhaustion on the face of every man. And there were the wounded to think of too—they needed help if they were to avoid gangrene and septicaemia.

A middle-aged man with grey hair appeared at the door. He listened to Larsen for a while, then stepped from the house and walked towards the barn. Larsen beckoned. 'Follow him,' he said. 'He wants us all in there.'

The farmer opened one of the twin doors, then swung his arm in a sweeping motion—*in you go*—until the men followed.

Larsen said, 'His wife and daughter are coming. They're bringing bread and soup first, then hot water and bandages.'

It was dark and dusty inside, the smell of dried hay and straw mixing with the stench of animal dung. Tanner joined Sykes and eased off his pack. He felt in his haversack for Zellner's pistol, a Walther semiautomatic that fitted comfortably in his hand. The men were quiet, too exhausted to speak. Tanner noticed that a Frenchman was already asleep on the straw. So, too, was Sandvold. Tanner thought about the professor. Had he perhaps invented some new terror weapon—one that would change the course of the war? If so, the sooner Britain got to use it the better.

He lay back against his pack and closed his eyes, sleep a luxurious release. Then, all too quickly, he was being shaken awake. Next to him were Sykes and a pretty girl with an oval face, pale eyes and straw-coloured hair.

'This is Anna Rostad, Sarge,' said Sykes. 'She's brought us some food.'

'It's not much, I'm afraid, Sergeant,' she said, in fluent English. She passed him a bowl of soup and a piece of bread.

'Thank you,' said Tanner. The warm meaty stock tasted good.

'My mother and I have done what we can for the wounded men,' she continued, 'but they need to be seen by a doctor. We could take them tomorrow.'

Tanner thought. 'Where would you take them? Tretten?'

'Yes. There's a doctor there.'

'The Germans would have surgeons too.' He paused. 'But you'd be questioned. What would you say?'

'That we found them. What else would the Germans expect us to do? If the men stay here, they will probably die. In Tretten they at least have a chance.'

Tanner smiled. 'You're very brave. Thank you.'

Anna shrugged. 'It's the least we can do. My brother, Jonny, was called up two weeks ago. We have heard nothing since. He is my twin.' She wiped the corner of her eye. 'Really, it is too terrible.' She stood up.

Tanner grabbed his rifle and got to his feet. 'Where are Larsen and Chevannes?' he asked Sykes.

'I think they're in the farmhouse.'

'They're talking with Father,' said Anna. 'I will take you to them.'

Anna led him across the yard and into the house. The three men were in the kitchen sitting round a large table. A lamp in the centre of the table flickered gently, lighting the men's faces.

'What do you want, Sergeant?' said Chevannes.

'To talk to you about what we're going to do.'

'You're not an officer. It's up to us to make such plans.'

'You might be the officer in charge here, sir,' Tanner retorted, 'but I still have ten men to look after.'

Larsen looked at Chevannes. 'He has a point.'

Chevannes sighed. 'You may stay and listen, Sergeant, but our decisions will be final. Understood?'

Larsen spread his map on the table.

'We have to head north,' said Chevannes.

'We need roads,' said Tanner, 'a vehicle of some kind. I've no idea how far the Allies have fallen back, but whatever distance they've retreated, we'll never be able to walk faster through the mountains than Jerry can through the valley. And he's got M/T.' Tanner leaned over the table. 'What about this road? It goes from Tretten, cuts over the mountains into this valley here. If we can get there and find some transport, we could maybe get all the way to here—Otta—without seeing any Germans at all.'

Chevannes shook his head. 'Brilliant, Sergeant. Just how will we get past the Germans in the valley and across a three-hundred-metre-wide lake? And where exactly will we find a vehicle that will take us all?'

'We don't cross the lake. We cross at Tretten and we go at night. We have German uniforms now.'

'There is a place you could cross,' said Anna. 'Just north of the village, there is a small spur that juts out into the river. The crossing is only about a hundred and fifty metres wide at that point and on the bank are boats.'

Good girl, thought Tanner.

Anna spoke hurriedly to her father, who nodded. Then Larsen spoke to her in Norwegian. For a minute an argument ensued.

'She wants to come too,' said Larsen. 'I told her it is out of the question.'

'But my brother and I hiked over the Oppland Mountains last summer.' She looked imploringly at Tanner. 'Please,' she said. 'I want to help.'

'It is far too dangerous for a woman,' said Chevannes, 'and especially for a pretty girl like yourself, mademoiselle.'

Tanner groaned to himself, then said, 'But she knows these mountains and being a woman, the Germans would be less likely to suspect her.'

'And I speak German,' she added.

'She'll slow us down,' said Chevannes.

'I will not,' said Anna, defiant now.

Her father interjected angrily.

'He says she is twenty-two,' Larsen translated, 'and old enough to know her own mind. He also says he is proud of his daughter for wanting to help.'

Chevannes sat quietly. 'I want to think about it. I am not at all convinced that we should even try to cross the valley. In any case, are you proposing that we stay here until tomorrow night?'

'There is a cave in the forest above the farm,' said Anna. 'It is a secret place. We could show you in the morning.'

'And we need to move the wounded,' added Tanner. 'Anna and her father are proposing to take them in their cart to Tretten.'

'And hand them over to the enemy?' said Chevannes.

'They will die if they stay here,' said Anna. 'They need proper attention.'

'Sir?' said Tanner. Chevannes picked at his lip. Come on, thought Tanner. Make a decision. 'Sir,' he said again, 'we need to make a plan.'

'Be quiet!' Chevannes snapped. 'I need to think.'

'But what about the wounded?' Tanner insisted. 'You're the commander here. Mr Rostad and his daughter are willing to risk their lives to save them. Tell them what you want them to do.'

'All right, damn you!' Chevannes ran his hands through his hair. 'Take the wounded men. In the morning. Thank you, mademoiselle, monsieur.'

Larsen placed his hands flat on the table. 'I think we should get some sleep. The situation may seem simpler when we have rested.' He stood up and without a further word, Chevannes and Tanner followed him outside.

WHEN TANNER AWOKE, it was nearly six in the morning. He sat up and looked round the barn. Most of the men seemed to be still fast asleep. Then he noticed the wounded men were no longer there; neither was Larsen. Grabbing his rifle, he crossed the yard to the farmhouse. Anna and her mother were there, as was Larsen, drinking coffee. The smell of fresh bread filled the room.

'Good morning, Sergeant,' said Anna. 'You slept well?'

'Too well, thanks, miss. Where are the wounded men?'

'We moved them in the night,' said Anna. 'They were crying out.'

'Christ. I didn't hear a thing. And how are they now?'

'We gave them brandy. Riggs is not good, though.'

Anna's mother passed him some bread and gave him a mug of coffee.

'We need to post guards,' he said to Larsen, and then to Anna, 'When will you take the wounded into Tretten?'

'My father is tending the animals. Then we will go.'

'I'll come with you some of the way,' said Tanner, suddenly. It occurred to him that reconnaissance, however crude, would improve their chances of success. 'We need someone to recce Tretten.' He pushed back his chair. 'Thank you for breakfast. Call me when you want help with the wounded.'

Outside, the morning sun shone gold, casting long blue shadows over the mountains. He could already hear melting snow dripping from the pines.

He wondered whether Zellner and his men had escaped and when more German troops would be sent to search for them. And he wondered how he could best manage Chevannes. Tanner felt certain that his plan to cross the valley was the right one. Meanwhile, it was time for the men to be up. As he neared the barn, Larsen emerged from the house and called to him.

'Sergeant,' he said, walking over to Tanner. 'You know, you should try to patch things up with Lieutenant Chevannes.'

'With respect, sir, his judgment is terrible. He makes bad decisions and he undermines my authority with my men.'

Larsen smiled. 'He feels threatened by your greater experience. We are all finding out that what is taught in peacetime bears little relation to what we discover in war. We are not warned about the difficult decisions we are forced to make.'

'That's the nature of command, sir,' said Tanner. 'We should have left the *seter* two nights ago when it stopped snowing. Sandvold would have been whisked away to safety by the Allies.' He sighed. 'If I keep quiet, Chevannes will lead us to disaster.'

'How can you be so sure?' Larsen asked.

'Sir, there's no road this side—other than that in the valley—for more than twenty miles and that leads away from the coast. We have neither the time nor the strength to catch up with the Allies. Our only chance is to find transport and use roads as much as we can. We have to cross the valley.'

'You are probably right,' said Larsen. 'But it feels as though we are heading into the lion's den. Sandvold must not be taken by the enemy.'

'I won't let that happen,' said Tanner grimly. 'Perhaps you should talk to Chevannes. He's more likely to listen to you than me. It would be useful to have Anna Rostad with us too. It's about survival, not honour and decorum.'

Larsen smiled. 'All right, I will do that. I am glad we have had this talk.'

THAT MORNING, Tanner and Chevannes avoided each other. There was no need for Tanner to argue his case further because, with the men roused, Chevannes stood in the barn and outlined the plan exactly as he and Anna had suggested. They would cross the valley that night, he announced, and would spend the day resting and getting ready. The wounded men would be taken into Tretten. 'It means they will become prisoners,' he added, 'but they will also have a chance to live.' Neither did Chevannes object to Tanner's suggestion that he accompany Anna and Erik Rostad part of the way.

'He's hoping you'll get caught, Sarge,' said Sykes.

Tanner grinned. 'You might be right, Stan.'

First, however, Anna would lead them to the cave above the farm, where they would lie up until evening. No more than a quarter of a mile away, it proved to be ideal.

Tanner left Sykes in charge of the men. 'You know the drill, Stan. Don't let Sandvold out of your sight.' He left his jerkin and helmet behind, taking the German wind-jacket and field cap.

It was an old, creaking cart, led by a plodding mule. Erik sat up front with his daughter. Sitting in the back with the three men, Tanner saw Saxby contort with pain at every jolt. 'Not long now,' said Tanner.

'I don't want the Jerries to kill me,' Saxby mumbled.

'They won't. They'll make you better. Be brave and you'll get through.' He knew he sounded trite. He hoped that the enemy would show compassion to the men but, really, he had no idea whether they would or not. Hell, he thought, and moved away from Saxby's misery to draw alongside Anna and her father. 'Thank you for doing this,' he said.

'I wish we could have looked after them ourselves,' said Anna. 'I am training to be a doctor, so I feel bad that I cannot help more. The war has interrupted my studies in Oslo and, in any case, I don't have the equipment or medicines.' She glanced at Tanner wistfully. For the first time, he began to realise what a terrible thing the invasion must be for the Norwegians.

'I'm sorry,' he said. 'It must be a very difficult time for you.'

'One minute I feel overcome with grief, for Norway, for me, for Jonny; the next just very angry. It's one of the reasons I want to come with you. I don't want to sit at home feeling sorry for myself. I want to *do* something.'

'I had a word with Lieutenant Larsen this morning,' he told her. 'He said he would speak to Lieutenant Chevannes again.' For a brief moment, he held her gaze. Those eyes, he thought. 'I think you'd be a great help to us.'

She smiled. 'Thank you for saying that.'

Tanner stayed with the cart until they had the first glimpse of the valley road below. Pasture and forest jostled for space along the lower slopes. By keeping within the tree line he was confident he could remain hidden.

'You won't have to go far,' Anna told him. 'You'll soon see Tretten.'

Tanner thanked her and wished them luck. As he watched the cart rumble on down the track, doubt flooded over him.

THE TELEPHONE in the hotel room rang shrilly, shattering the silence in which Reichsamtsleiter Scheidt had been lying for the past three hours. Kurz was asking him to come over right away. Scheidt looked at his watch. Seven forty, twelve hours since news had arrived that the mountain troops were closing in on Odin. Scheidt had waited, on tenterhooks, ever since.

He almost ran to Kurz's office.

The SS major looked up, his face grave. 'We need to go to Tretten.'

In the car Kurz gave him the bad news. Zellner and just eight of his men had reached von Poncets' new HQ in Tretten a short while ago. Stripped to their shirts and trousers, wearing British army boots, they had stumbled into the station house in a terrible state.

'Needless to say,' added Kurz, 'they did not bring Odin. However, Engelbrecht's boys did take Tretten. The British were crushed yesterday.'

'I don't give a damn,' snapped Scheidt. 'We have to find Odin, Kurz.'

TRETTEN WAS a hive of activity. Kurz drove slowly, weaving through the troops and vehicles, passing bombed-out houses, piles of rubble and charred timber. The smell of the recent battle was pervasive.

Eventually he turned off the road and down to the station. Inside, clerks and staff officers were busy organising the next German thrust down the valley. Scheidt and Kurz were led upstairs to see Major von Poncets.

'Congratulations,' said Scheidt. 'Another victory, just as you predicted.'

'Thank you. I'm sorry I don't have better news regarding Odin. Those men the Norwegians are with have more steel than we had appreciated.'

'What now?' asked Scheidt. 'When will you mount another search?'

Von Poncets smiled. 'The Tommies have fallen back a long way, it seems. Our recce boys have been flying up and down the valley since first light and there's little sign of them. We're moving most of our men out today. Nearly all will be gone by this evening, so we'll have a little respite on our hands.'

'Which means you have time to find Odin?' asked Scheidt.

'I'm going to give one of my own companies this task. I'm sorry—I thought a platoon would be more than enough. I was wrong.'

'An under-strength platoon,' added Scheidt.

'Well, we won't make that mistake again.'

There was a knock on the door. Zellner entered, freshly shaved and wearing a new uniform. His right eye was blackened, Scheidt noticed. Zellner began quickly, 'I would like to say, Herr Reichsamtsleiter and Herr Sturmbannführer, that I apologise unreservedly for failing in my duty.'

Scheidt nodded. 'All right, Hauptmann. Now tell me who was there.'

Zellner had seen a middle-aged man with spectacles and a moustache. There were two other Norwegians, a few French mountain troops and the rest were British. A French officer, Chevannes, seemed to be in charge. 'He's weak, though,' Zellner told them. 'His interrogation was pathetic.'

'You told him nothing?' asked Kurz.

'Of course not, sir. He wouldn't touch me—a fellow officer. He's too concerned with behaving honourably. There was a British sergeant there who would have had us killed, I think. The Frenchman was horrified.'

'So how did they defeat you?' Kurz asked.

Zellner bristled. 'The sergeant is good. His name is Tanner. About my age. He has a sniper rifle with sights. It was how he ambushed us. And he has explosives. He has been decorated. I saw a ribbon on his tunic, striped blue, white and red.'

'The Military Medal,' said Kurz. 'A gallantry award for men in the ranks.' He turned to von Poncets and Scheidt. 'We've had Poland in which to hone our battle skills, but the British have had their empire.'

'It appears to have done them little good,' said von Poncets. 'Perhaps they were expecting us to attack with spears.'

At that even Zellner managed to smile.

'Is there anything else we should know?' Scheidt asked.

'Two of their men were killed and three wounded. They are now sixteen strong, not including Odin.'

'Very good, Zellner, you may rejoin your men,' said von Poncets.

'Sir, I would like your permission to stay here and help find Odin.'

'Thank you, Hauptmann,' the major replied, 'but that won't be necessary.'

'Wait,' said Scheidt. 'There is logic in continuing to use Hauptmann Zellner and his men, Herr Major. His knowledge of the enemy would be useful, surely?'

Von Poncets nodded. 'So, Zellner, you may continue the hunt for Odin.'

Zellner thanked them. 'I vowed I would kill Sergeant Tanner, and I will,' he explained. 'And I will also bring you Odin. You have my word.'

'Hauptmann,' said Scheidt, 'I don't care about your personal vendettas, but I cannot stress enough the importance of finding Odin—alive.'

NOT UNTIL THE AFTERNOON did Tanner return to the cave above the farmstead, by which time Anna and her father were safely home. He had learned much, and reported his findings to Lieutenant Chevannes. Tretten was now quieter. Soldiers had been leaving all day. The boats that Anna had mentioned were by the jetty and there was an approach that would enable them to stay within the cover of trees almost to the river bank. The only open ground was the last seventy-five yards.

Chevannes dismissed him without a word, so he went to find Sykes.

'Are we going to be all right, Sarge?'

Tanner nodded. 'It's not going to be much fun crossing the river, but if we hold our nerve . . .'

''Course,' Sykes said. 'We've been having a gander at some of that Jerry kit.' He passed a rifle to Tanner.

Tanner lifted it to his shoulder, aimed, then pulled back the bolt. 'Don't like this much. I'd rather have my old Enfield. What about the shells?'

'Fractionally larger. Almost nothing in it.'

'We'd better make sure no one mixes this ammo up.'

'Don't worry, I've warned everyone already. What's the pistol like?'

Tanner passed it to him. 'See for yourself. I don't really feel that comfortable with pistols, but useful for clearing a room, I suppose.'

'Close-quarters stuff?'

'Exactly.' Tanner watched as Sykes loaded and unloaded the magazine, cocked and uncocked the pistol, then examined the safety catch. Not far away, others played cards or slept. All the Rangers were on the same side of the cave. It was strange how attached to them he now felt.

He hoped he had made the right decision to cross the valley, hoped he wasn't wasting these men's lives. They trusted him—but was it justified? Was he leading them to capture—death? He looked at Sykes again. He barely knew his corporal, a man he considered in many ways a friend.

'I've been meaning to ask you,' he said at length to Sykes. 'Where did you learn how to handle explosives like that?'

'In the army, of course.'

'Not handling gelignite.' He looked Sykes in the eye. 'Spit it out, Stan.'

Sykes glanced around to check no one else was listening, then leaned forward. 'Before I joined the army, I . . . I used to rob stuff. Houses, offices. I could crack most safes, but they didn't always have combination locks, you see. So that's when I learned how to use explosives.'

Tanner raised an eyebrow.

'I'm not proud of it, but when you're doing offices and banks, you persuade yourself they can afford it.'

'When did you join the army?'

'We was doin' an office in Islington, and before we knew what was going on there was police everywhere. One of the lads pulled out a gun. He was caught but me and the other two got away. I decided there and then that my criminal days were over. I got on a train to Leeds and joined up. That was October 1938. And I haven't stolen anything since—except what I nicked from that dump in Lillehammer.' He looked at Tanner. 'You won't say anything, though, will you, Sarge? Not even to the other lads?'

''Course not. You're a good corporal, Stan. I don't care what you did before the war. Anyway, I'm in no position to judge.'

'How come you ended up in the Rangers, Sarge? Where did you say you were from again?'

'Wiltshire,' said Tanner. 'In the southwest. My father was a gamekeeper.' He smiled. 'I reckon I had a rifle in my hands from the age of about five.' He picked up the German rifle again. 'I left home and joined the army as a boy soldier. Straight out to India with the 2nd Battalion.'

Sykes nodded thoughtfully. 'So we're both outsiders, aren't we? Southerners among all these northern bastards.'

Tanner smiled. 'Yes, Corporal, but I think we're licking them into shape.'

IN LILLEHAMMER, Scheidt was waiting for news with mounting frustration. Reconnaissance aircraft had reported nothing despite countless sorties up and down the valley. He snatched the photographs delivered by the Luftwaffe an hour before and peered at them intently.

'I couldn't see anything in those,' said Kurz.

'They're taken from too high up.' Scheidt flung them onto the desk.

Absent-mindedly, Kurz picked the photographs up again. 'And I suppose the Luftwaffe do have to find the British positions.'

Despite Scheidt's comments, the photographs were both clear and detailed, but no tracks could be seen in the snow. High on the mountain plateau there was nothing but an undulating whiteness. What was most striking, however, was the rapidity with which the snow was melting along the valley floor. 'Spring has come,' said Kurz, almost to himself.

Scheidt stepped outside into the cool evening air. Norway. By God, he loathed the place. He wished he could be back in civilised Berlin.

He walked into his hotel.

'Brandy,' said Scheidt to the man at reception, then walked through to the lounge and sank into an armchair. His brandy arrived and he took it without a word to the waiter, drank it in one and called for another.

He knew there was a large area in which to search for Odin, but even so, there were practical constraints that limited the opportunities for manoeuvre. He knew the Luftwaffe had flown many sorties up and down the valley, and von Poncets' men had been trawling it too, yet they had found nothing.

Then inspiration struck. Suppose they had stayed where they were, lying low somewhere, while von Poncets' troops wasted time hunting for a false trail? He finished his brandy and rushed back to Kurz's office.

'They're going to cross the river!'

Kurz looked at him. 'You've lost me, Herr Reichsamtsleiter. Who is?'

'Odin and the men with him. They're still on the mountain above Tretten. Tonight, when it's dark, they'll try to cross to the other side of the valley.'

Kurz seemed doubtful.

'Listen to me,' said Scheidt. 'They know they can't travel through the mountains faster than us, and they know the Luftwaffe will be looking for them. They're stuck on the same side of the valley as the road and the railway line. But what's on the other side? Nothing! If they can get over there, they have a better chance of shaking us off their trail. They'll try tonight.'

Kurz was nodding now. 'Yes, I think you might be right. And all we have to do is make sure von Poncets' mountain troops are waiting.' He stood up and slapped Scheidt on the back. 'Smart thinking, Herr Reichsamtsleiter.'

As Kurz disappeared to send a signal to von Poncets, Scheidt leaned against the desk and examined the photographs once more. Perhaps, at long last, they really were just hours from snaring their prey.

AT A LITTLE AFTER half past ten that night, a small column of French, British and Norwegian troops, with two civilians, began to head down through the trees towards Tretten. The Tommies had put away their helmets and greatcoats and replaced them with German field caps and wind-jackets. The French had stuck with their own clothing, while the two Norwegian officers had replaced their kepis with captured field caps. The idea, Tanner had suggested, was not necessarily to pass themselves off as German troops but to throw seeds of confusion should they be seen.

Tanner, with Anna beside him and his men behind, led the way, following the route he had worked out earlier that morning. They had been fortunate to find such accommodating hosts. They were setting off with full stomachs, and bread and cold meat in their haversacks. Erik Rostad had told them that most Norwegians in the Gudbrandsdal Valley would share their own antipathy towards the German invaders. If this was so, Tanner reflected, it would give them an important advantage in the days to come.

They paused on a crest that gave them a view down through the trees towards the beach-like spur that jutted out into the river. Tanner, with his German binoculars, scanned the ground in front of them. Most of the village and the river as it entered the gorge were hidden. He glanced at Anna.

'It seems quiet,' he whispered.

'But we can't see the bridge or the church from here.'

'Then no one can see us.'

He signalled to them all to crouch and they moved down the last slope. A hundred yards ahead lay the road. The snow had gone from the ground, replaced by thin grass and a carpet of russet pine needles. Tanner waved them forward until they reached the edge of the tree line beside the road. There, long grass returned. A soft bank overlooked the road and beyond, 100 yards away, was the water's edge.

Tanner lay down in the grass and signalled to the others to fall in beside him. He could see the mass of the mountains on the far side of the valley, and the inky river ahead.

Chevannes slid beside him. 'It seems quiet, no?'

Tanner nodded, but no sooner had he done so than he heard a rumble coming from the direction of the village. In a moment, the noise increased—vehicles accelerating and changing gear. Trucks.

'I knew this was an imbecile idea,' hissed Chevannes.

Tanner could think of no reply. The vehicles were getting closer. Then he saw the first rumbling along the valley road. Everyone keep still, he prayed.

They were most likely troops on their way north. The lead truck was only fifty yards away and, to his horror, he realised that it was slowing down.

The first truck passed them and stopped just thirty yards beyond. The second also ground to a halt—so close Tanner felt he could almost reach out and touch it. Orders barked, then troops were jumping out of the back onto the road. Hardly daring to watch, Tanner saw half a dozen men, rifles in their hands, look directly towards him, then cross the road.

There were now just yards between him and the leading enemy rifleman.

5

At his new headquarters in a farmhouse at Heidal, fifty miles north of Tretten, Brigadier Morgan was bracing himself for General Ruge's visit. Most of 15th Brigade had now landed at Åndalsnes and had been reaching the Gudbrandsdal Valley throughout the day, but they had brought little relief. Major General Paget, due to take over command of both brigades, was not due until the following evening. So Morgan was still responsible for stemming the flow of the German advance.

He felt so tired he could barely think. He had been writing a note when he had felt his eyes close and his pen drop from his hand. One of his staff officers had hurried into the room and he had immediately woken.

'Sir?' said the young captain. 'Are you all right?'

'Fine, thank you,' muttered Morgan. 'What is it, Grayson?'

'The Norwegians are struggling to hold the enemy.'

Morgan sighed. 'Do they know another battalion is on its way to them?'

'Er, that battalion's already there. They say they've already lost two-thirds of their strength, sir.'

Morgan laughed. 'And how much have we lost, eh, Grayson? About seven-eighths of ours, I'd say, wouldn't you? Tell them to stay where they are. Tell them if they don't, the whole front is likely to collapse.'

Captain Grayson had barely gone before General Ruge was announced. The Norwegian commander-in-chief strode in, as immaculate as ever.

'A present for you, Brigadier,' said Ruge, placing a bottle of whisky on the kitchen table that was now Morgan's desk.

Morgan found two tumblers and poured generous measures into each.

Then he spread the map across the table. He pointed out where the Norwegians were attempting to hold the enemy, and where, six miles further back, the newly arrived 15th Brigade were preparing to make a stand.

Ruge nodded thoughtfully. 'And what about 148th Brigade?'

'General, there's nothing left. About four hundred and fifty men, but they've taken even more casualties today. Is there any news of air support?'

'Actually, yes,' replied Ruge. 'I thought you had been told. A squadron of Gladiators landed north of Dombås earlier today.'

Morgan could not believe what he was hearing. 'Gladiators,' he muttered, 'but they're biplanes. What good are they against the Messerschmitts, Junkers and Heinkels? And one squadron! It's risible, General, an abominable disgrace.' Morgan shook his head. 'I'm sorry. What must you think of us?'

Ruge looked at him grimly. 'I do not blame you, Brigadier, or your men. But I do blame London. Inadequate planning has cost many lives.'

Morgan poured himself another whisky. 'Your troops at Vinstra will fall back earlier than I'd hoped but 15th Brigade are building up their position at Kvam and, God willing, they'll put up a good fight. Still, the hard fact remains that Jerry has as many as nine thousand troops, while we have only three thousand. And, of course, he's got tanks and armoured vehicles and a frightening amount of air power. Our boys are funnelled into a valley that's never more than a mile wide, with one road and a railway line as our only line of communication. To make matters worse, we've no way of preventing an outflanking manoeuvre because of the lack of mountain troops.'

'I'm sending you more Norwegian ski troops,' said Ruge. 'We'll put them up in the mountains to watch over our positions.'

Morgan sighed once more. 'Well, that's something.'

'You are tired, Brigadier, I know. But at least it is not your country that is about to fall. At least your King and Government are still in London.'

Morgan was chastened. 'You're quite right, General. I'm sorry.'

Ruge said, 'This morning I saw the King at Molde. There is a matter of great concern to him: the whereabouts of four of His Majesty's Guard.' Under a Colonel Gulbrand, Ruge explained, these men had been entrusted by the King not only with some priceless crown jewels but also the safe passage of an important scientist, Professor Sandvold. After the invasion these men became separated from the royal party. Two days ago a message had been intercepted by British Intelligence, indicating that Gulbrand was dead, but Sandvold and two of His Majesty's Guards were being escorted by a group of British and French troops.

'British and French?' said Morgan, incredulously. 'Where were they?'

'Just south of Tretten. Apparently they defeated an entire platoon of German mountain troops. I have some names: a Sergeant Tanner and a Lieutenant Chevannes. He's from the 6th Battalion, Chasseurs Alpins.'

'Ah, yes,' said Morgan. 'We had a company of them at Øyer.'

'Chevannes was on mountain patrol when he and his men went missing.'

'Presumably Sergeant Tanner and his men were doing much the same. Tell me, why is the King so concerned about Professor Sandvold?'

'That I cannot say. But I can tell you he would be very valuable to the Germans. However, there are concerns about him. In the early thirties he was a member of the National Party—he was a friend of Quisling.'

'You doubt his loyalty?'

'It would be potentially catastrophic were he to fall into German hands. I want you to keep a lookout for these men. The King is determined that they should be found. I just hope to God they are not already in German hands.'

THE LEADING GERMAN soldier walked to barely five yards in front of Tanner and Chevannes. Tanner held his breath. Then, to his surprise, the soldier fiddled with his fly buttons and began to urinate. Two of his comrades followed suit. By the trucks, soldiers were talking, lighting cigarettes, laughing.

Five minutes later, orders were barked and the men were clambering back into the trucks. Engines started and they were off, making for the front.

'A lucky escape, Sergeant,' whispered Chevannes. 'Now for the crossing.'

Gingerly clambering down the bank to the edge of the road, Tanner reminded each man of the drill: Anna was to lead. Lieutenant Chevannes would wait on the far side of the road while he himself would give each man the signal to cross.

'All right,' Tanner said. 'Let's go.' He took two deep breaths, patted Anna lightly on the shoulder, saw the fear in her eyes, then watched her disappear into the darkness. Chevannes followed, then his men and the Norwegians, running across the narrow road and down to the edge of the river. Damn it, they were so loud, he thought. Metal studs on tarmac.

It was the turn of Tanner's men now. More noise, jarring, from the river. The boats were being righted and taken to the water. Footsteps on the pebbles; someone tripping. Tanner groaned inwardly. 'For God's sake keep quiet!' he whispered. He knew they were trying, but they were heavily laden and most were carrying not one but two rifles—their own and the captured German Mausers. And, of course, there were those metal-studded boots—brilliant on the mountain, but hopeless for crossing a pebble beach.

With Kershaw the last across, Tanner followed. Anna and the Norwegians were in the first boat, two French troops rowing. Six in the boat—the dinghy looked worryingly low in the water.

Chevannes, his remaining two Chasseurs, Erwood, Moran and Bell, clambered into the second and pushed off as Tanner, Sykes and the last of the Rangers struggled into the third, the craft tilting and lurching from side to side.

'For God's sake, try to keep it steady,' hissed Tanner.

Sykes whispered, 'Where are the oars?'

Tanner glanced around. The light from the stars cast enough of a glow to show him there were no oars to be found. Tanner could feel himself beginning to panic. 'We'll have to use the Mausers like canoe paddles.' He took his own from his shoulder and plunged it into the ice-cold water.

FROM THE UPSTAIRS dormer window of Tretten Station, on the west bank of the Lågen River, Zellner had a fine view of the bridge below to his right. He looked at his watch: eleven twenty-three. Will they come? he wondered. He had agreed with Kurz that Tretten Bridge was the most likely crossing place. He had told his men to keep out of sight: the aim was to encourage the fugitives in their belief that the village was unoccupied.

Suddenly he thought he heard something from away to his left—further along the river. He turned to Lieutenant Huber, the platoon commander. 'Listen.' There it was again, a scraping sound—almost inaudible. 'What *is* that?' He peered through his binoculars towards where the river widened into Lake Losna. He could see the water, smooth as glass, twinkling, the mountains looming behind, but nothing out of the ordinary.

'Shall I investigate?' Huber asked.

'And give ourselves away? No,' said Zellner. 'Keep listening.'

He continued to stare through his binoculars and, at last, something caught his eye. A faint ripple on the otherwise smooth water.

A moment later he saw a boat as it passed in line with the valley and was silhouetted against the sky. Zellner smiled. 'Yes!' he said. 'I think we have them. Quick, Huber. We haven't a moment to waste.'

TANNER'S BOAT soon caught up with the one in front. Ahead, the far bank still seemed an interminably long way off.

'Come on, boys, keep at it,' he snapped. His body was tense, waiting for the sound of shouts and machine-gun fire. He'd never liked being on open water. It made him feel exposed and vulnerable.

The lead boat was drawing near to the shore. Tanner allowed himself a sigh of relief. Perhaps they would make it, after all.

The sound of an engine shattered the illusion, then another, both from the direction of the village but on opposite sides of the river. 'Quick, lads, quick!' said Tanner, plunging the Mauser into the water furiously.

Ahead, the first boat was drawing onto the gravel shore. There were splashes as the occupants stumbled out. The beam from the trucks cut across the water. The first lorry had stopped on the side from which they had come. Moments later shots rang out, bullets whining over their heads. A warning, thought Tanner. Don't try to turn back.

The lights of the second lorry, curving round the river's edge, were only a few hundred yards away now. Tanner heard the grinding of gears just as their own boat scraped against the stony shore. 'Get out, quick!' Tanner shouted. 'Cross the railway and head for the trees!' The third boat was closing on the shore too. One of the Frenchmen jumped but the water was deeper than he'd thought, and he flailed trying desperately to free his pack.

'Keep going!' Tanner shouted, kneeling to take aim as the vehicle turned towards them. He fired once, missed, then fired again and hit the windscreen. A screech of brakes, and the lorry came to a halt 100 yards ahead. A German voice yelled orders, and enemy troops hurried from the back of the truck. The Frenchman in the water was drowning, but Tanner ignored him and grabbed the prow of the dinghy. 'Jump!' he yelled, as Chevannes leapt out. Bullets ricocheted off the stones. Tanner was conscious of someone beside him. 'Go!' he shouted.

'*Non!*' came the reply. '*Mon ami. Vites, Henri, vites!*'

'He's gone, mate,' said Tanner, but the Chasseur stepped into the water to rescue his friend.

'For God's sake,' said Tanner, grabbing him. 'Go! Now!' A machine gun opened fire, raking the water. At this, the Chasseur gave up and both men were running for their lives, off the pebble shore, across a grassy verge and over the railway line. Tanner could hear the footsteps of enemy troops running towards them. He ran on into the trees.

'Sarge, is that you?' called a voice.

'Stan!' said Tanner. 'Where the hell is everyone?'

'Up ahead. Are you all right?'

'I think so. Thank God for dense forests.'

Suddenly a machine gun opened fire again. Tanner crouched behind a tree as the bullets flew. He saw a flickering torch beam, so he stepped out from behind the tree, aimed towards the light and fired. The reply was another burst of machine-gun fire, but this time the bullets cut through the trees above their heads.

The firing lessened as they climbed higher and eventually, 200 feet above the lake, they reached a clearing in the trees.

'Sergeant, is that you?'

Larsen. Tanner breathed a sigh of relief and peered into the darkness. He could just make out the shape of several people in a group. All six from the leading boat—Sandvold included—were still together.

'We made it, sir,' said Sykes, breathlessly, to Chevannes.

'Yes,' replied the Frenchman. 'A miracle.'

A head count showed that two men were missing: Chasseur Bardet and Private Moran. Both had been in the last boat. 'I'm sorry, sir,' said Tanner to Chevannes, 'but Bardet drowned. Chasseur Junot tried to rescue him but . . .'

Junot himself was not in a good way. Soaked below the waist, he was shivering. He was inconsolable at the loss of his friend.

'He needs to change his clothes,' said Tanner. But no one had any spare trousers, only jackets. Neither had they seen Moran. 'Tinker?' he said to Bell. 'You were in the boat with him.'

'We jumped out, Sarge. There were lots of bullets. He may have been hit.'

Tanner hated to leave Moran behind, but they needed to get going. He peered into the trees. Nothing. Damn you, Mitch, where are you? he thought. Then, turning to Chevannes, he said, 'Sir? We have to move off.'

'I know, Sergeant,' snapped Chevannes. 'Mademoiselle Rostad, where should we be heading?'

'Straight up the hill through the trees,' Anna said. 'At the top there is a track that leads to the hamlet of Svingvoll at the head of a valley.' She was cut off by a hiss as a flare shot into the sky, followed by several more, showering the mountain with light. Then they heard troops below them.

'*Vite!*' whispered Chevannes. He waved his arm and the men clambered onwards as rifle and machine-gun fire cracked behind them. Tanner paused to fire, then took out a grenade and hurled it down the mountain, in the hope of blinding their pursuers. As it exploded, Tanner heard a German cry out. He clambered on, until it seemed that at last the pursuers had given up.

Cresting the hill, Tanner paused. Across the valley, he could see the looming mountains, the formidable mass of rock and snow over which they had struggled the past few days. Now they had made it successfully to the other side. A miracle, Chevannes had called it, and for once Tanner was content to agree with the French lieutenant.

Beneath them, Tanner heard the sound of an engine revving.

'You know what that is, don't you, Sarge?' said Sykes beside him.

'Yes, Stan.' Tanner grinned. 'Jerry's got his wheels stuck.'

As ANNA HAD PROMISED, there was a well-trodden track, which wove its way past a number of farmsteads, hidden from the valley floor.

They reached Svingvoll, skirted the lip of the shallow valley, then joined another track that led across a forested plateau. Shortly after two in the morning, the first hint of dawn spread pinkly across the horizon behind them. Tanner was relieved to be able to see his surroundings, the men—and Anna—walking in front.

She had already more than proved her worth. He had been impressed by her cool-headedness: her first time under fire and she had not panicked.

He drew alongside Sandvold. 'How are you, Professor?'

'Too old for making daring dashes across rivers,' he replied. 'I don't mind telling you, Sergeant, I found the experience terrifying.'

Tanner smiled. 'I can't say I enjoyed it much either.'

'And all those bullets . . . How do you keep calm in such situations?'

'I find that in the heat of the moment there's no time to be frightened.'

Sandvold eyed him. 'That is why you are a soldier and I am not.'

Soon after, Junot collapsed. Crouching beside him, Anna felt his brow. 'His temperature's dropped,' she said.

'He's got hypothermia,' said Tanner. 'We need to wrap him in something warm.' He took off his German wind-jacket. 'Fold this round his legs.' Another makeshift stretcher was assembled and Junot hoisted onto it.

'He's going to need help,' Anna said, turning to Chevannes.

'And we can't walk all the way to the front with a stretcher,' added the French lieutenant. '*Merde*. How far is it to the valley?'

Anna shrugged. 'Five kilometres, maybe. There's the village of Olstad. We can get help at a farm.'

It was nearly half past eight in the morning when they reached the crest of the mountain plateau and were able to look down over the narrow Jøra Valley. On the east-facing slopes, the valley was thickly wooded with a blanket of snow still on the ground, but on the west-facing sides, the snow had all but gone. On the valley floor, a narrow river wound away to the northwest. Beside it there was a road, little more than a rough track.

Chevannes called a halt. Beneath them lay a settlement of scattered farms and a small church. This was Olstad, Anna told them. Junot was now ghostly white, his lips and ears blue. 'We need to hurry,' she told Chevannes.

They pressed on until they reached the first farmstead. Several dogs ran into the yard as Anna walked ahead with Larsen. Tanner watched apprehensively. A few minutes later, Larsen reappeared and signalled to them. The men hurried into the yard. The farmer watched them suspiciously as they trooped past him into the dimly lit, low-ceilinged kitchen.

The farmer's wife ushered the stretcher-bearers to an armchair by the fire, then barked at her husband, who grudgingly began to stoke the fire with more wood. His wife disappeared, but soon returned with a pile of blankets. Junot was stripped from the waist down, swathed in wool and the woman began to rub his hands and feet, talking to Anna as she did so.

'She knows how to deal with hypothermia,' Anna said. 'Her cousin had it once, but she is worried it is too late.'

Suddenly the woman felt Junot's neck. She sat back and looked up at Anna and Chevannes.

'He is dead?' said Chevannes to Anna, disbelief on his face.

Anna nodded. 'I am sorry, Lieutenant.'

Chevannes put his hands to his face. '*Mon Dieu*,' he muttered.

Tanner's first thoughts were what they should do with the body. They needed to cover not only their own tracks but those of the farmer and his wife. Then they had to consider what they would do next.

The farmer and his wife were arguing now.

'The farmer wants us to take Junot with us,' Anna explained. 'His wife is saying we should carry him to the church for a Christian burial.'

'That's ridiculous,' said Tanner. 'We need to take him up to the trees above the farm and bury him.' He turned to Chevannes. 'Don't you agree, sir?'

Chevannes nodded. He seemed distant and distracted.

As a shallow grave was dug, Tanner gazed down at the valley below. It looked peaceful, as though the war could never touch it.

Sykes was standing beside him. 'Do you reckon Jerry knows about our professor, then?'

'I can't work it out, Stan. The other evening that German patrol seemed to be coming after us for a reason. Why else go to all that trouble just to catch a few soldiers on the run? And last night I could have sworn those men at Tretten were waiting for us. There's another thing, too. Did you notice most of their shooting was high? Not a single one of us was hit. Except possibly Mitch. But maybe I'm imagining things. With any luck they won't come looking for us here.'

'We could do with some transport, Sarge,' added Sykes. 'Perhaps one of these farmers here has got a truck.'

'Perhaps.' Behind him the men had finished covering Junot. 'Come on, boys,' said Tanner. 'Let's get back to the farmhouse.'

As they reached the yard, they saw the farmer hurry outside. He glared at them as they passed him.

'What's the matter with him?' said Hepworth.

'Maybe he doesn't like having a bunch of soldiers turn up for breakfast,' said Tanner. They went inside to find the others putting on their packs.

'The farmer is nervous,' explained Anna. 'He is worried about what the Germans will do if they find out we've been here.' She looked at the farmer's wife. 'She is furious with him. She called him a coward and a traitor.'

'Have we asked whether anyone in the village has any transport?'

'Not yet.' She turned and spoke to the farmer's wife, who replied after a moment's thought, then pointed and gesticulated.

'Uksum Farm,' said Anna. 'A man called Merit Sulheim. She says he has a truck he uses to take livestock to Lillehammer.'

Tanner's spirits rose. 'Perfect,' he said. 'Where is this farm?'

'Not far. About a kilometre.'

As they continued down the track towards the valley, they heard the sound of aero-engines thrumming faintly over the mountains. A little louder, then a Junkers roared into view a few hundred yards ahead.

'Everyone, take cover!' shouted Chevannes. They flung themselves onto the track's bushy bank. Tanner watched the aircraft swoop across the valley, then turn, curving, so that its bulbous nose pointed directly towards them. Moments later, the Junkers thundered over them. They watched as the aircraft flew on, then banked again, arcing across the valley before turning for another run above them.

'Here, Dan!' Tanner called out to Lance Corporal Erwood. 'Have a crack with the Bren, will you?'

'And give away our position?' called Chevannes.

'Sir, he's seen us. The only way we're going to stop him bleating is by shooting the bastard down.'

'No, Sergeant, and that is an order!'

The Junkers was approaching once more, no more than 100 feet above them. Again it roared overhead. Tanner cursed, then watched as it began to bank yet again. 'Sir, he's bloody well seen us! Let's have a pop at it. What have we got to lose?' Chevannes said nothing. Tanner smiled, aware that the French lieutenant's silence was the authority he needed. 'Aim off, Dan,' he called to Erwood once more. 'Give yourself plenty of lead.' Tanner had his own rifle to his shoulder now and saw that the rest of his men had followed his example. He knew a .303 round would probably make little impression on an eight-ton monster such as a Junkers 88, but it was flying so low he reckoned it had to be worth a shot.

He watched it straighten and its wings level. Tanner pointed his rifle vertically in the air. 'Ready, Dan?' he called. '*One, two—fire!*' he yelled, and as bullets pumped into the sky the aircraft swept over them.

Then a miracle happened. The starboard engine spluttered and, as the aircraft banked over the valley, flames appeared, followed by a long trail of smoke. As one, the men on the ground stood up and watched, open-mouthed. They followed the plane as it headed north up the valley, rose over the mountains, then plunged earthwards. A ball of flame erupted briefly followed by the dull rumble of destruction a few seconds later. For a moment the men were dumbstruck, then raised their rifles and cheered.

'Good shooting, men,' said Chevannes. 'Very good shooting.'

'And a very good decision to let us fire,' said Tanner. 'Come on, lads!'

They walked on quickly, past farmers who had emerged to see what the commotion was about. Two young boys stood on a gate to watch them pass and several of Tanner's men cheered at them, the boys grinning back.

'That's enough!' Tanner warned.

'It is amazing to see everyone's spirits lift like this,' said Anna.

'Mine will be even higher if this truck works out,' Tanner replied. He barked at his men: 'Come on, you lot! Get a bloody move on!'

'We were just saying, Sarge,' said Erwood, 'what a shame it is that Mitch isn't with us, him being on my Bren crew an' that. He'd have loved to have seen that Jerry plane come down. I wish I knew he was all right.'

'I'm sure he is. I expect he just tripped and fell,' said Tanner. 'You'll probably find he was picked up by the Jerries.'

'I'M TELLING YOU,' mumbled Mitch Moran, 'I don't know anything. We were just trying to get back to our lines.'

Sturmbannführer Kurz looked at the pitiful figure. A swollen eye, so puffed and blackened it had closed, cracked lips, a line of congealed blood from nose to mouth. With his arms tied behind the chair, his head hung down as though it were too heavy for him.

Kurz sighed. Beating someone to within an inch of their life always struck him as crude. And this fellow was just a simple boy. A few cigarettes, a bit of friendly chat and the Englishman would have been eating out of his hand ages ago. Now it was probably too late. Ah, well, worth a try. He lit a cigarette and ordered the guard to untie Moran's hands.

'A smoke?' he said, and placed the cigarette between Moran's lips. 'I'm sorry you've been so roughly treated. Hauptmann Zellner was—well, he was a bit frustrated. I'm sorry he took it out on you.' He saw Moran lift his head a fraction, then raise a shaking hand to the cigarette. Kurz smiled. 'War . . . what a waste of time it is. You know, I used to teach English. I travelled in England when I was a student. You are from Yorkshire, I believe?'

Moran nodded.

Kurz stood up and walked to the cabinet where he now kept his Baedekers. He picked up the England edition. 'Which part?'

'Knaresborough,' mumbled Moran.

'Knaresborough,' said Kurz, flicking through the pages. 'Near Harrogate, is it not?' He paused, as though lost in a happy memory. 'I recall a wonderful English tea at Betty's in Harrogate. Do you know it?'

'My grandma took me there for my tenth birthday,' Moran mumbled.

'I remember it being quite charming,' said Kurz. He leaned closer to Moran. 'Look, I want to help you. You would much rather be at home in Knaresborough with your family, just as I would rather be at home with my wife and baby daughter in Ludwigsstadt, but there is a war on and that is all there is to it. I cannot get you home but I can get you cleaned up and looked after, and I can promise you there will be no more beatings.'

'Thank you.'

'I was wondering why you were crossing the river. It seems rather a risk. And difficult to walk through those mountains. There's still plenty of snow.'

'Not in the valley beyond.'

Kurz smiled. Really, he thought, this was almost too easy. 'No, I suppose not. So your plan was to head north down the Jøra Valley?'

Moran nodded.

'And what,' Kurz added, 'made you cross where you did? It showed remarkable local knowledge.'

'Our sarge had recced the area earlier and found the boats,' said Moran. 'And a Norwegian girl showed us the way.'

'Ah,' said Kurz. *Now I understand*. 'Well, I'll let you rest now, Moran. And good luck.' Two guards came over and took Moran away.

Scheidt, who had been sitting silently in the corner, clapped. 'Bravo. A virtuoso performance. I had no idea you had been a teacher.'

'I wasn't.'

'Ah. And you don't have a wife and baby daughter?'

'Of course not. Nor have I been to England and certainly not Betty's Tearooms. Baedeker's a useful friend.'

Scheidt smiled, but then his expression changed. The British sergeant was proving a thorn in their side. And they had a guide with them. Damn them, he thought. And damn Zellner. Odin had slipped through their fingers again. He ran a hand wearily through his hair.

'Cheer up, my dear Reichsamtsleiter,' said Kurz. 'We're closing in now.'

'You keep saying that,' snapped Scheidt, 'yet Odin repeatedly eludes us, and for two days we've heard nothing from our source.'

'Yet we know where they have headed. The Jøra Valley is narrow. Zellner and his men will be able to search it with far greater ease than they could the Gudbrandsdal Valley.'

'Zellner,' muttered Scheidt. 'Hardly a man to inspire confidence.'

AT TRETTEN STATION, Zellner was anxiously awaiting a call from the Luftwaffe. At ten o'clock, they had told him, he could expect a report from their morning reconnaissance. Yet it was now nearly half past and there was still nothing. One plane was back, he was told, and had found nothing. The other was late and out of radio contact.

Zellner cursed Odin and Tanner, and every one of those miserable fugitives—men who were making a fool of him. He could not believe they had got away. He had replayed the events of the previous evening over and over in his mind, and every time his anger and despair grew. He could feel the career for which he had worked and trained so hard was slipping away from him.

There was one small consolation. The rest of the division were now further north, fighting at Kvam. That had meant a reprieve for him and his company. It was not yet too late. If he could capture Odin successfully, all else would be forgotten and the upward path of his career would continue.

He made a decision. His men were ready and waiting. They would begin the search now without the Luftwaffe's help. Kurz had told him they had been heading for the Jøra Valley. Well, if that was so, someone somewhere must have seen them. And he would make sure they talked.

TANNER COULDN'T HELP feeling that things were looking up. Shooting down the Junkers had probably meant their whereabouts would remain secret for a while longer. Then they had safely reached Uksum Farm, where Merit Sulheim was far more helpful than the farmer they had encountered earlier.

A heavily built man in his thirties, Sulheim ran a successful logging business and had invested in the latest machinery, including a large Morris-Commercial truck. The farmhouse was equipped with electricity, a modern range in the kitchen and a radio. Because of this the farmer was able to tell them there was heavy fighting at Kvam, forty-five miles to the northeast. German-backed radio had reported that they were advancing virtually unopposed up the Glåma Valley, parallel to the Gudbrandsdal. On hearing this Tanner had glanced at Chevannes. *And you reckoned we could head north in that direction.*

But Sulheim reported something more. That morning an announcement had been broadcast that a dangerous band of British, French and Norwegian troops was at large in the Gudbrandsdal Valley. There was a reward for securing their capture, but a warning too: anyone offering these men help could expect 'the severest' punishment. That made one thing clear, thought Tanner. The Germans knew about Sandvold.

The threat of punishment did not seem to perturb Sulheim, who professed his desire to help his country against the Nazi oppressor. He offered them his truck. Petrol was scarce but he produced two four-litre cans. 'You should have enough for maybe fifty kilometres.'

'Then we should leave right away,' Tanner said.

Chevannes shook his head. 'In broad daylight? It would be better to head off this evening when all is quiet.'

'I agree,' said Larsen.

Tanner sighed with exasperation. 'Look, it's clear Jerry knows about the professor. We should get going while we've got the chance to stay ahead. Mr Sulheim has offered us his truck. Let's head north, towards the Allies.'

'Sergeant, not for the first time, I would like to remind you that I am the senior officer and I am ordering us to stay where we are.'

'But this is madness!' said Tanner. 'Do you think those Germans who attacked us last night are going to sit quiet all day? They'll be swarming all over this valley. Please, sir, I implore you. We can't afford to lose another whole day. We have the chance to drive away from the enemy.' He turned to Sandvold. 'Professor, surely you see that?'

Sandvold shrugged. 'Please—I am not the one to make such a decision.'

'We will hide in the mountains and come back down this evening,' said Chevannes.

Sulheim coughed. 'I have a suggestion,' he said. 'I have a *seter* up in the forest. I don't think any German would find you. I can take you there now. Tonight I will come and get you when the coast is clear.'

'That settles it,' said Lieutenant Larsen. 'We stay here today and head out tonight. I agree with Lieutenant Chevannes.'

So, thought Tanner, that's that.

Chevannes called the men together. 'Today we wait up in the mountains. Tonight we continue our journey in Monsieur Sulheim's truck.'

Tanner could see the expression on Sykes's face. 'Don't say it,' he growled. 'That man has no brain. Neither does Lieutenant Larsen.'

THE FUGITIVES LEFT Merit Sulheim's farm and made their way into the dense pine forest that covered the steep western slopes of the valley. By following a brook they were able to reach the heart of the forest without a trail of tracks in the snow. The *seter* was overgrown with young shoots of alder and pine. As a place to hide, it was hard to fault. A short distance below, a clearing offered a good view of the river and the cluster of farmsteads at Olstad. Tanner settled to watch any activity in the valley.

A truckload of German soldiers reached the church just before midday, and Tanner watched as they began their search of the farms. Tanner wondered whether that morning's old farmer had squealed. He could see through his binoculars that soldiers were now searching the place. Not long after, a number of troops hurried down the track and made for Sulheim's farm. Tanner hoped Sulheim would hold his nerve. Then he remembered the truck. Surely the Germans would requisition it? He cursed.

ZELLNER BANGED his fist on the table. 'I know they were here, Herr Sulheim,' he said. He was pleased to see that both the farmer and his wife flinched.

'And so they were, but I turned them away. I heard the announcement on the radio. I am a patriot but I didn't want to put my family at risk.'

'But you have a truck, do you not?'

'Yes, but it's not working. Something is wrong with the alternator.'

'Show me.'

Sulheim led him across the yard to the truck.

'Lift the bonnet,' Zellner ordered and called one of his men to examine the engine bay.

'And where is the alternator now?' he asked, turning back to Sulheim.

Sulheim pointed to a cylindrical block of metal lying on a workbench.

'And where did they go when they left?'

'Up the road. North,' said Sulheim. 'I made it clear I didn't want them here.'

Zellner couldn't decide whether or not the man was lying. The Norwegian's answers certainly seemed plausible. He ordered a search of the entire farm. Nothing was found. After an hour, he posted half a dozen men in the church—the bell tower was to be used as an observation post—then ordered the rest back into the trucks and headed north.

TANNER WATCHED these events carefully. During the afternoon more trucks arrived. Planes hummed overhead. On the far side of the valley, he followed a platoon of troops with skis on their backs as they climbed out of Olstad and up into the mountains. He was painfully aware that the men in the church had remained where they were.

The hours ticked by. As the evening drew on, there was no sign of Sulheim or of the German observers leaving the church.

After ten, Chevannes shuffled down the slope beside him.

'They're still there, sir,' said Tanner.

Chevannes peered through his binoculars. '*Merde*,' he said.

'I take it we stay here for the time being,' said Tanner.

The Frenchman turned away. 'Yes, Sergeant,' he snapped.

As the brief hours of darkness passed, Tanner's anger rose. He could not help thinking about the Allied front line. Was it still at Kvam? By now they must have been pushed ever further away. A whole day wasted, and now, perhaps, several more. Not for the first time Tanner wished he had never set eyes on Colonel Gulbrand and his men.

WITH RELIEF, Brigadier Morgan saw Major General Bernard Paget standing before him at his headquarters at Heidal. The fierce, intelligent eyes, the long, aquiline nose and the thin lips somehow contained so much authority.

'General, how very good to see you,' said Morgan, stepping forward into the dim light and clasping Paget's hand.

'Good to see you too, Harry,' said Paget. 'Although I wish the circumstances might have been different. This is a hell of a bloody mess, isn't it?'

'You've seen General Ruge?'

'Just come from his headquarters south of Dombås.' Paget chuckled mirthlessly. 'Not very impressed with we Brits, is he?'

'No, sir.'

'And with reason. I'm afraid it's the bods back at Whitehall who are to blame. Lack of planning, lack of thought. Not enough kit. Not enough air cover.' He sat down in front of Morgan's desk while the brigadier poured two tumblers of whisky from the bottle Ruge had brought.

'Tell me what the news is here. How are 15th Brigade doing?'

'We've held off the enemy so far, General.'

'Good,' said Paget, then raised his glass. 'Cheers.'

Morgan raised his in turn, then added, 'But I'm afraid there are only four serviceable aircraft left. I don't think we'll survive another night. Our best hope is to keep the enemy at bay until evening and withdraw overnight.'

Paget nodded. 'All right, Harry. I'm going to report back to London tonight, if I can, and you should know that I'm going to recommend our withdrawal. Your brigade's already had a savage dusting.'

Morgan finished his whisky, then said, 'Did General Ruge mention anything about a missing patrol of British and French troops?'

'Is this the scientist?'

'Yes, sir. Professor Sandvold. The King's anxious he should be found.'

'I know, but we can't hang around here on the off chance when this fellow might already be dead,' Paget said.

'I don't think he is, sir. London intercepted a radio signal broadcast by the Germans. Apparently they've warned Norwegians to report any sightings. It seems Jerry's onto them.'

Paget stroked his chin. 'Well, we'd better hope they get to us quickly. I'm sorry, Harry, but the King has to face facts: we can't stay here much longer.'

6

There had been no movement by the Germans all night, nor as the morning wore on. Tanner's mood was not improved by Chevannes, who had joined him and Sykes at the lookout. Trying to ignore him, Tanner watched another German army truck trundle down the valley. An aeroplane droned above.

Chevannes pursed his lips. 'Perhaps we should go over the mountains.'

It was something Tanner had thought about. Behind them there was a range of snow-covered peaks, 6,000 feet high. Anna had confirmed that it was a barren wilderness with no roads. Perhaps they could cross successfully and reach the valley beyond, but there was no knowing how long it might take. 'Sir, I think we should sit tight and hold our nerve,' Tanner said. 'Sulheim's truck is still there.'

Without another word, Chevannes left and returned to the *seter*.

'A real decisive one there,' said Sykes.

'Oh, I don't know, Stan,' said Tanner. 'He was pretty decisive yesterday when he ordered us to stay here. His problem is that he digs his heels in when he shouldn't and not when he should.'

The hours rolled by slowly. At around four, the German troops left the farm, yet there was no movement from the church.

'What are they playing at, Sarge?'

'I suppose they're assuming we're still somewhere in this valley,' Tanner said. 'After all, we were seen by a number of Norwegians, and they haven't spotted us crossing the mountains. I suppose they think we'll have to show ourselves soon and are waiting to pounce when we do. My hunch is they'll think we'll come down tonight when it's dark.'

Shortly after six, three trucks of troops pulled into Uksum Farm. The men made a show of searching the entire settlement at Olstad once more. Three hours later, with much revving of engines, they drove away again.

Chevannes appeared at the lookout shortly after. 'So they are leaving,' he said. 'We set off as soon as it is dark.'

'It's a trap, sir,' said Tanner. 'They've still got men in the church.'

Chevannes' expression changed. 'Are you sure, Sergeant?'

'Yes.' Tanner observed him. The only consolation, he thought, for the delay was the discomfort it was causing the Frenchman. 'As I said earlier, sir, we need to keep our nerve.'

Chevannes snorted, then sharply turned away.

Not long after, Anna joined them at the lookout. 'I want to know whether either of you has had any sleep. We need you fresh and alert.'

'I have, miss,' said Sykes. 'Took forty winks earlier.'

'Not today,' admitted Tanner. 'And how about you?' he asked. 'The lads are minding their manners, I hope?'

'Well,' she said, 'they swear often, but they do apologise afterwards.' She laughed. 'Now remember, Sergeant, sleep. It's very important.'

She was right, Tanner realised, and once she had gone, he lay back, his pack as a pillow, and closed his eyes. He was asleep in moments, despite the discomfort, and by dawn he felt refreshed. He watched the sun rise over the mountains on the far side of the valley, casting a golden light on the snow.

A little after three he saw troop movements at the farm. Bringing the binoculars to his eyes, he watched the men disappear behind a shed. Soon after, a small truck he had not noticed the day before emerged and turned onto the road, heading south.

Tanner reported this to Chevannes. 'It could still be a trap, though, sir.'

'What about the soldiers in the church?'

'That might have been them. But I couldn't say for certain.'

Chevannes nodded. 'We'll wait here a while longer.'

At nearly half past four, Tanner spotted Sulheim emerge from the farm-house. Glancing around, he hurried out of the yard towards the trees. When he reached the *seter*, his eyes were wide with excitement. 'They have gone. You have been spotted back over on the other side of the mountain. They think you crossed into the Gudbrandsdal Valley again.'

'And the men in the church?' asked Tanner. 'Did they leave earlier?'

Sulheim nodded. 'Yes. The officer was convinced you would appear when it was dark. He was on the point of leaving when he had the signal.'

'How could we have been spotted?' Chevannes asked.

'A Norwegian reported seeing you.' He grinned. 'You see? We are mostly patriotic countrymen around here.'

They loaded their packs and headed back down the mountain to the valley. No shots were fired, neither did enemy troops appear. At the farm, anxious minutes ticked by as Sulheim replaced the alternator in the truck. His wife gave them bread and cold meat, but Tanner's appetite had left him.

At last they were ready to go. It was some time after six o'clock on the morning of Saturday, April 27.

'What will you say if the Germans return and see the truck gone?' Tanner asked Sulheim.

'That you came back and forced us to hand it over.'

'Perhaps we should tie you up. Otherwise you'd be obliged to contact them the moment we left.'

Shortly after, with Sulheim's family left bound in the house, they walked to the truck. 'I'll drive,' Tanner told Chevannes. 'I know these vehicles. The British Army's got hundreds of them.' As he stepped into the cab with Anna and Chevannes beside him, the driving mechanism felt familiar. He turned the ignition key, pulled out the choke and pressed down the starter in the footwell. The engine fired into life and Tanner eased the truck out of the yard.

IN LILLEHAMMER, Scheidt had spent another wretched night railing against their continued inability to capture Odin. With the arrival of morning and his return to the Sicherheitsdienst offices, his mood had worsened when a signal arrived informing him that the night's search had been fruitless and that misinformation had sent them on a wild-goose chase back to the western side of the Gudbrandsdal Valley.

'Please stop fretting,' Kurz told him. 'Get some fresh air.'

Scheidt was contemplating doing as Kurz suggested when a clerk knocked at the door. 'A signal, sir. It's just come through.'

Scheidt snatched the thin transcript paper. As he read it, a smile broke across his face. 'At last,' he said.

'Atmospheric conditions have changed, then?' Kurz said, grinning.

Scheidt nodded. 'It would seem so, Sturmbannführer.'

A DIFFERENT MESSAGE was tapped out to Zellner back at Tretten. He read with mounting excitement: ODIN LOCATED IN JØRA VALLEY. THEY HAVE M/T AND ARE HEADING NORTH. STOP THEM. DO NOT FAIL. KURZ.

TANNER GLANCED in the mirror. He could see Erwood and Hepworth manning the Bren, its barrel resting on the tailgate. Next to them Larsen was scanning the valley to the south with his binoculars. The steep, wooded slopes above gave Tanner a claustrophobic feeling.

They drove in silence at first, which suited him. He wanted to concentrate without distraction, but at length Chevannes spoke. 'Tell me, Anna,' he said, 'have you always lived here in the Gudbrandsdalen?'

'My family have, yes,' she said, 'but I have been studying medicine in Oslo for the past three years at the university.'

'A doctor in the making. You must be very clever.'

Anna looked down, embarrassed. 'Perhaps I will not be able to finish now. Everything has stopped with the war.'

'It will not go on for ever. In any case, people will still need doctors.'

'I will not become a doctor under the Nazis,' Anna replied.

'No, no, of course not. Anyway, I am sure we will turn the tide.'

'I hope you're right.' Anna sounded doubtful.

'I am. France has the largest army in the world. I know we have all seen pictures of Nazi rallies, but that is for show. They might have swept aside Poland, but the Polish cavalry was still on horseback. France has an army of more than two million men, and more tanks and guns than Britain and

Germany put together. So all will be well, you'll see.' He patted her knee.

Tanner felt her flinch. Shut the hell up, you French bastard, he thought. This was no time to sweet-talk Anna Rostad.

'Of course,' said Chevannes, 'I never went to university myself, but I did study at St Cyr, our national military academy near Versailles.'

'All clear at the back?' yelled Tanner.

'All clear, Sarge,' came Sykes's reply.

'And Versailles is magnificent, of course,' continued Chevannes. 'The—'

'Where are we now, sir?' interrupted Tanner.

Chevannes opened the map on his lap. Anna peered over his shoulder.

'We are here.' She pointed a finger. 'We are climbing to the Espedalen where there is a mountain lake.'

The truck laboured as the track steepened. 'Come on,' muttered Tanner.

They inched round a hairpin bend and hit a pothole. Amid groans from the back, Anna was knocked against Chevannes. 'Sorry,' she said.

'Why would I mind having you thrown against me?' Chevannes smiled. 'I must say, I do admire your brave decision to come with us.'

'What's that noise?' snapped Tanner.

'I didn't hear anything,' said Chevannes.

Of course not, thought Tanner. You're yapping too much. He strained his ears. Yes, there it was again, unmistakable. 'I can hear an aircraft!' He turned to Chevannes. 'Sir, can you see anything?'

As he spoke, Hepworth shouted, 'Got them! Two aircraft at five o'clock. Coming up the valley.'

'Get some bloody binoculars on them!' Tanner shouted.

Chevannes leaned out of the window, glasses to his eyes. The truck was gaining momentum once more. Tanner searched ahead for a place to shelter at the side of the road, but there was nothing. Rather, as the road straightened he could see the ravine to their left rising towards the lake. They were even more exposed up here.

'Single engine, Sergeant!' Larsen called out. 'Two.'

'Stukas!' said Chevannes. '*Mon Dieu.*'

Tanner tried to think. *Keep going. If they know about Sandvold they're not going to hit us.* He could hear them clearly now. The road was rough, but clear and straight. He put his foot down hard on the accelerator.

'What are you doing?' said Chevannes. His eyes were wide.

'I'm going to bloody well keep driving. The faster we move the harder it'll be for them to hit us.'

The two Stukas flew on, small but distinct. It was hard to know how high they were, but he guessed at least 6,000 feet.

'They're flying past us,' said Hepworth. 'They're getting a bead on the truck before they dive.'

Sure enough, the aircraft turned onto their backs and dived at about a ninety-degree angle. As the lead Stuka seemed about to plummet into them, it levelled out. A dark cigar-shaped bomb detached itself from the belly and fell. A split second later a deafening explosion behind them rocked the truck. Tanner righted it as the second aircraft pulled out of its dive and there was another explosion, this time ahead.

Tanner felt the brakes lock, and momentarily lost control of the front of the truck, then regained it and straightened the Morris. With a screech of burning rubber, it slid across the stony road and ground to a halt in a swirling mass of smoke.

'Are you mad?' yelled Chevannes. 'Now we are sitting ducks!'

'Not in this smoke. Anyway, they're not trying to kill us. They're trying to stop us.' Tanner wound up the window, coughing as dust, grit and cordite choked him. 'They want Sandvold alive.'

The two Stukas had gone without strafing. It was the confirmation he needed that the capture of Sandvold alive was the enemy objective.

As the dust dispersed they could see a large crater ahead. It covered more than three-quarters of the road; debris was scattered for yards around.

'Bollocks,' said Tanner, hurrying to the crater's edge. Chevannes followed him and, from the back of the truck, came Sykes and Larsen.

'Can't help but admire it, can you?' said Sykes.

'Bloody fine marksmanship,' agreed Tanner.

'I knew we should have waited until this evening when we would have been out of sight of the Luftwaffe,' said Chevannes. 'Now we're stuck.'

'Well, sir.' Tanner winked at Sykes. 'If you'd take your men and keep a watch out for any trouble, the corporal and I will get us moving again.'

Sykes delved into his bag and produced two cartridges of Polar dynamite. 'See, sir?' Sykes beamed at Chevannes.

'You wish to make another crater?' The Frenchman was clearly appalled.

'No, sir. We'll blast a bit of the bank. Then we can drive round the hole.'

Tanner hurried back to the truck where the other men were waiting. Grabbing his pack, he said, 'Get ready with your shovels. Bomb crater in the road. We need to get past it, pronto.'

He took out his safety fuse, which Sykes tied round the dynamite and placed in a small hole in the bank that he had already dug. 'You might want to take the truck back a bit, Sarge.'

Tanner nodded, cut the fuse and ran back to the truck. After he had reversed it thirty yards, he saw Sykes put a match to the fuse and run down the road towards him. He kept an eye on his watch, following the seconds ticking by. A breathless Sykes reached him. 'Any moment now, Sarge.'

An earsplitting crack rent the silence of the valley, the report echoing across the lake. Once the rain of rock, stone and grit had settled, Tanner and Sykes hurried back to see that a six-foot-wide chunk of the bank had been blown into the existing crater. The road would soon be passable once more.

'Stan,' said Tanner. 'You're a genius.' He ordered his men to start clearing debris from the road. Less than ten minutes later, Tanner began to inch the truck forward. The offside wing ground against the bank and then the truck lurched ahead. A moment later, it was safely on the other side.

The men got back in the truck and they set off once more. Tanner wondered how long it would take the Stuka crews to warn the ground troops of their position. They might meet Germans at any moment. Perhaps Chevannes had been right, after all. Perhaps they should have waited.

'In a couple of kilometres, the road climbs again,' said Anna. 'You can see a long way from up there.'

'What about snow?'

'There will be snow on the mountains but the road will be clear by now. There are quite a few farms—they will make sure the road can be used.'

A mile, then two. Suddenly the end of the lake appeared and the climb began. The road was winding, so their forward view was never more than 100 yards at most. 'We're nearly there,' said Anna, as Tanner drove round yet another sharp hairpin and the road levelled at last.

'How far ahead can you see now?' Tanner asked her.

'Three or four kilometres at least. The road's empty.'

'See anything at the back?' Tanner yelled.

'Nothing,' came the reply.

Where were they? Tanner wondered. There were a number of farms along this high mountain route, but not a soul stirred. The road was empty—not a cart, person or animal. The place seemed lifeless; it was almost impossible to think a war could be going on. Tanner strained his eyes. Fatigue was getting the better of him.

A glint in the distance snapped him out of his reverie. 'There!' he said. 'What was that?'

Chevannes and Anna had their binoculars trained. Another glint.

'It's them,' said Chevannes. 'A convoy of four trucks. Seven kilometres, maybe eight.'

'What are we going to do?' asked Anna, fear in her voice.

'Stop and head into the mountains,' said Chevannes.

'Here?' said Tanner. 'There's no cover at all.' He glanced at the map. 'What's this valley here?' He pointed to a dogleg in the road.

'It's not far,' said Anna. 'Look, the road turns just ahead.'

'Good. We can ditch the truck there and take cover in the trees.'

To his relief, as they turned the corner and lost sight of the enemy, Tanner saw that the landscape was covered with forest. At the corner of the dog-leg, the road crossed a stream and Tanner stopped.

'Everyone out! Quick!' shouted Chevannes. 'Head for the trees!'

'Sir, wait!' Tanner ran after him. 'If you and your men take the professor and Miss Rostad, my men and I will try to hold the Jerries off for a while.'

Chevannes paused then said, 'Very well.'

'Miss—Anna,' said Tanner. 'Where will you head for?'

'Here,' she told him. Her finger was shaking as she pointed on the map. 'Skjedalen. There are several mountain huts where we can shelter.' She swallowed, her eyes searching Tanner's face for reassurance. 'There are two peaks above us. Keep those on your right and head almost due north.'

'All right,' he said. 'Wait for us there.'

Wide-eyed, frightened, she turned and ran on.

'Lads, quick,' he said, calling his men to him. 'We need to halt these Jerry bastards. There are four trucks, and by my reckoning that's around seventy men.' The men's faces were ashen. 'Stan, the time has come for us to use up a bit more of our explosive. Can you start rigging the truck? You've got five minutes. Dan, head upstream a bit, then cut into the trees on the right-hand side. Look for a good view down here, where you can see the road both sides of the bridge. The rest, follow Dan and find some cover. Now, get going.' Erwood and the other five hurried off.

Sykes was already rigging together four cartons of Nobel's gelignite. 'What have you got, Sarge?' he asked, deftly tying a length of fuse.

'Five more packets of Nobel's and about ten sticks of Polar. Oh, and half a dozen grenades. Where are you going to put them?'

'Round the fuel tank. And a packet of Nobel's in the engine bay.'

'How are you going to trigger it?'

'Grenade on the door?'

'Sounds good.'

'It seems a real shame to blow her up,' said Sykes, as he set the booby trap on the passenger door.

'All for the greater good, Stan.'

'I s'pose so. Even so.' He handed the fuse back to Tanner. 'I see Mr Chevannes has buggered off.'

'I told him to. Someone has to look after the professor and Miss Rostad.'

'He didn't need much persuading . . . anyway, it's just us now, Sarge.'

'Yes,' said Tanner, 'and I feel happier already. Right. All done?'

Sykes nodded.

'Good. Let's get the hell away from here.'

They scrambled off the road and up the side of the stream. Tanner looked back to see the leading enemy truck turn the curve in the road a couple of hundred yards behind them. His heart was thumping. 'Here they come!' he called, and scrambled up through the snow and into the trees. Erwood, with Hepworth beside him, lay behind a rocky outcrop, a clear field of fire on the road below and the stream beneath them. The other riflemen were nearby, most behind trees but making good use of the undulations on the steep slope rising from the stream. They were learning, thought Tanner. The forested slopes would protect them as they fell back.

'Stan, you stick back on the lip of the ravine. And here,' he said, taking off his pack and gas-mask case, 'keep these by your feet.' He now realised how foolhardy he had been in keeping so much high explosive about him during the firefight at the *seter*; he didn't want to chance his luck a second time. He grabbed two sticks of Polar dynamite and three grenades, then stuffed them into his haversack and ran over to Erwood and Hepworth.

'Hep, move back. I'm going to man the Bren with Dan.'

Along the road ahead the trucks were drawing near. Tanner undid the fastenings on his magazine pouches, felt in his haversack for his grenades and .303 ammunition clips, then pulled his rifle into his shoulder.

'Don't fire until I say.' He took a bead on the truck. The pack of Nobel's strapped to the fuel tank was out of sight, but he had a clear view of the bonnet. His body was tense as the first enemy truck drew alongside the Morris-Commercial, then pushed on across the bridge. Damn, he thought, then saw that the two trucks following had halted alongside Sulheim's wagon. Troops were jumping from the back of the lorries. Tanner watched with bated breath as two men approached the Morris. Then, to his annoyance, they stepped round to the far side and opened the door.

'Sod it,' whispered Tanner. 'They've opened the wrong door.' The soldiers were shouting now. 'They've found the grenade.' Tanner pulled back the bolt on his rifle. He knew that the moment he fired the battle would start. Would any of them survive? He squeezed the trigger.

The first bullet missed, but the second slammed into the bonnet, puncturing the thin metal, tearing into the packet of gelignite and igniting it. A split second later, a vast ball of orange flame erupted round the Morris, incinerating the men who had been examining the cab and engulfing the second German truck. Now the third truck was aflame, the engine exploding.

'Bloody hell, Sarge!' whistled Erwood.

'Start firing, Dan,' said Tanner. 'That's only half the job.' The Bren began to chatter next to him, empty cartridge cases clattering onto the bare rock. Men were falling in disarray at either side of the burning vehicles, but Tanner knew this advantage would soon pass. What concerned him now was that the men from the first and last trucks, either side of the carnage, would try to infiltrate round the side of their position. Thick, black smoke covered the road and lead truck too. It gave the enemy from the lead truck perfect cover to make an advance up the slope on the far side of the stream. We should make use of it too, thought Tanner. A moment later he heard a whistle and twenty yards to his right there was an explosion.

'What was that?' shouted Erwood.

'They're firing mortars from behind the smoke screen!' Two more followed. Bullets were now zipping through the trees as the enemy troops from the first truck found their composure and their aim. 'Quick, Dan, get off a few rounds towards that first truck! Fire through the smoke!' Blindly, he fired several rounds in succession. A man cried out and a spectral figure fell, but Tanner knew it was now critical that he and his men move back. Machine-gun fire raked the ground around them. Even with half the force destroyed or out of action, enemy firepower was already proving too heavy.

'Come on, Dan.' He pulled out a grenade. 'One, two, three! Go!'

Erwood stood up, then fell back with a cry. 'He's got my arm!'

'Right,' said Tanner. 'Hand over the Bren. I'll cover you.' He rammed another thirty-round magazine into the breech and pulled back the cock. 'Go, Dan!' he shouted, as he opened fire, the butt of the Bren pummelling his shoulder. 'Fall back! Everyone, fall back!' More mortar shells fell among them, but the enemy machine gun was now silent. Out of the corner of his eye, Tanner could see more enemy troops working their way round the lead truck; he fired another burst from the Bren. The first truck was drawing all their fire, yet he knew the men from the last must be working their way behind them. 'Stan!' he yelled and the corporal looked across. Frantically, Tanner waved his arm—*fall back!*—and Sykes nodded. First, though, the corporal pulled a stick of Polar dynamite from his haversack. Tanner saw Sykes light the stick, count, then hurl it across the stream at the enemy troops. More mortar rounds rippled across the slopes. Then Sykes's dynamite exploded, and for a brief moment, the enemy fire stopped.

Tanner scrambled out of his position to be met by bullets fizzing past his head. Frantically he searched the ground above him for cover. Trees ahead and, to his left, a fallen trunk. He gasped, lungs straining. More bullets. Yards to go. Feet losing their grip. Where were the others? Another mortar shell, followed by another. He plunged over the fallen tree, then rolled and lay sideways. As debris pattered on his helmet he fired another burst of the Bren, just as yet another mortar round hurtled towards him. Tanner ducked, heard the explosion, then felt the blast knock him back against a tree trunk.

When he came to he was aware that he was surrounded by half a dozen enemy troops. As his eyes focused, he realised he was looking up at none other than Hauptmann Zellner.

Tanner had a pounding headache, his ears still rang shrilly and his mouth was drier than sand, yet he had the presence of mind to glance at his watch. Nearly fifty minutes had passed since Chevannes had led Sandvold into the trees. Well, that's something, he thought.

Two men pulled him to his feet, so that he was face to face with Zellner. The German smiled, then rammed his fist into Tanner's belly. The sergeant gasped and doubled over, only to be pulled up again.

'Where is he?' Zellner hissed.

'Who?' said Tanner.

Zellner punched him again. 'Where is he?' he repeated.

'I couldn't say,' murmured Tanner. 'We're just the holding force—holding you up, that is. And we are right now. So, let's chat some more.'

'Enough!' said Zellner, and then struck him a third time. 'We do not need to know. We will just follow the tracks and we will catch him.'

'You won't. He'll be shot before you get a chance.'

Zellner pulled the pistol from Tanner's holster. 'Mine, I think.' He checked the magazine, then cocked it and pointed it at the centre of Tanner's forehead. 'I said I would kill you and so I will.'

Tanner smiled. 'You're a fool, Zellner.'

Zellner glared back. 'Tanner, you have said your last.'

IN THE TREES on the slopes above, Sykes crouched, watching his sergeant and wondering what on earth he could do. Having seen Tanner knocked backwards, he had immediately thought to follow the others, but as he had turned he had seen enemy troops pull Tanner to his feet. Knowing he was alive, Sykes felt compelled to stay and help. But how?

He decided that a diversion was his best option. He still had a few packets of Nobel's 808 as well as several sticks of dynamite, and he had Tanner's pack too. He climbed a bit higher, then saw what he was looking for: a jutting outcrop of rock, like a giant boulder. If he could get enough explosives behind it and force it to tumble down the mountainside, he might help Tanner escape or, at worst, give the enemy a further headache.

He glanced back at Tanner and froze. The officer had his arm extended with a pistol pointing at Tanner's head. 'No!' mouthed Sykes, under his breath. He turned his head, not daring to look.

Then came the sound of a single pistol shot.

TANNER HAD EYED the men gathered round Hauptmann Zellner. There were six. Three had their rifles slung on their shoulders, two clutched them loosely with one arm, while a sixth had a machine gun slung by his side. It looked to him a similar if somewhat more sophisticated weapon than those he had seen after the firefight at the *seter*. The cock, he noticed, was on the right of the breech. The crux of the matter was whether or not the magazine was empty. Surely no machine-gunner would wander around with an unloaded weapon while the battle still had a chance of continuing?

Tanner was glad he had kept Zellner talking long enough to take all of this in, but accepted that the moment had arrived to act. Holding Zellner's stare, he brought up his left hand quickly and knocked away the German's arm. Zellner fired harmlessly into the air as Tanner rammed his right fist straight into the man's mouth and nose. As the unconscious Zellner fell backwards, Tanner lunged for the machine gun and slid it down the stunned soldier's arm. Pulling back the breech, he fired.

The recoil of the machine gun nearly knocked him backwards but a rapid burst of bullets from the barrel neatly scythed through the six men so that only Zellner, who had slumped backwards, escaped being nearly sliced in two. Firing another quick burst at the startled men behind, he grabbed a rack of two-drum magazines, then spotted his rifle lying on the ground. He snatched it up and raced for the trees. 'Act decisively, act quickly,' his first sergeant had told him. It was an adage Tanner had not forgotten.

Bullets pinged and zipped either side of him, but the trees were closing protectively round him. On he ran, driven by instinct alone, until an explosion shook the ground and made him stop. Below and away to his left, he could hear the blast of rock. Screams followed and he heard someone call: 'Sarge! Sarge!' Corporal Sykes was scrambling towards him.

'Stan, you're alive!' Tanner grinned and held out a hand, which was shaken gratefully. 'I thought you'd been killed back there.'

'And me you, Sarge!'

They kept running until they reached the edge of the tree line, where they emerged into a wide expanse of snow.

'Look!' said Sykes. 'The others! All of them! We made it!'

Away to their right, a peak emerged magisterially. 'That's the first of the two peaks that Anna mentioned,' said Tanner. 'It's bloody exposed, Stan.'

Moments later Tanner and Sykes had caught up with the rest of the men. 'Dan, what's the damage?' said Tanner, as he reached them.

'The bullet just nicked me, Sarge.'

'Good,' said Tanner. 'Any sign of the others?'

'Only tracks. Easy enough to follow,' said McAllister.

'I'm about done in,' said Hepworth.

'Me too,' said Bell. 'Tell me it's not much further, Sarge.'

'Stop bellyaching,' said Tanner. 'We're all tired, but we've got two, maybe three miles of this, and then we should be among the trees again. Come on, boys, we've seen off those Jerries. We can't let ourselves down now.'

He said this for his own benefit as much as his men's, for exhaustion had swamped him too. On his shoulders, he still carried his rifle and the German machine gun, as well as the drum magazines, his pack, gas-mask case and haversack. The weight seemed agonisingly oppressive.

And what of the enemy? There was still no sign. He thought of Zellner and reckoned he'd judged the punch about right. It would take him a while to wake. Whether they followed now or regrouped depended, he guessed, on whether other officers and NCOs were present and still fit.

Tanner fumbled in his pack and found a piece of bread. Chewing it slowly, he tramped onwards, his men following. At least, he thought, it was nearly May. These mountains would be deadly during the depths of winter, but with a high, warm sun, they presented less danger. No one would succumb to exposure. Exhaustion was their main enemy now.

Already Tanner could see the second peak Anna had mentioned and then he heard the distant boom of guns. His spirits rose. The battle at Kvam—the

Allies were still there! New reserves of energy found their way into his legs. 'Lads!' he said, grinning. 'Hear those guns? We're nearly there.'

McAllister cheered. 'Hoo-bloody-ray, Sarge!' he exclaimed.

Ahead, a figure emerged from the darkness of the trees. Those pines certainly offered good cover, Tanner thought. The man could not be seen until he was well clear and standing in the snow. He put his binoculars to his eyes. 'Lieutenant Nielssen,' he said, and waved.

'You made it!' said Nielssen, grinning as they reached him.

'Where are the others?'

'Sheltering in a *seter*. I've been waiting to guide you there.' He patted Tanner's back. 'It's good to see you safe.'

He led them through dense pine until they emerged into open snow once more, then reached the crest of the next valley. A vast view stood before them.

'The Gudbrandsdalen once again,' said Nielssen.

Guns were booming dully and, away to the right, a pall of smoke hid the valley and the Lågen River. Above, they heard the faint drone of aircraft.

'Heavy fighting, Sarge,' said Hepworth.

The *seter* stood beneath the crest of the valley, hidden by trees but with a view of the village of Sjoa and the curve of the river. Stretching away to the west from the Gudbrandsdal was a lesser valley.

'You're alive!' said Anna, smiling as Tanner entered the hut.

'What happened?' asked Chevannes.

'We destroyed two of their trucks and killed a number of them, I'm not sure how many. They don't seem to have followed us.'

'Your Bren?'

'Lost,' admitted Tanner. 'But I found this Spandau.' He tapped the German machine gun. 'Sir, we need to hurry. We need to keep going.'

Chevannes gave orders for them to move.

'There's a bridge across the Sjoa River about a kilometre west of the village,' said Anna.

'Very well,' said Chevannes.

They stumbled down the steep valley sides. Tanner disliked walking down mountains more than he did climbing them, and now his knees felt particularly weak, as though his legs might buckle at any moment. They headed diagonally across the valley, in a northwesterly direction. The sounds of battle had now all but died away.

By seven o'clock they were standing above the bridge over the Sjoa and now all could see that the bombers were dropping their loads further north.

Clearly the main Allied effort had fallen back. Tanner spotted enemy forces blocking the road south of Sjoa. He lowered his binoculars and stood silent, numbed by the knowledge that again they had missed their chance of freedom by a sliver.

'We've missed them.' It was Sandvold, and Tanner turned to him. Defeat and despair clouded his face. 'They're bombing them as they retreat.'

'A couple of hours earlier and we'd have been safe,' Tanner growled.

'I did what I thought was best for all of us,' said Chevannes. 'Lieutenant Larsen agreed with me. So did Professor Sandvold.'

'For pity's sake, man,' snarled Tanner, 'you're in charge. It's your decision, not theirs, and it's your fault we've missed the chance yet again to rejoin the Allies.' He had to think clearly and rationally. 'We must work out a new plan,' he said. 'What do you suggest, sir?'

'The map,' said Chevannes, icily. 'We must look at it.'

A rough track followed the southern side of the Sjoa Valley as it ran northwest. There were no villages of note, but scattered farmsteads all the way to Heidal, some ten miles on. A couple of miles south of Heidal there was a bridge. If they kept going now, Tanner suggested, they could cross when it was dark, then try to find a farm to rest for a few hours before heading into the next ridge of mountains. Beyond the next range lay the Otta Valley and the town of Vågåmo. 'Look,' he said, pointing to the map, 'there's a road leading north. It bypasses Dombås and joins the Åndalsnes road further north—here. It means we keep well away from the main German advance but we still run parallel to it.'

'What if the enemy is already past Dombås by then?' asked Larsen.

Tanner shrugged. 'Do you have a better idea, sir? Perhaps we'll find some more transport. Maybe in Vågåmo.'

'Good,' said Chevannes. 'This is what we'll do. First, we rest for a while and eat what food we have left. Then we head for the bridge.'

The men delved into their packs and squatted on the ground. Tanner saw that Bell and Kershaw were shivering. 'Listen, boys,' he said, 'this is a blow, I know, but we need to look forward now. Come on, I know we can do it.' Tanner watched the resigned nods, the faces blank with exhaustion.

He wandered away and leaned against a tree. His words had seemed fatuous. He wondered how long they would be content to follow him. What reserves of strength were left in the tank?

The crack of a twig made him turn. 'I'm sorry to disturb you, Sergeant,' said Sandvold, 'but I wondered whether I might talk to you a moment.'

'What is it?' asked Tanner.

Sandvold now wore a full beard, grey at the chin. It made him seem more venerable. 'I want to apologise. I should have backed you up at the farm. If I had we might have persuaded Lieutenant Chevannes. Then we would have reached the Allies before it was too late.' He cleared his throat. 'It was weak of me, but I thought I should not get involved in military decisions.'

'What's done is done, Professor,' said Tanner, 'but there will be other difficult decisions to make. You could back me up. If we work together, we'll have a better chance of succeeding.'

Sandvold nodded. 'All right, Sergeant,' he said. 'I will do my best.'

Soon after, Chevannes gave the order to move off. Tanner tried again to rouse his men. 'We'll still make it, boys,' he told them. 'Don't lose heart.'

'It's easy to say that, Sarge,' said McAllister, 'but I felt knackered before and I'm even more done in now.'

'Listen, Mac,' said Tanner. 'We'll be at the bridge by nightfall and once we've got across we can have a rest. It's not far. You can do it.'

They were strung out in a patrol line. Of the enemy there was still no sign. The track passed through dense forest that ran almost all the way to the river's edge, giving them good cover.

'Don't worry, Sarge,' said Sykes, drawing alongside him. 'They're good lads. They'll be all right. We've got a bit of grub inside us now. That helps.'

'Perhaps.'

'Sarge,' said Sykes, after a short while, 'how did you get away from those Jerries? I saw that officer pointing his pistol straight at your bloody head and the next minute I heard a shot. I thought you was a goner.'

Tanner smiled. 'I brought my arm up quickly and simply knocked the gun to the side of my head. By the time he'd pressed the trigger the shot was already wide. I gave him a right hook to remember me by.'

'Did you kill him? The officer, that is?'

'Zellner? I don't think so. Broke his nose. Possibly his jaw.' He grinned. 'Any explosives left after your little diversion?'

'Not much. A carton of Nobel's and a few sticks of Polar.'

'It's thanks to you those bastards aren't at our backs now. You did well.'

'Sarge?' Sykes said. 'I'd just like to know how those Stukas knew it was us. And how did those trucks know where we'd be?'

'They've had aerial reconnaissance buzzing over nearly nonstop.'

'Yes, but we didn't see anything before them Stukas turned up, did we?'

'What are you saying?'

Sykes said, in a hushed voice, 'I'm hoping we haven't got a spy among us.'

'A spy?' Tanner gaped at him. 'Are you joking, Stan? Who?'

'I don't know, do I?'

'I mean, how on earth would anyone be contacting the enemy? We've been together all the time.'

'Not *all* the time, Sarge. There've been times when we've been kipping, when we've wandered off to—you know . . . We don't know what those Norwegians are carrying in their rucksacks. Perhaps they've got a radio.'

'But how could they use it without anyone else seeing?'

'I don't know. I keep thinking about how those Jerries dog our every move and that makes me wonder whether someone's tipping them the wink. I mean, you yourself thought those Jerries were waiting for us in Tretten.'

'We keep this to ourselves and watch everyone, Stan. The Norwegians at any rate.' They walked on in silence, Tanner deep in thought. It seemed so fantastical, yet there was no denying that the enemy did seem to have been second-guessing their movements. He shivered, whether from the cold or the suspicion that the corporal might be right, he couldn't say.

THEY REACHED the bridge safely. A sliver of moon appeared, but the valley was dark and still. Once again, Tanner was struck by how far away the war seemed, yet only a dozen or so miles to the southeast a two-day battle had been fought.

They crossed the bridge, Tanner cringing at the sound of the studded boots on the wooden struts. They were bunched up now, walking together so they didn't lose one another. They walked in silence along the soft verge that ran close to the northern bank of the Sjoa River to deaden the sound of their footsteps. Tanner sensed the men were dragging their feet; he was too. Every step was harder. In the faint creamy night light, he could see that Sandvold was almost falling asleep as he stumbled on.

'Sir,' he said to Chevannes, 'we should stop soon.'

'And this from the man who thinks we should never rest at all.'

'I need to rest,' muttered Sandvold. 'I cannot go much further.'

Chevannes struck a match and squinted at Anna's map. 'We're near Heidal, I think. We will look for somewhere to rest for a few hours.'

Only a short distance further on a farmhouse loomed. It was dark, with no light showing, but in the yard there were signs of vehicle tracks.

'Larsen, go and have a look round,' said Chevannes. Larsen, with Nielssen accompanying him, walked forward cautiously.

When the Norwegians returned, the news was good. 'It's empty,' said Larsen. 'Someone's been here recently, though.'

'Sergeant,' said Chevannes to Tanner, 'organise guards. The rest, follow me into the house.'

'Hep, you can take first watch with me,' said Tanner.

Hepworth groaned. 'Sarge, why does it have to be me?'

'This way you get it over with. Stay here and watch the road.'

Tanner left him and, taking his machine gun, crossed the road. There was only one way the Germans could come, he reasoned, and that was from Sjoa. He had his rifle and the MG set up on its bipod. The night was so quiet that if any vehicles approached he knew he would hear them a long way off.

Satisfied that should there be any sign of the enemy he could raise the alarm, he sat down on the bank, thinking of what Sykes had said earlier. He felt sure it couldn't be Sandvold, yet the professor had been in Oslo during the first days of the occupation. Perhaps the story of his mother was a lie. Perhaps he was working for the Nazis after all. Then he considered Larsen and Nielssen. Again, it seemed unlikely. If one was a spy, he could surely have killed the other two and taken Sandvold to the Germans.

He thought about Anna. In truth, he'd thought about her quite a lot over the past two days. There was no denying she had been very keen to help them—perhaps overly so. But if she was a traitor, how was she passing on information? She carried a rucksack, but was it big enough for a wireless? And what was her motive? It didn't make sense.

And, of course, there was Chevannes. No one, in his view, had done more to hinder them at every turn. And yet it couldn't be the Frenchman—of that he was sure. Sleep was what he needed. Perhaps he'd be able to see the situation more clearly after that.

AN HOUR LATER Sykes and Bell relieved him and Hepworth. 'Get inside,' Sykes told him. 'We found a whole load of tins of Maconochie's stew and a few bottles of vino too. Some of our boys were here not so long ago.'

Inside, Tanner found Chevannes and Nielssen sitting at the table, one empty and a half-drunk bottle of wine between them.

'Where's the professor?' he asked.

'Upstairs,' said Chevannes, pointing above his head. 'Don't worry—he's sound asleep.' His eyes were glassy, his words somewhat slurred.

'I'll just get something for me and Hepworth to eat. I hear there's some stew about.'

'*Oui, oui*. Heat up another tin. And have some wine.' While Tanner found two tins of stew and vegetables, Chevannes poured out a chipped tumbler of wine, spilling some. 'A toast, Sergeant,' he said, pushing the tumbler in Tanner's direction. 'A toast to surviving so far.'

Tanner scowled at the Frenchman. 'No bloody thanks to you.'

'What did you say, Sergeant?' slurred Chevannes.

'You heard,' Tanner retorted. He went back to heating his tins of stew.

'How dare you?'

'How dare I what?' said Tanner. 'If it wasn't for you, we wouldn't be sitting in this hole. Get drunk if you want to but in a few hours' time we'll be off again and I'm not waiting for you.' Tanner grabbed the heated tins.

He found Hepworth almost asleep on the stairs, then entered another room on the ground floor. He lit a match and saw a half-burnt candle on a desk, which stood before a fireplace. Lighting it, he looked around, while eating his stew. In the grate he found the remains of a number of papers. Tanner picked up the top of a sheet entitled WAR DIARY, beside which had been scrawled in pencil: *148 Inf Bde*. So, this had been Brigadier Morgan's headquarters, he thought. Missed by hours.

Tanner lay down on the floor by the fireplace and, using his captured jacket as a pillow, closed his eyes and slept.

HE WAS BEING shaken roughly. 'Sarge! Sarge! It's me, Bell. You need to come. The corp sent me.'

Tanner got wearily to his feet, grabbed his rifle and stumbled outside. Sykes was by the gate. 'What is it?' Tanner asked.

'Someone came out of the house,' Sykes whispered. 'I couldn't see who it was, but they went into the barn. Whoever it is, they're still there.'

They crept towards the barn. The door was ajar and they paused. Tanner's heart was hammering. 'Cover me,' he whispered, then pushed the door and went in.

He listened intently but could hear nothing. Sykes and Bell were now behind him. He felt in his pocket for his matches and struck one. The flame gave only a little light, but it was enough to show a row of animal stalls in front of them. He lit another match and walked slowly along the row. There, asleep on a pile of hay in the last stall, was the mystery person.

'Miss!' said Tanner.

She woke with a start. 'Sergeant, what's the matter?' She sat up, blinking.

'We heard someone leave the house,' said Tanner. Suddenly he felt rather foolish. Sykes lit another match. There was nothing beside her: no rucksack, and certainly no radio.

'I'm sorry,' she said. 'It was the lieutenant. He was drunk.'

'What did the bastard do?'

'Nothing, really.' She made to stand up and Tanner stepped forward to offer her a hand. 'He—well, he was drunk and making a nuisance of himself.' She took his hand. Her fingers were cold but gripped his tightly. 'I didn't want to make a scene.' The match went out but her hand stayed in his. 'I just thought it would be quiet out here.'

With his heart still hammering, but now for a different reason, he said, 'It would be safer if you came back inside. If anything should happen . . .'

'I'm sure the lieutenant will be sound asleep by now, miss,' said Sykes.

'Yes, of course,' she said. 'I understand.'

Back outside the barn, Tanner turned his watch to the light of the moon. 'Just gone one,' he said. 'Stan, you and Tinker are on until half past, then get Mac and Kershaw out for an hour, and they can come and get me again. We want to be away by half three. All right?'

'Got it, Sarge.'

Tanner led Anna back into a silent house, showing her to the office. In the dark, he bumped into her, apologised, then whispered, 'Over here.' He crouched and heard her settle next to him. 'Would you like my jacket?'

'No, no. I'm fine. Thank you. I've got my own.'

'Try to get back to sleep, then,' he said. He closed his eyes, then felt her hand take his, squeezing it. Was she genuine, or playing a part? To hell with it, he thought. In less than two hours he had to be awake again. For now, the soft warmth of her touch was a much-needed comfort.

WHEN MCALLISTER WOKE him, Tanner was alert in an instant. He went out to watch the road. Not for the first time since arriving in Norway ten days before, he watched the sun rise over the mountains.

Soon after three, he went back into the house, woke Sykes and ordered him out on watch, then stoked the fire and roused Anna. 'I need your help,' he said. 'Can you heat some more tins of stew for me?'

She nodded sleepily.

'Are you all right?' he asked, as she stretched and yawned.

'Yes, I think so. This is harder than I thought it would be. I had not realised we would get so little sleep.'

He smiled. 'It's an occupational hazard, I'm afraid.'

'I know.' She looked up at him. 'Jack, do you think we'll make it?'

'Of course. We have to.' He went to wake the others.

One by one, the men stumbled into the kitchen, stretching and yawning. Chevannes was the last to appear, eyes narrow and puffy.

While the others ate the remaining tins of Maconochie's, Tanner spread the map on the floor. 'Anna, do you know this stretch of mountains?'

'I know Bringsfjellet, the peak above Vågåmo, and I've been to the town.'

'What about here?' He pointed to a narrow, steep-sided valley that ran north from Heidal. 'Do you think it will be wooded?'

'Almost certainly.'

'It looks as though there's a track through it. It's mostly southwest-facing so with luck there won't be much snow. I think we should head down there.'

'Excuse me interrupting,' said Chevannes, his voice laden with sarcasm, 'but it is not up to you, Sergeant, to decide.' He leaned over, stale wine fumes heavy on his breath. 'We should find some transport. The men are still exhausted. Their welfare is clearly not of concern to you, Sergeant.'

Tanner took a deep breath. 'If we see something we should take it, but I don't think we should waste time looking. It's no more than a day's march to Vågåmo where we'd have to ditch any M/T we had anyway.'

'And the fact that the men are exhausted?' said Chevannes. 'We should find a vehicle.'

'We need to get going while it's still safe, sir. We're by a main valley road, and it's not long before Jerry will be here. I've had a look at the sky. It was clear three-quarters of an hour ago, but the cloud's building and it looks like rain. We need to get away and under the cover of the forest as soon as possible. We can rest later. Better to do so where we can post proper sentries and prepare a decent escape route. We should aim to get to the mountains above Vågåmo. Anna knows those peaks.'

'There are good views of the River Otta, the lake and the town from the Bringsfjellet,' added Anna.

'So from there,' Tanner continued, 'we can look down on the town. It may even be that we'll get there before the Germans do, in which case we'll be fine. If not, we can work out how to join the road north of the town. I agree, we'll need some M/T then, but we don't have time to look for it now.'

'The track we take this morning should be fairly easy going,' said Anna.

Chevannes turned to face her. 'Oh, I see, you two have—how shall I put this?—a little understanding.'

Tanner reddened.

'That is charming,' continued Chevannes, 'but, Sergeant, you must not let your feelings for Miss Rostad cloud your judgment.'

Something inside Tanner snapped. Without further thought he clenched his fist and swung his right arm at Chevannes. The movement was executed with such lightning precision that the Frenchman had no time to react. The force of the punch knocked him backwards in an unconscious heap.

For a moment, no one said a word.

Damn, damn, damn, thought Tanner.

'Sergeant,' said Larsen, eventually. 'What did you think you were doing?'

'He pushed me too far.' He glared at the Norwegian.

Chevannes groaned, then came round. 'Tanner,' he hissed, 'you struck an officer!'

'You insulted me and Miss Rostad, sir.'

'You had better apologise, Sergeant,' said Larsen.

Tanner sighed, then said to Chevannes, 'Sir, I apologise for hitting you. And now can we get the hell out of here?'

'Don't think that's the end of it,' said Chevannes. 'Because when we get back to our lines, I'm going to report you, Sergeant, and you will be court-martialled. I'm going to make sure your career is finished for—'

'Enough!'

The professor had stepped forward. 'Enough of this,' he said again. 'Lieutenant—please. Ask everyone to wait outside. You, Sergeant, and you, Larsen and Nielssen, stay here.'

Chevannes was plainly surprised by the professor's intervention. 'Yes, all right,' he said. 'Everyone—out. Now!'

'Listen to me,' said Sandvold, once the door had closed. 'I'm not interested in your squabbles. What I *am* interested in is successfully reaching the Allies, and it is your task to help me. If you want to bring charges against the sergeant once this is over, that is up to you, but for now you must put aside your differences, because if I may say so, Lieutenant, your desire to undermine Sergeant Tanner is, to my mind, undermining our chances.'

Tanner smiled to himself. Good lad, he thought.

'Now, Sergeant Tanner has clearly studied the land carefully and it strikes me his plan is the right one.'

Chevannes sniffed. 'Professor, you should leave any such decisions to me.'

'I am not under your orders, Lieutenant. We must stop bickering and go.'

Chevannes glanced at Larsen and Nielssen, hoping for support, but found none. 'Very well,' he said stiffly. 'We leave now.'

7

Reichsamtsleiter Scheidt could hardly believe it was only six days since he had last stood in this corridor at the Bristol Hotel; it seemed like a lifetime ago. As he waited to see the Reichskommissar, he paced uneasily. Coming back to Oslo was a gamble and he was uncertain how Terboven would react.

At last the door opened and an SS officer ushered him into the suite where he and Quisling had first seen Terboven.

The Reichskommissar was writing at his desk and did not look up as Scheidt entered and stood before him. The silence was so complete that Scheidt could hear the nib scratching the paper.

It was an old trick to impose one's authority by keeping a subordinate waiting. Nonetheless, Scheidt reflected, it was still effective. He could feel the greasy sweat on his palms. A further minute passed, then Terboven stopped writing, carefully replaced the lid of his pen, laid it on his desk and said, 'Ah, Reichsamtsleiter Scheidt—you are the bearer of good news?'

Scheidt looked Terboven directly in the eye. 'I'm afraid not.'

Terboven leaned back and raised an eyebrow.

'We have located Odin several times and have been within a hair's-breadth of capturing him but, alas, he has always eluded us.'

'How can this be possible?' Terboven snapped.

'The most General Engelbrecht could spare was a reconnaissance company of Gebirgsjäger. These troops met stiff resistance from a company of British and French troops who have joined Odin and his Norwegian guardians. Killing them has not been the difficulty; killing them and rescuing Odin unscathed has, however, proved more challenging.'

Terboven nodded. 'And what about your "source"?'

'The information has been crucial, but sporadic.'

'You have until tomorrow, Herr Reichsamtsleiter, until our deal is over. I don't mind telling you I'm surprised to see you here. I'd have thought that your time could have been used more profitably.'

'I'd like your help, Herr Reichskommissar. I'm here to ask you to speak with General Engelbrecht. The company of Gebirgsjäger have suffered heavy casualties yet he refuses to give us more troops.'

Terboven pursed his lips. 'My difficulty is that you are asking me to order a general in the field to redirect some of his forces at a time when he is engaged in heavy fighting but without my being able to give him much reason. There is nothing to stop General Engelbrecht from contacting the Oberkommando der Wehrmacht in Berlin and complaining vociferously about such interfering. When the supreme command demand an explanation, I will have to tell them that Reichsamtsleiter Scheidt has assured me these troops are needed for a very good yet unspecified cause.' He leaned forward. 'The time has come to stop the games, Herr Reichsamtsleiter. Before I speak with General Engelbrecht, I want to know who this Odin is and why you think he is of such enormous importance.'

Scheidt knew he was cornered. Odin's secret would be his no more.

THAT MORNING IT POURED, soaking the men and turning the track to mud. But with the rain came low cloud. Aero-engines could briefly be heard droning across the sky, but they never saw the planes. More importantly, as Tanner was well aware, the aircraft could not see them.

It had done nothing to improve his dark mood. How dare Chevannes talk about him and Anna in front of his men? The thought of the others looking knowingly at him and Anna infuriated him. He had avoided her since. He could not deny that he found her attractive but now was not the time to be distracted. They had a mission to complete.

The valley climbed gently and, with the rain, the snow was receding almost before their eyes. Tanner turned up the collar of his battle blouse, but still water dripped down his back, while the rain pattered noisily on his helmet. His battle dress was now sodden. He wrapped his remaining packets of Nobel's and sticks of dynamite tightly in the German wind-jacket and stuffed them into his pack. The canvas of their webbing protected the remaining rounds of ammunition, but the possibility of losing it to the wet was another thing to worry about.

So too was Professor Sandvold's condition. He saw Anna and Larsen speaking with him, and Larsen put a hand on his shoulder. Alarm bells rang in Tanner's mind and he hurried along the wet track. 'What's the matter?' he said, as he reached them.

'He's got a temperature,' said Anna. 'Feel his brow.'

'A slight one, perhaps,' said Sandvold, but his teeth were chattering.

What next? Tanner thought. 'Are you wet through?' he asked.

Sandvold shook his head.

'How much have you drunk?' asked Anna.

'Enough, I think. I don't feel thirsty.'

'Water helps to bring a temperature down,' she said. 'I'll get some from the stream.' The others had gathered round them.

'What's going on?' demanded Chevannes.

'Nothing—please, I'll be all right,' said Sandvold.

'He needs rest,' said Anna. 'We should look out for a *seter*.'

Chevannes glared at Tanner, his implication clear. 'Very well,' he said. 'Let's hope we find somewhere soon.'

Luck was with them. Soon the western side of the valley folded away to reveal a mountain lake and an isolated farmhouse.

Thank God, thought Tanner, then prayed they might find refuge there. Chevannes halted them and sent Larsen, with Anna, towards the farm. As they waited, Tanner walked away from the others and signalled to Sykes. 'If one of them is a spy,' he said, 'this will give them another opportunity to make contact. We need to keep a close watch, Stan.'

'Why not talk to the others?'

'I don't want to frighten them.'

'Better that than Jerry turns up.'

Tanner thought for a moment. 'No, they'll chatter among themselves. If there is a spy we want to catch them, not put them on their guard.' He patted Sykes's shoulder. 'You and I are going to have to take responsibility here.'

Larsen returned. 'The farmer has gone to fight, but his wife is there with two small children and her father-in-law. She says we can come in.' He smiled wistfully. 'Two girls, they have. Beautiful children.'

Tanner and Nielssen helped the professor to his feet. He staggered. Tanner caught a glance from Anna: there was fear in her eyes, but what could he say? The professor was ill, and they could go no further.

HURRYING BACK to the Gudbrandsdal Valley in Kurz's black Citroën, Scheidt had instructions to report to Engelbrecht's headquarters at Vinstra. The general, Terboven had assured him, would be far more compliant this time; the Reichskommissar had made it clear that he was to give every assistance to Scheidt in the quest to capture Odin. Terboven had spoken with General Geisler, the commander of the Luftwaffe in Norway, too. 'If you have any problems, Scheidt,' Terboven had told him, 'let me know.'

He looked out at the passing countryside through the rain-streaked window. The snow was melting in the valley, leaving drab grey-yellow fields. His gamble, he supposed, had paid off, but although he now had the support he had gone to Oslo to ask for, he felt no elation. It was as though he had reached the endgame, not only for Odin but for himself.

In Lillehammer, he picked up Kurz and together they drove on to Vinstra. They found Engelbrecht, the commander of the 163rd Infantry Division, in a large building a few hundred yards south of the railway station. He was in conference with several of his commanders, including Major von Poncets, and insisted they be ushered into his planning room.

Reconnaissance reports that morning had suggested the British would be making a stand in battalion strength only. The first attack had been made a few hours earlier, but repulsed with heavy casualties.

'I had hoped we would force a way through quickly,' said Engelbrecht, 'but we must now wait and deploy in strength.'

'It's always easier for the defender to get away quickly, General,' said one of his commanders. 'The road between Sjoa and Otta is badly damaged.'

'The engineers are working flat out,' said another officer.

'Good,' said Engelbrecht, rubbing his hands together. 'The Luftwaffe will bomb the British positions once more, followed by a short but concentrated barrage. Then Infantry Regiment 307 will attack on a wide front with von Poncets' men sweeping round the eastern flanks.' He smiled. 'That should do the trick. But there must be no letup.'

He dismissed his commanders, then turned to Scheidt and Kurz. 'Forgive me, gentlemen,' he said, shaking their hands and leading them into a room he had established as his office. 'I've spoken with the Reichskommissar and I assured him I will do what I can to help. So where do you think this elusive fellow is?'

'We had contact yesterday to the west of Vinstra, then received a signal that they were heading for Sjoa,' said Kurz.

'Then I'm sorry to say they've most probably reached the British.'

Kurz shook his head. 'I don't think so, General. Yesterday evening we intercepted a message from the British brigade headquarters in Otta to their HQ in Dombås. They are as in the dark as we are.'

'Even so,' said Engelbrecht, 'you may have to accept that this fellow has already reached safety.'

'It's possible, yes,' admitted Kurz.

'The point is, General,' said Scheidt, 'that we must be ready to strike if and when we do hear news. Assume Odin is still at large and that there is much to be gained by his safe capture.'

'Yes, yes,' said Engelbrecht. 'I've heard all this from Terboven. Of course we will do what we can. But my forces are engaged in a battle at Otta. This afternoon, or perhaps this evening, the town will be in our hands. Thereafter, I will be in a better position to help.' He smiled again. 'So it might be better for you if Odin is not only still at large but that he waits for us to clean up at Otta before making his whereabouts known.'

AS IT HAPPENED, Odin was no more than twenty-five miles from Engelbrecht's headquarters. He was lying in the dark with a high temperature and a crushing migraine. He had vomited repeatedly.

In the barn, the men had been fed—boiled eggs, chicken, bread and stewed apple. The old man and his daughter-in-law had been generous hosts. The men had rested too, and the straw had helped to dry their clothes.

Tanner leaned against some straw, carving a small aircraft from an old piece of wood with his bayonet and clasp knife, watched by the two little girls who sat beside him, crosslegged.

Larsen wandered over. 'You're a natural, Sergeant.'

'It's something to do. Anyway, you should have seen Corporal Sykes earlier. Had the girls captivated with his coin tricks.'

Larsen spoke to the children, then smiled. 'They want to know which of them will have the plane. Perhaps you should make two.'

Tanner smiled. 'I've nothing better to do.'

'I have two girls.' Larsen sighed. 'I do not mind telling you, Sergeant, that I miss them terribly. This war is a dreadful thing.'

'But you're a soldier, sir. One of the few Norwegian professionals.'

'Yes, but if I am honest, I never expected to fight. I thought I would remain a member of His Majesty's Guard in Oslo, not that Norway would find itself at war. We are neutrals, Sergeant.'

'Yes,' said Tanner, 'we British are a bit more used to it.'

Tanner finished the first model and gave it to the elder child. He had just begun a second when their mother entered the barn and spoke with Larsen. The fear in her eyes that had been so evident when they had first descended on the farm had gone, but the anxiety was still there. Tanner couldn't blame her. It was brave to take in Allied soldiers with the Germans so close.

'What news?' Tanner asked Larsen, once she had left them.

'The professor's asleep. Anna has put her medical training to good use.'

On their arrival at the farm, Tanner had stationed guards. One was in the attic, from where there was a clear view of the valley, while the other stood guard outside Sandvold's room. Each man did two hours on, four hours off. Later, when Tanner and McAllister went into the farmhouse to relieve Kershaw and Erwood, he had a chance to talk to Anna.

She looked tired, Tanner thought, as they sat on the floorboards of the second-floor landing. 'You must get some rest too, you know,' he told her.

'I will.' She leaned her head on his shoulder. 'I could fall asleep now.'

For a moment there was silence between them.

'Professor Sandvold's going to be all right,' said Anna at length. 'It's exhaustion more than anything. He's twenty-five years older than most of us and he's been on the run for days without proper sleep or food. Oh, and he has migraines. If you get a bad one, you can do nothing except lie in a dark room until it passes. It should have gone by the morning.'

'Will he be able to walk?'

'He'll be a bit weak, but possibly.'

'We could always make a stretcher.' Tanner sighed. 'But the moment he can move again, we must leave.'

'Let's pray he sleeps well tonight, then.'

'You too, Anna.' Her face was lovely, he thought. The eyes, the gentle arc of her eyebrows, the curve of her lips. She moved her head, her eyes turned to his. Leaning down, he kissed her. Suddenly it seemed the most obvious and natural thing in the world.

A LONG NIGHT and an even longer morning. The rain had passed and so had the professor's fever, but the migraine was proving more stubborn. Tanner had taken over guard duty outside Sandvold's room at noon. He had felt more at ease on the mountain at Uksum Farm, where at least he could see the valley spread before them and watch the enemy's movement. Here they were hidden.

At one, Anna checked on the professor again. Reappearing a few minutes later, she said, 'The migraine has subsided. We can leave.'

Tanner breathed out heavily. *At last.*

The old farmer helped make a stretcher from wood and a tarpaulin. The professor protested that he was capable of walking, but after nearly collapsing down the stairs that led from the farmhouse, he acquiesced.

'Are you sure he's fit to travel?' Tanner asked Anna.

'He is weak, but if he is on a stretcher he will be fine.'

At least the others were now refreshed, Tanner thought. The sloping shoulders and foot-dragging of the previous morning were replaced by a renewed vigour that was clear from the moment they set off.

They skirted the lake, then turned northwest, back under the protection of the forest and beneath the snowcapped peak of the Bringsfjellet. By evening they were only a few miles from Vågåmo.

They found a boarded-up *seter* among the trees beside a mountain brook, shielded behind a wooded outcrop. It was a good place to base themselves while they prepared the crossing. Hidden from the air by the dense covering of surrounding birch, alder and pine, it was also shielded from the valley. In addition, the outcrop half a mile beyond would provide an ideal observation post from which they could watch the town and the lake.

Tanner had barely spoken to Chevannes since the day before, so he turned now to Larsen. 'We need to have a look round from this knoll.'

As he had hoped, Larsen suggested this to Chevannes, who silently concurred. They climbed through the trees, scrambling over patches of bare rock, until they reached the summit. From there the valley before them and the mountains on the far side stretched in sharply defined clarity. With his naked eye, Tanner spotted the bridge crossing the river, and the road along which he hoped they could escape. He peered through his binoculars. The bridge was seventy to 100 feet wide, he guessed. The town itself was set back from the river and, he now realised, spread round a lesser river coming down from the valley beyond. He'd not noticed that on Anna's map. Dark timber-framed buildings lined the main road and there was a wooden church with what looked like a separate bell tower next to it, with trucks and German military vehicles parked round an open area by the church.

'The enemy is here,' said Chevannes. 'We will never get across.'

'Not in daytime,' said Tanner.

'What should we do?' asked Larsen.

Chevannes said nothing, so Tanner went on, 'Sir, with your permission I'd like to carry out a reconnaissance tonight.'

'What are you thinking? Crossing further east downriver?' asked Larsen.

'No. I was considering crossing the lake. Look.' He pointed westwards. 'See that spur jutting out? There's another on the other side. What's that? Two miles from Vågåmo? The crossing would be quite narrow there. I reckon we can get across tomorrow night when it's dark, then double back and cross into the valley. With any luck we'll pick up some M/T there.'

'It means another long delay,' said Larsen.

'We need that road beyond,' Tanner said. 'It's the only clear route to Åndalsnes. I admit it's a risk, but what alternative is there?'

Chevannes nodded. 'Very well. Do your reconnaissance tonight, Sergeant, and then we will decide.'

Tanner smiled to himself. A plan had already formulated in his head. A plan to solve all of their problems.

'SARGE,' SAID SYKES, after Chevannes had told them they would be remaining at the *seter* for the time being. 'What's going on?'

'You and I are going out on a recce tonight.' He walked away from the hut and crouched on a rock beside the stream.

'But what about keeping an eye on the Norwegians?'

'Don't worry about that.' He winked.

Sykes looked at him suspiciously. 'What you up to, Sarge?'

'All in good time, Stan.' He took off his backpack. 'What explosives have we got left? I've got two packets of Nobel's and four sticks of Polar.'

Sykes delved into his own pack. 'Two packets of Nobel's and two sticks of Polar. You got some fuse left, Sarge?'

'Yes—I've got the tin here.'

'We can still do some damage with this lot,' said Sykes.

Sandvold was walking towards them.

'How are you feeling?' Tanner said.

'Not so good, but better than I was.' He cleared his throat. 'I must apologise, holding you up like that. I feel we have done more to stop ourselves reaching the Allies than the Germans have.'

'My old mum used to get migraines,' said Sykes.

'Yes—well, hopefully the Allies are not yet out of reach.' He shuffled his feet, then said, 'I wonder, Corporal, would you mind if I had a word with Sergeant Tanner alone?'

When the corporal had gone inside the *seter*, Sandvold and Tanner walked along the stream until they were almost out of sight. 'Sergeant, you and your men have sacrificed much to help me get away. You have kept your promise to Colonel Gulbrand without complaint and without once thinking to save yourselves first. Yet you have no idea what this is all about.'

'One day I'll get to the bottom of it.'

'Actually, Sergeant, I would like to tell you now. It is only fair that you know why you have put your lives at risk on my behalf.' Sandvold glanced around. 'Do you know what modern armed forces need most to fight a war?'

Tanner shrugged. 'Men. Weapons. Machinery. Lots of aircraft.'

'But what is it that enables those machines to work?'

'Petrol—oil?'

The professor smiled. 'Yes! Black gold, it is sometimes called. Now, Germany lacks its own oil. Without it Hitler will be unable to continue the war. It is true that I am a scientist, Sergeant Tanner, but my field is geology. So far, man has tapped only a fraction of the world's oil resources. Most of it lies underground and, more specifically, under the sea. The problem is how to find it and then how to get to it. My career has been dedicated to solving these problems.'

'And you've been successful?'

'More so than I could possibly have hoped. I believe there are large oil fields waiting to be mined on the Norwegian continental shelf.' Sandvold smiled. 'The point is, Sergeant, that on the continental shelf, the sea is shallow—at least, shallow compared to the ocean. And in the North Sea off the coast of Norway it is only around a hundred metres deep, sometimes less. The question is, how to get the oil out. The answer is by making a drilling platform. You make a platform and its accompanying legs on land, tow them out to sea and embed them in the sea floor. Then you begin drilling.'

'And you think this is possible? What happens to the oil once it is drilled?'

'Siphoned into waiting tankers. And, yes, I do certainly believe it is possible. Last year I applied for a royal grant, which was awarded.'

'Which is why the King has taken such a personal interest.'

'He realised the implications. But he also appreciated that war was coming to Europe and that these discoveries could be a cause of potential trouble for Norway should Germany—and, I might add, Britain—find out about them.'

'How did they?'

'I do not know. I work mostly alone. Only I have the blue papers. But the King knows, and presumably so do some of his advisers. When the war is over, Norway will become very rich. But now the Germans want me so that I can help them produce the oil they will so badly need if this war goes on for any great length of time.'

'Why don't you just burn the blue papers?'

Sandvold laughed. 'Do you have any idea how much work has gone into them? Believe me, Sergeant Tanner, reaching a stage where oil might actually be extracted from below the seabed has taken years of work. If it comes to it, I will burn them, but I have been hoping that with your help it will not.'

So, Tanner thought. It's all about oil. 'Tell me one last thing, Professor.

Wouldn't such a platform be vulnerable to attack from the air and the sea?'

'You surround it with minefields, and it would be within easy reach of land. In any case, you're forgetting, Sergeant, that the Nazis fully expect to control all of Europe. And who is to stop them? Not the British.'

'We're being defeated here, but that doesn't mean we'll lose the war.'

'Maybe you won't *lose*. But can you defeat the Nazis? And I think Hitler is looking beyond Europe. To America and Russia.'

'But they're allied with the Russians and America isn't even in the war.'

'It is only a matter of time. And then Germany will need vast amounts of oil—which the Soviet Union and the United States have in abundance.'

Tanner shook his head. 'What happens next month, next year, is beyond me, Professor. All I want to think about now is getting us out of here. Getting you to safety.'

'But you see now why that is so important?'

'Yes. Thank you, Professor. I thought it must be some secret weapon.'

Sandvold chuckled. 'In a way it is. Without oil, the Nazis won't win.'

IN THE DANK CONFINES of the *seter*, Tanner and Sykes prepared for their reconnaissance mission. It was nearly half past ten. From their packs they took out the German uniforms they had captured and put them on.

Tanner turned to Chevannes. 'We'll have a look at the town, then we'll head west down the lake and try to find a good crossing-place.'

'Yes,' said Chevannes. 'Now go.'

In the darkening light, they headed towards the valley, Tanner explaining his plan. They reached the lower slopes directly above the bridge into Vågåmo, with just enough light for them to study it sufficiently. Two stone pillars jutted out from the banks at either side, and across it there was a simple iron construction.

'What do you think, Stan?' said Tanner.

'It can be as strong as it likes, but if it's got a wooden roadbed, we're going to be able to put it out of action. Simple as that.'

There were just two guards on the bridge, both on the southern side. 'That'll make life easier,' said Tanner.

'What I want to know, Sarge, is why Jerry's here anyway.'

'Because of that road, I should think,' said Tanner. 'It gives them another line of advance north towards Åndalsnes. But they're not using it yet.'

They moved away through the trees until they were a safe distance from the bridge, then dropped down onto the valley road. Stars twinkled above, reflected in the inky darkness of the lake. A crescent moon stood high over the valley, enabling the two men to see the shape of the road, the lake, the mountains. A few miles to the west the road forked.

'Where's that lead?' whispered Sykes.

'Back to Heidal and Sjoa,' said Tanner. 'It's a long way round, though.'

They walked on until they reached the headland that projected into the lake. There was a wooden jetty and, as Tanner had hoped, a few small boats.

It was a little after midnight. The dawn of a new day, the last of the month. Twelve days they'd been in Norway. It felt like eternity.

WITH THE FIRST STREAKS of dawn, the *seter* stirred into life. As the soldiers woke, they stumbled outside, some to urinate nearby, others to wander further. One of their number, an agent of the Sicherheitsdienst, wandered away from the hut, safe in the knowledge that it was possible to break away from the others for a few minutes without arousing any suspicion. At least, it was now that Tanner and Sykes were away. They suspected someone, that was certain. *But not me*, the agent had decided. There was now a clear chance for him to send another signal.

He headed into the woodland until the *seter* was out of sight. Finding a wide tree, the agent took two small metal boxes from a haversack. One was a transmitter, the other the accumulator. From a pocket, three leads were produced, each with crocodile clips. The agent attached the two boxes together, then turned a black knob at the front of the transmitter causing a faint light within to glow. A long length of wire was connected to the back of the box with trembling fingers. This done, the person took the weighted end and threw it high into the tree above. With a hammering heart, the agent glanced round, then took a quick look at the transmitter. The light was glowing brighter now, as the valves warmed up. Half a minute more.

The agent prayed this message would get through. Instructions had been to send as many as was possible without jeopardising the mission. The transmitter was a device for sending Morse signals and not a receiver, so there was no way of telling whether the messages had been read. Until the Stukas had arrived three days before, the agent had begun to think that the transmitter could not be working: a specific message from the Rostads' farm had been sent and several from the Jøra Valley, yet despite troops arriving at Uksum Farm, they had made no attempt to act on his information.

'No one will suspect you,' Kurz had said. 'We will whisk Odin away before anyone has the chance.' Perhaps that would have been so, had it not been for

Tanner and his men. The agent cursed him. Thanks to Tanner, several golden opportunities for Odin to be captured had been foiled. Now perhaps all would be well, for the sergeant appeared to have let down his guard.

The agent leaned back against the tree, eyes closed, then checked the time once more. Just a few more seconds. Taking a deep breath, the figure held a finger above the Morse button and began to transmit. Less than a minute later, the message was completed. Having rolled up the wire and put the boxes back into his pack, he walked steadily towards the *seter*.

SCHEIDT WAS SHAKEN awake, and rolled over to find Kurz leaning over him.

'What the devil is it?' he croaked.

'A message—good news!'

Scheidt snatched the paper from Kurz: IN MOUNTAINS ABOVE VÅGÅMO. CROSSING PLANNED OVER LAKE WEST OF TOWN WHEN DARK APRIL 30.

Scheidt's face broke into a grin. 'Excellent,' he said. He looked at his watch. It was only half past four, but he knew there could be no more thought of sleep. 'We've got him this time.'

Having shaved and dressed, he hurried downstairs to the conference room of Engelbrecht's spacious headquarters in Vinstra. Three men were standing by the map pinned to the wall—Major von Poncets, Sturmbannführer Kurz and Hauptmann Zellner.

'Ah, good morning, Herr Reichsamtsleiter,' said von Poncets.

Scheidt nodded, then looked at Zellner. A bandage had been strapped across his nose, his cheek had blackened, his eye had turned yellow. 'Hauptmann Zellner, what are you doing here? Shouldn't you be in hospital?'

'I'm well enough, thank you, Herr Reichsamtsleiter,' he replied.

Scheidt stared at him with contempt. 'You have come off worst against those men no less than three times, which should have put paid to your chances of taking any further part in the operation.'

'We suspect the men will be wearing German uniforms,' said von Poncets. 'The Hauptmann will be of help in identifying them.'

'I suppose there's something in that. What forces has the general given us?'

'There's a company of the 324th Infantry Regiment and two companies from my own battalion of Gebirgsjäger.' He pointed to the map. 'The 324th boys are already based at Vågåmo. They moved in after the fall of Otta.'

'As you know,' put in Kurz, 'the general agreed to leave them there in case there was any sign of Odin.'

Scheidt nodded. 'Will that be enough?'

'More than enough.' Von Poncets smiled.

'I recall that we had the same conversation some days ago, Herr Major, and it seems both you and the Hauptmann underestimated the enemy.'

Von Poncets said, 'Numbers are not the issue. Execution is what counts.'

'Which, so far, has left much to be desired.'

'This time we have firm intelligence. It is no longer a guessing game.'

Scheidt felt annoyed that the operation appeared to have been left to von Poncets and Zellner, men who had lost his respect. He wished General Engelbrecht would join them. Turning to the major, he said, 'So, what are your thoughts?'

'We have to assume,' von Poncets said, pointing to the mountains south of Vågåmo, 'that they will be able to observe the town at the very least.'

'So the difficulty is laying the trap without the enemy spotting it first.'

'Exactly,' said von Poncets, 'which is why a large number of troops is not necessarily the key. I suggest we use this route—here.' He pointed to a road that ran west of Sjoa, linked with another that ran roughly north–south until it joined the valley road several kilometres west of Vågåmo. 'They can approach by truck and debouch out of sight of the town or of anyone in the mountains, for that matter. Assuming there's good cover, I see no reason why this movement should be seen at all.'

'And what about the troops in Vågåmo?'

'It's important the enemy believe it's still strongly held, so I propose we leave most of the company there.'

'Isn't that rather a waste of these men?'

'Don't worry, Herr Reichsamtsleiter, we shall show the plans to the general. And in any case, we may receive another signal.'

THEY DID, just after ten o'clock that morning. STILL ABOVE VÅGÅMO. CROSSING TONIGHT AT MIDNIGHT 6 KMS WEST OF TOWN AFTER FORK IN ROAD. Scheidt's spirits rose, and he was invigorated by the activity at Engelbrecht's headquarters. This time, thought Scheidt. It had to be.

When the general arrived, von Poncets explained his plan to the assembled officers. They would be leaving directly after the briefing and would then make their way to lying-up positions. Scouts would be sent forward to reconnoitre their ambush positions, and to mark where they would place spotlights. The men would move into these positions at 2300 hours.

Hauptmann Dostler of the 324th Infantry stood up. One platoon was to drive along the opposite bank of the lake. The road could easily be seen from the mountains opposite. Thus, they were to drive beyond the crossing-point, after which the road was hidden by forest. They would then head back through the trees, close to the crossing-point, where they would set up another spotlight. The remaining three platoons would stay in Vågåmo to give the impression that the town was still heavily occupied.

Scheidt raised his hand. 'Surely, Herr Hauptmann, the town *will* be heavily occupied if there are three whole platoons there?'

'Not particularly,' said Dostler. 'All our units are now under strength. There will be about sixty men.'

The general cut in. 'Which is more than enough. There will be vehicles and equipment in the town as well. Let's get on with the briefing.'

Chastened, Scheidt said no more, and after Kurz and Zellner had briefed the room about Odin and the accompanying fugitives, Engelbrecht addressed them. 'I can't stress enough, gentlemen, how important it is to capture Odin alive. The fear is that they will shoot him before you can get to him, which is why it is essential that none of you makes a move until they are almost in the boats. They will have travelled through the darkness and that is where the lights come in. Caught in the beams, these fugitives will be momentarily blinded. That is the time to strike. The men must be killed and Odin left standing.' He clapped his hands together. 'Right, gentlemen, off you go. And good luck.'

Scheidt followed the men on their way out, watching them get into the trucks. A bark of orders and engines rumbled into life.

Kurz paused beside him and offered a hand, which Scheidt took.

'Exciting, isn't it?' He grinned. 'If only we'd had this kind of intelligence and preparation five days ago.'

Scheidt smiled thinly.

'See you later,' added Kurz. 'With Odin, of course.' He trotted down the steps and along the road to von Poncets' waiting Kübelwagen.

Scheidt took out a cigarette. Exciting? He supposed so, although he did not share Kurz's obvious relish; he would save that until Odin was sitting before him. He struck a match, brought the cigarette to his lips and realised his hands were shaking. 'It's out of my control now,' he muttered.

TANNER WAS NO LESS apprehensive as he watched the hours tick by. He had left Sykes alone on a ridge overlooking the road from the south with instructions to return only if he spotted any German troops, and had returned to the *seter* around seven that morning.

Chevannes had accepted his story without question. When he explained that he had left Sykes on guard above the bridge, the lieutenant had merely nodded. 'Did you see whether there were enough oars this time?'

'Yes, sir—there are.'

'Good.' Chevannes had ordered him to organise lookouts on the knoll and dismissed him.

Tanner had spent most of the morning there, and was keeping watch with Larsen, when a staff car arrived from the direction of Otta. There was no further movement of vehicles until after four when two trucks headed west along the far shore of the lake. A couple of miles later, they disappeared. Tanner was puzzled, yet relieved to see troop movement from the town. He counted the remaining vehicles: five troop-carrying trucks, two further lorries and two staff cars.

Shortly after, Hepworth arrived to relieve Larsen, with Anna in tow. It was now nearly half past four and Tanner wished Sykes would reappear.

'Here,' said Larsen, handing Hepworth his binoculars. He got up and picked up his rucksack. 'Let's hope the town stays quiet, Sergeant.'

'Here's hoping, sir,' Tanner replied, then turned to Hepworth, 'Get the far side of the knoll, Hep. Try to work out where those troops are.'

With Hepworth gone, he and Anna were alone. 'Everything all right at the *seter*?' he asked.

'The resting has done the professor good,' she told him. 'He's been eating and he's even shaved his beard in the stream. He's not going to need the stretcher.'

Tanner continued to peer through his binoculars. Anna sat behind him on a loose rock. A few small patches of snow remained, but grass now sprouted between the pines and birches.

'And Chevannes?' said Tanner at length.

'He's been quiet. It's since the professor spoke up on your behalf. That undermined his authority.'

'Hm,' said Tanner. 'I'll still need to watch him tonight.'

'Jack, will the crossing be all right? We were lucky last time.'

'We'll be fine, I promise.' It was a promise he was in no position to make. Where the hell was Sykes? He looked back at the town. Nothing stirred. How many troops were down there? Fifty? Eighty? So long as the enemy weren't expecting them there, all would be well. But there was no Plan B. He trained his binoculars on the trucks next to the church. Whatever happened, they had to take one.

By six o'clock, Tanner was finding it increasingly difficult to maintain his outward composure, although he knew that to betray his mounting anxiety would be a grave mistake. Having returned to the *seter*, he now busied himself cleaning his rifle and the Spandau.

At around twenty past six, his corporal finally appeared.

'Well?' said Tanner, hurrying to him.

'They're there. A company, maybe two, of mountain troops.'

'Ha!' said Tanner, laughing. 'We were right, Stan!'

'*You* were right, Sarge. Zellner's with them. And they've got searchlights—small ones, but lights all the same.'

Tanner grinned. 'Perfect. And *you* were right all along—there is a spy.'

'I've got the nose for it, Sarge. You watch my back and I'll watch yours. 'Cos together, I reckon, we make a good team, you and me.'

Tanner slapped the corporal on the arm. 'Stan, you're on.'

The final hours were interminable. At half past nine, accompanied by Chevannes and Larsen, Tanner left the knoll for the last time. The town was as quiet as ever, the trucks still parked next to the church.

'It looks calm,' muttered Chevannes. 'And you've seen nothing, Sergeant, to make you think they're up to anything?'

'Apart from the trucks and staff car earlier, there's been no movement.'

'I saw nothing, either,' said Larsen, 'and the crossing is nearly six kilometres away. No one from the town will hear or see us rowing across from that distance.'

Chevannes nodded. '*Bon.*'

They walked in silence back to the *seter*, where the rest of the men were waiting outside, wearing German tunics. Tanner rolled his jerkin and battle blouse into the bottom of his pack. He had already transferred most of his explosives into his haversack and gas-mask case. Having wedged his tin helmet into his pack, he placed the last two packs of Nobel's on top.

Chevannes looked at his watch. 'Three minutes past ten. Let's go.'

Tanner glanced at Sykes. 'Actually, sir, I'd like to say something.'

A flash of irritation crossed Chevannes' face. 'What, Sergeant?'

'I don't think we should cross the lake after all.'

Chevannes and the Norwegians looked aghast. 'What?'

'I think we should go through the town.'

'Have you gone mad, Tanner?' said Chevannes.

'No, sir.' Say this right, he told himself. 'It's just that there are only fifty or so men in the town. They're not expecting us. I reckon we can take out the guards quietly enough, then march up to those trucks. You speak good German, sir, and so do the lieutenants here. At night, when all is quiet, they wouldn't suspect a thing.' He could see some of his men nodding now.

'Except that every German soldier for miles seems to know about us.'

'I'm sorry, sir. I hadn't considered it before, but as we were walking back . . .' Chevannes was rubbing his chin. Good. Indecision again. 'The thing is, sir,' Tanner continued, 'it's the far side of the lake that's bothering me. We're going to have to climb over the mountain. Those trucks are just sitting there. This time tomorrow we could be in Åndalsnes.'

'I think there's something in what Tanner says, sir,' said Nielssen. 'I'm certain they're not expecting us. I think it's a risk worth taking.'

'I'm not so sure,' Larsen said. 'We know the coast is clear at the crossing. Going through the town seems to me too big a risk.'

'We need M/T straight away,' said Tanner. 'The crossing will hold us up. I'm convinced that we should head down the hill and go through the town.'

'I think we should do it, Henrik,' Nielssen said to Larsen.

'Me too,' said Tanner. 'Come on, sir. Those trucks are just sitting there. It'll be dark, we're wearing German uniforms—it'll work, I know it will.'

'Let me think—' said the Frenchman.

'No,' said Larsen. 'We should stick to the original plan.'

Now, Tanner thought. 'Why, sir?' he said, stepping towards Larsen. 'Do you know something we don't?'

'What do you mean?' Larsen's eyes darted briefly, almost imperceptibly, to either side of him. But Tanner saw.

'Exactly that, sir. Are you hiding something from us?'

'What the hell are you talking about, Sergeant?' Chevannes frowned.

'I'm just wondering if he can explain why the best part of two hundred German mountain troops are lying in wait for us in the trees beside the crossing-point.'

'*What?*' Chevannes was incredulous. Larsen simply stood where he was, the colour draining from his face.

'No, Henrik!' said Nielssen. 'Say it is not true!'

'I—I do not know what you are talking about.'

The professor stumbled forward. 'Henrik?'

'You—you are wrong,' stammered Larsen, 'I know nothing about it. You are lying, Sergeant. How dare you?'

'The only one lying is you,' said Tanner. 'Someone has betrayed us.

Those Stukas didn't come from nowhere. Neither did those trucks on the pass. But this confirms it.'

'It was a set-up,' mumbled Larsen.

'Yes,' said Tanner. 'We'd suspected for a while but when those Jerries turned up this afternoon we knew for certain. All we didn't know was who.'

'Men!' called out Chevannes. 'Hold him!' But Larsen already had his pistol in his hand. He grabbed Sandvold, the gun thrust towards the professor's stomach.

'Get back, all of you!' said Larsen, dragging Sandvold towards the *seter*. The professor gasped. 'Stop this madness, Henrik!'

'Quiet! Now get back—or I will shoot!'

Tanner took a step towards him. 'Sir, put the gun down.'

'Get back, Sergeant!'

Tanner took another step towards him. 'Sir, put down the pistol.'

'Tanner, don't be a fool!' There was panic in Chevannes' voice.

'Don't worry, he won't shoot. The Germans want Professor Sandvold alive. If all the lieutenant can offer them is a body they'll not thank him.' He took another step forward. 'It's over, sir. Put down the pistol.'

Larsen suddenly pushed Sandvold forward so that he fell. 'You were right, Sergeant,' he said, 'I wouldn't shoot the professor, but I *will* kill you.'

Tanner was now only a few feet away. His mind was clear. Timing was everything, and although he was fairly sure no shot would be heard in the town, it was a risk he would rather avoid.

Then Nielssen stepped forward. 'Why, Henrik?' he said, and for a fraction of a second Larsen turned his head towards him.

Tanner grabbed Larsen's wrist and pushed the lieutenant's arm backwards hard. The pistol fell from his hand and Tanner drove his left fist into the Norwegian's head. Larsen's eyes rolled back and he toppled over.

For a moment no one spoke. Then Tanner picked up the pistol, and said, 'Treacherous bastard. And to think I liked him.'

'Have you killed him, Sergeant?' asked the professor.

'No,' he said. 'He'll come round in a minute.' The others gathered beside the prostrate figure. Tanner felt Anna take his hand. Tears ran down her face.

'I cannot believe it,' she said. 'I just cannot believe it.'

Larsen groaned and Nielssen squatted beside him. 'Why, Henrik?'

Larsen mumbled in Norwegian to Nielssen. Tanner hoisted the Spandau onto his shoulder. It was twenty past ten, and he was anxious to leave so they could reach a position above the bridge before dark. And there was another reason: the next changeover of the guards was due at eleven thirty. Tanner reckoned eleven o'clock was the right time to deal with them—when their alertness was diminishing but well before the fresh shift arrived.

He was about to ask Chevannes what they should do with the traitor when he heard a strangled cry. He pushed through his men and saw Larsen dead on the ground. Nielssen was cleaning his short bayonet grimly on Larsen's tunic, then put it back in its sheath. 'I had no choice,' he said.

Tanner nodded. 'How did he do it?'

Nielssen rolled the dead man over and took off his pack. He pulled out two metal boxes with a length of wire.

'What the hell are they?' asked Tanner.

Nielssen looked at them. 'From these dials, I'd suggest this one must be a transmitter of some kind. It's tiny.'

Tanner turned to Chevannes. 'Sir, we need to go.'

'Yes, of course,' he said. 'Right, men, we will go through the town. We must forget about this traitor. We need to concentrate on the task ahead: successfully getting into Vågåmo and taking one of those trucks.'

As they finally set off, Tanner did not glance back. Larsen's body was left where it lay: unburied on an empty mountainside.

8

From the upstairs window of the newly requisitioned farmhouse beside the lake, Zellner had a grandstand view of the headland that jutted out into the water, and of the boats roped to the wooden jetty. Beside him were Kurz and von Poncets. A field telephone had been rigged up, linking them to the men crouching in the trees and along the shore. His nose and cheek still throbbed, but the pain of being cheated by the British sergeant a third time hurt him most of all. Yet the prospect of Tanner's imminent death had improved his mood. The last light of the day was fading in the west. He looked at his watch. An hour—that's all, he thought.

Kurz was telling them about their source. 'We pinned him down the day after the invasion,' he said. 'He didn't need much persuading, I must say. He's got a wife and two small girls in Oslo. I'm not sure how much it had to do with it but we did mention that we might not be able to guarantee their safety should he decline our offer.' He chuckled. 'Actually, I must give Scheidt some credit. He's a bit of an old woman, but he's sharp. He's been grooming that buffoon Quisling on the say-so of the Führer. It was Quisling's men who put him onto Larsen. Apparently he was a secret National Party man.'

'So he was primed,' said von Poncets.

'Primed—exactly. And then with a bit of persuasion we had our spy. A massive stroke of luck, of course, that he was chosen to go back and fetch Odin. Initially we had planned to use him to get to the King and the gold.'

'Why didn't he lead you to Odin in Oslo?' asked Zellner.

'He didn't know. It wasn't until later. We ransacked Odin's offices. We didn't find any blue papers but we found enough to know what he was trying to do. Trust me, if this fellow can truly get oil from under the seabed, we'll have the eternal gratitude of the Führer.'

The thought cheered Zellner even more. Well, it wouldn't be long now. This time nothing had been left to chance. He was certain they could not fail.

IT WAS MINDLESS WORK, patrolling a bridge. One man walked one way, one the other, up and down, back and forth. Pieter Greiger was tired. The fighting at Dombås had been gruelling for his company and they had lost several men. Half his platoon had been killed or wounded. One of the dead had been a friend since boyhood. He'd tried hard to put his loss out of his mind, but sentry duty gave him too much time to think.

He reached the north end of the bridge, then began to walk back, the rhythmic clump of his boots loud on the thick wooden planking. He had passed Reitmann when a sound pulled him from his reverie. A short distance ahead, he saw a column of men marching towards the bridge. Seeing the outline of their field caps, he relaxed. He called to Reitmann and they strode towards the southern end of the bridge.

'Halt!' said Greiger, as the men approached. The officer brought his men to a standstill and waited as Greiger and Reitmann walked towards them.

'Good evening,' said the officer. 'We've come from the crossing-point. We've been ordered to help man the bridge.'

Greiger stared at him but it was hard to see much in the darkness. Then he noticed the white *Edelweiss* on the side of the cap.

'Gebirgsjäger?' he asked. The officer nodded. 'May I see your orders, sir?'

The officer said, 'Of course,' then made for a leather satchel at his waist. Instead of producing papers, though, he pulled out a short bayonet and thrust it hard under the sentry's ribs. Pieter Greiger's short life was over.

As NIELSSEN was ending the life of the second man he had dispatched within an hour, Tanner had used his fist to knock the second sentry out cold.

'Quick,' whispered Tanner to his men, as he grabbed the first man's Mauser. 'Get their weapons, ammo and helmets and drag them off the bridge. Mac and Hep, put these helmets on and take over sentry duty.'

Chevannes was standing beside him. 'Good work, Nielssen,' he said to the Norwegian. 'Now for the truck.'

'Sir?' said Tanner. 'Sykes and I are going to blow the bridge—prevent any of those mountain boys coming after us.'

'You don't think it might alert the enemy?' Chevannes' voice was heavy with sarcasm.

'We'll set a delay with the safety fuse.'

He dithered, then said, 'Well, be quick about it.'

Tanner hurried over to Sykes, took out a packet of Nobel's and passed it to him.

'Sarge, open it, take out two cartridges and tie them together with a small length of the fuse.'

'You think that'll be enough?' He could just see that Sykes was doing the same with another packet.

'Yes.'

Taking out two cartridges, Tanner put the remainder of the packet back into his gas-mask case, then took out the tin of fuses. With his clasp knife, he cut a strip and tied the two cartridges together.

'Good,' said Sykes, fumbling with the detonators. 'How long do we want to wait?'

'Six hundred yards to the church,' Tanner muttered to himself, 'but we need to get in the truck and start it. On the other hand, the distraction of the blast might be useful. Ten minutes? No—let's say eight.'

'All right—cut me a sixteen-foot length.'

Using his forearm as a measure, Tanner did so, then passed one end to Sykes who managed to crimp the fuse to the detonators with his teeth.

'And another length the same, Sarge,' whispered Sykes.

Suddenly Chevannes was beside them. 'Have you finished?'

'Almost, sir,' said Sykes. Chevannes disappeared back down the bridge as Tanner measured another length of fuse.

'I've run out, Stan. I'm three foot short.'

'Bollocks,' said Sykes, then scratched his head. 'All right, here's what we do: we tie the explosives each side of the bridge, rather than at either end, and run a length of fuse from one on to the main fuse. Here, give it me.' A few moments later he dusted off his hands and said, 'All set, Sarge.'

In a whisper, Tanner called to McAllister and Hepworth, then Sykes lit the fuse.

'About time,' whispered Chevannes, as they rejoined the others. 'Same marching order, all right?'

'Sir,' said Tanner. He held the face of his watch to the sky. Fourteen minutes past eleven. Christ! he thought. This'll be close.

A couple of minutes later they had still not reached the first houses of the town. He realised they needed to increase their pace if they were going to reach the truck before the gelignite detonated.

'Sir,' he whispered to Nielssen, 'we need to speed up.'

As they reached the edge of the town, two figures emerged in front of them. Tanner tensed, but the men merely saluted and walked on. Replacement sentries, thought Tanner.

23.20 hours. Six minutes gone. Either side of the road, sleeping houses, the night as still as ever. The church getting closer. Tanner struggled with the overwhelming desire to run. Two minutes until the shooting started. Would they make it? Or was he now facing the final moments of his life?

He held up his watch to the night sky again: *23.21. Seven minutes.* And there they were, two trucks parked together, a third the far side of the church. Nielssen halted them.

'Sir, we might as well take both these trucks,' whispered Tanner to Chevannes, who was behind him. 'More fuel and in case anything happens.'

'*D'accord*,' said Chevannes.

Suddenly figures appeared before them, calling out. Sentries, thought Tanner. Nielssen spoke to them. How many? Tanner couldn't see but he had his rifle off his shoulder and felt in his haversack for a grenade.

A German soldier stepped forward, his tone aggressive. The moon drifted clear of a cloud. It did not have much light to offer but it was enough for Tanner to see half a dozen men round the trucks. *23.22. Eight minutes.* Where the hell was the explosion? Had the fuse gone out? Had he miscounted? *Come on, come on.*

The German NCO walked towards Tanner. He was looking at Tanner's rifle and the Mauser slung on his other shoulder. Damn it, thought Tanner. Now just a few feet away, the German addressed him directly, pointing angrily. What was he saying? Where did you get that Tommy rifle? Tanner had no idea.

Sod it, he thought. 'I'm sorry, mate, I don't understand a word you're saying,' he said, as he squeezed the trigger. The German crumpled to the ground, and at that moment, the bridge blew. Tanner started, but so did the enemy soldiers, who ducked involuntarily and looked south as an orange ball of flame mushroomed into the night sky. Seeing his chance, Tanner sprinted towards them. *Pull the bolt back and forward, fire.* Another man fell. A third fumbled at his rifle as Tanner swung the butt of his own into the man's head. The soldier cried out as Tanner kicked a fourth to the ground, all before one had fired a shot.

Shouts now from the surrounding houses. Tanner yelled, 'Into the trucks, quick!' Pistol shots—Nielssen and Chevannes. Screams from another man. Tanner grabbed Lance Corporal Erwood's shoulder. 'Get into the second truck and fire that bloody Spandau from the tailgate!' He searched frantically for Anna and the professor. 'Get in! Get in!' he yelled, when he saw them running, crouching, towards the first truck.

'Sir,' he shouted to Nielssen, 'drive the second truck!' Tanner grabbed Anna's arm, shoved her towards the cab of the first and hastily jumped in beside her. It was dark and the Opel was unfamiliar. 'How do you start this bloody thing?' he muttered. Chevannes now clambered in next to Anna.

'Come on, Sergeant!' shouted Chevannes. '*Merde!* Get us out of here!'

Troops were now running out of the houses, shots cracking apart the night. From the back of the truck, their own men were firing.

'I can't get it started!' he yelled across to Nielssen. 'There's no key!'

'Use wire, or a screwdriver—it's above the ignition button.'

Bullets smacked into the truck as Tanner fumbled in his haversack for his tool wallet. He found what he was searching for—a set of five different-sized reamers. The first he tried was too large for the hole. 'Hell,' he muttered, then felt the second slide into the ignition. Immediately a small red light came on, revealing a sign that said ANLASSAR and what had to be the ignition button. Pulling what he hoped was the choke, he pressed the button and the engine coughed into life. Yanking the reamer upwards to keep it in place, he shouted to Nielssen, 'Tell Erwood to spray the other vehicles, sir!'

A bullet cracked through the windscreen. Anna screamed, and Tanner thrust the truck into gear, released the handbrake and the Opel lurched forward. 'Professor?' he shouted. 'Professor, are you there?'

'Yes! Just go!'

Chevannes fired his pistol through the window. More bullets rang out. Tanner found the headlights, switched them on—just slivers of light, but enough. Out of the church square. Ahead, troops kneeling in the road. Another bullet cracked through the windscreen and Anna screamed again. Tanner charged at the men. Figures scattered but he felt a thump as he hit one, heard a scream. Behind him now the men were still firing. He was conscious of the Spandau's short, clattering bursts. Ahead the second bridge. *No time to blow that.* He dropped a gear, turned, rumbled across the short expanse, then drove left towards the valley road that led north. 'Keep going, Tanner, faster!' screamed Chevannes, then grabbed Tanner's Mauser and fired off five rounds in quick succession.

Changing up a gear, Tanner pushed down again on the accelerator as they reached the edge of town. He was vaguely aware of Chevannes reloading the Mauser and preparing to fire, then suddenly realised what the lieutenant had done. 'No, sir, don't fire!' he shouted.

With a loud crack, the rifle jerked upwards, Chevannes screamed and his head and shoulders were flung backwards.

'Sir!' shouted Tanner. 'How bad is it? Anna, see if you can find out. I can't stop now.' The town was now behind them, the shooting receding.

Chevannes groaned.

'Rest your head on my lap,' Anna told him. 'Try to bring your legs up.' Slowly, the Frenchman did so until he was lying across half the seat and her. 'There's a lot of blood,' she said. 'He needs dressings as soon as possible.'

Tanner began taking off his German tunic. 'Here,' he said, 'have this. I'll stop as soon as I can.' Then he called, 'How are you in the back?'

'Tinker's hit, Sarge,' McAllister yelled, 'but I don't think it's serious.'

'Yes, it bloody is!' called Bell. 'My arm's agony!'

Almost too late, Tanner saw the road ahead fork. 'Which way?' he said, bringing the truck to a halt.

'I can't get to my map,' said Anna.

'Hold on,' said Tanner. He jumped out of the cab and ran to the other truck.

'What's happened?' asked Nielssen.

'We don't know which way—left or right? Do you have your map, sir?'

'A moment, Sergeant.'

'Any casualties?'

'Your lance corporal. Erwood. Shot in the head. Dead.'

'Damn,' said Tanner. 'He was a good man.'

'What about you, Sergeant?'

'The lieutenant's hit in the face. He needs dressings and attention soon. And Bell—not serious.'

Nielssen looked at the map. 'Turn right. We've a bit of a climb, then in thirty kilometres we reach the main road to Åndalsnes.'

'It would be good to be on the main road by first light,' said Tanner. He paused to get some field dressings, then hurried back to the cab. Passing the bandages to Anna, he pushed the stick into gear and rolled forward.

ZELLNER HAD SEEN THE EXPLOSION before he heard it: a bright orange glow lighting the sky to the east. A moment later, the report. Then a sickening feeling swept over him. An almost speechless von Poncets had immediately sent a signal to Vinstra. A quarter of an hour later the truth was revealed: around fifteen men, dressed in German uniforms, had infiltrated the town and stolen two troop carriers. And the bridge had been blown to pieces.

Zellner was overcome by the weight of despair. Tanner, he thought.

MAY DAY, 1940—Wednesday—and the dawn rose to their right, the sun gleaming over the mountains amid a cloudless sky.

'Damn it,' said Tanner. 'What we want is a bit of rain and low cloud.' The speed with which winter seemed to have passed had surprised him. 'What happened to spring?' he asked Anna.

She laughed. 'We don't have one. Winter then summer. Now it's summer.'

Tanner glanced down at Chevannes' bloodied head, wrapped in stained bandages and strips of lining from a German tunic. 'Stupid bugger,' he said.

'What happened to him, Jack?' Anna asked him, the Frenchman's head still resting in her lap. 'Was there something wrong with the rifle?'

'He put a clip of French ammunition into a German breech. The French rifles use a fractionally smaller cartridge. It's enough to bugger up the firing mechanism. When he fired, the bolt sprang back and hit him in the face.'

They had emerged into a deep, narrow valley, with mountains towering steeply at either side. Chevannes moaned.

'Jack,' said Anna, 'we need to stop. He needs attention.'

'We'll pull in at a farm. Perhaps we can find out what's happening.'

They reached a settlement called Lia nestling beside the river. Approaching a red farmhouse with white fencing, Tanner slowed. 'This looks smarter than most.'

'You think they will have a wireless?'

'That's what I'm hoping.'

The farmer and his family had been asleep but seemed untroubled to be roused by two trucks of fugitive troops. Since the fighting at Otta had ended, troops had been streaming past, the farmer told Neilssen. The British were evacuating. 'You're the last,' he said. 'You'd better hurry.'

The farmer and his wife brewed coffee and gave them bread while Anna examined Bell and Chevannes.

Bell's wound was clean enough—a bullet had gone through his upper arm. Chevannes' head, however, was a mess. His right cheekbone had been smashed, and a large gash had been torn in the side of his face. As Anna removed the bandages he screamed. 'He needs pain relief,' she said.

'I don't have any,' said Tanner.

Neither did the farmer but he did have whisky. 'Take it,' he told Anna.

They made a bed of sorts for the lieutenant and laid him in the back of the first truck. 'Change back into your own uniforms,' Tanner told his men.

When they continued on their way north, Tanner and Anna were alone in the cab. She yawned and leaned on his shoulder. He could feel the warmth of her body against his. If they managed to reach Åndalsnes, he wondered whether she would come with them to Britain. He hoped so.

'How are you feeling?' he asked.

'I don't know. Tired. I can't stop thinking about last night. And about Larsen. I thought he was going to shoot you.'

'He didn't have it in him. What was he saying to Nielssen at the end?'

'He said they had threatened his family. And then he kept saying, "I should have turned you in at Økset, but I was trying to protect Stig." Then Nielssen said, "Some protection that was." And that's when he killed him.'

'What did he mean by that?'

'I asked Nielssen. Apparently they had been hiding at a farm in a village called Økset, north of Elverum. It belonged to Larsen's cousin. The Germans had turned up, led by Zellner.'

'Zellner? Bloody hell.'

'Nielssen hadn't seen him, but Larsen did and recognised him in the fight above our farm. Anyway, although Larsen had the perfect chance to betray them there and then, he hadn't wanted to get his cousin into trouble and kept quiet while Zellner and his men searched the place. After the Germans had gone, they took his cousin's truck, crossed the river and headed north. But at that point Larsen realised the Germans would have seen them from the other side of the river.'

'And put two and two together,' said Tanner.

'Exactly. And since then he worried not only about the fate of his wife and daughters but also his cousin and his cousin's family.'

'What a bloody mess.' Tanner sighed.

'Enemy aircraft!' A shout from behind.

'Damn!' cursed Tanner. They were hopelessly exposed. He felt Anna grip his arm. 'There's no cover,' he said. 'We'll have to hope for the best.' He pressed his foot on the throttle. 'Can you see them, Mac?' he shouted.

'Yes, Sarge. Four of them coming up behind, Messerschmitts, 110s.'

The four planes were upon them now, two lines of bullets kicking up the ground to their left. More bullets cut a swath across the road from right to left, clattering and pinging into the bonnet. Tanner swerved, then righted the truck, but the Opel was spluttering, steam hissing from the radiator.

The four aircraft hurtled onwards down the valley.

'Will they come back, Jack?' asked Anna.

'Doubt it,' he said. 'They've probably gone on to attack Åndalsnes.'

With the engine coughing, he rolled the truck off the road and brought it to a standstill. He jumped out of the cab and ran to the other.

'We are all right,' Nielssen called out. 'They missed us entirely.'

'That's something,' said Tanner. 'Our truck's had it.'

'Get into this one quickly,' said Nielssen.

Within ten minutes they were on their way again, Tanner and Anna now beside Nielssen in the cab. 'How much further is it?' Tanner asked.

'About sixty kilometres,' said Anna.

'We can't stop,' said Nielssen. 'We've got to risk it.'

A few more miles slipped by, and then a few more. Tanner wished he was driving; it would have given him something to do. The valley no longer seemed beautiful; rather, he saw it as little more than a deathtrap. At any moment more enemy aircraft would be upon them.

They passed a settlement called Brude. 'How far now?' he asked Anna.

'About forty kilometres, I think.'

'Aircraft!' yelled Sykes from the back. 'Lots of them!'

Tanner leaned out of the window. They were only specks on the horizon, but he could see two formations, one higher than the other. A hundred yards ahead the road curved and beside it the forest reached the road's edge.

'Can we make the curve of the road?' A thought, but said aloud. Leaning out of the window, he saw the lower formation swooping down towards them.

'Now!' he said. They were close enough to the bend. 'Sir, get the truck to the side of the road. Out, everyone, quick, and into the trees!' He leapt from the cab, hurried round to the back and, with Sykes, hoisted Chevannes onto his shoulder and sprinted to the trees. He had barely stepped away from the road when the first line of bullets spat a line behind him. Laying Chevannes on the ground, he crouched behind a tree, aircraft roaring overhead. Bullets hurtled through the branches and along the road. A line pinged across the truck. A second later there was a boom and the vehicle was engulfed in flames, the canvas cover and wooden rear crackling loudly.

It was over in moments, the six aircraft thundering onwards. A miracle: no one had been hurt.

Twenty miles, thought Tanner, give or take. They could walk it, but would the enemy catch up before they reached safety?

They made another stretcher, this time for Chevannes, and on they went. For a while no one spoke and all that could be heard was the tramp of boots. They had come so far . . . Tanner cursed.

'Come on, boys,' he said at length. 'Let's lift our heads. We're nearly there. Just a few hours' hard march, that's all.'

'Sarge!' said Sykes, suddenly. 'Look!'

They followed his outstretched finger and there, a few hundred yards ahead, they saw the unmistakable sign of a roadblock. Hastily, Tanner brought his binoculars to his eyes.

British troops.

'They're ours, lads!' he said. 'They're bloody well ours!' And he began to run towards them.

The roadblock was manned by a detachment of Royal Navy Marines, whose commander stepped forward as Tanner stood gasping, his hands on his knees.

Immediately he straightened and saluted. 'Sergeant Tanner, sir, of the King's Own Yorkshire Rangers.'

'Lieutenant Lindsay,' the Marines officer replied. 'Where in God's name have you come from?'

AT LIEUTENANT LINDSAY'S command post—a roughly built sangar made from stones and branches—Tanner gave a brief account of their journey from the Balbergkamp, and stressed the importance of getting the professor away as quickly as possible.

Lindsay, a thin-faced Scotsman, said, 'Although the port is only eighteen miles up the railway track, it would be suicide to attempt the journey now. A mile behind us, though, there's a small village and a four-hundred-and-eighty-yard tunnel. That tunnel's the reason we're here. Most of our forces are already at Åndalsnes, but what's left are in the tunnel.'

'How many, sir?' Tanner asked.

'One company of Green Howards, plus various other loose strands. The aim is to hold off the enemy here, then slip away tonight. The chaps in the tunnel are going by train—it's in there, ready and waiting—and we've got seven trucks hidden here. There are ships coming for us tonight—assuming they haven't been sunk.' He paused. 'It's pretty grim, I'm afraid.'

Tanner turned to Nielssen. 'What do you think, sir?'

'We should wait until this evening. If we are caught out in the open we could be in big trouble.'

Tanner nodded, then walked a few steps away.

'Sarge?' It was Sykes. 'What are you thinking?'

'That a handful of Marines won't stop a concerted effort by the Germans.'

'We've still got a few explosives. Could always put them to good use.'

'You're right. Sir,' he said to Nielssen, 'why don't you go with the professor and Chevannes and take cover in the tunnel?' Then, to Lieutenant Lindsay, he said, 'If we can help here, sir, we'll stay. We have some explosive.'

Lieutenant Lindsay smiled. 'I'm afraid demolitions aren't my line. But we've got a two-inch mortar, one Lewis gun and two Brens. There is an ammunition train as well in the tunnel, so you can get some if you need it.'

Tanner's spirits rose. He thought quickly. 'With your permission, sir, I'd like to take one of the trucks to the tunnel, leave Lieutenant Nielssen and the professor, then load up with a few supplies.'

'I'll get a couple of my men to help you.'

THE TUNNEL HAD BEEN blasted through the steep valley side. It was dark and narrow, the air close. Although most of the troops were already on the train, a number were milling about at the tunnel's entrance. Tanner asked a Green Howards corporal if there was an regimental aid post.

'Aye,' he replied, pointing into the tunnel. 'On the train.'

They woke an orderly who was asleep on the carriage steps. 'All right,' he said, 'bring him in.' Tanner and Nielssen hoisted Chevannes aboard.

'What are you bringing me?' asked a doctor, his overalls bloodied.

'A smashed cheek,' said Tanner.

'Put him there,' said the doctor, pointing to a space in the corridor.

At long last, thought Tanner, as he helped to lay the lieutenant down.

They pushed on alongside the dimly lit train until they found the adjutant of the Green Howards. After a brief explanation, the Norwegians' names were added to his list.

'You take the train when it leaves,' Tanner told them.

'Thank you, Sergeant,' said Nielssen, 'for everything.'

'What about you?' asked Anna.

'We're going to help the Marines,' he replied. 'We've got to make sure that that train can get you to the port.'

'But you'll be able to escape in time?'

'I hope so. We'll find you at Åndalsnes.'

She looked up at him, biting her lip. 'Good luck, Jack.' She kissed him, then stepped up onto the train.

He walked back slowly towards the others.

'Cheer up, Sarge,' said Sykes. 'At least you've still got us.'

'Yes, give us a kiss, Sarge,' said McAllister.

'I'll give you a bloody sore gob, if you're not careful.'

The ammunition train was further towards the tunnel entrance. Twenty minutes later, they were back at the truck, clutching a wooden crate of gelignite, another of grenades, four tins of safety fuse and another of detonators. Their pouches were stuffed with clips of .303 rounds.

'You took your bloody time,' muttered the Marines' driver. 'Come on, load up and let's get the hell out of here.'

Back at the Marines' position they unloaded and reported to Lieutenant Lindsay.

'A successful trip, Sergeant?'

'Very, sir,' Tanner replied. 'Now, perhaps you could show me round.'

It was, Tanner recognised, a naturally strong position. The valley sides were steep and rose sharply from the river's edge on both sides. Just behind them, a smaller river cascaded down the mountainside to join the Lågen, while the valley road and the railway line had been cut away from the mountain. Lieutenant Lindsay's Marines had been spread out between the northern side of the valley and the Lågen, which ran swiftly, full of melted snow. The mortar team and machine-gun crews were dug in behind hastily built sangars, while the rest of the men had made use of what cover there was.

The tour over, Tanner gathered his men. 'What are your thoughts, Stan?'

'Well, Sarge, we should blow the road in a couple of places, then set up a few booby traps—wires between trees, that sort of thing. As soon as they come we want a clear field of fire, but also to leave ourselves time to scarper.'

'So, how far down the track?'

Sykes shrugged. 'Six hundred yards?'

Tanner agreed. 'That should do it. Let's be quick about it.'

IN VINSTRA, Reichsamtsleiter Scheidt was having one of the worst days of his life. In the early hours, he had received the shattering news that Odin had eluded them again. Only as the morning progressed did the extent of their failure become apparent. First, Henrik Larsen's body had been found, then reports had arrived from Luftwaffe headquarters that two trucks had been spotted and strafed heading northwards. Either Odin was already dead, or he had made it to Allied lines.

Scheidt was granted an interview with Engelbrecht shortly after noon.

'General, about time—'

The general put up a hand to silence him. 'A moment,' he said, and led Scheidt into the briefing room. He pointed to the map. 'There are three blown bridges, Herr Reichsamtsleiter. This has considerably slowed our advance.' Engelbrecht sighed. 'Our troops will reach Verma around seven o'clock this evening. The Luftwaffe are harrying their positions and bombing Åndalsnes too.'

'But what about Odin? You must make another attempt to—'

Engelbrecht turned on him. 'We're not going to do anything about Odin,' he said. 'I'm sick of him. I'm sick of you! I've already wasted enough time and men on this, running around as you asked me when I've got a battle to manage. And what do I discover? That your intelligence is about as reliable as snow in a desert! The enemy are evacuating and it's my task to make sure that as few as possible get away. So, please, leave this headquarters. Go back to Lillehammer or Oslo or wherever, but stop bothering me.'

'You can't talk to me like that!' Scheidt retorted. 'I'm going to speak to Terboven about this.'

'Save yourself the bother, Herr Reichsamtsleiter. I've already spoken to him. Believe me, he's not very happy. Now get out of my sight!'

TANNER AND HIS MEN had blown the road and the railway line three times with fifty yards between each crater. They had also felled a series of trees and linked a web of booby traps among them so that when anyone tried to move the barriers one or more cartridges of gelignite would explode. In addition, they made liberal use of grenades and safety fuse, preparing a variety of tripwires between trees further up the slopes from the road.

Since midday, two more waves of bombers had headed over, dropping loads at either end of the tunnel, then going on to paste Åndalsnes. But the tunnel had not been blocked and the tiny port was still open for business.

There had been no sign of the enemy on the ground, which had given

Tanner's men the chance to put some finishing touches to their devil's nest of explosives and booby traps. At well-spaced intervals, they were now placing single cartridges of gelignite, propped up on rocks, and wedged atop mounds of earth. All, however, were visible from vantage points along the Marines' positions.

'A bloody good idea of yours, this, Sarge,' said Sykes, as he handed over his last cartridge.

'Waste not, want not, Stan. Got the box?' He upended the wooden box in the middle of the road, then placed the last cartridge on top. 'Now, where's Hep? I need some tracer rounds. Hep?'

Hepworth hurried over from one of the other jelly-mounds—as the men had christened them—and gave him a handful. Placing them in his haversack, Tanner put his binoculars to his eyes and gazed down the valley.

Sun glinting on glass, a few miles away. 'They're coming!' he yelled. He took out his Aldis scope and screwed it onto his rifle.

Sykes hurried over. 'How many, Sarge?'

'Eight trucks—company strength, I suppose.' He watched as the trail of vehicles drew ever closer. Then, when he judged them to be a little over 400 yards away, he rested the rifle on Sykes's shoulder, took careful aim and squeezed the trigger.

Five rounds slammed into the leading truck, which swerved off the road and crashed into the river. Tanner's men cheered. Tanner watched men pour out of the remaining trucks and spread out in a wide arc.

'Time to go,' said Tanner.

They ran back to the Marines' lines and watched as the enemy approached. Germans reached the gaps in the road, then spread out through the trees.

Tanner took a bead on one of the jelly-mounds. A short distance beyond he could make out some enemy troops darting from tree to tree. 'Come on, Jerry,' he muttered, 'a bit closer.' *Now.* He squeezed the trigger and the tracer round smacked into the cartridge of gelignite and exploded instantly. Several men disintegrated with the blast, while others were flung through the air. A half-minute later, Tanner had detonated a second. Trees caught fire, enemy troops screamed and then, as the Germans came into range of the Marines' Lewis and Bren guns, the chatter of small arms rang out.

A tank was now squeaking forward. It was larger than any Tanner had seen. He followed it as it edged its way towards the first of the fallen trees.

'Come on, my lovely,' said Tanner. 'A bit closer.'

The tank drew within twenty yards of the first of the felled trees, then opened fire. Immediately a huge ball of flame erupted into the sky followed by a second explosion as the tank's magazine detonated. Thick black smoke engulfed the road and, as indistinct figures emerged through the smoke, the machine guns opened fire again. But the enemy infantry pressed on. Half a dozen ran straight down the road towards them.

'The mad bastards,' said Tanner, taking aim at the gelignite box now directly in front of the advancing soldiers. He fired, the gelignite exploded, and when the smoke cleared, the six men were gone. So, too, were the rest of the attackers, who had slipped back behind the cover of the smoke.

The small band of Marines and Rangers now waited. Tanner peered ahead through the smoke and haze, straining his eyes for any sign of the enemy. The tank still burned, thick black smoke pitching high into the valley. 'Where are those bastards?' he muttered and strode towards Lieutenant Lindsay's sangar. 'Any news, sir?' he asked.

'None, Sergeant, I'm afraid. Perhaps Jerry's called it off for the night.'

'Maybe,' said Tanner. 'I just wish that damned train would leave.' He walked back to his men and, as he approached Sykes, stopped suddenly.

'What is it, Sarge?' asked Sykes.

'Listen.' The faint, but increasingly distinct sound of aero-engines.

They could all hear them now, the sound rising to a deafening roar. The aircraft were above them, a formation of Stukas. The first flipped over onto its back and dived, then the next, and the next, until the air was rent by the crescendo wail of their diving scream. Tanner lay flat on the ground as bombs hurtled towards them.

He was lifted clean off the ground and smacked back down again, the air knocked from his lungs. Suddenly he could no longer hear. He could feel the pulse of the bombs rippling through the ground, could see the flash of orange and thick clouds of smoke, but there was no sound. Daring to look up, he saw two Marines crouching in their sangar not forty yards from him as a bomb seemed to detonate right on top of them. Tanner ducked as debris sprayed him. When he raised his head again, he saw the men had gone, their sangar replaced by a large hole in the ground.

His ears began to ring, a high, piercing whine, then sound returned. The sirens of the Stukas had gone but shells were now ranging in towards them from the south. 'Rangers!' he shouted, and began to run between the trees. He found Hepworth vomiting, then saw Sykes and McAllister. 'Where are the others?' he yelled.

Sykes pointed to Bell and Chambers, taking cover a short distance behind, then spotted Kershaw.

'Keep looking out for the infantry,' Tanner shouted.

Artillery shells continued to smash through the trees and there were mortars, too, blasting deadly shards of shredded metal.

'We can't hold out here much longer, Sarge,' said Sykes.

A whistle blast rang out and the Marines hurried backwards.

'Rangers!' shouted Tanner again, at a second whistle blast. 'Fall back!'

As Tanner began to run, he turned to see shadowy figures emerging through the smoke. 'They're coming,' he yelled, then paused to aim at one of the remaining jelly-mounds as troops materialised through the smoke. A ball of flame erupted. He turned and ran, bullets hissing and slicing around him.

A searing pain scorched his neck and he crashed to the ground. Gasping, he put up a hand. It came back red with blood. Someone grabbed his shoulders and yanked him to his feet.

'Can you still run, Sarge?' yelled Sykes.

Tanner nodded.

They sprinted through the trees until at last the bullets were no longer following them. Ahead was a clearing and Tanner saw trucks pulling out.

He stumbled again. A hand grabbed his collar. 'Come on, Sarge, nearly there!' *Sykes*. Tanner's neck stung like hell, his chest was tight and his legs felt as though they had turned to jelly. A shell whistled over. The trucks were leaving. *One left*. Men leaning out, arms outstretched. Suddenly his hand was clutching the tailgate and he was being pulled aboard.

He collapsed onto his back as the truck sped onto the road, away from the carnage. Sykes and Lieutenant Lindsay were staring down at him.

'The trains? Have they gone?' he asked.

The captain nodded. 'Yes, Sergeant. They have.'

Tanner closed his eyes briefly. 'Thank God for that.'

'Here, Sarge,' said Sykes, handing him a field dressing. Tanner hoisted himself onto the wooden bench. As he pressed the bandage to his neck he saw that all six of his men were among the Marines.

'It's just grazed you,' said Sykes. 'Let me wrap that bandage round it.'

As Sykes bandaged him, Tanner gazed at his men: Hepworth, Kershaw, McAllister, Bell and Chambers. McAllister and Hepworth were by the tailgate, scanning the skies for aircraft; he'd not even asked them to do that. They were soldiers, he thought. Not kids any more.

'You did damned well out there,' said Lieutenant Lindsay. 'If it hadn't been for your pyrotechnics, I'm not so sure we'd have held them off.'

'Thank you, sir.'

They fell into silence as the truck rumbled on.

At last, after nearly an hour, they emerged from the valley, and there, nestling at the water's edge beneath a thick pall of smoke, stood the tiny port of Åndalsnes. The town was a wreck, with hardly any houses standing; most had been reduced to little more than charred, blackened remains. The harbour teemed with exhausted troops, but there was no sign of the ships. Tanner and his men jumped down from the truck.

'Thank you, sir,' he said, offering his hand to Lieutenant Lindsay, 'but we must leave you here. We need to find the Norwegians.'

Lieutenant Lindsay shook his hand. 'Good luck, Sergeant.'

They headed down a rubble-strewn road towards the quayside. 'Keep your eyes peeled, boys. We've got to find them.'

'Why, Sarge?' said McAllister. 'They'll be here somewhere.'

Tanner turned on him. 'I'll tell you why, Mac. Because we've lost good men for that professor. We've been strafed, bombed and shot at, and I'm damned if I'm going to leave this godforsaken place without knowing that they're here and safely on a ship.'

Ahead, as they reached the quayside, all he could see was a sea of men. How are we ever going to find them? he thought. They pushed their way through. 'We're looking for three Norwegians. Two men and a girl? Anyone seen them?' It was hopeless, he knew.

They pushed on and then ahead, inching its way towards them, a destroyer. As it sounded its horn, the entire throng let out a massed cheer.

Tanner looked up at the skies. The light was fading.

'Another ten minutes,' said Sykes, 'and then it'll be too dark.'

'I know, Stan,' said Tanner. 'That's what worries me. Come on, come on,' he muttered, 'where are you?'

'I didn't mean that,' said Sykes. 'I meant too late for the Luftwaffe.'

They reached the end of the quay, but there was no sign of the Norwegians. Doubts were creeping into his mind. What if they had never got aboard that train, after all? Perhaps they had been turned away.

As the destroyer berthed and a gangway was pushed out onto the quay, Tanner lurched forward, forcing his way through the throng, amid angry cries from equally exhausted and irritable men.

'You don't understand,' pleaded Tanner, 'I've got to make sure someone gets on that ship.'

'Sarge!' Tanner felt a hand on his shoulder and turned to see Professor Sandvold, Lieutenant Nielssen and Anna standing before him.

Then he was laughing.

''E's been getting in a right flap,' Sykes told them. 'Worrying 'is pretty 'ead that you got left behind.'

'You need not have done, Sergeant,' said Professor Sandvold. 'We have been here for over an hour and a half, quite safe.'

'We were worried about you, though,' said Nielssen. 'We heard there was heavy fighting.'

Tanner looked at Anna and pushed his way towards her.

'You're wounded,' she said, reaching out to him.

'A nick, that's all.' He squeezed her hand. 'Anna, I'm very glad to see you. Will you come with us?'

A wistful expression crossed her face—the same he had seen on the morning they had headed towards Tretten. 'I cannot leave my family, Jack. I have to find my brother. If I went with you, I would feel as though I am running away. Deserting my country.'

Tanner nodded. He took both her hands in his. 'What will you do?' he asked.

'I don't know. Try to get home. Continue the fight.' She looked at him. 'The war will not go on for ever. One day . . .'

They had almost reached the gangway. Professor Sandvold was now walking onto the ship.

'I'll miss you,' she said.

'And me you.'

'Sarge?' said Sykes.

She kissed him, her lips lingering a moment on his. 'Goodbye, Jack.'

Tanner swallowed hard and felt her fingers let go of his. Someone pushed into him and then he was walking up the gangway, looking back. He stumbled, steadied himself and then he looked back once more. She had gone.

As the destroyer pulled away, Tanner gazed at the black outline of the mountains. It was little short of a miracle, he thought, but they had made it. Sandvold was safe. He and six of his men were safe. But far too many had been left behind.

'Cheer up, Sarge,' said Sykes, beside him. 'We're going home.'

'Yes, Stan.' He patted Sykes on the back. 'I suppose we are.'

JAMES HOLLAND

Born: June 27, 1970, Salisbury, Wiltshire
Former career: publishing PR
Website: www.secondworldwarforum.com

RD: What are your strongest childhood memories?

JH: I was lucky that I had a very clever brother, two years older than me, so we played at being Romans and Ancient Britons a great deal and, when we were older, lots of cricket. Our garden wasn't huge but we managed to squeeze in a net and during the summer played from dawn to dusk. And I remember we always had holidays in Britain: beaches in Cornwall and Northumberland; canals and castles in Wales. It was idyllic.

RD: And your best and worst memories of your school days?

JH: My best were of the Scout Camps that our school troop went on at the end of every summer term. Long walks, wide-games, making stuff, cooking on open fires, the smell of canvas and grass. My worst memory was being dropped from the 1st XI cricket team in my penultimate year of school before we'd even played a game. I was heartbroken.

RD: You read history at Durham, graduating in 1992. Was it the course there that first sparked your interest in the Second World War?

JH: No, not at all. In fact, both my dissertation and special subject were aspects of seventeenth-century England. I've always loved the Restoration and I also hugely enjoyed the Anglo-Saxon course. I've never studied any twentieth-century history.

RD: What is it about Second World War history that particularly fascinates you?

JH: It was a period of intense human drama and every single person in the country was involved. I was fascinated by thoughts of what I would have done—which of the services would I have joined? How would I have coped with having to go into combat and with being away for such potentially huge periods of time? The human experience of war was the starting point. I find it endlessly interesting.

RD: Is Jack Tanner changing and developing as you get to know him better?

JH: Definitely. War does change a man. He's also becoming a better soldier. The books allow me to chart the progress of the British Army during the war. In 1940 it was behind the times and, on the tactical level, a bit bereft. Slowly but surely the commanders learned. Also, the war changed the social landscape. Later in the series Tanner will win a commission in the field, which will make a working-class boy an officer. Social boundaries, so tight before the war, were broken down significantly by its end.

RD: Is Tanner a reflection of you in any way?

JH: We share a love of the countryside, but that's about it. And, as you can probably tell, I can talk for Britain while he's pretty taciturn on the whole.

RD: How much of the book is true, and how much is fiction?

JH: It is fiction based around real events. The campaign is depicted pretty much as it was, the commanders are real, and the places in which it is set. I picked the Norwegian campaign because it was the first in which the British Army came up against the Germans and not many people know a lot about it.

RD: Your website includes an oral history archive packed with first-hand experiences of the war. How did you gather so many?

JH: I've been writing nonfiction books about the war for a while now and every time I do a new one I interview people who were actually there. My research has taken me to some pretty far-flung places. I've recently been in Germany interviewing Luftwaffe Battle of Britain pilots. It was fascinating.

NORWEGIAN ROYALS IN EXILE

In April 1940, the situation in Norway was exactly as it is portrayed in *The Odin Mission*: the Allied defence of Lillehammer was crumbling in the face of the better equipped and seemingly unstoppable Nazis. Oslo, and several major Norwegian ports, had fallen, and in June 1940, King Håkon VII of Norway fled his country hotly pursued by the Germans. He found asylum in Britain and set up a Norwegian Government in exile.

The king's monogram, H7, became a clandestine symbol of the Norwegian resistance, and could be found chalked on buildings and worn as a lapel badge. In 1945, King Håkon (pictured waving, right) and his family returned to Norway on the HMS *Norfolk* and were greeted by cheering crowds. So grateful were the Norwegian people for Britain's support that they decided to send an annual gift of a majestic Norwegian spruce. The first tree was forty-eight foot tall and was erected in Trafalgar Square in London just before Christmas in 1947.

COPYRIGHT AND ACKNOWLEDGMENTS

THE FINAL RECKONING: © Jonathan Freedland 2008.
Published at £6.99 by HarperCollins*Publishers*.
Condensed version © The Reader's Digest Association Limited, 2008.

SILKS: Copyright © Dick Francis, 2008.
Published at £18.99 by The Penguin Group.
Condensed version © The Reader's Digest Association Limited, 2008.

LOST & FOUND: Copyright © 2007 by Jacqueline Sheehan.
Published at £6.99 by Ebury Press, an imprint of Ebury Publishing,
a Random House Group Company.
Condensed version © The Reader's Digest Association Limited, 2008.

THE ODIN MISSION: © James Holland 2008.
Published at £12.99 by Bantam Press, an imprint of Transworld Publlishers.
Condensed version © The Reader's Digest Association Limited, 2008.

The right to be identified as authors has been asserted by the following in accordance with
sections 77 and 78 of the Copyright, Designs and Patents Act, 1988: Jonathan Freedland,
Dick Francis, Jacqueline Sheehan, James Holland.

4 (top) © Krestine Havemann; 4 (middle) www.horsephoto.com; 4 (bottom) Joann Berns;
5 courtesy of James Holland. 6–8 Main image: Joe Sohm/Digital Vision; illustrator: Benjamin
Savignac@advocate. 164 © Krestine Havemann; 165 © Corbis/Bettmann. 166–7 illustrator:
Olly Howe@advocate; 306 (top) © Apex; 306 (bottom) and 307 courtesy of Dick Francis.
308 Image: Shinya Sasaki/NEOVISION; 309 Image: Sharon Montrose/The Image Bank;
308–9 illustrator: Darren Walsh@velvet tamarind; 420 © Joann Berns; 421 © Science Photo
Library/Sovereign, ISM. 422–3 illustrator: Michael Worthy@advocate; 574 courtesy of James
Holland; 575 © Imperial War Museum/A29155.

Printed and bound by GGP Media GmbH, Pössneck, Germany

020-257 DJ0000-1